THE GREATEST
HORROR
FROM
NEWFOUNDLAND

Published in Canada by Engen Books, Chapel Arm, NL.

Library and Archives Canada Cataloguing in Publication information is available upon request.

Print: 978-1-77478-171-5
eBook: 978-1-77478-172-2

Distributed by:
Engen Books
www.engenbooks.com
submissions@engenbooks.com

First mass market paperback printing: January 2025

Cover Image: Kit Sora

THE GREATEST HORROR
FROM
NEWFOUNDLAND

'Jacobi Street' dedicated to 'Ellen'
- Matthew LeDrew

'After Dark Vapours'
'is dedicated to Ben
My father, my teacher, my friend'
- Brad Dunne

'Carcharodon' dedicated to
'Mom and Dad,
For introducing me to the joy of reading.'
- Paul Carberry

'Variety Show' dedicated to
'all you theatre nerds. And for Matthew,
who created such a great world that I had to steal it.'
- Ali House

'That Halloween' dedicated to
'Baz – All of this is because of one tweet eight years
ago. I'll let you judge if that's good or bad,
but thanks all the same.'
- Mike Hickey

CONTENTS

JACOBI STREET

MATTHEW LEDREW

CHAPTER ONE

Chelsea walked into the gift shop a full half hour later than usual, carrying a big gray paper bag with rope handles that stuck up of their own accord. She was wearing a deep-red blazer with two large black buttons just below her central plexus that stared out at him like the bulging pupils of a heavily stoned person.

Bob closed his eyes and tried to make the image go away, turning toward the candy dish alongside the cash. There were a dozen or so chocolates in the shape of the Mona Lisa there. They were wrapped in tinfoil that was supposed to color her curves and contours correctly, but usually just made her look as though she were wearing someone else's skin, like Leather-Face. Once Bob had tried to fix them and had ended up buying twenty or so when the foil had become ripped irreparably.

"Good morning!" Chelsea chimed, laying her bag down against the floor so she could shake the cold out of her hair.

Bob turned and smiled at her, but kept fiddling with the order of the chocolates. "What kept you this morning?"

"Woke up with a hangover," she grinned, rolling her eyes a little. "Stopped by the market to get me a little Vitamin C from Booster Juice and ended up stopping in this quaint little boutique that's opened up there. You know the one?"

"I don't know *all* the boutiques."

"Of course. Well, they had this marvellous little shawl there that I had to try on, and when I was paying for it I saw they had these adorable little handmade necklaces for sale."

"I don't know *any* of the boutiques."

"I told them they should bring a dozen or so by for us to sell. Put them out when they get here, twenty per cent markup. They'll sell."

Bob forced himself to stop fiddling with the chocolates and wiped his palms on his jeans.

"Make it twenty-five. They'll sell. I bought five."

"I'm sure they will. Speaking of, it is the tenth so—"

"Right, the new shipment comes in today. Fuck me, I'm gonna need more coffee in me before I deal with that!" She laughed, shrilly and honestly, slapping the glass counter top. Her hand made her way to the Mona

Lisa chocolates then, and when she took one out, she displaced the large semi-circle around it.

"Yes," Bob nodded, letting out a deep sigh. "Yes, definitely. But in addition to that, the tenth is when you said you'd—"

"Actually, can you handle it when the shipment comes in?" she asked, not meaning to interrupt. Not even acknowledging that he had spoken, really. "Don't tell them where to put them, I'll handle that, just make sure everything that's on the list are in the boxes. Remember the Monet shipment? I swear, if I ever have to deal with that much red tape again, I'll puke like a freshman."

"Charming. Now, I was wondering if we could discuss—"

"I'd love to sweetie, but I've got to go." She smiled and picked up her bag again. The handles bent into odd shapes. "I can't just stand around here talking all day. Some of us have work to do!" She laughed again, then reached over and clasped another chocolate.

Bob reached out and plucked it from her fingers, pressing it back down into its plastic nest. "We're running low."

Chelsea paused and looked at him a moment, their hands touching over the small milk chocolate. After a tense moment, she smiled. "Yes," she said finally, smiling wide. "Duh, Earth to Chelsea, right? Lol."

She actually said 'lol' in speech, making it rhyme with 'doll.' It made Bob cringe every time.

Her fingers parted with his and fluttered deftly away. "Ta," she said, scanning the rest of the candy before leaving the way she'd come in.

Bob watched her go, cursed under his breath, and started arranging the chocolates properly again.

CHAPTER TWO

Bob leaned against the rotting guardrail that surrounded the unused back stoop of The Menagerie, looking out at the windowless red brick buildings and right angles that made up the back-alley of Jacobi Street. Overhead the sun beat down, reflecting off the stone and asphalt all around him and bathing him in the last of the summer heat. His vision was wavy near street-level, making the lower bricks of the buildings sway to and fro while the rest of them stayed ridged and upright, like old folks dancing the tango. He smiled thinking of that, and made a mental note to paint that at a later date.

Bob had lived on Jacobi Street for the last ten years, his entire life. He was older than ten, was in fact secretly thirty-five, but did not consider those first twenty-five years to have been living. They were more of an extended incubation period, as though he'd walked through his early childhood and teenage years and early adulthood in a fragile shell. Then Jacobi Street had just shattered it, with Bob emerging newly born: naked to the wonder and culture and the extreme heat.

Jacobi Street was famous for exactly one thing: not being famous. It was less than half a mile in length and existed as a side street just to the south of 14th Street. It was a one-way with both the exit and entrance to Jacobi being off 14th, giving it the impression of an appendix or small tumor. It was so small that it was often left off of maps entirely, and Google Maps refused to acknowledge its very existence. When it *was* acknowledged as existing, which was a rarity, it often was in the context of having the most street vendors, markets, theatres, and art galleries per square foot of any street in North America. They'd all been pubs during prohibition, when the small entrance and exit to the street had been false front houses to hide from the local constabulary. The streets were made with beautiful cobblestones, and five years ago the city had passed ordinance to lower the speed limit on Jacobi Street to 10 mph to preserve its natural beauty. That, and its narrowness, contributed to why the only vehicles ever seen on Jacobi Street were delivery trucks. It was the only area in the city where children could still play in the street without fear. There was no need for cars anyway: everyone who lived on Jacobi Street worked on Jacobi Street, though the only apartments were above businesses.

There was a hiss from down below him, a static sound that was nothing like a snake or a cat. He took a puff of his cigarette—the first he'd had in five months—and bent over the precarious wooden railing to see to the bottom of the alley, squinting his almond eyes against the strain of the sun.

Sloan Barkhurst was standing in front of the red brick wall scratching one of her pale cheeks. She had a can of spray-paint in each hand and was absorbed in the paper stencil on the red brick before her, already partially covered in pink and purple and baby blue. Her long brown hair was matted and tied off in random places and was clumped with spots of paint that had gone in wet, stuck together, and since dried.

She wiped her cheek with the back of her hand, smearing pink just under her right eye. She was wearing a white tank-top and camouflage pants filled with pockets that sagged because they were used to carrying cans of spray-paint. She held the a can of purple in her left hand and a can of pink in her right, both at her hips like a gunslinger ready to draw at any moment.

"Jeffrey Dahmer?" Bob called out, taking a puff of his cigarette.

Sloan scratched at her scalp and made a pensive face, though she did not turn for him to see it. "No, Dahmer was last month. Ran out of the yellow I needed for the M for the last few stencils and they just looked weird. Only had five left at the end so I scrapped them."

Bob nodded, leaning to try and get a better look at what she was doing until he felt the rail shift slightly beneath his weight.

Sloan was a self-proclaimed Street Artist. Officially, the state deemed her a 'Graffiti' artist, but she rejected that term as easily as she had rejected most of the terms the state had chosen to bestow upon her, including (but never limited to) terms relating to outmoded codes of gender identity, sexuality, and (briefly) humanity as a whole.

At any given time there were up to twenty street-artists calling Jacobi Street their home base, from which they spread their art throughout the city, each in their own unique style.

There was a Native American man who called himself Emilio, who lived above Cooper's General Market. He made wooden shoes and tied them together and hung them from lamp-poles. Because they were out of the way and took up a space unused by most other artists, they had an extended longevity. Bob had gone for a walk with him once and he'd pointed out a pair of shoes in a colour he hadn't used in seven years. When he put them west of 59th Street the locals had gotten uppity until they realized who had made them, as they had become 'in' in some markets. Now they were still taken down in well-off areas, but instead of ending up in trash bins they ended up on eBay with price tags of two grand and up.

Another street-artist, who was also a self-imposed street-urchin, was Obi. He could usually be found outside The Oz Theatre. He refused to tell anyone his full or real name. When pressed too much for it by those he called 'the authority' he would chuckle "Obi-Wan Kenobi, Motherfucker," typically with a marijuana cigarette clasped between his dried lips. He looked as though he'd time-travelled straight from the 90s punk scene, with three barbell-piercings in each eyebrow and bright jade hair. He made art out of trash, typically fast-food cartons. At one point he and Sloan had broken into The Menagerie late at night and added his plastic cup men to the Memorial Day display, and it was a week before anyone noticed.

Sloan did stencils, a complex form of art that involved paper, paint, knives, and lots of agility. The process began with the purchase each month of a ream of 200 sheets of thin canvas joined at the north end, which Sloan got a special discount on because she had once dated the manufacturer. When the mood struck, but usually once a month, she took her knife to the ream and carved an image into it, employing negative space, carving out the silhouettes or shadows in a face or the space around a letter, much in the way one would carve a pumpkin. The cuts would go all the way through the sheets, and she would have her stencils for the month. She would spend the next thirty days sticking them in strategic places around the city, painting them quickly, then ripping down the stencil and leaving only the color filling in the formally-negative space. The result was 200 hundred identical, yet unique, works of art. There were three websites dedicated to tracking her art, though none were affiliated with her or knew who she was. Last month's stencil had been of Jeffery Dahmer eating a Happy Meal, his cheeks plump and fat. She'd called it *You are what you eat.*

Bob had met her three years ago when she had borrowed a ladder from Eddie and he'd ended up going with her to the freeway at three o' clock in the morning to paint over all the ads and billboards with whitewash, giving commuters an advertisement-free drive to work for the first time in most of their lives. The billboards were back up by ten of course, but anyone driving into work that morning had driven free of what Sloan had called "the capitalist nightmare." Bob had come home to them both covered in white paint and drunk on cheap wine and laughing all over one another. When he'd come in, he'd raised a thick eyebrow at them and that had made them laugh even harder. After several minutes, Eddie had managed to get out the words: "This is Sloan," and that was how he met Sloan Barkhurst.

Sloan made two final sprays with each of the paint cans, repeating the same hissing sound that had gotten his attention in the first place. Her final statements made, she peeled off the paper stencil to reveal her newest masterpiece: a stern-faced Barack Obama giving the viewer the finger. The exaggerated and protruding middle digit had a plump top to it, giving it the impression of a phallus. The pink, purple, and baby blues came down in three stripes all around him and highlighted in various other points.

"Nice," Bob said, taking a quick puff of his cigarette. It was down to the butt now and he was burning the filter, the sick taste of roasting fibreglass filling his mouth. "Does it have a name?"

"*No, We Can't,*" she smirked, stepping back from her work as she shoved one of her cans into her pocket. She turned and looked up at him for the first time since he'd noticed her, just as he was flicking his cigarette out towards the mouth of the alley. "You smoking again?"

"Nope."

"Eddie's gonna kill you."

"Eddie can suck my dick."

"No he won't. He says cigarettes make your cum taste like death," Sloan smiled.

Bob fought the urge to laugh at that and failed. After a moment of chuckling he coughed twice, and the pleasant bubble of his laughter transformed into the sound of his throat rending.

A dull vibration filled the alley. Bob reached into his pocket and pulled out his phone. "Speak of the devil," he said, unlocking it with a swipe of his thumb. There was no need to lock it. He'd lost it twice since living on Jacobi Street, and both times it had been in his mailbox by morning, untouched save for accessing his address. It was a good neighbourhood.

"What's he saying?" Sloan asked, back to examining her work.

"'Bring Twizzlers,'" Bob read aloud, even as he punched in his response.

"Movie night?"

"Movie night." He waited for his answer to send, then put his phone back into his pocket. When he withdrew it it was holding another cigarette.

"Jesus Christ Billy-Bob, what's the deal?"

He took several quick, halted puffs to get the cherry started. The smoke billowed upward and joined the cloud cover that was finally starting to come in. It would rain later, the type of hot rain that could only happen at the end of a hot summer in the city. He could smell it in the air even now.

Sloan watched him and waited for an answer. When she didn't get one, she picked up the baby-blue can of spray paint and added a quick line to the bottom right-hand corner of her piece, giving the hint that Obama was standing in front of something. A podium? Who knew, that was up to the interpreter. If it was a podium, who was he giving the finger to? The American People watching at home? The Conservative Media? She didn't say and didn't want the piece to say: so much of the meaning of art was on the viewer, and she'd said too much already.

"Today the tenth?" she asked finally, willing the newest mark she'd made to dry before the rain came.

"Yeah," Bob said curtly, tapping the ash from the end of his smoke to punctuate it.

She nodded. "Talk with Chelsea didn't go well, huh?"

Bob snorted. "The talk didn't happen. We talked about the new shipment coming in that I have to inventory, because apparently I'm Receiving now, and we talked about some kitschy little necklace that I'm gonna have to find a place for in the gift shop, but that was all we talked about." He took another puff of his cigarette, and then threw it away in disgust, only half gone.

Sloan pursed her lips and nodded, but said nothing.

Bob was a painter. Not a street-art painter like Sloan, Bob worked on traditional canvas. He did landscapes and portraits and the occasional commentary or mood piece. He used a wet-on-wet style with oil paint in a similar fashion to another famous Bob who was also a painter. His work couldn't go on walls as quickly or easily as Sloan's: it had to be bought and mounted and framed and placed purposely on the wall in someone's home or office. So far in his career he had painted at least two-hundred paintings and sold ten. Most of them now occupied a storage unit on 59th Street that he shared with Sloan and Eddie. Sloan kept her name off the lease, and the most incriminating of her art supplies in the unit.

Eight years ago Bob had taken a job at The Menagerie, an art gallery dead in the center of Jacobi Street, as a way of getting his foot in the door and get his art on the walls. As of yet The Menagerie had yet to feature any of his work. It had had a tree with Emilio's wooden shoes hanging from it for a month in the main lobby and, for one glorious month last year, had had Obi's plastic-cup men on display (even though nobody had known), but never his. Chelsea, the gallery curator, had always managed to avoid the topic, although she had bought one of his pieces herself.

His phone buzzed again. He took it out, smiled, then typed something back.

"What'd he say?" Sloan asked, happy for the topic change.

Bob smiled. "He said, 'Shawshank,' with five exclamation points."

"That's a lot of exclamation."

Bob sighed, then chuckled despite himself. He had a throaty chuckle, with a cadence of a machine gun heard while underwater. When he tucked his phone away and looked down again, Sloan had finished putting her paint into her pockets. "Where you headed?"

"UES. Got a score to settle there at one of the Liberal Political Offices."

Bob saluted her, said "Stay safe," then opened the rusted back door to The Menagerie and stepped back into the darkness of the back hall.

CHAPTER THREE

The shipment was larger than most that came through the doors and took hours to sort out. When he was only a third of the way through the inventory, Bob began to hear the telltale pitter-patter of raindrops against the roof of The Menagerie. By the time he was halfway done, the pitter and patter had morphed into an all-out downpour.

There were three works by Pardy and four by Boone, the last of the latter of which was a ten-foot by eight-foot canvas that took three delivery-men to unload. The frame on it seemed thick, and he doubted that the studs in the wall where it was planned to go would hold it. They'd have to find somewhere else. Not only that, but Chelsea had earmarked it for the third floor, and he didn't envy the person who had to scale the narrow staircase with that particular piece.

There was a print by a young kid named Flaherty from the west coast that was quite good. Bob had taken the front off the crate, not recognizing the name. It showed a girl bathed in fire and the brushwork on the flames reminded him of that one William Blake: pale but lively. The bio card said he was a student, but Bob didn't recognize the name of the Institute as any art school he knew of.

There was a Pollock on loan from MoMa, as part of a series they were doing to commemorate some anniversary. It would replace their current piece, which had its own special room, and was kept locked except for tours. There were three Lairds and five works by Marsh. He didn't look, but assumed they were from her cat period. There was too much, he realized soon, to fit where Chelsea had allocated the space for the collection. They'd have to rearrange the Corben pieces to be all on the same wall to get some of these in.

As the deliverymen became frustrated, he began checking down the inventory list in front of him, making small ticks alongside each entry in pencil. When he was done, there was only one that had no tick next to it, an untitled work credited to O.K. Mal.

He paused and looked around to see if he'd missed something. Three Pardys, four Boones, a Flaherty, a Pollock, three Lairds, five Marshs, but nothing by anyone by the name of O.K. Mal.

"Hey, we're missing one," Bob said, raising his pencil into the air and stabbing at the humidity.

The deliverymen continued wheeling their carts back toward the front entrance.

"Hey," Bob said, looking up from his clipboard and annunciating. A small amount of colour had risen to his cheeks. "I said we're missing one."

A sleepy-eyed deliveryman with the name Nelson embroidered onto the breast of his uniform stepped over and took the clipboard from Bob, scanning his eyes down it. "It's all... here," he said, pausing before the last word for no discernible reason.

Bob tapped the line that the missing painting was on. "This one. I'm looking and not finding it, if I'm not finding it, you can't leave."

Nelson frowned with his big lips, his lower lip sticking out and revealing a thick purple vein running across it. He stuck it in and out contemplatively as he scanned over the assembled crates, then finally made a sudden *pop!* sound with it that made Bob jump. He walked over to where the four Boones all stood in a row, leaned against one another. There was a gap between the first and the second, and he carefully separated them and reached between them, returning with a small thin rectangular crate. He held it up triumphantly, and then handed it to Bob.

The inventory sticker on the lower right side indeed said the piece inside had been done by O.K. Mal, and that the title was unknown.

Bob looked from the sticker to the man, then back to the sticker. The colour left his cheeks and they returned to their normal shade. "You can go," he said flatly, signing the inventory and passing it to the deliveryman.

They left without another word, at least none that Bob heard, as he slowly stepped into Receiving. He walked by memory as he kept looking at the small rectangular crate. The crate was indeed much smaller than any that he had ever taken in at The Menagerie before. It couldn't possibly have held anything larger than an eight by twelve, once the frame was accounted for. It was heavy in his hands though, somehow having weight that belied its small stature: it must have had a very ornate frame or a very thick canvas, or both.

He reached the Receiving office and took out the original copy of the order. On it were the orders for Three Pardys, four Boones, a Flaherty, a Pollock, three Lairds, and five Marshs. He paused, squinted, then read the order again. Three Pardys, four Boones, a Flaherty, a Pollock, three Lairds, and five Marshs. There was nothing on the order form about an untitled piece by anyone named O.K. Mal.

This would not have been the first time this had happened. Shipments came from all over, and sometimes the entries for one order were mistakenly put with another: human error was a problem no amount of technological interference could truly ever account for. Usually Chelsea would report the error and track down the museum it was supposed to have been shipped to, but typically they'd just make room for it, and when the next shipment came in thirty days, it would leave with the deliverymen. Only once had a mistakenly-delivered order not gone on The Menagerie wall, a Georgia O'Keefe that had been desperately needed elsewhere and whose owners had been beside themselves by the time Chelsea had called.

Bob picked up the small crowbar with yellow stripes that usually sat on the desk of Receiving and worked it carefully into the groove of the small crate, steadying it on the desk and rocking the bar back and forth until the nails came loose. With one steady, practised pull, the front of the crate came free and packing tumbled to the floor, revealing the small painting that had caused him so much anxiety just a few minutes before.

It looked to be wet on wet from what he could tell, and quite old. He recognized the brush strokes, the hurried movements, from his own work. Wet on wet was a delicate art, requiring speed and precision and many, many spare canvases for all the versions you ruin. The image was of what looked to be an old style opera house, from the point of view of the singer looking out onto the audience. There were hints of thick red curtains along the sides and across the top, each with gold trimmed rope. The clarity of them was amazing for something so small, though still limited; there was only so small a brush could get.

The dominant features of the piece were the lifelike theatre seats, the perspective of which sloped in for a three-dimensional affect, which was done perfectly. The tone of crimson on each seat was marvellously crafted, slowly getting darker as it went further and further back into the cheap seats and finally faded into a patterned, murky back row, made not completely dark only by the golden pillars that held up the upper balcony, just out of frame.

The audience was not full. It held only nine patrons. In the front there was a portly man with tiny spectacles and a white wig sitting in the left of the second row whose face was blurred, as all faces are on a canvas of this size. Even though it was blurred it had a subtle, whimsical hint of expression on it, one that reminded him of someone who had just had their rear-end pinched on a crowded subway.

Bob smiled, taking out his phone and unlocking it with a swipe of his thumb. He quickly snapped a picture then sent it to Eddie with the caption: 'Check this out.'

The text went through with a small *wooloop* sound. A moment later he got back the reply: 'Thats cool! :) Twizzlers / Shawshank.' He snorted.

He laid the painting upright against the desk, then took out a post-it notepad and pen. He scribbled "find out who—" and stopped, unable to recall the artist's name.

He turned and looked over his shoulder at the painting's reflection in the mirror opposite it, the proportions of at least one patron looking not-quite-right when reversed. Still unable to make out the signature in the reflection, he leaned forward so he could see the painting again, and noticed that the artist had signed his last name first, followed by initials.

He finished his note: "find out who Mal O.K. belongs to" and stuck it on the ornate silver frame before heading back out into the lobby to deal with the rest of the inventory. Outside the rain came down hard.

CHAPTER FOUR

Bob walked into the living room and stopped right in front of the couch. He was dripping wet with the rain outside and carried two gray grocery bags that were as well. There was water pooling in the bottom of them and they reminded Eddie of the way water balloons looked when they were half-full, their contents sloshing around unevenly.

Eddie looked from the bags to Bob, and then back again. A slow, wide grin spread across the lower half of his face as the soft blue light from the television caressed it magnificently. "Did you get them?"

Bob glared at him, his almond-shaped eyes fuming and the pupils within them becoming tiny little needlepoints. His nostrils flared and his lip curled, and Eddie had to keep himself from cracking up with laughter as he pictured little rivets of steam shooting out from each of Bob's ears.

"If you didn't get it, I'd understand."

Bob let out a breath through is nose, rainwater still dribbling down it, fuelled by the wet mop of thinning black hair that lay atop his egg-shaped head like a rug.

"It's hellish out there. Sixty-mile-an-hour winds, at least that's what it said during a commercial." Eddie's grin got larger. He stifled a laugh by tossing a handful of popcorn into his mouth. When most of it had been swallowed, he took a single fluffy piece, clasped it between his thumb and forefinger, and flicked it into the air. He caught it in his mouth, chewed for a moment, then motioned back toward the tv. "You missed your favourite part, by the way. When Andy asks Boggs if he can read."

Bob held out one of the bags before him, his arm meeting his torso at a ninety degree angle. Little spots of water dribbled off the plastic for a moment until he let it go, the bag crashing down onto the couch with a splash.

Water flickered onto Eddie, coating his lap and making him look as though he'd just had a rather embarrassing accident. The bowl of popcorn got it too, soaking into the fluffy kernels and turning them into soggy dead tarantulas.

Eddie looked at him for a moment, not even really noticing the water that was even now penetrating the fabric of his boxers. He turned and craned his head over the top of the bag, peeling away one of the handles to carefully look inside. He smiled, snatched up the bag and brought it to his lap. Humming happily, he reached inside and pulled out a bag of Twizzlers. "They did have them!"

Bob narrowed his eyes at him, then slowly sat down next to him on the couch. The cushion he sat on squished audibly as his bottom found the apex of the puddle he himself had just made, though aside from the sound he barely noticed it. He was already soaked.

He sat there for a moment and then let out a long sigh. The colour on his cheeks almost changed as he did this, going from the pale red it had become back to its typical jaundiced yellow hue. When the breath was complete, he bent over and reached into the remaining bag, his fingers getting wet again as he did so, and withdrew a bag of Lays chips. He opened it and shoved one into his mouth, crunching down hard.

Eddie looked at his unopened bag of Twizzlers, then at Bob's chips, then back again.

Bob turned, noticing this motion as it repeated once again, and rolled his eyes. He tilted the opening of his bag toward Eddie.

Eddie smiled happily, reaching in and grabbing a healthy handful of chips and piling them onto the top of his popcorn. He leaned in and gave Bob a quick kiss on his cold, wet lips. "Thanks Bob."

Bob had met Eddie halfway through his first year on Jacobi Street. He had lived on the Street alone just long enough to realize that he loved it, and not just his life with Eddie. He loved them both equally, with each taking up the same room in his heart. He felt as though he'd learned a lot about himself through his contrast with Eddie. From Eddie's messiness, he'd learned that he was neat. Through Eddie's humor, he'd learned that he could sometimes be uptight. Both things he'd managed to let go of a little, and found himself less stressed as a result. Eddie hadn't just been the ideal partner for him; he had made him better as a person, simply through the virtue of having been there.

It was also through his relationship with Eddie that he had learned that his parents were bigots.

His parents were first generation Asian-Americans, though their parents had not been from Asia. His ascendants had been Asian-Canadians, having been brought from China to help work on the great Canadian Railway in 1892. His grandfather used to tell him there was "one dead Chinaman for every mile of that track." Asians were used to doing dangerous jobs, like bringing nitro into mines to be exploded, or climb caverns with cables slung over their shoulders to set up a pulley system. He looked it up once out of curiosity. The track was 14,000 miles long. He thought of this whenever Canadian friends attempted to postulate their moral superiority over Americans, stating that race relations were so much better in Canada for never having had a slave trade: "Just because your slaves were yellow and not black, doesn't make them any less slaves."

Bob's parents had not had a problem with he and Eddie's relationship purely out of homophobia. Although he'd dated women while he was young and had lost his virginity to his first (and only) girlfriend, he'd realized his true lifestyle preference before leaving home. His father had caught him in bed with David Woodworth mid-way through senior year and they hadn't spoken for a week. At first Bob thought it was out of shame... only to realize it was the natural awkwardness that came from any parent catching their child in bed with any-one when, after a week of silence, his father had poked him proudly in the ribs with his elbow and had said: "Captain of the Football team, huh?" with pride in his voice. For the rest of the year there had been many Football-related sex puns; trying out for the team, going over manoeuvres. They'd even continued into Bob's next relationship, Tim Fowler, until Tim had found out what they were in reference to and had put a stop to it.

Bob had dated several men in college, none of whom his parents had taken issue with. One had even been a house-painter, someone with a 'low' job like Eddie had now. Had it not been for that, he might have given his parents the benefit of the doubt and assumed their disapproval for his relationship was based on class or concern for the well-being of their only son's future: if Bob was going to be a painter, he needed a partner that could bring in the money, a breadwinner. But it wasn't that. In truth he had dated men long enough and prolifically enough in his more promiscuous youthful days that there was only one mitigating factor left as the reason behind his parent's prejudice.

Eddie was Mexican.

Eduardo Alvarez, a third generation Mexican who had begun work at the Quaint Little Theatre. That was the actual name of the theatre, and also quite apt. His job had consisted of constructing and painting sets during a short run of a play called *Marks*, a musical about a detective who was tracking a killer based on the marks he left on the body, and who was also a Marxist. It hadn't lasted three shows, but the sets had been fantastic: so much so that the theatre director had hired Eddie on full-time. He'd commuted back and forth from the East End for the first year he'd had the job before meeting and moving in with Bob, in the big studio-esque apartment above the Hemp Emporium. He'd joked to Bob that he'd "left Mexico to get *away* from the drug-trade" while they were moving his couch up the narrow flight of stairs that led from street-level to the apartment, to which Bob had stone-face humourlessly replied to him: "You've never even *been* to Mexico."

Despite Eddie having never been to Mexico, Bob's parents had had a strong dislike of Eddie from the start and had never let go of it. And it wasn't because of disapproval of his sexuality or that he was with someone not considered economically stable, the reason came down to one thing and one thing only: every other boy Bob had brought home had been white and Eddie wasn't. First-generation Asian-Americans, whose ascendants had been brought to North America to work as slaves in all-but-name on the Central Pacific Railway, who had endured the internment and persecution of Asians by Canadians all through the 40s and who had raised their son with the old canard that all races were equal: racists themselves. One of the last things he'd ever said to his father had been on that very subject: after accusing him of his bigotry, his father had whipped out that old chestnut that all races were equal. "You say that," Bob had said, standing in the back yard of their retirement home in Western Maine, "But what you mean is, *your* race is equal." They'd never spoken again.

Bob squeezed Eddie tight to his shoulder as the rain came down outside.

CHAPTER FIVE

The Corben Popart pieces on the second floor had indeed needed to be moved, just as Bob had thought they would. Previous to the arrival of the large shipment, all ten pieces had been in a horizontal line along the south wall of the second floor corridor. Now they occupied a space less than half that length in the western corridor. They were hung vertically, one on top of the other, their index cards stuck together on the wall just down from them. Bob had hated it: the pieces on top couldn't be appreciated, you couldn't really get up close, but Chelsea had overruled him.

Corben had been a popular part of their Popart series for well over a year and had steadily become the public face of it. Popart was an upper-class way of saying comic book art, although none of the art presented in any of the Popart showings had been remotely to do with comics and had merely been drawn by some of the betters in the medium: your Alex Rosses, your Richard Isanoves. Richard Corben was a mostly underground comic book artist known for heavy inks and tones. He'd worked on comics like *Grim Wit, Slow Death, Fever Dreams,* and had done some fill-in work for the original *Teenage Mutant Ninja Turtles* volume. He was best known, however, for his work on *Heavy Metal* magazine where his realistic portrayals of human anatomy and shading brought the larger-than-life fantasy images on the covers to life, making them leap off the page. He'd won the Spectrum Grand Master Award and had been indicted into the Will Eisner Award Hall of Fame, but no matter how many times Chelsea had to tell that memorized line to patrons visiting The Menagerie, when no one else was around Corben was still 'that comic-book guy.'

Bob had fallen in love with the line work from the moment he'd seen it, and couldn't have been happier when Corben had been one of the artists that had been brought into regular rotation... save of course, if Bob's own art had been. His favorite piece of Corben's was a large landscape that featured a unique Executioner's block. Four women stood around the block bare-breasted, wearing ceremonial headdresses, and stern, dower expressions while another hung back in the shadows. One was reminiscent of Cleopatra, another of Aphrodite. In the center was a tall, proud woman wearing only an executioner's hood and gloves, gripping an axe with both hands at crotch-level. She stood next to a stump and basket used for decapitations, and opposite her was a muscular man in the style of the perfectly-proportioned Greek statues. The nameless figure stared up at her as though in question, but she never returned his gaze. Though it was clear he was meant to place his head upon the stump, from his current position his manhood hovered precariously just above it and to the right of the axe's sharp blade.

The tones of the piece were what had captured Bob's attention at first: that was the key to lifelike human images, it was all in shading and tone. A man could be fully anatomically proportionate, but without a light-source and tone it laid flat.

Bob walked past the piece now, taking a bite of the hummus sandwich that was his lunch. There was a break room but it wasn't necessary: the gallery was all but vacant from noon to one on most days, and any patrons who were wandering about wouldn't mind. Patrons of the arts who found their way to Jacobi Street and to The Menagerie were typically not the type to turn up their noses because someone ate a sandwich in front of them.

Adjacent to the Corben art were the Marsh pieces he'd taken in only a week before during the big shipment. He'd been right without even having to have opened the crates: the pieces had been from her cat period. All five pieces were portraits of cats on vibrant coloured backgrounds: primary colours like yellow and blue and red that made the images they sat behind pop out at the viewer. Her brush strokes were clean and precise, with thick black lines accenting the figures of each fantastical feline. His favorite was a white cat with a Mona-Lisa-smile and a pink eyepatch covering its right eye. Bob smirked as he stepped past it and checked the card, noting the title of the piece: "Butterscotch." He snorted, and the sound echoed throughout the tiled hallway.

He turned at the end of the hall and stepped down the southern corridor, where the Corbens had been until last week. It was a long straight hall that terminated in a dead-end, unless one counted the fire escape hidden on its right. The terminating wall had been the best place to hang something eye-catching. It was where the Corben landscape of the Execution had been, with a small spot-light above it illuminating the piece. It served to create anticipation: when Chelsea did her tours the eyes of the patrons would always go to where she directed them at first, then slowly drift back to the piece highlighted at the end of the hall: "I wonder what that is?"

Now one side of the hall was home to the three new Pardys and the other to the four Boones that had come in. Pardy was a painter that used quick, expressive strokes to tell her stories. She was often called an expressionist, but dabbled in pop from time to time, and had become famous for constantly tweaking her works until they were out of her possession, sometimes even when they had been already paid for by a buyer. The most famous example of this had been a mood piece she'd titled 'fall' in the style of Pollock with oranges and reds and yellows splashed about the canvas with reckless abandon. It had been seen at a show and a young starlet had fallen in love with it and had paid the twenty-thousand dollar price for it on the spot, ordering it to be delivered to her flat the next week. When it arrived, Pardy had added a large triangular 'rip' painted into the center of the canvas, from which a man in a 60s era spacesuit poked his helmeted head out, his stubbly fingers holding onto the canvas to escape the star-field behind him. When the starlet had called, angry about the addition, Pardy had cooly answered: "The astronaut had always been there, she just hadn't painted him yet."

At the end of the hall now, in that coveted, spotlighted place, was the unnamed and unclaimed wet-on-wet of the theatre by O.K. Mal.

The formerly dull silver frame had been polished to a mirror shine since the last time Bob had seen it, and it glinted in the ambiance of the spotlight. The light reflecting off it moved and morphed as he got closer to it, bending and taking on new shapes as it travelled along the warped bends and creases on the weathered frame.

Bob put the last of his sandwich into his mouth and sucked the bit of excess hummus from his finger as he closed the gap between himself and the subtle white line on the floor that indicated how close one should get.

The man wearing the wig in the front row still appeared as comical to Bob as he had the first time he had seen it. Though his eyes were normal, they were overshadowed by the spectacles he wore and the glint from the light-source of the stage on them. The artist had made it seem as though these were his eyes, which made the already miniscule pug of a nose seem shorter still. His flabby cheeks seemed to vibrate, his mouth curled open in a bow as he just slightly turned around, adding to the overall expression that he was reacting to someone laying hands on his backside. The only person behind him was a large black man in overalls and a faded yellow shirt patted with dust and debris.

Bob smiled and furrowed his brow. Could this be a comment on race relations? When had this painting been produced? He had at first assumed it to have been at least a hundred years old from the style, but if that sort of message was in play that early on and it was intentional, then that would be quite impressive. So much so that he wasn't sure how he'd missed it before.

He checked his watch. He still had fifteen minutes of his break left. He smiled, wiped his finger on his pant leg, then brought his hand to his mouth contemplatively and looked back at the black man.

He was sitting alone in the third row, despite the fact that there were eight other patrons in the theatre. His shoulders were hunched over and his jowls saggy and depressed. There were red rings under his eyes and he stared out at the viewer forlornly, looking impossibly tired. He did not address the man in the front or seem to acknowledge him in any way, though now it seemed clear that the man in the wig was looking back in his general direction with concern.

Bob locked eyes with the large, bald black man, and for a moment the painting was almost so real he could step inside it. The man looked angry and sad all at the same time, yet resigned somehow. That racial tension, that anger... was that what this was about? He'd always tried to take what bothered him most about a piece and use that as a way of considering what the piece was actually *about*. With effort, he tore his gaze away from the steely eyes of the African and moved them up to the next row.

Just over the black man's left shoulder was a slender, gaunt woman with short cropped hair. She looked like a flapper girl, but couldn't have been. She was wearing a loose top that hid her breasts almost completely, and there were shimmering sequins down either side of the neck. She was dirty-blonde like Sloan, and had a hint of a smile somewhere behind her cheeks. It teased and played: a reference to the Mona Lisa, or a coincidence of the brush? It was hard to say.

Behind the flapper girl was a rough looking, scruffy man with sunken eyes. He had a long length of dark brown hair and wore a proper suit for the time period: that sort of puffy shirt that poofed out from the neckline. The hint of his belt, visible over the woman's shoulder and the seat in front of him, gave the impression that it was large and gold. His face was curled up in a sneer and his eyes were black. His cheek had been bloodied with a series of scratches.

Several seats to his right were a mother and child. The child was at its mother's exposed teet, the neckline of her dress hiked down to accommodate it. Its gender was ambiguous. It was nude and facing away from the stage. The woman however looked out at the viewer pleadingly. There were brush strokes down the face that were not present on any of the other patrons... the hint of tears? Her mouth was open in a wail to add credence to this. She wore a bonnet, pulled back to show the auburn hair on her sweat-strewn face.

Bob shivered, unnerved. The woman stared right into him, pleading with him, as her child drank from her. His eyes turned, involuntarily, back to the black man in the third row. He was angry about something, and this woman was scared. She seemed scared for her life, although the only reference Bob had for such things was in fiction.

On the next row up, seated almost an equal distance from the woman and the grim man, was a knight. He wore mail and had his helmet at his side and the sort of long blonde hair and unshaven gruffness one would expect of a classic portrayal of a knight. He wore a long white sash with a red cross on it and stood upright and straight, his eyes dead ahead but looking at nothing, as though he were standing guard over the five sitting below him. His chin was tight in a magnificent representation of a 'stiff-upper-lip.'

Finally, there were two women on either side of the knight in the row behind him: a nurse and a prostitute. The prostitute looked salaciously toward the stage with a wry smile, sitting in her seat lengthwise with one foot in the air. Her squared blouse showed her bosom to excess, almost as much as the mother who was feeding. The nurse sat quietly forward with her hands in her lap, the way people used to sit for portraits before cameras were invented. She wore a small paper hat and looked forward, but her eyes betrayed her: they darted to the right, towards the whore. Were these the angel and the devil on the Knight's shoulders? Bob looked back at the it, suddenly reminded of the Knight from the Wife of Bath's Tale from *The Canterbury Tales*. Did the women represent the Knight's choice between a hag and a maiden? Were they his warring morality, his desires as a man which had gotten him into trouble versus his virtue as a knight?

Behind the two women was only the darkness and shadow of the back of the theatre, framed by gold, inlayed pillars that matched the picture's frame itself.

The dark had seemed so fully dark when he'd seen it in the Receiving room, but now he saw that there were hints of purple in it as well. One winding S-shaped brush stroke, almost a semi-circle but not quite, was particularly noticeable. He squinted and leaned in, raising his hand to block the light from the spotlight to make sure it wasn't some trick of the light or reflection.

"The distributer doesn't know where it came from," Chelsea said.

Bob jumped slightly, pressed his hand to his chest, then smiled. "You startled me."

She smirked, then nodded toward the painting. "I decided to hang it until they sorted it out."

Bob turned back to the piece and nodded. Absently, he asked: "What do you tell people on tours?"

She shrugged. "That we don't know. Adds to the mystery."

Bob nodded. His eyes had gone back to the black man, who still stared out at him with an anger that would have been better described as vengeful fury. Bob noticed, for the first time, that there were three small gashes on the man's barrel of a chest.

He stepped back from the piece, realizing he'd inadvertently stepped over the white line while examining it, although Chelsea hadn't seemed to mind. The picture as a whole told a story, like the Hogarth etchings and portraits. These paintings of multiple figures always told a story and interacted with one another and said something about the society they came from: like ethnographic time capsules, perfectly capturing the culture and mood of that moment and place in human history.

"Remember to leave the key with Mr. Cooper tonight on the way home; he's going to deliver some refills to the gift shop once he closes up the General Market, okay?" Chelsea asked, checking something on her clip board. Bob kept looking at the picture, finally drawing her attention. "Hey? Your break's over."

He looked at his watch, nodded, and apologized.

CHAPTER SIX

Bob and Eddie stood on either side of the stage painting, with Sloan dead in the center. She was sitting cross-legged with her hair tied into a quick-and-messy bun that protruded from one side of her head, munching on dried mango with a sheet curled around her. She was wearing a black tank top that may well have covered no more than a sports bra on more-endowed women, showcasing just how miniscule she really was. She ate her mango and almonds mostly in silence, turning her head from one side to the other depending on who was speaking to her but otherwise remaining relatively still.

Had anyone been in the theatre to see, it might have looked like a scene from an indie comedy play. "Three's A Crowd" or "Odd Woman Out" would be the title, the story of a free-spirited young manic-pixie dream-girl who bridges the gap between two dissolved lovers. But the theatre was void of presence except for the three of them, and the distance between the two men was practical, not emotional: they were both painting.

To stage left, Eddie stood with a large, broad paintbrush making wide, firm strokes on the wooden figure he'd cut out not twenty minutes before from wood. He was applying a cream base before adding details to what would, eventually, be an image of Buckingham Palace for a small play titled *Et Tu Berlusconi*, which told of an alternate history in which Silvio Berlusconi had married the aging Queen Elizabeth in 1982. It starred an all-female cast, and the image of the twenty-something star bound and dressed as Berlusconi in the rehearsals made Eddie crack up every time he saw it. Twice last week he'd woken from sleep laughing about it, rousing Bob at the same time.

To stage right, Bob had sprayed the spatter from his oil paint all over the mat they'd laid down over the entire stage. There was a metal spiral at his feet between the legs of the easel that he used to beat the excess paint off of his brush when he was done with a colour for the moment. His palate was held out in front of him with a steady left hand, always at his side. It was a large circular piece of Plexiglas, its translucence worn away from years of use and scrapes with his knife. The knife sat on the tray of the easel now, one side of it caked in the adobe red he'd created.

He was painting the red brick walls of the ally he'd seen the other day with Sloan while having a cigarette. The buildings arose out of nothing, over the fog and ether of the smog and continued up past where the eye could wander. With great effort, he had used the edge of his knife to shift the paint on the lower halves of the tenement buildings back and forth until it had the same wavy, hot appearance it had had that day. Now he painted frantically, adding 'street art' to the red bricks of the buildings to give the impression of an elderly couple dancing, their legs blurred by the same waves of heat.

Sloan leaned back as far as she could, until she could see over Bob's shoulder. "Nice," she said, crunching on an almond. "Alley outside The Menagerie?"

Bob nodded, a motion barely perceptible from Sloan's point-of-view.

"The window on the right building looks amazing. It's like a photograph of the real thing."

Bob smirked. "Thanks," he said, turning toward her slightly, but not enough to even see her. He was working quickly, trying to get enough of the paint down before it started to dry. This was the hectic nature of wet-on-wet, and it was what made him not understand how others found it so relaxing. For him it was stressful, but a good kind of stressful: the type that amazing art was born from. He entered the first stroke tentatively, and by the third he had worked himself into a fury. Each painting was like a baptism through fire, and the image that came out the other side was better having survived the warzone of its creation.

Eddie turned to watch Bob for a moment. Bob had paint in his thinning hair, Eddie had paint on his cheek. Bob's energy of activity made him smile: there was something about him in the zone of creation, although it appeared so stressful, that brought a kind of serene calm to him. He took a deep breath, and then turned back to the leisurely pace with which he painted on the white base of Buckingham Palace. "You know Allie went home with that girl from the Fall Festival, right?" he said, absently.

Sloan's head whipped around so fast that her ponytail shifted its precarious placement. "Pardon?"

Eddie smiled. "Yea she went back with her and they spent the weekend together upstate."

"Poor Martin."

"Oh, Martin knows."

Sloan started to raise her eyebrow, then caught herself and laughed, shaking her head with bemusement. "Only Martin could justify staying with a girl that so clearly has no interest in him."

"You know they haven't been together in a year?" He bent down and got his drink cup and slurped through the straw.

"For real?"

"What I heard."

"Man."

"What I heard."

Bob pushed the canvas gently with one finger and let it crash to the floor, making the other two jump.

"What the heck?" Eddie asked without accusation.

Bob looked down at the piece which had landed upright and looked up from the dirty sheet at him. "It won't come out right. The couple... they look like marionettes."

"I thought that was intentional," Sloan smirked, playing with her own hair. "It's what I like about it."

"It wasn't."

"I swear I can see the strings, and their little joints where the pins get stuck like in the Robaxacet commercials."

"It wasn't though."

"Sloan," Eddie coughed, stepping away from his work. He passed the distance between stage left and stage right until he was just a foot from Bob, where he stopped suddenly as if Bob had a shield around him. He waited there as Bob took several deep breaths, his back and shoulders rising and falling, then stepped forward and put a firm, gentle hand on his neck.

Bob stirred briefly, twitching. Eddie kept his hand where it was, and eventually Bob brought his own hand to it and clasped it, giving it a tight squeeze.

Sloan arose; distressing the cloth at her feet until it inadvertently looked like an eggshell had risen in the center of the stage. She stepped lightly on her toes like a ballet dancer, her hair falling against her shoulder wildly until she'd found her way around Bob and Eddie, to where the picture lay. She picked it up gently by the dry canvas on one side and turned it until it was right-side-up, regarding it with a clenched brow and strumming her finger against her upper lip.

"It's a good painting," Eddie said finally, tapping the heel of his hand against the nape of Bob's neck.

Bob huffed through his nostrils, then calmed, massaging Eddie's hand with his own and leaning his head back. "It's not good enough. It looks like an assembly-line painting."

Eddie smirked. "Maybe that's why I like it. They're all the rage back home."

Bob rolled his eyes, but laid his head on Eddie's hand.

Sloan continued pressing her lips between her index and middle fingers. Her eyes moved from one part of the painting to another, finding each new element organically and lingering there. "It really is good," she said, mostly to herself. Her voice was far more critical than it typically was: there was no padding to her comments but no barbs either. The free-spirit had gone for a moment, to be replaced by the traditionalist buried deep within. "The brushwork is immaculate. The bricks are porous and catch the light correctly... it looks like you could step into it."

Bob turned and smiled at her. "Thanks, really. But it's not good enough." He reached for it and Sloan pulled it back. She withdrew a spray-paint can from her cargo pants and held it outstretched towards him like a weapon.

"Back!" she yelled, laughing. "Thou hast assaulted this maiden before! Not again!"

Eddie laughed as Sloan started to back up, spidery legs walking back towards the center of the stage while pinning the painting to her chest and keeping the spray-can aimed in Bob's general direction. When she was back to the eggshell rose she'd created, she stopped and pulled back the painting, checking it quickly to make sure she hadn't damaged it.

Bob looked at her, sighed, then started to laugh despite himself.

"You can have it back when you're in your right mind, and not before!" she said, thrusting her fist into the air when she said *and not before,* and yelling as though she were at a pro-choice rally. She tucked the painting under her arm guardedly. She looked like a cartoon character, her hair moving as though independent of the rest of her, her motions translating to it until long after she stopped.

Bob smirked, and then shook his head. He set up a new canvas on his easel, but after several minutes of staring at it, he moved to stage left to help Eddie, and did not start a new piece.

CHAPTER SEVEN

Frederick Cooper put the last of the tiny artisan chocolate Mona Lisas into their cardboard cradle, fastening the plastic crate that held them closed. The cooler had already been filled with carbonated drinks—there had been more Mountain Dew than he'd expected to be gone this week for some reason—and the gelatin-based candy packets had been topped up. Maps and pamphlets had been placed correctly and a bin of assorted brand-name chocolate bars had been topped up to its fill-line. The postcard rack had been filled and rotated. The ice-cream cooler had had its old stock rotated out and the new rotated in. He straightened the last of the stubborn Mona Lisa chocolates and then stood with his hands on his hips, surveying the gift shop in the glow of twilight until satisfied that he was done. He nodded once to himself, twitched his bushy white mustache, then picked up the remainder of his supplies and left the gift shop for Bob to contend with in the morning.

Frederick had lived on Jacobi Street for almost forty years, and for most of that time he had run Cooper's General Market. It hadn't always been *called* Cooper's General Market, but it had always been there in one form or another. For the first ten years he'd owned it it had been Davidson's General Store, a testament to his father-in-law from whom he'd inherited the business. After enough people had told him he'd honoured the man for long enough it had become Cooper's General Store for twenty years, until he saw the changes in the buying habits of those that lived on the street (and indeed, even in himself) and decided to make the change to Cooper's General Market. There was something about saying "I'm going to the market" that his clientele found cathartic when contrasted with "going to the store," and he found that he liked the way it rolled off the tongue as well. He sold seeds and artisan goods and unpasteurized pickles. He sold blankets made from wool from cruelty-free farms upstate that were hand-woven by local working mothers, bought and sold at living wages. He had embraced the sustainable market wholly and found that while he'd never felt bad about himself before, he felt good about himself now. His wife however had loved the change, embracing it fully and doing much of the product research herself. It was she that had struck the deal with The Menagerie, making sure to keep the highest-selling candy items available in The Menagerie and out of the Market's shelves to make sure they maximized profit without compromising what they held in their space.

The hallways of The Menagerie were long and dark in the evening. Sunlight was damaging to most paintings so there was very little natural light allowed in. When the running-lights were brought down and only the sleepy blue emergency lights were left, the halls had an impression of being permanently shadowed.

Frederick stepped down the dark second-floor hall now, unwrapping one of the chocolates absently as he did. He brought its milk chocolate head to his mouth and took a bite. The echo of his footfalls bounced and reverberated off the walls before finding their way back to his ears, the sound foreign to him by the time they did. Each footstep sounded like three in the cool light. The lights placement was such that the shadows cast on the paintings by the frames made each painting seem like a pitch black canvas.

They weren't though. As Frederick passed each one, he saw details come into view, muddied through the fog of his poor vision in the evening, but there all the same. The harsh whites of the Corben illustrations came out even clearer now, the pale nude women in it shining like beacons in a sea of shadows. The black hood of the executioner sunk into the blackness surrounding it, giving the eye and mouth holes a skeletal appearance.

This had been the true perk of doing business with The Menagerie, Frederick had long thought. Not getting the carbonated beverages and gelatin off his shelves while still making money off them, not expanding his shelf space without having to pay for more real estate, this: for a brief period of time once a week, once he was done filling the stock, he had The Menagerie all to himself: his own private art gallery. What was more, he had it as nobody else in the world could have it; for the paintings were one thing in the day and quite another when under the veil of shadow. If anyone needed any proof of that, he referred them to play with the brightness and contrast on any photo they owned digitally and note the results.

He'd learned that Jackson Pollock was haunting in shadow, those bright oranges and yellows becoming eerily still. If colours could lie in wait for you to look away, that was what these colours did. The yellow hung back between the red and the orange, thinking it was camouflaged, like a predator convinced you cannot see it. Either action: proving you know it's there, or turning away, could prove fatal. He'd learned that Boone sometimes used fluorescent paints to change her images, making them mirrors of themselves when viewed in the dark. He'd never seen that in any of the literature he'd tried to find on her, and had decided to keep it his secret, something intimate that only he and the artist knew.

That was the truest word for this feeling: *intimacy*. He knew the paintings the way no-one else did, for he knew them as they looked at night when no-one else was around. To see someone in the dark, bathed in the blue light that was all-too like that of the moon was to know them in their flesh alone, to see them vulnerable, their secrets laid bare. When he had these paintings alone for a few minutes each week, they were his. He had never once contemplated cheating on his wife, seeing The Menagerie at night was as close as he'd ever gotten.

At the end of the hall there was one light still on, spotlighting the portrait oil of the theatre and casting black shadows on all the paintings around it. Frederick stopped and tilted his head at the piece, brushed the last of the chocolate from his nose, then stepped closer to examine it.

Nine figures sat in the seats of an old theatre. They were arranged in a way that was seemingly random at first, and Fredrick was sure it was meant to seem as though they were random, but thought they must have been arranged to say something by the artist.

Seated the furthest back were a Knight and two women, each of the females sitting behind and to either side of the Knight.

The Knight was wearing chainmail and clasped a sword, the hilt of which was gripped at his central plexus, the blade disappearing into the chair below him. He was square-jawed with pronounced cheekbones, and long blonde hair that came down in front of his eyes as far as his nose. His head was tilted upward and his mouth was not quite straight, giving the appearance of a sneer or a half-opened yell.

His eyes were almost invisible under that mop of sweaty blonde. They each appeared as large white splotches, almost too big for the rest of the features of the face.

Fredrick stared at the man made of oil and lead for a moment, then pulled his eyes away with some effort, swallowing hard.

The woman on the left wore a low-cut blouse and looked like the prototypical barmaid, of the type one was likely to see during Oktoberfest. Her body was leaning against the seat in front of her, showing off her ample bosom, leaning both toward the viewer and the Knight. Her face was turned away though, back towards the black in the back of the theatre, exposing the nape of her slender, supple neck.

The woman on the right side of the Knight appeared to be a nurse. She wore a small paper hat with a cross indicated on it in a shade just off from the rest of the hat. Her hands were in her lap and her body positioned forward, but she was turning back as if caught in mid-motion looking at the shadows behind her.

Fredrick bent closer, his nose almost touching the canvas.

In the dark blues and blacks that made up the vanishing point of the back of the theatre were a series of several small, purple swivels and one large S-shaped line. The swivels looked like something out of a Van Gogh: several small brushstrokes making something whole when viewed together. The small strokes were grouped below the large, slanted S-shape, contained by it.

Fredrick squinted.

Above the swivels were two deep red dots, almost so faint they weren't visible.

CHAPTER EIGHT

The static hiss of Sloan's paint-can filled the alley behind the theatre, along with the antiseptic stench of aerosol paint. She moved her hand back

and forth in precise motions, pasting the stencilled outline of Barak Obama
to the granite accent with bright blue paint until it was impossible to tell
one from the other. She missed a large triangular section jutting in from the
left side into Obama's suit.

"You missed a spot," Bob said from his vantage point over Sloan's
shoulder. He was pinching his nose to dissuade any fumes from the spray
can. It made his voice higher and more nasal than usual. In his opposite
hand he held two more of Sloan's stencils, rolled up and tucked under his
arm.

Sloan shrugged, not bothering to move the millimeter it would take to
aim her spray-can at the void dagger currently stabbing into the heart of the
forty-fourth President.

Bob twitched, shifting from foot to foot.

Sloan wiped some of the sweat from her brow, leaving a small trace
of paint between her eyebrows. Her hair was wild. She had taken it down
before dragging Bob outside the theatre with three of her stencils in tow. It
had stayed mostly in place on the left side of her head for a few minutes,
held together by some magic or (more likely) clumped together with paint,
but it fell apart when a gust of wind had touched it and was now all around
her like a lion's mane. She kept forcing it out of her line of sight, pushing it
this way and that, never forcing it into the same position twice.

She caught him twitching out of the corner of her eye, moved her can to
far east, and pressed the trigger. A line of blue paint not congruous with the
rest of the picture appeared, jutting out from where Obama's raised middle
finger would eventually be.

Bob huffed under his breath.

Sloan smiled. "What was up with the painting in there anyway?" she
asked. She shoved the blue can into her cargo pants, still oozing paint, and
withdrew the hot pink.

"What do you mean?"

She smirked and hunched her shoulders. When she spoke her voice
was artificially deep and had an accent like a cave-man. She was doing an
impression of Bob that was actually just an impression of all men in general: "Not good enough. Not good enough."

Bob lowered his eyebrows. "Droll."

"Thanks," Sloan smiled, making several calculated lines with the pink
paint that would, when done, be the shadows on Obama's face and tie.

Bob watched her, knowing that right now it looked like a blue rectangle
(with too little paint in a triangle on one end, and too much in a phallus on
the other) with a few lines of hot pink spattered on, but that soon when
she peeled away her original stencil it would transform into a recognizable
representation of Barack Obama, giving the finger with a stern, paternally

disapproving face.

"Well?" she asked, making one last mark with the pink before shoving it away and bringing out a can of deep black, almost the colour of India Ink. The pocket she took it from had a large sticky blotch of it along the bottom.

Bob twitched, then frowned, his ears moving along with his lower lip. "The painting was fine I guess. It was just too cartoony. It wasn't good enough for the gallery... for Chelsea."

Sloan looked at him for a long moment, then shook her head and turned back to her art, making several small, precise lines deftly to accent the President's features. "Bad reason to do art," she said finally, and not without a modicum of judgement.

She grasped the stencil by a corner she'd deliberately left loose and peeled it away in one quick motion, the excess paint falling away to reveal Barack Obama giving the finger to any who passed by. She'd drawn sunglasses on him with the black can at the last moment, leaving gaps in the frame to show through the pink paint, giving the impression that they were actually reflecting something pink in front of him.

Bob smiled.

"You like?" Sloan asked, wadding up the stencil for disposal. "I call this variation, *Cool Obama Don't Give a Shit*."

"You've been watching too much Randall."

She laughed. She turned and looked at it for a moment, watching as some of the paint from the sunglasses ran and dripped down Obama's face, a periodic consequence of doing spray-paint wet-on-wet. She ran her fingers back through her hair, not out of frustration, but because she loved the feeling of her nails on her scalp. "You know there's the Print Shop over on Anderson that has this great wall... great wall, adobe and shale base, all the street artists that know about it use it. It drives the owner nuts, he goes out every morning with a can of pressurized water to beat it all off. But the wall faces the morning traffic and catches the light just right, so it's almost worth it: you've gotta be quick. You've gotta get your thing up there in the night and know that by eleven AM the owner is gonna have it down, but you'll definitely get seen by that seven-to-eleven traffic so it's almost worth it. Anyway, I put *Where Are the Ponies* there and I liked the way it looked even though it ended up in a puddle at the guy's feet a few hours later, so when I did *Revenge of the Nerds* with that Sheldon guy as the nerd standing on Bush's head I put it up there too. Eleven AM, down it comes. I spray it on, he sprays it off, circle of life."

Bob nodded. "There a point to this?"

"Sure is. So I do three more pieces there: I do *Fuck Jonas* and *Why Stop Dreaming Just Because You Wake* and *Print is Dead*. I skipped the *Fuck for*

Chastity pastiche because I think I remember someone telling me the guy's brother lost a leg overseas and I didn't want to be a dick."

"Big of you."

"Yeah. So I stuck around at the coffee shop across the road after I do *Print is Dead* and get a scone and a red eye, and as the sun comes up and people start to walk back and forth I see people start to notice the piece. I don't usually stick around to see people see it. It was the one with Rupert Murdock with the little black Charlie Chaplin 'stache."

Bob lowered his eyebrows. "Chaplin. Right."

Sloan laughed. "So these people start to look and they point and they start to talk. Some of them take pictures of it: I guess they know it'll be gone before too long, so if they want one they'd better take it now. I see a lot of people taking pictures, and I noticed a few of them show up on those 'Street Art' apps, with the location tags? Well, the owner must have noticed too, because when I came back to do *You Are What You Eat* last month, it wasn't gone. The guy had framed it, with glass and everything so that nobody else could go over it. There was this little engraving on the bottom edge of the frame: art by Sloan. They'd even tried to do my name like my signature, they screwed the N though."

Bob nodded, his brow furrowed. When she held out her hand for the stencils he handed them to her. "I suppose I'm supposed to get some kind of message from this? Do the art you want and the recognition will come?"

Sloan smirked. "I broke the glass and spray painted over *Print is Dead* in deep black. I don't think I'll go back there again, fucker can keep his nice wall. I kept the engraving though: pried it off and stuck it to my headboard. It trips the shit out of guys I have over when they notice it."

Bob paused in mid-step, shaking his head. "Why?"

"Because they're about to cum and I'm sucking on their neck, and all of a sudden they look up and see 'Art by Sloan' there with my signature on it. It's funny as shit."

"No, I mean—"

"I know what you meant," she smiled. "Because the moral of the story is: fuck recognition. The art is the art, and if I'd wanted it in a frame I would have painted it on a canvas."

They walked to the apartment tenement across the street and Sloan started pasting up her next stencil.

CHAPTER NINE

Fredrick Cooper hadn't been home in three days. His wife had tried to call the police for the first time on the first evening, when he'd been too late coming home from The Menagerie, but they'd told her that he'd have to be missing for at least twenty-four hours before they'd open a case file. At the end of the second day they had, in fact, opened a case file and found that Chelsea had already prepared the relevant security camera footage into a DVD for them: most of the cameras inside The Menagerie were dummies, with only a few protecting the entrance and some of the more expensive pieces. The footage showed Mr. Cooper finishing up for the evening in the gift shop and then turning to go through the halls, which Chelsea told the officers was common and not a problem, and his wife confirmed. Several shots taken from cameras targeting prominent pieces showed Mr. Cooper, either in shadow or in partial, passing by them. There was no footage of his leaving The Menagerie, but Chelsea assured the officers that she'd looked high and low for him, and that he must have left through the back exit.

The entire next day there had been no sign of him, nor had there been today. It was past the forty-eight hour mark when things were the most likely to turn up, and some people had already begun to assume that poor, sweet Fredrick Cooper had been the victim of a mugging gone wrong and were just waiting for someone to discover the body in some obvious-yet-overlooked corner of Jacobi Street.

Bob stared at the MISSING poster that Chelsea had put up on the sliding glass door of the Gift Shop, right at eye-level where people could see it. Usually there were several posters there, advertising upcoming exhibits or local shows on The Street or future events, but Chelsea had removed them all so that nothing could detract from the photo of Fredrick Cooper, cropped from a family photo taken while on vacation in Hawaii last summer. She'd printed it on high-quality paper in bright true-life colour, the pinks and blues of the festive tee he'd been wearing showing against the bright blue of the day. There was another version pasted to the front of the cash register, that one in black and white. She'd printed hundreds of those herself and had given them to Mrs Cooper, who had attempted to pay her for the printing cost and had been shooed away.

He picked up one of the small chocolate Mona Lisa dolls that Fredrick delivered every week, feeling the supple milk-chocolate body become pliable under the heat of his fingertips almost instantaneously. He reached into his pocket, produced two dollars, and then put it in the till without taking his change. He unwrapped the chocolate, cutting through the famous smile inadvertently, and ate the candy while staring out into the void space of the hallway.

"It's your break," Chelsea said as she stepped past his field of vision on her way to the drink cooler.

Bob straightened, startled. He should have heard her heels approaching all the way from her office, but he hadn't taken notice of her until he couldn't avoid her anymore.

She took a Mountain Dew from the cooler and pressed it against her brow, bosom, then back to her brow again before opening it. She took a long swig and motioned to him.

He took out a small booklet from under the cash, opened to a page with a green tab, and put a tick under 'Mountain Dew.' The page was headed 'Chelsea' and currently there were nine ticks under the heading Mountain Dew.

Once a quarter of the bottle was gone she gasped and released it from her lips. "Sorry," she said, wiping her lips. "I was out for a run this morning, took some of the posters with me. Did you put up any?"

"All around my building. I gave some to Sloan, she's going to take them when she goes out into the city and put them wherever she puts her art."

Chelsea nodded, then eyed the chocolate wrapper and the book.

Bob made the 'money' motion by rubbing his fingers together, nodding toward the register.

She nodded and took another gulp of her drink. "Go. It's your break."

He stepped out from behind the register and was about to walk past her, when he stopped himself. "Actually I was hoping we could talk again about maybe getting some of my stuff into the gallery."

She stopped on her way behind the cash to cover for him, turning back to him and looking him up and down.

"We said we'd talk about it on the tenth, but with the shipment and everything and getting in the new stock, we got distracted." *She* got distracted, he'd wanted to say, but restrained himself.

She took another, smaller, more contemplative sip of her drink, and then laid the bottle down on the glass postcard display. She paused to swallow, so long that she could have shot-gunned the entire bottle. "What do you have?"

He forced himself not to look hurt. She knew well and good what he had, had seen it multiple times. Had she forgotten or was this just a tactic to delay the conversation? The latter he suspected, but he couldn't back out now. "The cityscape landscape is still my best I think. There are a few good Natures and Still-Lifes I did while I was vacationing upstate. I've

done a few quick portraits of the old men playing chess down at the park...
I painted them but only in greys and blacks, so it's a painting that *looks* like
those charcoal sketches, kind of experimenting with mixed-medium, but
not really."

Chelsea nodded. "The cityscape has potential, and the men playing
chess. I can see that all in a line, you know?"

Bob nodded, smiling.

She took a sip of her drink again, swishing it back and forth between
her cheeks as she thought. "What's on the wall now is staying there for at
least thirty days, or at least until we find out what's up with that mystery
piece. I think I've still got some of your stuff on my phone. Tell you what,
go to your break and I'll think it over, but it'd be best to wait until the tenth
to talk to me, when we can actually do something about it."

His smile faded. He nodded again, then turned and made his way out
into the hall.

'The Tenth' was the death knell of anything happening with any acquisition at any time, whether Chelsea knew it or not and he suspected she did.
The tenth of every month was the arbitrary date which the previous curator
had decided that any changes to the lineup would happen: old works came
down and new works went up. It was chosen to coincide with the end of the
business month, and although Chelsea had changed *that* when she started,
the tenth had become recognized as the day when The Menagerie changed
its displays by the community and she had kept that the same.

No new works could be decided upon until the old works were taken
down... the problem was that by the time the new works had been taken
down, Chelsea had already toured the city and seen the new pieces she
wanted and hand-picked and ordered them: the wall-space a new artist
was to enquire about was already spoken for and as such was unavailable.

She'd taken in the Boones and the Pardys after an extended stay at a
bed and breakfast where a few of the pieces had hung. She'd seen a poster
with Corben's art on it advertising his appearance at a local comic-book
convention and had decided he would be perfect for her pop-art exhibit
without knowing much more about his work with *Heavy Metal* or anything
else about him: she saw something she liked out in the world and decided
she had to have it.

That was how Richard Corben, a wonderful artist to be sure but a glo-
rified funnybook painter to most who knew him, and a relative unknown
to the rest of the world at large, had gotten an all-but-in-name permanent
exhibit in the only art gallery on Jacobi Street while he still had yet to get a
single piece on the wall. Bob had considered running off some cheap prints
at Kinko's and pasting them around town in places he knew she frequent-
ed, perhaps advertising a fake convention, but had decided against it. For

one thing, the money spent on prints was better off spent on rent.

Even someone literally unknown, like O.K. Mal, had managed to get a piece in the gallery, simply by virtue of a shipping error.

Without being totally conscious of it, Bob had auto-piloted his way to the hall with the majority of the Corben's exhibited, including the one with the feminist executioner he enjoyed so much. He had already passed that piece though, and was almost binocularly presented with the piece by O.K. Mal that had been the subject of his ire just moments before. He stared at it, in its ornate but worn silver frame, the simple picture of an audience of nine and their interactions as some unseen play went on beyond the artist's point-of-view.

Ten.

There were ten people in the audience, he now realized. To the far right side of the third row, his shoulder partially obscured by the frame, was a gaunt man in a green apron. He was wearing a powder blue long-sleeve shirt underneath with one arm rolled up to reveal a thin, hairy arm. The brush-strokes on the arm-hairs were perfectly in sync with one another, and Bob wondered if Mal had used a single brush with most of the bristles taken out to achieve the affect. He'd done something similar when he'd done a portrait of Obi, to make sure all his hair was tossed to the side in unison.

The man's cheeks were gaunt and sallow, his skin so pale that one would be forgiven for thinking the artist had used the same colour for the man's hair as he had for his flesh, though Bob noted a slight tonal difference. His eyes were sunken and dark, turning back and to his right, the small bushy white mustache underneath looking as though the artist had caught it in mid-twitch.

Bob squinted, raising an eyebrow. There was something familiar about the mustache, though it was just a single white line under the hint of a nose the artist had given the figure. Had he seen a similar technique used before? Perhaps in one of the Hogarth's he suspected that Mal was, in some way, aping?

He leaned back out, adjusting his neck and frowning. He let his gaze follow that of the man in the green apron to see what had him so worried, finding that he, like the man in the wig, was throwing a concerned look at the African man several seats away.

Bob stopped, startled. He looked at the piece again, letting his eyes move from the pale man to the black man and back again. Eventually he held up his finger at eye-height to use as a makeshift level, making sure that both figures were in the same row, the third row back from the stage. The African man still looked out through the painting and into the reader with exhausted, bloodshot eyes, returning the gaze of neither man.

Hadn't the black man been alone in his row? Hadn't that been a part of his entire thesis as to why the work as a whole was some commentary on racial tension specifically and tension in society in general: that the rest of the theatre had been so troubled by the presence of this black man that they all turned and stared at him in horror and disgust, *without* anyone sitting in the same row as him, effectively segregating him?

He leaned back further, frowning, taking in the picture as a whole after having focussed in too close.

"Hey," Chelsea called from behind him. He had once again somehow ignored her heels. Although it hadn't startled him this time, he decided that it meant he needed more coffee. "Your break's over."

He nodded, but did not turn away from the piece. Eventually she made her way up alongside him, her heels clacking on the tile floor and echoing with every step along the way.

"Earth to Bob," she said, with some mix of humour and seriousness only possible by a boss who considered themselves 'the fun boss' in their own mind. "You're needed back at base, Bob."

"It's different," Bob said quietly, almost to himself. He motioned to the third row and cleared his throat, repeating himself. "The painting. It's different."

She snorted, glanced at the painting, then back at him. "Take a moment to get some coffee from Receiving before you go back, would you?"

"I'm serious."

She laughed again.

"Look," he huffed, digging into his pocket and producing his phone. He unlocked it and opened up his photo album, which brought up the latest picture taken: the shot of the art of O.K. Mal he'd taken to show Eddie the night he received it. He brought it to full screen and pinch-zoomed in to the third row, revealing the large dead-eyed black man... and the skinny, pale white man in the green apron several seats down from him.

He stared at the pixilated, poorly-lit image on his phone screen for a moment, then turned back to the painting, then back to the phone again.

"Get some coffee, Bob," Chelsea smiled, placing a hand on his shoulder. She stepped away from him and started walking down the stairs.

Bob continued to stare at the painting for a moment, his jaw slackened. Now that he looked at it as a whole he saw details in the shadows in the back of the theatre that he'd missed as well: the purple S-shaped brushstroke he'd seen before, but also several purple semi-circles of the same colour and two red splotches, where it looked as though Mal may have dripped some of the paint for the velvet curtains, and attempted to cover it up hastily with black.

CHAPTER TEN

Bob sat on the couch with his legs and feet spread out over it, almost lying down except for the haunch of his back and shoulders. He rested a large hardcover book against his stomach and read, his eyes darting back and forth in quick succession. The book was the deep maroon that it seemed like all hardcover texts from the 80s had to be by some unknown bylaw, the gold of the spine's text long since chipped away and the dust jacket misplaced. Wedged between the couch cushion and his side was his tablet, opened to a web browser and radiating heat. Next to the couch and within arm's reach were three more hardcover texts, which had been stacked haphazardly and were currently functioning as a coaster for Eddie's drink cup.

All four books were on art history, one of the few courses Bob had taken towards his major before realizing—thankfully before spending too much money—that one did not study art history to become an artist: one studied art history to become someone who looked at art and said 'Hmm.' The one currently resting on his stomach was titled *Hogarth and his Influence* by M.E. Way, who he had learned since was a female academic who'd shortened her name to initials as some women did to be taken seriously, but he still could not hear the voice in his head as anything other than a British man. He supposed that was a part of the same prejudicial system that had led to Way making the name change choice to begin with, but he considered it a benign sexism on his part. It was less, he thought, to do with systemic sexism and more to do with his long standing crush on Ian McKellen.

The other three books were *Art of the Seventeenth Century and Beyond*, *Sociology on Canvas*, and *Opera Houses of the World* by Thierry Beauvert, which he'd borrowed from the public library two streets up before coming home. It was the book that was now at the top of the pile, bearing the weight of Eddie's drink.

Eddie took a long, loud sip through the straw, laughed heartily at something on the television, then placed the cup back down on top of Beauvert's work.

Bob's gaze shifted from the page to the cup, then to the back of Eddie's head where he sat next to the couch. "If there's a stain on that book when I bring it back, I'm not going to be paying the fine," he said dryly.

Eddie nodded without turning away from his show. "Nor should you, fines are bullshit."

"What I mean is, you'll be the one paying the fine."

"Oh. I don't see that happening."

"Don't get anything on the book."

"I won't."

"It can come from more than a spill you know. Condensation can make a ring on the hardcover that you can't get out."

"I know."

Bob sighed, finally tearing his eyes back away from Eddie and continuing to read. Finding nothing on the page he was looking at he turned it, then two more, coming upon more text to scan through. Eddie reached up behind him and squeezed Bob's leg just above the knee, giving it two quick, gentle, affectionate tweaks before letting his arm fall back into place. As soon as he did he laughed at something on the screen again. Bob glanced up to see that it was a young man's head being bisected by a cleaver. He grimaced and turned back to his book.

Eddie loved horror movies. It was one of the few places where their interests divided and had never waxed or waned in the last eight years; Eddie's love never diminishing and Bob's revulsion never sating. There were a few other examples, such as Bob's love of brussels sprouts, his need to watch any movie starring Nicolas Cage, and his rubber band collection. Their shared bookshelf then was a study in contradictions, with the top shelf being regulated to books on art and the study of art, which was currently flopping to one side as it missed three volumes, and the bottom shelf being filled with classic monster movie DVD box sets like the Universal Horror set, classic novels, several hardback Stephen Kings, and many coffee-table books on the art and images of those early films. Once, as a gag gift for an anniversary, Chelsea had gotten them a book on the historical art of horror clichés. Eddie had loved it, Bob had ordered it wedged between two larger volumes as the cover itself had been enough to make his skin break out in gooseflesh.

Eddie had seen his first real horror movie when he had been just seven years old. He'd snuck in with his sister, Marlene, after they'd both paid the price of admission for a dime-a-dozen children's movie about sharing and working together, which had been nonsense kid's stuff to their jaded minds. Neither of them remembered what the movie was called or even much of the plot, but one scene stuck out in both their minds: a man entered an empty room and the camera panned around slowly, showing the entirety of the room before coming back to his face. Slowly and without him seeing, the door closed shut behind him to reveal an oozing old hag brandishing an axe. He'd never forgotten that tension and terror as the old woman slowly raised her implement without the protagonist's knowledge and without so much as a sound to warn him... Adding to the height of the terror in retrospect, was that the memory cut off before he could find out if the man made it out alive or not, probably because he'd ducked his head into his jacket at the last moment.

He wasn't even sure if Marlene truly even remembered that much of the film so much as she remembered him talking about it so many times over the years, as their memories started and stopped at the exact same frame. Whatever the case, the unnamed film had started them on a life-long journey towards cheap thrills and a love of horror. They saw every movie they could, renting and sneaking into theatres and staying up late to catch dirty horror B-movies on cable. Eventually the terror gave way to calm as the plots and jump-scares became more and more predictable and repetitive, and the props became more and more recognizable. Calm had given way to humour, the over-the-top kills being transformed into the punch-line of a twisted joke that the suspense was the set-up for. Every so often he and his sister, either in person or via Skype, would still sit and watch a horror movie together, seeking thrills but finding catharsis in the laughter instead.

Eddie wiped tears from his eyes as he laughed, the machete on the screen dripping corn-syrup blood in the center of the frame.

"What are you even watching?" Bob sneered, trying to keep his attention on the text but unable to completely.

"One of the Wrong Turn movies, I'm not sure which one," Eddie smiled, his laugh fading into a hum as he took another sip from his cola. He turned back to Bob, his grin so large it seemed to threaten to escape his broad face. "You?"

Bob turned his gaze on Eddie. The spine of the book he was reading, clearly imprinted with the name 'Hogarth' and the name of the author, stood between them. He waited a long moment to see if Eddie would pick up on this fact on his own. When either thorough ignorance or spite he did not, Bob replied: "It's a book on Hogarth."

Eddie smiled. It had been spite then, the sort of humour only he could get in asking something he already knew the answer to, just for the joy of having Bob answer it. Bob wasn't sure where the humour in that was, and in all these years Eddie had yet to adequately explain it to him. "He's the engraver right?"

"Among other things," Bob nodded. "I'm not looking for him though, I'm looking through the people that came after him. Someone he influenced."

"Who?"

"Not sure," Bob muttered, turning the page. "Remember that painting I sent you a pic of?"

"Oh, yeah," Eddie nodded. He paused a moment, the memory catching up to him. He turned and nodded more enthusiastically. "Oh yeah. Yeah, it was a little like his stuff. Kind of *Gin Lane* meets *The Analysis of Beauty*."

Bob shot him a wry look.

"I can know stuff."

Bob smiled. "So yeah, I'm thinking it was a contemporary of his, or someone aping him: your John Colliers, your Andrew Dykes. But for the life of me I can't find anything like the painting by this O.K. Mal guy in here anywhere, or any reference to him." He stopped himself, realizing that he had once again assumed that the abbreviated name was masculine instead of feminine, but then decided that for the purposes of his search it didn't matter.

"You try the web?"

Bob nodded toward the tablet, still wedged between his side and the couch cushion. He turned the page absently, no longer reading. After a moment longer he gave up, marked his place, then turned toward the screen. "What's the movie about?" he asked, his head on the heel of his hand.

Eddie raised an eyebrow but did not turn around. "A wrong turn."

"Yeah, but what's it about?"

"This isn't art history. It's a movie called Wrong Turn about yuppies who take a wrong turn and get killed. That's all."

Bob smiled. He reached down and picked up Eddie's cola, pretended to take a sip, then placed it down on the floor away from his books.

CHAPTER ELEVEN

Bob and Sloan sat cross-legged at the end of the second floor hallway, with several boxes of home-fries and burgers in front of them from LiLi's, a small take-out restaurant on the corner that did American food in Asian styles. The food had been served in the sort of square folding boxes one expected of Chinese food. They sat, mirrors of one another, and stared up at the painting of the theatre in front of them, sipping their colas in reverent silence.

The gallery had been closed for an hour. Chelsea was still in her office making calls about donations. They could hear her over the hum of the cooling fluorescent lights, the sound of her high-pitched voice refracting off the walls and making its way through the entire building. Sloan had come by just as Bob had been settling up his cash for the evening, with a hot turkey sandwich burger and a tofu express burger in each if their own individual boxes, with fries. The fries were the main attraction of any meal from LiLi's, as anyone on Jacobi Street knew. Sometimes if the wind was right you could smell them from one end of the street to the other, a fact which nobody ever complained about.

"The brush work is incredible," Sloan said, munching on her fries without taking her eyes off the painting. They both had to crane their heads up to see it, like people sitting in the very front row of a movie theatre. "Immaculate even."

Bob nodded. "You see what I mean though?"

"Mmm. Yes, definitely inspired by Hogarth. The way all the characters are interacting... it tells a story through caricature, and the story is different depending on which figure you start with and which you end with. But it's telling a story, like Hogarth. I'm surprised there's not a little yappy dog in there somewhere."

They both stared at it, spotlighted against the dark by its own light fixture.

"So if Hogarth died in 1764, this painting had to have come after, we're saying?" Bob asked, consulting the notes he'd taken on his phone.

"Oh, way after."

"Oh?"

"The theatre they're all in... it's based on the Salle des Capucines, or some derivation from it."

"You're sure?"

"Absolutely. I've been there, it's like it was plucked from my memory. And The Salle wasn't completed until 1875."

"So it's a turn-of-the-century artist aping Hogarth."

She ate another fry, this one dipped in mustard. "There were more than one."

Bob nodded curtly, returning to his notes.

Sloan stared at the piece, taking her hand out of her fries and resting them on her lap, as though without life. "What's that in the back?"

"Oy?"

"There's something in the shadows in the back of the theatre."

"Nn," Bob dismissed, waving his hand. "It's a trick of the brush. When you do wet-on-wet you mix many colours together to get black. Sometimes when it dries you'll see swirls of the colours in with it."

"He mixed purple to get the black then?"

"Stands to reason."

"There's no other purple in the piece."

Bob looked up at that. The curtains were red, the seats were red, the stage was lined with gold. The patrons wore pinks and blues and whites and blacks, but none of them wore a stitch of purple. He opened his mouth, searching the canvas, working his jaw open and shut several times before speaking. "It's the blue and the red. The dark red of the curtains mixed in with a dark blue, made the black more purple than black."

Sloan shook her head and pursed her lips, scanning the piece from side to side. "The Salle is in Paris. Are we thinking this was a French painter?"

Bob rubbed his chin. "How exact is the image?"

"Like I said, plucked from memory," she said, her voice haunted.

"If we're saying this was done prior to photography then he would have had to have been there. He would have had to have sat on the stage with his easel and looked out and sketched it and drawn it."

Sloan leaned in, holding her hand up above her eyes to block the glare off the frame.

"What?"

She frowned, hesitated, then pointed: "You've got this guy down in the lower left, he looks like he should be a member of the Whig Party. Then you got this woman in the fourth row," she moved her pointer finger to indicate, "Who dresses like it's the Roaring Twenties."

Bob raised an eyebrow. "How's that?"

Sloan smirked, cupping her own breasts and bouncing them for effect. "She doesn't have any of this. She looks like she's doing the breast-binding thing that was all the rage back then. Flat chests were in." They laughed. She moved her finger. "Just up from her you have the Knight, who looks—"

"Medieval."

"Appropriately, yah. And the woman in the top right looks like she stepped right off the battlefield during World War One. *Maybe* 1812, but the little square hat has me thinking World War One."

Bob checked something on his phone quickly. "There were some like that in 1812, but mostly it was bonnets."

Sloan tapped her head. "Not just a hat rack."

"I'd assumed the aerosol fumes had killed any functioning brain cells long ago."

She shot him a dry look, then motioned back to the painting. "Finally there's this guy in the front, wearing a green apron. He looks like your stereotypical grocer... the type that didn't really show up on the scene until the 40s or 50s, in *America*."

Bob had begun to jot some of this down into his notes app.

Sloan looked from one end of the painting to the other, then motioned with both hands to encapsulate it all. "It doesn't make any sense."

Bob counted off points on his fingers. "It's a wet-on-wet oil painting by a French painter in the style of an English engraver and using subjects from European and American iconography." He paused. "And it had to be painted in the 50s at the earliest, because it includes reference to the 50s. It's one thing to have a piece of art look back, quite another to have it look forward."

Sloan winced. "Could have fooled me. I thought it was older."

"Yeah..." Bob whispered, "Me too."

Sloan shrugged, popped the last of her fries in her mouth and started to get up. "Well, if it wasn't until the 50s than it wasn't painted at The Salle." Bob looked at her quizzically. "In name I mean. By that time it had been changed to The Palais Garnier."

CHAPTER TWELVE

There was one cheap pub on Jacobi Street, which also happened to be its only eat-in restaurant. *The Belle Verde* was a name that didn't make much sense to anyone on The Street, and that in itself had become a part of the joke and its charm. The rapid shift from English to French, and from French to Spanish, left most people blaming Gordon Bowker for the state of American language, and roughly translated to *The Lady Green* or *The Green Lady*. While most patrons observed that *The Green Lady* was the more likely of the two intended meanings, there were a scant few who insisted on calling it *The Lady Green*, often to results that they themselves found humorous.

Eddie Alvarez was one of those people.

"How are y'all doin' tonight?" asked the waiter, a twenty-something named Gradey who seemed to be in a perpetual state of being in mid-grin. His lips had the sort of natural pinkish hue that most beauticians would kill to be able to reproduce, with a complexion always clear and radiant, his eyes always deep water blue. He only said colloquialisms like "y'all" when first greeting someone who walked into the restaurant: at all other times, he spoke in a perfect television-trained American accent.

"I'm feeling a bit peckish myself," Eddie said with a wry grin. Even as he said the set up, Bob's head fell into his hand and he rubbed the bridge of his nose. "I'm so hungry I could even go for a munch at the lady green!"

Sloan said a single 'ha' and Gradey laughed with that polite, bottled laughter that only those in the service industry can truly ever master.

Eddie had had two lagers at Sloan's before they'd decided to go out, and was feeling a bit loose. He walked between Bob and Sloan as Gradey showed them to their booth. He turned to Bob conspiratorially, speaking in a stage whisper: "First time for everything, hey?"

This time Bob did chuckle, more at the ludicrousness of his partner than the quality of the joke. "Stop it," he laughed, finding his seat. "Just stop. I can't handle you until I've had some carbs."

The restaurant, like most of the buildings on Jacobi Street, had been transformed from the conjoined tenements and low-income homes of years past through a gradual process of evolution, each likely starting as a home business and slowly becoming more a business than a home, until finally someone applied to have the lot re-zoned and the city tried to say "you can't put a business there" to which the owners and community likely said "you can't take that business away, it's been there for twenty years." It was the "easier to ask forgiveness than permission" style of business management, and in large cities it too often worked.

The building was one of the few on Jacobi Street which was *not* duel-zoned and did *not* have a living quarters on its second story. The second story was taken up by the kitchen and manager's office, and a small break room. Although the building seemed small from the front – barely fifteen feet across – it stretched far back past the property lines of its adjacent neighbours, interrupting the small alley that existed behind most of the buildings and stretching out until it met 14th Street. It had its own, rarely-used entrance on 14th Street, which was how most people discovered that Jacobi Street even existed: "Let's go out the back way... hey, did you know there's a whole different street back here?"

The majority of the restaurant's seating were booths that lined every wall. The bar was in the middle like an island and there were stools surrounding it and, while there were a few high tables scattered around, nobody wanted to be the unlucky soul who came late on a busy night and had to sit at them, with servers pushing back and forth and patrons heading to and from the bathroom or to get drinks. The booths were the way to go, with Bob and Sloan's favorite booth being dead center on the right wall. Eddie was ambivalent towards the choice in booth, and was more apt to weigh in on the choice of tequila on the rare night he felt the need to attend.

All the colours of the bar were maroon red and a woodsy brown, with the occasional mustard-yellow thrown in for flourish. There was something calming about those colours: not bright and exciting like primary tones, but subdued and earthy. A forest-green wouldn't have been out of place here, although it hadn't yet appeared. Bob had painted it once and had added in a small tree in the corner next to the men's room, and had decided that it looked good there. The owner had yet to take him up on his suggestion.

"What can I get you guys tonight?" Gradey asked, the 'y'all' conspicuously absent from his speech. He was Southern exclusively in greetings.

Neither of the three had to look at the menu. "Vegan Medley," said Sloan, taking off her coat and loosening her hair. "Fish," said Eddie, with a deep breath. "Like a lot of fish. Whatever the biggest fish you have is. You don't even need to put it on a plate, just throw it at me." The only fish they served was bass, and all parties already knew that.

"We'll manage to get it to you on a plate, I'm sure," Gradey smiled politely, writing down 'fish' in large block letters on his pad just as Eddie had said it.

"The Buddy Burger," Bob finished, handing Gradey the unused menus. "Hold the lettuce, regular onions instead of red onions, add chipotle mayo and extra mustard."

"Coming right up! Beers all around good?"

They all nodded, Eddie enthusiastically.

The Belle Verde was the sort of restaurant where beer, not water, was the assumed default drink of choice. The type of beer was never specified: it was assumed that the wait staff would bring whatever was local, artisan, and on-tap. If there came a time when for some reason that option was un-available, though it never had, Hennessy was an acceptable substitute.

The menu was pages upon pages long, the sort of thing that would make any professional chef tear out his hair in frustration. Flipping through its pages was an archeological dig into food trends: there was an entire page of carb-free pub grub like burgers without their buns, which some cleaver person had repurposed as an impromptu gluten-free menu two years ago, checking two fads at once. There was a gelatin dish with pimento olives and cheese that would have been at home at a dinner party in the 50s but had no place on the menu of a restaurant that hadn't even existed during that time period. There were deep-fried pizzas and deep fried meatballs, which had started as an experiment but had become a house staple, with one small meatball accompanying everything but the vegetarian dishes. There were salads and shrimp and shareable fondues: a dish, it seemed, for every man woman and child living on Jacobi Street. And in practice, that was true. Nobody that lived on The Street had had to look at the menu in years, and it was easy to spot a tourist by looking for someone with theirs open. Every-one had their dish, and it was most likely the same dish ordered time and time again. When it came to The Belle Verde, everyone on Jacobi Street was an irregular regular.

"That was quite an order," Sloan teased at Bob, battling with her hair elastic. "I'm surprised you didn't specify how the cow was fed."

Eddie snorted.

The beers were delivered. Bob took a swig that drained the neck of his bottle all at once, said *ah* satisfyingly, and then put the bottle down on the table. "Nothing wrong with knowing what you want."

Sloan hadn't noticed. She looked as though she were doing a complex mathematical equation in her head, her fingers twitching as she counted items off. When it looked as though she was done she twitched, making sure, then turned to Bob and squinted. "A Buddy Burger with chipotle may-onnaise, extra mustard, regular onions, and no lettuce or red onions?"

Bob stared at her for a long moment. "Yeah?"

"That's a Southern Belle Burger, just with a little extra mustard. Why not just order that?"

"Because I didn't want a Southern Belle Burger," he replied in a matter-of-fact tone. "I wanted a Buddy Burger."

Eddie and Sloan both laughed, Sloan hiding her eyes behind her palm as she did so.

By the time the food arrived, Bob and Sloan were almost done their beers and Eddie had been long finished his, and so Gradey returned not long after with three more. It was good food, the type that could only be gotten at a local, non-chain, mom-and-pop style eatery close to where you lived. In many ways *The Belle Verde* was less a restaurant than it was a kitchen for the entire community; a place where the family could meet as a whole before heading out to their lives, with the assurance that they would meet back there again at the end of the day.

The patty on Bob's burger was almost three inches thick and the sort of juicy moist meat that was just the right shade of brown to be appetizing. The tomatoes they put on the Buddy Burger were fried before they were added, crunchy and crisp on the outside and warm and soft on the inside. It was the majority of the reason he got it sans lettuce: so that the greens would not detract from the crunch of the tomato's flesh. The chipotle sauce was spicy and succulent when mixed with the tangy dill mustard, the only kind that the cook employed. Both sauces soaked into the grilled poppy-seed bun they made special three blocks over, packed with so many seeds it would likely have registered on a drug test. Bob's eyes fluttered every time he took a bite of it, having to open his mouth so wide it aggravated his TMJ every time, but he didn't care.

Eddie's bass was served whole in a bed of strawberry-spinach salad. He'd only been at *The Belle Verde* once when it had not been served whole, the first time, and when he'd been asked how he had enjoyed his meal he had complemented them, but said: "It's just hard to get used to not eating it whole, like my mother cooked it." Since then Eddie had always gotten his bass whole without asking. He had inquired about this once, and was assured that 'the first time had been an aberration.' There were candied lemon slices in a line along the bass' plump body, the slit from gill to tail exposing the soft pink meat inside stuffed with a thin line of pico. He ate it slowly and reverently, taking a small bit of bass away with his fork and knife, pairing it with spinach or strawberry, and then repeating. He had two beers while he ate, taking the time to enjoy every morsel as the restaurant became more and more alive around him.

The Vegan Medley was a Vegetarian burger patty prepared and served as a part of a salad with cucumber, large tomato chunks, soy bacon, crisp lettuce, and black olives. The entire bowl was drizzled in sweet chili sauce and seasoned with lime, which Sloan gleefully added to her second beer when it was delivered. She ate each bite humming, her smile so infectious that everyone that passed her table said hello to her. Half way through the plate she became so relaxed that she had to loosen her hair even more.

A guitarist had started to play, sitting on a high chair below a lone spotlight in the far corner. He wore an auburn toque and large thick glasses that covered half his face, with stringy hair covering the other half. Only his large nose, bigger on him than his face or body would have implied, stuck out. He played soft jazzy guitar riffs with a Latin-American spin that made Eddie clap at one point. One song flowed seamlessly into the next, and the only way one could be totally sure they were actually different melodys was that some had lyrics and some did not. Those that had lyrics were kept simple, just one or two phrases repeated, often in French.

When the trio had finished their main meals and were eating the waffle fries that Gradey had placed in a large bowl between them, Emilio came in. Sloan called his name with a smile that was uncommonly wide even for her, and got up from her seat to give him a hug. He had hugged her back with equal enthusiasm, picking her off the floor slightly as he did. He'd talked for a minute about Fredrick Cooper and his wife. He'd asked Eddie how things were at the theatre and had taken the time to shake Bob's hand he hadn't seen him in so long. He'd come to play a hand drum for the last half of the guitarist's set, and when Eddie turned around to watch, he was shocked to see that the place had become full of life.

Obi had come in just after ten and Sloan borrowed another patron's hat and used it to collect small donations from the crowd to buy him a hearty meal. Gradey took the money even though it wasn't enough even with a major contribution from Eddie and Bob but served Obi anyway—they typically did. He was served a single beer and a Buddy Burger with two patties and a seemingly endless amount of waffle fries.

After her fourth beer Sloan had discovered that, underneath the removable glass top, the table for the booth was solid wood. Without asking, she had handed Bob and Eddie their drinks and had removed the glass covering with the rubber feet, and had begun using a small knife to etch a design into the table's surface. It was a collage of small images cascading and swirling out from a larger image in the center, a cartoonish representation of a French waiter, cross-hatching on his nose indicating an alcoholic's bulge. Eddie laughed when he saw it, and the faux Captain America shield just up from it, with a beer in its center replacing the star.

After his fifth beer and the third time Gradey had come around to fill their basket of waffle fries, Bob had begun to laugh. Not the practiced, polite laugh that he had honed for use on patrons who thought they were funny, but his real laugh: a loud, rattling, nasal snark that sounded like a machinegun blast. Eddie had just made some snide comment at his brother's expense and, unexpectedly, Bob had let out a long "Heh-hehehehe-hehehehehehe" that in turn made the entire crowd laugh, although they hadn't heard the joke that had set it off.

That was the unspoken signal for when it was time to leave. They slowly made their way from the table (Sloan replacing the glass cover over her masterpiece) and settled their tabs.

They walked Sloan home despite her protestations and then Eddie and Bob walked home themselves. By the time they arrived, the last of the alcohol had set in, and Bob was thoroughly drunk. Eddie helped him out of his clothes and into bed, somehow miraculously still sober himself despite imbibing more, and the both of them settled in for a restful, peaceful, at ease slumber.

CHAPTER THIRTEEN

When Bob was in college, he'd written an essay about Munch's *The Scream*, which had included the phrase 'uncommonly deceptive.'

"The work," he had written, "Is uncommonly deceptive in its popular consensus in popular consciousness. The public at large believe they know what *The Scream* is about and what disturbs them about it: the balding, misshapen and incongruent head of the screamer, his skin the same pallid yellow as my own, staring out into the viewer is long thought to be the focus of the anxiety. This could not be further from the truth. We do not fear the screamer; we fear what we see in him, for we see ourselves.

"Of the twentieth century authors, only Phillip K. Dick seems to understand this, when he writes of the painting: 'The painting showed a hairless, oppressed creature with a head like an inverted pear, its hands clapped in horror to its ears, its mouth open in a vast soundless scream. Twisted ripples of the creature's torment, echoes of its cry, flooded out into the air surrounding it; the man or woman, whichever it was, had become contained by its own howl.' The word to note, here, is *oppressed*. With this single word, Dick illustrates that what we fear in Edvard Munch's masterpiece is not the screamer himself, but those that chase him."

Bob had had nightmares about *The Scream* after first having been exposed to it as a child. To have called them nightmares would have been to dismiss them though, they had been more like full-blown night terrors, the sort of recurring torture that plays on the mind and stays with it, like Hag Dreams or dreams of the Man in Black. His parents had told people, repeatedly, that he'd been scared by the screamer, but they'd been wrong.

He hadn't then been able to articulate what he had thought Dick was implying so well, that the terror in *The Scream* did not come from the screamer... it was in fact a terror you shared with the screamer, for the two shadowy men behind it.

The Scream featured the titular screamer on a long bridge overlooking a calm lake near sundown. Behind him, always at or near the edge of the frame, were two men draped in shadow against the light of the setting sun. Both men wore tall hats, either cowboy hats or fedoras, and were walking toward the screamer.

They were The Oppressors, as Dick had so cleverly coined. They walked at a brisk pace, somehow keeping time with The Screamer despite the way he ran. If it hadn't been drawn in the 1890s, Bob would have sworn that it was a piece of Vietnam art: the yellow man screaming in terror from the Americans as they bore down on him, the cowboy hat and fedoras long-standing symbols of American masculinity.

The Oppressors were what scared him, not simply in the way they looked or what he felt they represented... but in how they *moved*.

There were five known pieces by Edvard Munch known as The Scream. There was an 1893 pastel on cardboard, possibly the earliest version, in which Munch was still mapping out the composition. There was the most famous, the 1893: oil, tempera and pastel on cardboard. There was the 1895 lithograph, of which only 45 prints existed. There was an 1895 pastel on cardboard, and finally the 1910 tempera on cardboard.

In almost all five works, The Screamer remained the same... while The Oppressors stepped forward.

They did not move in order. The frames may not have come to Munch that way, or he may not have drawn them in order. Or he may have, and not released them in order. It was impossible to know.

When Bob arranged the paintings, he placed the 1910 piece first. Here The Screamer was looking out at the viewer, his pupils blank in abject terror. The Oppressors are stepping in time with each other down the long hall of the bridge: high above the water below, The Screamer cannot turn left or right, he has only the option of outrunning The Oppressors. He is trapped.

Next came the 1893 oil, tempera, and pastel. In this piece The Screamer has started to turn. His pupils are visible now, and it is only through this that we know he is turning his head back toward The Oppressors, who are closer.

The lithograph was third. The Screamer's face is more defined here, as though he knows his fate. The Oppressors are farther back than before: perhaps The Screamer has picked up his pace?

The 1895 pastel on cardboard was the most disturbing, and still sent gooseflesh down Bob's spine when he thought of it: The Screamer's head was fully turned back toward the man following him now, and one man was closer than the other, leaning against the rail of the bridge. His hand was up contemplatively, as if he were resting on it or hiding his face... that was what Bob saw when he looked at the piece, which had once sold for over one hundred and twenty million dollars: that the man on the right had recognized that The Screamer had spotted him and tried to shield himself, to turn and look casual, and appear as though he were not in pursuit. The body language was too ridged though, and the second Oppressor just stared forward ever-the-more menacingly. It did not appear casual, it appeared haunting.

Still, it was not so haunting as the final image, the first drawn, the 1893 pastel on cardboard. The man who had leaned on the rail was closer now, having sped up. They were closing in on The Screamer, but the man to the left stayed behind... but The Screamer's eyes did not latch onto them now. Though he seemed to scream louder than ever, his pupils stared to the right, off the part of the bridge and the page we could never see.

"What," Bob had written, "Could possibly be there that was more terrifying than the two dark, shadowy men looming down on him over the course of five frames?"

CHAPTER FOURTEEN

Sloan looked up at the blank ream of paper before her, which hung from a hook in her living room. She could see the image that would soon be cut away from it even now, before she had made her first slice: just as sculptors claimed that the sculpture had always been in the stone, they had just removed the excess so that everyone else could see it, so too did she see the stencils that would eventually emerge from each new ream.

She made her first cut not thirty minutes after Bob and Eddie had dropped her off over her protests that Jacobi Street, despite its proximity to streets where it was not safe for a young woman to walk alone, was not 'one of *those*' streets.

She cut the pulp away again and again, making tiny slits and then pausing before making another, constantly in motion. She pruned and preened like a gardener, adjusting every fragment down to the smallest detail until it was absolutely perfect. She worked long into the night, until her stomach panged with hunger and the sweat that beaded off her brow had rolled down and soaked into the neck of her shirt. Until she expended the last heat of the summer in one glorious cut of ecstasy that came from her wrist and up her arm, and flicked through the blade with beautiful terror, making one last ripple across the night sky she'd made.

She stepped back and looked at her work: it was a high tower with pillars on a hill. She had no idea why she had carved it.

CHAPTER FIFTEEN

The precarious and teetering fire escape of The Menagerie rocked even under the scant weight of Obi Caste. He paused on the third rung from the top of the ladder, feeling it give slightly under his foot, then skipped it and made it the rest of the way up the ladder without incident. Even the stoop itself rocked back and forth slightly, shifting to and fro beneath his Doc Martins.

When he felt as though he were steady, he brushed his mop of green hair back out of his face. Sweat licked from the tips out toward the brick beneath. He smiled and took a deep, satisfied breath of the late night air. He wished he had a cigarette.

The brick buildings of the next street that surrounded The Menagerie rose up in the dim moonlight, towering over him like stern gargoyles. They leaned in and looked down on him, erect and phallic and strong. He winced and looked away. Although the night was hot with the last sweat of summer, he felt a chill rise through him as he pried open the warped steel back door of The Menagerie and disappeared within.

The hall that the back door opened into was stubby and wide, like a tunnel facing the wrong way. In the day, light from around the disfigured borders of the door kept the room in silhouette, but at night there was nothing. The room was as black as pitch, as though someone had placed a veil of thick velvet over Obi's eyes without his knowing. There was a mop and a small shelf he couldn't see on the wall next to him. He reached out and touched them both to make sure they were there. Once they had not been where he'd expected, and he'd tripped on them and badly hurt his foot. Secure in their position, he peeled away his jacket and lowered himself to the floor, curled into a small ball, placed his jacket under his head, and shut his eyes.

There were three places on Jacobi Street where Obi felt it was safe to spend the night. The Menagerie was not his first choice of the three: that was the small storage closet above The Soper Boutique. They sold scarves and some hand-crafted jewelry, but he'd never take anything. The building had once been a small hostel, and the owners had since piled the old un-used mattresses into a storage closet for a rainy day. Three perfectly good mattresses sat in the back storage closet, one atop the other, and on the rare instance that Obi could make it in to one, his back turned to gelatin upon touching that soft fabric, and he fell instantly to sleep.

A less favourable option, usually when it was raining and the ladder of The Menagerie fire escape was too treacherous to ascend, was the back porch of *The Belle Verde*, which was covered with a tarp on stormy nights and at least provided protection from the elements.

There was a homeless shelter on Eleventh Street, but he didn't feel safe there. It was run by evangelists, and he hadn't trusted evangelists since he had been twelve. There were transitional homes on D that had turned him away too often, and had made him feel like a louse. He wasn't a louse and he wasn't a thief. Nor was he a drug-addict or a pedophile, all of which their eyes had told Obi they thought he was.

The Menagerie was warm and quiet and nobody used the back hall due to the disrepair of the fire escape. He never took anything, nor would he ever, he simply needed a place to sleep. In the humid night air of the crowded room, sleep began to haze over Obadiah Caste's anxious mind.

Through that same foggy humidity, he heard the faint, watery sound of music beginning to play and opened his eyes.

It was a piano, of the type his father used to play when he'd gone on tour with a jazz troupe. They'd never gone outside The City, but there was a lot of money to be made circling the local bars and pubs and trendy spots at that time, if you knew how to play. And if there was one thing his father had known how to do; it was play.

The notes came in slow, haunting tones, one at a time and without trail-ing into the next, as though whoever was playing them was skillfully man-ning the instrument with one finger. They were high quarter notes that sounded as though they should have been played much faster. They should have been swift and playful, but had been slowed to the din of barely being heard.

Obi rose up onto his palms, his arms erect. "Hello?" There was no pause in the music, it neither increased nor decreased tempo. "Is someone there?"

He rose to his feet and listened, tilting his ear toward the unused hall-ways of the gallery. The sound rose for three notes and then fell one, then started again, over and over. A B C B, A B C B, timed with a low thromb travelling through it all that he hadn't heard while he had been lying down. It wasn't one-fingered playing after all, there were chords playing under-

neath it all. One two three, fall. One two three, fall. It played over and over
again, then suddenly rose higher for a moment in a small flourish, before
returning to its steady pace again.

It was in that moment that Obi knew he wasn't imagining things.

The sweat that had been on his forehead a moment ago rolled down his
neck and into his shirt, tickling the soft flesh it found there. He'd had hair
on his chest at one point, but it had fallen out. His green coif was pasted
to the right side of his head, his left devoid of anything but natural brown
stubble. His eyes bulged in the dark, unable to see anything. His pupils
were large, soaking in all of the light they could and still he was alone in
the pitch blackness of the closet. His world was void, all except that soft,
light music, sneaking in from under and around the corners of the door to
The Menagerie.

He swallowed hard, then reached out and turned the knob. He'd never
spun it before, but it moved freely. When the door was open even a crack,
the dull, shadowy light of the hallway cascaded into the closet and screamed
at his pupils harshly, but the sound of the piano was no clearer.

When his eyes adjusted, the brightness became the dark blue haze that
was The Menagerie hallway at night. Those dim lights looked so much like
moonlight – artificial moonlight, in a city that rarely saw the genuine moon
for the blazing sheen of neon and electricity. The turquoise light fell over
the tops of the picture-frames and turned them into Morse Code: glowing
dashes in the blackness of the night, interspersed with the small dots from
where the lights originated.

The door to the storage room closed suddenly, making Obi jump. He
turned back and tried the knob, making sure he wasn't trapped in the main
section of the gallery. Finding that he was good, he allowed himself a thankful sigh before turning back to the long hallway before him. In the low light
it seemed to go on forever, vanishing into the low-lit darkness just beyond
his vision. He took one cautious step forward, then another. On the third,
he noticed that the hard walls and floor of the gallery refracted the sound
of his steps back toward him: but not the piano. The piano came to him
whole, not distorted by bouncing off one wall and another before reaching
his ears.

He could hear now that every second note was two notes, played is
such quick succession that they had been almost indistinguishable from
one another from behind the heavy door to the closet. He stepped forward
slowly, straining his ears to hear, until he caught the far away caw of a baby
crying.

"Hello?" he called, his voice hoarse from too many nights spent on the
street. "Does someone need help?"

The music added the flourish that came every few notes on time, but did not respond. The baby either stopped crying, or couldn't be heard anymore.

"I was just trying to stay warm, but does someone need help?" he cried again. He could hear his own voice bouncing off the walls, echoing back at him, but the music still played as though it were coming from somewhere close by and devoid of distortion.

"Someone," came a voice from around the corner. It was gone as soon as Obi turned to it, the light just bright enough to convince him that whoever had spoken was not just beyond the power of his vision, hiding in the shadows. It had not been a voice like the voice of a child, it had been a man's voice: deep and guttural. It hadn't been the only word spoken either, just the only word that Obi had heard. The voice had faded in until those two syllables, and had then faded back out again, like a single line of a song heard while tuning a radio dial between stations.

Was there a radio on in Chelsea's office? Or a television? That might have been more reasonable at first, but the same melody—Russian, he thought, but couldn't be sure—had been playing for several minutes now without change.

Obi stepped with the sides of his feet, as he'd been taught while he had been in the service. Now his feet made less of a sound as he turned another corner, keeping his back as close to the wall as he could without disturbing the paintings. There was someone else here, likely more than one person. He wasn't one to judge, he shouldn't be here either, but what if they were doing something they shouldn't? A fire on Jacobi Street could take the whole street down to ash; the houses were so close together.

"Run," came another voice, this one had an odd accent. Not American, though not Russian either. It was something foreign to Obi's ear. The word hadn't been an imperative: the speaker wasn't telling his fellows to run, it was a part of a larger sentence that was unknown to him.

The music had reached a normal pace now. Its tempo seemed to shift the closer he got to it, rather than the volume. He could almost recognize it now, though he wasn't sure from where. It was haunting to recognize something so mysterious and yet not know from where: like recognizing a smell and not knowing if it meant there was danger.

He stepped down the east hall, silently stepping past two adjacent halls after looking down them to make sure there was nothing there.

"Help," came a woman's voice with a thick New England accent.

"Who's there?" Obi called out again, his voice returning to the resonate tenor it had once always employed.

All at once the baby started to cry again, louder now, deafeningly loud. It was a scream that came from everywhere all at once, and the music became so fast that one note bled into the next; ABCBABCBABCB over and over again without a break or flourish. The baby screamed so loud Obi thought that his ears would bleed, and no matter how hard he pressed his hands to them, it wouldn't even dull the sound. It was like it was coming from inside his own head, as though his brain was screaming at him while some tiny Russian sat on his cerebellum and practised his cords.

Obi screamed as he ploughed forward, but he couldn't even hear his own above the baby's. It was a scream beyond hunger or loneliness or fear: it was pain, the sort of torturous pain that only a child can experience, when they have no frame of reference or social context from which to frame it: when a child feels pain, the whole world is pain... and right now the whole world was its scream. There were no other sounds on the entire planet, Obi was sure: just the ear-shattering scream of that babe and the soft undercurrent of a Russian piano melody existed.

And then, suddenly, it stopped.

Obi stopped in his tracks, his breath heavy and hard. He thought at first that the blare of the scream had rendered him deaf, but he could hear the air whistling out through his nose and the drip of his sweat on the tile floor. It wasn't just quiet, it was deathly quiet. It had gone from so loud that he thought he would die to no sound at all in a fraction of a second, without even the echo as the sound travelled throughout the rest of the gallery.

Obi took one long breath in, shut his eyes, and then let it out again.

He turned, and down at the end of the hall was the one single painting in all The Menagerie which still had a light spotting it, even now in the wee hours of the night. It was a painting of a theatre from the point-of-view of the stage, he could see the red drapes falling on either side of the canvas.

With one green eyebrow raised, Obi stepped forward.

There were people in the aisles of the theatre. Not enough to call it filled, just a few in each row. Some were Caucasian, some were African. Some were men, some were women. Some were young, some were old.

All stared straight ahead.

They stared straight ahead in that way that still pictures sometimes did, looking directly at the focal point of the piece so that their eyes seemed to follow you everywhere. Indeed, as Obi stepped down the hall closer and closer to this, the first significant source of light he'd seen since entering The Menagerie, he swayed slightly and found that yes, the glossy globs of paint they had for eyes fixated on him.

At the far left of the fifth row was the only patron not staring at him: a babe at its mother's breast, crying so hard its face was flushed and red.

Obi stopped and stared at that a moment, the echoes of the screaming child still hanging in the back of his mind. A shiver went down his spine as he looked at the child's face, its cheeks a deep blood red.

Aside from the child there were ten sets of eyes staring back at him;

four women, five men... and in the shadows in the back of the theatre, one pair of large, circular, deep red eyes.

When they blinked, Obi screamed long enough and loud enough to have put the sound of the infant to shame.

CHAPTER SIXTEEN

They were after him, the tall men in the dark hats, always ten or twelve feet behind. They walked with a tepid, casual gate and yet no matter how fast he ran, whenever he turned around, they were there.

Bob woke up with a gasp in a flop of sweat that had nothing to do with the diminishing heat of summer. His mouth was open and moist, and had a salty taste in it as he took several deep, panicked breaths in a row.

The morning light shone in through the window and reflected the faded red brick building that was their only view. Eddie wasn't next to him, but Bob could hear him in the kitchen. Still breathing hard, he reached for his phone without looking, patting for its place on his nightstand three times before finally laying his hand on it.

He opened his phone and his photo album app, and suddenly his breath stopped. The colour rushed from his cheeks and his eyes went wide with fear, and he felt his unused hand start to tremble and shake.

"Hey you want some—" Eddie started, coming into the room with a simmering pan in hand. He stopped when he saw Bob's face. "What's wrong? Is it your Mom?"

Bob did not speak, his lips pursed tight. Slowly, he turned the phone around to face Eddie.

Where there had been ten seats filled in the audience, there were now eleven. In the fourth row on the far left side was a gangly man with sunken cheeks, red blotches on either side of his neck, and green hair.

CHAPTER SEVENTEEN

Eddie, Bob, and Sloan all stood before the painting, regarding it with their hands on their chins the way one would when appraising the brush-work of a new artist at a showing. Except here their hands frequently went to their mouths, registering their shock and horror as they stared at the newest addition to the portrait: a green haired man, slumped towards the frame and sullenly looking back behind his shoulder.

Sloan stepped forward with her hand out, as though to touch the new paint, then thought better of it. "It's...Obi."

"It wasn't there before," Bob said as a statement of fact. He knew this was the thing to get over, the hanger on which all their disbelief must be hung. It had to be addressed first, or there was no point in continuing. "We can agree on that, right?"

Sloan nodded. Eddie did as well, but he had taken a step back from the painting without even realizing it.

"We would have noticed it. We would have discussed it. When we were talking about the time period of the painting and all the people in it, we would have mentioned the guy with green hair. He's Grunge, it would have placed our estimate into the 80s and—"

"We get it Bob," Sloan swallowed, stepping back and touching him on the arm.

Bob closed his eyes and nodded, composing himself.

She moved back in to the picture of Obi. There was a red ring all the way around his throat, but it was not solid. It was thick on either side, but in the middle there was a single red line, between which one could see the pale hue of his flesh.

"What made you take out your phone and look?" Eddie asked, his voice small. He crossed himself. The others didn't see.

"I had the nightmare about *The Scream* again." They all knew of it. "I did a paper on it when I was in college, and I talked about how it wasn't just the people chasing The Screamer that changed position, his eyes do too. And I followed the line of sight of The Screamer to make my case."

Bob stepped forward so that he was level with Sloan. Pointing without actually touching the canvas, he started with the stuffy man in a wig in the bottom left. He motioned to indicate his line-of-sight, then followed it with a straight-line into the back of the theatre. He did the same with the grocery store clerk, then the woman with the baby, and the Knight, and both women in the back row. Finally, he did it with Obi. "The only one who doesn't do it is the black man, that's what threw me off at first. He's just staring straight ahead at the viewer... he's not scared, he's just resigned to his fate."

Sloan swallowed, finding it hard to breathe.

In the back of the theatre, at the junction where all the lines-of-sight had converged, were large, purple shoulders. It was just a hint, barely visible in the dim light, but they were there: large shoulders and a hunched back with a wild mop of black hair that hid it from the light and blended it with the shadows... and two large, perfectly round red eyes that stared bleakly out at the viewer.

On the seat just behind the Knight, almost directly between the whore and the nurse, rested its large purple hand. The knuckles on it were deeply defined and dry looking, and it had long, black nails that were tinted with the same red that had been on Obi's neck.

Eddie crossed himself again.

Sloan's eyes fluttered over the painting, taking in every tiny detail, looking for things she hadn't noticed before or that may not have been there before.

"Come on," Bob said, turning around and stepping down the hallway with great purpose. Eddie turned and followed immediately, while Sloan lingered for a moment on the red stain in the center of the black man's chest. When the two men were almost at the end of the hall she looked up and saw the fire-red eyes of the thing behind the seats again, then turned and quickly made her way down the hall to catch the others.

The three of them moved through the halls, turning this way and that past Boones and Pardys and Corbens until eventually arriving at Chelsea's Office, which he opened without knocking. She looked up from whatever she was doing on her computer and smiled. "Nice to see you in on a day off."

Bob nodded, his voice and purpose suddenly gone. He'd stepped down the hall knowing exactly what he needed to say... but now it was gone, sounding ridiculous in his mind.

"Sloan," Chelsea beamed, getting up and reaching out a hand to her. "A pleasure, as always. The new piece of Obama is yours?"

Sloan smiled despite herself, but didn't agree, merely tapped the side of her nose.

"Of course," Chelsea winked.

"The O.K. Mal," Bob blurted finally, so quickly it made Chelsea jump. She smiled from the start it had given her. "The picture, the one unaccounted for... of the theatre."

"Yes," Chelsea nodded. "I know the one. Yes?"

A long silence hung in the air that felt like an eternity.

"Have you found the owners yet?" he asked finally.

"No one's claiming it," Chelsea shrugged, looking back toward a pile of shipping invoices as if the stack itself could confirm her. "But it seems to be doing well. I like the way it—"

"You need to get rid of it," Eddie said, just as fast as Bob, his accent coming through in a way it only did when he was excited.

The smile slowly faded from Chelsea's lips. "Pardon?"

Bob sighed, rubbed his hands against his face, then stepped forward and sat at the seat across from Chelsea, hands forward. "I know how this is going to sound."

Chelsea raised an eyebrow.

"But there's something wrong with that picture. It changes. It changed last night, there's a man in it with green hair now." He took out his phone, unlocked it, and showed it to her.

She squinted, the shrugged. "It was always there."

"No, it wasn't."

"Well," she smirked, mockingly. "It kind of would have had to have been, wouldn't it?" She looked back at the photo. "This was taken in Receiving."

"The picture changed as well."

She smiled forcibly, composing herself and squaring her shoulders.

"It changed before, remember? Right after—" he stopped, more of his colour leaving him. He turned around and looked at Sloan and Eddie. "Right after Mr. Cooper went missing."

"Oh no," Sloan said, tearing up. Eddie took a moment longer, and Sloan turned to him. "The man in the apron." He cursed.

"Well, I do have a lot to do," Chelsea said in a high, too-polite tone. "Good seeing you all, as always."

"Please," Bob said. "You can dock my pay you can change my hours you can do anything you want but please, just take the painting down. Put it in storage, at least until we can find out who's supposed to have it and where it came from."

Chelsea folded her fingers together and smiled again, which did nothing to hide her unease and annoyance. "Well," she said finally, it that same too-chipper tone that revealed the opposite meaning of the words. "I do have a lot to do. Good seeing you, as always."

Bob closed his eyes, took a deep breath, then nodded.

CHAPTER EIGHTEEN

The three sat in their booth at The Belle Verde, each with a cold cup of coffee in front of them. Despite the early hour, Gradey had given them an odd, side-long glance when they had deviated from the typical drink of beer. He had taken longer than usual to come back with the coffees, as though he had had to take both the grounds and the machine with which to percolate them out of some long-forgotten storage bin.

All three of them had taken it black, despite only Eddie taking it that way normally. They sipped the bitter, salty liquid sparingly until it had gotten quite cold, with Gradey coming over every thirty minutes or so and topping it back up but with the new hotness by no way having enough energy to warm the rest of the cup by a measurable margin. Still they thanked him absently, and each time he walked away with his pot mostly full and a grim sensation that there was something on his back.

Eddie looked as though he were ready to speak, stopped, then crossed himself again.

Bob's phone was on the table next to him. Every few minutes he would press a button or scroll or pick it up and type something, slowly becoming more and more irritable.

"I keep thinking of other things it could be," Sloan said quietly, finally breaking the silence. "Like maybe someone's kidnapping people and then painting them into the painting or... something. I don't know. Anything."

"Bad episode of CSI," Eddie said under his breath.

"I know right? But anything's more realistic than... well, what we're thinking." She paused, taking a deep breath. "But the pictures on Bob's phone. Every time I come back to that: the pictures on the phone changed too."

Eddie nodded, and the three of them again descended into silence.

"Damn it," Bob cursed, slapping his hand against the table and making the both of them jump. Sloan let out a small yelp, her cheeks flushing when she did from embarrassment. "I've searched for this painting everywhere. MoMa and Google and Engraved, everywhere I can think. I can't find it anywhere. There's no mention of the painting, and no mention of the paint-er." He put his phone aside and ran his fingers through his hair. "How does that happen? How does something just not exist online? There's scads of work by unknown artists everywhere that I can find with three clicks. Your stuff!" He gestured to Sloan. "You don't even sign your stuff but there's three websites where I can search your name and find it and find where and when it was with GPS!"

Sloan nodded knowingly.

"But this guy, we have his damn name! We have his name and I still get nothing, from anywhere, when I search O.K. Mal!"

He buried his face in his hands, and the three of them sat there in silence. Eddie reached out and touched Bob's shoulder, tenderly massaging the muscle.

Sloan's brow was furrowed.

"What?" Eddie asked, raising an eyebrow.

She opened her mouth, closed it, then opened it again. "Why do you keep calling it O.K. Mal?"

Bob looked up. "That's the name."

She shook her head and reached for his phone. "No it isn't." She turned it on and looked through his pictures. "You're turning it around, which some artists do, but there's no punctuation between the Oh and the Kay."

She turned his phone back to him, having pinch-zoomed to the bottom right hand corner of the picture. Sure enough, in purple paint, were the letters: but there were not periods or dots between the letters. It was a trick of the light.

What there was, was an apostrophe before the Oh, so faint in the shadow of the dark red curtain that it was almost invisible.

The name, as presented, was Mal 'Ok.

"Mal 'Ok," Bob said aloud, zooming back out so that the picture was fully framed on his screen. He closed the image and brought up a browser again, and began to type. "I don't even think it's the artist... I think it's the name of the painting."

Sloan nodded, leaning forward in her seat to see what Bob was doing and tilting the glass surface when she did so.

Eddie's jaw had gone slack.

"There's nothing," Bob frowned. "Nothing relevant anyway. There's some gun and a weird Latin page, but nothing—"

"Malloch," Eddie said, his voice a ghost. "Type in: 'Painting' and 'Malloch.'"

Bob turned to him, looked as though he were about to question it, but then typed the words into the search window.

The page filled with hits, each one lighting up in blue. There were images of landscapes and cityscapes and a bright, lurid sunset that looked like something Munch himself might have done had he lived an extra century. Eddie leaned in, his face now so pale that he was almost unrecognizable, and touched the screen. "That one."

The page that opened wasn't an image, but a page of text.

Bob scanned down through, frowning. "How do you know that this is it?"

Eddie took a swing from his coffee. "Because it's on my shelf at home."

CHAPTER NINETEEN

Horror in Historical Art had sat on Eddie and Bob's bookshelf for nearly five years, having been gifted to them as an anniversary present. It was a thick hardcover with glossy pages and had a wrap-around dust-jacket with the image of an 18th Century engraving of a shadowy goblin perched on a sleeping child's bed, an image so disturbing that Bob had ordered it to be wedged between two thick books so that it wouldn't be seen.

The pages were of the sort of thick, heavy paper that coffee-table books typically were: the sort that made the book seem to have more pages than it did. The edges were bevelled, every second period of ten pages alternatively a quarter inch short, then long, then short again. The images in it were glossy and tracked the light, especially along the black ink, giving the impression that the light was somehow coming from the shadows of the image as Eddie tilted the book.

"There," he said, planting his finger into the page with force. He was sitting cross-legged on the floor with the book in his lap, Bob and Sloan behind him on the couch. They both leaned in.

It was a full page on the right-hand side, page sixty-seven, across from an artist's rendering of Jack the Ripper. The heading, in scrawled Tosca Zero font like something from a B-horror movie, was *Malloch*. Unlike the page it was facing or every other page in the book, what followed the heading were two long columns of text.

"How do we know that's it?" Bob asked.

"Listen," Eddie replied, following his finger along the text as he spoke. "...Believed to be the common ancestral thread of many urban legends and suspicious beliefs, such as moving pictures and the idea that pictures or images steal souls."

Sloan sat up straight, a chill having found its way to her spine.

"Reports of The Malloch painting reputedly go back as far as 1475 in Wallachia."

Bob furrowed his brow. "That can't be right."

"What it says. It says that for a hundred years after tales of it popped up all over Western Europe. They have fragments of diaries and excerpts from manuscripts—" Bob took out his phone and started searching. Eddie continued. "Most are in Middle-English. A few are in German and Slovakian, and at least three are in Latin. Most of them are all but destroyed, but some accounts remain. Most surviving accounts reference silver, darkness, and no reflection prominently. 'No Reflection' has been found in many translations, although language historians debate this interpretation and authenticity. The Malloch painting then dropped from sight for over fifty years before resurfacing in France in 1898."

Bob grunted, clearing something on his phone with a swipe and then typing again.

Eddie stopped, looking over his shoulder. "There's more... about the different cultures that believe images steal your soul... should I...?"

"The dates don't match up," Bob frowned so deeply that it altered the line of his jaw.

"What do you mean?"

"Theatres like the ones in the painting didn't *exist* in 1475. They were... simpler. They weren't these grand, operatic things, just... stages in parks, essentially." He started typing again. "Sloan said she recognized the the-

atre in the painting as being an opera house in France, The Palais Garnier...
that matches up with what you're saying about the picture turning up in
1898, but you can't type in 'Palais Garnier Picture' into Google because it'll
just come back with pictures *of* The Palais Garnier."

Sloan leaned in over his shoulder to look at the screen. She pointed, accidentally touching it and stopping the scroll. "It wasn't called Palais Garnier in 1898," she corrected absently. "That wasn't until later. It was called
Opéra Garnier at the time."

Bob stopped, then scrolled back up to the search bar and typed. "Same
thing, just pictures."

"Try Mallock Opéra Garnier," she said.

"They list Chiapas here..." Eddie said softly, still reading from his book.
"That's not far from where my parents were born."

"There," Sloan said, pointing and again inadvertently clicking. "Sorry."

"What is it?"

Bob squinted, skimming the article. "It's an account by a one Jean
LaCrainte. Says he worked at the Opéra Garnier during the turn of the century."

CHAPTER TWENTY
THE ACCOUNT OF JEAN LACRAINTE

June 10th

*The walls have been repaired in the east wing, as well as the roof re-shingled.
The signs of weathering are all but gone, and only a crack in the stonework remains
to show where it once was. Julian has begun to decorate again and new textures
and tapestries make it into the Opéra Garnier daily: fine red cloth and velvet and
the finest oak this countryside has ever seen! We are rebuilding.*

Eddie gestured with his hand outstretched. "Rebuilding from what?"

Bob shrugged.

*Maria has given birth to a fine young boy, healthy and strong, the first son to
bear the name LaCrainte since I was born no less than two and twenty years ago.
He will be named Philippe, after my father before me and his grandfather before
him, and will be a good, strong boy. He will grow in the shadow of The Opéra
Garnier: his manger will be the soft tails of curtains, his nursemaids will be the
seamstresses, and his schoolyard chums those who come to watch him on the stage.
I see him now, taking his first bow as the crowd cheers: Bravo, Bravo! And toss the
same flowers they did as for the Romans and William before him.*

The labour was hard on Maria—

"Vote to skip," Eddie said, raising a hand into the air. Sloan silently raised hers as well.

"Fine," Bob relented, scrolling down. "Here we go."

New paintings have been hung in the east wing to hide the faults in the reconstruction and the cracks in the walls. There is a large portrait of Shakespeare that is like nothing I have ever seen, Mama. He glares out at me with eyes lit with fire and a rueful, baneful sneer... and for once there is no doubt that this could be the man that did write those words, Will all great Neptune's ocean wash this blood clean from my hand? That man has contempt for the world in him, and shall see it down around his ankles as ash and soot.

There is yet another painting though that disturbs me yet more. This is small and sits across from the main stage, on the wall which divides the balcony of the east wing from the balcony of the west wing. From the stage it is center in one's view at all times if one knows to look for it, although I admit it is small enough that one would be forgiven for mistaking it for a part of the wall if not.

It is of a field of tall grass in the fall of the year, the grass turned dull and dead and yellow. The portrait faces west, the sun in the sky behind it low yet still visible. There are no mountains or trees or fiords to disrupt the ceaseless march of the grass blades across the canvas: nothing but dead leaves and sky, and the men who wait upon it.

Bob furrowed his brow. "Maybe he gets into it later. This isn't the painting."

"Keep reading," Sloan said in a hushed tone.

Four figures stand in a line across the field in perfect sections. Each stands before a long pole that stretches skyward behind them, and each stares down at their feet before them like a man awaiting his fate at the gallows.

The first is a Knight Templar if ever I have seen one, in such detail that I fight the urge to stand at attention each time I see him. He stands square-shouldered and clasps his sword before him, but its tip is to the ground and he will not raise it. Hair peeks from his helmet in grimy tuffs and there is blood mixed with the red cross of his sash: he is worn from battle, this Knight.

The second is a Knave. A Knight and a Knave? The Knave is filthy with soot and grime, his eyes darkened with it. He wears thick leather that has cracked in the sun and he, too, holds a sword: again, the sword is lowered to the ground. The battle has been fought and the judgement awaited, but in what battle did Knight stand with Knave and both reach their folly?

A broad dark man is third, and though he holds no weapon, nor should he, it is clear that he joined in the battle as well from the three cuts down his chest, soaking blood into the tufts of his shirt collar. There is water on his cheeks that has dried in the harsh sun only to be provided again.

The last man, I swear to you as clearly as I sit here today, is the image of that

First Earl of Orford, Sir Robert Walpole! He stands, plump and saggy, with his bushy brows and white wig before his pole, awaiting punishment with all the rest, as though standing in condemnation of all the Whigs in the Church of England!

I must admit it fascinates me. Surely this could not be the end of any real battle, for in what battle did Knight fight along Knave? White fight along Black? Commoner fight along Politician? None of which I am aware.

And the poles behind each man, dear sister, the poles that seem to mark the end for each man and raise high into the evening sky, as I look now I see that they are not poles at all. Each comes to a sharp point that I at first took for a trick of the brush, but they remain spikes or pikes or javelins: They are fierce weapons each for these men, who stand prostrate and await the punishment for the crimes of war.

And in the grass at their feet there is a fifth being, hidden among the blades. I see him only from the corner of my eye it seems, like some trick of the clever painter's stroke. Between the dark man and the Whig, nestled crouched like a tiger, a royal demon sits in wait for these four men to accept their fates.

I admit that of all this, nothing unnerves me more than the signature inscribed upon the canvas: Mal 'Ok.

"What does he mean 'royal demon'?" Eddie asked aloud.

Sloan looked pensive, her eyes flitting over the books still of their shared shelf until she came to one with a dark Tyrian Purple soft-bound cover. "It's the colour," she said, her head snapping back to the boys so fast her hair whipped around. "A demon coloured Royal Purple."

Bob thought back to the purple swirls he had first seen in the shadowy background of the painting.

June 25th

Philippe has been stricken with colic and Maria has been wrestling with Mother's Dread, the same that PaPa used to tell us took our poor grand-mère from us. I try to bring her 'round but she does nothing but sulk most mornings, leaving me to tend to Philippe. I apologize for my tardiness in returning your letter – yes, October will be fine for you and Robert to visit, of course. Will his sister Anna-Maria be joining you as well?

July 2nd
Dear sister,
The painting hung between the east and west wings has changed. The Manager and Producers believe I am mad, that I have come down with exhaustion from too many nights with Philippe without Maria's aid, but I swear it is true. Do you still have the letters I sent in June? Please keep them and bring them when you visit in October, they are the only record of my sanity.

What was once described to you as a wheat field has been replaced by a painting of the Opéra itself, as though the artist sat upon the stage and gazed out upon the empty seats and marked his brush in kind. When I try to tell anyone that it has changed, they mock me and say that it has always been this way: they only didn't look at it as I did.

I hear you in my mind even now, dear patient sister, how is it that it was not reported that the picture was merely moved or stolen and replaced with this forgery of the Opéra? Why would I say that the work itself must have been changed when such a more logical explanation presents itself? Discounting the ornate frame, which remains the same and shows no sign of tampering... the men, my dear sister. The four men I described to you in the wheat field are the sole occupants of this new theatre, and they no longer look down, but out at me.

The Knight sits near the back, still grasping his blade, the Knave just below him at his left. Seated near the front is the dark man, where he ought not to be, and he stares out at me with red-ringed eyes of warning. The Whig sits in the second row, and has grown a coat of flop-sweat since I 'ere seen him last.

I thought the Demon gone at first, until I caught a glimpse of it in the back of the theatre... where I then stood. Where the Demon appeared was where its painting hung, and when I realized this, chills ran through me. It was hidden by deep blacks and I admit to losing it more than once as a trick of the eye, having to follow the gazes of the patrons of the theatre to find it again, for all but the dark man glare back at it.

The Demon, however, glares at me.

The name has changed too sister. Still it says Mal'Ok, but now it is in the same royal hue as the monster itself, not the sheer black I first saw.

"Did he say the signature was black?" Eddie asked.

"Would you?" Bob shrugged.

It changed so as to still be visible against the shadow of the aisles I am sure.

Sister, this portrait has unnerved me in ways I cannot even put to pen. I have vowed not to approach that wall under any circumstance, to approach those wings through alternate means, but always I feel its red eyes on me when I am in its view: on the stage or between the seats. Late last night, I swear as I write this to you, I was alone in the theatre and heard a Prussian piano melody coming from that floor – where there is no piano. It was 'Standing Still,' a children's melody. The notes are in me now even as I write. The painting is with me at all times, sister. It haunts me as a phantom of the Opéra.

"Wait, what?" Sloan said, turning the screen toward her.

Eddie almost laughed, then didn't. Sloan took his phone from him without asking.

"It's a coincidence," Bob said, still staring at the phrase. "Has to be."

Sloan frowned. "It might be a coincidence, but there's more than one: "The Palais Garnier has been called the most famous opera in the world, a symbol of Paris like Notre Dame Cathedral, the Louvre, or the Sacré Coeur Basilica, at least partly due to its use as the setting for Gaston Leroux's 1910 novel *The Phantom of the Opera."*

Bob turned to the word again. "Ten years later," then scrolled up.

Sloan shuddered.

July 12th

The Painting, I feel, has brought me to the edge of madness, and here it intends to leave me. It shifts and bends the few times I must see it: the patrons moving seats, the demon pacing to and fro in its shadowy den, as though pondering when to strike.

I attempted to sketch the beast, to provide some proof until October, but became quickly frustrated.

I inquired, with some distress, as to its origin. At my most recent request the director at last relented, and his logs revealed a long providence which ended in Wallachia, where it appears my original assessments of the demon have found credence. The picture came bathed in blood, I know that now, and more than the blood I have found on each o' the patrons.

"Blood?" Eddie asked.

"Shh," Sloan hushed, bringing a finger to her lips.

Four it has and thirteen it needs; that most unholy number that first came to the fall of the templar knights... like the Knight himself, the first. This I have found with the Director, but have mostly heard through the whispers in the night... at night the painting comes to life, and those four poor souls speak to me from their living hell.

Bob paused, then took a screen-shot of that section before moving on.

Dear sister, I may not be able to wait 'til the fall of the year. If I can implore you, send the letters now that I might prove myself and end my torment.

July 20th

Dearest Emilia; it is with great sadness that I write this passage. You may disregard my request for the letters if you have not already sent them. Keep them with you, or burn them if it suits your designs. It matters not.

Philippe and Maria had walked to the Opéra. I had been encouraging Maria to find herself outside more often, to lift her spirits. They were there for me... and there, they will remain. The Demon Mal'Ok has them, a part of the living hell which is his canvas.

"The mother and child," Sloan said, her voice quavering.

They cry out to me as though they can see me, their arms outstretched. I can see the tears on their faces and in their eyes as though they were moving and falling dear sister, the anguish and the pain on them is too much to bear, even before the blood. My Maria has her mark against her breast, a tally-marked herringbone calling her his fifth. And my poor sweet child – his sweet face is marred with three lines a cheek, salt water staining them.

It is with agony, my sister, that this will be my final letter and that I shall not be available to host you in the fall... not only for my deep sorrow... but for my fear. Seven more the demon needs, and though my last act may see me in hell, I take solace in that it will not be the hell that hangs on the wall of The Opéra Garnier.

CHAPTER TWENTY-ONE

The three sat in silence for a moment at the end of the passage, the air hanging still between them, thick with the dread of it.

Eddie crossed himself.

"Jesus," Sloan said under her breath. Then again, louder: "Jesus!"

"It's not true," Eddie said, kissing his cross nonetheless. "I won't believe it."

Bob's brow was furrowed, the flesh there clenched so tightly that his bushy eyebrows all but joined in the middle. He had closed the browser with the account of Jean LaCrainte in it and had opened his photo albums. He opened the screen shot he had taken first, repeating it out loud: "Four it has and thirteen it needs, that most unholy number that first came to the fall of the templar knights... like the Knight himself, the first."

"The mother was the fifth," Sloan said. "The man said she had a herringbone on her breast. That's what they used to call it when you made four marks and then crossed the fifth over it, a herringbone."

"Nana used to call it Making a Book," mumbled Eddie.

Bob opened the picture of the painting and zoomed in. The babe, Philippe, was still feeding in his version of the painting – but he could see the red smudges along her breast and his face where they met, as though hiding them from the viewer. "The marks are there," he said, his voice a low growl. "This is the one."

He scrolled over to the Knight, who had a single gash in the center of his chest. Next to him, the scruffy man who Jean had called The Knave, had two such marks on his neck, almost hidden from his collar. He realized that he'd seen the black man's when he'd first viewed the piece: the three red lines in the center of his chest, as if from a lynching, he'd thought at the time.

The man with the white wig had four slashes. The Prostitute had seven, the Nurse eight. The thin woman who sat in front of The Knave had nine, one herringbone and four scratches alongside, and he wondered how he hadn't seen them before.

His friend, Frederick Cooper, had two adjacent herringbones. And poor, lonely Obi had the same two bones and an eleventh strike besides.

"Ten," Eddie sighed.

"Eleven," Bob corrected. "We keep not counting the baby, from when we thought they were figures, Madonna and child."

Eddie nodded, his face pale and his eyes watering. After another long moment he said, hoarsely, "We don't go back there no more."

Bob turned to face him, then leaned in and kissed him, but did not respond.

Sloan took his phone and opened his search engine.

"What is it?" Bob asked, rubbing Eddie's shoulder rhythmically.

"He mentioned Wallachia... that was in Romania – yes, Romania," she said, clearly finding the evidence that she was correct. "A long providence that ended in Wallachia... and that his original assessments were true."

"What's providence?" Eddie asked.

"The history of who owned a thing," Bob said. "Like a record of owners."

Eddie worked his mouth and wiped his eyes. "Our record ended in 1490."

"1495."

"Whenever. It was maybe the same record?"

Sloan nodded, and typed 'Wallachia 1490' into the search bar. Articles regarding the History of Romania appeared. She frowned.

The three of them were silent for what felt like an age.

Bob picked up his phone and scrolled over the painting. The creature had moved from the last place he'd seen it, he noted. He scrolled to the bottom right, found the signature, and stared at its purple hue for a long time.

"Royal was the only thing he'd said about the creature," Bob said absently, turning the phone to face Sloan. "Royal Purple he'd been referencing – but unless we're missing letters, that's the only 'assessment' Jean made about it."

Sloan nodded, and amended her search to: 'Wallachia, 1940, Royal.'

A new article appeared, dedicated to Vlad the Third, the Prince of Wallachia from 1431–1476.

She went white even more than she already had as she scanned the selected article.

"What?" Bob asked, as Eddie sat up straight. "What is it?"

With a quavering voice that they'd never heard from her, she read aloud. "Vlad III served as the Prince of Wallachia from 1431 to 1475 or 76, as a member of the House of Basarab, also known as the House of Drăculeşti." She stopped and looked at them.

"I don't get it," Eddie said, tapping his hand on his knee.

"After his death, he was given another name; Vlad the Impaler."

Bob felt his throat run dry. At once the image of how Jean had first described the painting came to him: four men standing with their heads lowered as if they were at the gallows, each standing before a long, sharp stick, as the creature watched in the distance.

Eddie found his voice first. "Vlad the Impaler. *The* Vlad the Impaler? That was a real guy?"

Sloan nodded. "They made up stories about him. Said he was a cannibal, which is how some other stories about his family name got popular. You'd have recognized him by those anglicized names as well: when he was Vlad Dracula."

Bob felt his body start to curl and stopped it. He zoomed out of the photo and took a long look before closing it.

It was a portrait of a demon, whose first record came from Romania in the same year as Vlad Dracula's death. Since then it had travelled from region to region, feeding on the living, only moving at night. It needed thirteen souls, and it had eleven.

He stared at the image of The Knave, with the two gashes alongside his neck, with renewed horror, then turned off the screen.

CHAPTER TWENTY-TWO

Chelsea Whitmire stepped out of the receiving office into the dark halls of The Menagerie, the fierce brightness she was leaving making it hard for her eyes to adjust. When it came to the evening lights at the gallery, she had always been of two minds: one voice in her head told her to leave them on, at least until everyone was gone. The thought of the liability alone—financial and personal—if Bob or one of the movers was in and tripped during the low light, was enough to birth that thought within her. The second voice, the voice she'd heard as her father's ever since she had been a child, responded with: "Just burn your money, it'll cast more light."

For as long as she could remember, Chelsea had been contending with those two voices. Was her father's voice the voice of her conscience? If he'd been alive and someone had asked him, he'd have likely said so. But too often the things his voice whispered in her ear were not truisms or nuggets of good advice or even good deeds: too often they were miserly, sensationalist, or downright wrong-headed. It was the voice that told her to round up the cost of admissions rather than down, to charge extra for the concessions, and to keep the most prized parts of their collection sheltered away for 'restoration' whenever a group of children came through the gallery on a field trip.

It wasn't that Hans Whitmire had been a radical or a racist—far from it, to her recollection. But he always erred on the side of caution, and often that overt caution too easily became xenophobia. She would receive warnings about her friends growing up: "You can hang out with that one, it's no problem, but keep your eye on him." There was never more said than that: just keep your eye on it. Despite the arguments and the distance it created between them in her teens and beyond, she found that voice, much to her dismay, at work in herself. When she met someone new, she heard that voice inside her: "She seems nice, but keep an eye on her to be sure." It had happened when she had met Bob, it had happened when she had met Eddie, it had happened when she had met Sloan. And as much as she tried to pin the blame on her father, in the end, the voice in her head was her own, just aping his tone.

She corrected the tilt of a Boone piece in front of her, which had somehow been knocked to the right. There had been children in earlier, and despite her father's warnings, she hadn't watched them. They had looked like children, but they had behaved more like wild cats and herding them had been roughly the same experience. They had all had sticky fingers no matter how many times she and their chaperone had tried to clean them. The fingers had been a mystery until they discovered one particularly gummy little boy had had a pocket full of gelatin worms and had been sharing them with the others.

She stepped back from the Boone and eyed it, tilting her head to one side, then the other, until she decided it was good. "Alarms, you should have these," the voice of her father said in his thick eastern-European accent. "If someone can bump, someone can take."

She smiled, shrugged the thought away, then reached back into the receiving room and got her coat and shut off the light. The darkness of the hallway was now near-total, with only the blue caress of the emergency lights to guide her way the short distance to the exit.

She was half way across the hallway when, far in the distance of the halls of The Menagerie, she heard the faint notes of a piano.

Chelsea turned and stared into the darkness of the hallway, then slowly laid her jacket down to rest on the tiled floor.

Deep in her mind, her father's voice told her to go; to not see where it was coming from; to leave.

As with most of the cautions he gave her, she pushed them aside.

Bob brushed past Emilio, knocking shoulders with the man without even so much as acknowledging him.

Emilio turned and frowned and muttered something under his breath, turning back around just in time to see Sloan and Eddie coming up behind him.

"Sorry," Sloan said between rushed breaths, her eyebrows tilted up in apology. "So sorry."

Emilio frowned and nodded, then turned and continued his way down Jacobi Street. He was pushing a small shopping cart filled with the wooden shoes he made, and had clearly chosen tonight as one of his nights to 'plant.'

The Menagerie was in view, just at the end of the street, its stairs silhouetted by the setting sun. Bob kept his eyes trained on it, even as the glare from the last ebbs of twilight burned at his eyes, as if afraid that it too would move or twitch when he wasn't looking.

Despite his exhaustion, he picked up his pace.

The Corbens framed Chelsea's shoulders as she stared down their hallway to the one light that had been left on in The Menagerie: the bright light that shone down upon the unknown painting by O.K. Mal.

It was brighter than she remembered it, the iridescent purple flesh of the figure in the background standing out against the dull, natural hues of the rest of the audience. It was like a mound or a hump, all back and nothing else, like a hunchback turning away from offending eyes. It looked back over its shoulder at her, with eyes that seemed to follow her wherever she went. Some people found that artist's trick unnerving, but Chelsea had always enjoyed it: she would sit with her art book as a child and speak to the Mona Lisa and the Van Gogh, each of them listening intently with their eyes trained on her.

All of the members of the audience had their eyes trained on her, each and every one of the eleven seated, and the thing that was behind them. The man with the funny wig that reminded her of a judge, and the scruffy boy with the green hair watched her intently. The green popped out, like a patch of fresh grass where all the rest was drab and dead.

The music had stopped. It had reached a fever pitch of sorts, the melody coming to a head and reminding her of the transitional music in what she had once described to her father as 'Russian Line-Dancing,' much to his amusement. Now the hallway was as silent as a tomb, save for a small skittering, like a mouse, but not a mouse. It had the structure and cadence of language, but was too faint for her to hear, faint whispers barely understood through a thick hide.

Her mouth opened as she stepped down the hallway, one foot in front of the other, the illuminated painting slowly enlarging in her view.

Bob reached the doors of The Menagerie and tried the push-bar knob with a loud clang. The door jostled on its bearings and he brought up a knee into its bulletproof Plexiglas, but it did not budge. He cursed, then banged his fist twice on the glass.

"Chelsea!" he hollered into the door, rapping again and again as he stared into the faded blue light of the hallways. "Chelsea, open up!"

Eddie came up behind him and started hammering on the glass as well, hard enough that normal glass would have broken.

Bob stepped back and pulled a large ring of keys from his pocket and started to cycle through them.

Chelsea heard the banging on the door somewhere far away, but did not take her eyes off of the painting. "It's someone who doesn't realize we're closed," the pragmatic voice in her head told her, while the other voice—the voice of her father that she'd long trained herself to ignore—told her to check. It could be burglars. It could be vandals. It could be anything aside from this painting, with the spotlight shinning down on it and the people staring out at hear.

There was an old man in an apron that seemed especially upset, looking up at the stage and at the viewer with great distress. He had half risen from his seat, as though he wanted to stand and warn the person on the stage, but that something was holding him back, although she couldn't foresee what it was. It certainly wasn't the pale woman with no tits behind him, she didn't look like she could lift a pound let alone hold back a fully-grown man.

Her gaze returned to the amethyst haunch at the head of the piece, shyly lording over all the patrons as it stared out at the viewer with its elongated teeth.

...Had there been teeth before?

"There must have been," came that calm, pragmatic voice within her again, as she stepped so close to the painting that she could have touched it without fully extending her arm.

"Got it!" Bob yelled, hip-checking Eddie and Sloan away from the door and sliding in the key. It turned and the lock slid into place with a loud ker-chunk, and when he next pressed the latch down, the door slid open easily.

Bob was through the door and into the lobby like a bolt. "Chelsea!" he screamed, his voice echoing off the walls, over and over again. But he wasn't heading toward her office or the receiving office, no, he was heading straight for that dead-end hall that capped the Corben exhibit.

"Bob wait!" Sloan screamed, seeing what was happening and heading after him.

Sloan and Eddie followed Bob through the winding hallways of The Menagerie. It had never seemed so much a maze as it did this night, with Bob far enough ahead that he only came into view as they rounded every corner, only to disappear from view again around the next.

They turned the corner to go down the Corben hallway and had to stop abruptly, almost slamming into Bob's back in the shadowed darkness. He had begun to sob softly, his shoulders bouncing with each laboured breath, silhouetted in the spotlight at the end of the hall.

He turned suddenly and screamed something inaudible, punching the wall between two paintings as hard as he could. There was a small dent where it had landed, but nothing that would be noticed unless one were looking for it.

Eddie pulled him back from the wall and Bob collapsed into his arms, his face a tortured mix of terror and anguish.

Sloan moved around them and stepped forward, walking the same path that Chelsea had mere moments before.

There was a twelfth patron of the Opéra now.

Chelsea sat in the back row, directly behind The Knight. Her auburn hair was matted and clumped, as though she'd rung her fingers through it and tangled it and not been able to get it out. Her hands weren't in her hair though: one gripped the armrest as though trying to put her nails through its plush fabric, and the other was palm-outstretched toward the viewer. Tears and terror streamed down her face, her mouth open in a scream so wide that Sloan could see the pink of her uvula.

Her throat was slashed and gnashed where it met her collar, a herringbone on either side. Two further strokes travelled from the center of her throat to the areola of each breast, the blouse there ripped and soaked with red paint.

Sloan fought back tears. Despite the shivers that seemed to have made a permanent home on her spine, she couldn't turn off the analytical part of her psyche that still loved artistic composition. Chelsea sat in the back row, behind The Knight, yes, but directly between The Whore and The Nurse. Something about that lingered in the back of her mind, because wasn't that what Chelsea was: neither Madonna nor Whore, but rather somewhere in between? Wasn't that what all women were, all people; neither the good that was expected of them, nor the ill?

Her mind snapped back and she forced herself to look beyond Chelsea.

Behind her, the creature, Mal 'Ok as she now thought of it, stood in full view now. It no longer hid in the shadows. One of its heavy, misshapen hands lay on Chelsea's shoulder, and its glowing red eyes peeked out from over her other shoulder, pale with blood-drained flesh.

It was in the light now, no longer shy as it had been. The light source seemed to come not from anywhere in the painting, but from the spotlight on the ceiling of The Menagerie itself, as though the outer world were affecting the lighting of the piece. She was tempted to move it and see if the hue of the creature would change, but dared not.

Mal 'Ok stared out at her, not with malice of ill intent: it just watched, its hand resting heavily on Chelsea's tense shoulder.

It was mocking them, she realized slowly.

She backed away from it, not wanting to turn her back on it as she moved back up the hall to meet Bob.

CHAPTER TWENTY-THREE

Bob sat on the very edge of his stool, his feet resting on its metal braces and an untouched cup of cold coffee in his hand. His eyes had thick red bags beneath them and he hated himself for it. He wanted to be sterner, but every time he tried to summon a stiff-upper-lip he saw Chelsea's pale hand, her fingers splayed as she reached out to him for help from her world of oil and canvas.

Sloan sat on the floor next to him, her head just slightly touching his leg. The remnants of three juice boxes lay at her side and she moved her blade, the one she used to cut her stencils, back and forth from one hand to the other absently.

She hadn't cried. She wanted to, desperately. She felt as though the tears were just beyond the well of her ducts but refused to come forward; timid, tiny drops of salt-water. She didn't cry often and hadn't even as a child, but when she did it was followed by a deep catharsis. She craved that catharsis now, and it was denied her.

Eddie sat on the kitchen table, away from the two of them, his legs resting on the seat of a chair in front of him. He did this to face them rather than turning the chair around or sitting on it backwards. He'd cried. He had wept openly from The Menagerie to here, but by the time they had unlocked their door, the tears had gone. His jaw was set now, so set that it would have taken a crowbar to force it apart. He stared at Bob, the source of his rage, though not its focus. Every tear demanded blood, his grandfather had told him once, his accent thick and his breath smarmy with gin. When someone you love is hurt, for every tear there is blood that must be paid.

He sat, lip curled, unable to focus his rage on anything concrete for the first time in his life.

"She didn't deserve this," Bob said, breaking a silence neither of them had consciously built but that had hung around them for nearly an hour.

"Nobody deserves this," Sloan correctly reflexively, her voice a whisper.

Bob nodded, and another tear fell to his jeans. Unconsciously, Eddie marked and counted its passing.

They sat in silence into the night, finding sleep not far from where they sat.

CHAPTER TWENTY-FOUR

Bob ran in the dimming hours of twilight, but no matter how fast he ran, they stayed behind him. He could hear the panting of his own breath and feel it in time with the heat in his cheeks, the lap of the waves far in the distance, and the steady plunk of old boards beneath his feet.

He'd been running for what seemed like forever, the splintered guard-rails on either side of him going into the horizon. The wood creaked and moaned beneath his weight, threatening to bend and break with each foot-fall.

There were low men behind him, Low Men in tall hats. They were in shadow, silhouetted against the bright oranges and pinks and yellows of the setting sun, but each time he turned around he could see them. They were never moving when he turned, yet not matter how fast he pumped his legs, they were always behind him. Closer behind him each time as a point of fact, gaining. Not by much, not by enough that his heart would give and his legs might stop and he would turn to face them: just enough.

They moved as if playing a children's game of spotlight, only moving when he turned away from them and remaining as still as stone statues when he turned to look. Was he running in place? He couldn't see their faces and yet knew they bore no expression, as stern and emotionless as the face of his father the last time he'd seen him.

He made a sound, a dull N-sound, deep within his throat that was supposed to be a word but it wouldn't form. One of the Low Men was resting against the rail when he turned back next, looking out at the sailboats along the water. The sound of the waves thundered and roared in response to this, but the water itself seemed calm and placid.

The other one, the larger of the Low Men, had been caught in mid-stride with his left foot thrust forward. His fists were clenched and his jaw was set with determination. Eyes that weren't there stared into Bob, not at him but through him, daring him to attempt a false front of bravery because he could see through it all into the terror and the panic that lay just beneath the flesh.

Bob turned back around to the front reluctantly, and when he did he saw a lumbering, hunched purple mass in front of him, so large that it blocked the entire bridge. He screamed, long and loud, and then thrust himself up off of his pillow.

Sweat came from his brow in great round bullets, running down his cheeks and off his chin and down his back. He felt soaked in the sheets that barely covered him, the blankets having been kicked off. He'd been running in his sleep some part of him acknowledged, those sort of jerky bicycle kicks your legs managed during restless slumber.

He gasped for air he hadn't been able to get on the bridge as his heart raced. Somehow there didn't seem to be enough air in the world.

Next to him, by some miracle, Eddie remained asleep.

He didn't seem peaceful as he normally did. Typically Eddie managed to laugh off the troubles of the day by the time his head had hit the pillow, and managed to sleep with regular ease. Now his brow was tense, and Bob could see where lines might form in the years to come.

Bob watched him sleep for what felt like forever, allowing Eddie's presence to guide him back to reality. Eddie was never a part of *The Scream* Dream. He couldn't be. *The Scream* was about tension and fear and the unknown, and with Eddie everything was a known quantity. That, perhaps, was what calmed him the most about staring at the way the moonlight grazed the slope of Eddie's brow: his incompatibility with the world Munch had made. The two could not coexist, and if Eddie was real, then *The Scream* was the fiction. It was dubious logic, he knew, but the panic and anxiety of the dream world was not logical, it was visceral, like the world of art.

He got up slowly as he thought of this, bringing his jeans up over his bare buttocks. He took his eyes from Eddie only when necessary, as though his gaze kept him from stirring as it had the Low Men in the Big Hats. Eddie flitted and moved in his sleep though, the steady rise and fall of his broad chest teaching Bob's breathing how to return to normal, until slowly his anxiety had dissolved itself into a trembling tingle in his fingertips.

When he was dressed he stared at Eddie for a long moment, all of the blankets still curled around him, snug and sound despite the stress on his face. His black hair, thick and full and wild with the mess of the bed, shimmered in the ambient light filtering in from Jacobi Street.

Moments turned into minutes and he still stood in place at the foot of his bed, staring at Eddie and unable to move, until he began to wonder if the dream had really ended. Then finally, some part of him reached the decision he knew he would from the moment he'd jolted from his pillow, he stepped forward and kissed Eddie at his temple, then left the apartment they shared without waking him.

CHAPTER TWENTY-FIVE

He'd had to walk to FDR to find a gas station; there were no gas stations on Jacobi Street. The bright red gas can had cost him $8.97 and the gas to put in it had rounded it up to an even ten. He'd paid with a twenty and not stopped to collect his change, walking back out onto the street without a word to the attendant, even as he called out, waving his lost ten-spot back and forth. In the end he'd decided that Bob couldn't understand him, and had made some vaguely ethnocentric remarks before he was out of ear-shot.

He didn't feel himself again until he'd crossed back onto Jacobi Street. The air was different here somehow, although he knew this was foolish. The air everywhere in the city was dank, the smog like the thick fog surrounding a haunted castle in a Hammer horror classic.

The gasoline sloshed back and forth in the gallon canister. He hadn't filled it even a quarter of its way, and hadn't needed to.

Bob entered The Street on the south end of 14th Street, legs moving like pistons the entire way up: past the home that he and Eddie shared, past Cooper's Market that wasn't really a market, past *The Belle Verde* and up the stone steps of The Menagerie.

He found his keys without difficulty this time. He stared blankly at the 'closed' sign that had hung, without comment, for days now in the front window of the gallery. He put the key into its lock without looking at it, staring instead into the dull blue darkness of the halls behind the sign. Dust had settled on the floor in a way it had never had a chance to do until the past few days, and when he pushed the door open it wafted up in a kinetic wave, the dust particles catching in the soft light and billowing into the darkness beyond his sight.

He closed and locked the door behind him. He stepped forward into the darkened hallway, then almost as an afterthought, turned back and faced Jacobi Street as he reached around the side of the entrance and hit all eight switches there. Lights blazed to life all over The Menagerie, the florescent hum noticeable only for its absence a moment before.

Somewhere in his vacant, almost entranced mind, it occurred to him that this could have been in defiance of Chelsea Whitmire. He could hear her voice behind him now, telling him to not to waste the electricity and the lifetime of the bulbs when there were not patrons in the gallery. He shrugged this thought away though. This wasn't about Chelsea, at least not wholly.

He turned to the left and set down his sloshing container, again producing his keys and unlocking the gate to the gift shop. The drink coolers buzzed with electricity. He didn't turn on the lights. He stood amidst it all in the darkness for a moment, surrounded by sugar and toffee and salt. Then he reached out with a hand that was almost a phantom, and picked up the chocolates shaped like the Mona Lisa. He placed one in the pouch of his hoodie and then went back for another, and another, until all five that had been left in the display were on his person. He left the gift shop without a sound or utterance, and without paying for the chocolate, stepped back into the hall and picked up the can he'd left sitting there, then stepped quietly into the halls of The Menagerie.

The halls were not as labyrinthine in the light, their white walls and colourful portraits seeming lively and bright. The colours complemented each other into a rainbow of thoughts and feelings and experience, and on any other night he wouldn't have been able to walk down those halls without stopping every few feet, his head swivelling, looking from side to side at the works of a community he had longed so desperately to be a part of a lifetime ago.

He reached the Corben hall. The spotlight at the end was no longer special now, the other lights stole its illumination from it. When all things were equal, it was just another painting in a building that saw them come and go with systematic regularity. The mauves were no different than the mauves used by Boone, the gold no different than the gold used by Pardy.

Bob made his way down the hall without turning to look at the fine pencil work of Richard Corben. The Mal 'Ok came slowly more and more into view, the glisten of the spotlight off its oil brushstrokes becoming less and less until the small piece seemed enormous in his vision.

He laid down his can.

Chelsea had settled back into her chair since he had last been to the gallery. Her hand was no longer outstretched, and he was glad for that. Even in his determined state, he wasn't sure his composure could have withstood that. She sat back with her head and neck rested on the back of her seat, as though exhausted and about to fall victim to sleep. Her eyes were wide though and she stared out past the fourth wall, to the painter or to Bob or to whatever it was they saw.

Mal 'Ok stood behind her, the light off his thick shoulders casting deep shadows on the rest of his frame. One shoulder was pushed forward, as though the artist had caught him in mid-stride, just as Munch had one of the Low Men in his 1893 pastel on cardboard. Could the creature move when it was watched, or did it just choose not to? It amounted to the same. Bob watched it, close enough to touch his nose to it, close enough for his breath to make the canvas flap in his wind, all but daring it to move.

Without taking his eyes from the canvas, he removed a long paint-brush from his pocket. It was a two-inch background bristle with a wooden handle, made of badger hair and stiff with its newness. He had chosen it over the other brushes, the ones he had used to create his tiny failures and masterpieces over the last few months: they had been used to create, and just as Eddie had been antithetical to the world of Munch's Scream, those brushes that had been used to make art seemed antithetical to the duty that lay before him.

He unscrewed the cap of the red plastic gas can and tipped it over the brush, splashing it onto the floor as the foul-smelling liquid soaked into the hair and was caught between the bristles. When it glistened with the moisture of it he stopped and stood upright, his dripping implement at his side like a gunslinger's revolver.

Had the creature's lidless red eyes gotten larger in the brief moment he had looked away, or was it his imagination?

He reached out and flopped the brush into the centre of the creature's face, spattering it with gasoline. Some of the paint smudged, but not much. He dragged the brush downward, soaking through Chelsea and The Knight and then through the African man, all of whom stared out with that same resigned, tight-lipped sternness that Eddie had had while sitting on the table some nights ago.

When his brush touched the frame, he brought it up and to the left, in the same motions he would when applying a base white to a fresh canvas, applying firm, steady pressure. It was like second nature to him now, muscle memory, the only thing breaking him from his trance the stench of the gas. He pushed the blade up through Fredrick Cooper, his green apron smearing into his face. He pushed it through the woman with the bound breasts and The Knave and The Nurse, who smiled sweetly out at him even as he doused her in gasoline.

He brought his brush back across Mal 'Ok then down over The Prosti-tute, the Mother and Child who were no longer screaming, Obi's green hair and the fake hair of the man of the Whig Party. He coated the canvas until it was all glistening with the flammable paint-thinner, the faces blurred and distorted in the glimmer of the spotlight.

Without a word, he reached into his pocket again and found a small lighter, of the sort bought for a dollar at any convenience store. Not breaking eye contact with the demon he reached out to the bottom right of the piece, the empty chair in front of Fredrick Cooper where he had first seen the words he'd mistaken for O.K. Mal, and sparked the flint.

The flame travelled up almost instantaneously, cascading up from lower left to upper right, defying gravity like a wave. There was a sound like skittering, chattering teeth, or the harsh buzz of voice heard through dense fabric.

Bob watched it and the paint began to curl and break, then stepped back and kicked the silver frame with the toe of his shoe. It came up from its mount easily, picture and frame crashing down to the floor as the flames overtook the Opéra de Paris, turning its seats to ash and its aisles to smoke and flame.

Bob stepped back a pace and then sat cross-legged on the floor. One by one he took all five Mona Lisa chocolates from his pouch, unwrapped, and ate each one as he watched the painting burn. He ate them all, the heat melting the milk chocolate before it had found its way past his lips and leaving its gooey residue on his fingertips.

He ate the chocolate and watched the fire burn until there was nothing left but the smouldering, charred silver frame.

He stared at the scarred pattern of the flame-kissed wall behind it, its stone unhurt by the flame but for the burn marks. The silver framed it and made it seem intentional, as framing something often did, just as Sloan had commented when the store owner had framed her street art.

The fire had been his brush, the flame his final statement.

After all his work, his art was finally on display in The Menagerie.

CHAPTER TWENTY-SIX

The Officer that had come to ask Bob about the fire had been named Stanley, and had been Latino. He had a thick goatee and bushy eyebrows so thick that they all but covered up his eyes. Bob had never seen him on The Street before, and he found himself looking at those bobbing brows as he answered the man's questions.

"Where were you?"

"Here."

"Have you seen her?"

"No."

"What was the painting?"

"Couldn't say."

"Nothing missing from inventory?"

"No."

They'd come to the conclusion that Chelsea had set the fire, due to her disappearance. Bob wanted too much to correct and contradict them, but he could not. He would not have been able to change their minds anyway. Officer Stanley left Eddie and Bob alone in their apartment as his partner questioned Sloan in the hall.

The Menagerie was closed until the owner could find a new manager.

CHAPTER TWENTY-SEVEN

Bob sat with his copy of *Opera Houses of the World* open on his lap, flipping the newsprint-thin pages one by one as he looked through the marked section. He was sitting cross-legged on a thick stone coffee table in the center of Sloan's living room studio, and not five feet away she was staring blankly at a long slice she had made in her newest canvas without knowing fully why she had made it.

She had heard his story of what had happened to the Mal 'Ok three times since he had burned it, each time at her request. There was something about how he viewed that last part of the story, the art that had come from the fire in patterns on the wall, that had changed how she viewed the way she worked with her blade. Was her art truly creative? She wasn't adding paint to the canvas to create the art, she was removing anything that was not the art from the canvas: her art, she was finding, was in its own way as destructive as the flame and the gasoline had been.

She had told the police what she had known: nothing. Bob had purposely not told her what had happened until after her interview was done, making it impossible for her to lie badly. She thanked him for this, though not aloud. There was a lie to it that she was glad to get away from, as though he had allowed her the take her blade to the parts of her life which were not art as well.

Eddie's brush went back and forth on the plywood board he'd leaned in front of him at an angle, painting the cedar-brown the dark gray of the walls of a medieval castle. The variety show that took over the theatre every second Thursday had requested it as a part of a sketch on Disney Princesses – each one being taken back to the castle to find the others there, the Prince Not-So-Charming having collected them all polygamously. From what he'd been told, or rather, from what he'd understood from the thick French accent of the Director, the skit was tentatively to be called 'Sister-Princess-Wives.'

He stepped back a pace from the castle to look at what he had done, his tongue sticking out the side of his mouth.

Sloan cut a third piece away from her canvas, completing a large semi-circle which she was beginning to believe was going to be the top-half of a rip-off Kirby's head, but wasn't quite sure yet. She looked up when she heard Bob make a loud huff, in time to see him lay aside his copy of *Opera Houses of the World* and pick up another, a thick text called only *Hauntings*.

Her face twitched. "What is it?" she asked, tentatively.

He frowned. "Net nikakogo otrazheniya," he said, touching a red-bound text behind him with a hammer and sickle on the spine.

"Pardon?" she asked, raising an eyebrow and lowering her knife.

"Pas de réflexion," he said in the same matter-of-fact tone, resting his hand on the copy of *Opera Houses of the World* he had taken from the public library. Finally he motioned to the book that was now on his lap. "No reflection. It's everywhere, it's the one commonality in any book that even hints at the painting. No matter how garbled or lost the rest of the text is, somewhere it will say the painting has no reflection, or something that seems like it was there, *something*."

Sloan looked at him with pity. "Does it matter?"

He looked at her, then went back to his book. Several minutes later, after turning a few pages and becoming frustrated again, he finally replied, his voice low. "Yes," he said firmly. "It matters because it doesn't fit. Everything else... fits, this doesn't."

In the moments between she had made another cut, having decided that it would be Kirby, devouring all the money of the middle-class, and that she would use a separate stencil to give Kirby a Trump-style hairpiece. She put her knife down again, loosened her hair, then folded her fingers together and turned to listen to him.

"Look," he said, turning the *Hauntings* book toward her. It was an anthology book with no author listed. There was a small piece that seemed to be about the Mal 'Ok painting, or something like it, as an addendum to a piece detailing how early propaganda of Catholic cannibalism had contributed to the creation of popular myths regarding creatures who drink blood. "Everything else makes sense, and even this makes sense. The Romani reference, the blood, all of it. Even the no reflection makes sense, it's like that's where that part of the myth came from."

She glanced at the page, but mostly listened. "So then what's the problem?"

"It *did* have a reflection," he said with stress, remembering how it had looked that first day in Receiving. "And if it had a reflection then that can't be the basis for the myth and there's no reason for it to be in this book. But it *is* in this book, it's in *all* these books. It's the one part of the presentation that never changes."

She shrugged. "And lack thereof."

He turned back to his book, turned the page, then stopped and turned back. He looked up at her, brow furrowed. "Pardon?"

"You know, the presentation. The other thing they all have in common. There's no sketch or drawing or engraving of the picture; that was what took us so long to find it in the first place."

He nodded, and once again went back to his book.

Eddie finished painting a tree, having gotten far too into the intricacies of the leaves that nobody in the audience would ever be close enough to see. Painting trees had always brought him a certain amount of calm though: he could always hear the soothing voice of Bob Ross in his mind when he made them, expositing about "Happy Little Trees."

His phone went off on the mat a few feet away, its screen lighting up. It was an alarm or a call, he wasn't sure which, but the tone was unfamiliar to him. He let it ring until it went to voicemail, not wanting to touch it with its paint-covered hands.

Bob closed the book slowly, and laid it aside. Sloan was working on the large round eyes of Kirby-Trump now, and was paying little attention to him.

She didn't see how pale he had gotten, as he stood up so that he could reach his phone.

He fished it out of his pocket and unlocked it, scrolling through his apps until he found his photo album and opened it. He went back several rows of images, found what he was looking for, and felt his legs turn to rubber.

He sat quickly, almost at free-fall, next to Sloan's canvas.

"What?" she said suddenly, seeing his cheeks with no colour. "What is it?"

"No reflection," he said, holding up his phone to her. "It wasn't a statement."

The ringtone blared through the theatre again and Eddie huffed loudly. It was a tinny piano melody that sounded European, not something he would have put on his phone. Bob must have done it, he decided. He stepped over to it and picked it up tentatively by the brushed band edges, turning the screen toward him.

There was no alarm or call notification, just the mp3 screen showing that a track called *Romanian Folk Dances - Standing Still* was playing. He frowned, and then unlocked the phone to stop it.

As soon as the screen was unlocked, it was filled with two glowing red eyes and the scant hints of the purple flesh which contained them.

Eddie screamed and dropped his phone.

Bob held the phone out toward Sloan, revealing that the Opera's patrons were still there, all twelve of them. The back of the house was empty though, Mal 'Ok was nowhere to be seen.

"No reflection was *instructional*," he said hoarsely.

CHAPTER TWENTY-EIGHT

The Quaint Little Theatre, as it had been ironically rechristened several years ago, was empty. The only light came from the stage lights, which shone down on wooden reconstructions of a knight, a castle, and an intricately designed tree.

Bob and Sloan made their way down through the aisles slowly, their brows thick with sweat and their breath strong but laboured as they stepped down the sloping aisle, row on row, until finally they were at the rickety staircase that led up to the stage.

There was a phone in the center of the stage.

Bob stepped over to it slowly. When he reached it, it lay between his feet and he stared down at it, daring it to move or make a noise of cease to be altogether. After a tense moment with Sloan standing back with her hands clasped to her lips, he bent down gingerly as if he were going to touch his toes and picked up the phone.

He unlocked it with Eddie's code, and as soon as he did the photo Bob had sent Eddie the first time he had taken the painting out of the box emerged, although it was so different now that it was almost a totally new piece.

Gone was the Paris Opera, replaced instead with the very seats that the stage now looked out upon: the audience of The Quaint Little Theatre on

Jacobi Street. The house lights were on, not as they were now, and all the rows were in view. Chelsea, The Nurse and the Lady of the Night were in the farthest row back and seemed to be conversing about something privately. The Knight stood watch over everyone but them in the next row, followed by Maria and little Philippe and The Knave. Obi sat with the slender woman in the middle row, while Fredrick Cooper and the African American man both faced the audience (and away from each other) in row three.

To the far left of the first row was the man wearing a white wig. Two seats to his right, Eddie Alvarez sat with his fingers laced in front of him. He looked calm and ready to enjoy a show, were it not for the herringbones cut into each bicep and the three additional strikes on his forehead, marking him as thirteen.

There were no shadows for a demon to hide, and no demon presented itself.

Bob felt his eyes well up with tears even as he saw what he thought might be a playful smirk on Eddie's face. He handed the phone to Sloan who took it then fell to the mat, hysterical sobs escaping from her tear-stained lips. Bob did not hear them.

He stepped to the edge of the stage and hopped down, then stepped the short distance to the first row. He counted the second seat from the left and sat there, closed his eyes, and laid his hand on the arm rest.

For a moment he thought he could feel Eddie's warmth on the seat beside him. He leaned his head onto where the phantom shoulder would be and waited for time to catch up to him.

EPILOGUE

Sloan walked into the gift shop of The Menagerie, her hair pulled back in a makeshift – and unconvincing – ponytail, a full half hour later than usual. She was carrying a large sheet of canvas and was wearing a blue blazer that didn't suit her over a tattered Rolling Stones t-shirt, which did.

Bob looked up at her and smiled weakly, then finished arranging the chocolates on the cash. They were ears now: tiny chocolate ears with raspberry filling called "Van Gogh's Delight," which Sloan had found hilarious and Bob had found in poor taste, but delicious.

"Good morning!" Sloan chimed, laying her canvas down against the floor so she could shake out her hair.

Bob smiled at the patrons that walked by the gift shop entrance. The Menagerie was full, with more patrons on this Tuesday than it used to have on any given Friday. "What kept you this morning?" he asked, turning back to Sloan.

"Was out late putting up new pieces," she grinned, rolling her eyes a little. "Stopped by The Belle Verde to get me a little coffee." She handed him one.

He took it graciously, nodding in thanks.

She turned back to the large piece that was framed and hung in the center of the hallway, the first piece people saw when they entered The Menagerie, advertising one of its new exhibits. She watched as people walked past, each and every one stopping to stare up at it before moving on. "The piece is doing well," she said, almost smugly, or as close as Sloan could ever get to that.

Bob smiled, and nodded.

"Take your break," she smirked, slapping the desk to annunciate her point.

"Yes boss."

Bob stepped out into the hall with his coffee, still steaming heat. He walked up alongside a small elderly lady who was admiring it, gazing up with some difficulty but without complaint. He took a sip of the caffeine, grateful for it even though it burned his mouth. He stood alongside her and stared up at the painting, a slow smile spreading across his lips.

It was the last piece he had worked on while Eddie was alive, the wall of the alley with the old couple dancing the tango on the bricks.

In front of it was a small sign that read, 'Haung Exhibit - Third Floor.'

The old woman turned to him and smiled. "Lovely isn't it?" she beamed. He nodded, and blushed a bit, but did not respond. "It's almost like they're moving."

He forced his smile to remain, but broke away to enjoy the rest of his coffee outside in the early winter air.

"Lever ça là," came the thick French accent from the front row, waving his hands like a conductor.

"What?" a man with a bushy beard and a large belly said, turning back precariously on the ladder he stood on.

"Lever ça là," the man repeated, frustrated.

"English please, Jim."

The Frenchman frowned, so deep his wrinkles found their way off his face. "Raise that up, here," he said, biting each word.

The man on the ladder chuckled, then rolled his eyes and got up higher on the ladder.

Off from stage right, a thin man with a hooked nose and deep tan sunglasses chuckled to himself. He puffed on a cigarette that he knew he shouldn't have lit, as a large blonde woman beside him coughed and waved her hand in front of her face, glaring at him side-on. He pretended not to notice.

They watched as the man on the ladder raised the moon higher.

"You hear that?" the man in glasses asked after a moment of silence.

"Hear what?" the woman replied, not looking away from the ladder.

The man stepped back into the shadows behind the stage, the thick curtain blocking out all light, and reflecting sound as well to help with the acoustics. From here Jim's taunts and French curses sounded distant.

For a long moment there was nothing, and then, all at once, there was a sound again in the depths of The Quaint Little Theatre on Jacobi Street.

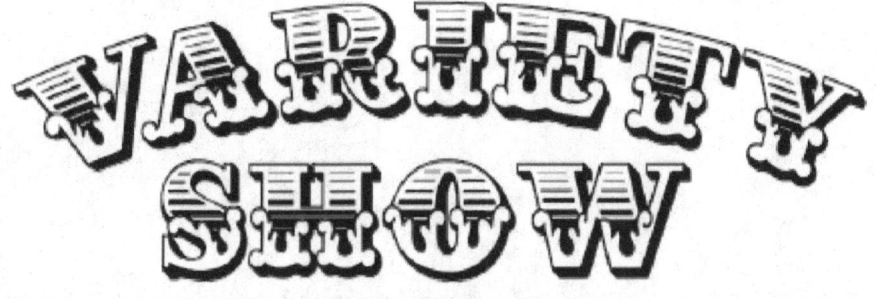

ALI HOUSE

CHAPTER ONE

"You hear that?"

Francesca didn't bother turning to look at the thin man to her left, but she did roll her eyes at his question. "Hear what?" she asked in a bored voice. They had been standing in the off-right wing for the past fifteen minutes, waiting for their scene to finally start rehearsing, and she hadn't heard anything other than the director angrily giving instructions to the set designer on how to hang the moon. It was a scene that everyone at the theatre was well versed in, as it happened at least four times during every stumble-through. Jim, the director, would find some fault in the set or lights and instead of communicating it in English, he would give all his instructions in French, knowing full well that Billy, the set and lighting designer and resident stagehand, couldn't understand him. Billy would then politely ask Jim to speak in English, and the mere suggestion would cause Jim to fume angrily for at least a minute before reluctantly replying in English.

Watching such a scene was an entertaining enough way to pass the time while waiting for rehearsal to continue, but as Jim continued to fret over the precise location of the wooden moon, Francesca began to wonder if she and Gerard would be standing here forever.

"Hear *that*," Gerard repeated.

Sighing, Francesca turned to him, wishing that he'd put out that damn cigarette. The scent reminded her of days and nights spent on the smoke-filled verandas of Paris, drinking with famous actors and directors, and right now it wasn't a memory the large blonde woman wanted to revisit.

Before she could speak, he put one finger up to his lips, the tip of which rested under his large, hooked nose, indicating for her to be quiet. She glared at him, which he pretended not to notice. Moving backwards, he stepped away from the stage and further into the wing. He was careful to step around the prop-tables, costume racks, and set pieces that were cluttering the area. By tomorrow everything would be neatly placed and easy to manoeuvre around, but right now the area was more akin to an obstacle course set up by drunkards.

As Gerard moved further away from the stage, the director's cursing grew more distant, until it was barely noticeable. Once he was far enough back, he listened and waited. For a long moment there was nothing, and then there was a sound, a low, deep knocking sound that seemed to come from the depths of the theatre.

Gesturing for her to come join him, he watched as Francesca reluctantly came over. After another moment, the sound repeated itself. She raised an eyebrow. "Do you think something's gotten in the pipes?"

Gerard frowned and paused to think. "It's probably something to do with the furnace," he said dismissively, taking a puff from the cigarette he carelessly held in his right hand. Now that the mystery had been solved, he'd instantly lost interest. Was it too much to ask that something *interesting* happen in this theatre?

"Perhaps you should make yourself useful and go fix it," Francesca shot at him.

"You shouldn't be smoking back here," a nasally voice called out.

Gerard rolled his eyes at the intrusion. "It's only a cigarette, Scott."

The young, red-headed man stepped out from behind a large set piece and tried to glare at Gerard through his bottle-thick glasses. Unfortunately, the effect wasn't anywhere close to what he was hoping to achieve.

"He has a point," Francesca remarked, using her hand to wave the smoke away from her face. "And if Ari sees you, they'll tear a strip off you. You're in costume, after all."

The threat of the stage manager's wrath was enough to make Gerard second-guess his obstinate determination to break all the theatre's rules. However, he was not going to show weakness in front of a lackey like Scott. Taking a long drag, he smirked at the young man before blowing smoke in his direction.

Scott coughed and tried to wave the smoke away with his clipboard. "Monsieur Le Faull says that we'll be starting the 'Amore' sketch in two minutes, so be ready."

"Just call him Jim," Gerard said impatiently. "Everyone else does."

Scott clenched his jaw and exited through the door, heading to the green room to warn the other actors.

"What an annoying little twerp," Gerard muttered to himself. He waited until Scott was out of sight before putting his cigarette out on the back of a nearby set piece and slipping the unfinished portion into his pocket.

"Do you think you'll remember your lines this time?" Francesca remarked as she smoothed her costume, her pleasant pitch tinged with hostility.

"Francesca, please," he said, putting on his most flattering tone. "Shall we have this tiresome conversation all over again? You know I always get it right by the night of the show."

She crossed her arms over her ample chest. Despite the many years she'd worked with Gerard, she had yet to get accustomed to his various "methods." He claimed that it was part of his routine to never say his lines correctly until there was an audience in the house, but she knew that he was bluffing around his terrible memory. Perhaps if he spent more time with his script and less time with a certain young actress…

The knocking sounded again, but this time it was louder and sharper.

"Are you sure it's the furnace?" Francesca asked, resisting the urge to glance towards the backstage door.

"Probably," Gerard shrugged. "What else could it be?"

She didn't know why the noise unnerved her, but it did. "I swear I've never heard it do anything like this before. Do you think something's wrong with it?"

"Perhaps you should concentrate less on the furnace and more on the skit we'll be doing in a few seconds, once *le Director* stops cursing."

"Gerard, please," she scoffed. "Of the two of us, I'm *never* the least prepared. All I'm suggesting is that maybe someone should go back there and make sure the furnace isn't about to explode."

He rolled his eyes. "It's likely nothing."

"But maybe it is."

"But maybe it's not."

"Maybe it's a ghost!"

Both of them jumped at the sudden exclamation.

"*Merde*," Francesca swore under her breath as she turned around to see two young women standing behind her, both dressed in black pants and white shirts, their hair pulled back into ponytails. Despite their similar costumes, the two women looked nothing alike, with the taller of the two having dark skin and curly black hair, and the shorter having pale skin and long brown hair. It was Stacey, the taller woman, who'd startled them, and her lips parted in a wide smile as she relished how she'd managed to spook the two elder actors. The other, Wendy, managed to keep her face neutral, but there was the slightest hint of amusement in her eyes.

Francesca hadn't heard either of them approach and resented the fact that she'd been startled this close to performing. This kind of thing never would have happened in Paris—the ensemble would have known better.

"There's no such thing as ghosts," Gerard said, curling his lips.

"C'mon," Stacey prodded. "Every theatre has a ghost. It's tradition."

"Not this theatre," Francesca replied confidently. "Jim has owned and operated it for the past fifteen years and there's not been even the slightest supernatural activity." Stacey opened her mouth to speak, but she quickly interrupted her. "Any strange occurrences you may have witnessed are merely the product of your own imagination."

"Bor-ing," Stacey replied under her breath.

Wendy wouldn't admit it, but she was glad to hear Francesca say that.

This theatre was full of dark spaces and strange noises, and she'd much prefer if there wasn't a spirit hanging around, causing trouble.

A string of French curses rang out in the distance and the group moved towards the stage. The director, a short, thin, bald man who was frowning so hard that there were deep creases on his forehead, was standing in the front row of the audience, glaring at them.

"*Que Dieu me vienne en aide*... If I have to ask one more time for actors to take their places..." Jim rumbled. "*Sommes-nous prêts?*"

"English, Jim!" Billy called out. Although he'd said the phrase at least a hundred times today, there was no exasperation in his voice.

Jim frowned and rubbed his temples. "Places for 'Amore.'"

The actors quickly took their places for the top of the scene. Stacey remained in the off-right wing, while Wendy hurried through the cross behind the stage to the off-left wing. Francesca and Gerard moved onstage to the table and chairs Billy had set up after finally hanging the moon to Jim's satisfaction. Once everyone was ready, Jim called for the scene to start.

The sketch was a comment about how the song "That's Amore" makes no sense and was probably written by someone who was hungry and near an Italian restaurant. Francesca's character was a doe-eyed lover asking Gerard's character to write a romantic love song for her to prove his love. He'd start out fine, but, every time he became stuck, he would look around for inspiration, at which point Wendy or Stacey would cross the stage with some kind of Italian food or drink, which he would add into his song. Francesca would alternate between romantic, confused, and irritated, while Gerard would grow hungrier and more distracted.

Wendy hoisted her first prop, a large cardboard pizza, and prepared for her entrance. As soon as Gerard said her cue line—or, at least, something resembling her cue line—she walked across the stage as if she was delivering the pizza to a couple sitting in the other wing. Stacey gave a nod as Wendy walked past before lifting her own prop, a tray of plastic wine bottles. Her cue came shortly after, and Stacey walked onto the stage, crossing to the other side.

Placing the pizza on the discard table, Wendy looked for her next prop, an imitation of pasta fazool that was quite realistic despite being made of packing peanuts and paint. As she reached for the comically large bowl, she was startled by a sudden loud knocking sound and almost knocked the prop off the table. Shaking it off, she tried to tell herself that it was merely the pipes and it was nothing to worry about, but as soon as she started to relax another knock startled her, this time louder than the first. Taking in a deep breath, she picked up her prop and reminded herself that it was only a mechanical issue. Jim would get someone to check it out soon and then the noise would stop.

Still, as she moved to the wings to listen for her next cue, she couldn't help feeling as if a pair of ghostly eyes were staring at her, watching her hungrily.

CHAPTER TWO

After they finished running through the remainder of the skits, Jim called for the cast and creative to gather in the audience for notes. It took time for everyone to make their way from the various sections of the theatre, but within fifteen minutes the entire troupe had settled into the red, well-worn audience seats.

Wendy had been on her way to sit with Stacey and Carina, but after spying a familiar face she made a detour to the fourth row on the left, where Betty Snow, the props designer, was sitting by herself. Betty was tall and thin, with chin-length red hair that often stuck out in strange directions—usually a result of her nervously playing with it while she worried about a million different things. She was holding a pad of paper and a pencil, ready to take down any notes that Jim might have about the props.

"Nice pasta fazool," Wendy remarked as she neared. "It looked good enough to eat."

Betty smiled and her cheeks flushed at the compliment. "Thanks. It was fun to make. I just hope Jim thinks it's good enough."

Jim, who was standing in front of the stage, chose that moment to clear his throat loudly. He stared out at the sea of faces before him, a grim look on his face.

Quickly taking a seat, Wendy trained her attention on the short man. She'd thought that the stumble-through had gone pretty well, considering that this was the first time they'd worked with certain props and sets, but the look on Jim's face told her that he didn't feel the same. Not that his expressions had any relation whatsoever to reality—Wendy had been working as an actor for The Quaint Little Theatre for the past six months and had yet to see Jim actually pleased with *anything*. Even if something went well, his expression could only be described as not-angry. It was as if his face was missing the necessary muscles required for smiling.

He quickly launched into his notes about the many things that had bothered him tonight—from the lighting in 'Shakespearean Stories,' to the lack of detail in their current set pieces, to the costume changes not being effective enough in 'Reverse House Party.' Wendy listened carefully as Jim ranted and railed, now familiar enough with this routine to know the difference between general ennui and an actual note. Jim was burdened with memories of grandeur, and most of his comments boiled down to him wanting things to be better but not being able to afford it.

When he reached the end of his list, Jim took a deep breath. "We will start the dress rehearsal tomorrow afternoon at exactly 2:00 pm, and I expect us all to be perfect in preparation for the show tomorrow night. Now go, rest, and be better tomorrow."

Wendy held back a laugh. Inspiring as always...

It had been a long day for the troupe, with the cue-to-cue taking up the morning and afternoon, and then the stumble-through in the evening. Most of them rose wearily to their feet, eager to go home and rest before starting again tomorrow afternoon, but before anyone could leave the room, Francesca stopped them in their tracks.

"Jim, you haven't yet announced which show we'll be doing at the end of the month," she said, her voice projecting loud enough that everyone in the room could hear every word perfectly, no matter where they were standing.

Those who were on their feet quickly sat back down. Although the theatre made most of its money by putting on a variety show twice monthly for a rich benefactor, every month Jim would cast a "legitimate" play for them to rehearse and perform. The variety shows were fun, but the cast and crew enjoyed the chance to work on something serious; something that would exist for more than one night. Their last play had been *Glengarry Glen Ross*, which was an interesting choice for a theatre company that only had six actors—two-thirds of which were women. But with a little script tweaking, Jim had made it work.

Usually, the new play was announced the Monday after the previous show closed, but now it was Wednesday, and Jim still hadn't revealed anything. The cast and crew had spent the past two days wondering if Jim had forgotten to find a new play or if he was withholding the information because he delighted in tormenting them.

Jim grimaced in a way that only a man who constantly had to deal with his ex-wife could. "I am still finalizing *le scénario*. But if you are all so eager to know, I am adapting *Le Fantôme de l'Opéra*." He paused so that they could all murmur excitedly, and once the noise died down a little he continued. "Auditions will be on *Vendredi*, with casting to be announced *juste après*."

Although Wendy wasn't fluent in French, she'd picked up enough to understand that auditions would be on Friday and the casting announced shortly after.

Despite Jim's having lived on Jacobi Street for the past fifteen years, he was still reluctant to let go of his native language. Francesca had adapted and now only spoke the odd phrase or two of French, but on certain days it was impossible to convince Jim to speak even a single word of English.

It was a sore point for some of the troupe, as most of them didn't speak French, but Wendy was thankful for it. Her heritage was half French and half Inuit, but her parents had wanted to assimilate into their very-white, very-American neighbourhood and refused to speak any language other than English. Wendy's paternal grandparents had died before she was born, and every bit of French she picked up from Jim and Francesca made her feel closer to them.

Now that his announcement was complete, Jim gave a heavy sigh and walked away, heading towards his apartment above the theatre.

"Guess I'd better put the props away," Betty said, giving Wendy a small wave goodbye.

As she watched Betty scurry away, Wendy had a feeling that she would spend the next hour or so trying to fix all the problems Jim had pointed out. While everyone recognized Jim's flair for the dramatic, Betty took most of Jim's notes to heart. She worried about a lot of things—theatre related and otherwise—and didn't want to risk losing her job over the colour of a prop. Others, like the costume designer, Paloma, would merely address one or two notes and call it a night. Paloma knew that no matter how much Jim railed about imperfections, he didn't have the energy to fire them all and hire a brand-new cast and creative.

Wendy looked over and noticed Stacey and Carina talking animatedly in their seats, so she made her way over to them.

"I can't believe he's doing *Phantom*!" Carina exclaimed.

"I know!" Stacy added eagerly. "It's such a great story. So romantic."

"I wonder how different the book is from the musical," Wendy said, leaning on a nearby seat. "I've only ever seen the movie."

Stacey shrugged the comment off. "Knowing Jim, he'll steal a bunch of stuff from the musical and add it in. The musical's super popular, and all he really cares about is making money, which means keeping the audiences happy."

The three of them continued to talk as they made their way backstage, heading for the large dressing room they shared on the lower floor. They were all wearing their final costumes of the night, which was for the skit 'Vamp-liar High.' It was about a girl who arrives at a new high school and discovers that some of the kids are vampires, but who later learns that they're actually humans who are lying in order to seem cool. Stacey, who was playing the new girl, was wearing jeans and a t-shirt, but Wendy and Carina were dressed as wannabe vampires, with dark clothing cut at weird angles and lots of black eyeliner. Although Wendy didn't have many lines in the skit, she was glad that she at least got to wear an elaborate costume.

As they talked about the upcoming auditions, they were very careful not to mention how much each of them wanted the part of Christine. They

all knew that only one of them could get the part, and although they secretly hoped the others would fail, nobody would admit it out loud.

Wendy wanted to play Christine more than anything else, but as the
newest member of the troupe she wasn't sure if she'd "earned" a role like
that yet. Stacey had been working at the theatre for three years, and Carina
for two and a half, so the role of the young ingenue in every play went to
one of them. Meanwhile, Wendy rarely managed to get a lead role in one of
the eight to ten skits they performed every second Thursday. She couldn't
help feeling self-conscious sometimes, with Carina's carefree spirit, bronze
skin, and long legs; and Stacey's theatrical background off-Broadway,
million-dollar smile, and ability to act any part put in front of her. Often
Wendy wondered what she brought to this troupe other than her ability to
be another body in the background.

Still, it didn't stop her from wanting the part of Christine so bad that
she could almost taste it.

"Who do you think is going to play Raoul?" Carina wondered aloud
as the group entered the dressing room. It had been built for four people,
so it didn't feel cramped when the three of them were inside at the same
time, bustling around. There was a long counter along one wall with four
mirrors above it, each one lined in large light bulbs that heated the room to
an uncomfortable degree if they were left on for too long. Along the other
wall were four closets where they could each hang up their clothes and
costumes, and store personal items. There was also a shower and bathroom
at one end, opposite the entrance. Next door was another dressing room exactly like it, which had been assigned to Gerard and Sam. There were four
private dressing rooms on the main floor, behind the stage, but those were
reserved for people with lead roles or who had been named Francesca.

"We can all agree that it won't be Samuel, right?" Stacey burst out
laughing. "I mean, he's old enough to be our grandfather."

"Maybe it'll be Gerard," Carina suggested as she wiped the heavy
make-up from her face.

Wendy and Stacey exchanged a look. Although Gerard was younger
than Samuel and looked younger than his fifty years of age, neither of them
wanted to play his love interest. They knew that Carina, however, wouldn't
have any qualms about that.

"I don't know," Stacey said as she quickly changed into her regular
clothes, "I mean, during *A Streetcar Named Desire* he kept changing up his
blocking and lines, and I never felt like I knew where I was."

"That's just his process," Carina replied diplomatically.

"Well, I wish he'd get another one," Stacey muttered.

Wendy held back a laugh. "Do you think Jim might try to get Billy to do
it?" Although Billy had enough to do with designing the sets and lighting,

he had no problem stepping in for a bit part occasionally. While he'd never expressed a desire for a bigger part, she'd feel more comfortable with him in the role instead of Gerard, even if he was nearly fifteen years her senior.

"Or Scott?" Stacey pretended to gag. "That would be the worst."

Carina wrinkled her nose. "I bet he'd do it if Jim promised him the chance to finally assistant direct something."

"Maybe one of us will end up playing it," Wendy interjected, quickly changing the subject. Although she didn't like the way that Scott skulked around the theatre, acting as if he owned it (or *should* own it), she didn't want to say anything that he might hear. It was well known that he had a habit of listening at closed doors, and while some people didn't care one bit about what he might think, she didn't want to make enemies of anyone at the theatre. "I mean, we've certainly played enough male roles in the past. Besides, Raoul and Christine are supposed to be childhood friends and we're closer in age than any of the men."

"Well, let's just hope that Jim isn't planning on casting Francesca as Christine," Stacey said bitterly. "I wouldn't be surprised if she demanded to play the part."

"Oh, that would be the worst!" Carina cried, slumping against the counter. "I mean, losing that part would be terrible, but it'd be even worse if it was to *her*."

Wendy finished hanging up her costume and picked up her purse. She hadn't managed to get all her eyeliner off, but the gossip was starting to overwhelm her. "See you two tomorrow afternoon," she said as she stepped into the hallway.

She could hear noises farther down the hall as designers cleaned up their workspaces or discussed Jim's notes with each other or adjusted certain projects. A smile broke out on her face as she thought about how lucky she was to work in a place that was so full of life, where people truly enjoyed what they did.

As Wendy made her way to the staircase, she kept an ear out for the strange noise that she'd heard earlier in the wings. At first it seemed as if the noise had gone away, but, as she started to ascend the staircase, she heard a sharp knock and instinctively looked towards the door to the basement.

It was a perfectly normal door, located next to the staircase, leading to a large room that housed the furnace, and which they also used to store backdrops and furniture. She'd walked past it hundreds of times, but, as she looked at it now, it took on a sinister quality. The dark red paint seemed redder and more chipped, with jagged pieces sticking out and flaking off, like dried blood. As she continued to stare at the door, a sudden, ear-splitting knock from within rattled the door and caused her to jump. She quickly hurried up the stairs, her heart pounding in her chest.

CHAPTER THREE

Stepping outside The Quaint Little Theatre, Wendy took in a deep breath of the cool night air. Now that she was away from the basement door, she felt a lot better. Shaking her head, she chided herself for being so easy to scare. It was probably one of the other actors playing a joke.

As she took in her surroundings, she saw that even though it was late evening, the street was alive with people heading to and from the many businesses that occupied Jacobi Street. Despite the short length of the street, it was packed full of vendors, markets, galleries, and theatres, with plenty of apartments tucked around. Most of the people who worked on the street lived here, creating a harmonious, symbiotic feeling within the neighbourhood. That magical feeling was likely helped by the fact that the street rarely existed on any maps, making it more difficult for ordinary folk to find. This street belonged to the people who lived on it, and they all knew it.

A smile crossed Wendy's face as she thought of how lucky she'd been to discover it.

She had grown up further north in the city, completely oblivious of Jacobi Street and its charming ways. Although she'd dabbled in high school drama, Wendy had never once considered becoming an actor. Her parents had always wanted her to go to college and become an accountant like her mother or a data analyst like her father, but neither option sounded ideal. In fact, the whole notion of college was unappealing to her. So, despite her parents' objections, Wendy decided not to go. She found a full-time job working at one of the restaurants downtown, and once she'd earned enough money she moved out of her parents' home and away from their expectations. Deciding that life was good enough for now, she spent three years working at the restaurant, enjoying her freedom from her parents' rules and assumptions.

It wasn't until she noticed a paper sign taped to a light pole on 13th Street that the course of her life changed dramatically. The sign was eye-catching in its simplicity, with hand-drawn curtains and a stage framing the notice. All the other signs had been printed on glossy paper and looked professionally designed, so this one stood out like a sore thumb. The name of the theatre sounded vaguely familiar, although she'd never been to it, and the sign said that it was looking for an actor for its bi-weekly variety show.

At that moment, she began to wonder what it would be like to be an actor. The plays she'd been in during high school had been fun, and although she suspected that this would be a lot more work, it had to be better than occasionally getting yelled at for the soup not being warm enough or for getting an order wrong—even though it was exactly how the customer had ordered it. After an hour of debating the matter with herself, she decided to try out and see what happened. If she got in then perhaps she'd give acting a try, and if she failed horribly then she'd still have the restaurant to go back to.

Finding Jacobi Street hadn't been easy, but after a few false starts Wendy finally discovered the entrance off 14th Street. She must have walked past it many times over the last few years, but never once noticed where it led. On the day of the auditions, she stepped onto the cobblestone street for the first time, keeping an eye out for The Quaint Little Theatre, but also getting distracted by this strange, wondrous street that she had never known existed. There were no cars, and it was crammed full of tall, thin houses that had been converted into businesses. Everyone seemed to know everyone else. For a minute she wondered if she had suddenly started hallucinating. No other street in the city looked or felt like this.

When she found the theatre and stepped inside, she was surprised that such a luxurious place could exist in such an unassuming building. The long hallway she found herself in was carpeted and ran the length of the building, with another door at the end, likely leading back to 14th Street. There appeared to be a small Box Office window further down on her right, and on her left were two large wooden doors that were propped open. They led into the auditorium, which was even more surprising. The room was huge, easily able to seat 200 people, and the style was baroque, with elaborate wall-fixtures and a gilded frame around the raised proscenium stage. The theatre had definitely seen better days, but it was still grander than any other theatre that Wendy had been to. There were large red curtains framing either side of the stage, and the orchestra was filled with fold-down chairs in a similar red.

An older, bald man with a round head was talking to a large blonde woman and a larger man with brown hair and a bushy brown beard near the stage. She wondered if they were also auditioning or if they worked here. There hadn't been any number to phone and ask questions, so Wendy had decided to show up and hope for the best. However, she could feel uncertainty growing inside of her as she walked further into the auditorium, passing by row after row of red chairs. This theatre looked way more professional than she'd been expecting, and now she was worried that she was completely out of her league. Coming to a stop, Wendy wondered if she should continue to the stage or turn around and go back home before anyone noticed her arrival.

Before she could decide, the group realized that a newcomer was in their midst and all eyes turned towards her.

"Hi...?" she called out nervously. "I'm here to audition..."

"*Venez ici,*" the bald man said, waving her forward.

Wendy wasn't sure what the man had said or which language he'd spoken, but she assumed that he meant for her to come closer. With a ton of butterflies fluttering in her stomach, she walked towards the group of three, and what commenced was the strangest experience she'd ever had.

Although she'd come prepared with a monologue, she had no idea that she needed a professional headshot or resume (nor had that information been included on the poster). As she tried to remember the few plays she'd been in during high school, she could see the French man becoming more and more impatient, and she began to regret her impulsiveness. She fumbled the beginning of her monologue but managed to push through and finish stronger, and when they asked her to sing, her mind blanked for a few seconds before she hastily brought out a pop song she'd last sung in the shower that morning. The other man and woman, who had introduced themselves as Billy and Francesca, tried to keep the mood friendly and light, but they weren't entirely able to combat Jim's obvious hostility.

When Wendy left the theatre, she was certain that she'd never be able to show her face on this street ever again, which was a bit of a shame. She'd love to go back but wouldn't want to risk the chance of running into the angry director again. He seemed like the type that would hold a grudge. However, the very next day she received a call from Francesca saying that if she wanted to become a part of their troupe, they would hire her. Then Francesca told her what kind of work the theatre did, what would be expected of her, and named a price that was less than she was earning at the restaurant, but still seemed ridiculously high for an actor in a bi-weekly variety show. Although Wendy suspected that she was being hired because she was the only person who'd auditioned—and she was still a little afraid of Jim—she also knew that she really wanted the job.

And thus she became the newest troupe member of The Quaint Little Theatre. Mostly she worked background and bit parts, learning what was involved in putting on a show, and eventually she began to grow and get better. After her first month with the troupe, she moved into a small studio flat above the Oz Theatre, an old movie house that only showed Technicolour movies—except on April Fool's Day when they'd play black and white movies.

Since then, the rest of the world began to fall away. Her relationship with her parents, which was tense due to her unwillingness to follow their plans, became further strained by her new career path. The friends she'd made at the restaurant didn't understand why she would quit a well-paying job to work in a theatre and earn less, and they had no desire to even look for Jacobi Street, let alone watch her perform. But Wendy didn't care. She found new friends within the troupe and a new life that challenged and excited her. The more time she spent on Jacobi Street, the more convinced she became that this was where she was meant to be.

CHAPTER FOUR

"You did wonderful work tonight, darling," Francesca said, coming up beside Wendy and pulling her from her thoughts. "You've come a long way in the past few months."

She paused expectantly and Wendy knew exactly what she wanted to hear.

"It's all thanks to you," Wendy replied. It was something she would have said anyway, but Francesca didn't like to rely on chance whenever a compliment was involved.

A little over a month after Wendy had joined the troupe, Francesca decided to take her under her wing and provide acting and singing lessons—something she'd never offered to anyone else. Although *la grande dame du théâtre* was intimidating as hell, Wendy was cognizant enough to realize that she desperately needed the help if she ever wanted to be considered an asset to the team. The best part was that Francesca didn't ask for money, she merely asked for an opportunity to share the wealth of knowledge she'd amassed over many years as a professional actor in Paris. And—although Wendy would never admit it out loud—she was sure that Francesca did it because it gave her the chance to revisit her heyday and wistfully reminisce about all the wonderful parts she'd played in the past.

"Now, darling, tell me that you've been keeping up with your practice," Francesca said as they walked away from the theatre. She rented the one-bedroom apartment on the floor below Wendy, so they sometimes walked home together. In fact, Francesca had been the one to suggest to Wendy that she should move onto the street and let her know that the apartment upstairs needed a tenant.

"I have," Wendy replied, being careful to make her pace slower to match the older woman's.

"Good, because the part of Christine is basically yours if you want it."

Wendy stopped in her tracks, her eyes widening in surprise. "Really?"

"Of course, darling," Francesca said, sounding as if she was stating a fact that everyone knew. She paused and turned to Wendy, regarding her fondly. "With all the training I've been giving you, you've become quite the star in hiding. All you need is the perfect audition to show Jim just how talented you are. Give me a few hours and I will find you the perfect piece. Trust me, Wendy. After all, I played Christine in *Les Joueurs de Paris'* performance of *The Phantom of the Opera* musical by Andrew Lloyd Webber, so I know exactly what's required."

"I guess that means you want to play Carlotta?" she said carefully.

Francesca laughed. "Of course. Carlotta has a much more expressive role and lends itself to more humour. I've played so many ingenues, my dear, that these days I crave variety. You'll see once you've gotten more roles under your belt."

As they continued walking, Francesca spoke of her time with *Les Joueurs de Paris*. Every so often she would pause to say hello or wave to someone on the street, but then immediately pick the story back up right where she'd left off. They soon reached the Oz Theatre, which was currently playing *Viennese Nights*, and headed up to their respective apartments.

"Have a good night," Francesca said with a wink, before disappearing into her apartment.

Wendy smiled at the closed door before continuing up the staircase. Because her apartment was on the fourth floor, she basically lived in the attic. The walls went about four feet high before the ceiling sloped inwards on two sides, but the rent was cheap enough that she didn't mind occasionally knocking her head. It was a bachelor apartment, but she'd found some folding screens to place around her bed to give the illusion that there was some kind of separation between the "bedroom" and the "living room." It gave the room a quirky, bohemian quality that fit in with the rest of the buildings on the street, and it made her feel more like an artist.

Walking over to the fridge, she took out a bottle of white wine that had been chilling since the morning. Taking two glasses from the cupboard, she left one on the counter and poured wine into the other. Putting the bottle back in the fridge, she picked up her glass and walked over to the couch, turning on the television.

Her glass was almost empty when there was a knock on her door.

"It's open," Wendy called out.

"Sorry I'm so late," Betty said as she entered the apartment. She walked over to the couch and greeted Wendy with a kiss. "It took me longer than I thought to get everything ready for tomorrow."

"It's okay," Wendy said. "I know you're a hard worker. There's wine in the fridge if you want."

Betty's smile grew as she moved into the kitchen area. "If I want? When have you ever known me not to want wine?"

"Better top me up while you're at it."

Once the wine was poured and snacks were retrieved, they settled on the couch together. Wendy sat at one end while Betty curled up next to her, leaning her head on her shoulder. They settled on a channel playing *The Princess Bride*, which they'd already seen a hundred times but still loved watching.

"Oh," Betty said suddenly, sitting up straight and turning to Wendy. "On my way up here, Francesca stopped me and told me to tell you..." she paused and screwed up her face as she struggled to remember. "Mina after she drinks Dracula's blood in... Dietz's *Dracula*, and Christine's song from the *Phantom* musical."

Wendy paused for thought before nodding. "That makes sense."

Betty reached for some chips. "Do you want to explain what that means? Or would you rather I spend an hour guessing?"

"Francesca's helping me choose a good monologue for the *Phantom* auditions. I guess since Christine's a singer it'll be smart to have a song ready."

Betty nodded approvingly. "I still can't believe she hasn't said anything to anyone about us yet. I keep expecting her to shout it from the rooftops."

Wendy smiled. "Turns out, Francesca knows how to keep a secret."

Wendy and Betty had been secretly dating for two months, although they'd been secretly flirting for longer. Neither was sure how the other actually felt until late one night, after an incredibly inebriated cast party, when the two had managed to sneak away from everyone else and get some things straight—or, actually, not-so-straight.

Betty took in a deep breath. "I almost told Galia yesterday."

Wendy sat up straighter and gave her an encouraging smile. She knew that Betty desperately wanted to tell her sister about the two of them but was too scared. Their parents had been extremely conservative and had a lot of strict rules and racist opinions, which is why the sisters decided to move out of the house after both of them finished high school. They ended up on Jacobi Street, almost as if by providence, and had jobs at the theatre within two weeks. Even though it was only the two of them in their small apartment above Pangea Market, Betty said that it felt more like home than their parents' house ever had.

Wendy suspected that Galia would be okay with the news that her little sister was dating someone of the same gender, but Betty wasn't sure enough to say anything. She didn't want to risk her sister freaking out and kicking her out of the apartment they shared or refusing to talk to her. She didn't want to lose the only family she had left.

Although Wendy didn't have any strong familial connections, she knew what it was like to hide a part of her true self. She had never come out as bisexual to her parents, figuring that it would disappoint them as much as her lack of college ambition or—even worse—that they'd think it was a phase she'd grow out of once she met the right man. Though she wanted to be able to hold hands in public and cuddle up together at the theatre, she would never push Betty to do anything she didn't feel comfortable doing.

"We were having supper last night and Galia remarked that I'd been spending more time with my 'paramour,'" Betty said, filling Wendy in. "She said that she knew our place was small, but it'd be okay with her if the two of us spent time here, at the apartment. I almost told her right then and there, but she said something else." Betty paused, a pained look crossing her face. "She said, she'd love to meet *him*."

Wendy put her arm around Betty and pulled her close. "It's okay," she said softly.

"I'm sorry, Wendy. I don't want to keep you a secret, but..."

"It's okay," she repeated. "It's okay."

They sat together in silence for a while, the movie playing in the background, Wendy's arms wrapped protectively around Betty. At least in this apartment they didn't have to hide.

"You know, you did good in rehearsal tonight," Betty said, changing the subject to something lighter. "Jim really should give you better parts."

"Well, other than Carina, I've been there the shortest amount of time."

"Yeah, but I'd put talent above time served."

"I don't think the other girls would see it that way," Wendy remarked, reaching for her glass.

Betty scoffed. "If Stacey doesn't like it then she can go straight back to off-Broadway, like she keeps threatening to do. She's good in some parts, I'll give her that, but she's not that great at playing vulnerable. And Carina thinks that fucking Gerard is the best way to get better parts, but she's actually not that versatile of an actor. She needs to spend more time on her script and less time on Gerard's dick."

Wendy considered those observations. "I won't agree with you, but I also won't argue."

A wide smile broke out on Betty's face. "Because you know I'm right!"

"I think the wine is making you smarter," Wendy laughed.

"Then I'd better get some more," Betty said before tipping her glass back and finishing off the contents.

Wendy joined her, quickly finishing off what was left in her own glass. As she reached for Betty's to get a refill, Betty leaned in for a kiss, and soon all thoughts of wine were pushed aside.

CHAPTER FIVE

Scott held his clipboard close to his chest as he stepped through the basement door. The light from the furnace gave the room a red glow that seemed to signify that you were about to descend into hell. He turned on the light switch near the door, but only half of the large bulbs in the ceiling lit up. He wondered if Billy knew about this or if it was another one of Jim's cost-saving measures.

As he made his way down the metal stairs, the steps clanging and shaking slightly under his feet, Scott could feel animosity rising up within him. Jim didn't care one bit about the strange noises the furnace was making, but the matter had been brought up by Francesca, and he knew that she'd never give him a moment's peace until it was resolved. This led to Jim barking at Scott to go check out the furnace after rehearsal, and when Scott mentioned that he knew nothing about furnaces, Jim let out a string of curses that only ended when Scott agreed to go and take a look.

It was difficult not to feel sour. He knew that the only reason he had a job at this theatre was because his uncle was the theatre's benefactor and had pulled some strings, but he'd always hoped that eventually Jim would give him a chance to prove that he could be valuable. Unfortunately, Jim only saw him as an extra body, available for all the jobs nobody else wanted to do. This was a perfect example—Billy would be a much better choice for checking out whether a furnace was okay or not, but Jim didn't care enough to send the best person for the job. He simply wanted to give the impression that he was doing something about it.

Some days, Scott wondered if he should ask his uncle to step in and make Jim give him a better position. When he'd learned about his uncle's activities, Scott decided that it would be great if he could become a director. Of course, he didn't expect to start directing shows straight out of the gate, but he'd been hoping that Jim would let him be an assistant director and show him the ropes. Instead, he became the person who fetched coffee and set up tables and got shoved into an ill-fitting costume whenever they needed a silent body on stage. It would be easy enough for him to make the suggestion, but he didn't want his uncle to have to step in. He wanted to prove that he didn't need someone else to solve his problems—he could solve them on his own.

As Scott stepped off the staircase, he took a deep breath and walked towards the back of the room, where the furnace was located. There was something about the low, intermittent knocking sound coming from the back of the room that unsettled him. He looked around, but nobody else seemed to be down here. There was nothing but stacked backdrops and set pieces on either side, leaving a crude hallway in the centre of the room which led to the back, where the furnace angrily glowed red. Scott had been ordered down here many times to fetch items, but he'd never gone as far back as the furnace and he wished that it could remain that way. Maybe he could lie and tell Jim that he'd taken a look and nothing was wrong. No, that wouldn't be smart. If something went wrong later then he'd be to blame, and if Jim found out that he hadn't taken this request seriously, it could hurt his future in the company.

A particularly loud knock almost made him drop the clipboard. Tightening his grip on it, he slowly walked forward. Another noise startled him, but it wasn't a knock this time, it was a low scraping sound. Scott paused. He'd been told that a furnace could make knocking sounds if air or an animal was trapped in the pipes, but what could make a scraping noise? Was there any part of a furnace that could scrape? Had something come loose?

He took a tentative step forward. The horrible scraping sound grew louder. It was like something sharp was being dragged along metal, and it almost sounded as if it was moving towards him.

"Hello?" Scott called out. "Is anyone back there?"

He tried to remember who had been upstairs when Jim sent him down here. He wouldn't put it past anyone in the troupe to hide down here and scare him. Some of them enjoyed playing tricks on him, like the time someone stole his clipboard and put it in Jell-O.

Summoning up all his courage, Scott moved forward.

"I know you're down here, so there's no point trying to scare me."

Another scrape made him jump, but at least he didn't cry out in fear.

"You might as well show yourself," he continued, putting as much false confidence into his voice as he could muster.

Scott continued towards the furnace, preparing himself for the jump scare that would come. However, nothing could have prepared him for the large shape that stepped out of the shadows and moved his way.

His clipboard fell to the ground as a terrified shriek escaped his lips.

CHAPTER SIX

Backstage at the theatre, the energy was almost too much for the building to contain. Designers were rushing around, making sure that the props

and costumes had been placed correctly, that the set pieces were all in order, and that everything was ready for tonight's show. Some actors paced
the hallways as they went over lines, while others were meticulously following pre-show rituals in the hopes that it would make tonight perfect (or
at least minimize the number of mistakes that could happen).

All throughout the chaos was Ari, the stage manager, who was calmly
going through their final checks while actors randomly approached to ask
them questions about cues, and entrances and exits, and other information
which had been forgotten due to pre-show nerves.

Wendy tried to keep out of the way as much as possible while doing her
pre-show checks. Some people would have no qualms about running her
over if she got in their way for even a second. The desperate need to have
everything perfect for the show seemed to make people more frantic and
self-obsessed than normal. Well, other than Scott, who seemed to be doing
his best to avoid everyone else. Normally he'd at least try to project a bit
of authority and give someone a pointless order, but tonight he seemed to
have given in to the fact that he had no real power, except for the tiny bit
that Jim allowed him.

Turning her attention away from everyone else, Wendy continued her
pre-show ritual, which involved going through her script one last time before making sure all her props and costumes were in their correct places.
There were five sketches before intermission and five afterwards, so it was a
lot to keep track of, even if she wasn't in every sketch. At least this time she
only had two quick-changes that she'd have to do in the wings. There was
enough time between her other costume changes for her to go down to the
dressing room and get ready in a less hectic mode.

There were a few sketches that were one or two people, but most
sketches involved four to six actors, so everyone had lots to do during the
show. Jim made sure to pace the larger skits with the smaller, to give some
people a chance to catch their breath, and had even created some skits, like
Billy's "Stagehand Shuffle," to give the actors time to gear up for a bigger
sketch. Everything was carefully planned so that the cast and crew could
move easily and effectively from one sketch to the next—barring any kind
of unexpected disaster.

Wendy used to wonder why they bothered being be so elaborate with
the show and the sets, especially since they were only sketches and only
existed for one night, but then someone informed her that if it wasn't for the
money that J.P. Lodge shelled out for these shows, the theatre wouldn't be
able to hire half as many people or produce any other works.

After confirming that her props and costumes were properly set, Wendy walked over to the curtain and peeked outside. There were about 30
people in the audience, which was good, all things considered. In the be-

ginning the variety show had been attended only by Mr. Lodge and a few of his friends, but then Mr. Lodge began inviting more friends, and then the residents of Jacobi Street began attending and it became something like a community gathering. That was the way of the street—those who lived here supported the local businesses whenever possible.

The past few months had been hard on the street, with several disappearances that still remained unsolved. Some suspected that the people had simply run away, likely due to embezzlement (the owner of The Menagerie gallery) or affairs (Mr. Cooper, of Cooper's General Market) or getting into serious trouble that they needed to disappear from (one of the local street artists, Obi). Although the reasons were sound, others weren't so sure. It would have been strange enough for one person to disappear without a word, but for so many to go within a couple weeks... Whatever the reasons, it was difficult for many residents to accept. There weren't a lot of people who lived on the street and they were all quite familiar with one another, so it was a shock for someone to just up and leave without notice, even if it wasn't entirely out of the realm of possibility.

Tonight's audience seemed like they were in a good mood and ready to laugh, which helped calm Wendy a little. She always felt nervous before a show, no matter how prepared she was. It was the thrill of live theatre, where anything could happen—and often did. Someone might bring on the wrong prop, say the wrong line, or wear the wrong costume. The joy of the variety show was that there was always a way to pretend that a mistake was a part of the act, even when it wasn't.

Stepping away from the curtains, she headed back to the dressing room to get into her first costume.

Jim settled into his seat near the back of the theatre, a frown on his face and his arms crossed over his chest. During rehearsals he sat closer to the stage, to get a better idea of how the show was going, but whenever there was an audience in the house he wanted to sit as far away as possible to try to avoid recognition. Not that his choice of seating mattered, since everyone in attendance knew that he was the writer and director, but over time the patrons had learned to think of him as an eccentric creative and give him some space. A few still waved hello to him, but they all refrained from trying to start discussions.

A few minutes later, Scott came out from backstage and hurried over to a chair that was near the back and on the opposite side of the theatre, nowhere close to Jim. Jim frowned as he thought about the annoying young man with the coke-bottle glasses. As much as Scott wanted to be a director, Jim knew that he was all wrong for the part. Sure, he sometimes had "ideas," but he had no concept of the "big picture." Whenever Jim mentioned it to him, Scott would narrow his eyes and act as if such a thing wasn't important.

Scott also had no authority whatsoever and let the actors and designers run all over him, which would only lead to chaos in rehearsals. Jim had a feeling that the kid had never been involved in theatre before being hired here, and had simply woken up one day, realized that his uncle was patron to a theatre, and decided to jump in head first. If it weren't for Lodge's patronage, Jim never would have considered hiring the slimy young man, but Lodge was thankful for Jim's giving his nephew something to do and actually gave more money to the theatre because of it. So, although Scott was a twerp, he at least had *some* value.

As Jim looked up at the red velvet curtains that currently hid the stage from view, he could almost imagine that he was back in Paris, waiting for the premiere of one of his plays. It had been so much easier back then, to bask in the glory of the applause and recognition. Back then he'd created *art*, and people had been more than willing to throw money at him, eager to contribute to such an honoured and highly esteemed craft. In those days, if you'd asked what he thought the future would be like, he never would have entertained the idea that he'd end up in some strange American city, desperately pinching pennies, and performing ridiculous sketches for people who'd never been in a theatre larger than two hundred seats.

Perhaps he'd been too proud in his earlier life, but since then he'd had more than enough humility for nine hundred lives. How he wished that he could snap his fingers and be back in Paris, among the opulent theatres where the red curtains were soft and not worn bare in places, where the gold accents were shiny and untarnished, where the ropes always worked and the joists were well-oiled, and where whatever he wanted was within his grasp.

Nowadays, it was the small things that kept him going. Soon he'd put the finishing touches on his script for *Le Fantôme* and show this street how real theatre was done. He'd wanted to perform this show for ages, but there hadn't been enough money to do it properly. Over the past few years, he'd scrimped and saved in order to bring this show to life in a way that did it justice. He'd show everyone what the theatres of Paris were like, and how terrifying and breath-taking a theatrical experience could be.

The door next to the stage opened and Rhonda entered the auditorium, walking over to the upright piano beside the stage. Jim was pleased to see that she was wearing a long-sleeved black dress with no embellishments. For the first few shows after she was hired, she'd worn bright and colourful clothing, assuming that it would be appropriate for a show like this, and Jim had to inform her that the audience was here to look at the stage and not her. She caught on quickly, and although she'd successfully argued for the right to wear costumes during any "themed" variety shows they put on—like Halloween and Valentine's Day—she at least gave him less of a headache than most of the other crew.

Rhonda sat in front of the piano and began to play the introduction music for the show. Taking a deep breath, Jim steadied himself as the curtain rose.

First up was Samuel, whose job it was to welcome the patrons. Jim had hired him because he fit the image of a typical paternal character, and it was always handy to have someone like that around. Samuel had worked in professional theatre for a long time, until the roles started drying up. Jim suspected that it was because Samuel considered himself the greatest actor to have ever lived—a notion that grew old quite fast. In Paris, Jim would have kicked him to the street, but here he had to take what he could get. Samuel was useful as the show's greeter, as he lent gravitas to the introduction and provided a proxy in which Mr. Lodge and his friends could see themselves and imagine what it would be like to be on stage.

After a few words, Samuel introduced the first sketch, and as he left the stage the curtains opened, revealing a restaurant set with a small table and two chairs. The skit was about two people who were in love, except one person was a vampire and the other wouldn't give up garlic. As Jim watched Gerard and Stacey perform the skit, he observed that Stacey had indeed taken the note he'd given her about exaggerating her expressions more. He also noticed that Carina, who was playing their waitress, had hiked her skirt up a couple extra inches, and that Gerard was constantly sneaking glances her way, despite his character's love for the vampire seated across from him. The skit ended with Gerard swearing that his love for Stacey was the most important thing in the world, and that he would give up garlic forever to be with her, but as soon as she'd left the stage, he ordered a large plate of garlic bread. Holding the bread close, he swore that he'd give up garlic tomorrow before pretending to dive in. The audience clapped and a black curtain descended, covering up the back half of the stage and the set, giving the illusion that the stage was empty.

The lighting changed to something more joyful, and Francesca walked onstage wearing a shimmering blue and white dress with a short skirt. She began to sing "Anything Goes" from the Broadway musical of the same name, engaging the audience with her energy and character. While she sang, a smile crossed Jim's face, and for a moment he fell in love with her all over again. As she enchanted the crowd with her voice and talent, he was able to see the young woman he'd married those many years ago. But all too soon the song ended, and she disappeared offstage, and the reality of his life came rushing back.

The black curtain flew up, revealing a skit about two co-workers finding a birthday cake in the break room and not knowing whose birthday it was. It starred Wendy and Carina, who ended up realizing that they knew absolutely nothing about their co-workers, including most of their names. Eventually they decided to go and pretend that they hadn't seen the cake, but before they could leave, Samuel's character walked in and started asking questions. The two of them convinced Samuel's character that it was a surprise for him, and that the name on the cake being someone else's was part of that surprise, before quickly running away and ending the scene.

The black curtain dropped again. After another lighting change, Francesca walked onstage wearing an elaborate Elizabethan outfit and began to retell "Goodnight Moon" in the Shakespearean tongue. Other actors, dressed all in black, moved props across the stage, animating the story.

The final skit before intermission was 'Mad House Party,' which was about two college kids and their desire to throw a rager of a party. Although it started out crazy, as more people showed up, the party became tamer and tamer, until it finally turned into a Victorian tea party—much to the chagrin of the hosts.

As the curtain came down and the audience applauded, Jim breathed a small sigh of relief. The first half of the show had passed without any major issues and the audience seemed to have enjoyed it. There was still the second half to get through, but it looked like the troupe was having a good night. Then again, he knew better than to assume everything would be okay. Some people relaxed when a show was going well, which often led to mistakes.

When the lights to the auditorium came on, most of the audience headed out to The Orchestra Pit, the bar next door. It was the smallest bar on Jacobi Street, and was run by a Scandinavian man who spoke with an extremely thick accent that was difficult to understand most of the time. The man attended all their shows, and during intermission he would turn his living room into a bar, providing a limited assortment of alcoholic and non-alcoholic drinks to patrons, along with some snacks. Jim had to hand it to him—the man had noticed an opportunity and seized it.

As much as Jim wanted a drink right now, he didn't want to stand in line with the common public; shoulder to shoulder with someone who'd likely offer him a "brilliant" idea for the next show. He briefly toyed with the idea of going upstairs and pouring a drink from his personal bar, but he had an odd feeling that if he took his eyes off the stage something terrible would happen. Instead, he stayed in his seat and waited for the minutes to pass.

Finally, everyone arrived back in the auditorium and it was time for the second half of the show to begin. It started with a skit of two reviewers talking about the show so far, giving a humorous review of the first act's skits. As it played, Jim glared at the back of Walter Astoria's head, hoping that the reviewer for the local paper would be able to see that 1) the troupe could take a joke and 2) reviewers were ridiculous. It was something Jim absolutely hated about this city: the fact that there was only one theatre reviewer who came to this theatre, and that he was a terrible, twisted man who couldn't understand the value of variety shows. Astoria seemed to think that *all* theatre needed to be some grand fantastic message, so while he was sometimes fond of their actual shows, he constantly eviscerated the variety show. Thankfully, Mr. Lodge didn't care about reviews—all he wanted was to be entertained.

Next was a skit about Benvolio and Balthasar from *Romeo and Juliet* falling in love behind the scenes of the play as tragedy ensued around them. It quickly moved into the 'Amore' sketch, after which the black curtain descended, and Billy came onstage to tell jokes and charm the audience while everyone else set up the scene for the final skit. The 'Stagehand Shuffle' had started out as Billy buying time to cover up an incident backstage that slowed the set-up of the next scene, but it turned out that audiences liked Billy so much that Jim had to make it a regular part of the show. The jokes Billy told were rarely funny, but he had an endearing warmth that people liked.

The 'Shuffle' went well, as it always did, and then it was time for 'Vampliar High.' The skit commented on a lot of current pop-culture trends and made fun of tired, old franchises, and the audience absolutely ate it up.

Finally, the actors took their bows and the curtain closed for the final time that night. Jim took in a deep breath and affixed a smile to his face. First, he'd talk to Mr. Lodge about the show, and maybe a few other audience members, but then he'd be able to retire to his apartment and continue working on a script that actually mattered to him.

CHAPTER SEVEN

There was something about applause that brought a wide smile to Wendy's face. After all the hard work they'd done putting the show together, it was nice to know that their audience had enjoyed and appreciated it. Sure, it seemed like a silly little show full of sketches and jokes, but it made people laugh and forget about their troubles for a while, and that made it worth all the trouble.

The red velvet curtains closed, and the actors made their way offstage. The wings, which had started the night meticulously organized, were now a mess. Props had been thrown in and around discard boxes, costumes were hanging over every available surface, and set pieces had been shoved any place that they could fit. Despite the discord, there was a jubilant feeling amongst the entire troupe. The show hadn't been entirely perfect, but they'd gotten through it and the audience was none the wiser.

As the actors made their way to their dressing rooms to change, the designers started clearing up, gathering the items from their departments quickly and efficiently. Now that the show was over, it was time for everyone's favourite part of the night—the cast party. The faster everything was put away, the sooner they could start celebrating a successful show.

"Did you see how I almost dropped that pizza?" Stacey said as she tossed her costume into the laundry hamper Paloma had placed in their room earlier. "I mean, I thought it was going to fly out of my hands and brain that guy in the first row. He'd have deserved it for sitting in the front row, but still..."

"At least you didn't drop a book on Francesca's foot," Carina countered, shimming into a tight red dress. "I thought she was going to kill me after the house party sketch."

"She still might," Stacey warned. "Better watch out or she'll push you from the top of The Treehouse!" Stacey waved her fingers in Carina's direction and made spooky noises.

Wendy held back her laughter and tried to keep a straight face as she straightened the neckline of her dark blue sweater dress.

Carina scoffed and tossed her hair to the side. "I'm sure I could take her in a fight. Zip me up?"

Wendy walked over and zipped Carina into her dress. "I'd stay away from any windows, nevertheless," she warned playfully.

"Hey, if you die," Stacey said, abruptly turning away from her make-up routine, "can you come back and haunt the theatre? I still can't believe we don't have a ghost. I mean, *every* theatre has a ghost. It's so lame."

Carina rolled her eyes. "When I die, which will be a long time from now, I hope that I'll get to rest in peace. Although, if it happens that one of the actors here kills me, I might see about sticking around for a day or so to torment them."

Smiling, Stacey gave her plan two thumbs up before returning to her lipstick application.

When they were finished, the three of them exited the dressing room, eager to party. Wendy glanced down the hall, where the costume, special effects, props, and carpentry rooms were located. She knew that it would take Betty a while to get to the bar since she had to put away all the props that were used tonight—and there had been a *lot* of props. Since the two of them weren't "official," she had no valid reason to stay behind and help

Betty, and so she continued walking with Stacey and Carina.

When they headed up the stairs, Wendy couldn't help glancing at the basement door, which looked exactly the same as it had last week. There had been no strange knocking tonight, which relieved her. Hopefully, the furnace problem had been solved.

"I still can't believe that a person genuinely laughed at Billy's joke about the hedgehogs," Carina remarked as they made their way into the street.

"Did they? I couldn't hear anything over the groans," Wendy said.

Stacey smiled widely. "I have it on good authority that the guy who laughed might be Billy's current paramour."

Carina gasped in mock horror. "You mean there's two men out there who have a sense of humour like that? How terrible!"

"At least they've found each other and are sparing the rest of us," Stacey pointed out, to which the others had to agree.

They quickly reached The Treehouse, but that was the way of Jacobi Street—no matter where a person started, it never took long to reach their destination. The building was three-stories tall, with the first floor set up as an art gallery devoted to the owner's father's artwork. The main bar was on the second floor, and there was a private room on the third, where people could go to get away from the crowds or rent for parties. The troupe had a great relationship with Calie, who owned the building and lived in the basement, and Calie would always hold the third floor for them after each show. Wendy suspected that Calie did this because she knew they'd spend an obscene amount of money on alcohol and snacks.

The gallery was closed this late at night; not that any of them would have suggested skipping the party to go inside. Wendy sometimes thought about going in and checking out the artwork, but often it was a fleeting thought she had while on her way to the bar. Calie worked both businesses, so when the bar was open, the gallery was closed, and vice versa.

Climbing up to the second floor, the group headed over to the bar, which was a semi-circle set against one of the walls. Behind the bar were shelves that were designed to look like tree branches, holding the bottles. There were a few stools around the bar, a couple of which were already occupied, but the rest of the floor contained long tables and benches, where people could sit and mingle. The atmosphere of the bar was casual and respectful, and it was meant to be a place where people could hang out and have a good time. Wendy had never seen anyone step out of line, but she'd heard that Calie kept a baseball bat behind the bar just in case.

Standing behind the bar was Calie, who greeted them upon their arrival. As usual, she was wearing jeans and a striped shirt, with a backwards baseball cap perched on her short blond bob.

"How'd the show go tonight?" she asked as she poured their drinks.

"It was fabulous," Carina gushed.

"Went about as good as expected," Stacey said, waving a hand non-committally.

"The audience enjoyed it," Wendy added helpfully.

"You'll have to check it out sometime," Stacey said.

Calie laughed. "If I ever decide to hire some help here, I'll do that."

Once they had their drinks—white wine for Wendy, red wine for Carina, and a Jack and cola for Stacey—they headed up to the third floor. This room had a more casual atmosphere, with chairs and small tables that could be arranged in whatever way was preferred, and the wooden floor was filled with scrapes from furniture being pulled here and there. There wasn't much about the room that resembled a treehouse, other than the wood panelling on the walls and a few lanterns hanging from the ceiling, but the windows offered a fantastic view down on Jacobi Street.

Music played lightly in the background, loud enough to provide atmosphere but low enough for people to carry on conversations without shouting. Samuel, Gerard, and Rhonda were already seated in a semi-circle, discussing their previous experiences in theatre, and the young women grabbed chairs and joined the group. The conversation opened to include them, but it soon became apparent that not everyone was interested in the dialogue anymore. After exchanging a few not-so-sly glances, Gerard and Carina made flimsy excuses to break away from the group and move to one of the more intimate corners of the room. The others exchanged knowing looks but continued with their conversation.

A short while later, Francesca showed up, and she instantly turned the focus her way. Carina and Gerard stayed in their corner, with Carina nervously glancing at Francesca every few seconds, but the blonde woman ignored her and joined the larger group, changing the topic of conversation to the show they'd just completed. Wendy noticed that Francesca was always her best self at the cast party, when she was celebrating with the others. Her energy was high, her mood positive, and it was one of the few times other troupe members found her approachable. Did it have something to do with the fact that Jim never went to these parties? Possibly, but Wendy couldn't be sure.

The group drank and laughed about the things that had gone wrong and mistakes that had been made, gently poking fun at each other. At first, Wendy used to be mortified every time she made a mistake, but then she realized that as long as the mistake didn't result in injury or damages, it was okay. In fact, some actors saw them as a challenge—a way to stretch their acting muscles. If something went wrong on stage and they were able to cover it up in such a way that the audience thought it was part of the show, then that would be worth a large pat on the back.

Eventually Betty, Galia, Billy, Paloma, and Ari arrived. The top floor became more crowded, the voices more animated, and the party swung into full gear. The alcohol was flowing and inside jokes were tossed around with no explanation. Occasionally they'd play a theatre game, or someone would try to teach someone else a dance from a show they'd once been in, but everything was always in good fun. The troupe worked hard to get the variety shows up and running, so they partied even harder.

While Francesca regaled the group about the time she'd accidentally walked on for the wrong scene during *The Importance of Being Ernest* and had to pretend that it was deliberate until she could find a good time to scurry offstage, Wendy chanced a look over at Betty. She was standing next to Galia, holding a glass of wine. When Betty caught her gaze, Wendy smiled and raised her glass in a cheers, and although Betty smiled and gave a cheers back, she remained at Galia's side for the rest of the night.

The party went on for a few more hours before people started breaking off to go home. Some of the actors would remain until Calie kicked them out in the wee hours of the morning, but others were concerned about the auditions tomorrow afternoon. Despite being able to cast a show in two seconds due to the small troupe size, Jim took auditions very seriously and expected everyone to show up and do their best. Tales were told of the time Gerard arrived at his audition and said, "I'm going to get the part anyway, so I won't bother wasting your time," then walked offstage. Jim had been so angry that he rewrote the entire play, taking out the character Gerard would have played and casting him in a non-speaking background role.

Wendy wasn't feeling particularly tired when she excused herself from the party, but she wanted to spend an hour or so practising her monologue before going to bed. She'd done as Francesca had suggested and created a monologue from *Dracula* by cutting out the other character's lines in between Mina's. It was short, about one minute long, but it showed Mina's vulnerability, fear, and strength—qualities which were reminiscent of a certain character in *Phantom*.

Although she still refused to say it out loud, she really wanted the part of Christine—wanted it so badly that she could feel it ache deep inside. As new as she was to acting, she desperately craved a chance to be in the spotlight and prove that she was more than a secondary character.

CHAPTER EIGHT

Before heading home, Paloma went back to the theatre to empty the dryer. There was always a large pile of costumes that needed to be washed after one of these shows, and there was only one washer and dryer in the entire building. Most of it could wait until tomorrow, but some pieces needed to be washed immediately so that they didn't sour, and then hung up after drying so that they wouldn't wrinkle. Luckily these were the kinds of tasks that she didn't need to be sober to perform.

Paloma was the only person in the theatre's costume department and had been for the past ten years. All the design teams were comprised of one person, and although the variety shows were insane and complicated, it wasn't anything that they weren't able to handle on their own. The theatre had a good-sized wardrobe collection that was comprised of outfits Paloma had discovered at second hand stores and costume sales from larger theatres, as well as pieces she'd created herself. She enjoyed being the master of costumes and having it all to herself.

After Jim announced that he was planning on doing *Phantom*, her mind went wild with all the possibilities. She'd attended the musical when she was younger, and the costumes were so rich and extravagant. It was the complete opposite of *Glengarry Glen Ross*, where she'd merely needed suits and a police officer outfit. Although Paloma didn't yet know the particulars of the script that Jim was writing, he'd have to be a fool to remove the masquerade scene. Just like the dramatic chandelier fall, you couldn't have a *Phantom* story without it—it would be almost as bad as leaving out the Phantom himself.

Using her key to enter the theatre, she locked the door behind her, just as she'd promised Ari. All the design team had keys to the theatre, but they'd only received them after swearing to their stage manager that they wouldn't mess with anything, and that they'd be thorough when locking up. At times Paloma thought that Ari was being unreasonable with how much control they had over the theatre, but then she'd think about what it would be like if everyone came and went whenever they wanted and had to concede that this way was better.

The lobby was dark, except for a few soft night-lights that were plugged into the walls. As fun as it was to have a hive of activity around her, Paloma enjoyed those peaceful times at the theatre, when it was quiet and unassuming. It was like the entire building was hers and hers alone (although in the back of her mind she knew that Jim was upstairs drowning his sorrows in alcohol). Sometimes there were so many people bustling around that it was difficult to think, but in the darkness and solitude it was all hers.

Making her way into the auditorium, she saw the ghost light shining on the stage. The stage was empty except for the light, which stood at the centre—a single light bulb on a four-foot stand. Paloma didn't understand why they needed to put out a ghost light every night but had to admit that there was a kind of beauty about it.

Once she made her way to the lower level, she began turning on lights to see. Although she knew this floor well, she also knew that people were likely to leave things lying around in strange places, and it was better to see where you were going than to risk tripping over something and turning an ankle—especially when one's reflexes had been properly dulled.

After taking the clothes out of the dryer and hanging them up, Paloma looked at the racks of clothing lining the costume room. She'd have to do up some sketches and start thinking about fabrics. The dresses that she'd need for *Phantom* would have to be made from scratch or pieced together from older costumes. She'd also have to find a way to source formal tuxedos that didn't cost an arm and a leg but also looked expensive. For this show, she was definitely thinking tails.

A loud knocking noise startled her and she jumped. Taking in a deep breath, she told herself that it was only the furnace. Whatever they'd done to stop it from making the noise earlier must have worn off. She'd have to remember to tell Jim about it the next time she saw him.

Although the night was already growing late, Paloma pulled out one of her many bins of fabric and started looking through the contents, hoping to find some inspiration. She was holding up a bolt of pink satin fabric when there was another loud knock. She jumped again, and then laughed at herself for being so easily startled. However, when a third knock came soon after, she began to feel uneasy. The noises before had always been spaced out, with enough time in between to forget you'd heard it in the first place. Another knock sounded, and she began to wonder if there was something terribly wrong with the furnace. Was she in danger of it exploding? Perhaps it'd be best to go home.

She put the fabric down and stepped out of the costume room, turning off the lights after her. As she approached the staircase, she noticed that the door to the basement was ajar and that there was a red light coming from inside. She couldn't remember if the door had been open when she first passed it, but it must have been. She must not have noticed.

Suddenly a loud scraping sound startled her. She paused and listened. It sounded like someone was definitely down in the basement. Walking to the door, she opened it a little wider and listened again. It was hard to make out, but there were clanging sounds, like tools hitting metal, and something that almost sounded like a man muttering to himself. A feeling of ease washed over her. It was probably Billy. He was the resident handyman after all.

He must have come in after her, and she'd been too preoccupied with the costumes to hear him. That was what those noises were—Billy trying to fix the furnace. It didn't sound like he was being particularly successful, but what did she know about that kind of thing? Taking in a breath, Paloma turned to the staircase to leave.

Suddenly she heard a crash, like something heavy breaking off and falling to the floor. Instinct kicked in, sobering her up almost instantly, and she hurried to the basement. When she turned on the lights, only a few of the bulbs lit up. Some of them flickered in a way that indicated they would soon burn out, but it didn't slow her descent. Thankfully, the red glow from the furnace provided enough light for her to make out most of the room.

Stepping onto the floor, she called out Billy's name, letting him know that she was here and to tell her where he was. He didn't answer, but she could hear groans coming from the back of the room, where the furnace was. As she neared, she could feel the temperature of the room rising. She called out Billy's name, but still couldn't see him, and it was getting harder to hear him as the furnace's hissing and churning grew louder and louder.

"Billy? Where are you?" Once she reached the furnace, she saw nothing that looked like it could have caused that noise. Nothing seemed to have tipped over or fallen. Had she imagined it?

Suddenly there was a knock, the loudest one she'd heard yet, as if someone had slammed a baseball bat into the side of the furnace. Before the sound had a chance to finish reverberating, there was another and then another. The knocking was almost deafening, and even though Paloma tried to cover her ears with her hands, the noise wouldn't lessen. It felt like the room was going to fall in on itself, crumbling with her inside of it.

She tried to turn around and leave, but her feet wouldn't obey. Suddenly, the lights overhead started to flicker, and Paloma felt a shiver of fear run through her body. Her heart beat faster, and though she desperately wanted to run away, her body still wouldn't obey her mind. She needed to get out of here. She needed to get out of here now.

A deep, ragged breathing sounded behind her, and although the last thing she wanted to do was look at whatever could make a noise like that, her body moved of its own accord. In the dim red light, she could just make out a large shape that rose from the shadows. The being was much too tall for an ordinary person—too broad and big and hulking. Her heart leapt in her throat as the creature began to move towards her, and a terrified scream escaped her lips.

CHAPTER NINE

When Wendy woke up the next morning, she knew that she'd had some kind of strange dream during the night, but the details started slipping away the moment she opened her eyes. Images that were once so clear started getting fuzzy and dissolving into nothingness, leaving her with only vague recollections, but she could definitely remember standing on a stage in a long white dress that looked similar to a nightgown and hearing music.

Was this a sign that she was going to get the part of Christine? The stage was empty and so was the audience—no, actually, there were some people sitting in the seats, but she couldn't make out any faces. She knew that they were staring at her, but there was something strange about them. Were they wearing costumes? Maybe it was Stacey and Carina watching her, jealous because she'd gotten the part that they'd wanted.

Deciding to leave it alone, she told herself that it was likely a sign she was spending too much time thinking about the show. Her time would be better spent warming up her voice, instead of trying to interpret a half-remembered dream.

After eating a light breakfast—which was more like brunch, considering that it was closer to noon—she did a few vocal exercises and stretches before going over her monologue and song. Once she felt comfortable about both of them, she went to her closet and stood in front of it, trying to figure out what to wear. She didn't want to give the impression that she was wearing a costume, but wanted Jim to think of her as a young ingenue, so settled on a light blue dress with cap sleeves. After that decision had been made, she went over her monologue and song again before doing some breathing exercises as she anxiously waited for her audition time to get here.

When it was time to leave her apartment, she felt a thrill of excitement and a sense of trepidation. She usually felt nervous walking to an audition, but this time was different. It felt like there was more at stake. Normally she wouldn't care what part she received, but Francesca's encouragement had made her believe that she could get the lead. If she didn't, she'd be letting down not only herself but also Francesca and all of her teachings.

She arrived at the theatre early and quietly sneaked into the auditorium to sit in the back row. Samuel had just started his monologue, with Jim watching from the third row. Rumour had it that Samuel only had two monologues—one for comedy and one for drama—and this was the dramatic monologue. As he performed, Wendy figured that Samuel would be good as one of the managers of the theatre but definitely wasn't right for the Phantom. His posture was too stiff, and he wasn't menacing enough. Gerard would be a better Phantom, plus it'd keep him from being cast as Raoul. She smiled as a thought struck her. Maybe Raoul could be written out and the love story could be between Christine and Meg Giry. Then Betty could audition for Meg and the two of them could be together in front of everyone...

She heard her name being called and realized that she'd missed the end of Samuel's audition. Taking in a deep breath, Wendy stood up and made her way to the stage, preparing herself for what was to come.

And then, in a matter of minutes, it was over.

As she walked off the stage, she couldn't help noticing how many hours she'd spent agonizing over something that only lasted a few minutes. First Jim asked her for her monologue and, when that was finished, he asked her to sing. Then he thanked her for coming, and suddenly it was all over.

Wendy felt like she'd done a good job. There were no stumbles or forgotten lines, and the emotion she'd brought out had felt real enough. Jim hadn't shown much, but he did raise an eyebrow in surprise when she started singing. If she didn't get the part of Christine, at least she knew that she'd done her best.

On her way out of the auditorium, she was so relieved to be finished with her audition that she ran right into someone in the lobby. Backing up, she looked at a young man with dark, shaggy hair and darker eyes. He was wearing ripped jeans, a white t-shirt, and a black motorcycle jacket, like he'd just walked out of a James Dean movie.

"Sorry," she said, stepping out of his way. "Wasn't paying attention."

"Don't worry," he replied, shrugging one of his shoulders. "I'm a little lost. This is The Quaint Little Theatre, right?" He gestured at the lobby.

She nodded. "Yeah, it is."

"Great. Thanks." He moved past her and disappeared into the auditorium.

Wendy frowned at the space where he'd been standing. It was strange to see someone who wasn't part of the troupe in the theatre on a non-performance night. She thought back to the audition sheet, but there hadn't been any unfamiliar names on it—someone would have commented if there were. So, what was this guy doing here? Was he a walk-in? Then she remembered the strange knocking from a few days ago. Maybe he was here to check out the furnace and make sure everything was okay.

An involuntary shiver ran through her at the thought of the knocking, and she quickly made her way out of the theatre and into the bright afternoon sun.

CHAPTER TEN

As usual, Jim kept the casting secret until the very last minute. By early Friday evening everyone had received a message telling them that the read-through was at 1:00 pm on Saturday, and nothing else. Jim had once explained that giving actors the script or their parts beforehand gave them ill-conceived notions, but never actually explained what that meant or provided examples. Nobody felt strong enough about it to battle him on this matter, so they all let it go. It was simply one more quirk for an already quirk-laden director.

Wendy felt almost electric as she made her way to the theatre for the read-through. This was the moment she was both anticipating and dreading. The world wouldn't end if she didn't get the part she wanted, but she'd feel like a deflated balloon. It would be almost unbearable having to watch Stacey or Carina perform the part she so desperately wanted.

She arrived at the theatre five minutes before 1:00 pm. The stage had been cleared away of all set pieces and had a large square table in the centre, surrounded by chairs. In front of each chair was a pile of paper—the much-anticipated script. Despite the constant curiosity around it, nobody was sitting down or flipping through the pages. Instead, they huddled in groups, circling the table like sharks, wary of seeming too eager or getting too close.

Standing near the edge of the stage were Stacey and Carina. Wendy went over and, after a quick greeting, asked how their auditions had gone. It was partly because the conversation was expected, but also because she was hoping to gauge how well they'd done in relation to her. Carina had been surprised by the request for a song, but otherwise thought her audition had gone well, and Stacey felt that hers had been great. They asked Wendy about hers, and she said it had gone well, and then talked about how she'd caught part of Sam's audition, quickly changing the subject.

"Who is *that*?" Stacey interrupted, staring between Wendy and Carina. The two of them immediately turned around and Wendy saw the same young man she'd run into after her audition. He was wearing a similar outfit as yesterday, which was almost identical except for the jeans being slightly more faded. A cautious expression crossed his face as he looked around the theatre, taking it all in.

"*Me gusta...*" Carina said with a hungry smile on her face.

Wendy frowned in confusion. "What's the furnace guy doing here?"

"Wait, do you know him?" Stacey demanded, swiftly turning to her.

After shaking her head, Wendy shrugged. "I ran into him after my audition. Like, *literally* ran into him. I thought he was here to look at the furnace, but maybe not." Yesterday he'd walked around like he owned the place, but now he was more trepidatious.

"I hope he's playing Raoul," Carina said, watching as he made his way to the stage. "I don't even care if he can act."

The stranger walked over to Jim and they talked quietly as everyone else pretended not to stare. Wendy was certain that every conversation was now focused on this new addition.

The mood was broken as the auditorium doors swung open, and everyone turned to watch Francesca make her way towards the stage. Wendy had to give it to her—Francesca knew how to make an entrance.

"Seats, everyone," Ari called out.

Jim took his place at the "head" of the table, between Ari and Billy. He motioned for the new guy to take the seat closest to Ari, while everyone else made their way to their usual seats. Wendy normally sat next to Ari, so she was a bit put off by the new guy taking her seat, but then she noticed that this side of the table had four chairs instead of three. She'd been so entranced by the script that she hadn't even picked up on the change.

As she sat down between the new guy and Stacey, the young man turned to her and gave her a slight nod before looking down at the script in front of him.

Francesca arrived on the stage, taking the seat across from Wendy. She always showed up exactly five minutes late to every read-through, so it never started until she arrived. When Wendy asked her about this, Francesca said that the first five minutes was always filled with inane chatter and gossip, so she preferred to skip it.

Clearing his throat, Jim stood up and looked around the table. "I know that you have all been waiting impatiently for the cast list, but it happens that we have a new cast member joining us for this show." He gestured towards the young man, although it wasn't necessary. "So today will be a little different. I shall be introducing you at the same time as your character, and I will also be introducing the crew."

Jim stepped back from the table, and everyone kept their eyes on him as he moved around the stage, introducing each person.

"This is Ari, they are our stage manager. Billy, he is our set and lighting designer. Francesca, she will be playing Carlotta, Sorelli, and the nurse. Gerard, he will be our Phantom, as well as Monsieur Poligny. Samuel, he will be Monsieur Moncharmin. Scott, he is basically a gofer."

Wendy noticed that Scott's eyebrows furrowed at the job description and his head bowed even lower than it already was, attempting to hide his frown.

"Rhonda, she will be our accompanist and musical director. Paloma, she is our costume designer. Galia, she is in charge of special effects. Betty, she is in charge of props. Carina, she will be Mrs. Giry, Meg Giry, and Man One. Stacey, she is playing Remy, Jammes, and Man Two. Wendy, she will be Christine."

Wendy's eyes widened as she realized that she'd actually gotten the part of Christine. Although Carina and Stacey were playing other characters, Wendy hadn't realized what that meant for her until Jim had actually said it. A large grin broke out on her face, which she was quick to dial back to a modest smile, lest the others think she was gloating. When she glanced over at Francesca, the blonde woman gave her a proud look, and she had to fight to keep a blush from creeping up into her cheeks.

"And Vance, he will be our Raoul. I am Jim, he/him, and I am your director. And now that the introductions are out of the way, it is time for us to get to the script."

At the end of the read-through, Wendy couldn't wait to start rehearsals. Jim had created a script with all the expected romance, horror, and tension. He'd cut out a lot of characters from the novel and simplified the story and language, making it a tight, energetic show. There were some hints to the musical in it, but, according to Jim, it was still very much like the book.

Jim talked for a while about his vision for this show and what he expected of everyone. He mentioned that a few of the designers would be expected to dress up and stand around for the retirement and masquerade scenes to make the stage look more crowded. He also explained that since the opera in the show is *Faust*, Rhonda would be working on adapting the music into something more accessible for both the actors and the audience. The rest of the musical numbers would be songs from the musical version of *Phantom*, so that they would be familiar to both the singers and the audience. He intended to have all of the cast singing "Masquerade" for the masquerade scene but was prepared to use a recording of the song, should it not sound the way he wanted it to.

"Good to know we've got the rights," Rhonda said, a half-smile on her face that was more akin to a half-smirk.

Jim gave her a tired look but didn't respond. A few people around the table were holding back laughter, trying to hide their amusement. For theatres to perform certain shows or musicals they had to pay for the rights to do so, ensuring that those who created the works received compensation, but Jim never did. At first, he'd tried to do original works or plays that had no rights, but when he realized that nobody really knew or cared about the theatre, his morality went right out the window. Rights were expensive and the theatre wasn't exactly resting on a bed of money, so he figured that he was owed a certain level of oversight. Rhonda first enquired about it during a pared-down version of *My Fair Lady*, and Jim had told her that if the rights holders wanted him to pay, then they could march right down to the theatre and demand the money in person. He knew that this theatre was small enough to go unnoticed—both a blessing and a curse. And, sure enough, he'd gotten away with it so far. While Wendy didn't know much about producing theatre, she also wasn't the person making the decisions, so if anyone got in trouble, it wouldn't be her. If anything, she was glad that the music for this show would mostly be songs she already knew how to sing.

Jim finished his ramble and declared the read-through over. Before everyone could leave, Ari handed out a rehearsal schedule, reminding them all to pay close attention. Jim warned them that tomorrow would be their only day off next week, so they should spend the time going over the script to be prepared for when rehearsals started. They only had two and a half weeks to rehearse, so the sooner they were off-book, the better. Then he asked Vance if the two of them could have a word, to which Vance nodded.

"Let's go," Stacey said to Carina and Wendy, and the two nodded, grabbing their scripts as they stood up from the table. Wendy glanced towards Betty, but she was deep in conversation with her sister, probably about the many effects and props that the show would require.

The group left the theatre and headed to The Belle Verde for their traditional after-read-through meal. They were early for supper, which was good because they'd stand a chance of getting a booth and not have to sit at the bar, which was smack in the centre of the restaurant, or one of the tables around the room, which were always too cramped. Gossiping was best done in a booth, where you didn't have patrons and staff constantly manoeuvring around you and possibly listening in.

Gradey, one of the waiters who always seemed to be at the restaurant no matter what time of day it was, greeted them with a Southern-twang-tinged "How y'all doing?" As had become their custom, Stacey replied in English, Wendy in French, and Carina in Spanish. Gradey gave them a half-grin and showed them to a booth along the right side, giving them menus despite the fact that nobody who lived on Jacobi Street ever looked at them. The menu was basically the size of a phonebook and it was almost guaranteed that whatever meal you wanted was inside, no matter how obscure it might be. And if it weren't there, there was a good chance that you could cobble together a few different dishes to make it.

"What can I get you?" he asked, his voice now a more neutral accent than the greeting had been. Not that he needed to ask, since everyone basically ordered the same thing every time, but he always did anyway.

"*Ropa Vieja*," Carina said.

"Pastrami on rye," Stacey ordered. "With lightly salted potato chips and carrot sticks on the side."

Wendy paused. "I'll get the cranberry spinach salad with chicken."

Gradey raised an eyebrow. "Sounds like *someone* got a good part in the next play." He smiled at her and walked away, not bothering to wait for a reply.

"Nerves getting to you?" Stacey asked. "It's your first big role, after all."

Wendy nodded. "A bit." Normally she'd order *navarin d'agneau* with a side of bannock, but after all the excitement today her stomach needed something lighter. It had become a tradition for Stacey and Carina to go to The Belle Verde after every read-through, and after Wendy joined the troupe, they'd invited her to come along. Most of the time they'd get their usual dish, but once in a while Stacey or Carina would order a salad after getting cast in a really good role, being too nervous and excited for their usual order. The first time it happened it had thrown Gradey for a loop, but he quickly caught on. Wendy realized that this was the first time she'd been able to do this, and that satisfaction helped calm her nerves a little.

"You'll be fine," Stacey said. "Jim wouldn't give you the part if he didn't think you could handle it. I mean, it'd only be more work for him."

"Um, thanks?"

Stacey waved her hand, dismissing her words. "Just chalk what I say down to being a jealous bitch because I wanted to play Christine. Especially since you get the new hot guy to be your Raoul."

Carina sighed wistfully. "He's got a real James Dean vibe going on. It's so hot."

"It's a good thing I have a weak spot for broody guys," Stacey added.

Although those two seemed enamoured of the new arrival, Wendy wasn't sure what to make of Vance. He'd barely said anything that wasn't written in his script during the read-through and didn't try to get to know anyone. At least he sounded good reading the lines, which hopefully meant that he could act.

While the others gushed about how hot Vance was, Wendy found it difficult to join in. Perhaps she'd have found it easier if she only had to admire him from afar, but he was her main scene partner. If he turned out to be a major jerk or a terrible actor, her dream role would quickly turn into a nightmare.

Gradey arrived with their drinks, placing each one down with emphasis before moving on to another table. Unlike food, they never bothered ordering drinks. Beer was the assumed libation of The Belle Verde, and Gradey always knew what to give them. Wendy had a light, white beer with citrus notes, Carina had a Mexican beer that came in a tall green bottle, and Stacey had a beer so dark that light couldn't penetrate it.

"You know, Paloma seemed tired today," Carina said, sipping her drink in a way that seemed to suggest she'd take in fewer calories if she took smaller sips. "There were bags under her eyes, and she looked pale. Do you think she's coming down with something?"

"I hope not," Wendy frowned. If one person in the theatre got sick then it was bound to spread to everyone else, and she didn't want to come down with a cold or flu this early into rehearsals. She made a mental note to stock up on vitamin C. "Hopefully it's just a hangover or a bad night's rest."

Stacey nodded in agreement. "Oh, did either of you notice that Scott seemed extra squirrelly today? That guy is so weird."

"It probably had something to do with Jim calling him a gofer," Wendy said, laughing at the memory.

Carina joined in. "I swear, the day that Jim describes him as his assistant director is the day that I keel over dead from shock."

"If that ever happens, I'm sure Jim will be the next one to keel over," Stacey added as they all laughed.

"I wonder what the chandelier drop is going to look like," Wendy said, trying to picture something so crazy happening in their small theatre.

Carina nearly snorted. "We'll be lucky if it doesn't drop on our heads."

"You know Ari wouldn't let anything like that happen," she replied pointedly.

"I also know that Galia is insane," Carina deftly countered. "Remember the time she caught the stage on fire during that wrestling skit?"

Wendy winced at the memory; the past five months having done nothing to dull it. The skit had been about a fearsome wrestler whose only fear was fire, and it was supposed to have four pyrotechnic charges go off while he was gloating about his big win, reducing him to a quivering, weeping mess. But instead of the small charges that Ari had approved, on the night of the show Galia decided to make them extra theatrical. It resulted in actual surprise from Gerard, who was playing the wrestler, and then real fear as the ropes making up the wrestling ring around him caught on fire. Ari had to bring in the fire curtain while Billy ran for a fire extinguisher. Luckily, the audience thought it was all part of the show and Gerard escaped with no injuries.

That stunt had almost resulted in Galia getting fired, but instead she'd been given a severe talking to and a second chance. With the watchful eye of Ari hanging over her, Galia had been much less reckless ever since.

Stacey took a long drink from her glass before bringing it down onto the table with a thump. "I wanna talk about the theatre ghost!"

Wendy and Carina exchanged a confused look.

"What ghost?" Carina asked.

"The ghost of The Quaint Little Theatre!" Stacey looked at them expectantly but received blank looks. "Look, I've been doing some digging and although I haven't found anything about a specific ghost that haunts the theatre, I've found allusions to a few people who've died there over the years. A stagehand here, an actor there, an audience member once in a while. There are a lot of ghosts that could be haunting the building."

Carina gave her a sceptical look.

Wendy frowned. "But Francesca said that there hasn't been a ghost at the theatre since Jim bought it fifteen years ago. You'd think someone would notice if there was."

"Ah ha!" Stacey exclaimed, pointing a finger at Wendy for emphasis. "I have a theory about that! See, I think that the ghosts within the theatre have been lying dormant, probably because they don't have enough energy to manifest. But when Jim decided to do *Phantom*, it woke them up. Like some kind of invocation. That's why we're hearing that knocking—it's the spirits trying to communicate with us!"

Carina burst out laughing. "You are *realmente loca.*"

"The knocking was just the furnace, and it hasn't been heard since Wednesday," Wendy added. She was trying to sound flippant, but deep down she knew that there was something about the noise that unsettled her. Could it actually be ghosts trying to communicate with them by tapping on pipes? Didn't ghosts throw stuff or move things around? What kind of ghost knocked?

"Look, I can tell you're both sceptical," Stacey said, refusing to back down, "but I know that's what happened. Jim called up some kind of spirit and now it's trying to talk to us. We need to have a séance or something to communicate with it and find out what it wants, and then once we've helped it, it'll be able to rest."

Wendy exchanged another look with Carina. Both were equally doubtful about Stacey's theory, but before they could say anything, Gradey arrived with their meals. They all tucked in and Wendy hoped that it would put an end to the ghost talk, but Stacey seemed to take their silence as acceptance and continued to ramble while they ate, hypothesizing which ghost would be the likeliest to come forth. There had been a stagehand who'd fallen from the lighting grid and died, an audience member who'd had a heart attack during a show, an actor who'd killed themselves in their dressing room, an actor who'd killed another in a fit of jealousy, and a director who'd hung himself on stage.

Wendy tried to ignore Stacey while she ate, but it wasn't easy. She was glad that she'd ordered a salad, since the more Stacey talked the less she felt like eating. Thankfully, Stacey didn't go into any of the gory details, but she did speculate a lot about each ghost, making up stories about how they'd all met their demise. At one point, Wendy wondered if Stacey was suddenly so into this ghost theory because she didn't want to talk about how Wendy had taken the part they'd all wanted.

By the time they'd finished eating, the restaurant was starting to fill up with other inhabitants of Jacobi Street, so they quickly paid and left.

"See you later," Wendy said as they broke apart and went their separate ways. Carina and Stacey shared an apartment above The Soper Boutique, which was in the opposite direction as Wendy's apartment. They waved back to her before turning away, heads bent towards each other as they talked in low voices—mostly likely gossiping about Jim's casting choices.

Wendy couldn't help feeling relieved now that the other women were gone. Although she liked them, they hadn't given her much of a chance to feel excited about getting the lead role in the play. Stacey had hit the nail on the head about them being "jealous bitches," but it still would have been nice if they'd let her gush for a bit.

Taking in a deep breath, Wendy cleared away all thoughts of ghosts and jealous co-workers and allowed herself to think of how she'd finally managed to get a role that she'd desperately wanted—that everyone else had desperately wanted. A wide smile broke out on her face, and, as she walked towards her apartment, she felt a bounce in her step.

CHAPTER ELEVEN

Billy whistled to himself as he looked through the old set pieces stacked in the basement. Even though it was their day off, he'd come into the theatre to show Jim his preliminary sketches for the sets for *Phantom*, in order to get started on them right away. After Jim approved them (with only a few minor changes suggested), Billy had decided to go to the basement in the hopes that there would be some old pieces in storage that he'd be able to re-use. The show had nine different sets and Jim wanted them all to look luxurious and professional, so if Billy didn't have to make everything from scratch, it'd save him a lot of time.

Ever since their former scenic painter, Eddie, had decided to walk out on the job, Billy found himself having to fill in the role. He'd called Eddie's apartment to find out why, but his partner said that Eddie had gone and wasn't coming back. Billy wasn't sure why he would quit, especially right in the middle of a project, leaving behind a half-painted set piece and open cans of paint around the stage, but it was probably something serious like a family emergency. Jim hadn't found a satisfactory replacement yet and, knowing him, he was using this as an excuse not to spend money hiring someone. Although Billy wasn't as good a painter as Eddie, he was good enough for Jim not to complain.

As Billy searched through the large boards, he could hear a low knocking sound coming from the furnace. Shaking his head, he wondered when Jim would get someone in to look at it. It probably wasn't anything serious, but it wouldn't hurt to fix whatever was making the sound and reassure everyone that the place wasn't about to blow up. It was likely a cost issue, as Jim hated spending money on anything that wasn't show-related, but keeping the building in tip-top shape was important. It'd be hard to stage a play in a building that was falling apart.

He pulled out a large board that had been painted to look like a stone wall and set it aside with the other pieces he'd pulled. So far, he had pieces that could be used for the manager's office, cemetery, and now the catacombs. It wasn't much, but it was a start. And the less time he spent painting sets, the more he'd have to work on Box 5, the eponymous box that the Phantom requested be held for him for every performance.

Suddenly Billy stopped whistling. He thought he'd heard something, but when he paused to listen all he could hear was the sound of the furnace. Shrugging, he went back to his work, looking through the flats. When he was finished with that, he moved over to the set pieces on the other side of the room. He needed to find something that could be used for the mirrored cabinet in Christine's dressing room. It had to be big enough for people to travel through, and sturdy enough to stand up to a lot of activity, as well as whatever Galia had in mind for that effect.

Pausing again, he stepped out into the middle of the room and looked towards the back, where the furnace was. He'd definitely heard something that time, but who could be back there? Nobody else had been around when he'd arrived at the theatre.

Maybe Jim had come down earlier to look at the furnace and had injured himself. It wasn't likely, but who else could it be?

"Jim? Is that you?" Billy called out.

There was no answer, other than a sharp knock. He nervously ran a hand through his thick brown hair, before tugging at his bushy beard. The knock sounded again.

"Is anyone back there?" he called out.

Another knock.

He was about to turn back to his work when he heard a pained moaning.

"Don't worry, I'm on my way!" he said as he hurried to the back of the room. When he approached the large metal furnace, he scanned the area for the injured person, but there were only shadows amongst the glowing red light. Looking up, he noticed that some of the fluorescent lights in the ceiling were dark, and he made a quick mental note to replace them later.

"Where are you?" he called out. "Am I close?"

There was no answer except for a loud knock, and Billy was hit with a sudden realization that the knocking might have been someone crying out for help. All this time they had no idea that a person was down here, hoping that someone would come and help them.

Another knock followed that one, and Billy stepped closer to the furnace, moving in the direction of the sound, keeping his eyes out for an arm or leg trapped underneath something. The knocking grew louder and more frequent, which he took as a sign that he was on the right path.

"Don't worry," he called out, trying to be heard over the knocking. "I'm here to help!"

The air began to grow hotter as he manoeuvred around the large metal furnace, moving towards the back wall. Wiping the sweat from his brow, Billy searched desperately, but it was almost impossible to make out anything in the dim red light.

The knocking increased in intensity and suddenly seemed to be coming from everywhere at once. The heat was getting worse, but he had to find the person in trouble and help them.

"Where are you?" he asked, resisting the urge to put his hands over his ears and drown out the noise.

Looking around frantically, he suddenly noticed movement in the far corner.

"Just hold on!" he called out as he headed towards the corner, walking deeper into the thick, dark shadows, which quickly rose to swallow him.

CHAPTER TWELVE

Wendy woke up twenty minutes before her alarm went off and nearly jumped out of bed with excitement. Unlike when she'd first started at the theatre, today she felt both prepared and qualified for the job she was about to do.

There was a vague notion in the back of her mind that she'd had the same odd dream of her standing on stage and being watched by an invisible audience, but she tried not to give it any thought. Now that she'd gotten her desired role, the dream had probably transformed into the kind where she'd forgotten her lines in the middle of a performance or came to rehearsal only to discover that Jim had replaced her with someone else, and she didn't need any negative thoughts or insecurities influencing her mood today. Today was about being positive.

She'd read through the script multiple times on Sunday, even though it was her day off, because she wanted to prove to Jim that he hadn't made a mistake in giving her this role. Not only was she well on her way to memorizing all her lines, but she had a good glimpse into Christine's motives, actions, and emotions.

Some of her preparedness came at a small cost, though. Betty had come over last night to spend a few hours, and while the two were watching a movie, she caught Wendy constantly sneaking looks at her script instead. Thankfully, Betty understood the situation, and after some playful chastising, she turned her attention to the movie and said nothing more about Wendy's inability to keep her eyes off her lines.

As Wendy approached the theatre for her first day of *Phantom* rehearsal, she could feel her heart racing with anticipation. Stepping into the lobby, she noticed that Scott was sitting in a chair near the door to the auditorium, holding his ever-present clipboard with one hand and a pen in the other. He was attempting to sit up straight and proper, but his shoulders were slumped and there was a wash of irritation on his face—likely from having to be the designated door-watcher. She gave him a smile before walking past but didn't say anything because she didn't want to give him an invitation to complain.

Swiftly making her way through the auditorium and the backstage area, she only slowed down when she reached the staircase. Pausing for a moment, she was unable to stop herself from looking at the door which led down to the lower level, where the door to the basement was located. Stacey's words about the many ghosts that might be haunting the theatre and trying to communicate with them echoed in her mind, but she quickly pushed them aside and ascended the stairs.

The rehearsal hall was the only room above the backstage area. It was as wide as the stage (including the wings) and one-and-a-half times as long, so it didn't feel crowded unless all of the actors and set pieces were piled inside. The floor had already been marked with different colours of spike tape that outlined the stage area and showed where certain set pieces, like the infamous Box 5, would be located. The floor was relatively clean, but Wendy knew that more pieces of colourful tape would make their way onto the floor as they rehearsed, marking the location of furniture and other smaller pieces.

Ari and Jim were already in the room, with Ari sitting at a table near the back, in the "audience" section of the room. Their giant binder was open in front of them, containing the full script, paper for notes, and more paper—just in case. Next to it was a case holding pencils, pens, erasers, and more labels and tabs than Wendy would ever know what to do with. Ari was in discussion with Jim, who stood in front of the table, his back to the door. Wendy greeted them both, and although Ari said "hello," Jim merely looked at her and nodded before turning back to the conversation.

When Wendy first met Ari, she didn't know what to make of them. They were five foot eight and broad, with a muscular physique that made you suspect that you shouldn't underestimate them. Their hair was bright pink, straight and long, and the right side was shaved down to the skin. They usually wore their hair flipped to the left, exposing the shaved part, and revealing an ear that had piercings all the way from the bottom to the top. There was something so punk about the ear piercings, especially when paired with the silver hoop pierced through their lip. Ari usually wore tank tops, jeans, and steel-toed boots, no matter the season, which only added to their tough aesthetic. Wendy sometimes felt jealous of Ari's style, although she knew she'd never be able to pull something like that off.

Usually, Ari didn't say much during rehearsals, which made the occasions when they spoke all the more important. Oftentimes they'd mutter to themselves in German when annoyed or irritated, but they never let their emotions boil over—unlike certain other people in the troupe. Everyone respected Ari, and nobody crossed them. Despite all of this, Ari had a great sense of humour and was great to talk to outside of rehearsal. They had all kinds of stories about working in theatres in Berlin—from classical to modern to extremely experimental. The parties at the Treehouse didn't usually pick up until they arrived.

Wendy spotted two empty chairs facing the table, which were likely for her and Vance. More chairs were stacked along the side of the room, and although there weren't any set pieces up here yet, there was a stack of black wooden boxes in one corner that they could use in place of items. Rhonda wasn't needed at this rehearsal, so the piano was tucked away in the far corner. Taking a seat, Wendy opened her script and went over her lines as she waited for Vance to arrive.

He showed up a few minutes later, just before the call time. He gave a quick hello to everyone in the room before taking the seat next to Wendy.

"Well, let's get started," Jim said, sitting down next to Ari.

Ari tapped their pencil on a nearby piece of paper, drawing Jim's attention. He looked down at the paper, frowned slightly, and cleared his throat.

"Before we get down to business," Jim said, addressing Wendy and Vance, "you should take a moment to get to know each other. You two will be sharing a lot of scenes together, so I don't want either of you feeling uncomfortable. Take the next five—"

Ari coughed loudly.

"Take the next *ten* minutes to get comfortable with each other." Jim took in a breath and attempted a smile. "After all, trust behind the stage leads to greater trust on stage."

Wendy noticed that one corner of Ari's mouth had quirked up into a half-smile. No doubt they'd been the one to let Jim know that it wasn't wise to hire a stranger and drop them into the troupe without any introductions. She wouldn't have been surprised to find out that Jim was quoting Ari for that last bit.

As Jim and Ari started talking amongst themselves again, Wendy turned to Vance and gave what she hoped was a warm smile. He looked at her, his mouth moving up into a quick smile before going back to neutral.

"I'm Wendy," she said, holding out her hand. "I've been with the troupe for about half a year, and I live on Jacobi Street."

He looked at her hand for a few seconds before shaking it. "I'm Vance. I did some acting in high school, but this is my first professional role. I mean, if this counts as professional. I know it's not Broadway or anything, but..." he paused. "I live up on 28th."

"So, how did you get involved in all of this?" she asked.

"I saw a flier on 13th Street."

She waited for him to elaborate, but he didn't. "That's how I got here, too," she said. "I used to work at East of Sicily, but I saw a flier and decided to audition."

He nodded and Wendy had to resist sighing. This guy really wasn't giving her much to work with.

"I wasn't much of an actor when I started," she rambled, "but they hired me anyway. After a few shows I realized how fun this was and how much I enjoyed it, so I started taking lessons and stuff. So, why'd you decide to accept the part?"

"Well," he said, his voice uncertain, "I wanted to try something new. Work's been a bit... tedious. Like I said, I used to act in high school but had to give up after graduation. And I like the novel, so I figured this might be fun to try."

Wendy nodded and smiled, thankful to get more than a few words out of him. For a guy that wanted to do something fun, he was surprisingly lacklustre. But being stuck with a dull scene-partner was still better than getting stuck with Gerard or Sam, or—heaven forbid—Scott.

She asked a few more leading questions, and it felt like he was starting to warm up to her by the end of the ten minutes. She'd learned about some of the parts he'd had in other plays, and how the garage he worked at was owned by his father, and even that he was currently seeing someone. It was a lot of surface-level information, but at least she had a better idea of who he was. Although she doubted that they'd ever be best friends, she was fairly certain he wasn't an axe murderer.

"We'll read through the scene once," Jim instructed them. "When we are done, you may ask questions, and I will give notes. Then we'll read it again. And then we'll get up on our feet." He looked at them for agreement, and they both nodded.

Wendy and Vance read through their first scene together, which was the first time Raoul and Christine meet. It was a great scene because Raoul was so excited to see his childhood friend, but Christine had to pretend not to recognize him because the Phantom was nearby, listening. The scene had more to it—with Raoul coming back to try and talk to Christine one more time, but instead he hears her speaking with the Phantom, and then he sees two men carrying a body along the hall—but those parts would be rehearsed later, when the other actors were around. Instead, they moved on to the next scene with the two of them, when Raoul finds Christine in a cemetery, going to lay flowers on her father's grave.

Their rehearsal had been scheduled for four hours, with a break in the middle, and by the end of it, they'd loosely blocked all of Christine and Raoul's scenes. Wendy was sure to take meticulous notes in pencil, knowing full well that Jim might end up changing everything during the next rehearsal. She'd been surprised by Vance, who seemed to become a whole other person during their scenes. His first read wasn't anything to call home about, but by the time they got on their feet he was much more comfortable and warmer. She could see why Jim hired him.

After their rehearsal time was over, Ari informed Wendy and Vance that Paloma would be expecting the two of them at wardrobe for their costume measuring. Wendy thanked Ari and headed out of the room.

"Um... Wendy?"

She paused at the top of the stairs, turning around at the sound of her name. Vance was standing behind her, looking sheepish.

"Can I ask you where the wardrobe room is?" he said.

"Just follow me," she replied.

Vance didn't say much as she led him down to the lower level and through the hall, so she tried to fill up the silence by talking about the theatre and pointing out where everything was. When they reached the costume room, she was thankful for the opportunity to stop talking.

Paloma informed them that she'd measure Vance first and asked Wendy to wait out in the hall, to give them some privacy. While she waited, Wendy tried to distract herself by thinking about where she'd get something to eat for lunch. It'd be in her best interest to learn how to cook better, but she was always missing some vital ingredient in her cupboards or she'd read a recipe wrong and it would always taste a little strange. It was much less hassle to let someone else do the cooking, especially when they were much better at it than her.

A loud knock startled her from her thoughts and her heart jumped. Memories of Stacey's ghost stories started to creep forward, filling her imagination with images of spirits desperately trying to communicate, but she shoved them back into the far recesses of her mind. It was only air in the pipes, nothing more.

Another knock sounded, and it was so loud that it seemed to reverberate throughout the building. Wendy looked around, but she was the only person standing in the hallway and nobody else poked their head out from any of the rooms. How had nobody else heard that? For a brief moment she considered asking Paloma and Vance if they'd heard the sound but decided that they might think she was being paranoid.

She tried to calm herself down and tell herself that there was nothing supernatural about the sounds, but the knocking continued the entire time she was waiting. Sometimes it was sharp and quick, and other times low and deep. It sounded like it was coming from different places, and sometimes all around her. Still, nobody else came out to enquire about it, making her wonder if only she could hear it.

Was it possible that Stacey's crazy stories were true? Was there some kind of strange presence in the theatre? If so, what was it trying to say? Did the different knocks mean different things?

But if it was simply a lonely ghost with unfinished business, why did every sound unnerve her? Why did it feel like there was some kind of malevolent spirit watching her with unseen eyes? Wendy wrapped her arms around herself and tried to tune out the noise.

When Paloma poked her head out to tell her it was her turn, she was so relieved that she could have kissed the woman. Vance thanked Wendy as he left, heading down the hallway, and she hoped that he'd be able to find his way out okay. She hurried into the costume room, finding Paloma leaning on one of the tables.

"How was rehearsal, my dear?" Paloma asked, grabbing her tape measure and pushing herself upright. There were dark circles under her eyes and her movements were slower than usual.

"It was good. How are you, Paloma?" she asked gently.

"Good," Paloma said, before realizing that Wendy hadn't asked just to be kind. "I've had some trouble sleeping, but it's nothing, *mi querido*. I have too many costumes to make to let something like that bother me."

Wendy smiled. "Well, I hope your sleep troubles end soon."

"They usually do."

The two chatted as Paloma measured her, comparing her current measurements with the ones from last month's show and overwriting anything that needed to be changed. Although Paloma was clearly exhausted by the time they finished, she decided to show Wendy some of the sketches she'd made for Christine's costumes, which seemed to breathe new life into her and renew her energy. Wendy gushed over the costumes, growing even more excited about the role, and she could see that Paloma was delighted by her reaction. When they were done, Wendy wished her a peaceful sleep tonight and headed out.

As she walked along the hallway, Wendy kept her ears open and her guard up. The knocking seemed to have stopped, but she quickened her pace anyway, hastily making her way upstairs.

CHAPTER THIRTEEN

"Betty! I need your help testing the noose!"

Betty jolted up from the book she was diligently working on, almost knocking it to the floor. Despite having spent the past hour carefully distressing the pages to make it look like it was from the early nineteen-hundreds, she immediately lost interest in her project and rushed into the hallway.

"No, no, no, no, no," she muttered under her breath as she hurried to the special effects room. When she entered the room, she saw her sister standing on a chair, a noose around her neck. "Galia!" she cried out a split second before her sister stepped off the chair.

The noose tightened around Galia's throat and she started to flail as her airway was constricted. Betty rushed forward and grabbed her sister around the legs, getting a few kicks to the midsection before containing them, and guided her back onto the chair.

"What were you thinking?" Betty scolded her sister once she was breathing again. "Jim said that it's supposed to be a dummy in the noose, not a real person!"

"I was testing the weight capabilities," Galia said, taking the noose off and rubbing her throat. She'd only been hanging for a few seconds, but her voice was strained. "If it can hold me without breaking, then it should be able to hold whatever dummy you come up with, provided that it's under my weight." She paused. "Although the dummy will be hanging for a while, so I should test it for longer."

"Dammit, sis," Betty cried out. "Test it with a dummy, not yourself! What if I hadn't been here? Or hadn't heard you?"

"I had a backup plan," Galia said flippantly, smoothing her chin-length blond hair with both hands. Her response didn't inspire much relief. Although Galia was older and taller and more confident, Betty often felt that she was missing the gene for self-preservation.

"Shouldn't you be working on the chandelier?" Betty asked. "That's going to be way harder to coordinate than a noose."

Galia looked up at the rope and grabbed it with one hand, giving it a tug. There was a bit of slack, but not much, and the rope stayed strong. She nodded satisfactorily, put her other hand on it, and lifted herself off the chair. After swinging for a minute, she smiled broadly before dropping to the floor.

"I mean, hanging by an arm isn't the same as hanging by a neck, but if it can support that kind of weight, we should be okay..." her voice trailed off as she did a few sums in her head.

"The chandelier, sis?" Betty prompted.

"Yeah, I'm working on it..."

"Good, because that drop at the end of Act 1 needs to be fantastic."

Galia's green eyes widened with excitement. "Oh, it's gonna be *so* cool."

Shaking her head, Betty watched her sister lose all interest in the noose and wander over to her drafting table. Now that her attention was somewhere else, Betty moved the ladder from the corner of the room and climbed up it to untie the noose. The knots were difficult to untie, due to the stress having tightened them, but eventually she managed to get the rope down from the beam without cutting it. The entire time she worked, Galia said nothing to her, her head filled with thoughts of chandeliers falling.

"I'm taking this with me so that I can test it on the dummy," Betty called out as she descended the ladder with the noose.

Her sister gave a half-hearted wave, not bothering to look up.

She sighed and put the ladder away before heading back to the props room. She wished that Jim hadn't decided on a play with so much going on. There were a lot of different and dangerous elements involved, and she was worried that her sister was going to destroy the theatre—or herself—trying to pull these effects off. She still remembered last Christmas when Galia was trying to figure out a pyrotechnic effect for their production of *A Christmas Carol* and accidentally set herself on fire—four times. In order to prevent her sister from ending up in the hospital or burning the theatre down, she'd had to get Ari to intervene.

Placing the noose somewhere her sister wouldn't find it, Betty went back to work on the journal. Once it was distressed enough, she'd be able to start writing in it. Jim had given her detailed notes on what the journal should look like and she knew that he expected her to follow them to the letter, even though ninety-nine percent of the audience wouldn't be able to see any of those fine details. She could have made a few pages look great and skimped on the rest, but she didn't want to risk Jim seeing those bad pages and thinking she was lazy.

After thirty minutes, she looked at her watch and saw that it was getting close to dinnertime. Wendy would be expecting her soon. Betty put away her work and started to leave, but she paused outside the special effects room. Peeking in, she could see that her sister was still hunched over the chandelier plans.

"Umm, I've got plans tonight, so I won't be home," she said through the doorway. Her right hand absent-mindedly tugged at the hair around her ear.

Her sister gave a half-hearted wave, but then her head popped up. "You'll be gone the whole night?"

"Yup. So, don't go blowing anything up, because I won't be standing by with the fire extinguisher."

Galia rolled her eyes. "Any idea of when I'm going to meet this paramour of yours? You've been staying over a lot more, which must mean it's serious."

"Well..." Betty paused. "Maybe..."

"I mean, I don't care if he has two heads or five eyes. Although I will judge you if it turns out to be Gerard." Galia smiled easily at her joke, but Betty had to force her own smile.

"I'll see," she said. "We're just waiting for the right time."

"Well, let him know that I'm a terrible cook, but would love to have him over some time."

Betty forced her smile wider and nodded. "I'll pass along the message to *him*," she said before quickly saying goodbye and hurrying off.

She barely noticed anything on her way to Wendy's apartment, surprising herself when she realized she was standing in front of Wendy's door. Taking a breath, she smoothed her hair and knocked.

"It's open!" Wendy called out from the other side.

It was always open, but Betty still always knocked and waited for a response. She walked into the apartment and headed straight for Wendy, who was in the kitchen, looking through the cupboards. Betty walked up behind her and wrapped her arms around her, resting her forehead on Wendy's shoulder.

"I'm a wuss," Betty said sadly.

Wendy took hold of her hands and leaned her head on Betty's. "I refuse to believe that."

Taking in a deep breath, Betty held Wendy closer, enjoying the warmth of her body and breathing in her vanilla and coconut scent. She wished that the rest of her life could be as easy as this. After a few minutes, she loosened her grip and Wendy turned around to face her.

"Rough day?" Wendy asked, wrapping her arms around Betty's shoulders.

"Mostly fine. I got a lot of work finished on the journal."

"Well, that sounds good."

Betty leaned her forehead against Wendy's. "It's also hungry work. Have you found anything that might resemble a meal yet?"

Wendy smiled. "I've found a takeout menu for The Penguin's Monocle."

"Pad thai?"

"Pad thai."

The two smiled and Wendy gave her a quick kiss before breaking away to find her phone and order them some food.

Galia was determined to make the chandelier fall the best effect this theatre had ever seen. Her current plan was to hang the chandelier over the audience and let it drop straight down, so that when it fell everyone would think it was going to fall on them and crush them all. It was going to be brilliant.

Well, it would be brilliant if she could figure out a way for it to not actually hit the audience, and if she could figure out what it would do once it stopped falling. But that's what rehearsals were for—trial and error. She paused. Hopefully her sister was making the chandelier out of something that wouldn't shatter.

Her major problem was that she couldn't get gravity to bend to her will. Another problem was that she was having trouble concentrating because of the loud knocking sound in the hallway. At first it was merely an annoyance, but then it started getting louder—loud enough to pull her out of her work. And before she could get back in, it sounded again, and again. Galia sighed in annoyance. Putting down her pen, she frowned deeply. She hated being distracted.

Grabbing her mp3 player from her backpack, she stuck the earbuds in her ears and turned on some music, hoping to drown out the knocking. It was impossible to work under these conditions.

CHAPTER FOURTEEN

She was standing in a dark, empty hallway. In her left hand was a wrought-iron lantern with a candle inside, but the light coming from it was weak, and she was only able to make out a few feet in front of her. As she took small, tentative steps forward, the lantern's light illuminated nothing except for the bare earthen floor and the dark walls of the hallway. There were no doorways or windows or other objects to be seen. The air around her was chilled and slightly musty, like that of a tomb.

She turned around to see what was behind her, but there was only darkness, as if the hallway was falling away with each step she took. Even the dim light of her lantern couldn't penetrate it. She wondered what would happen if she tried to turn back. Would her foot find an earthen floor, or would it disappear into the darkness?

Facing forward, she continued to walk. She could hear a noise in the distance, something that grew louder as she approached. Was it singing? Was there another person at the other end of the hallway singing a slow, mournful tune?

Soon she came to the end of the tunnel, which contained a large black door. The music was coming from within, and as she reached for the handle she wondered who was behind it.

A loud sharp knock startled her and she jumped back. The edges around the door began to glow a deep red and she watched as a dark red liquid began to bleed down the front of the door, coating it and changing it to the dark crimson colour of the basement door.

Another knock—but this time it came from behind the door, causing it to shudder violently. A small cry escaped her lips as the lantern fell from her hand and she turned away, running into the darkness.

She could no longer see anything, but still she ran, desperate to escape the terrible thing she knew was waiting for her behind the door. The knocking increased in intensity until it felt like it was coming from everywhere. Putting her hands over her ears, she closed her eyes and screamed for it to stop.

When she opened her eyes, she was standing on the stage of the theatre, wearing a white, old-fashioned dress. The audience was empty, but she could feel eyes staring at her, watching her. Her heart was still racing, but she didn't move. She had no idea what she was supposed to do or what her invisible audience expected, so it felt safer to do nothing.

But then the knocking started up again, sharp and quick at first, but growing louder each time. As she looked out at the auditorium, she noticed something red gently glowing behind the last row. As the object took shape, she realized that it was the basement door, shuddering with each knock, as if it was going to blow off its hinges.

The knocking came faster and louder and though she placed her hands over her ears again, it was so loud that it felt like it was inside her head, rattling her skull.

"LEAVE ME ALONE!" she screamed, but the knocking wouldn't stop.

Wendy woke up with a start. Her heart was pounding in her chest, but there was enough light coming through the window for her to see that she was in her own bed, safe in her apartment, with Betty sound asleep beside her. Taking in a deep breath, Wendy tried to slow her heartbeat and calm down.

It had been a while since she'd had a full-fledged nightmare and she didn't miss the feeling. As a child, she used to have nightmares whenever she was feeling particularly nervous or anxious about something. Her parents used to brush them off, telling her that she had nothing to fear from dreams, but it was her maternal grandmother who helped her work through them. Her *aanaga* explained the importance of symbolism and meaning, and whenever Wendy had a nightmare, the two of them would talk through it, figuring out what it meant, until the nightmares went away.

Wendy felt a pang of sadness as she remembered those moments. Although her mother refused to acknowledge her Inuit heritage, her *aanaga* had secretly taught her about their culture. It had to be kept secret, otherwise Wendy knew that her mother would stop letting her visit, but that made it even more exciting. Wendy's grandfather had died shortly after her mother was born, and her *aanaga* never remarried. She was strong and independent, and although she respected her daughter's decision to blend in, she also respected Wendy's desire to learn everything. In her youth, Wendy often wished that she could live with her *aanaga* instead of her parents, but never said anything because she knew it wouldn't be allowed.

Since her *aanaga's* passing seven years ago, Wendy had lost the one person she most wanted to talk to; the person she felt spiritually connected to; the person who loved her—faults and all. That was when her relationship with her parents began to fracture.

Taking in a deep breath, Wendy stared at the ceiling and conjured up the memory of her *aanaga*. She told her about the nightmare, hoping that the memory would provide some help, but all she could hear was her voice saying: *You know what this means. Think about, make it real, and acknowledge it.*

The music behind the door seemed to be some strange version of "Angel of Music" and she'd ended up on the stage at the end, so it was obviously related to the show. Maybe it was symbolic of her nervousness about getting the part of Christine. The only problem was that she didn't feel very nervous anymore. Her first rehearsal had gone well, and she knew deep down that she could do this. Any nerves she still felt were no different than the ones she had before the variety shows. Frowning, she wondered if those parts of the dream actually meant nothing and were simply weird bits cobbled together from the past few days.

The most important part of the dream was the knocking, so it was obviously related to the sounds at the theatre. Was it possible that the knocking was no longer limited to the theatre and was now invading her dreams? No, it was more likely that what had happened earlier outside the costume room was still lingering in her subconscious. It wasn't bad enough that she was scaring herself during the day—now her unconscious mind had to get in on it.

Looking through the window, she saw that the sky was starting to lighten with the dawn. Beside her, Betty slept peacefully, undisturbed by the events within Wendy's head. Turning towards her, Wendy gently placed her hand over Betty's, feeling the warmth and comfort of her touch, and closed her eyes.

CHAPTER FIFTEEN

"Gerard, *pour la dernière fois*, we are not putting a spotlight on you in the catwalk."

"But how will the audience know that it is I, the Phantom, up there?"

Jim huffed and counted to ten under his breath while the rest of the room watched silently. Wendy wondered if Ari was going to interrupt and take control of the situation, but she could see by the look on their face that they were enjoying the moment. Considering how temperamental Jim could be, sometimes it felt good to watch him be tormented.

"The audience will know it is you, because they will know your voice," Jim said sternly, the wrinkles on his forehead standing out prominently against his bald head.

But Gerard still wasn't satisfied by this answer. He cupped his chin with one hand and thought about it for a few seconds. "Are you suggesting that the Phantom should have some kind of catchphrase?"

Wendy forced back a laugh and tried to keep her shoulders from shaking with amusement. Jim's face instantly turned red and she could almost see smoke coming out of his ears. Although Gerard had started this conversation earnestly, she knew that he was now being deliberately obtuse. Bowing her head, she tried to concentrate on the scene they were supposed to be doing, but she could see out of the corner of her eye that Vance was still watching Jim and Gerard with an expression on his face that was equal parts confusion and uncertainty.

They weren't supposed to be working on scene 9 today, but Gerard had felt that his opinion was needed on every single scene in the script. He simply couldn't be expected to move on to scene 12 without first discussing scene 9.

Jim pinched the bridge of his nose and closed his eyes. "I am saying that the audience will not be full of idiots, and that if you give your character a catchphrase then *je vais vous assassiner et laisser votre corps dans une poubelle.*"

Gerard put his hands up in surrender and sighed. "Fine, Jim. I will trust that the audience will be smart enough to recognize my dulcet tones. Now, shall we discuss the Phantom's motivation for being at the masquerade?"

Wendy thought that Jim's head was actually going to explode as his face turned from a tomato red to a deep crimson.

Ari cleared their throat, holding back a laugh. "Gerard, we'll discuss the masquerade tomorrow afternoon, as the rehearsal schedule indicated. For now, let's move on to scene 12, *danke*."

Gerard nodded and opened his script to the appropriate scene. Everyone busied themselves as they waited for Jim to calm down enough to continue with rehearsal, which—considering the colour of his face—didn't take as long as expected.

For the rest of rehearsal Gerard behaved and there were no other incidents. Still, Wendy could tell that Jim was relieved once they'd finished the final scene, and when Ari signalled that rehearsal was over, he was the first one out the door.

Wendy gathered her things, but her day wasn't over yet. Instead of going home for lunch, she grabbed some fries at LiLi's and ate them in the back of the auditorium while going over her script. Normally she'd go down to the dressing room, but she wanted to stay as far away from the knocking sound as possible. Every time she'd gone to the lower level over the past couple of days, she could hear the strange knocking, low and sinister, almost as if it were teasing her, so she'd decided to avoid that part of the theatre as much as possible. As long as she was careful not to leave a mess, she knew Ari wouldn't mind her eating in the auditorium.

As much as she tried to keep her mind off morbid things, she couldn't help looking around the room, remembering all the ghosts that Stacey had mentioned. There had been more than a few deaths in this area, and yet lately she only heard the knocking in the lower level. Her eyes moved over the empty seats, up the walls, to the darkness above, where the lighting grid was. Perhaps the knocking wasn't caused by one of the people who died in this room. Maybe it was someone who'd died on the lower level. Thinking back, she recalled Stacey saying that there was one actor who'd killed themselves in their dressing room, and a second who'd been killed by another actor. Unfortunately, Stacey hadn't elaborated on those incidents, so the first could have happened in the backstage or downstairs dressing rooms, and the second could have happened anywhere.

Munching absentmindedly on her fries, she thought back to what her *aanaga* had told her. There were two kinds of spirits: those who had unfinished business and couldn't let go of the material world, and those who wanted to cause pain and suffering. Was it possible that there was a spirit in the theatre who couldn't let go? Maybe that person had died during a production of "Phantom" and now that they were doing a similar show, it had re-awakened. Maybe all they needed to do was figure out what the ghost wanted and then it would leave them alone.

And yet, there was something about the knocking that made her think it wasn't as simple as that. What if it was the second kind of ghost? What if it was knocking to torment them, to make them feel scared? But why was it here now? And how could they get rid of it? What if it didn't want to go?

Giving herself a shake, she tried to clear her mind of all uncertainty and focus on her upcoming music rehearsal. Although there'd been no nightmare last night or the night before, this line of thinking would assure she'd have one tonight.

Finally, it was time to head up to the rehearsal hall again. This time it was only Ari and Rhonda, as Jim had other things to do. Wendy wondered if those other things happened to be avoiding Gerard for the next few hours while secretly plotting his death. Although Gerard wasn't here yet, Wendy had a feeling that he'd take this rehearsal more seriously.

When he showed up, Rhonda led them through a quick warm-up and then they sang "The Point of No Return." They didn't have to do any acting or blocking, which made it easier to concentrate on getting the right notes.

They sang through it a few times, with Rhonda making corrections and adjustments. Then Gerard left and it was time for Wendy to work on "Think of Me." After that song, Francesca arrived and Rhonda talked to them about the songs she'd created for the opera within the show. Rhonda didn't bother leading Francesca through a warm-up, rightfully assuming that she'd warmed up at home.

Wendy knew nothing about *Faust*, but she was glad that Rhonda had created something that was in English and was more in line with the other songs they were singing. She had no idea how close it was to the actual opera but took Rhonda's word that it was quite similar.

When they finished the musical rehearsal, Wendy couldn't wait to get home and relax. They were only four days into rehearsal, but this show was much more involved than any other show they'd done. While Jim usually made the plays simpler, in order to fit within their small budget, he'd gone all out for this one. No wonder most of the designers looked haggard.

"You're doing fabulous, dear," Francesca said as they headed out of the theatre.

"Thanks," Wendy smiled. She had a feeling that she was doing okay, but it always helped to have someone else verify it. "I had no idea Jim was going to be so intense about this script. I mean, he wrote it, sure, but I've never seen him so particular about every little thing."

Francesca gave a bitter laugh. "He's always loved this story. He directed me in it a year before leaving Paris. Probably thought he'd never get to do it again."

Wendy nodded, and when she didn't say anything else, Francesca began to talk about the terribly conceited woman who'd played Carlotta in that production, and how much of a nightmare she was to work it. Wendy was thankful for the subject change. Sometimes she forgot that whenever she mentioned Jim she was talking about Francesca's ex-husband. There were decades of experiences shared between the two of them, but a sourness had tainted the memories, leaving them both with bitter tastes in their mouths. Although they tried to play nice in front of the rest of the troupe, at times it was impossible to ignore the past that weighed them both down like shackles.

It had taken some time, and many bottles of French wine, but eventually Wendy learned about the circumstances that brought Jim and Francesca to Jacobi Street.

Francesca Pettit had been a big star in Paris, acting in more plays than Wendy could name. She'd started out as a child actor, quickly becoming a theatre darling with her brilliant smile and sweet attitude, and the roles never stopped coming. Theatre soon became her life, and directors fell over themselves trying to cast her in their productions.

And then Jim Le Faull came along. When they met, he was also at the height of his fame as a talented director, and once Francesca caught his eye there was nothing that could turn his gaze away. Francesca was in her early twenties and Jim was seven years older than her, but the two quickly hit it off. Jim lavished her with gifts and prime theatrical roles, giving her everything her heart desired, and they dated for two years before marrying. For almost a decade they were a theatrical power couple, dominating the Parisian theatre scene.

But then came the fall. Over time, people became suspicious of Jim's ability to always be able to afford whatever he needed for a show, no matter the cost, and a small group of rivals began to dig into his business practices. They soon realized that Jim's covert business partners were not only involved in distasteful business practices—such as arson, blackmail, and smuggling—but that they may also have been responsible for the downfall of many others within the theatrical community—others who threatened Jim's rise to the top.

Jim swore to Francesca that he knew nothing about his backers' terrible business dealings, and at that time she had no reason to think he would lie. But even if he was innocent, the speculation was out there and the damage was done. Since Jim was unable to prove his innocence, it was decided that the best thing for them to do would be to leave Paris and lie low for a few years, until the whole thing blew over. Francesca didn't want to give up her home or her life, but her husband assured her that all they needed were a few months or maybe a year away, and then they'd be able to return to their normal lives.

Jim moved them all the way across the Atlantic Ocean. He purchased a small theatre and called it *Le Petit Paris*, managing to give them a home and a place to work in this strange new city. Although Francesca found the street charming, the body of work that the theatre did was less than desirable, and the small apartment on the third floor only reminded her of how far she'd fallen. Not only was she thousands of miles away from her home and friends, but she had been reduced to performing bare-bones theatre for nearly empty houses. She was certain she'd end up working as a waitress within a year.

But then Jim's magical ability to find money came through. In less than a year, he found the theatre a benefactor with more money than brains, but the money came with a catch. This man loved old vaudeville theatres and variety shows and only agreed to give Jim money if he promised to put on a bi-monthly variety show for him. If Jim did that, the theatre would have enough money to hire full-time actors and crew, and even a little left over to put on an actual show once a month.

While Francesca regarded this as a giant leap backwards in her career, she tried to look on the bright side. Performing in the variety show gave her a chance to explore different characters, and she was still with Jim and in love. They hired more actors and designers, and the theatre seemed to spring to life. Some days, if she closed her eyes and added a few embellishments, it was almost like the good old days.

But no matter how good things got, she still longed for home. After two years on Jacobi Street, she asked Jim about returning, but he said that it wasn't time yet and they needed to wait longer. Every year after, she'd asked him about going home, and every year he'd say no; they needed more time. After a while she felt as if she would never get home. She stopped following her rigid diet, stopped practising her talents every day, and fell into a dark mood. After ten years of their self-imposed exile had passed, she told Jim that he had ruined her life, that she would never see Paris again because of him, and that she wanted a divorce.

On the day she moved out, Jim rechristened *Le Petit Paris* as The Quaint Little Theatre.

CHAPTER SIXTEEN

"I just had a brilliant idea!"

Betty looked up from the mask she was painting with an expression of alarm on her face. It was never a good thing when her sister had brilliant ideas. Great ideas and awesome ideas were okay, but brilliant ideas usually resulted in hospital trips.

"What is it?" Betty asked cautiously.

Galia was standing in the doorway of the props room, a large, insane smile on her face. "What if we let the chandelier actually fall on the audience?" She opened her arms wide, expecting an enthusiastic response, but Betty's mind was too busy trying to work through all the health and safety issues with that idea to respond. Eventually Galia put her arms on her hips and stared at her sister.

"Wouldn't that be... dangerous?" Betty finally managed to say.

"You're not thinking about it the right way," Galia said, walking over to her. "We kill a few seats in the house, the ones directly underneath the chandelier, so that when it falls it doesn't hit anyone. The chandelier would have to be smaller, and we'd have to move it to the front of the audience so that everyone sees it, but wouldn't it be so cool to have the chandelier *actually* fall? I mean, what other theatre has the guts to do something like that!?"

Betty wanted to say that it wasn't guts that stopped other companies from doing such a thing, it was more like insurance and liability, but she refrained. "Are you sure Jim would be okay with not selling a portion of the audience? You know that sometimes a lot of people come to our shows."

Galia waved her hand dismissively. "When Jim hears about this idea, he's going to have to add extra performances!"

"I mean, you'll have to run it past Ari first," Betty said, thankful that she could hide behind the stage manager. If Ari said no then Galia would have to let it go, and if Ari said yes then it meant there was a safe way to do the stunt.

"I'm sure Ari will see reason. I mean, they know a brilliant idea when they hear it."

Betty nodded. "Well, whatever happens, let me know ASAP. If I have to change the design of the chandelier so that it's foam instead of wood or plastic, I'll have to know soon."

"Foam?" Galia laughed maniacally. "If we're going to drop this sucker, I don't want to hear a soft 'thud' — I want a *crash*!"

And that was it — the moment that Betty realized she would do just about anything to not have this effect approved. Maybe she could text Ari to warn them... or bribe them to say no...

"You're ridiculous, sis. Have I ever told you that?" Galia laughed the entire way out of the room.

"I'm worried that Galia's going to kill the audience," Betty said as she stepped into Wendy's apartment.

Wendy had been lying on the couch, but at Betty's words she lifted her head up and looked in Betty's direction. "How is this different than any other show we've worked on?" she asked.

Betty crossed to the couch and leaned over the back, looking down at her. "On the other shows I'm usually worried that she's going to kill herself or one of the actors. This time I'm worried she's going to take out half the audience."

Wendy sat up and gave Betty her full attention. "What's she doing now?"

Sighing deeply, Betty filled her in on Galia's 'brilliant' plan to drop the chandelier on the audience. By the end, Wendy's eyes were wide with surprise.

"Ari wouldn't let her," Wendy said. "I mean, she'll end up killing someone. If not with the drop, then maybe with shrapnel."

"I know." Betty sighed again. "I really hope that Ari says no."

Wendy gave her a reassuring smile. "Ari's smart. They'll say no. I mean, it's not like we need any more ghosts at the theatre."

A quizzical look crossed Betty's face. "More ghosts? What does that mean?"

Wendy realized what she'd just said. "Nothing, I just..." She paused. "Stacey started it. Well, the knocking started it. You know that knocking from the furnace?"

Betty nodded. "Francesca said something about it last week."

"Well, Stacey said it's probably a ghost trying to communicate with us, and then went and dug up a bunch of stories about people who died in the theatre."

"Huh..." Betty's brows furrowed. "But it's just the furnace knocking. Why would she think it was a ghost?"

Wendy shrugged. "According to Stacey, any theatre worth its salt has a ghost hanging around. Francesca tried to tell her that there weren't any ghosts here, but Stacey latched onto the idea and ran with it."

"Someone really needs to tell her that ghosts aren't real," Betty said, shaking her head.

Her voice was so matter-of-fact that Wendy suddenly felt ashamed for her earlier thoughts about spirits. The feeling went away quickly, but it was there long enough for Betty to notice.

"Oh no, did I say something wrong?" Betty's face fell. "I don't mean to say that you're wrong if you believe in ghosts. I might be wrong. Maybe ghosts really do exist."

Her sincerity was almost enough to make Wendy laugh, but instead she smiled and placed her hand on Betty's. "It's okay. My grandmother taught me to believe in spirits, so although I've never seen one, I'm open to the idea. But I don't think there's a ghost at the theatre." She paused. Her resolve wavered as the memory of the sinister knocking loomed in the back of her mind, and a frown crossed her face.

"Wait," Betty said, moving around the couch so that she could sit down next to Wendy. "Do you think there might be a ghost in the theatre?"

Cursing her face for being so easy to read, Wendy figured that it would be best to be honest. "I don't know, but I get a really creepy feeling about the knocking. Sometimes it's low, sometimes it's loud, and sometimes it's enough to split to my head open. If it were consistent then maybe I'd think otherwise, but it almost seems to have a mind of its own. There's something that's just... not natural about it."

Although she'd thought this numerous times in her head, it was strange to say the words out loud. Wendy half-expected Betty to make fun of her superstitious ideas, but instead she nodded.

"That does sound weird. I can't say I've had the same experience, but I tend to zone out when I'm working, so I haven't really heard any knocking. And even if I had, I'd think it was the furnace." Her face suddenly went serious as she reached forward and took Wendy's hand in hers. "However, if you plan on trying to confront this ghost and you need a non-believer to hold your hand, I'll be there." She winked and smiled.

Wendy burst out laughing. "I'll be sure to remember that."

CHAPTER SEVENTEEN

Rehearsals for the rest of the week went well, with most of the show getting blocked except for the four big crowd scenes. Everyone gathered on Thursday afternoon to read through the scenes and ask any questions they might have, so that Jim could devote all of Friday and Saturday to blocking and choreography. Almost every actor was involved in the scenes, which meant that everyone was going to have a couple of very long days. Even the designers were expected to attend, so that they'd have a better idea of what those moments would look like and, possibly, to fill in as extras.

Group scenes were always harder to block because there were so many moving pieces, and it didn't help that Jim was so exacting with his ideas. Friday morning was scheduled for the opening gala for the new manager, and the afternoon was for the masquerade where the Phantom makes an appearance. Then on Saturday they'd take on the performance at the Opera House where the chandelier falls, and the performance where the Phantom abducts Christine.

By this point they had all the "stand in" set pieces, which they'd use until the actual set pieces were ready or until they finally started rehearsing on the stage. They also had a number of "stand in" props to use, like letters and swords. Their costumes were still being worked on, but Paloma had provided certain actors with a few basic costume pieces to help with spacing and characterization—vests or pants for the male characters, and full skirts for the characters performing within the Opera House.

As Wendy pulled her rehearsal skirt on over her jeans, she told herself that today was too important to mess around. It could be awfully easy to become distracted or lost in thought while Jim was working on a part of a scene she wasn't needed in. As a lead character, it'd be best for her to set an example, like Francesca did, and be on her best behaviour.

Jim and Ari were sitting at the table along the back wall, but seats had been put out on either side for the designers, so that they could get a good view of what was going on. The only exceptions were Rhonda, who sat at the piano in the stage-right corner, and Scott, who was sitting in a chair that had been pushed back into the far corner of stage-left, his head ducked low over his clipboard, as if trying to avoid being noticed. As Wendy took in the designers, she noticed how tired most of them seemed.

Once everyone had arrived and was ready to rehearse, Jim got down to business. The opening scene didn't involve much choreography, as most of the characters stayed in small groups, celebrating the new manager of the Opera House, and gossiping about theatre business. The crowds parted to the sides as Christine came on stage to perform in place of Carlotta, who turned down the opportunity in a fit of ego. After Christine was mobbed by her adoring fans, she withdrew from the stage, and Raoul, having recognized her, followed. The party continued until Stacey burst on as Jammes, a ballerina who'd spotted the Phantom near the dressing rooms. There was a moment of panic, which would be increased by the special effect of a body dropping from the ceiling, sending the scene into total chaos. Although they couldn't drop the body in this room, Ari described the effect to everyone, giving them a cue when it was supposed to happen.

Wendy found herself thinking back to Stacey's stories about the director who'd hung himself and the stagehand who'd fallen from the lighting grid. She tried to remind herself that those spirits seemed to be gone and hoped that they'd made peace with their deaths. She didn't want any more of them waking up because of this show.

Billy and Betty were expected to be extra characters on stage, to make the party look more full. When Jim mentioned that one of them would have to say a line, Betty's eyes had widened in fear, so Billy stepped forward and said he'd do it, earning a grateful look from Betty.

Within two and a half hours, they'd finished blocking the first scene and had run it a couple times (skipping over the song for now). After a short break, Jim quickly moved on to the masquerade, which he knew would take longer because it involved choreography. There wasn't much dialogue, but Jim wanted a grand song and dance to start the scene. It involved all the actors, except for Wendy, who would enter shortly after the dance ended. There were a few moments of Jim muttering about how in the old days he'd have a professional choreographer to work with, but Wendy could see that he enjoyed creating the dance, even if he found some of the actors less than ideal to work with. As she watched, Wendy imagined what it must be like to work in a theatre where you could have twenty or thirty actors, all dancing together on a large stage. She liked her little troupe but couldn't help picturing how spectacular this show would be if Jim had been able to hire twice as many people to work on it.

Since there were no special effects in the scene, Galia had been roped into being a background body with Billy and Betty. They didn't have to dance or sing, but they'd get to wear costumes and masks and move about to "fill the space."

The dance took almost an hour to instruct, mainly because of Samuel's two left feet, Vance's being new to this kind of dancing, and Gerard spending most of his time looking at Carina instead of his dancing partner, Francesca. Wendy was determined not to grow bored or impatient, and spent the time going over her lines while sitting in the area of the room that had been designated as the off-right wing.

When it was time for her to enter the scene, she was excited at the opportunity to finally do something. The dance partners changed up as Raoul moved over to join her, and Gerard went backstage to prepare for his next entrance as the Phantom. Jim had those who were still onstage perform a much simpler dance, but there was a lot of careful blocking that needed to be done, so that nobody ran into anyone else. With so many people on stage, and Christine and Raoul trying to have a private conversation, there were a lot of things to focus on.

They hadn't yet made it to the end of the scene before it was time to break for dinner. Wendy, Stacey, and Carina decided to go to Curds & Whey, a local street vendor who specialized in tofu and vegetables. They were all hungry enough to eat a horse but knew that the healthier alternative would keep them from wanting to take a nap during the rest of rehearsal.

Before everyone knew it, it was time to start up again. Jim finally finished blocking the masquerade, and then had them run through the scene a few times, before going back to the opening scene.

By the time rehearsal ended, everyone was exhausted. And they all knew that there was still one more long day to go.

CHAPTER EIGHTEEN

After rehearsal was over, Carina caught Gerard's eye, huffed, and turned away. She quickly gathered her things and headed downstairs, not exiting at the stage level like everyone else, but going all the way to the lower level. She walked into Sam and Gerard's dressing room, knowing that it was less likely for Sam to show up in there than for Wendy or Stacey to show up in the room the girls shared.

Although they rarely used the dressing rooms during a show's rehearsal period, it still smelled like Sam's cologne—which she referred to as "old man smell." Carina wrinkled her nose and lifted herself up to sit on the counter, being careful not to sit too far back because of the lightbulbs framing the mirrors. While she waited for Gerard, she looked around the room, which was mostly empty. There were no costumes hanging in the racks on the other side of the room, and other than a few skincare odds and ends that Gerard kept on his side of the counter, the space was quite empty. The girls usually kept their stage makeup in their dressing room, so they didn't have to keep trucking it back and forth between shows, which made their room look much more cluttered. At least it smelled better.

Voices on the other side of the door let her know that some of the designers were in the hallway—likely going to their offices to get some more work done before calling it a night. She crossed her arms and let out an angry sigh, hoping that Gerard had gotten the message. Tomorrow was going to be another long day, and she didn't want to waste most of her night waiting for him to show up. Thankfully, less than a minute later, Gerard walked into the room.

"Carina..." he said, rolling the "r" and putting as much seduction into her name as the three syllables would allow. "Why have you been so distant lately?"

She pouted and turned her head away from him. "You promised me that you would get me the lead role in *Phantom*. Yet here I am, having to play an old woman." She said the last two words as if they were the saddest words in the English language.

Gerard walked closer, stopping in front of her. "Darling, I talked to Jim, but he was worried that your beauty would distract from the story." A smile played along his lips. "How could I not agree with such an indisputable observation?"

She huffed again, but in a haughtier manner, turning her head in a way that elongated her neck. "You said that last time..." she pouted, pushing out her lower lip.

"Because it was true last time, as well." He gently laid a hand on her face and she allowed him to turn her head back to him. "Carina... my *querida*. You know I'm your biggest fan."

She pouted again, but there was a glint of a smile in her brown eyes. Gerard only spoke Spanish when there was a particular activity on his mind.

He placed his other hand on the other side of her face. "Do you forgive me?"

"This time," she said before leaning in for a kiss. Eventually he lowered his hands, moving them down her body until they rested on her thighs.

She pulled away. "Not here."

Less than a minute later, they were in the basement, tucked away behind a pile of rarely used set pieces in the far back corner. It wasn't their favourite place to fool around within the theatre, but with so many people still wandering the building, it was the least likely place for anyone to walk in on them.

Carina let out a soft moan as Gerard slipped his hands under her shirt, sliding them up to her chest. Yes, she was disappointed that she hadn't gotten the part of Christine, but the truth was that she'd figured out how useless Gerard was a long time ago. He only cared about one thing—himself. His focus was getting himself a good part, and with Sam as his only competition, it meant he basically had to do nothing but continue dying his hair and working out. Sure, he would try to convince her that he'd spoken to Jim about giving her better parts, but she knew that he was lying.

The whole situation was folly on her part. Five months after joining the troupe, she'd decided that the only way to get better parts was to seduce someone important and convince them that it'd be a great idea to cast her in the lead roles. Setting her sights on their resident leading man, Gerard, she began to pursue him. It had been much easier than she'd originally thought, and the fact that Gerard was a self-serving narcissist made her feel much less guilty about using him. Getting the lead roles, however, wasn't as simple.

She could have called off this useless charade many times, but the truth was that she needed an excuse to see him and this was better than anything else she could come up with. As much as she hated to admit it, Gerard was one of the best sexual partners she'd ever had—not that she'd ever tell him. His ego was large enough for now, and she sure as hell wasn't going to be the reason it increased.

There weren't a lot of eligible bachelors around these parts, and it was helpful to have someone she could call if she ever got an itch. She'd thrown a few advances at Vance, hoping to hook the newcomer with her charms, but he seemed to be made of ice. Meanwhile, every time she threw an advance at Gerard, he was more than ready to catch it.

Pulling him closer, she kissed him deeply, closing her eyes and picturing Vance's face instead of his. Her smile spread wider as one of his hands travelled down her thigh and between her legs, but her thoughts were quickly interrupted by a loud knock. She jumped and let out a startled cry.

"It's just the pipes," Gerard said, trailing kisses down her neck.

Laughing it off, she closed her eyes and arched her body towards him. He let out a low moan and quickly reached for his belt, undoing his pants.

When the next knock sounded, they were too involved to notice. They didn't notice the one after that, or the next one, or the next. And when the lights in the basement started to take on a deep red glow and the shadows began to rise around them, it was already too late.

CHAPTER NINETEEN

Saturday's rehearsal seemed easier than Friday's, although Wendy wasn't sure if that was because they'd already been through one gruelling day or if it was because there weren't as many bodies on stage at the same time.

First, they worked on the scene where the chandelier falls, which was the final scene of Act 1. It took place during a performance of *Faust*, and some characters were watching the show, while others were performing the play within a play. Before the show, the Phantom had tried to scare Carlotta from performing, but ended up only making her more determined to go onstage. Meanwhile, Christine was distracted because she was torn between the Phantom and Raoul; she's unable to escape the Phantom and doesn't want to involve Raoul in her difficult situation, but she's also unable to ignore her heart and turn Raoul away. The new owner of the theatre and his aide, Moncharmin and Remy, are watching the opera from the infamous Box 5, with Moncharmin eager to prove that this Phantom business is all nonsense, while Raoul watches from another Box.

The scene started with a short dance by Meg, as a kind of introduction to the opera. Then Meg left and Christine came on stage to sing. This scene took place right after the one where Carlotta accused Christine of using the Phantom to try and scare her away from performing. Shortly after Carlotta's departure, Raoul appeared and a fight ensued about the Phantom, so Christine's emotions were quite high as she stepped onto the stage.

Jim informed Wendy that Christine would try to sing well at first, but then her resolve would falter, and her performance would suffer. After-wards, she'd step into the background and Carlotta would come on stage to great applause and begin singing. But Carlotta's joy would be short-lived as the Phantom had other plans, taunting her from above. The scene ended with the chandelier falling from the sky, interrupting the opera and bring-ing the show into intermission.

As Ari described how the chandelier would drop from the ceiling be-fore being caught on a safety line, Wendy glanced over at Galia, who was trying to hide her frown. She was quite thankful that Galia's insane idea to actually drop the chandelier on the audience had been vetoed.

Other than Carina's choreography, the scene was quite easy to block, and they quickly moved on to the final group scene, which took place dur-ing the Opera's performance of *Don Juan*. It was the performance between Christine and the Phantom, although nobody was supposed to know that it was the Phantom until his cover was blown.

First there was a dance by Jammes and Meg, and after that Christine would come onstage to start "The Point of No Return." The Phantom would join her, in disguise, and she wasn't supposed to realize that her scene partner was actually the Phantom until his voice began to sound fa-miliar to her, about two-thirds through the song. At the end of the song, she would rip off the Phantom's mask, revealing his scarred face, and then the lights would go down. When the lights came back up, she and the Phantom would be gone, and a knife would be driven into the stage where they had been standing.

After the blocking had been figured out, Jim had them rehearse the scenes a few times. Then there was enough time to go through Friday's scenes again, to help cement them into everyone's brains.

By the time rehearsal ended on Saturday, they had officially blocked the entire show. Wendy wondered if this was what it felt like to scale Mount Everest. She had no idea what the scenes she wasn't in looked like, but if they were anything like hers, then this was going to be a show to remem-ber. They still had to add in costumes and sets, but even without them Jim had managed to outdo himself. It was amazing what the team had accom-plished so far.

Before everyone left, Jim handed out the scripts and cast list for next week's variety show. Even though tomorrow was a day off, everyone knew that Jim would expect them to spend part of the day learning lines for the variety show and the other part learning lines for *Phantom*. Wendy was glad that this week-long overlap only happened once a month.

"Supper?" Stacey asked, as she gathered her stuff. Carina and Wendy nodded emphatically. They headed to The Belle Verde, managing to grab the last empty booth seat in the half-crowded restaurant.

"Well, that was fun," Stacey said as she took a long sip of the beer Gradey had quickly placed in front of her. He had noticed the exhausted looks on their faces and fetched their drinks faster than usual. "We need to stop doing group scenes. Like, forever."

"At least it was easier than yesterday," Wendy said. "That masquerade dance at the top of the scene is insane."

Carina nodded. "You should be thankful you only have to learn the easier one."

"I am," Wendy replied honestly.

Stacey's eyes narrowed. "How's it working with Vance? You cracked that nut yet?"

Wendy wasn't sure what Stacey was asking but was pretty sure it was lewd. "He's okay. I mean, we don't really talk that much outside of rehearsal, but he's not a jerk. And he's a good actor."

"He's extremely cold," Carina added, stifling a yawn. "But still definitely hot."

Stacey raised an eyebrow. "Oh, is someone tired today? Perhaps had a late night yesterday?"

"I am an adult and will do what I wish," Carina shot back.

Stacey turned to Wendy and gave her a knowing look. "She didn't get in until after 2am," she stage-whispered, making sure her voice was loud enough for Carina to hear. Carina glared at her.

Wendy smiled, but didn't say anything. She'd noticed the dark circles under Carina's eyes and knew that the most likely answer was that Carina had been out late with Gerard, and she didn't want to think about that before eating. It was bad enough that her nightmare had come back last night—she didn't want to risk thinking about things that might give her different nightmares.

Before Stacey could say anything else, Gradey arrived with their food.

"Has anyone heard any knocking from the furnace lately?" Stacey said as they all tucked in.

Wendy paused, trying to figure out if she should admit to hearing the knocking and how strange it was, or if it was better to keep quiet and not encourage Stacey.

"I heard it the other day," Carina said flippantly.

"Excellent," Stacey nodded, her hand hovering over the chips on her plate. "That means the ghost is still in the theatre and is still trying to communicate with us!"

Carina laughed. "No, it means that Jim's still too cheap to hire someone to look at the furnace."

Rolling her eyes, Stacey picked up a chip and popped it in her mouth. "It means that the ghost is still around and that we should hold a séance to try and communicate with it."

Carina laughed out loud as Wendy shook her head.

"Come on," Stacey pleaded. "I don't want to do it alone, and you're my best hope. I've got the Ouija board and everything. We just need to pick a night."

"My grandmother taught me not to mess with spirits," Wendy said, tucking into her food and hoping that Stacey would let the subject drop.

Stacey turned her gaze to Carina, pleading.

Carina shook her head. "I've got better things to do with my life, *querida*."

"You two are the worst," Stacey muttered.

CHAPTER TWENTY

Galia stomped down to the special effects room, all the while muttering about being surrounded by philistines. Betty was close at her heels, sensing her sister's mood and knowing that she'd need to be calmed down.

"Plan B is just fine," Betty said gently, trying to sound upbeat.

Galia gave her a stern look. She'd tried three times to communicate how amazing her idea was and why it would be the best idea ever, but each time she was told that it was too risky and would take too many seats out of commission. After rehearsal she'd tried for a fourth, knowing that their current plan was way too simple, but she'd been shut down by Ari before she could even open her mouth

Betty knew that eventually she'd get over it, but left to her own devices, Galia would grumble for weeks instead of hours, and with a show this elaborate, they didn't have time for that kind of tantrum.

"Plan B is fine if you like *boring*," Galia shot back. "I mean, any theatre can make a chandelier look like it's falling, but we could've had the most amazing effect *ever*. I mean, it's not like we ever sell out a performance, so what's wrong with killing a few rows? We even could've put a dummy in the row, and that could've been the person who gets the chandelier dropped on their head, and then medics could come in, and it would be totally immersive..."

Sighing, Betty tried to think of what she could say to get Galia's head back in her work. The chandelier was never going to drop at all if she didn't start working on it soon. They had fewer than two weeks before the show opened, and they still had a variety show to prep and perform. Maybe she could distract her with another effect to work on, but that wouldn't solve the problem. Galia needed her interest in the chandelier renewed and rein-vigorated.

Looking out into the hallway, Betty noticed Billy walking past. "Hey, Billy!" she called out. "What do you think about the catch line for the chandelier being lower?"

Billy paused and turned around, and when Betty saw the exhausted look on his face, she felt guilty for disturbing him. She opened her mouth to apologize, but he interrupted her.

"Depends on how low you're talking about," he said, walking into the room. He leaned heavily against the doorway, but otherwise seemed mentally alert. "How much more of a drop are you thinking?"

Betty glanced over at Galia, who was muttering quietly to herself, and raised her voice. "What about four feet above the audience? That'll give most of the audience time to notice it and look up."

Billy absently stroked his beard with one hand. "I don't know. It might be too risky. What if someone stands up?"

"Good point." She paused to think. "How else can we make sure that everyone notices the drop? The current set-up's pretty quick."

"What if we had it swing down and towards the stage? We could use a catch line before it reaches the stage, perhaps shut the curtains as it swings, just in case anything flies off?"

"It's supposed to fall *on* the audience!" Galia turned on them angrily, standing with her hands on her hips and giving them a look that suggested their idea was beyond stupid.

"I know," Billy replied gently, "but if we injure a patron, even by accident, we're all going to be out of a job."

Galia opened her mouth to argue, but then shut it again. Betty and Billy waited patiently as she frowned, tilted her head, frowned harder, and then stared up at the ceiling. Billy started to speak, but Betty put a hand on his arm and shook her head.

"Okay, new plan!" Galia said. "We hang the chandelier over audience centre. When the Phantom finishes doing his thing, we let off a few fireworks—*harmless* fireworks," she added after seeing a look of alarm cross Betty's face. "The chandelier drops and swings down towards the stage, the lights go out, the chandelier swings into the stage, curtains close, lights back on, and then we remove the chandelier during intermission?"

Betty thought over the plan. Then she thought about it a second time. It sounded... reasonable. "The fireworks would draw the audience's attention... I like the idea of making it 'disappear' with the lights going down, and it would be easier to clear away if it's on the stage at intermission."

"Sounds good," Billy nodded. He suppressed a yawn. "I can help you with some of the details if you need."

Galia nodded. "I've got a few things to figure out first, but I'll let you know what I come up with. Then you two can help me convince Jim and Ari that this is the best idea ever." Moving over to her drafting table, Galia picked up a pen and started scribbling.

Billy and Betty exchanged a look and exited the room, leaving Galia alone with her work.

"Thank you for that," Betty said softly as they walked down the hall.

"Anytime," Billy smiled, but the smile didn't quite reach his eyes.

"Hey, are you sleeping okay?" Betty asked. "You seem tired."

He shook his head. "It must be something in the air. I'm sure it's nothing."

"Well, take care of yourself. Spend your day off relaxing. I don't know what this theatre would do without you, so don't get sick, okay?" she teased, smiling at him.

He gave her a big smile. "I'll do my best."

But as he walked away, Betty couldn't help worrying that there was something Billy wasn't telling her.

CHAPTER TWENTY-ONE

Jim had been drinking steadily since mid-afternoon. Although rehearsals for *Phantom* were going about as well could be expected, there was still so much more that needed to be done. He didn't just want this show to be perfect, he *needed* it to be. If he could show Lodge how a real show looked, then maybe he'd be able to squeeze some more money out of the old fogey and finally get this theatre operating at its full potential.

Stumbling down the private stairs from his apartment and into the lobby, he wondered if there was any alcohol hiding around the theatre. He'd just finished his last bottle of scotch and didn't want to leave the building to buy more. Inebriation of this level was best kept to oneself and one's best friends—if such things were possible to have. He should have restocked days ago, but rehearsals had been taking up so much of his time.

The theatre was empty and dark, with the ghost light shining brightly on the stage. Although he preferred for a theatre to be full of people and movement, over the years he'd come to appreciate the quieter moments. Perhaps it had something to do with the current company he'd gathered. In the old days nobody would have dared talk back to him, and if he gave an order it would be followed to the letter. *Merde*, he needed a drink.

Ari probably had a multitude of spirits pocketed around the booth, but he'd bet they were too well-hidden. Even though he'd owned the theatre for sixteen years and Ari had only been hired seven years ago, Ari knew more of the building's secrets than he did. If he cared about things like that, it might bother him, but he didn't. Besides, taking Ari's secret alcohol wouldn't be worth the trouble that he'd get if they found out, so there was no point in trying. Billy never drank at the theatre, and although Jim wasn't sure if Betty drank, he figured she must not because she'd be a lot more relaxed if she did. He hoped that Galia didn't drink at the theatre, because she was unstable enough sober, although it would explain a few things. So that left Paloma...

Wandering through the empty auditorium, Jim brought up a vague memory of Paloma pulling a bottle of something from behind her sewing machine. Hadn't she mentioned something about using vodka to clean costumes? Stumbling past the empty seats, he manoeuvred to the backstage area, using the ghost light to guide his way. It was late Sunday evening and although a few designers had come in during the day to work, they were long gone by now. There was nobody to disturb him in his quest.

He muttered to himself as he made his way to the lower level. When he moved to this godforsaken city, he'd intended to spend a few years here before returning to Paris, but it turned out that while he was away even more dirty laundry had been aired. He never told Francesca about these new revelations, or how it was likely that he'd never be able to show his face in Europe ever again. He'd die in this damned city, his name tainted by his own ambition.

And Francesca... Perhaps it had been selfish to insist that she come with him, but he couldn't imagine starting over on his own. He couldn't blame her for eventually leaving him — he only wished that he'd been brave enough to be honest with her about everything. Instead, they were trapped in this quaint little purgatory, never rising further, yet never falling.

When he reached Paloma's office, he was careful not to disturb too much, and to right anything that he accidentally knocked over. It took a bit of searching, but eventually he discovered a bottle of white rum tucked behind the serger. Smiling to himself, he took a long drink from the bottle and left the office.

He'd have one hell of a hangover tomorrow, but right now all he wanted to do was drink more to numb the pain. This theatre was making him feel like Sisyphus — working so hard to reach the top only to have to start over at the bottom again and again. If he could get more money or another benefactor then he could hire someone else to deal with the variety show and spend his time working on real art, but it was almost impossible to make money in this city. People on this side of the world didn't care as much about the arts — especially when it came to the smaller theatres. Maybe it'd be better for him to give it all up and try again in a new city, but he'd doubt that his team would follow him, and he was getting too old to start over from scratch. Again.

Taking another swig, he tried to focus on *Fantôme* and how wonderful it would be once everything came together. If he could pull this off, then it would prove that he'd always been an amazing director and visionary. If the right kind of people came to see the show, then he'd be one step closer to reclaiming his future.

Approaching the stairwell, he suddenly realized that the door to the basement was open. Turning and squinting at the door, he tried to remember if it had been open when he'd come downstairs. He was sure he'd have noticed if it had, but perhaps he'd been too drunk.

Walking over to the door to shut it, he noticed that there was a dull red light emanating from within. Peering into the room, he wondered if the alcohol was affecting his vision as the red glow began to pulse.

As if in a trance, the hand holding the bottle lowered to his side and Jim stepped into the basement.

CHAPTER TWENTY-TWO

She was standing on the stage of The Quaint Little Theatre. It was completely empty, with no set pieces, backdrops, or other people around. In front of her were rows of plush red seats, and even though there was nobody sitting in them, she could sense people out there, staring at her.

Squinting, she tried to make out any shapes or forms, but there was nothing except for that feeling of multiple eyes watching her from different areas of the room. Who were these people? Why couldn't she see them? Were they waiting for her to do something? Acting? Singing?

She wanted to leave the stage and get away from the invisible eyes, but it felt as if her feet were glued to the floor. She opened her mouth to speak, but didn't know what to say, so she closed it without a word. She didn't understand why she was here or what was going on.

A loud knock startled her. She turned to her head to the right, still unable to move her feet. Behind her she could see the door that led backstage, except it wasn't that door, it was the basement door. A red glow was around the edges, bleeding into the room. The knock happened again, shaking the door violently. As it happened again and again, growing louder each time, she realized that it sounded like it was moving closer.

A sudden chill gripped her and she wrapped her arms around herself. Some-

thing was coming—something bad. She couldn't see it and had no idea what it was but knew that it was evil.

The knocking grew louder as it approached; her eyes stayed fixed on the basement door. Fear enveloped her heart in an icy grip. What was coming? What did it want? Why wouldn't it leave her alone?

The feeling of being watched grew stronger and she wondered if this was what the audience was waiting for. Was this the show? Were they here to witness her demise? She wanted to turn and see if the audience had suddenly materialized, but her eyes refused to leave the basement door. Something inside told her that if she looked away, she'd regret it.

All she could do was stand and wait for whatever was coming. She could do nothing to stop it.

Wendy woke up with a start, her heart pounding loudly in her chest. Moonlight illuminated the room, letting her know that she was in her apartment, but she still pinched herself to ensure that she wasn't still asleep.

Turning on her side, she pulled the covers around her and tried to fight the chill that the nightmare had brought on. The dream had been so unsettling and fearful, but already it was starting to slip away, and the details were fading. She tried desperately to cling onto whatever she could—the theatre, unseen eyes watching her, and the evil coming towards her—but most of the details were gone within seconds.

Taking in a deep breath, she tried to tell herself that it was just a dream. She'd been spending too much time thinking about ghosts and evil spirits, and now it was invading her dreams. It was merely her brain being overactive—too full of this nonsense to know what to do with it. It wasn't anything to be afraid of.

But what if it was? What if the dreams were trying to tell her something?

Wendy closed her eyes and tried to shake those kinds of thoughts out of her head. The theatre was safe, there were no ghosts, and it was simply her imagination blowing things out of proportion. It was stress—nothing more. Nothing more.

CHAPTER TWENTY-THREE

The next week at the theatre was a grim one. Everyone was feeling stressed and overworked, and many of them had dark circles under their eyes and yawned whenever they thought nobody was looking.

Although this wasn't the first time the troupe had rehearsed two shows at the same time, they'd never tried to pull off such an elaborate full-length show. To accommodate for this, Jim had simplified the variety show slightly—re-using some sets, having a few simpler skits, and giving the biggest parts to those who weren't as prominent in *Phantom*—but it was only barely less complicated than last week's show. He still needed it to be as detailed and interesting as it usually was; otherwise, they'd run the risk of annoying their benefactor and getting their support cut off.

As Wendy made her way to the downstairs dressing room on the night of the variety show, she noticed how haggard everyone was looking. There were a few people who didn't seem as affected by the amount of work piled on their shoulders, like Francesca and Ari, while everyone else ran the gamut from "exhausted" to "dead on their feet." Wendy wondered if there was some weird flu going around. Nobody was coughing or had a fever or had asked for a day off, but she made a mental note to take even more vitamin C, just in case.

While doing her pre-show ritual of checking on her props and costumes, Wendy couldn't help observing how different the atmosphere of the theatre was. Instead of the excited and frantic energy that usually radiated throughout the building, there was a sluggish exhaustion hanging over them. There was no more gentle mocking or running around; instead, people were barely speaking and were leaning against walls or sitting on any surface they could find. It seemed that some of the troupe were doing as little as possible in order to save up enough energy to make it through the show. Even Gerard and Carina were too tired to flirt.

Wendy's usual nervousness increased to an almost unsettling point. They'd done shows where a person or two were having an off night and the rest of the troupe had to compensate, but never had there been so many people at one time. There was an actual potential for everything to crash and burn, despite their best efforts.

Jim would be furious if they messed this up and displeased their patron. Although he seemed just as exhausted as everyone else, there was no limit to his energy when it came to being upset.

Wendy desperately hoped that they'd make it through the show unscathed.

The first act went well, all things considered. Francesca was on-point as always, although Wendy suspected that she could be two seconds from death and still give an amazing performance. Gerard was more forgetful than usual, but Francesca covered it well, having had many opportunities to deal with his lack of line-learning. There were a few flubs and errors throughout each of the sketches, and Carina seemed spacier than usual, sometimes staring off absently when she was supposed to be listening to another actor. Even Billy appeared to move slower during the scene changes.

However, it wasn't the train wreck that Wendy had been predicting. The audience sounded like they were enjoying themselves, even laughing when they caught someone messing up. Despite the low energy, everyone had been able to pull it together (for the most part), pretend that everything was fine, and get the job done.

When she thought about it, Wendy had to hold back a laugh. Wasn't that what actors did best? Pretend?

The second act had a rough start after intermission, with 'Mime the Musical,' which was a strange enough concept anyway, but at least it didn't require any set or props or dialogue. The pace picked up with 'Dating Sports,' where commentators provided a running commentary for two people training for upcoming dates, and continued to increase right up to the final skit. Thankfully, the show ended on a high note with 'The School of Hard Knocks,' a skit about a no-nonsense teacher whipping her students into shape by teaching them important life skills, like doing taxes and reading up on rental laws. Part of the reason for the success was that the teacher was played by Francesca, who was giving a perfect performance, walking a fine line between tough and knowledgeable.

Although the show ended with roaring applause from the audience, as soon as the curtains closed, it felt as if the entire stage exhaled wearily. Actors stopped smiling and let out sighs or yawns, and designers leaned against walls or collapsed into chairs, no longer able to stand. Instead of the mad rush to get everything put away before the party, there was a weary recognition that there was still more work to be done.

Wendy followed Stacey and Carina down to the dressing room, being careful not to show too much energy, lest they get annoyed at her for having some.

"We've earned this party," Stacey said, pulling off her costume. "This has been the week from hell and back again."

Carina nodded and yawned, leaning against the counter. "Next time I think I'll ask Jim to write me out of all the skits."

"Hopefully the next show will be a lot simpler," Wendy said as she changed. "If it isn't, the entire troupe might revolt against Jim."

"Now that sounds like fun," Stacey smirked.

They finished getting ready in silence, but Wendy noticed that Stacey was starting to get her second wind and her mood was improving. Carina, however, was still slow and lagging behind. Wendy wondered how many late nights she'd had with Gerard. Surely it wasn't worth the two of them being this tired and rundown.

The designers were still busy putting things away as the three women left the theatre. Wendy expected a few of them to make jokes or talk about the cast party, but nobody said anything. They all kept their heads down and did their jobs. Suppressing a shudder, Wendy tried not to think about how the theatre had changed so completely in only two weeks. Hopefully, now that the variety show was over, they'd all get a chance to rest and feel better. *Phantom* was going to be tough enough, and it'd be best for everyone if they had a chance to recuperate from the past week.

When they reached The Treehouse, the atmosphere was just as subdued, but at least they could all sit down with a drink in hand and didn't have to worry about performing. The conversation wasn't as animated as usual, and their voices barely rose above a level tone, but Wendy could see people perking up and genuine smiles on their faces.

Although Wendy felt fine, she was thankful for the quieter party. This week had been even more stressful than when she'd first joined the troupe, and she wasn't sure she'd make it through tomorrow's rehearsal if she partied too hard. As fun as their usual gatherings were, she was grateful for the chance to conserve energy.

As she glanced around at the tired, cheerful faces in the bar, Wendy hoped that the troupe would manage to find some of the life and energy that the past two weeks had sapped from them.

CHAPTER TWENTY-FOUR

Ari walked through the lower level slowly, keeping an out to see if there was anybody still down there. Normally they'd go to the cast party with the last few designers, but the show seemed to have worn everyone out, and they wanted to make sure nobody got left behind. It wouldn't be too surprising to find someone curled up, asleep, in one of the rooms.

It was incredible that the show had gone as well as it did. Ari had noticed that some strange virus seemed to be making its way through the troupe, lowering people's energy and creating a lack-luster effort backstage. Either that or people were getting tired of Jim's crazy rehearsal schedule—which was a very plausible excuse. Jim was getting dangerously close to the edge with this project, putting so much pressure on everyone to make *Phantom* the best thing the theatre had ever done, while refusing to cut back on the variety show. They made a mental note to keep a close eye on everyone over the next week to make sure Jim didn't push the cast or crew any harder.

As Ari walked through the hallway, they heard the knocking of the pipes and made a second mental note to remind Jim to get someone in to look at the furnace. Although they were sure it was nothing, they didn't want to risk this being part of a bigger problem and causing more trouble in the future.

Making their way towards the stairs, Ari heard the knocking increase as they passed by the basement door. Shaking their head, they started to go up the stairs, but then they heard a sound, almost like someone groaning.

Rolling their eyes, Ari pushed open the door to the basement and stuck their head through.

"If you're mucking about down there, get your act together and go home! I don't have time for this nonsense!"

The noise instantly stopped and the theatre fell deathly silent. Ari headed up to the next floor, frowning and shaking their head.

CHAPTER TWENTY-FIVE

Tapping her pencil absent-mindedly on the side of her desk, Betty tried to concentrate on her work, but her mind kept going back to the strange mood within the theatre. Normally when she passed people in the hallway they'd smile and say "hello," but these days they were barely able to raise their head and grunt some kind of greeting. Everyone seemed to be lost in their own world, occupied by thoughts of their work, with no room for anything else. She wished that there was a way for everyone to take a break for a few days, so that they could get some rest and catch up, but there wasn't enough time.

She was also feeling stressed by the amount of work before them, but for the first time in a long time she had a notion that other people were worse off than her. It wasn't a good feeling.

It didn't help that her thoughts were also preoccupied by her worries about Galia. The chandelier effect had consumed her sister's every waking thought. Even with help from Billy and her, Galia wasn't yet satisfied with the effect and so wasn't able to let it go. She'd finished all the other special effects, so her brain was entirely focused on this one. As the days passed, Galia stayed at the theatre later and later, and whenever she was at the apartment, she walked around like a zombie—her mind totally consumed by thoughts of falling chandeliers.

Betty tried to tell herself that the effect would soon be complete, and her sister would go back to normal, but those thoughts provided little comfort.

It would be impossible for any of them to relax until the show's run was over.

Tugging at her hair, she tried once more to focus on her work. She still had to finish staining the barrels of gunpowder for the scene in the Phantom's lair, and there were plenty more letters for her to write, but the multiple worries bobbing around in her head refused to let her concentrate.

Finally she realized that if she didn't get some actual work done, it would stress her out more and she might end up a walking zombie like everyone else. Taking in a deep breath, she put her head down and made a list of four things she needed to accomplish today. Once the list was real and tangible, she made a promise to her worries that she'd get back to them soon and got to work.

When she finished two hours later, she didn't feel any better. There should have been some relief at completing her list, but something was bothering her, poking at the insides of her brain. Tapping her pencil against the desk again, she wondered if it was her worries about her sister or everyone else in the troupe, or if it was something deeper.

The answer hit her like a ton of bricks. It was Wendy. It was keeping their relationship secret from her sister. Being constantly on edge and worrying that she might let something slip or say the wrong thing was exhausting; so was worrying that her sister might say something to make her feel even worse. That anxiety had been slowly gnawing away at her, ripping her up inside, and had been doing so for a long time.

A part of her brain told her that she was overreacting and that all this worry and build-up was for nothing. Surely her sister wouldn't care who she dated. There were plenty of people in the theatre who dated all kinds of people, so if Galia didn't mind that, surely she wouldn't mind her sister dating someone of the same sex. Right?

But then her mind flashed back to her parents and all the terrible things they'd said about anyone who didn't fit into the "norm." What if all their poisonous rhetoric had settled into Galia's subconscious? What if what was okay for other people wasn't okay for her family?

Unfortunately, there was only one way to find out.

Taking in a deep breath, Betty rose to her feet, sending her chair scraping back along the floor. That was it—she was going to do it now and get it over with, and she'd deal with the fallout later. (She really hoped that there wouldn't be any fallout.)

Marching into the hall, she headed to the special effects room, finding Galia leaning against her drafting table, her chin resting in one hand, and her eyes half-closed.

"Galia?" Betty took a tentative step into the room, all her determination getting pushed aside as concern for her sister rose to the surface. "Are you okay?"

Galia looked up, and Betty could see the dark bags under her eyes. "Just tired. Still trying to figure out a way to make that chandelier fall look good."

"I thought it looked good yesterday when you tested it."

Galia rolled her eyes. "It looked *okay* yesterday, if you think a boring chandelier fall is good enough."

"I don't think there's such a thing," Betty countered.

Galia sighed and leaned back in her chair. "It's still too slow. I want the audience to feel like it's going to fall on their heads and that they're going to be smashed under it. I know I can do it. I just need to figure it out..."

Betty walked over to her, standing near the desk. "Sis, I know you want to do a great job, but I don't want you killing yourself over this. Maybe you should go home and sleep. In fact, when was the last time you had a full night's rest?"

Galia shrugged. "When have any of us slept a full night ever?"

"You know, that's probably something we should change," Betty said hesitantly. "If we're not careful, the whole troupe's going to pass out from exhaustion."

"It's nothing we haven't done before," Galia replied, waving off her concerns with her hand. "We'll rest when we're dead."

Betty frowned but didn't respond. She'd never liked that phrase.

"So, what do you need my help with?" Galia asked.

"What?"

"I'm assuming you're in here because you need my help. Or are you checking up on me?"

Betty looked down at her feet. She tried to bring back the determination that had brought her into the room, but she could only muster up fifty percent of it. It would have to be enough. "I..." she paused and looked up at her sister. "I want to talk to you about my relationship."

Galia sighed. "When are you moving out?"

"What?" She was so taken aback by the comment that she almost physically took a step backwards. "No, I'm not moving out."

"But you're spending more time away from home." Galia suddenly sat up straighter. "Oh, am I finally going to meet your mystery man?"

Betty felt her entire body crumple. Her face fell and she was filled with the urge to run from the room and never come back.

"What's wrong?" Galia said, slowly standing up from her chair. "Did I say something wrong?"

Betty sighed, frustration filling her body and propelling her forward. "You know what? Yeah, you did. And you keep doing it, and that's the problem."

Galia stared at her as concern and confusion crossed her face, but Betty didn't allow herself to stop.

"You keep saying things like 'him' and 'man,' and I keep getting crushed under the weight of those expectations. You have such a clear idea of things in your head, and I can't live up to them. I wanted to tell you ages ago, but I couldn't stop myself from drowning in all the terrible things that might happen if I did, and I didn't want to risk our relationship if I didn't have to. I didn't want to lose you, like we lost mom and dad." Betty saw Galia's expression fall as she started to put the pieces together.

"Betty, I would never toss you out because of who you love..." Galia put her hands to her head. "Was I really that narrow-minded? Oh my god, I can be such an idiot sometimes. I'm so sorry I did that to you."

"So, you really wouldn't care if I wasn't dating a guy?" Betty asked, her voice quiet and small.

Galia went over and wrapped her up in a big hug. "Sis, I don't care who you're dating, as long as they treat you right and you're happy."

Betty wrapped her arms around her sister and hugged her tightly. "Thanks."

When they broke apart, Betty felt a giant wave of relief wash over her. She'd been so nervous for so long, and it had all been for nothing.

"So," Galia said, smiling, "who is the person you're dating?"

"It's... Wendy."

Galia paused. "So, you're dating an actor?"

Betty burst out laughing. "Shut up."

"I'm just saying... they're notoriously crazy."

"Well, I've had lots of practice from living with you."

"Touché."

The two of them looked at each other and large smiles broke out on their faces.

Betty took in a deep breath. It felt as if the air was clearer and easier to breath. "Now that that's over with, I want you to promise me that you'll take care of yourself. Get some sleep tonight."

"I'll try, sis," Galia said, sitting back at her table. "Maybe if I add another safety line, Ari will let me drop it faster..."

Betty started to leave, but then she turned back. "Oh, do you know if there's any extra spray paint in the basement? Jim suddenly wants the lantern spray-painted silver, and I used my last can on the knives, so I need more."

"The basement?" Galia immediately stood up from the table, almost sending her chair to the floor. "No, there's nothing down there. Don't bother looking."

"Are you okay?" Betty said carefully, taken aback by Galia's violent reaction.

"Yeah. Just don't go down there, okay? Promise?"

"Why not?"

Galia paused. "I've got a feeling. It's hard to explain. It's like a skin-crawling, terrible, horrible feeling. Just avoid the basement, okay? Please."

Betty didn't understand why her sister sounded so wary. If she didn't know any better, she'd say that Galia sounded scared. "All right, I won't go down there. I mean, the furnace and the knocking are creepy enough, right? I'm more than happy to stay away."

Galia nodded, but it was an absent-minded movement. She pulled the chair back and sat down, her energy suddenly low and subdued. "Yeah..."

"Galia?" Betty said cautiously.

It was like a switch flipped and instantly her sister was back to her old, tired self. "Thanks for finishing the chandelier so quickly. And so far, the pieces are all staying on, so good work. I'm going to do some more thinking, but I'll let you know when we're ready to do another test."

The change was so sudden that Betty wondered if she'd been mistaken about before, but the unease of her sister's words about the basement still resonated in her mind. Deciding not to bring it back up, she nodded. "Thanks. I can't wait to see what you come up with."

Betty turned to leave again.

"Oh, one last thing."

"Yeah?" Betty turned around, curious about what her sister might say. Was it another strange warning?

"I'm genuinely happy for you and Wendy." She smirked. "Even if she is an *actor*."

Unable to hold back her grin, Betty nodded and left the room.

Before Wendy had a chance to call out that the door was open, Betty burst into the apartment. The sudden arrival startled Wendy, and she instinctively backed up against the kitchen counter, wondering what had gone wrong. When she saw the look of elation on Betty's face, however, she quickly realized that everything was okay.

"I did it!" Betty said, raising her hands in triumph. She bounded over to Wendy, her eyes bright and sparkling with joy. "I told Galia!"

Wendy's mouth dropped open in surprise. She could tell by Betty's reaction that the conversation had gone well and grinned widely. "Congratulations!" she said, sweeping Betty up in a big hug.

Betty's lips found hers, and when they kissed it felt just as magical as the first time.

Wendy was overjoyed that they no longer had to keep their affection hidden. They could hold hands at the theatre and walk down the street together. She could even visit Betty in the props room more often.

"I'm so proud of you!" Wendy said. "And I'm relieved she took it well."

Betty smirked. "Well, she is a little disappointed that I'm dating an actor, but she'll get over it."

Wendy rolled her eyes, but the smile never disappeared from her face. "We should celebrate!"

Although they were both feeling invigorated by the good news, they decided to stay in and order food, and celebrate on their own. But instead of one of them picking up the food, this time they went together.

There was a chill in the winter air, but there was no snow on the ground. They held hands as they walked past the streetlights that illuminated the small cobblestone street, and Betty filled Wendy in on how her conversation with Galia had gone. Wendy was surprised that Betty had lost her temper, but she was glad that it had helped her get over her nerves. She was also relieved that Galia had been so accepting, because she knew how much it meant to Betty to have her sister on her side.

They picked up their food at Electric Lunch and then headed to Rainbow Bites to get something sweet for dessert. One of the many perks of living on this street was having a small bakery that stayed open late to satisfy any sweet cravings that might pop up.

Still holding hands, they smiled brightly as they walked along the cobblestone street, back to Wendy's apartment.

CHAPTER TWENTY-SIX

She was standing on the stage, all alone, with an empty audience in front of her. It was like the last time, with numerous unseen people watching her, but there was one big difference. Hanging above the invisible audience, glittering in the dim light, was a gigantic chandelier.

There was something beautiful, yet ominous about it. It was made of razor-sharp pieces of crystal, keen enough to slice the air in two. The audience it was perched over seemed oblivious of the danger above them.

A knock sounded behind her and she felt her heart jump in her chest.

"Stop!" she yelled at nobody in particular; her voice filling the empty room. "Go away! Leave us alone!"

Silence.

The eyes continued to watch.

Breathing heavily, she realized that she could make out faint shapes in a few of the seats. Transparent black smoke had somehow appeared and formed human-like shapes. It was still impossible to make out any features, but she could see that there were thirteen people watching her. Were they the spirits of everyone who'd died in the theatre?

The knocking started up again, but instead of coming from behind it was now coming from above. Her gaze moved up to the chandelier. The crystals began to glow an ominous red, reminding her of drops of blood. With each knock the entire structure shook, and the hundreds of crystals making up the chandelier rattled violently.

She knew what the chandelier was supposed to do. It was supposed to fall, to kill someone, just like the Phantom wanted. He had warned them that they needed to obey, and they hadn't. Now they were going to pay the price.

As the ominous chandelier continued to shake with each knock, pieces began to break off, falling into the audience like drops of blood spilling from a wound. None of the dark shapes seemed disturbed by it, and she could still feel their gaze on her, never wavering. They weren't afraid of the chandelier because they knew that it couldn't hurt them. They were made of smoke, not flesh and bone.

Her however...

Was that why they were here? To watch her be crushed by the chandelier? Did they want to see her die?

A loud noise shook the entire building, including the stage underneath her unmoving feet. The rigging holding the chandelier gave a loud creak and she could hear wires snapping. Her eyes widened as the chandelier dropped and began to swing towards her.

"Wendy! Wake up!"

Her eyes snapped open. She was in her bed, the room half-lit by the rising sun. "What...? Betty?"

Betty was leaning over her, concern filling her green eyes. "You were tossing and turning and seemed really scared. What was going on? Were you having a nightmare?"

Wendy tried to think back to the dream, grabbing onto as many details as she could before they disappeared.

"It was bad," she said, piecing together the fragments as she pulled herself into a sitting position. "I was at the theatre, on the stage, but nobody else was there. But there were people in the audience, except they weren't people, they were more like spirits..." She shook her head, wondering if Betty was able to make any sense of what she was saying. "There was a chandelier. The knocking started and it was loud enough to shake the whole building. The chandelier was shaking, and pieces were raining down on the audience, but then it fell and started swinging right for me."

Betty let out a breath. "That sounds terrifying."

Wendy nodded and sighed. "I think I'm just nervous about the show."

"You shouldn't be. You're doing great."

She wanted to smile, but those words filled her with dread. "But how else am I supposed to explain these dreams? I keep hearing that I'm doing great and I feel good about what I'm doing, but these nightmares won't go away." Fear suddenly overwhelmed her and an image of the basement door glowing red flashed in her mind. "I know it sounds weird, Betty, but I feel like there's a monster in the basement. There's something at the theatre that isn't right. Everyone's walking around like zombies, and I don't think it's because Jim's pushed us too far. Something's really wrong."

When she looked over at Betty, she noticed a conflicted expression on her face.

"I don't know what to say," Betty said carefully. "I mean, I don't believe in ghosts, but I agree that everyone seems more rundown than usual. If it's the flu, then it's the weirdest strain I've ever seen." She paused, suddenly remembering something from yesterday. "There was something Galia said, after I talked to her. I mentioned going down in the basement and she told me not to. She didn't have a good reason for it, but she seemed scared."

Wendy's eyes widened at this new information. Did Galia also suspect that there was an evil spirit in the basement?

"She couldn't explain it, and I don't know what to think about it," Betty continued. "There's got to be a logical explanation for all of this, but I don't know what it is, or why the basement creeps out so many people when we've been around it for years."

"I'd love for there to be a logical explanation," Wendy said, sighing. It wasn't a lie. She wanted nothing more than to make things go back to the way they were, and if all this ghost talk turned out to be nothing, then she'd be relieved. However, the evidence seemed to be lining up in favour of something that couldn't be easily explained. "...But I think we should both avoid the basement either way."

Although Betty didn't think that there was anything down there to be afraid of—other than a temperamental furnace that might explode—she nodded. When the two people she cared about most told her to avoid a place, she had no choice but to do so.

CHAPTER TWENTY-SEVEN

Their show opened in two days and Wendy wasn't sure if they were going to make it. They'd run through the entire show twice yesterday, but there was a lot that needed to be fixed. Gerard still didn't know his lines, Carina and Stacey were low energy and late for entrances, Billy had so many cues that he missed half of them, and most of the costumes still needed work. Jim's note sessions after each run-through went on for so long that even he seemed tired of hearing his own voice.

Wendy had been optimistic about Monday's rehearsal, seeing as how the day before was their day off and everyone would have a chance to sleep in and get some rest, but there was so much to be done that she doubted anyone rested. Even she had spent half of the day going over her script at home.

Although they'd run through the show on stage instead of in the rehearsal hall, they didn't run most of the effects, including the chandelier drop, for which Wendy was thankful. Even though Francesca would be in a much more precarious position than her when the drop happened, her nightmare had made her particularly nervous about that effect.

Betty, Galia, Billy, Ari, and Jim had come in early that morning to run it a few times, so that it'd be ready for the afternoon's cue-to-cue. While Wendy knew that Ari wouldn't let any potentially dangerous effects happen, she couldn't help feeling on edge every time she looked up at the massive chandelier hanging above them.

Normally Wendy found cue-to-cues extremely long and boring. They involved running through the show, but only going from one cue to the next, and although most of the dialogue was skipped, it often took twice as long as a run-through. Even though the creative team worked hard beforehand to get the cues ready, there was always a risk that Jim wouldn't like the timing or that something would need adjusting. Since the actors were needed to perform their entrances and exits and give out cue lines, they usually spent a lot of time standing or sitting around, waiting for their next cue.

This show was so elaborate that Wendy had suspected they'd be here for twenty-four hours in order to run through all the light, sound, and effects cues, but it was moving along at a good pace. It likely had to do with how tired Jim looked. Whenever he was too exhausted to nitpick, Ari would quickly move everyone on to the next cue.

When she wasn't needed on stage, Wendy managed to keep busy by watching everyone else, looking for signs of illness or something more sinister. Some people seemed tired but fine, but most were looking even worse than before. Whenever they weren't needed, they usually sat around, not doing anything, acting like listless zombies. Was it her imagination or did their skin look grey?

She wondered if they'd opened some kind of Pandora's Box when they decided to do this play, releasing a curse over the theatre and everyone inside.

Betty nervously watched as Ari gave the cue for the chandelier. They'd run through the drop three times earlier and everything had worked great, but this was their first time running it in sequence. Ari had suggested that they run the cue first with nobody on stage, to give the actors a chance to get used to it, and then reset and run it a second time with the actors. There was a groaning from a few people about having to do such an elaborate cue twice, but that wasn't enough to stop it from happening.

Even though Betty was already looking at the ceiling and knew exactly what was going to happen, the popping and sparking of the small pyro charges around the edge of the chandelier startled her. After the charges finished, the chandelier dropped down and started to swing towards the stage in a wide arc. The theatre plummeted into darkness as the lights went out, and when they came back on a few seconds later, the curtains were closed and the chandelier was nowhere to be seen.

There was a round of applause from everyone sitting in the auditorium. Even though Betty knew that Galia had pushed herself to the point of exhaustion to get this effect perfected, it didn't stop her from jumping up and pumping a fist in the air in triumph.

Breathing a sigh of relief, Betty slid down in her chair and allowed herself to relax a bit more. It was a good thing she'd taken extra care to attach the fake crystal pieces on the chandelier, as not a single one of them had fallen off all day.

Now they just had to try it with the actors on stage.

The curtains opened and Galia moved on stage to help monitor the chandelier's rise, while Billy and Ari headed to the lighting grid to pull it back up to the ceiling. Betty was glad that she was able to witness this effect from offstage. If she'd been an actor and had to stand there, watching that swinging towards her, she'd freak out.

Suddenly she was reminded of Wendy's dream on Sunday morning, about being on stage and watching the chandelier coming straight for her. Her mind wandered back to that conversation, and how sure Wendy had seemed that something wasn't right at the theatre. Betty had been so certain that there was a reasonable explanation behind it all, but over the past few days she'd found her confidence wavering.

She'd seen illnesses pass through the building before, and the cast and creative had been overworked many, many times—especially when she'd first been hired—but this was a completely new occurrence. Watching people closely, she could see that it was almost like they were having their energy sucked out of them. It had bothered her so much that she'd gone online to see if there were reports of a strange new flu that was affecting people in this way, but there was nothing. Nobody else on Jacobi Street seemed to be affected by it. It was like it was limited to their building.

Every rational explanation she came up with didn't fit. She'd even asked Ari about the possibility of there being mold in the building, but Ari said that it had been inspected four months ago and passed. But what else could it be? Even if ghosts were real, they couldn't affect people like this. Or could they?

When the cue-to-cue finally finished, Jim declared that there was enough time to do a full run of the show before calling it a night. Although the day had been a long and tedious one, he said that going through the show would help further cement everything in their minds.

It wasn't a smooth run by any means. Cues were missed, lines were forgotten, and props were mislaid, but they managed to get through it all without any serious incidents. By the end even Jim was too tired to give notes. He merely looked at everyone and told them, "You know what you did wrong," and called it a night.

They all trudged to their various workshops and dressing rooms, too tired to say anything. Wendy's thoughts were swirling around in her head as she made her way to the private dressing room backstage that she'd been given because she was a lead role. Francesca had her usual room, while the other two had been given to Vance and Gerard. She noticed that Francesca seemed fine, other than being annoyed at the imperfect run, and so did Vance, but Gerard was flat-out exhausted. In Wendy's mind there were two groups of people: those who were tired but healthy, and those who seemed to be having their energy sucked out by some unseen ghost. She didn't like how long the latter list was.

After changing out of her costume, she sat down at the counter, and tried to make sense of what was going on at the theatre. Could it be a curse? Or was it a vengeful ghost, hiding in the basement, draining everyone else's energy to make itself stronger? It sounded impossible and ridiculous, but also made more sense than anything else she could come up with. If it were an illness, then surely there'd be some kind of medicine that would help them feel better. There was no way that so many people would feel so terrible and not do anything to help themselves.

But how was a person supposed to fight against a ghost?

Putting her head in her hands, she wondered how things had gone so wrong. This was supposed to be her dream role, but how could she enjoy it when so many people were feeling terrible? How was she supposed to help when she had no idea what was going on?

There was a knocking on her door that startled her, but she quickly realized that it was a person knocking and not the terrible sound from the basement.

"Come in," she called out, quickly pulling herself together.

Betty poked her head in through the door. When she noticed that Wendy was alone, she slipped into the room, closing the door behind her.

"I think you're right," Betty said, her voice full of uncertainty, as if unable to believe what she was saying. "Something's wrong here. I've seen people sick and tired and overworked, but this is completely different, and I don't know what it is, but it's unnatural."

Normally Wendy liked being right, but this time she felt no satisfaction. "I don't know what it is either, but I think it might be a spirit. Something in this building is draining the life from certain people, and I don't know why it's attacking them and not everyone, but maybe it only has a limited reach?"

"So, what do we do?" Betty walked into the room and leaned against the counter. "There has to be something we can do to fix it. Right? We need to figure out what's going on and make it stop, and then everything will go back to normal."

Wendy was about to say that she had no idea what to do, but then the image of the basement door popped in her mind. "I think we need to go to the basement," she said cautiously. "I think there's something down there that's causing all of this."

Normally Betty wouldn't be scared to go anywhere in the building, but Galia's warnings about the basement were still fresh in her mind. Her certainty that supernatural creatures did not exist had been shaken, and she was actually feeling afraid.

Pulling herself together, she summoned up all her courage. If Wendy could suggest such a thing when she was obviously scared, then she could handle it. After all, she'd promised Wendy that if she needed her, she'd be there to hold her hand.

"Should we go down now?" Betty asked.

At the suggestion Wendy felt her heart leap in her throat and her pulse quicken. She was definitely not prepared to face the basement right now.

"No, this day's been too long and insane. Let's do it tomorrow night, after midnight, when everyone's gone. That'll give us time to prepare."

Betty nodded. "Tomorrow, then. What should we take with us? Crosses and holy water?"

She shrugged. "Salt, lighter fluid, and matches? Your guess is as good as mine."

"I'll do some research." Betty paused. "What do you think we'll find?"

A thousand terrible things raced through Wendy's mind, but she didn't want to say any of them. Instead, she decided to be honest: "I don't know."

CHAPTER TWENTY-EIGHT

On the night of the dress rehearsal, the whole troupe gathered in the audience to listen to Jim's motivational speech. He gave the same speech every time, no matter what they were doing—whether it be a play or a sketch show—so most of them knew it by heart. But there was something about the way Jim was speaking this time that wasn't the same. He sounded tired, just like everyone else looked. Instead of the excitement of being one day away from opening night, it felt as if he was trying to ward off an ill omen.

Once the speech was over, Wendy hurried to get into her first costume. She tried to tell herself that it was only a rehearsal and that she was prepared for almost everything. And even if things went wrong, wasn't there a saying in the theatre: "bad dress rehearsal, good opening night"? She quickly changed into her costume and put on her make-up. When Ari gave the places call over the speaker, Wendy felt her breath catch in her throat. She took a few deep, calming breaths and left her dressing room.

As nervous as she was beforehand, it didn't affect her performance, and whenever she was on stage she felt confident and prepared. However, the minute her character left a scene, everything seemed off. The wings looked darker than usual, everyone's attitude was quiet, and the overall mood was more intense. Normally she'd spend most of her free time watching from the wings, but today she stayed in her dressing room until it was close to her next cue, away from everyone else and their strange behaviour.

She was thankful when the show ended. As amazing as it was to be playing this part, she wanted to shake off the unsettled feeling that had increased during the dress rehearsal. She felt that she'd done well, but other actors had forgotten lines and missed cues, and even though everyone had tried to compensate for it, she knew that it had been a terrible performance. If Betty and she weren't able to figure out what was causing this strange behaviour, then this show was doomed.

She'd just finished changing into her street clothes when there was a knock on her dressing room door. She opened it to see Vance standing on the other side.

"Yes?" she asked, startled by his appearance. They'd gotten along well enough during rehearsals, but he'd never made much of an effort to talk to her before or after.

"I know I'm new to this," he said, looking around to make sure that nobody was listening, "but are we actually ready to open this show or is it going to get cancelled?"

She opened her mouth to say something flippant, but then thought better of it. She also thought better of telling him her suspicions.

"No," she shook her head. "This is some kind of weird flu or something. I think everyone's saving their energy for tomorrow."

"I hope so," he said, a concerned look on his face. "My partner's got a ticket for tomorrow, and I'd hate for it to not happen."

"It was a pretty bad run," Wendy admitted, "but I've seen worse when it comes to our variety shows, and we always manage to pull it together by showtime."

He seemed slightly reassured. "That's good to hear. I've been having fun doing this, and I'd hate for all our hard work not to pay off."

"You've been having fun?" Wendy said before quickly slapping a hand over her mouth. She couldn't believe she'd said such a rude statement out loud. "I'm sorry! I didn't mean to say that! It's just that in rehearsals you don't... I mean, it's not obvious... Oh god..." She wanted to crawl under the counter and die.

To her complete surprise, Vance laughed. "I get it, okay? I haven't been the most outgoing person." He gave a half-shrug. "You're all so familiar with each other and sure about what you're doing, and sometimes it feels like I'm on the outside looking in."

Taking a moment, Wendy thought about how it must have been for Vance to come into this crazy troupe. She'd had an easier time, but it was mostly because Stacey and Carina had decided she wasn't much of a threat and added her to their group, and because Francesca helped her out. Gerard and Sam were too self-centred to help anyone, and she'd been so preoccupied with her own role that she hadn't thought to check in on him.

"Do you have a moment?" she asked. "Because if you're interested, I can tell you a bunch of gossip about everyone in this building. It'll be like you've known them forever."

He looked at his watch and nodded, a large smile crossing his face.

"I've got some time."

As Wendy motioned for him to enter her dressing room, she felt a grin cross her own face. First, she was going to make Vance feel like more of the team, and then later tonight she and Betty were going to find that evil spirit and kick its ass into the next century.

CHAPTER TWENTY-NINE

The bright glow of the ghost light's single bulb was almost blinding in the darkness, but its reach wasn't far enough to illuminate the entire auditorium. Instead, it lent a faint glow to any objects farther than four feet away, outlining the shape but not providing any detail.

The theatre was dark and silent as Betty and Wendy made their way through the auditorium, using Betty's keys to let them in. They'd checked that all the lights in Jim's apartment had been out before entering the building, not wanting him to accidentally wander down and find them. If someone dared question what they were doing, Wendy had a feeling that she'd lose all nerve and run away, and she wanted to get this over and done with. Whatever *this* was.

Wendy was carrying a purse that contained multiple lighters, candles, filtered water, a steak knife, and some salt. Meanwhile, Betty had decided to bring a large pipe wrench that was almost as long as her arm. Hopefully it would be enough.

As they walked, Wendy thought she could see people sitting in the audience out of the corner of her eye, but when she turned to look at them, the seats were empty. Outlined by the glow of the ghost light, Wendy wasn't sure if her feeling of being watched by an invisible audience was real or something that she was creating all on her own.

The two of them made their way through the backstage and down to the lower level, exchanging an uneasy look as they stopped in front of their destination. The door to the basement looked more innocent than it had in months. The colour had gone back to a faded dark red and looked nothing like blood. There was no eerie glowing coming from behind, and even the chipped paint looked more like normal flaking and not something being forcibly peeled back.

"You okay?" Betty asked, her voice low and soft even though they were the only people in the building.

Wendy nodded. "I hate it, but I'm going to do it anyway." She reached out for the door, but before she could put her hand on the doorknob, it creaked open. She looked back at Betty, whose eyes had gone wide.

"It's just the air, it's just the air, it's just the air..." Betty muttered to herself over and over, her breath coming quickly. She lifted the pipe wrench higher, holding it like a baseball bat.

Taking in a shaky breath, Wendy gripped the flashlight tighter and stepped through the door. She'd half-expected the landing to crumble as soon as both of her feet were on it, but although it let out a low groan, it stayed up. Swallowing hard, she flicked on the light switch near the door. Instead of all the overhead lights turning on, only the ones in the middle of the room lit up, creating a path for her to follow to the back of the room. She didn't like it.

Every step she took, she expected something terrible to happen, like for her foot to break through the step and get stuck, or for something to grab at her legs through the stairs. The fact that nothing happened was almost worse. Other than the door opening on its own and the strange way the lights had turned on, there was nothing out of the ordinary. Was the basement trying to lull her into a false sense of security?

"Where to?" Betty asked once they'd both stepped off the stairs and onto the floor.

Wendy shone her flashlight to either side, illuminating the darkened areas. Around them were old backgrounds and set pieces. Although being down here gave her the creeps, there was nothing about this area that was particularly chilling, so she pressed forward, following the path of the overhead lights.

They moved at a slow pace, with Wendy shining her light over everything along the sides, making sure that nothing was going to jump out at them. Perhaps this was an elaborate joke orchestrated by Stacey and Carina, to make her think she was crazy as revenge for her getting the role of Christine. Maybe they'd involved the entire troupe, except for Betty, and now they were waiting in the shadows to jump out and laugh at how gullible she was. If that was the case, then she'd be relieved. Furious as hell, but still relieved.

Unfortunately, as they neared the furnace, Wendy realized that perhaps it wasn't a joke.

"What is that?" Betty whispered, drawing closer to her.

"I don't know." Wendy stepped forward and stared at the large red circle that was painted on the floor of the basement, tucked into the space between the furnace and the wall. There was a large triangle painted in the middle of the circle, with each point touching the edge of the circle but not going outside. Another circle had been drawn in the middle of the triangle, separating the three points, and inside each point were strange squiggly lines. Each squiggle was different, and she had no idea what any of them meant or what language they were supposed to be. In the centre of the circle was a low metal bowl filled with something that looked like ash or dust.

Betty frowned. "Is this a joke? Is someone trying to play a prank on us?"

Wendy wasn't sure what to say. She wanted to take a closer look, but she also wanted to run as far away from here as humanly possible. She'd seen enough movies to recognize that this had to be some kind of magic.

"Maybe it's a spell to sap people's energies..." Wendy said uncertainly.

A loud *bang* startled them, and they both jumped.

"What are you two doing here?"

They jumped again, but when they turned around, they saw Scott standing about six feet behind them. His eyes were narrowed and he looked like he hadn't slept in days. He was holding his clipboard loosely in his left hand.

"Oh, it's you, Scott," Betty said, lowering her pipe wrench. "What are you doing down here?"

"I heard you two talking last night. I wanted to see what you'd find."

Wendy frowned. Had he been listening outside her dressing room? It was creepy, but entirely in character for him. Maybe he also suspected that something weird was going on and was trying to figure it out.

"Look what we found," she said, pointing to the circle. "What do you think it is? It's got to have something to do with the crazy stuff happening around here, right?"

"Who do you think did it?" Betty asked as he glanced towards the circle. "I can't imagine anyone else doing something like this. Maybe it was Vance? We've known him the least amount of time."

Yesterday Wendy would have been on the same page, but now that she'd had time to get to know Vance, she was pretty sure he wasn't malicious enough to do something like this. But who else could it be?

Scott rolled his eyes. "Of course, you think it's Vance. He's all anyone thinks about these days."

Wendy and Betty exchanged a look. Was this really the time for jealousy?

"Vance didn't do this," Scott said angrily, absentmindedly tapping his clipboard against his leg.

"How do you know?" Betty asked.

"Because I'm the person who drew it!" Scott yelled, glaring daggers at them. "It's a summoning circle, you morons. And before you ask, I did it because I'm sick and tired of being treated like trash. You all look down on me as if I'm a useless bug. Jim refuses to let me assistant direct, the crew only acknowledges me when they need something, and the actors barely even know I exist. Unless I'm in the way, in which case you have no problem telling me what a waste of space I am. So I summoned this demon and trapped it down here, and once it's strong enough, it'll kill you all."

Wendy's mouth dropped open. She knew that Scott didn't like having to do menial tasks around the theatre and that some people gave him a hard time, but she had no idea that he was filled with so much hate. "What did you summon?"

Scott laughed. "As if I'm going to tell you."

Betty looked around, worry creasing her face. "Is it here?"

As if in answer to his question, a deep knocking sound reverberated throughout the basement.

"Fuck..." Betty muttered under her breath. "Fuck, fuck, fuck..."

"Get rid of it!" Wendy yelled. "Un-summon it or whatever."

Scott laughed bitterly. "Why would I do something like that?"

"Because it's hurting people!" Betty shouted as her eyes darted around the room.

"You've made your point," Wendy argued. "We get it, and we'll tell the others to stop giving you such a hard time. Now, get rid of that thing."

The sound reverberated again, louder this time. Scott rolled his eyes. "Whatever." He turned around to leave, but Betty raced forward and grabbed him by the shoulder, bringing him up short. His clipboard fell to the ground, clattering against the concrete.

"Take your hands off me," Scott ordered.

She tightened her grip. "Not until you get rid of this... thing."

Scott narrowed his eyes at her. "*Ad constringendum, ad ligandum eos pariter et solvendum: Et ad congregandum eos coram me.*"

The temperature in the room suddenly heated up. There was a scratching sound, like sharp objects being dragged along the side of the furnace. A low growl filled the room and Wendy had a bad feeling settle in her stomach.

"I'd ask you to take your hand off me again, but it's too late," Scott smirked.

Betty's hand dropped from Scott's shoulder as she noticed a large shadow rising behind him. The shadow seemed to be made of swirling air, black and dark purple, with two glowing red eyes.

"Oh, fuck fuck fuck fuck fuck..." Betty muttered, backing away from the shape.

Wendy' eyes widened in fear. She didn't know what the thing could do, but she wouldn't be surprised if its mouth was full of sharp, deadly teeth.

"HUNGRY," the creature said, its voice low and dark as death.

"Then get eating," Scott ordered, retrieving his clipboard. "Eat these two, and then I'll see about getting the rest of them down here."

"HUNGRY."

Scott rolled his eyes and started walking towards the staircase.

The beast looked down at Betty, its red eyes glowing menacingly. "HUNGRY."

Panic rose inside of Wendy. She didn't know what to do but knew that she had to do something. If she didn't, then she and Betty would never make it out of here alive. Turning back to the summoning circle, she made a split-second decision and kicked over the bowl, spreading ash all over the floor. When that didn't cause the beast to disappear, she drew the steak knife from her bag and started scratching at the paint on the circle. First, she'd un-summon this stupid demon, and then she'd deal with Scott.

The growling of the beast increased. Betty backed up almost to the wall, holding the pipe wrench in front of her, but the beast hadn't yet moved. It looked down at what Wendy was doing and then back at Scott.

Wendy scraped harder, desperately trying to scratch a line all the way through the paint and effectively breaking the circle. As soon as she did so, she was knocked off her feet by an invisible burst of energy.

"FREE."

Wendy stood up and scrambled over to Betty. Betty was still holding the wrench, but the beast was no longer looking at her. It had turned to Scott, who'd frozen in place, two feet away from the stairs.

"FREE."

Scott turned around and started whimpering as the beast approached. "No! You can't hurt me! I'm the one who summoned you!"

"TRAPPED."

Frantic noises escaped Scott's mouth. "No! Don't! Please! I'll get everyone down here faster! I'll send you back after you eat them all! I promise! Please!"

The beast drew closer. "HUNGRY."

Wendy watched in horror as the beast descended upon Scott. The screams he made would haunt her for a long time, but she didn't want to say or do anything that would put herself in the way of the beast.

When the screams stopped, she hoped that the beast would disappear, but instead it turned around, its glowing eyes watching her and Betty. The black and purple swirling air that made up its body were joined by swirls as red as blood. Wendy's breath came faster as she prepared herself for what was coming, but then the demon suddenly disappeared.

The basement went silent. There was no knocking, no screaming. Only quiet.

After what felt like an hour, Betty broke the silence.

"We should go."

Betty's words seemed to break the hold that was upon her and Wendy found herself able to move again. She took Betty's hand and they headed towards the stairs, ignoring the dark stain on the floor that was all that remained of Scott.

CHAPTER THIRTY

"Wendy?"

Wendy slowly opened her eyes. She felt groggy, as if she'd drank too much last night and was in that strange middle-ground that existed between drunk and hungover. When her eyes finally came into focus, she saw that she was lying in her bed, Betty sitting beside her, sleep still in the corners of her eyes, her red hair sticking out to one side.

"Did that happen last night? Was that real or a dream?" she asked.

Wendy tried to clear the fog from her mind as she pulled herself up into a sitting position. "Was your dream about us going in the basement, finding a demon, and watching it murder Scott?"

A grim look was on Betty's face as she nodded. "Dammit." A pained look crossed her face. "So, demons are real, and so is witchcraft, and our friends were having their life-force drained by a demon that Scott was keeping in the basement because he resented us all. How am I expected to do anything after all of that?"

Wendy reached out and took Betty's hand in hers. Last night was weird and terrifying, but she'd grown up believing in spirits, so while the appearance of a demon was surprising, it wasn't out of the realm of possibility. Betty, who hadn't believed in the supernatural until a few days ago, had to come to terms with the fact that she'd watched a demon appear out of thin air and kill a person in front of her very eyes.

"Betty, I don't know what to say other than what happened last night was fucked up."

"It was *so* fucked up," Betty said.

"I don't know if we should try to tell the others what happened or if they'll think we're totally nuts. But hopefully that *thing* is gone, and we can all go back to normal."

Betty's eyes widened. "Do you think it's released everyone?"

Wendy was hit with two possibilities—one: that after the demon killed Scott, it went for everyone else; and two: that when the demon disappeared, its hold on everyone disappeared with it and they were all free. She hoped and prayed it was the latter. They'd find out soon enough, anyways, once they went to the theatre.

She suddenly realized that tonight was the opening night for *Phantom*, and the dread from last night was pushed aside by nerves. Looking over at her clock, her mouth dropped open as she realized that it was almost five in the afternoon. They'd slept for over twelve hours.

"The show's in three hours!" Wendy said, jumping up from the bed. "But is it even going to go on? What if everyone's still a mess?"

Seeing Wendy start to lose her mind, Betty found herself gaining back some control. Pushing aside thoughts of demons and death, she focused on the show—something she understood and had a modicum of control over.

"I think we should go to the theatre early," Betty said. "I mean, most of us designers usually go early. I think I'm actually late, to be honest. But we should get ready and go see how everyone is."

Wendy took a few deep breaths. "Yeah, you're right. We should get ready and go. And hopefully everything will be all right and everyone will be back to normal."

The two of them exchanged a look that was meant to be hopeful, but a note of uncertainty hung in the air.

As they walked backstage, the theatre was once again a flurry of activity, with crew and cast moving about, searching for props or costumes. Wendy's eyes widened as she saw Billy humming to himself and smiling as he checked on the ropes that pulled the backdrops up and down. There were still bags under his eyes, but he seemed to be in the best health of his life. Paloma also seemed to be feeling better, muttering to herself as she quickly went through the costume rack in the wings, checking that everything was still in order.

Wendy couldn't help staring. It was almost as if the past few weeks hadn't happened. A smile crossed her face. She looked over at Betty, who looked astonished.

"We did it..." Betty said softly, a smile slowly crossing her face. "Everything's back to normal."

Everything about the show was perfect, even with Scott being a no-show. The first act went so smoothly that for a moment Wendy wondered if this was what it was like to be on Broadway or London's West End. Set pieces that might have been late coming in were perfectly timed, props that might have been moved accidentally were in their proper places, and lines that could have been dropped were said perfectly.

Now that the demon was gone, everything felt like a wonderful dream.

As they started the second half, Wendy threw herself into the performance. The masquerade scene was almost hypnotic. There seemed to be more people on stage than ever before, dancing and twirling. There was an intensity to the rooftop scene that she'd never felt before, and she heard audible gasps when the Phantom revealed himself at the end.

Wendy had never felt so alive. With the lights shining in her eyes, it was difficult to see the audience, but they made noises at the appropriate times, gasping and laughing whenever something astonishing or funny happened. One of them even shrieked when Christine ripped off the Phantom's mask, revealing the burned and scarred flesh that Galia had created from latex.

They finally reached the last scene of the play, after Christine and Raoul escaped the Phantom's torture chamber, running away as he screamed in agony. The stage was bare, but Jim had added a fake snowfall to provide atmosphere. Wendy saw Betty out of the corner of her eye, watching from the wings, before turning to Vance and saying her lines.

Finally, they kissed, and the play was over. The audience applauded loudly, cheering and jumping to their feet as the curtain came down. The designers and actors made their way onto the stage, ready for their bows. Even Jim joined them.

The curtain went up and Wendy stood near the centre of the stage, holding onto Vance and Gerard's hands as the group took a bow. But as they rose, her eyes caught something in the darkness, behind the audience. A cold, icy hand gripped her heart as the line of actors bowed again, taking her down with them. When they rose, Wendy looked back at the same area, noticing how one spot of darkness had taken on a purple and red hue, and how it almost seemed to be moving... swirling...

She glanced over at Betty and when their eyes met, she noticed that Betty also sensed something wasn't right.

Suddenly a number of stage lights went out, startling everyone. Wendy turned back to the dark, swirling purple smoke at the back of the room, but without so many lights focused on the stage, she was now able to see the audience better. She'd peeked out through the curtains before the show and noticed that the audience was almost three-quarters full, but now it seemed to be even fuller.

Some of the patrons looked strange, clad in odd outfits. There was someone dressed in full knight's regalia, another who looked like a nurse, another in an outfit from the 20s, and another in a powdered wig. It wasn't strange for people to dress up for shows, but these costumes didn't have anything to do with this show. Why were people wearing them?

Then she noticed that their former scenic painter was in the audience, along with the other people who had gone missing in the past month—Obi, the street artist; Mr. Cooper, the owner of Cooper's General Market; and

Chelsea, the former owner of the Menagerie. What were they doing here? Had they all come back?

The swirling in the back of the theatre intensified, and Wendy's heart nearly stopped as the shape formed into that of the beast; two glowing red eyes appearing in the smoke. Wendy's eyes swept over the crowd, who seemed oblivious to the monster behind them. Suddenly scratches appeared on the thirteen strange audience members, lines of dark red drawn upon their skin, blood running down their arms and faces.

"FREE."

Wendy's breath caught in her throat. Half of the room looked around, confused at the strange noise, while the other half simply stared straight ahead.

"FREEDOM." The beast's deep voice boomed throughout the theatre.

The costumed strangers and the missing people suddenly disappeared. Wendy felt Gerard let go of her hand, and when she turned to look at him, he was lying on the floor. Her breath caught in her throat as other people fell with him—Stacey, Carina, Billy, Paloma, Jim, and Galia.

"What's happening?" Betty cried out, falling to her knees beside her sister.

Wendy couldn't answer. Turning back to the beast in the shadows, she knew the truth. When she'd broken the summoning circle, the beast hadn't been banished. Instead, it had been freed. Without Scott holding it back, it was able to devour anyone it wanted. And it had.

The beast let out a growl and disappeared from the back of the theatre, leaving the room in utter pandemonium. Wendy stared at the darkness, unable to move, as tears filled her eyes.

EPILOGUE

The faint chords drifted down the alley and out into the night air. At the back of the alley running between The Rashomon Gallery and The Hidden Forest Market, were two people. They were sitting on the stairs of the fire escape, barely illuminated by the dim light above the emergency exit door at the top of the staircase.

"Play the one about the underground tunnel to China," the young woman, Maireni, said, taking a long drag from the joint in her hand. Her eyes were glassy and the smile never left her face. Her hair was a light blue-green and she was dressed in multiple layers of clothing, with tops, sweaters, skirts, and scarves in bright colours. Crystals hung from her neck and every finger had a ring on it.

Goni, the young man, smiled and obediently began to pluck out a tune on his battered guitar. The instrument was at least twice as old as he was and had seen better days, but it played well enough. It was his prized possession, and he was rarely seen without it.

He was dressed like the girl, with multiple layers, but less dramatically. His purple hair was cut short on the sides and left long on top, and he wore a vest over a sweater riddled with holes, much like his shoes and pants.

There were no words to any of his music, but Marieni knew all his songs. As he played on, she began to make up lyrics, waxing poetic about the feeling of travelling through tunnels deep into the Earth. In her imagination the tunnels travelled all over the Earth, branching off in hundreds of different directions. She liked to think that they were created by mysterious beings, whose only purpose was to dig tunnels from one city to another, to connect the Earth in an unseen harmony and help bring us all closer together.

Goni smiled at her words as his fingers moved from chord to chord. When he finished, he reached out for the remainder of her joint, but before she could hand it to him, the fire escape began to shake. They both looked up, curious as to who was coming out of the gallery so late at night, but they couldn't see anyone. Still the stairs continued to shake, as if someone were climbing down. Rising to his feet, Goni forgot all about the joint. He narrowed his eyes as he tried to see who was coming towards them, but there was only darkness. Actually, it was worse than darkness. The light near the back door should have illuminated the railing or the stairs, but it was obstructed by a large dark void that seemed to block out any light that might exist. A large, dark void that was drawing closer and closer.

Words escaped him as he reached out for Marieni, his hand closing around her upper arm.

"We need to go," he whispered.

She didn't seem to hear him, staring up at the darkness with a confused expression on her face. She didn't understand how it could be making such a commotion with its movements since it seemed to be made of swirling smoke. She tried to read its aura but there was only darkness.

The darkness seemed to stop and look at them, gaining shape and form, growing larger and more solid as they stared. A giant mouth opened, and sharp white teeth glistened in the moonlight. Goni felt his heart rise in his throat as two glowing red eyes looked down at them.

THAT HALLOWEEN

MIKE HICKEY

"Haunted houses up on the hill are fine to run past
and tell stories about, but if you ever ring that
doorbell then you're asking for it"
- Stephen Graham Jones, *The Babysitter Lives*

CHAPTER ONE

The Willow Woods isn't called as such because the forest is populated by willow trees, but rather that it's gated by them. When the town—then the village—of Granville was first settled by Mackenzie Hill in 1786, the landowner named the new community after his mother, Mary Blythe Granderson, and had two of her favourite trees, weeping willows, planted where his property met the sprawling timberland as a memorial to her.

The trees served as a beauty mark on the already picturesque landscape, not knowing the horrors that would eventually become synonymous with the place, although it would take some time before any of that happened.

With the exclusion of a mill fire that claimed a dozen lives in 1853 and a farmer who lost his crop to blight, his wife to a neighbour, and the lives of his wife, the neighbour, and himself to his own shotgun in 1907, the region was relatively free of tragedy until the spring of 1942 when Marcy Hart, prom queen, disappeared while walking home from babysitting for the Salter family three streets over. It would be five weeks until what was left of her body was found in the Willow Woods by two young boys on their way to their makeshift fort nestled in among the trees.

Daniel McIntyre followed. Like Marcy, he disappeared walking home alone at night, but his remains were discovered by a search team after a mere three days, thanks to their efforts being concentrated on the Willow Woods after the discovery of Marcy's corpse.

A horrific pattern emerged over the next two years. Every several months, usually coinciding with a clear night and a large moon, someone else would go missing. Not always residents of Granville, but always within Willow Woods County. The bodies weren't always recovered, but when they were it was always in the Willow Woods. The area was gripped in terror, held hostage by the stranger whose moniker came from a popular monster movie that also featured a killer who stalked his prey under the light of full moons, and thus, the public knew him only as "The Willow Woods Wolf Man."

The Willow Woods Wolf Man was born to an unwed mother who immediately brought him to the convent in Hollow's Cove two weeks before Christmas, 1913. The boy hardly spoke for the first eight years of his life but did form habits that drew concerns from the Sisters of Perpetual Penance who, after the cat kept at the orphanage to manage the rodent population was found with its neck twisted, found a gentleman willing to take the boy they had called Rodney Allan into his care.

Alphonse Barrett was widowed by a widow. Wealthy because of an inheritance from his estranged mother, he hadn't fathered children of his own but had tried to raise Nellie's two girls as if they were his. Both girls had always found Alphonse strange, never particularly warming to the man, only to his wallet.

The girls found him to be idiosyncratic and peculiar. There were rooms of the house that were always locked and off limits, and his hunting trips yielded the unusual spoils of small, gamey creatures that weren't particularly appetizing.

Once each girl had completed high school, she received a comfortable endowment and promptly disappeared into the city, only occasionally checking in when requiring a top-up of funds.

After some time alone, Alphonse decided that company would do him good and, discovering that the Sisters had a boy they found off-putting, Alphonse offered to take the child in.

Unlike his stepdaughters, Alphonse held no secrets from the boy and not only nurtured Rodney Allan's dark inclinations but helped integrate them with his own. Behind the doors Barrett kept the girls locked out of, he revealed to the boy a collection of oddities and amateur taxidermy projects that the pair would eventually take on the road as "Barrett & Son's Mystical Menagerie".

Using Alphonse's sizeable wealth as a means of independence, they freely roamed the countryside, often joining travelling carnivals until Rodney, who still rarely spoke, would eventually draw the ire of the head carnie with some infraction—usually involving a small animal that travelled with the company being discovered unnaturally dead—and the pair would be on their own again until they crossed paths with the next show.

It was early in 1936 when Alphonse Barrett died in his sleep while their caravan was somewhere outside Oklahoma. Rodney quickly discovered that while they had toured under the banner of "Barrett & Son," that didn't serve as a proper legal declaration and there were no other documents asserting the pair as such, and thus he had no claim to Alphonse's fortune. The absent stepdaughters inherited everything, and Rodney Allan Barrett found himself as a pauper whose only skillset was the small collection of odd jobs he had occasionally taken at different carnivals when Alphonse would be too deep into his bottle for them to run their oddity showcase.

He got on to the next show he found, but without Alphonse to serve as an intermediary between him and the rest of the carnies, and no one to keep an eye on him to keep his darker inclinations in check. Soon, Rodney found himself on the chopping block ready to be thrown back on the road by himself.

It was then he was offered the job anyone who's ever walked the midway knows to be the most desperate of positions, the geek.

The "temporary" position, always offered just until they could find a real geek, did what it always does: turn into a permanent position once time had slowly transformed the fake geek into a real geek and any semblance of humanity that was left within Rodney Allan Barrett disappeared.

When the carnival stopped in Hollow's Cove, echoes of his life at the orphanage and with Barrett came flooding back, sending him into a manic fit and the now feral creature broke loose from the cage that they kept him in.

Unable to track down the man they had driven wild, the show got on the road the next morning without so much as a warning to the local authorities. They moved so quickly that by the time the bodies and news stories of the horrors in the Willow Woods started to pile up, no one remembered the wild man they had left roaming the countryside.

That was April of 1942, less than three weeks before Marcy Hart disappeared.

***

October of 1944 was bookended by full moons.

By the time the earliest signs of the waxing gibbous appeared in the afternoon sky on the first of the month, the local sheriff's department was already on patrol along with reinforcements from neighbouring counties in response to the fifteen missing or murdered persons that had accumulated over the last two years, starting with Marcy.

A curfew was in place, as it had been for the six months prior. Fatigue had set in with the locals who began to question the curfew about two months in. But when parts of Cynthia Alfredsson were found in a ditch along the highway between Granville and Hollows Cove the morning after she had visited a friend just a few blocks from her parent's house and tried to walk home around 10 pm, it erased any doubt of the emergency measure's requirement. So now, another four months in, the streets were empty before the sun had even begun to set.

Walton Flynn wasn't new to the role of deputy, but it would still be another five years before Martin McGrady would retire and Walt donned the sheriff's badge for himself, mostly on the reputation he'd accrue over the next month. He, like the other men working in law enforcement in the area, was desperate to put an end to the reign of terror that had gripped Willow Woods County for the last two-plus years.

On October 1st, after he kissed his wife and baby daughter, but before heading out into the crisp autumn night, he touched his lips to the crucifix that hung around his neck and said a silent prayer that they'd catch the son of a bitch tonight, putting an end to all of it.

Tonight, he'd get closer than anyone had.

As he had done the week of each full moon for the past six months, he checked in at the sheriff's office and was given his directive for the night; he was to patrol Mason Avenue from where it intersected with Main Street and ran to the tree line of the Willow Woods.

Mason Avenue was commercial for the first few blocks, hosting several offices and shops before turning over to apartment buildings and eventually pleasant bungalows after crossing the old, covered Mackenzie Hill Bridge.

Flynn was joined by George Harris, a slightly older deputy who had been seconded from the neighbouring town of Hollows Cove. The two men paced the street, sweeping their flashlights behind benches, under the bridge, and anywhere else the glow from the electric streetlights, recently installed in the area as a deterrent for the madman, didn't reach.

They trudged back and forth along the same route for hours and were on their sixteenth pass of the night before anything that could be described as eventful happened.

Flynn had been standing at the window of Vincent's Drug Store, eying the electric hair dryer and curler set in the window and calculating the paydays between now and Christmas in hopes of getting it for his wife, Gertie. He figured he should be able to pull it off, providing their car decided to play ball with the dropping temperatures and not require any extra service.

The reflection of Harris' flashlight in the window snapped him out of his financial planning and back to the mission at hand.

He turned to see Harris crouched by Granville Laundrette, blocking the notice in the window offering full-service drop-off.

Harris tilted his head toward the alleyway the laundromat shared with the army recruitment office. Flynn duck-walked his way across the street, keeping his head low, and setting up in front of Uncle Sam, his freshly drawn gun mirroring the boney, outstretched finger of recruitment.

The two men waited with held breath, listening to the rummaging sounds coming from the alley.

Harris, also now brandishing his revolver, looked to Flynn and began a silent countdown.

Three.

Two.

One.

He leapt and spun, coming around the corner in a smooth motion, pointing his gun and flashlight down the dark alley while dropping his speaking voice an octave to declare:

"Police! Freeze!"

But the stray dog that was pulling half of a discarded bologna sandwich from an overturned trashcan didn't heed Harris' warning. Instead, he fled with the spoils of his pillaging to the other end of the alley.

Flynn buckled with laughter. The combination of the falsely deepened voice and the source of all this tension being a stray dog was just too much after the pins and needles of the hours of tonight's search alongside months of extra precautions and pressure to capture this killer. This was a breath of air that he didn't know he needed. Harris, first embarrassed, now couldn't help but join him in busting up and awarding the situation with more humour than it actually warranted.

When the pair finally stopped laughing, Flynn suggested that the dog had the right idea, and they clearly needed a break. It was time for them to eat.

They sat on a bench and each unpacked sandwiches that were wrapped in butcher paper.

"New daughter, I hear?" Harris asked.

"Yes, four months. Eva." Flynn produced a picture of his wife holding the baby from his wallet.

"Beautiful. Both of them." Harris complimented. "I've got a daughter myself. Just turned fifteen this past June."

"How's that?"

"You know how yours can't talk or walk and constantly needs to be fed and have her shit cleaned up?"

"Yeah?"

"Cherish this time." Harris laughed, only half serious, before adding, "Really though, she's not much younger than that first girl was when it happened. She's growing into this piece of shit's demo, and it terrifies me."

Flynn put a consoling hand on his shoulder. "We're going to get the bastard. Don't worry."

The lawmen shared the promise in silence for a moment before something caught Harris' eye.

"Did you see that?" he whispered.

"See what? Is Rover back?" Flynn chuckled.

Harris didn't answer. He put down his corned beef and picked up his flashlight. He turned back to Flynn, put a finger to his lips, and then beckoned to be followed. He crossed the road but signalled Flynn to stay on the opposite side. As they drew closer to the bridge Harris threw up a hand to stop and, straining forward to listen, unclipped the holster at his hip and withdrew his revolver.

Flynn's heart pounded so hard in his chest that he instinctively put a hand up to keep his badge from rattling. He drew his gun and flanked Harris at the mouth of the covered bridge. The deputies locked eyes as Harris pointed his flashlight at his stomach while turning it on to hide the light as he readied it and then whispered another countdown.

On one, they sprang around their respective corners, guns drawn. Harris filled the tunnel with light to reveal a dark lump in the middle of the bridge.

They shared a look and Harris motioned Flynn to inspect.

"You go look. I'll cover from here."

Flynn drew his flashlight, crossing his outstretched arms so the light and his gun pointed in the same direction, and cautiously moved forward.

He slowly approached the mass at the center of the bridge. As he got closer, he began to take stock and relay information to Harris.

"Looks small, too small for...y'know..."

"Christ, I hope it's not a kid," Harris called back. The thought hadn't occurred to Flynn. He drew back his gun arm and wiped his brow with the back of his sleeve.

"It's covered with something. A blanket, I think." With this, Flynn's head whipped to Harris, and they locked eyes as both men realized that they had walked this path well over a dozen times so far tonight and nothing was there, meaning that whatever was under the blanket was placed there deliberately. It had been laid there specifically for them to find, and it had been put there since their last sweep.

Flynn's heart sank but he was drawn to the shape to find out what it was.

"When was the last time we came through?" Flynn called back.

"Maybe a half hour?" Harris replied before calling through on his walkie, which was still a novelty for him. Granville had only acquired them in the last year because they were hunting a madman. Streetlights and walkie-talkies—who knew that all it took to embrace innovation was a killer on the loose?

"This is Harris. Flynn and I are at the bridge on Mason. We've got something here. We think he's close, send backup."

"Looks like blood," Flynn called back. He tucked his flashlight in the crook of his neck and reached out a trembling hand to pull back the grey woollen blanket.

Underneath was the scruffy mutt that Harris had almost put a bullet in not twenty minutes ago. It was lifeless with viscera congealing from a large, jagged wound at the side of its neck. Harris' slug would have been more humane.

The shock of it sent Flynn back on his ass. His flashlight dropped and he discovered himself fumbling in darkness, Harris' light suddenly absent.

"Harris!" he shouted towards the opening of the bridge. Nothing. "Dammit Harris, it's the dog." He called from the darkness, straining his eyes to adjust but just as they did Harris' light returned, briefly blinding him in its harsh glare. "Harris, it's the dog! The son of a bitch killed the damn dog. He's got to be close!"

He held his arm outstretched to shield his eyes, but the beam of light disappeared around the side of the bridge.

"Do you see him?" Flynn picked up his flashlight and ran out in pursuit. "Goddammit, Harris, answer me!"

He burst through the gaping mouth of the covered bridge, but Harris was nowhere to be seen.

He scanned the area with his light, shouting in a whisper.

"Harris? Harris!"

To his left, he heard a splash and he rushed to the side of the bridge, where his beam caught ripples in the water.

He braced himself to side-step down the embankment, but as he tried to shift his stance he tripped. Stumbling downward, his face splashed into the muddy shoreline.

He wanted to lie there, defeated, face down in the muck. Instead, he hauled himself up because he realized that not only was he prone and vulnerable but that Harris hadn't called back. One hand wiped the muck from his face while the other scanned his immediate vicinity for his flashlight. He was going to have to get a goddamned string for that thing. Once he regained it and as he pulled himself up, he pointed it back to see what obstruction had caused his fall, and he was met by a grisly sight.

There, staring back at him from the riverbed was half of the face of Deputy George Harris. Like when he saw the dog, the shock sent him stumbling back, this time into the water, but instead of falling straight in he landed on the rest of his temporary partner's body.

He leapt up and watched the remains rhythmically bob as the shallow water calmed, but heard splashing continue. He looked across the brook to see the assailant climbing up the embankment on the opposite side.

The Willow Woods Wolf Man, who in less than a month would be finally captured and revealed to be Rodney Allan Barrett, stared back at Flynn with Harris' flashlight pointed up from his chin exaggerating the maniacal grin on his blood-splattered face.

He clicked off the stolen flashlight and disappeared into the darkness of the Willow Woods.

CHAPTER TWO

With only two exceptions, there was a smattering of apprehensive applause from the class, the most apprehensive of which came from Ms. Vincent, the sixth-grade teacher at Granville Middle School.

"That was…" she looked for a word that would be more appropriate than the ghastly story the twelve-year-old in the Grim Reaper costume had just told her class of shocked pupils. "…that was very *afflictive.*" She bolstered the criticism with a wide smile, hoping the child wouldn't know the word.

This particular child did know the word and bounded back to her desk, frowning through the white greasepaint covering her face.

Dracula was waiting with an impressed look on her face as Grim Reaper plopped next to her.

"That was awesome!" she congratulated.

"Not 'characterized by or causing pain, distress, or grief?'" Grim Reaper replied, her braces causing a slight lisp around 'dithtreth'.

"Huh?" Dracula's face dropped from excited to confused on a dime, which often happened when talking to Grim Reaper.

"It's the definition of 'afflictive.' Ms. Vincent didn't think I'd know what it meant." The Grim Reaper slumped as she looked at the teacher. "She didn't like the story."

"She made it sound like a compliment." Hobo leaned forward from the desk behind Grim Reaper to join the conversation. "She probably liked it but thought it was too gruesome for a bunch of grade school kids and didn't want to encourage you."

"Too gruesome?" Grim Reaper shot back, offended by the premise that her story was anything but accurate. "We live in Granville, a town known for a series of ghastly axe murders, and she asked for stories about the town's history around Halloween. She can't possibly be upset by a story about ghastly axe murder."

"She probably wanted something about how they watered everything down in the 80s and started the Jack-o'-Lantern Festival," Dracula said.

"Ugh. I couldn't stand to be so pedestrian." Grim Reaper, whose costume was more specifically "Death from Bergman's *The Seventh Seal*," sat disappointed, fidgeting with the chess piece she had stashed in the pocket of the robe, the detail to really sell her identity.

Hobo suddenly looked even more defeated as she was called to the front of the class for her story.

CHAPTER THREE

In 1985 the town of Granville decided it was finally time to embrace what made them special, Halloween.

There had been a bunch of murders about forty years earlier, then there were a few more in the 50s, so people in the town had pretty much decided to ignore the holiday even though it was sort of their claim to fame.

Each October the cops in town had to run a bunch of young people away who had come to Granville to spend Halloween around the Marsters' house, which is this super creepy, old place out by the abandoned asylum where the murders that happened in the 50s happened. Anyway, eventually, someone with the town council or the chamber of commerce saw that a lot of other places had started holding harvest festivals or berry festivals or a festival celebrating whatever the town was famous for, and they decided that instead of running these young people out of town that they should start charging them two dollars for hotdogs.

They figured it was a bit gruesome to call it "Axe Murder Fest" or something like that, so they decided to make it a "Jack-o'-Lantern Festival" and made this big pumpkin carving contest the main event of the whole thing.

The first year was a really big success. In fact, while they didn't have a costume contest as part of the schedule, a whole lot of the people who came here just showed up in costume and several of the local businesses all chipped in prizes and made an unofficial one happen. According to the *Granville Gazette*, the grand prize that year went to a guy who dressed up as June Marsters, even with a big fake axe sticking out of his head. After that, the town wanted more control over the contest so they could downplay all the axe murder stuff and not have someone dressed like the thing they didn't really want to bring attention to as the big winner, so the costume contest was taken over and has become significantly more lame in the time since. Last year someone dressed as one of those little Tic-Tac-looking Minion guys won in a store-bought costume, which is stupid.

In the three and a half decades since, the Granville Jack-o'-Lantern Festival has actually become sort of cool, despite how corporate the costume contest has gotten. It brings thousands of people to town every year, so we get to see really cool underground horror movies play at the Popular Theatre, and we get a whole bunch of Halloween stores here that normally we would need to be a bigger town to have.

I've even heard that they're talking about having Tom Savini and Rick

Baker come to judge the costume contest next year when things go back to full capacity, which is why I'm conserving my energy and keeping things simple with this cool, old-school hobo costume this year.

In summary, the Jack-o'-Lantern Festival started kind of lame but has turned into something kind of cool.

CHAPTER FOUR

Grim Reaper felt terrible as Hobo made her way back down to her desk.

"I'm so sorry! I had no idea that's what you wrote about!"

Hobo shrugged apathetically as Ms. Vincent gushed her approval at the much more palatable story. Sure, it might not have been the best-written report on the town's Halloween history, but it was the one she was hoping more of the students would write.

The teacher scanned her class list and looked around the room, taking a quick inventory of who had presented and who she could fit in before the class ended and the costumed children in her charge scattered out into the magic of a late October sunset that seemed to start as soon as the school bell rings.

She saw Dracula's face beaming back at her, stark white with face paint and gripping a set of plastic fangs through a huge smile, her fists shaking as she excitedly held her report at the ready.

No. There's no way that Carrie Vincent could put the class through another report like Grim Reaper's. Dracula, a tried and true horror movie-loving "monster kid," was even more of a fiend for the grisly details of the town's sordid past and much more likely to bring a decidedly R-Rated story before her not quite PG-13 class.

The thing that Ms. Vincent didn't know when she called on Mark Jerrett, the kid in the back row who had dressed as Mark Jerrett for Halloween, was that Mark had put about the same amount of effort into his report as he had in his costume; he hadn't done it and had actually worked out a deal with Grim Reaper to present the sequel to her story on the Willow Woods Wolf Man, providing a conclusion to her harrowing tale of terror…

CHAPTER FIVE

A full moon on Halloween is shockingly rare despite how easy it is to conjure the image of ghosts and witches flying around dilapidated haunted houses on black and orange cardstock issued by Beistle. In fact, the actual full moon, and not just the especially gibbous nights on either side of it, only falls on October 31 about once every seventy years and, thanks to the four-week lunar cycle, is certainly the second full moon of the month, a blue moon.

The blue moon of October 1944 marked the end of the longest four weeks of Walton Flynn's life. Each night as he closed his eyes, he relived the events that culminated in the death of his temporary partner at the hands of the Willow Woods Wolf Man.

The scene played out in slow motion giving him an excruciating amount of time to second guess every move and decision he had made on that fateful night, punishing himself with details of what he could have done differently, what he should have done differently. But every time he thought it through, no matter what changes or measures were taken, Deputy George Harris ended up dead; a body floating in the creek behind Flynn while the dead man's eyes stared out from the decapitated head resting on the shore.

But alas, there wasn't time for Flynn to dwell on Harris' death because of the other event that night; the crazed lunatic known as the Wolf Man had gotten away and was still roaming the countryside in the moonlight.

In the weeks between that first moon and now, Flynn had been given time off, but he came back before it was up. He wanted to help catch the son of a bitch. Plus, there was a deadline now. A hard one.

The community had lived in fear for over two years and now the pattern of the killer—the same killer who taunted Flynn from across the brook as he had literally stumbled over Harris' body—had fallen in sync with Halloween. If they didn't catch the bastard tonight the sheriff's office would be forced to cancel the town's celebrations and enforce a hard curfew that would make trick-or-treating impossible for the children of the area.

He didn't want that to happen. He wanted to take this lunatic down. He owed it to the people who trusted him and the other law enforcement in the region. He owed it to Harris' wife and daughter.

"No one will judge you if you don't do this, Walt." Sheriff McGrady said putting a hand on his shoulder. "We all know what you've been through."

"Then you know why I've got to go out there tonight," Flynn replied. There was a determination in his words that let the sheriff know the issue was resolved. The consoling hand patted Flynn's shoulder.

"You're a good man, Walt. Good luck out there."

Sherry Johnson and Clem Rowland were driving back from Hollow's Cove in the jalopy that Clem's year of working at Patterson's auto shop had secured him. It had been a very conscious decision to take the job at Patterson's. Clem reasoned that while Patterson's paid him two cents less an hour than being a soda jerk at Vincent's drug store, the knowledge he'd accrue about cars would mean that he could get away with buying an older model for cheaper and fixing it up himself. It had paid off and he managed to pick up a twelve-year-old Ford De Luxe for a song and was slowly picking away at it.

The couple had tried to tell themselves that getting out of Granville for a night was because of the impending threat of the Wolf Man. That the looming danger of the killer was forcing them to seek refuge in the neighbouring town, but really their sojourn was because the bartender at The Ten Dollar Bill, the cleverly named roadhouse on the corner of Alexander Road and Hamilton Lane, didn't know that they were still high school seniors.

It was a trip they had made frequently through the summer, but this was the first time since the school year had begun. They were disappointed to discover that Hollow's Cove shared the sombre tone of Granville in the wake of George Harris' death. The local lawman had been on loan to their hometown to aid with the manhunt when he was viciously murdered just weeks before. What had served as their sanctuary had now been taken from them as well. Another victim of the Willow Woods Wolf Man.

The full moon cast a blue glow over the two lanes of blacktop that stretched out ahead of them, providing much-needed assistance to the dim yellow emitting from the Ford's headlights as it rumbled along.

Sherry and Clem had sat in silence for the drive. The disappointment of their inability to escape the gloom had drained the energy from a night out they had been anticipating for weeks. It was finally Sherry who spoke. She had seen the mile marker and realized they were coming up to the turn-off for Blythe Lake.

"The lake is just ahead."

Clem gulped when she said it. They had been going steady since May, and he had made suggestions of going to the lake over the summer, but they were always contorted by Sherry into trips with a group of friends, usually Cynthia Martin and Nick Rodgers. But now she seemed to be suggesting a trip, and she was suggesting it while they were alone at night.

For a moment Clem thought of the Wolf Man. The purported purpose of this trip was to get out of town because there was a deranged lunatic on the loose. Was it really a good idea for them to go off to a secluded lake in the middle of the night?

"It's a warm night for October, we could go for a swim," Sherry suggested and rubbed his leg. Immediately the logic and reason rushed out of Clem's brain along with every ounce of blood.

"I—I don't have my suit." He gulped again.

"Neither do I," answered Sherry. He whipped his head to her. She smiled a confirmation and the sides of his lips started to curl as he smacked his suddenly dry mouth.

He turned back to the road, adjusting and tightening his grip on the steering wheel as he pressed down on the accelerator, emboldened to get to the lake before Sherry changed her mind.

Walton Flynn cautiously eyed Deputy Gary Steevers. It was not from any distrust in Steevers, they had come up through the sheriff's office together and spent the summer taking turns hosting barbeques. He knew Gary and liked the man. His distrust was in himself. He hadn't been on patrol since the last man he was paired up with was brutally killed by the subject of their manhunt and the guilt he felt made him nervous for Gary. He blamed himself for what happened to George Harris, and now was feeling anxious about supporting Steevers, who he assumed drew the short straw to wind up with him.

Gary was a good cop and an even better man. He astutely picked up on Flynn's self-doubt and tried to deflate the tension.

"How're you feeling being back out, Walt?"

Flynn shrugged.

"I just want to get this bastard." He asserted.

At the lake, Clem skidded to a stop and threw the jalopy into park. He turned to Sherry, who flashed a coy smile. He leaned in to kiss her, but she was already hopping out of the car and moving toward the water, giggling.

Once she was in the car's headlights, she looked over her shoulder and locked eyes with him as she began to unbutton her cardigan.

Clem leapt from the driver's seat, kicking off his shoes as he pulled his Granville High School letterman sweater, which he had gotten for football and track, over his head before stumbling and falling to the dirt. He followed the sound of Sherry's giggles as he tried to pry his head out, but as soon as he got out of his sweater, her cardigan landed on his face blinding him again. He shook it off and followed the trail of clothes to the water, where she was gingerly creeping into the lake.

He took a deep breath as he watched her, glowing blue in the moonlight, slip into the inky pool.

Almost any seventeen-year-old boy would tell you that if you're about to have an axe driven through your temple, watching Sherry Johnson skinny dip in Blythe Lake would probably make a top five last things to see.

Sherry was underwater when it happened, so she didn't hear the crack as the Wolf Man swung his axe with the ferocity and accuracy of a batting champion. In another life, when tragedy hadn't beset his life and he hadn't been driven down such a dark path, Rodney Allan Barrett could've made the Majors.

Sherry also didn't see as Clem stumbled, arms outstretched, around the shoreline, his body instinctively grabbing out at the axe but never finding the handle to remove it. Barrett found the handle. He wrenched it out of Clem with such force that his skull split, and the top of the teenager's head popped off like a bottle cap and the rest of him slumped lifeless in the sand.

No, what Sherry saw next was just an empty beach. She came up for air and to look for Clem, who she expected to have joined her by now. She scanned the beach and didn't see him, but then the lights of the jalopy flashed on.

Knowing that the Wolf Man was on the loose, she panicked and assumed this was Clem trying to signal her back to shore. She quickly freestyled her way back, collecting her clothes as she emerged from the water. But she also noticed Clem's clothes were still lining the beach as well. What had made him rush to get back to the car without even dressing?

She quickened her pace, hastily hauling on items. When she got to the car, she expected to find Clem behind the wheel, but, instead, she found the jalopy empty. In fact, her door was locked and before she could check another door, she saw a glint in the reflection of the window and turned just to see Rodney Allan Barrett swinging his axe, with that big league swing, right into her midsection.

CHAPTER SIX

Carrie Vincent, who sat at her desk rubbing her temples, winced when the harsh shrill of the school bell cut through the story but readily accepted the end of the day.

As the kids all leapt from their seats to run out into the crisp October air, she called out to Mark and Grim Reaper.

"We'll talk about this on Monday, you two." Ms. Vincent said, "Especially the language."

"Sure, Miss! Happy Halloween!" Grim Reaper shouted back, choosing to ignore the pending punishment in light of being released to enjoy Halloween.

Children scattered outside the school. While some thought today was a waste because it was Friday, October 30th, and not Halloween, for Dracula, Grim Reaper, and Hobo it was even better. It meant that the magic of their favourite day of the year would be extended and this year they'd basically get two Halloweens.

As the mousy Cat joined them, their group was complete. The diminutive girl with giant glasses was two grades below the rest of them, but as Hobo's little sister she was conscripted to their makeshift monster squad whether she was ready to consume the bombardment of horror movies, novels, and comics or not.

"So, what's the plan?" Hobo inquired of the group's de facto leader, Dracula.

"Are you guys ready for this?" she asked as the rest of them looked on. "Tomorrow night is the first full moon on Halloween since the night Barrett was arrested in 1944."

"That can't possibly be true," Hobo retorted.

"It is. I looked it up! It's super rare and the last actual full moon on Halloween was in 1944. The closest since was in 1955 when it was like the day before and so it still looked full." Dracula beamed.

"Wasn't 1955 the year that the Marsters were killed?" Hobo asked.

"Yes, it was," an exasperated Grim Reaper confirmed. "All this was just in my story that Mark read. Didn't any of you listen to it?"

Dracula and Hobo looked blankly at her.

"We thought it was Mark's story so we kind of tuned it out," Hobo said.

"So anyway, I thought that in honour of such a momentous occasion we should…" Dracula paused.

"Go trick-or-treating then watch *Hocus Pocus*?" Cat finally chimed in, hoping her suggestion would be considered against whatever fright fest Dracula planned for them. In response, Dracula shot her a glare.

"We should go to the Marsters' house for ghost stories!"

The older two girls grew instantly excited about the idea, while Cat shrank even smaller.

"Yes!" Grim Reaper delighted. "I can finish telling you about the night Barrett was caught!"

"I still think we haven't given my whole trick-or-treating suggestion enough consideration," Cat pleaded.

"We're getting too old for trick-or-treating!" the twelve-year-old Hobo dismissed.

"You are not!" Cat argued. "And even if *you* are, I'm nine!"

"We'll sleep out in the clubhouse tonight for Halloween movies," Dracula said, referring to the detached garage that had been her dad's man cave until her parents' divorce and now served as the base of operations for their consumption of all things spooky. "And just because you're going to do the Marsters' place with us tomorrow, we'll do your movies tonight. *ParaNorman* and *Hocus Pocus* sound good?"

"I haven't said I'm going there with you tomorrow, but yes they do," Cat said as Hobo let out a displeased sigh at her little sister getting her way.

Dracula leaned in and whispered, "Don't worry, *Trick 'r Treat* and *Hatchet* as soon as she falls asleep."

"Original *Halloween* too?" Grim Reaper chimed in.

"For sure," and the trio simultaneously bumped fists to ratify their agreement.

If it wasn't for the modern flatscreen television, you would have sworn that the clubhouse was lifted straight out of an 80s movie. Posters for old monster movies, pages and covers from magazines like *Famous Monsters of Filmland*, *Rue Morgue*, and *Fangoria*, and Halloween masks covered the walls. An old couch and bean bag chairs provided seating, and what was once Dracula's dad's pool table was now lined with miniature figures from gaming campaigns.

All this was very deliberate on Dracula's part. She had carefully curated the space since her mom had allowed her to take it over, and she did everything she could to turn it into the shrine to her spooky obsessions.

It was in this very room that the obsessions had started. Curling up next to her dad on that same old couch for rainy day marathons of horror-inspired cartoons and Disney Halloween flicks like *Mr. Boogedy* and *Halloweentown*. It was fitting that now that he wasn't living there anymore that she'd be left to continue using the space to further her horror education.

The yellow sunlight pouring in through the windows at the top of the garage door landed squarely in the middle of the shaggy rug on the floor where the girls were plotting out their break-in for the next night.

"We'll actually start with some trick-or-treating just so we can be seen doing it," Dracula strategized. "And then we'll have some candy for when we get home, so our parents won't get suspicious."

"And also, because we're supposed to have candy on Halloween," Cat said as she lay on the floor pointed away from the other girls, facing the television where Huey, Dewey, and Louie were getting help from a witch to get revenge on their Uncle Donald.

Hobo rolled her eyes at her childish little sister before aiding with the plan.

"The doors are all boarded up, but some of the boards are loose and can be moved to get around them," she said.

"How do you know that? Have you been there?" Grim Reaper asked.

"No, but when Jenny used to babysit us, I heard her talking about it. She and her friends used to sneak in there to drink."

CHAPTER SEVEN

"Even if it isn't haunted, it should be condemned, and no one would ever be foolish enough to just go there for fun."

That's exactly the sort of thinking that teenagers assume adults have and leads to them breaking into a possibly haunted, definitely condemnable, house to sneak beers and soda bottles filled with an imperceptible amount of booze from a selection of their parents' liquor cabinets. Of course, these are the same teenagers that think that taking an ounce or so from a dozen different bottles so that there won't be a noticeable amount gone from any one bottle and then mixing it with Kool-Aid is a good idea, so that should tell you everything you need to know about their logic.

Jenny Baker and her friends weren't the first group of teens to sneak into the Marsters House for some underage drinking, and they wouldn't be the last, but that's not to say they shouldn't have been.

One thing about their trip to the Marsters' that should be noted is that they didn't go on a full moon or on Halloween. Because Barrett, the Willow Woods Wolf Man, was known to kill on full moons and his most famous crimes happened on Halloween nights, it would make sense, if you're someone who believes in the paranormal, that matching the circumstances around a particular haunting would make it more likely to occur. Likewise, a bunch of teenagers planning to split a six pack on a random Friday would be less likely to experience any supernatural activity.

So, Jenny and her friends should have been fine when they pried away the loose boards over the door to enjoy light beer amid the broken furniture and dead leaves.

Graffiti covered the walls of the living room, mostly relating to the legends of the house like "THE WOLF MAN LIVES" scrawled above a cartoonish werewolf or the random jack-o'-lanterns. But movie and music references also filled the place going from the faded logos of long forgotten local acts to rallying cries of fanbases for international bands that don't have any reason to know that Granville even exists.

Mon yous, mon us, but no them.

There were five of them. Jenny and her boyfriend, Steve, along with two of his friends and the new girl they were hoping to pair off with one of them to make couples nights more frequent.

The beers got popped open, the soda bottle of whatever booze Steve's dad wouldn't notice was missing was passed around and gulped from, jokes were told, and plans were made. The night was filled with all the things that you do as a teenager without a care in the world.

It was Jenny that first noticed the blood.

They should have realized that they were sitting in the living room, which, according to legend, was the exact spot where Frank Marsters was sitting when an axe was driven into his face. You can add that to the long list of things that should have kept these kids away from that house, but here they were.

"What's the deal with this place, anyway?" Chrissy asked, a recent arrival to town who Jenny was trying to set up with Steve's friend Eddie.

"You haven't heard about the Marsters?" Steve said. When she shook her head Eddie pounced at the opportunity to share the gory details

"It happened years ago," he started. "Right here."

"On a night just like tonight?" Russ, the friend being considered the backup plan in the event Eddie proved unappealing, asked, chuckling.

"No. Not like tonight. It was Halloween, a full moon. This guy…I forget his name…"

"Barrett," Steve added. "Rodney Allan Barrett."

"Right. Barrett." Eddie stood and began performing the story rather than just telling it. "So, this guy Barrett is in the mental hospital right over there." He pulled back the tattered curtains to point through the broken window to the old Granville asylum. "But he escapes on Halloween night and comes to this very house."

"There's so much more to the story than that, y'see…" Eddie said, interrupting Steve.

"That doesn't have to do with this house, Steve. She wants to know about this house," he said before diving back in. "There was a couple here, Frank and June Marsters. There are a whole bunch of stories that people tell that night, and honestly, no one knows exactly what happened except that by the end of Halloween night Frank, June, and Barrett were all dead inside these very walls."

"Barrett killed them and then the cops showed up and put a bullet in his head," Russ concluded, trying to take the wind from Eddie's story.

"Maybe," Eddie returned, "but maybe not. Many people of Granville, including yours truly, believe that's not what happened and that really happened was that…"

Before Eddie could unload his theory on the demise of the Marsters and the Wolf Man, Jenny cut him off.

"Eddie?" Her voice was trembling.

"Yeah?"

"Where did all this supposedly happen?"

"Uh, here in the living room and over in the hallway. Why?"

"So, someone got murdered with an axe where this pool of blood is forming?"

They all jumped back as they saw what Jenny was pointing to. A thick, dark liquid was forming a puddle in the middle of the living room, seemingly from nowhere.

"Jesus Christ!" Eddie exclaimed, quickly dropping his theatrics and letting his genuine reaction break through.

"Let's get the hell out of here!" Steve screamed as he collected the drinks and bolted for the door.

They didn't talk about the Marsters House after that night. Hobo only heard Jenny make plans to go, never hearing about the fallout of the strange occurrence that made her and her friends run from the place and never discuss it again.

If she had heard more, maybe she and her friends wouldn't have made their own plans to break into the abandoned house for their attempt at a memorable night. Maybe they wouldn't have gone in on Halloween, under a full moon.

CHAPTER EIGHT

There's a certain kind of magic that hangs in the air on Halloween as the sun sinks into the horizon and everything around you is cast in its orange glow, making everything feel exactly like it's supposed to as day turns to night. Sunset on that particular day feels like an allegory for the transition from the warm life of summer to the cold death of winter when the veil between this world and the next is at its thinnest. It makes you understand why that cultures around the planet for millennia have held this day in such esteem.

For four young girls amid their own transition from the youthful joy of trick-or-treating to the apathetic cynicism of just hanging around, this

Halloween, not unlike that Halloween that every small town has, would be their personal *that* Halloween. The one that would live on in infamy as the night everything changed.

Dracula and Grim Reaper had discussed heading to the Marsters' house early, making sure they could access it the way they intended, hanging some battery-powered lights, and setting the scene for the others. Dracula also considered setting up some gags around the house to ensure the others had a frightful experience, but, at twelve, she still held out hope that the house would provide all the scares they required without cheapening anything. She still remembered her dad telling her about the night he watched a Halloween special where a team of paranormal investigators did a live ghost hunt where, on camera, an unseen force tugged at the team leader's collar. Her dad swore that he could see the guy's hand move inside his pocket, tugging a string that had been run inside his jacket to make sure that the live hunt was eventful. Her dad told her how that ruined the credibility of the show for him, and he could never watch it again. She didn't want to sully her friends' experience like that, so she decided to just let things play out however they were to play out.

There was no school on a Saturday Halloween to hold them hostage until 3 pm, so the girls reconvened in their clubhouse just after lunch. Their parents, understanding the hold Halloween had over them, even gave each of them money to pop into the diner so they wouldn't have to break up the evening's festivities by something as lame as going home for dinner.

Dracula unfolded a map of Granville over the pool table, a black cross marking their location and a crude jack-o'-lantern roughed in over the Marsters' house.

"OK, so we'll head out of here at 3 o'clock. My mom said there was some sort of announcement in a parents' group online telling people not to start trick-or-treating until then." She began tracing the route with her finger along the map. "We'll hit the subdivision around Flynn Avenue first. Those houses are so packed together we'll be able to get a pile of stuff fast."

"Plus, they're big houses. Rich people," Hobo added. "Rich people give out the full-sized bars."

"Mackenna Morris told me that Mr. Davis gave out cans of soda last year!" Grim Reaper chimed in.

"It sounds like we should bail on this whole 'going to a haunted house' thing and just focus on trick-or-treating in the fancy neighbourhood," Cat said, still pleading her case.

Dracula reined them all back in.

"We should have every house in the subdivision done by 5 o'clock," she stated as she slammed her finger into the map. "Then, it's the diner for supper and we should be out of there and at the Marsters just before dark."

"Oh goody." Cat's sarcasm always felt so strange, the adult jabs coming from such a small child.

CHAPTER NINE

Flynn Avenue served them well. By 5 o'clock, they were able to complete the subdivision and be crammed into their booth at the diner, each with a pillowcase nearly full of cans of soda, full-sized bars, and bags of chips with not a single pack of Smarties, raisins, or a molasses kiss to be found, right on Dracula's schedule.

The four girls ate communally from a large platter of chicken fingers and fries while sucking down chocolate milkshakes, each mentally preparing for the next item on their agenda.

Cat, who still hadn't come around to the plan, tried to distract herself with talk of the haul so far.

"I can't believe Dr. Kelly gave us cans of Coke and full-sized Skittles. I was worried she was going to hand out toothbrushes or something!"

"It's smart business," Grim Reaper replied. "If I was a dentist I'd be trying to rot kids' teeth out too."

"Fair enough," Cat said as she took another gulp of her milkshake, her straw squealing defeat against the bottom of the empty cup.

Dracula was staring out the window in the direction of the Marsters' house, not seeing it above the tree line, only the old Granville Asylum looming beyond it.

"It looks like it'll be full dark in less than an hour. We should get going soon." She collected money from everyone and headed up to pay.

The kids wolfed down the last of their chicken fingers, Hobo smashed a fistful of fries into her mouth, then grabbed their pillowcases of candy and headed out of the diner towards the Marsters' house.

***

They trudged along in a haze of silent, apprehensive excitement. Dracula particularly was caught up in her imagination of how this Halloween was going to be something different than the usual, anti-climactic night of trick-or-treating she had grown accustomed to. Not that she didn't enjoy the haul of candy, just that she spent the time from November 1 to October 30 building up Halloween in her head, conjuring ideas of mythical Halloweens like the ones in the movies she watched and books she read. She hoped beyond hope that by putting herself in not only a haunted house but a house that was haunted because of events that happened on Halloween she was as guaranteed as spooky a night as she was ever going to get.

"So, what happened with Barrett?" Hobo asked in a deliberate effort to break the silence.

"Huh?" Grim Reaper asked.

"Your story, the one Mark was telling, how does it end?"

"Don't you want to wait to hear it at the house?" Grim Reaper replied, hoping to save it for the more atmospheric setting.

"I mean, it didn't happen at the house, did it?" Hobo retorted.

"No," Grim Reaper took stock of their surroundings. They were crossing the intersection of Main Street and Mason Avenue in the old downtown and coming up to the covered bridge.

"It actually happened over there."

"Well, that's perfect!" Hobo exclaimed and grabbed Cat by the arm as she led the group toward the bridge. "Let's go!"

CHAPTER TEN

Walton Flynn didn't know that Rodney Allan Barrett had already claimed two victims that night as he made his patrol in the same area where he was confronted by the madman just twenty-eight days earlier. It would not be until the next morning that Clem and Sherry would be reported as missing, hours again before Clem's jalopy was found abandoned in the Willow Woods not far from the bridge in Granville, and then another day before the search would find what was left of the teenagers at the lake.

Right now, Flynn just knew the task at hand was to find Barrett and stop him at all costs, even though, as far as he was concerned, there had already been too much cost.

"Where do you think we should go?" Steevers asked.

"He got George at the bridge. It's right at the edge of the woods and where he disappeared," Flynn answered. "I'd say it's around there that he'll come back into to town if—or when—he shows up."

"Alright, that makes sense to me."

The lawmen marched along Mason Avenue, the same route Flynn had walked with Harris toward the covered bridge. Flynn saw the dryer and curler set, still in the window at Vincent's drug store, and realized he hadn't thought about it since that night. He might still have time to stash a few dollars away to get it for Gertie for Christmas, even though that felt inconsequential right now.

He looked down the alley between the laundrette and the army recruitment office and chuckled remembering Harris nearly shooting the dog rummaging through the trash, but then he thought of how the night ended for George and the dog, and his laughter came to an abrupt halt.

"Walt!" Steevers called from a block down the street. Flynn jogged up to him. "There's not a breath of wind out here tonight, hey?"

Flynn took stock of the weather for the first time and noted that no, beyond it being unseasonably warm, it was a bright, cloudless night, and, as Steevers had noted, there was not even a breeze.

"No, I guess not."

"Then what's that?" Steevers drew his gun and without raising it gestured with his shoulders across the brook where the leaves on a group of lower trees were rustling.

Flynn's heart sank. He knew it was Barrett.

"It's him."

"I'll wade across the brook, you wait here," Steevers whispered. "We'll cut him off when he crosses the bridge."

Flynn nodded and watched as Steevers stealthily descended the embankment and waded through the water, reaching his chest at its deepest. He emerged on the other side and waited, lying soaking wet on the embankment with his gun readied.

Flynn tucked himself at the side of the bridge, trying to steady his breathing. Flashes of the night Harris was killed raced through his mind, and he remembered he was standing in the exact spot Harris was when Barrett got him and decided he should reposition.

There was an old wooden ladder nailed into the side of the bridge for town workers to use when the roof needed occasional repair. He climbed it and waited on the top of the bridge.

The rustling leaves got closer until Barrett emerged from the trees, dirtier and bloodier than Flynn remembered. With axe in hand, he lurched toward the bridge.

From his vantage point, Flynn could only listen as Barrett's footsteps echoed through the covered bridge, but he could see as Steevers climbed out of the embankment and step out gun drawn.

"Police!" he declared. "Put it down, you sonuvabitch!"

Flynn ran across the roof towards Steevers as a gunshot rang out. It missed and Barrett responded by throwing his axe back at Steevers who ducked clear and fired again.

"He's breaking for it!" Steevers called out, and Flynn ran back to the opposite side of the bridge, while Steevers, apparently a bad shot, kept missing the Wolf Man.

Barrett and Flynn both reached the mouth of the bridge at the same time and Flynn leapt off, tackling the Wolf Man to the ground. Flynn pulled him up by his hair and smashed his head into the ground, then rolled him over and started pummelling him with punches.

Barrett was unconscious by the time Steevers reached them, pulled Flynn off, and cuffed the Willow Woods Wolf Man.

CHAPTER ELEVEN

"Flynn was a hero," Grim Reaper continued. "He finally caught the Wolf Man and saved the town. They didn't even have to cancel Halloween. They had a big party in the street the next night."

"What about Steevers?" asked Hobo.

"They were both given commendations and stuff. I couldn't find much more on Steevers after. I think he moved away after the trial." The kids started walking from the site of Barrett's capture and were back on track towards the Marsters' house.

"That's crazy! He was a hero here. I definitely would have stayed if I was him," Dracula said.

"Flynn stayed. He was sort of a police rock star," Grim Reaper added. "No one even challenged him for sheriff when McGrady retired, and he stayed in the job for years."

"And they just put Barrett in jail?" Cat asked.

"His trial was a circus. He was found to be criminally insane and locked away in the asylum for life."

"So how did he get out?" Cat prodded.

"It was over ten years later. Weirdly enough, it was the next time Halloween had a full moon," Grim Reaper explained as the kids looked east to where the pale full moon was beginning to appear in the night sky. "They thought he was sick or something and were moving him out of his maximum-security cell to the infirmary for treatment."

"What is it with doctors moving serial killers on the anniversary of their big kills?" Dracula asked. "It's how every Halloween sequel starts."

"I don't know, but it seems really dumb," Grim Reaper agreed. "Turns out he was faking. He killed a bunch of guards and busted out during the transfer."

"And he came here," Dracula said, bringing a dramatic flair to their arrival at the Marsters' house.

"He came here," Grim Reaper confirmed.

"And we came here," Cat added, "like a bunch of dummies."

"Oh come on!" Hobo said, rushing up the overgrown path to the front door and starting to pry back one of the boards covering it. "Tonight is going to be epic."

CHAPTER TWELVE

A long time ago there was a house on the outskirts of town. In fact, the only thing around it was the old Granville Asylum for the Criminally Insane.

One Halloween night, Frank and June Marsters were home waiting for trick-or-treaters. Frank was sitting back smoking his pipe and reading the newspaper. He saw an ad saying that they were having a special, late-night Halloween triple feature at the Popular Theatre and thought that maybe he would bring June after they had finished handing out candy.

Down the hall, in the kitchen, June was peeling carrots for dinner. Just then, there was a knock at the door.

"I'll get it!" Frank called from the living room.

June smiled and went back to her carrots as she heard the door open to a chorus of "trick-or-treat!"

After a moment, Frank came into the kitchen.

"It was Howdy Doody and the Lone Ranger," he said, describing the trick-or-treaters as he cozied up behind her and kissed her on the cheek.

Their tender moment was interrupted by the bleating of a radio bulletin.

"Attention all listeners, attention all listeners: Authorities at the Granville Asylum for the Criminally Insane are advising of an escaped and dangerous patient."

June and Frank turned to each other, sharing a panicked look before bringing their gaze out the window to see the Granville Asylum rising from the tree line behind their house.

"Rodney Allan Barrett, known to the public as the Willow Woods Wolf Man."

June's eyes widened at the mention of Barrett's name.

"The axe-wielding Barrett was deemed criminally insane and sentenced to the facility for life following his arrest for the moonlit reign of terror that resulted in the deaths of at least seventeen persons in Willow Woods County with more victims suspected," the tinny announcement continued. "The public is advised that Barrett is considered extremely dangerous. Sheriff Walton Flynn has instituted an immediate curfew. Trick-or-treaters are to return home at once!"

They both knew who Barrett was, everyone in Granville did, and now he was loose, and their house was the closest place to him.

"Lock the doors!" Frank exclaimed, urging June towards the back door as he rushed to the front. "I'll see if I can catch those kids and get them to hold up here for safety!"

June, as instructed, moved to the back door, and turned the deadbolt. She looked out the window at the asylum again and then her attention fell to the axe sticking out of the stump in the backyard. She thought of going out and grabbing it, keeping it with her, safely, but her fear kept her inside.

She slowly moved to the hallway, watching the door Frank had charged out of in hopes of helping the kids, and waited for him to return.

Suddenly, he burst back in through the door, alone, latching it behind him.

"I couldn't find them," he told her as he went into the living room and began closing the curtains. "They're either going to be gone to the Folletts' or the Richards'. You go call them and make sure they heard the announcement and keep the kids safe if they show up."

But before June could go to the phone, they heard a crash come from the basement that stopped them both in their tracks.

"Go upstairs and hide," Frank said, changing the plan.

"What about you?" June asked.

"I'm going to barricade the basement door and call the police," he said, but June was frozen. "Go!"

She took off upstairs as Frank dragged the telephone table in front of the basement door, wedging it there between the door and the opposite wall.

As she ran into the bedroom, the lights in the house flicked off and June let out a yelp, the sudden darkness only adding to her fear. She looked out the window in the upstairs hall and could see Granville looking peaceful under a big full moon, but she could also see other houses in the distance with their lights on. It seemed it was only their house experiencing this blackout.

She continued to the bedroom and practically dove into the closet, curling into a ball with her arms hugging her knees, and waited.

And she waited.

And waited.

After what felt like an eternity of silence without any update, she emerged from the closet to find Frank.

"Frank!" she called out, as quietly as she could, from the top of the stairs.

Nothing.

She slowly crept down the stairs, with only the moonlight spilling in through the windows to light her way.

"Frank?" she called again, still with no response.

When she got to the living room it was total darkness, the thick curtains still drawn closed. She pulled a pack of matches from her apron pocket and lit one to inspect the room.

The light flickered across the room, creating distorted shadows along the wall as she slowly scanned the room before its glow landed in the corner and was what was left of Frank.

June gasped with horror and dropped her match, plunging her back into darkness.

CHAPTER THIRTEEN

"Bullshit!" Hobo exclaimed.

"You're saying the Wolf Man killed Frank?" Dracula interrupted Cat's telling.

"Yeah?" Cat nodded.

"Nope, June did," Dracula corrected.

"What? No way!"

"That's the way I heard it too," Hobo chimed in. "He was a dick, and she killed him. None of this lovey-dovey shit."

"You're wrong," Grim Reaper said. "I mean, the Wolf Man killed her father! I hardly believe that if her dad died that way she'd be so cavalier with replicating axe murder."

Dracula looked at Grim Reaper with exasperation.

"What?"

"The stories I told earlier. George Harris was June's father. He's the policeman that Barrett killed in 1944!"

"Oh, that's too convenient! It's just cheap storytelling," Hobo said.

"Next you're going to tell us you buy into the *Halloween II* thing where Laurie Strode is Michael Myer's sister," Dracula added with a laugh.

Grim Reaper rolled her eyes. "It was her father! He was the guy partnered with Flynn that Barrett killed by the bridge! If your father was decapitated by an axe murderer, would you really kill someone pretending to be the same axe murderer years later?"

"Maybe," said Hobo.

"Yeah, isn't that basically the plot of *Silent Night, Deadly Night*?" Dracula asked.

"Sure, it is," Cat added, "and that movie is so bad Gene Siskel called out the writer on television and said, 'Michael Hickey you should be ashamed of yourself.'"

The trio looked at Cat, not expecting her to drop obscure 80s slasher facts.

"...I saw it on YouTube."

"OK, we're going to come back to that later," Hobo said before turning back to Grim Reaper. "You're wrong about Harris being June's dad, though."

"I am not. He was her father and Barrett killed him! It would be more like..."

CHAPTER FOURTEEN

In the Marsters' darkened living room June cowered on the floor. A broken, overturned lamp was the only thing between her and the heap of viscera that was, until moments prior, her loving husband, Frank.

Her eyes were locked on the tall, thin man looming above her holding the axe from the backyard in his hands, now covered with Frank's blood.

"Ah, June..." Rodney Allan Barrett rasped, "seeing you cowering like this at the precipice of death, I must say," he raised the axe above his head, "you've got your father's eyes."

June screamed as the axe swung downward.

CHAPTER FIFTEEN

"No. Nope. You're full of shit." Hobo smacked her leg to accent her point.

"Then why did Barrett come here for them?" Grim Reaper asked.

"Because it's the closest frigging house to the asylum!" Hobo pointed out through a gap in the boards covering the window to the decrepit asylum building just beyond a small patch of woods.

"Now who's relying on cheap, convenient storytelling?"

"Oh, come on!" Hobo exclaimed. "You're trying to tell me that after eleven years of being locked away in a mental hospital Barrett had kept track of the daughter of a random policeman he killed and came here out of some sort of twisted attempt to end the family line or something?"

"More or less," Grim Reaper answered.

"That's the dumbest shit I ever heard!" Hobo was unrelenting. "Will you concede that Harris was a random killing? Barrett just killed him because he was there that night?"

"Yes."

"And Harris was inconsequential to Barrett, just one of the, like, seventeen people he murdered?"

"I can support that premise and I'm impressed you used 'inconsequential.'" The dig from Grim Reaper got a glare from Hobo before she continued.

"So then why would he make a point to come after the dead guy's daughter a decade later? Why her over any of the other victims' families?"

"Because it's the closest frigging house to the asylum?" Grim Reaper answered, quoting Hobo.

"Jesus Christ!" Hobo exclaimed while Dracula, tired of the bickering, was ready to chime in with her own story.

"You guys," she sat, eyes closed and rubbing her temples, subconsciously mirroring their teacher, Ms. Vincent's body language from the previous afternoon. "The story is that Frank was a real bastard..."

CHAPTER SIXTEEN

The afternoon sun of October 31, 1955, cast long shadows across the lawn of the two-story house, which loomed in a paradox of care and contempt. While the windows were clean and featured fresh dressing, the peeling paint and broken shutters demanded "go away" and the long, dying grass in the yard seemed like a deliberate choice to reinforce that sentiment.

In fact, if it weren't for the jack-o'-lantern that sat on the front step, you would probably assume that the Marsters' house was abandoned. But there it did sit, with dead leaves blowing across its face, its triangle eyes squinting against the sunset.

Inside, Frank Marsters sat back in his easy chair. It was in the middle of the room pointing at the black and white floor model television. Frank was alone in the living room, which was good because if there had been anyone else they wouldn't be able to see around Frank and his chair anyway. As he drank his beer, he rummaged through the candy his wife had intended for trick-or-treaters while watching Bela Lugosi in the old horror movie they were running on television as a celebration of the holiday.

Down the narrow hallway, June Marsters was in the kitchen, just as Frank believed she should be. A picture of 50s housewife grace, she stood over the sink scrubbing dishes in heels with a frilled flowered apron covering her crinoline dress. She didn't even take off her rubber glove as she reached for a cigarette from the ashtray next to the sink and raised the Lucky Strike to her delicate face, wiping her hair back as a tear rolled out of a fresh black eye.

She stood there, reconsidering all the choices she had made that got her here, with him, until a breaking news bulletin cut through the novelty Halloween song about the House of Frankenstein and stole her attention.

"Attention all listeners, attention all listeners: Authorities at the Granville Asylum are advising the public of an escaped and dangerous patient" the tinny voice poured from the AM radio. "Rodney Allan Barrett, also known as the Willow Woods Wolf Man, was deemed criminally insane and sentenced to life imprisonment following his arrest for the axe-wielding reign of terror that resulted in the deaths of seventeen persons from Willow Woods County with more victims suspected."

June raised her gloved hand to her mouth before turning her focus down the hall to where Frank let out indecipherable curses at the television.

"The public is advised that he is extremely dangerous."

Slowly, she turned back to the sink, looking through the kitchen window to where the Granville Asylum dominated the horizon. Then, her gaze drifted down to her backyard where an old, weathered axe stuck out from a large stump.

"Sheriff Walton Flynn has instituted an immediate curfew. Trick-or-Treaters are to return home at once."

June's hand moved to the bruise forming around her freshly wounded eye. She winced at the pain, but then her face turned from fearful to determined.

CHAPTER SEVENTEEN

"So, she just kills him in revenge for hitting her?" Cat, who had been silently watching the argument on which version of the story was more accurate, asked.

"Yeah!" Hobo enthusiastically replied in support of Dracula's tale. "And then she staged it to look like Barrett did it, but the real Barrett showed up and killed her. It's classic!"

"That isn't classic, it's cliché," Grim Reaper disagreed.

"Oh, so you won't get behind a good, ol' fashioned story of vengeance?" Dracula chirped, defensively.

"But she's right!" Cat added. "You called out my story for being too sweet or whatever, but yours is a total rip-off!"

"It is a bit like 'And All Through the House.'" Said Grim Reaper.

"No way!" Said Dracula, "In 'And All Through the House' she killed him because she was having an affair. This is a completely different motivation!"

"Yeah, she's defending herself here," Hobo pointed out. "She's way more well-rounded!"

"Not really." Cat pushed up the massive glasses sliding down her nose. "You just have her actions motivated by the man in your story. She still doesn't have any agency or depth."

"Him being a bad person doesn't make her well-rounded," Grim Reaper added to Cat's point before turning directly to Dracula. "It's just bad writing."

"OK, I am not going to be taking any criticism from 'precipice of death' over here!"

Dracula was cut off by the sound of radio static cutting through the house before being replaced by the sounds of an old novelty Halloween song.

Bum Bum Bum Bum Buuuuhhhh duhduhduhduh. All you kids gather 'round, 'cause in this house something special is going down!

The kids looked around and sourced the sound coming from the kitchen. They slowly climbed to their feet and moved toward the hallway as the song was interrupted by a tinny-voiced radio bulletin.

"Attention all listeners, attention...Granville Asylum for the Criminally Insane is advising...the Willow Woods Wolf Man...the moonlit reign of terror..." The kids' eyes were locked down the dark hallway toward the kitchen and didn't notice the glow of the TV that appeared in the living room behind them.

"More victims suspected..." the announcer's voice continued through the static as Frank Marsters appeared behind the girls, unnoticed, knocking back a can of Quittin' Time beer while watching the television. "Barrett is considered extremely dangerous...Trick-or-treaters are to return home at once."

"Alright then," Cat said as the sounds from the radio fell to silence, "let's return home at once."

She began to move to the door, but Dracula grabbed her arm, holding her in place.

The girls watched the end of the hallway for a tense moment until the click-clack of high-heeled shoes began to echo through the house. They shuddered at each click and each clack until the apparition of June Marsters appeared around the corner brandishing the axe from her backyard in her gloved hands.

She strode smoothly down the hall to the living room without noticing the girls, who dove back into the dining room when she reached them. They saw Frank sitting in the chair in the living room, but Frank didn't see June behind him as she drew back the axe and, after a deep breath, swung it down into the top of his skull.

Grim Reaper, Hobo, and Cat all clung to each other, trying to shield their faces from the horror, but Dracula couldn't look away. She barely managed to keep a smile from forming as she watched the haunting unfold in front of her.

She watched as the ghost of Frank instinctively tried to pull itself up from the chair, but its diminishing motor skills turned the action into a flailing that knocked over the table of beer and candy next to his armchair to the floor.

She watched the ghost of June pull the axe from the Frank-thing only to drive it back into its shoulder, and then repeat that action until Frank's body stopped trying to fight.

She watched the ghost of June pull out the axe and slam it back in one more time for good measure.

When the ghost was done and stepped back from her handiwork, Dracula lead her friends who were still hiding their eyes from the gore to the hallway, following June.

***

As June saw it, the blood dripping from the head of the axe was ruining her clean floors, but she didn't care. This time the floors not being up to standard wouldn't result in a beating, so the pool that started to form as the axe was laid beside the telephone table was of no concern.

She peeled off a rubber glove and was surprised by the elegant hand beneath. As she eyed her recently manicured nails, she couldn't help but believe that the bloodstained gloves were better at complimenting her lipstick.

Lifting the receiver to her ear, June tensed her entire body, forced herself into shallow breaths, and once she had herself adequately worked up, she dialled.

"You've got to come quick!" she blurted as soon as the call was answered. "It's my husband! I've just come home and he's been murdered! I think it was that Barrett man from the news! It's horrifying! You must come quick!"

The kids watched as she replied to the operator's questions.

"My name is June Marsters. Yes. No, I don't think so."

She told them the address, pleaded for them to hurry, and hung up, then stared into the framed wedding photo of her and Frank that hung above the telephone table. As her eyes shifted from the photo to her reflection in the glass, she adjusted her hair, put her glove back on, and smashed the photograph with the axe. Then she went back to the living room.

The kids had watched all of this unfold and dove out of the way as June carried the axe past them. They reformed on the other side of the doorway to the living room, an inversion of how they had stared down the hallway. In the room, June stepped around the chair, standing between Frank and the television, something she would never have dared while he was alive.

The mangled corpse was still facing the television even though his eyes were pointing at the chesterfield against the far wall and crushed to a gooey mess. Blood pooled from his wounds to the floor and ran into the candy dish, which was still surrounded by wax-paper wrappers.

June raised the axe again and the kids braced for more violence, but instead of inflicting more damage on the corpse, she brought it down hard through the coffee table. She then kicked over the pedestal ashtray next to Frank's chair sending cigarette butts and ash across the rug. She turned to the window and readied herself to swing the axe through, but stopped, plunged the axe into the adjacent wall, and left the room.

She proceeded down the hall to the kitchen where she opened the basement door, grabbed Frank's raincoat, and made her way back to the living room. The strength she apparently used to force the axe into the wall surprised her as she fought to remove it. How much harder had she swung at Frank? After a brief struggle it came free, and she headed outside. After all, the window shouldn't be broken from the inside.

The kids watched all this in confusion, dodging the June ghost while not sure exactly what she was doing. They didn't see her trash her nicely maintained home, staging the fake attack by the Wolf Man, they watched her inflict damage that had been in their version of the Marsters' house for the last sixty-five years.

As June opened the door, the wind immediately blew the hood of the raincoat back off her head forcing her to juggle the still bloody axe as she tried to pull the hood back up.

The costumed girls didn't understand. That door was boarded over when they'd pried back a plank to crawl in and there was no wind tonight.

Outside, in 1955, another strong gust pushed the hood down over June's face, causing her to trip and fall to the ground in front of the window. The wind, the hood, and her purposefulness all occupied her focus, so much so that she failed to notice that the basement window was open, and a dark figure was moving up the stairs to the main floor of the house.

Inside, in 2020, the girls were pinned against the hallway wall waiting for whatever June was going to do next when they heard the basement door creak open.

They held their breath as a mud-caked and bloody slip-on shoe appeared around the corner at the end of white pantleg, followed by the straps of a torn straitjacket hanging from underneath the tiny Eisenhauer jacket, stolen from the guard killed during his escape and much too small for the lanky man who the girls knew to be, or have been, Rodney Allan Barrett, the Willow Woods Wolf Man.

His wild eyes and yellow teeth practically glowed through the layers of hair, dirt, and grime that obscured the rest of his face.

They pressed themselves even tighter to the wall trying to create as much distance between themselves and the ghostly Wolf Man as possible. All, strangely enough, except Cat. The smallest of the girls, who had been the most apprehensive and frightened until now, found herself inexplicably fascinated by the apparition and reached out a tiny hand to test the plane. Thankfully, it wafted through a suddenly non-corporeal arm leaving a trail of ectoplasmic particles as it passed through.

But Barrett stopped in his tracks and quickly threw his head back, looking over his shoulder. He didn't see the four young girls cowering against the wall, he just saw the wall, the telephone table, and the recently smashed wedding photo.

Then the sound of glass smashing stole his attention back and he slowly made his way into the living room.

As soon as he was clear, the girls broke for the front door but stopped in their tracks as June flung it open and stepped back into the house. She propped the axe up on the porch and headed down the hallway.

Hobo rushed to make her escape through the door, but it was seized and she struggled with the knob.

"What are you doing?" Dracula whisper-shouted. "We've got to get out of here!"

"It's locked or something," Hobo quietly shouted back.

"It was just open!" Dracula dramatically flung her arms apart and knocked the axe over.

Not expecting to be able to touch the object from the haunting, the girls all froze. So did June, who turned and looked at the axe she heard topple over lying on the hall floor.

She didn't know why the axe fell, but she was distracted and dismissed it. While outside, she immediately realized that breaking the living room window was a mistake – no one would use it to get into the house and if they had it would have probably gotten Frank up from his chair. Shit. This was going to be a hole in her story. Still, there was an axe murderer on the loose, details could be missed. She'd be fine.

She moved back to the kitchen where she failed to notice that the basement door, which she had left partially open, was now closed and she had to open it to hang the raincoat back up. She closed the door then moved to the sink where she pulled a matchbox from the pocket of her apron and lit another cigarette.

In the hall, Grim Reaper was wrapping her head around Dracula knocking the axe over.

"Of course!" she finally exclaimed.

"What?" Cat asked.

"Spectral transcendentalism!" Grim Reaper proudly stated.

Dracula looked at her with bewildered disgust.

"I can't even with you sometimes."

"What the hell is 'spectral...'" Hobo began to ask, but Grim Reaper cut her off.

"We can, like, interact with them."

"But when I reached out?" Cat started.

"He turned! He felt something!"

"I don't understand," Dracula said. "If her hand went through him how could I knock the axe over?"

"I'm not sure, this seems like a residual haunting. I guess the residue..." Grim Reaper looked for the words, "...is getting *thicker*?"

"Gross," was all Cat could muster.

Hobo, getting impatient with her friends, began to head toward the kitchen in the back of the house.

"You guys, maybe this is a conversation for when we're not in a FRIGGING HAUNTED HOUSE."

"Where are you going?" Cat asked.

"There's a back door!" Hobo exclaimed.

"But June is down there!" Dracula said.

"I don't care!" But as she said it, Rodney Allan Barrett emerged from the living room where he had been appreciating June's axe-wielding skills. He stepped into the hall looking toward June in the kitchen, and, as he did, the kids all dove out of his way, landing on the staircase. Barrett, sensing the movement looked back to them but only saw the axe lying on the floor.

Unaware that the madman was in her house and now in possession of his weapon of choice, June stood at the sink slowly dragging on her cigarette. It was then that everything she had done tonight truly hit her and she began to weep.

Sure, Frank had been a son of a bitch who beat her and treated her like shit, but she had taken an axe and reduced him to a puddle of slop in the middle of the living room. She frantically pulled off the rubber gloves and began rinsing the blood in the sink. Her fresh tears mixed with Frank's blood as the liquid circled the drain.

Barrett watched June's shoulders shaking as she cried at the sink from the threshold of the kitchen, confused by her emotion. Rather than end her right then and there, he decided to have some fun, so he made his way back into the basement.

June managed to regain her composure. The police would be there soon, and she wasn't done setting her scene. She snuffed out the cigarette but didn't wipe her tears. She'd need them.

Leaving the kitchen, where the basement door was open again, she headed to the front porch to grab Frank's boots. So far, all the bloody footprints around the house were from her high heels and that didn't really help the narrative she was trying to sell.

"So does this spectral transmission thing mean they can touch us?" Dracula whispered to Grim Reaper as June moved down the hall.

"Transcendentalism."

"Whatever! Can the axe murderers murder us with axes?"

"I don't..." Grim Reaper stopped, "...maybe?"

Dracula gulped and turned back to watch June as she kicked off her heels and leaned on the archway into the living room and began to haul on Frank's boots. It was only when she looked down that she realized the axe wasn't on the floor where it had fallen.

She scrambled to the living room. Maybe she had left it there? Her eyes scanned the room just as a burst of wind blew through the broken window and threw the curtain over the bloody body that had recently been Frank, bringing her attention to the fresh footprints that circled the chair. Following them with her eyes, she watched as they left the room and paused to leave a thicker print where the axe had been. Before June had time to process any more than that, the house went black.

She gasped before remembering her matches. She fumbled in her pockets and eventually found the small box. Lighting one, she used it to scan her surroundings before her panicked motions waved it out.

With shaking hands, she managed to get another one lit and tried to get her bearings in the hallway, but it burned out too quickly and she had to light a third.

Outside she could hear a car pulling over the gravel driveway to accompany the ribbons of red and blue light that began to strobe through the house. Footsteps bounded up over the stairs, then Sheriff Flynn and his deputy burst through the doorway, stealing her attention so that she didn't see the face from the darkness blow out the match extended from her fingers.

"Get down!" Flynn shouted with his pistol drawn and flashlight blinding June. "June, I said get down!"

She dove to the ground, revealing the ghastly presence of Barrett with his maniacal grin and with June's axe in his hands, raised high above his head.

"Put it down, you sonuvabitch!" Flynn exclaimed.

The only sound louder than June's screams were the gunshots.

Between the sheriff and his deputy, five rounds were unloaded into Barrett's chest. The Wolf Man's feet were stable as the bullets forced his upper body to flail. With blood spilling out of his still smiling face he locked eyes with Flynn before bringing the axe down into June with a mushy crunch, immediately silencing her screams.

The deputy urged at the sight and was throwing up as Flynn fired a final round between Barrett's eyes, putting him down for good.

Flynn moved cautiously to inspect the bodies. The deputy did the same after wiping a stray dribble of vomit from his chin.

The sheriff kneeled at June's.

"Jesus, George, I'm sorry," he whispered. "I'm so sorry I couldn't protect her."

Grim Reaper's eyes lit up and she smacked Dracula to make sure her skeptical friend heard the confirmation of her hypothesis.

Cat, once again feeling oddly compelled despite her fears, pulled her flashlight from her candy bag, and pointed its light towards the scene which vanished in the beam.

"Is that all you had to do this whole time?" Hobo asked.

Cat nervously shrugged as Dracula pushed her way through them to the place where June's body had been. She crouched to the floor and ran her fingers over a darkened chip in the hardwood.

"It all really happened," she whispered. "It really happened right here."

"What. The. Shit," Hobo said as she climbed down the stairs to join Dracula.

"I thought it was just a legend?" Cat asked, scanning her friends' reactions.

"Wait." Grim Reaper said. "None of you believed it?"

They shook their heads.

"Then why the hell did we come here!" she shouted.

"It's a creepy old house on Halloween!" Dracula replied, matching her energy.

Before Grim Reaper could respond the radio burst back on.

Bum Bum Bum Bum Buuuuhhhh duhduhduhduh.

The kids swivelled toward the kitchen but suddenly the room was drowned in the light of television static, and they turned to the living room where the window smashed open, and wind billowed through the house.

They started to break for the door but were blocked by Sheriff Flynn and his deputy with their guns drawn.

"Put it down, you sonuvabitch!"

The girls looked back to see Rodney Allan Barrett, the Willow Woods Wolf Man, whose moonlit reign of terror in 1944, 1955, and now, 2020 resulted in the deaths of at least twenty-two people, charging down the hall, axe ready.

AFTER DARK VAPOURS

BRAD DUNNE

PROLOGUE (1967)

The pain reached down into Kate's stomach and pressed against her spine, twisting it. The doctor kept telling her to *push*, but she was afraid that if she did, her back might snap, and the baby would slip into her shattered tailbone and get mangled. Nothing in her life had prepared her for the pressure she was feeling in her lower back and abdomen. Tiny evil hands squeezed her like they were trying to wring the last bit of toothpaste from a tube.

"Push!" the doctor ordered again.

If he said it one more time, she was going to kill him, she knew it.

Time was without form; she no longer had any sense of how long these contractions had been going on. A terrifying thought formed in her mind: was this agony ever going to stop? Had she irreparably damaged something inside her, and now was going to feel like this for the rest of her life? Despite the mind-bending pain, she managed to somewhat convince herself that this was all totally illogical, just the usual neurotic anxiety she'd inherited from her mother.

"You have to start pushing, love," the nurse said.

Kate now had an incredible urge to go to the bathroom. Of all the indignities she was currently experiencing, splayed out for all these people to see her abominable vagina, she couldn't shit herself too.

"I have to go to the washroom," she said. "After that, I'll push."

"Sorry, love," the nurse said. "Can't do that. The baby might fall out into the toilet."

"Jesus Christ!" Kate yelled.

"Once you start pushing, the pain will subside," the doctor said.

Kate couldn't believe that rushing deeper into the pain would somehow lessen it. But she didn't really have any other choice, so she trusted the doctor and pushed. The pain shifted from her lower back, which at first was a relief until it felt like her vagina was being shredded by long, sharp claws.

"Your nails hurt!" she yelled at the doctor. "Stop it!"

"I'm not touching you," he said.

That was impossible. She was sure that red-hot pincers were spreading her vagina apart. However, with each push, the pressure decreased.

And the ring of fire in her vagina was actually preferable to her spine being crushed, so she kept pushing.

"The head is almost out," the doctor announced. "You're almost there."

She could feel the dimensions of the fireball. Reaching deep into a reserve of strength she didn't know she had, she pushed. She released a larynx-busting howl and pushed with every fibre of her body.

"Okay, the head is out," the doctor said. "A few more and we're done."

She kept at it. Each push brought a little more relief. The pain was subsiding. She couldn't believe it. A strange sort of ecstasy took over. She allowed herself to start feeling joy, something she hadn't felt since she first discovered that she was pregnant.

"The baby is out," the doctor said. "Just one more push for the placenta."

After the contractions and passing through the ring of fire, this final push was nothing. The pain had stopped. She looked around at this small team of people, their medical gowns soaked in blood -- her blood. One nurse was mopping it up off the floor. They were doing their best to be discrete, but there was nothing that could change the fact that the room was like a murder scene.

A nurse handed her the child: a writhing, purple mass screeching and bawling, covered in an orangey melange of blood and fluids. When Kate had arranged the baby's adoption, the agency had asked if she wanted to hold the baby before they took it away. It was a difficult decision. Kate wasn't sure if she could trust herself not to bash the baby's skull against the wall. However, holding it now, she was grateful to see up close what was responsible for tearing apart not only her body, but her marriage, her life, and her husband's mind -- and perhaps her own, too. Her fears of infanticide were allayed when she realized that, having come out the other side of a seemingly unending labour, she simply did not have the energy to wield a dozen-pound loaf like a hammer. And, looking at this oversized wrinkly plum, she realized that she didn't -- couldn't -- hate it. What was all of this for if it wasn't for love?

"It's a boy," the nurse told her.

Kate suspected as much. Derek was right after all. However, just because he was right, didn't mean he wasn't crazy. He'd began his descent into madness just as soon as she'd told him about the baby. He started disappearing for days at time. Coming home stinking drunk, incoherent. He lost his job at the hospital. Finally, Kate forced him to explain himself. He told her that when the moon was full he transformed into a monster, that he'd been cursed. He'd done something unforgiveable and this was his punishment. That she was carrying a son who would grow up to kill him. He said the only chance he had of surviving was to kill the baby, that maybe then he could stop the curse. He knew this because the moon had told him. He told her he knew how to "terminate the pregnancy." Kate would hear nothing of it. When she refused, he told her he'd kill her with the baby inside.

"How can you say these things?" she pleaded.

"I need my life so that I can save countless others," he replied.

She fled their house on Southside Road to her parents' house in George-town. She contacted the police, but they said they couldn't do anything because Derek hadn't actually hurt her and that it was just his word against hers. They advised she keep away from him if she felt threatened; to get a lawyer, get a divorce.

She stayed with her parents as she tried to get a handle on what her life had become, her stomach expanding as time progressed. One night, Derek called crying. This time she felt sorry for him and didn't hang up.

"Derek," she said. "You need help. You're having a mental break-down."

"You don't understand," he said. "I've done something terrible. This is my punishment. I'm not crazy."

"What did you do?" she asked. "When did this happen?"

"In Labrador," he said. "I killed her. Left her in the woods, to the wolves. They made me one of them. That's how I know. It's their idea of a sick joke. This is their revenge."

"I don't understand. You killed someone?"

He hung up the phone. Kate tried to decipher what he'd said. It seemed to her that he'd potentially murdered someone and the guilt was driving him insane. And who was this "they" he thought was after him? Wolves? Perhaps they were hallucinations, manifestations of his guilt. He was like Orestes being chased by the Furies. After that, her parents changed their phone number and were no longer listed in the phonebook. They pleaded with her to follow the advice of the police and file for a divorce. However, part of her didn't want to abandon him. *In sickness and in health.* She couldn't imagine him hurting someone. He was a doctor, a good doctor. He'd worked up in Cartwright, Labrador with the Grenfell Mission. Perhaps he'd made a mistake with a patient that ended up costing her life and now he'd driven himself mad punishing himself over it. It was all too much to think about with a baby on the way. She hoped that perhaps Derek would come to his senses when his child was born. She held on to that hope, secluded in her parents' house, staying away from anyone.

Then one night, not too long after that phone call, she realized that he wasn't entirely crazy. She was home, and her legs and back were cramping from sitting around for too long. She decided to take a stroll. There was a nice, little walking trail near her house that she liked to frequent. Her parents protested, but she assured them that she wasn't going far, and that she didn't like being treated like a prisoner. It was a clear fall night. The full moon had punched a hole in the night sky, a giant cataract keeping blind watch over the earth below. The walking trail wrapped around Bannerman Park. At the top by Military Road was the Colonial Building, the old seat of Newfoundland Legislation before Confederation. It was Kate's favourite building in St. John's. Whenever she walked by it, she liked to imagine the riot of 1932, when a crowd of ten thousand people protesting the thievery of the then Prime Minister Sir Richard Squires turned violent. They fought with police and smashed the windows, trying to get in to tear the heads off the politicians. It was like a scene from her favourite book, *A Tale of Two Cities* by Charles Dickens. It was fascinating to her to contemplate what it would take to drive normal people to commit acts of such violence. She was startled out of her reverie when she heard something rustle in the bushes behind her. Out crept what appeared to be a very large dog. But then it stood up on its hind legs and rose to the height of man. It arched back and howled. Kate ran out of the trail and into the street. She looked back and saw that the beast had disappeared. She tried to compose herself as she made her way back to her parents' house. She convinced herself that she'd imagined the whole thing, a product of the stress and lack of fresh air --and, of course, her mother's anxiety. A few days later, there was a letter for her. There was no return address, but she recognized Derek's handwriting. She opened it. *Now do you believe me?*

She knew then that she had to do whatever it took to protect the baby.

"We have to take the baby now," the nurse said.

Kate handed it over without hesitation.

He'd better grow up to make something of himself after what she was about to do for him, she thought.

Outside a weak winter sun was rising. How long had it been there? She searched the room for a clock and saw that it was eight in the morning. She came in last night just past midnight. It was impossible to conceptualize this passage of time. She knew that at moments the pain had felt endless, but now, trying to recapture the time span in her mind, it felt like it had passed so quickly. Parts of the labour were already fading from her memory, like trying to recall a dream that had felt so vivid at night but was now dissolving like smoke.

Kate's parents entered the room. Her mother's face was tight, but her eyes betrayed sympathy. Her father, the judge, was consulting his pocket watch, most likely wondering if he was going to be able to make whatever meeting was on his schedule.

"How are you, my dear?" her mother asked.

"I'm fine," Kate said.

"Your father and I are here if you need anything."

"I think I'd just like to sleep for awhile."

"Okay. We'll be here when you wake up."

Kate closed her eyes. There was one more thing she needed to do to make sure the baby was safe. Right now, she needed her rest for tonight was going to be a full moon. The full extent of her exhaustion made itself known. The nurses soon entered the room to change her sheets and gown. Her body was compliant but contributed no effort. Someone closed the curtains and shut off the light. She slid into a dreamless sleep.

It was night when she awoke. The window was full of inky blackness. She checked the clock: nine o'clock. Her parents were in the room with her. A voice from the radio described the play-by-play action of a match between the Montreal Canadiens and the Toronto Maple Leafs. The judge disapproved of television. He believed it was a threat to society, that it crippled people's intelligence and attention spans. Her parents did, however, own one. It was important that guests knew that they could afford it. Her father seemed to like having it around to demonstrate his renunciation of this modern temptation. The radio, on the other hand, was a perfectly civilized technology. After supper, he would sit by the radio and read his newspaper, and he was not to be disturbed. Her mother impressed on Kate the many demands of her father's career, first as a prominent lawyer and then judge. Kate supposed that she did have her father to thank for her love of literature. Her mother certainly didn't encourage reading, beauty tips from *Cosmopolitan* notwithstanding. Mrs. Emberly often fretted about how such a pretty girl shouldn't have her nose stuck in a book all the time. The judge countered that there were much worse things a young girl could have her nose into. And Mrs. Emberly never contradicted the judge.

Her father sat near the radio, considering his pocket watch. He cleaned and re-set that damned watch every night. It was an heirloom among his family's sons. Kate could easily sense the disappointment that he wouldn't be passing it down to her. She was their only child, her mother unable to conceive after her difficult birth. She was surprised to see her father here two days in a row, to take that much time away from work for the birth of a grandson he was never going to see. It nearly felt like a gesture of paternal love until she realized that he likely wanted to ensure this scandal didn't cause any more potential harm to his reputation. When Kate first told her parents that she planned to give the baby away, she expected resistance. But they supported the proposition. They were solemn in their acknowledgment of the decision's gravitas, but Kate sensed their relief. Without a child, her prospects for quickly remarrying were greatly improved. And they surely didn't want this little souvenir of sorrow crawling around their corridors.

"You slept all day," her father said, briefly taking his attention away from the game.

"Yes, and she earned it," her mother said.

"I'm still very tired," Kate said.

"Visiting hours are almost over," her father said, shutting his watch. "We'll have to be going."

"But we'll be back first thing tomorrow morning," her mother said.

"Okay," Kate said, fluttering her eyelids. "I'll see you then."

She kept her eyes closed then until she could hear her parents walk down to the elevator. She went to stand up out of bed, but the muscles in her legs cramped and she wobbled back down onto the mattress. Beside her was a tray with some food. She ate a cup of apple sauce and drank the glass of water. Her clothes were nearby. She took off her gown and discovered that she was wearing a diaper. She couldn't remember a nurse putting that on her. Her stomach had shrunk considerably already. She put on her dress and got into her winter coat and boots. She peaked outside her door. There were no nurses bustling about, so she made a break for the elevator. She passed by the nursery room. The babies were sleeping, cocooned in pink or blue blankets. She didn't feel the need to identify which one was her son.

The cold winter wind hit her as she opened the door and stepped outside Grace Hospital. A fleet of cabs were waiting, snow slowly accumulating on their roofs. She stepped inside the backseat of the nearest one. The stink of cheap cigarettes stung her nose. The dirty seats were infused with the fragrance of stale tobacco. Her father enjoyed smoking a pipe and the occasional cigar, but that was more like a rugged cologne compared to this stench. She'd only ridden in a cab a handful of times in her life and it was always this olfactory assault that first grabbed her. Then she considered all the other people who'd sat here. Sweaty men, messy mothers with their slobbering children. She did her best to hide her disgust.

"Where to, sweetheart?" the cabbie asked. He tapped a few more particles of ash into the car's heaping tray.

"Southside Road, please," Kate said.

"No problem, love," he said.

They drove through the centre of St. John's. The construction crews were finished up for the night. The wind pushed the snow around, gathering in piles around the equipment. Kate looked out the window at the moon, which stared at them like a great unblinking eye. As a child, she used to look out the window of her parents' car at the moon, thinking that it followed them like a benevolent guardian. Now it felt menacing.

"It's like a whole different city nowadays, isn't it?" the cabbie said. "I grew up on Wickford Street. The 'Central Slum' they called it. All them houses are torn down. The government moved my family out into the housing on Empire. They got their big, fancy city hall nearly built there now where the slums used to be. Got to impress the mainlanders, I s'pose."

Kate didn't understand the antagonism Newfoundlanders had towards Canada. Her parents and older family members still didn't consider themselves Canadians. Becoming a part of Canada brought all kinds of prosperity, as far as she could see. Having been born just a few years before Confederation, she couldn't remember a time in St. John's when it wasn't being ripped up and rebuilt. Whenever she took a trip to a big city like New York, Montreal, Toronto, or even Halifax, she was always struck by how much more modern everything looked. She was anxious to see her home become a real city. Now, though, she realized that she wasn't going to get to see St. John's finally join the twentieth century, nearly seventy years too late.

"Sure, they even shrunk the harbour," the cabbie continued. "I can remember when the streets were cobblestone. Much nicer, as far as I'm concerned. But, we had to tear all that up so the mainlanders would give us the buses."

Harbour Drive was built upon rocks that had been quarried from the Southside hills. The constant work helped lower property value in that area. Derek saw it as an opportunity. He bought some land and built their big new house there. He had bought some additional land and planned on developing that too. Kate didn't want to live on Southside. It was too far away from her friends and family in Georgetown. Most young couples from their circle were building houses in the recent Churchill subdivision, "the New Jerusalem," farther away from the downtown area. And Southside was too close to the harbour. Often, when the breeze was strong, the stench of cod, gasoline, and men's bodies came wafting through their windows. However, she had convinced Derek to settle in St. John's instead of returning to Labrador, so she thought this was a fair bargain. And she felt better about her home when guests came and marvelled at its size.

The cab stopped outside the house. Derek's Mercedes was parked in the driveway, but there's wasn't much sign of life inside. All the curtains were drawn and no light emanated from the windows.

"You have a nice night now, love," the cabbie said.

Kate paid the fare and got out. The bitter weather immediately made her miss the warm confines of the taxi -- what odds about the stench and the dirt. She ran to the protection beneath the front door's archway and searched for her key, which was still in her purse. To compensate for the poor location, Derek allowed Kate a great deal of control over the home's design. She wanted a Queen Anne style house, like her old dollhouses with elaborate trim and bright colours. Guests complimented her on her taste.

From the posh furniture to the custom-made bookshelf in the living room with the stone fireplace, the terracotta floor tiles, the wooden staircase with exquisitely carved railings, and the kitchen replete with the most modern appliances. The house was opulent without being too rococo or ostentatious. Derek had never haggled her about cost, but Kate understood now what he had actually been purchasing.

The cherry wood door opened as she turned the key in the antique brass door knob. The fetid stink of rot made her nauseous. She held a hand to her nose as she searched for the light switch. Her eyes watered. As her sight adjusted, she saw that the walls were covered with scars. Long ragged streaks tore across the damask wallpaper. Scraps of food, torn clothes, and what looked like smears of blood and shit canvassed the floor. Kate followed the destruction to the living room. Her beloved books were strewn about, most torn from their hardcover bindings. She saw that Derek was using the pages as tinder. The bookcase had been dismantled for fuel, along with the rest of the furniture in the house. On the fireplace mantle, she saw that Derek kept a beautifully illustrated version of Ovid's *Metamorphoses* intact. He'd bought her that book at Shakespeare and Company in Paris while on their honeymoon. Kate picked it up off the mantle and leafed through it. The pages were smudged by greasy fingers. Perhaps Derek had sought some comfort from his own accursed transformation in Ovid.

They bonded early in their courtship over their shared love of literature. Both loved nothing more than to curl up on a comfy chair and spend hours reading. Oftentimes, they'd go for coffee and read silently together, enjoying each other's solitude. At first, their relationship was like a long, happy dream for Kate. Ever since she was young, she had a crush on Derek. He was tall, broad-shouldered, and had rich brown eyes like a fawn. As a little girl, whenever their families spent time together for Christmas or other special occasions, she was so excited to see him. He looked at her in a way older people never did. Three years ago, Kate's mother had told her that Derek was coming for a visit. "I hear he's looking to move back to St. John's and start a family," she said, with a prodding smile. Kate remembered how she swelled with excitement. On their first few dates, Derek was a perfect gentleman. She was a virgin and Derek wanted to wait until they were married. Kate was nineteen at the time and the boys her age were exactly that: boys. His traditional ideas of courtship felt romantic to her. And after just nine months of dating, she said yes to his proposal.

For their honeymoon they went to London and Paris, the settings from her favourite book, *A Tale of Two Cities*. She believed that their honeymoon would be filled with passion, but sex brought disenchantment. Although Derek had never said whether or not he was a virgin, Kate had assumed that he had some experience. However, their lovemaking was awkward and quick. He approached their time in bed together as a chore that needed to be done, something to be endured not enjoyed. He thrust himself inside her before she was ready, and she endured the pain, not wanting to make him anymore uncomfortable. She hoped that things would improve as they spent more time together as husband and wife, that he'd allow himself to relax. But as time went on, Derek became increasingly dour. She noticed that he slept easier when she was on her period, the pressure of sex lifted. Kate was confused because she knew that she was an attractive woman. Men had pursued her even since she was a teenager. She became so desperate that she consulted her mother's heap of women's magazines. She learned about the strange kinks and fetishes that men often harboured but were too shy to volunteer. Wanting to be a good wife, Kate encouraged Derek to share his fantasies. And, still wanting to be a good wife, she obliged. She felt uncomfortable wearing the skimpy schoolgirl outfits and pigtails, but it was the few times Derek showed a physical lust for her. Their sex slowly began to improve, but then immediately evaporated once she became pregnant.

A plate fell and smashed in the kitchen. Kate grabbed a small splintered shaft of wood and went to investigate. She switched on the light. A dingy cat searched the counter for scraps. Kate exhaled with relief. The cat heard her and took off into the hallway and down the stairs to the basement. Kate shivered and clutched her coat close to her body. It was nearly as cold inside as it was outside. On the counter next to some rotten meat was a chef's knife. She dropped her wooden shank and picked up the knife. She walked out of the kitchen and took the staircase upstairs. The creaks under her footsteps made her aware of the crushing silence within the house. The wind moaned, and the sea sloshed against the rocks.

Two empty rooms mocked Kate with the children that would never occupy them. She went to the bedroom she and her husband once shared. Like the rest of the furniture, the elaborate bed frame had been broken up to feed the fire. The mattress was disemboweled, and goose down littered the floor. The bed had been ludicrously oversized for the room. It took the Sears movers hours to get it up over the steps. Kate suggested they return it and get a queen size instead. Derek insisted. "This is the bed you wanted, so this is the bed you'll get," he said. His dogged commitment to spoil her was endearing.

However, many nights alone on this bed revealed what Derek had tried to buy from Kate with this luxurious house: a silent and compliant wife. Derek worked indefatigably, an attribute she initially admired. She understood now that Derek in fact despised her, something she denied at the time. The dashing, romantic gentlemen that wooed her into marriage was an illusion, a trick to seduce her. Kate believed now that Derek needed something to hide behind. A pretty wife and a beautiful home were great disguises. But what was Derek trying to conceal? He believed that he was being punished for doing something terrible. What could it have been? This was the final piece of a puzzle that Kate would likely never finish. She didn't need to. He wanted to abort their child, and when Kate denied him that, he wanted to kill her. He told her that he needed his life so that he could save others. Someone with that kind of self-righteousness was capable of anything.

Kate knew she had to check the basement next to be sure Derek wasn't hiding there. Even under the best circumstances, she didn't like going down there. She gripped her knife tightly and tried to summon courage from some unknown source deep within her. Anxiety flashed throughout her body and she was desperate for fresh air. She ran to the window and opened it. A wintry wind kissed her face and chilled the boiling panic within her chest. She was about to leave the room and make her way to the basement when she heard a long mournful howl.

It was Derek, she knew it. It sounded like it came from Fort Amherst. She ran down the steps. Out of habit, she took the time to lock the door. After realizing what she'd done, she laughed to herself. She left the house and started walking up the hill. The cold and the pain soon erased her brief good humour. Her stomach and vagina ached. She was still bleeding. The wind curled up under her skirt and chilled the blood stain between her legs. She hoped the wind would carry her scent to Derek and draw him out. She was ready. All those feelings of self-pity were gone. This was her duty and she'd accepted it. She was sick of living in fear and she was sick of walking around in this cold.

She got to the top of Fort Amherst. Up the road, the lighthouse was spilling its light out over the Narrows and into the Atlantic. Beside it was the house where the lighthouse keeper's family lived. It was dark -- everyone was gone to bed it seemed. Gun emplacements and pillboxes from WWII clung to the cliffside, keeping watch over the slim passage opening up to St. John's harbour. The winter wind kicked up whitecaps on the water. The lighthouse's beam shimmered over the undulating waves. Above, clouds hid the stars, but the full moon burned right through. Kate clutched her jacket, the chef's knife in her hand. She had decided that she had to do this while he was the monster. For one, she needed that last piece of evidence to know she wasn't crazy. Mostly, though, she doubted whether she could kill a human being. She doubted she could kill anything. But a beast seemed within her capabilities.

She heard a growl behind her from the trees. A dog emerged from the woods, crawling on its knuckles like an ape. Spots of snow clung to its black fur. It paused before Kate and sniffed the air. She looked into the beast's earthy brown eyes. There was wild intelligence there, more than an animal but not quite human. She knew that somewhere in there was Derek. She was ready now. He shook the snow from his fur and stood up on his hind legs, snarling. Terror threatened to overwhelm Kate. She gripped the knife's handle so hard it began to hurt her grip. Her heart was working its way up through her dry throat. She swallowed hard and finally found the words to speak:

"You'll never get him," she said.

He lunged at her and tackled her to the ground. Kate wrestled away from his jaws as Derek fought to seize her neck between his teeth, gnawing at her shoulders. She plunged the knife in as many times as she could -- ribs, chest, stomach, back, never sure of where she was striking. He grabbed hold of her throat. Sharp teeth sunk easily into her flesh. There was a brief surge of pain and then everything went dark. The world rapidly drained into a black pool. Her grip fell limp with the knife left stuck in Derek's back. He whimpered and breathed roughly. Kate felt the furry body on top of her slowly transform into human skin. Derek slipped off her, naked, bloody, and dead.

It's done, she thought as her life poured out of her neck.

CHAPTER ONE (2015)

Tyler bit the smooth, fleshy muscle that ran from her neck to her shoulder.

"Oww," Julie said. "That hurt."

She generally tolerated Tyler's love-nibbles, but was quick to admonish whenever he got too 'bitey'. Tyler couldn't help himself. Normally a pale complexion year-round, Julie's skin in winter was white as a marshmallow. Tyler felt it screaming out at him, begging him to gnaw. On one occasion, he managed to pierce her skin with a particularly overzealous chomp. His teeth's indentations were speckled with little smears of blood, like strawberry and vanilla ice cream. Tyler tried to calm her—it was just a little scratch—but Julie insisted she go to the hospital. "Human bites have more germs than cats' or dogs'," she said. "I don't want your infection." They had a very awkward evening at the emergency room. He remembered feeling strangely disappointed: Why didn't she want his infection?

Tyler tried to bite her again, but she wiggled away.

"I'm trying to watch," she said

He hid his mouth amidst the messy bun of her long blonde hair and watched the final moments of *Where the Wild Things Are*. On Julie's parents' fifty-inch high-definition television, the boy pulled away from the surf in his little makeshift sailboat, waving goodbye to his big, hairy buddies. Then, just as he was pulling into the horizon, the boy's estranged friend ran out to see him off, howling a mournful goodbye, their grudges forgotten. The boy responded in kind. Now they were all howling together. No words needed. All was understood.

Tyler could sense Julie was having an emotional reaction. This was good. So far, the night had been a success. They needed a night like this. For the past year, a space had been growing between them, a space Tyler could not transcend. With each attempt to reduce it, it stubbornly endured and grew even more resilient. He soon realized that distance and absence were the conditions under which the space was allowed to flourish. However, Tyler was not a particularly manipulative person and quickly exhausted all his devices. He texted Julie constantly. He tried delaying his responses for hours, waiting for her to crack, and when she didn't, he went back to the high-volume approach. He now tried playing the part of the considerate boyfriend. The trick, he realized, was to be proactive, not reactive. Anticipate the space before it could catch hold. Draw on the past and look towards the future instead of staying in the present. Plan dates ahead of time, not a last-minute casual *You at?* Remember important events and bring them up in conversation before she could accuse him of forgetting. He asked her about essays that she was working on, books she was reading, ideas she was developing. Tonight their old chemistry was beginning to re-emerge and it seemed like his hard work was finally starting to pay dividends.

However, Tyler recognized that he was still only fighting the symptoms. He wasn't attacking the disease itself. What was the real cause here? What was the genesis of the space?

Undoubtedly, it had started last summer. Julie left in May to spend the summer semester in France as part of her French minor. And, by virtue of a largesse engendered by generous scholarships that she had accumulated over the years as well as additional funding from her parents, she made several trips to different countries in Europe. Germany and Greece were her favorites. This was the only significant stretch of time Julie and Tyler had spent apart. They'd toyed with the idea of Tyler coming over for a visit, maybe take a short little trip, but that never materialized. She got home in August and something was different. Her energy had changed. But they didn't get a chance to address it because just as soon as she got home they were on their way to Halifax with Tyler's friends to see NoFX. Julie was travel weary at that point, but she was still excited because this was a trip they'd planned before she left for Europe. NoFX was one of the bands Tyler had introduced to Julie when they first started dating. She fell in love with punk rock. However, in the years since she'd grown out of a lot of that skate punk stuff, and she didn't care for NoFX's new material. Nonetheless, she was looking forward to seeing them. It was the first time Tyler had left Newfoundland. He was nervous about flying so he smoked a massive joint before getting on the plane. He also hid another big one in the folds of his sweater's hood, knowing that he was going to need a hit as soon as the plane landed, even though it was a short flight. He didn't tell Julie about the concealed joint. The guys had a laugh when he retrieved it outside Halifax airport. They passed it around waiting for the bus to take them into the city. Julie was shocked that he would be so careless. Over all, Tyler thought the trip was a success, even though he didn't care much for Halifax. They all got black out drunk each night. He rarely got the chance to spend much time with his friends nowadays. Most of them were doing turnarounds in Alberta or other parts of the country. The show itself was incredible. NoFX even played "The Decline," which they rarely performed live. There were some minor dramatics. After the show, Tyler was wandering around Halifax alone, high on acid, and got mugged. Julie said he spent the night crying, howling about his father. Tyler was too high to remember. Julie tried to broach the topic several times. Tyler insisted that it was just drugged up nonsense. She didn't seem satisfied by this explanation, but she stopped pursuing it.

When they got back from Halifax, Julie still didn't move her stuff back into Tyler's. She started spending more nights at her parents' house. Once the fall semester started, the only time she stayed over at Tyler's was during the weekend, and they rarely saw each other during the week. Whenever Tyler expressed concern over this lack of shared living space, Julie explained that, this being her last year as an undergrad, she really needed to focus on school. A valid excuse, but Tyler couldn't help but dwell on the fact that school had never been an issue for Julie; she had a 4.0 and an 86 average. Indeed, Tyler was very respectful of her academic commitment. Whenever she needed to study, he would play video games and leave her be. Furthermore, Tyler's house was only a few minutes' walk from Memorial. Julie could practically roll out of bed and be in class. She was spending more time with her school friends, too. She worked at the university's Writing Centre and usually went there in the evening to have study sessions with some of her co-workers.

There was one guy Tyler particularly didn't trust: Nick. He was always tagging Julie in Facebook posts that she found hilarious. It was either political stuff, which Tyler didn't follow, or dorky humour, which he didn't understand. Julie told Tyler that Nick had a girlfriend back in New Brunswick, but that did little to assuage him. What bothered Tyler was that Julie was forming an emotional bond with a guy that Tyler couldn't infiltrate. His jealousy manifested as criticisms of Nick's character, such as his Native status and free tuition. "He can't be, like, anymore than one sixteenth Micmac," he'd say. "How could he have possibly been oppressed or disadvantaged?" Julie never engaged in those sorts of discussions.

He knew that the mature thing to do would be to have an open discussion with her about his concerns. However, something inside him prevented him from bringing this all up. He was afraid of where such a conversation might lead.

Where the Wild Things Are ended with the boy returning to his home, leaving behind his imaginary island of monsters to reconcile with his mother. Tyler felt something shift in his throat. He blinked hard a few times and coughed.

"I liked it," Julie said. "It's like a movie for the adults who grew up loving the story as a kid. What do you think?"

This, too, was something new: asking Tyler what he thought of things. Julie used to be too bashful to offer her opinion and was happy to speak at Tyler's level, a hyperbolic binary of best vs. worst movie ever. These days, Julie offered her critiques freely and pushed Tyler to engage more deeply. *What do you think?* It felt more like a challenge than a query, and his answers always seemed to disappoint. He usually just agreed with Julie. Tonight, however, he did his homework and had prepared an interesting factoid that should lead to some interesting discussion.

"Did you know," Tyler asked, "that Tony Soprano was the voice of Carol, the monsters' leader?"

"James Gandolfini?" Julie said. "No, I didn't realize. Cool."

She waited for Tyler to expand on his point, but he had nothing. She switched from Netflix to cable and turned on CBC's The National. There was a story about the big settlement for students who'd attended residential schools in Newfoundland and Labrador. The reporter interviewed a survivor who'd attended a school in Cartwright, Labrador. The old man detailed all the horrors they'd endured at school called Lockwood, run by the Catholic church.

"They always focus on the bad stuff that happened," Tyler said. "There must have been some good schools."

"Maybe," Julie said. "But that's not really the point."

"Then what is the point?"

"The point is that there were terrible injustices committed and there needs to be restitution."

"Sure we're always throwing money at these people. It never does any good."

"It's impossible for white people like us to appreciate the affect of colonialism and inter-generational trauma because we're so privileged."

"I'm not privileged. I never knew my dad and my mom's dead. Where's my bailout?"

"No one said your life wasn't hard. The difference is that none of those things happened because of your race."

"All that colonialism stuff happened a long time ago. Most white people now haven't done anything terrible to aboriginals. It's time they got over it and moved on."

"It wasn't so long ago. There are still a lot of residential school survivors who are still alive."

"But why is it always about money? That won't change anything."

"White privilege is based on racial exploitation. Our economic advantages are premised on depriving other communities. Reparations can help create a more just wealth distribution."

Tyler always baited Julie with this social justice stuff. He didn't really have a dog in the fight and actually agreed with her most of the time. He just liked to get her going. And he knew that she liked getting a chance to apply all the things she learned at school in a real discussion. She liked being challenged and he was happy to lay down the gauntlet.

"Well," he said. "What do you want to do now?"

"I don't know," she said. "I'm kind of tired."

"How about we go to my place?" Tyler suggested. "Smoke some weed. Listen to music."

"Okay," she said. "But, I'm probably going to fall asleep right away."

They walked upstairs and put on their winter coats. Julie's father was watching the Leafs play and her mother was busy with her Sudoku. Mr. and Mrs. Fitzpatrick never thought much of Tyler. Tonight was one of the rare occasions he spent time in their house. It was Julie's birthday, and they'd had family dinner together. Every year they invited Tyler and he usually declined because he knew it was just a nicety. Julie was always understanding because she knew how passive aggressive her family could be towards him. This time, though, he wanted to change the tone, make an effort. And it was moderately successful--only a few moments of awkward silence. That was progress, as far as Tyler was concerned. There was a lot of ground to make up. He didn't make much of an impression when she first brought him home four years ago, and their opinion, if anything, had declined in the time since. The fact that he was a Canadiens fan was the least of his problems. "So what's your plan?" Julie's father often asked Tyler. Initially, he intended to study computer engineering. He flunked all his courses his first semester and then dropped out in his second. That was his first and only year in post-secondary education. After that it was a series of half-baked ideas (graphic design, business school, game developer, and most recently chef), but nothing ever stuck. Not even Julie expected a "plan" from him at this point and Tyler was grateful for no longer having to continue the performance.

Mr. and Mrs. Fitzpatrick liked Keith Power, though, Julie's ex-, and only other, boyfriend. Keith was captain of the hockey team and Julie was one of the prettiest and popular girls in school. Their picture together in the yearbook was like Ryan Reynolds and Scarlet Johansson on the cover of *People*. The fact that they were dating seemed more a product of scientific laws than teenage courtship. Who else would either of them be dating? And yet, four years ago, at the high school graduation party that Tyler was hosting at his friend's cabin, Julie was there by herself. When Tyler saw her there, he was unsure whether he was having an acid flashback. No one knew what to make of her presence. She was never known to travel outside her tribe of Swedish swimsuit models and bovine jocks. Tyler had nursed a secret crush on her for years. They often locked eyes when passing each other in the hallways, but he couldn't remember ever having a conversation with her. In her eyes he believed he saw someone eager to get away from her stale niche--all she needed was a little push. Now was his chance, he realized.

He approached her. "Where's Keith?" he asked.

"Different party," she said. "This one seemed like more fun." Tyler smiled and got to work.

The party was at Leanne Whitten's cabin in Avondale, a few hours outside of St. John's. Leanne was a close friend of Tyler's. He and his friends organized the busses to and back from St. John's. Tyler had a reputation for throwing the best parties. Not the sort of parties, however, that Julie and her crowd would ever go to, of course (although Tyler sold them weed and the odd designer drug). He was popular, too, in his own way. He grew up without a father and his mother died of cancer when he was sixteen. He inherited the house and lived there by himself, his grandparents checking in on him intermittingly. He floated around, never touching down with a particular group of people for too long. Girls swooned over his easy charisma, undercut by his big brown eyes, so full of intangible melancholy.

When he saw Julie, he could not believe Keith allowed her to come alone. She had a flask of Smirnoff vodka mixed with Brookfield lemonade and was soon slurring her "Tylurrs." Most people interpreted her quietness for snobbery. Tyler was surprised to discover a fun-loving girl with few inhibitions who relished laughter. With Keith absent, Tyler figured he had nothing to lose. He offered her a line of cocaine and she agreed without hesitation. They went inside the bathroom and shut the door. He pulled out the baggy and drew two lines out on the sink, a big one for him and a tiny one for her. Julie wouldn't hear of it. She insisted they do equal shares. Tyler redistributed the allocation. He licked the card and rubbed it around his lips. He rolled up a twenty dollar bill and snorted his line. Julie, after watching carefully, repeated the process. Tyler tongued his numb lips while Julie bent and snorted. "It smells chemically," she said. Tyler laughed and agreed. She turned and kissed him. She pressed herself against him with enough force to push him backwards into the bathtub and they tumbled like felled trees. Tyler could barely feel her mouth inside his. He was surprised by her clumsy technique and obvious lack of experience.

She sat on top of him and took her shirt off. He pulled her towards him and flipped her over. She peeled off her jeans like a snake shedding her old skin. "I'm a virgin," Julie said.

"That's cool, but I don't have a condom" Tyler said.

"Whatever," she said. "Just pull it out and pop it on my tits."

Tyler's eyes widened at this sudden vulgarity. She giggled at his reaction, but then soon winced as he pushed himself inside her. Five minutes later, she was moaning. Tyler struggled to gain traction. He kicked the back of the tub, cracking it and cutting his heel in the process. Julie turned him over and straddled him. She screamed. A few people drunkenly banged on the door and then immediately left when they heard what was going on. Tyler and Julie laughed each time. They finished as Julie had instructed.

They cradled each other in the bathtub. The fractured porcelain was tainted with blood from Tyler's foot and Julie's broken hymen, like they were incubating inside an egg and were trying to burst out. They were too high from the cocaine and the sex to sleep so they talked for the rest of the night. In light of all that had happened in the past hour, it seemed natural to speak candidly to each other. They poured themselves into one another, each realizing as the words flowed how desperately they'd wanted someone to confide in. Tyler talked about the pain of losing his mother to cancer, that each morning he had to re-learn the choreography of going about the house in her absence. He talked about never knowing his father. That it was an ache he could never give a vocabulary, a void that refused to speak or be spoken to. She told him about her and Keith's asexual relationship. It was months before they kissed, and it was Julie who pressed the issue. And, after that, it was she who forced her tongue into his mouth. She was so self-conscious about her sexual frustration because her feelings did not seem to be reciprocated. Having little to no other experience, she figured this was how most people were and she was the one who was abhorrent. However, one night her and her girl friends had a sleepover and they began sharing stories. As the other girls laughed about embarrassing moments of spontaneous ejaculation and parents invading their escapades, Julie ran to the bathroom crying. A few nights later, she decided she would no longer wait for Keith to take initiative. As they were making out, Julie slid her hand under his belt and down into his crotch. She felt a fat, flaccid cock. He seized her wrist and pulled it away. Neither spoke of it.

Tyler could not get over his shock. "Why did you stay with him?" he asked.

"He's actually really kind to me," she said. "He's very gentle and sweet. He's a different person when he plays hockey. I don't know where all that rage comes from. He just transforms into a monster."

Keith's cruelty on the ice was well-known. A few years before, Tyler and Keith had played on a team together in house-league. During a game, they were skating down a loose puck, trying to seize it before the opposing goalie smothered the play. Keith used the opportunity to snow the goalie. The opposing defender gave Keith a shove with his stick. "Back off, faggot," he said. Keith cross-checked him viciously. The defenceman toppled over his goalie and fell into the net. Keith pounced and thrashed at him, beating his knuckles bloody against the guy's helmet. Tyler watched as the refs separated them, dumbfounded by the sudden eruption of violence.

He realized now that this could soon be his fate, too. He suppressed the anxiety. They lay there silently for awhile. "So what are we going to do about this?" she asked.

"Break up with Keith and get with me," he said. She agreed.

They passed out until Leanne ran throughout the cabin waking everyone to get on the bus. On the way back to St. John's, Tyler and Julie slept with their heads leaning on each other, holding hands. By Monday, everyone at school knew. Tyler walked the halls exhausted, fearful of the eventual encounter. He and Keith soon crossed paths. Tyler was prepared to take the beating of his life. A crowd formed. Keith stared into Tyler's face. When Tyler returned his gaze, some form of telecommunication occurred. Keith knew that Julie had told Tyler everything. Tyler saw that something had caught up with Keith, and that it was a long time coming whatever it was. There was no fight. Everyone gasped as Keith walked away. He quit hockey, and after he was done high school, he left St. John's. No one heard from him. Occasionally, Tyler would look for him on Facebook in vain. The guy had vanished. After school that day, Julie brought Tyler in through her parents' doors, which they were now exiting.

"I'm gone," Julie called to her parents.

"Goodnight," her mother replied.

Up above, a full, yellow moon was partly obscured by clouds. A light snowfall drifted in all directions. The sidewalks were only partly cleared, and they had to be careful of cars when they stepped out onto the street. It had been an icy winter. Snow piled atop peoples' lawn melted onto the sidewalk during mild days and then froze solid during the cold nights. They made their way out of Georgetown and were headed towards Rabbittown. At the cemetery on Bonaventure Ave and Empire Ave, Julie heard a dog bark. She gasped and stood frozen. Tyler laughed.

"It's just a dog," he said.

"Look!" she said and pointed towards the graveyard.

Creeping between the rows of headstones, a tall, broad-chested dog approached them. Its black fur glistened against the streetlights like stars in the night sky. The dog strolled towards them with long deliberate strides, then sat down before the chain link fence as if it had been expecting them and was now going to introduce itself. It considered Julie and Tyler with bright yellow eyes. Tyler knew that dogs who didn't turn away from a human's gaze were dangerous. It meant that they didn't recognize them as an alpha. Still, this dog didn't seem aggressive.

"What breed do you think that is?" Tyler asked. "It looks like a husky, but I've never seen one all black like that."

"His eyes are so yellow," Julie said. "What if it's a wolf?"

"Wolves have been extinct in Newfoundland for ages. And there definitely wouldn't be one in St. John's."

"Then maybe it's a coyote. I don't see a collar."

"It could be part wolf. Maybe someone got him in Labrador and brought him down here. Now he's out loose."

While he still talking, Tyler became nearly mesmerized by the dog's gaze. The night became impossibly cold and dark, and all semblances of joy and colour shrunk from his life. His chest caved in as he tried to squeeze out an exhalation. The hound's glowing eyes disappeared briefly as it blinked. It stood up then and ran off back into the graveyard. Tyler lost sight of it in the darkness. He began to feel like himself again. Julie clutched him close. Neither spoke as they continued down Bonaventure Avenue and then onto Whiteway Street to Tyler's house.

Tyler took out his keys and opened the door. The house was completely dark. He switched on the light and everyone yelled, "Surprise!"

Julie was nearly as startled as when the dog had barked. Her university friends just about filled the bungalow's small living room. In the kitchen there was cake. It had a picture of a pipe and below it was written, *"Ceci n'est pas un gâteau."* Everyone had a good chuckle at that except Tyler. He didn't get the joke. *Ahh, oui oui, très drôle,* he thought. As far as he was concerned, these people were a bunch of freaks and geeks. He would've preferred Julie's old high school friends over this crowd. At least he could understand what they were talking about. Half of what this crowd said weren't even words. *Phallogocentricism? Rhizomatic?* Julie explained these were what academics called "neologisms." Even words he did know, like "the Other" and "Deconstruction," seemed to take on special, encoded meanings for these people. Tyler thought it was all just a bunch of highfalutin gobbledygook.

Julie made the rounds, as everyone gave her a hug and wished her a happy birthday. The occasion was also special because Julie had recently been awarded funding from the Social Sciences and Humanities Research Council to do her Master's degree. A SSHRC was incentive for her to stay in St. John's for at least another two years, or so Tyler hoped. The subject of their shared future was rarely discussed. Julie had competing ambitions and desires. There was a professor in the Classics department that she always talked about working on a Master's thesis with. But on occasions when she grew frustrated with academia she considered the possibility of law school. And when she was really pissed off she said she wanted to spend a year travelling, this time in Asia. Tyler preferred to stay in St. John's. He had visions of her beginning her writing career once she finished her Master's. She could live with him while he supported them. It wasn't an outrageous idea. He only had to pay for insurance and utilities on his house. And if things got tight, he could gut his mother's old room and rent it out. Julie, however, was never very enthusiastic about these ideas. She was very bashful about her writing. Often she would reveal some grand idea for a novel or story, but when Tyler pressed her to follow up, she was evasive. He couldn't understand it. She had talent, intelligence, and a great work ethic. Why not go for it?

Julie was chatting with Nick. Tyler hoped that inviting Nick tonight signaled to Julie that he trusted her and was mature about these sorts of things. To demonstrate his maturity, Tyler went over and joined their conversation. He waited patiently for a moment to interject.

"We watched *Where the Wild Things Are* before coming over," Tyler said.

"Nice," Nick said. "Dave Eggers wrote the screenplay, I do believe."

"Are you serious?" Julie said.

Tyler recognized the name. Julie had a number of his books on her shelf. He cursed himself for not putting that together himself.

"Yeah," Tyler said, "and did you know that Tony Soprano did one of the voices?"

"James Gandolfini," Nick said. "Yeah, he's great."

The three of them stood in silence then for awhile. Some newcomers came in through the door and Julie shuffled off to great them.

"So," Nick said. "Are you going to be moving with Julie to Halifax?"

"What do you mean?"

"When she goes off to Dalhousie next fall for law school. Are you going with her or will you stay here?"

"No. She's staying here to do her Master's."

"Oh? Okay then."

"She wants to write about patricide in art," Tyler was about to explain before Nick interrupted him.

"She wants to focus on *The Aeneid* and connect it to Freud's Oedipus complex," Nick said. "The death of Anchises, mirrored by the fall of Troy, represents the opportunity for Aeneas to become his own man and build something for himself, i.e. Rome. The idea came from a quote from Picasso, who said, 'in art, one must kill one's father.' The desire to kill one's father isn't just about a sexual desire for your mother, it's more about wanting to get out from underneath his shadow and make something of your own. I think it's a great idea. I hope she writes it."

Tyler was silent. He took a lot of pride in being able to summarize Julie's thesis idea and Nick did a much better job than he ever could. That was bad enough, but the guy seemed like he wanted to rub it in that he had this deep personal relationship with Julie. Nick seemed to have recognized that he took it a step too far this time and bowed out to join some friends. Tyler shrunk away to go have a cigarette outside on the back deck.

The snow had stopped and the moon was out. There were two girls on the patio sharing a smoke, discussing the evils of gluten. Tyler looked out across the field behind his backyard. Out in the softball pitch was the same black dog they'd seen earlier. Its eyes glowed like two beacons. Tyler heard the door open behind him. Julie came out and joined him. She put her hand on his lower back and gave him a long, deep kiss. She smiled at him with love in her eyes. He couldn't remember the last time she'd been so affectionate. He was about to point out the dog, but he suspected that would ruin the moment.

"Think I could have one of those?" she asked.

Tyler smiled and handed her a cigarette. "Been awhile," he said.

"Special occasion." She took a small drag and exhaled. The smoke drifted lazily from her pouty red lips. "Thanks so much of doing this. I really had no idea you'd planned it. I didn't even think you knew all these people's names."

"The wonders of Facebook."

"How come you didn't invite any of your friends?"

"I didn't think they'd jive with this crowd."

"Yeah, good call." She took one last drag from her cigarette, then dabbed it out in the snow. She flicked the butt out into the yard. "I'm going back inside." She kissed him again then left.

Tyler looked out on the field. The dog was gone. Somewhere he heard a howl. He felt like responding in kind.

In the living room, Julie and her friends spoke passionately about something or other that Tyler couldn't follow. He fought the urge to check his phone. Instead, he sat there quietly, holding Julie's hand. He was sipping at a can of Blackhorse. Moderation was another goal he was working on. Usually at parties, Tyler got too drunk or high and Julie ended up babysitting him. He certainly didn't want that to happen tonight. So, he paced himself.

The night's topic of discussion was whether or not it could be said that Canada had a post-colonial literary tradition. Whatever that meant.

When the conversation slowed, he felt like it was an appropriate moment to take out his bong. To his pleasant surprise, Julie's friends chipped in some of their own weed. Tyler busted it up and mixed in some pinch from his cigarettes. He packed the bong routinely and passed it around. One of the nerds, Jay, went off on a tangent about various strains of marijuana from British Columbia. Tyler nodded along but didn't pay attention. He could remember going to one of Jay's parties where the guy had actually busted up a nugget using a mortar and pestle. Tyler couldn't even laugh he was in such disbelief.

Gradually the crowd petered out. Tyler puttered around the house and tidied up. For a supposedly sophisticated bunch, they sure made a fine mess. Probably used to their mothers cleaning up after them, Tyler thought. At least they left their bottles for Tyler to add to his recycling collection. Some of them were still half full. It was a small two-bedroom bungalow, so it didn't take long to clean. Julie often suggested he rent out his mom's room to a university student or even one of his buddies. Tyler considered it, but never did. She also suggested Tyler turn it into a gaming room. His "battle station" took up so much space in his room. Tyler thought that was a great idea. However, just thinking about gutting all his mother's stuff was exhausting.

"Psst," Julie said.

Tyler looked down the hallway and saw Julie standing outside his bedroom, naked. She summoned him with a finger. He dropped the garbage bag he was holding and followed her. She lay atop his bed. Tyler undressed. He started at her feet, leading a trail of kisses up her long, athletic legs, across her hipbones, through the middle of her breasts, and up to her lips. He reversed direction, working backwards. She pushed his face between her thighs. She was already wet. He growled, drawing air in through his nose as he licked furiously. She pulled him up by his hair and kissed him, her wetness now on both their lips. He slid inside her. It was the first time they'd made love in weeks. She came quickly. She dug her nails into the flesh of Tyler's back. He gasped almost in pain when he came. He lay down beside her. He knew she was smiling without having to look.

"I haven't even given you your present," Tyler said.

He rolled off the bed and opened a drawer in his computer table. He took out a small rectangular box and handed it to Julie. He turned on the bedside lamp so she could see it. It was a necklace. The pendant was a gold Phaistos disc with little esoteric hieroglyphs encircled each side of the coin.

"I found it on Etsy," Tyler explained. "It looked like something you raved about seeing when you were in Greece."

"It's beautiful," Julie said. "I love it."

"I love you," Tyler said.

"I love you, too," Julie said.

They embraced and made love again, longer this time, slower. Julie was on top. Her necklace jangled as she rode harder. The shimmering gold of the pendant reminded Tyler of the dog's yellow eyes. His body tightened as the climax neared. He heard the dog's howl in his own voice when he came.

CHAPTER TWO (1963)

"Alley over!" a voice shouted from the other side of the house.

The big, yellow ball soared over the top of the roof. It was Violet's turn to catch. She scampered around the yard trying to deduce the ball's trajectory, her sealskin slippers gliding across the grass. If she didn't catch it, she wouldn't get to play tag and would have to go to the back of the line, and she wasn't about to let that happen. The ball shifted with the breeze, dancing unpredictably. The wind pushed it away from her just as her fingers were about to grasp it, and she had to dive to catch it before it hit the ground. The kids cheered and laughed. She had grass stains all over her blue dress. Her mother wouldn't be happy about that.

She jumped up off the ground with the ball and took off to the other side of the house. Violet was small, but quick. The kids always underestimated her speed. They dodged her like a school of fish trying to flee a hungry shark. She was, however, very clumsy. She often tripped over herself, scratching her knees and getting her dress even more filthy. Some of the chubby kids were soon tired. Violet didn't want to pick on the easy prey, though. She liked to challenge herself and go for the bigger kids.

Luke was in her periphery. She could see him in the corner of her eye. He was so cocky. He acted like he played with the younger kids because he took pity and them and could just as easily go play cricket with the older crowd. Violet knew better, and she was going to strike that smirk straight off of his face. He was running away half-heartedly, not realizing the danger he was in. Violet let him think she was going for fat little Lucy but then she side-stepped and tagged him. Everyone laughed. She handed him the ball with a great big smile on her face. He took it sulkily.

"Alley over!" he yelled and gave it a good hard throw.

The kids had a desperate drive to have fun during the summer while they were on Spotted Island. On a warm, sunny day not even those nippy blackflies could bother them. They knew fly bites were infinitely better than being stuck inside a log cabin during the winter. Once the cod fishing was over for the summer, Violet's family moved to Roaches Brook. They packed all their stuff onto their boat and migrated to the sheltered interior of Labrador, where her father trapped fur six months of the year. It was the same for all the families on Spotted Island. They all moved inland for the winter.

Violet's paternal grandfather had built their log cabin in Roaches Brook when he came over from England to Labrador and married an Inuit woman. In the winter, the temperature dropped as low as minus fifty degrees, and a hard storm could sequester them inside for days, pushing them to the edges of starvation. Her mother tried her best to keep Violet and her siblings preoccupied with games to keep their minds off their hungry bellies and to keep them from losing their minds to boredom and cabin fever. So, during the summer, the kids did their best to take advantage of their six months on Spotted Island. The days were long, darkness waiting until almost eleven o'clock to set. When the weather was nice, and they had their chores done, the kids flocked outside to play together and make up games and have so much fun that they lost themselves and any sense of time.

As the game went on, the less fit kids dropped out as they got tired, but most of them kept playing, switching sides until a chorus of voices were heard on the wind: "Supper!"

Their parents were calling them in. Everyone dispersed, spread out over Spotted Island's naked, moon-like hills.

Walking home, Violet realized suddenly how hungry she was. Down on the shore, she could hear her father's boat. Each make-n-break engine had its own distinctive putputput, like a person's voice. She saw her father and older brother pulling the boat up to their wharf. Her brother, George, was sixteen and had a couple of summers experience now as a fisherman. George and their father plodded about the stage, heavy in their oilskins and hip rubbers. They moved sluggishly, visibly tired from a long day of hauling nets. But they still had work left to do. All the wharves were alive with the sound of splitting knives carving up cod and their skulls crunching under the fishermen's boots.

Violet walked past the outhouse, the sawhorse, and the vertical woodpile to the front door of her house. Colourful pages from catalogues and magazines lined the rafters. The floor's wooden knots stood up from all the dancing that happened during their famous parties. Violet's parents were both gifted musically. Many nights, Henry would take out his squeezebox and Darlene accompanied him with her acrobatic voice. Once the melodies started pouring out of their windows, people weren't long showing up. Neighbours came in through the door with bottles of homebrew and alchie.

Violet and the rest of the youngsters scuffled about, mimicking the adults' dance moves.

Her mother was in the kitchen, busy at the stove. She had to lean over her pregnant belly to keep it from the flame. Violet's sister, Cecilia, was minding their two-year-old brother, Bobby. He was babbling a blue streak while she mended some his clothes. Cecilia was fourteen years old and was learning how to keep house. She would soon be old enough to leave and raise a family of her own. Luke was coming around the house lately. He and Cecilia would sit together and listen to records under the gaze of Darlene and Henry. Violet often teased Cecilia, saying that they were going to get married and have ugly little babies that not even the fairies would want to steal. They teased each other constantly until their mother chased them from the house.

"What's for supper?" Violet asked her mother.

"Never you mind what's for supper," Darlene said. "You'll find out soon enough. And stay away from that pot."

Violet saw some duck feathers piled up beside the stove. The nauseating smell of scalding skin and scorched feathers permeated the house. Violet didn't like duck. It was too greasy and gave her a bad tummy. However, hunger was the best seasoning, as her father always said, and Violet usually gobbled up whatever her mother cooked.

Darlene had hazel eyes, olive skin, and curly blonde hair, just like Violet. She was short and slight, but strong. For their wedding, Henry had given her a rifle and a sewing machine, and Darlene made fine use of both. Each morning, she left the house before dawn with her .22 rifle and brought home a couple partridges, rabbits, or even a porcupine. The rest of the day consisted of sewing, knitting, making and mending new and old clothes, fashioning bedding from bleached flour sacs, chopping wood, and the innumerable other duties a fisherman's wife needed to perform to support the family.

"Mommy?" Violet asked.

Darlene didn't respond.

"Mommy?" Violet continued. "Can I go to school in the fall with Cecilia?"

"No, Violet. We've told you. We can't afford it. Little Bobby is a handful as it is and I'm going to need even more help when the new baby comes."

After Violet was born, Darlene had endured a number of miscarriages, stillborns, and even a couple babies who died during infancy. With each lost child, Darlene became harder with her children.

"That's not fair," Violet pleaded. "Cecilia gets to go to school."

"You wouldn't fit in at Lockwood," Cecilia said. "They're really strict. You're too disobedient. And you sook when you don't get your own way."

"How many times do we have to tell you?" Darlene said. "The price for furs is dropping and we simply can't afford it. Maybe once Cecilia is married and off on her own, we can send you for awhile." Darlene then turned and faced Violet. She saw the state of her daughter. "Your dress! I only just cleaned it!"

Violet had meant to try and clean herself up a bit before she got home, but she had forgotten. Darlene lashed out with her wooden spoon and rapped Violet across the knuckles, then the back of the legs. She was wicked with that spoon. Violet could never anticipate when an attack was coming.

"Ow! Mommy!" she cried. "T'wasn't my fault. I slipped."

"Bull. You were out playing alley over with all the other youngsters."

Violet sat at the kitchen table whimpering, which she knew drove her mother up the wall.

"Go on and take a piece of bread and get out of my sight until I'm finished supper," her mother said.

At the centre of the kitchen table was a bowl filled with molasses bread, cut into perfectly even slices. Beside it was a mason jar of cloudberry jam, Violet's favourite. She lathered a slice of bread with jam and was out the door before Darlene could see the grin on her face, which would surely induce another smack with the spoon.

"And don't go tormenting the dogs!" her mother cried out as Violet made her way towards the dogs.

The jam was sweet and the bread even had a few chunks of raisin in it. It helped soften the cries of her angry stomach. Cloudberry jam was usually preserved for the winter, but they used some of the fresh stuff for the late summer as a rare treat. Violet was always excited when the family went berry picking. She wasn't very good at it, though. She usually ate half of what she picked. The first time she convinced her mother to take her berry picking, she'd tried so hard to resist the temptation and after what seemed like hours she finally filled her tiny bucket. She ran to her parents to show off her hard work and tripped. The berries scattered, many of them squished beneath her hands and knees. Violet sat there and cried. "No sense bawling about it," her mother said. "What's done is done. Get up and salvage whatever you can."

Violet heard the puppies' yelps from underneath her aunt's porch. During the winter, the dogs pulled the trappers' komatiks, which contained all their materials. During the summer, however, they roamed free on Spotted Island. In the day, the dogs laid under porches or wherever else they could find to escape the flies and mosquitos. Some of the men upturned their old beat up boats and used them as kennels. The flies tormented the dogs so much that some of them had all the hairs on their tails piqued off. Young puppies born late in the summer had to be kept inside otherwise the flies would eat them alive. In the evening, the dogs ran wild. Oftentimes at night they could be heard howling, especially if the moon was big and full.

Violet loved the huskies, especially the little puppies that were born in the spring. It was late in the summer now, so they were big enough to play with. Many of the huskies had crossbred with wolves at different points so they were a little feral. Her mother and aunt often warned that a bitch was very protective of her brood and unexpectedly misinterpreted harmless gestures as threats, but Violet knew the dogs would never hurt her.

She started running towards the dogs. The mother perked up and watched her carefully. Violet went to take a last bite of her molasses bread and tripped up over a rock. She landed on her elbow and drove her fist into her mouth, which knocked out one of her teeth. She was bleeding from her mouth and she started to cry. Her elbow had a good knock, too, and was also bleeding. She sat up and saw that her dress was even more tattered. Her mother was surely going to give it to her with the spoon now. That made her cry even harder. She was about to pick herself up off the ground when she heard a growl.

She looked up and saw the huskies' mother. Her ears were pulled back and she was showing her teeth. Violet smiled to let her know she didn't mean any harm to her puppies. The bitch pounced. Violet curled up into a ball and covered her head, but the dog bit and tore at her scalp. Other dogs came over and started nipping and clawing at her arms and legs.

Violet screamed. Her body was on fire. They swarmed on top of her and attacked her from every angle. She could hear them snarling the way they did when her dad tossed them raw meat.

After what felt like ages, she heard her aunt yell at the dogs. She beat at them with a broom until they backed off. Violet hurt all over. She couldn't even distinguish the different parts of her body; she was just one big lump of throbbing pain. She tried to open her eyes, but something wet and sticky stung them. Her aunt wrapped a bedsheet around her. Violet wiped her face and saw that the sheet was covered with her blood. There was a group of adults standing around her now. They all looked horrified, holding their hands to their mouths. Violet heard her mother approaching.

"What happened?" Darlene asked.

"Don't look," someone said.

Darlene lifted the sheet and looked at her mangled daughter. She cried out in pain, the same pain consuming Violet's body. She pulled her daughter close to her, but Violet shrieked. Darlene slackened her grip and held her softly.

Violet slipped into blackness. She could hear voices -- familiar voices babbling, talking nonsense. A few times she heard her name.

The pain softened into a dull throb. People were touching her. She was being passed around. Someone rubbed something soft and warm on her scalp. The pain receded, and she reclaimed her head from the indistinguishable blob of misery. Once again, she was being passed around and then it felt like she was floating over water.

The entire time her mother was present. Her voice rose above the anonymous chatter and suffocating pain. "It's going to be okay, love," Darlene said over and over.

Violet opened her eyes. She was inside a dazzling square of light surrounded by women she didn't recognize. They wore masks. She was a big ball of yarn. The women were stitching her into a doll. Violet was scared, but then she realized the pain had stopped. They were turning her back into a girl. She understood. A man was there, too. He was examining her. She looked at the man's hands and saw that they were claws. Big furry ears poked out from his mask. She cried out for her mother. He snarled and revealed a mouth full of sharp teeth. One of the women covered Violet's face with a mask. Her quick, anxious breaths got slower and deeper. Her body was filled with soft warm air and she floated away.

She woke up alone in a strange bed in a strange room. There were a few other empty beds in the room, but she was alone. The strange visions were quickly evaporating from her mind. She remembered that she'd been mauled by the huskies, but couldn't recall anything specific or concrete about the attack. The last thing she could remember was falling down and seeing the angry mother husky growling at her.

She tore off the blankets and saw that she was wearing a gown. There were stitches and bandages all over her. As she surveyed the damaged topography of her body, she was reminded of each bite. She reached up and felt the top of head. It was buzzed and stubbly. All of her long, curly blonde hair was gone. Tracks of prickly stitches ran over her head like a baseball. She traced her fingers over the deep groves left from the bites. The details of the attack came charging back. She felt them sinking their teeth into her. She could hear them tearing away her skin. She saw the face of the mother, so angry and full of hate. And that strange wolf-man standing over her.

"Mommy!" she cried out. "Mommy!"

A nurse entered the room. "It's okay, love," she said. "You're alright."

"Where's my mommy?" Violet cried.

"She had to go back to Spotted Island," the nurse explained.

"This isn't Spotted Island?" Violet asked.

"No, we're in Cartwright. This is a hospital. You've been asleep the last few days, ever since the dogs attacked you. You're a lucky girl. Your mother did a good job dressing your wounds before she brought you to us. She made a poultice with boiled juniper boughs mixed with bread. Very clever. And it just so happened that Dr. Hunt was in town and was able to help you. You very nearly died."

"When can I go home?"

"It's best you speak with Mrs. Matthews about that," the nurse said. "I'll go fetch her."

Violet lay back in bed. She thought about the dogs that attacked her. They would all be killed, she realized. Once a dog had the taste of human blood, they were too dangerous to keep. Violet felt sad that they'd all be killed because of her. Those poor little puppies were going to lose their mother. It was her fault, she knew it. She upset the mother and she was just defending her puppies. Violet's mother and aunt were always warning her to stay away from the dogs, but she wouldn't listen.

She thought of Darlene then. Why did she leave? There was a lot of work to do on Spotted Island, and there was little Bobby, but how could her mommy just leave her here like that? She cried into her pillow. Whenever she rubbed her head against the sheets, she was reminded of her hair and she cried more. She thought of what her mother would say whenever she started sooking and bawling. "There's no sense crying about it," she'd say. "It's not going to change nothing." She wiped her tears in the blanket and tried to compose herself.

A new woman entered the room. She was younger than the nurses and had a big bright smile. A little girl, a few years younger than Violet, trailed behind her closely.

"Hello, Violet," she said. "My name is Mrs. Matthews. I'm the head-mistress at Lockwood. I'm told that you're a very brave and resilient little girl."

"Hi," Violet managed to say after sniffling away a few remaining sobs.

"And this is Ophelia," she said. "Would you like to say 'hello' to Violet, Ophelia?"

Ophelia hid behind Mrs. Matthew's legs, peaking out at Violet.

"It's okay to be upset," Mrs. Matthews continued. "You've been through so much. And you must be sad that your mother isn't here. Well, I have some news that might cheer you up. Your mother told me you've been very keen on coming to my school?"

Violet nodded.

"Then I'm pleased to say that you will be starting in the fall."

A big smile broke across Violet's face. She started to cry again, this time in excitement.

"You might have to start a little bit later than the other kids while you recover, so in the meantime you're going to have to wait here and recover."

"Will I be able to go back to Spotted Island?"

"I'm afraid not, my dear. School starts soon, and we don't want you to miss any more days than you absolutely need to. Okay?"

"But Mommy said they couldn't afford school for me."

"Well, we've decided to make a special exception for you because you're obviously a very special little girl."

Violet smiled. She felt very safe with Mrs. Matthews. She had so much warmth in her eyes. It was clear that she was a very loving woman.

"Now," Mrs. Matthews said, "be a good little girl and do everything the nurses tell you. They'll get you back to full health so you can be a good student."

"Yes, ma'am," Violet said.

The thought of not going home to Spotted Island until next spring frightened her. She'd never been away from her family before. As much as she didn't like Roaches Brook, she still liked being with her family. But she was a big girl now, she told herself. She was going to school. She thought about all the new friends she was going to make and all the great things she was going to learn.

CHAPTER THREE (2015)

He could always tell when she was faking it. All those phony *oohs, ahhs, yeaahs, babies*. Insincere porn was such a turn off. It disrupted the illusion. The last thing Tyler needed when watching porn was to be reminded that he was watching porn. Having refined his palette, he knew when a porn star was fucking as opposed to working. This required a familiarity with the particular actress. Tyler's ear was attuned to the different moans, grunts, and slurps of his favorite porn stars. He could read her body language: a curled upper lip, furrowed eyebrows, hands running through hair, floppy legs, flailing arms; or he heard it in the pitch of her moan, the space between sighs. Usually, when she was actually cuming, she descended into a kind of non-verbal language. Something primal and animalistic. And wasn't that true for everyone?

Tyler thought of what it was like when he and Julie were really going at it. They didn't need to talk to each other. And when they reached the point when it was all about pleasure and neither felt self-conscious, they just panted like dogs. They hadn't fucked like that since Julie's party a month ago. And before that? How long had it been since Tyler could expect Julie to rub the heels of her feet over his ass, crinkle the corners of her lips, and squeeze his shoulders until she screamed, then exhaled and giggled?

Tyler left work that night at around midnight. It had been a busy night. Servers dumped plate after plate onto his pile. At the end of the night, his raw dishwasher hands were peeling, and his shoulders ached from all the repetitive motion. It was a struggle just to get the garbage bags of leftover food out into the dumpster.

After the restaurant was cleared, he stood outside and had a cigarette. His hands shook as he flicked the lighter. He couldn't understand why he was so agitated. All night he'd had a raging appetite. He asked one of the cooks to make him a big bowl of fries, which he snacked on throughout his shift. He even took a few bites of uneaten chicken or beef from customers' leftovers. With just a few long drags, he'd finished his smoke. He lit another one.

It was a mild April night, so he decided to walk. A waxing gibbous moon followed him home, just a sliver shy of full. He was still hungry, so he ducked into a pizzeria near Whiteway Street. The place was sketchy, but they made great, cheap pizza. It used to be a confectionary too. Now the floor was empty except for a pyramid of two-litre soda bottles. Behind the counter was a closed-circuit TV recording the four surveillance cameras that surrounded the store.

The guy working cash had a tattoo of a spider descending from his left eye. "What'll it be?" he asked.

Tyler ordered a pizza the size of a car's tire. Extra cheese.

He got into his house, slipped off his sneakers, and went to his room. He tossed the pizza on his bed, stripped down to his boxers, then sat down to his battle station, although lately it was more of a masturbation station. He hunted for porn while digging his way through the pizza.

Since having picked up the habit over the past few months, he had developed a library of sorts. He didn't save anything to his hard drive, of course. He didn't need Julie stumbling over that. Rather, over the course of his many expeditions, he had compiled a mental map of websites, links, and URLs. Tyler had two divergent routes. One was the well-trodden paths of videos and clips that were tried, tested, and true. These always came in handy when time was an issue. The other route was when he wanted to go exploring. Tunnels and dark continents that had piqued his interest, but because he didn't have the time or wasn't interested in that particular moment he had made a note of to later revisit. Tonight, with nothing but insomnia and a blank schedule, Tyler turned Chrome onto incognito mode and went happily wandering.

He liked to start with girl on girl. That was foreplay. He needed to get warmed up before he could oblige the presence of another man's cock. He turned on an all-girl oil massage. This was great for the first twenty minutes or so, then a couple guys entered the scene and the whole thing fell flat. The girls stopped having fun and started performing. Oh well. Moving on. After a few more lesbian scenes, Tyler was ready to accept a man's company.

He followed up on a few leads, looking for the perfect blowjob. He liked watching a girl be overwhelmed by the size of a guy, unless it became comical. That was usually the case with black guys in porn. Tyler wondered if this confirmed the "big black dick" stereotype, or if porn selected the most horse-like black men to cater to the stereotype for the sake the industry's suburban white boy demographic. Either way, the black guys were always gigantic. Sometimes, this worked for Tyler, although he often felt bad for the girl. Apparently, the vagina can stretch up to two hundred percent (Julie once told him that), but what about her jaw? Or her asshole, for that matter?

Another quibble: why do male porn stars insist on groaning over the female's performance? You are not the main attraction, buddy. Let the lady do her thing. Also, chill out with all the violent gagging. Tyler liked it when the man pushed the actress' comfort zone to make things more interesting, but nothing too obnoxious. The best blowjob was when the male allowed the female do her thing; let her exhaust all her techniques and then take over.

Tyler was not too keen on the middle part; he was more interested in appetizers and dessert. Here he emphasized quality over quantity. He liked routines that did not feel the need to constantly change positions. When you have something good going, ride it out. What's the rush? For Tyler, sex was like cooking: just do the simple things well instead of messing up the complicated stuff. Doggystyle with a bit of hair-pulling was all he wanted. Sometimes porn stars got themselves into these absurd positions, arms and legs splayed out like they were playing Twister, which couldn't possibly be enjoyable. Tyler called this the porn-spider.

Now came the finish. Lately, Tyler increasingly needed something nastier, crueler. He liked forced orgasms and even dipped into some rape fantasies. For tonight, he selected a kinky dungeon video that he had been eyeing. The actress was strapped to a dildo machine and covered in electrodes. Here, with the girl chained and gagged, Tyler painted his masterpiece into a wad of Kleenex and tossed it into a nearby trashcan. He closed the browser. It was uncanny how quickly a scene that inspired such deep desire turned revolting moments after cumming. In that moment, Tyler saw with full clarity the sad state of his position. He was ashamed. He checked the time. Six in the morning. His body was a mass of Jell-O. He didn't even have the energy to get up from his chair. He closed his eyes and fell asleep.

Tyler dreamt he was walking in the woods. Snow crunched beneath his footsteps. He heard something groaning in the distance. He followed the sound and came upon a strange mass on the forest floor. It was a translucent red and grey embryonic sack. Something writhed inside. A bony claw stretched out from inside the sack until it pierced the webbed film that encased it.

Tyler ran away before he could see what emerged. He came upon a lake of black water.

"Help!" someone shouted. Tyler looked out and saw Julie drowning. She was fighting to stay above the surface. "Help!" she cried.

Tyler treaded out into the water even though he could barely swim. Julie was pulled underwater. Tyler doggie paddled desperately to where she'd submerged. He could not see anything beneath the surface of the water. Something wrapped around his feet and pulled him under. He was dragged underwater as if he'd been attached to an anchor. Cold darkness surrounded him. He looked for Julie, but all he could see was blackness. Two small yellow lights flickered. They grew as they approached him. Tyler tried to scream, but ink filled his mouth and throat until his entire body was numb.

He awoke in his computer chair with his limp dick sticking out from the elastic band of his boxers. The memory of the dream evaporated as Tyler rubbed the sleep from his eyes. He felt like getting in bed and going back to sleep, but his stomach had different demands. He opened the pizza box and saw that he'd eaten the entire thing. He fished his phone from his pants on the floor and saw that it was five o'clock. There was a text from Julie sent earlier today: *We need to talk.*

He sat back in his chair and stared at the ceiling until he couldn't ignore his stomach anymore. He got up and put on some clothes that he found on the floor that smelled acceptable. He went to the kitchen and turned the oven to 450 degrees. While he waited for the oven to heat up, he grabbed his bong. The interior of the glass was caked with residue. On the kitchen table he busted up a bud and loosened some pinch from a cigarette. His tobacco/weed ratio was tipping increasingly towards the former lately. He lit the melange and inhaled deeply. The water was old and stale. It tasted awful, but he didn't care. He took a few rips until the oven finally dinged. He opened his freezer and pulled out some fries and nuggets. He dumped a pile of each onto a pan and shoved it in. He grabbed out a cigarette and stepped outside. He still respected his mother's insistence that no one smoked in the house.

It was a typically mauzy April day. The dampness was dull and heavy. Fog squatted over St. John's with no wind to push it around. Tyler could feel the city's indecision over whether it wanted to let it rain or not. 'We all know what you're going to pick,' Tyler thought. 'Just get it over with.' He didn't mind the rain, drizzle, and fog. Certainly nothing worth moving over.

He lit his cigarette and considered Julie's text. *We have to talk.* Ominous words, always. He knew he'd hit a homerun with her surprise party. He had just needed to keep the momentum going. Then something sucked the energy from him. He couldn't muster the effort to be the considerate boy-friend anymore. Now he felt her drifting away further than ever, that this final failure was the last confirmation she needed to give him the boot. They hadn't seen each other since Julie's classes ended a week ago, and they rarely exchanged texts. He knew the way her mind worked. She wouldn't want the distraction of their breakup to interfere with her final papers and exams. She was probably done now and prepared to do the deed. Today was Saturday, so she was working all day at the pool.

Drop by after work, Tyler texted.

'Screw it,' he thought as he rubbed out his cigarette and went back into his house. 'Let's just be done with it.'

The fries and nuggets were nice and crispy. The brown pile of empty calories barely fit on the plate. Tyler took out some ketchup, mayonnaise, and hot sauce, and mixed them together in a cup. A little dipping station, as Julie called it. He sprinkled salt and pepper over his dish. He grabbed a can of Pepsi and returned to his room. He turned on *World of Warcraft* and worked through his mound of fried food.

After traipsing around Azeroth for a couple hours, Tyler grew bored. He was bored with all his games right now. He felt the need for something classic. *Grand Theft Auto III*? No, something deeper. Something engrossing and cathartic. Something tragic and archetypal. He thought of all the games that had left a mark on him throughout his life: *Ocarina of Time, Metal Gear Solid, Half-Life, Skyrim.* He settled on *Final Fantasy VII.* Tyler could find a torrent easily enough, but he wanted a physical copy. He still had his old PlayStation 2 kicking around the house somewhere. He also felt the need to get up and move around. It was eight o'clock now. Julie wouldn't be over until ten-thirty or so. He decided to walk to the mall to see if he could find a used copy of *Final Fantasy VII.*

He threw on his flannel coat and trekked out into the elements with his earbuds plugged in. His eyes strained against the little bit of light coming through the overcast sky. As he walked, he lit a cigarette. He didn't bother taking the bus because he could walk there faster, and it wasn't like the drivers ever followed a schedule anyway. The humidity had broken slightly with a light rain. Cars splashed tiny puddles of water, which were a minor annoyance but not worth dwelling on.

He arrived at the mall. The shopping dead wandered aimlessly. It never ceased to amaze Tyler the abundance of consumers every time he came. A lady bumped into him and he growled. He was just as shocked as she was by his reaction. He put his head down and made his way to the video game store. The garish lights combined with walls of blue, green, and red made him feel like he was tripping on acid inside Willy Wonka's factory. He dug around the used section. There was a copy of *Final Fantasy VII* for a shocking $70. He justified the cost by reasoning that it would help him through the soon to be breakup with Julie. He saw himself on his couch with his PlayStation 2 controller in hand, playing for hours undistracted. He brought the game over to the guy with a neck beard at the cash.

"Nice," buddy said. "Classic."

"Thanks," Tyler said.

Tyler never knew how to handle these sorts of mundane exchanges, although he instantly realized "thanks" was probably not the appropriate response in this case. He shrugged off that awkward exchange and left the store.

A colossal feeling of dread overcame him. Suddenly the mall and everyone inside it felt unreal, like there were no discreet entities and everything was just ooze melting into an indeterminate stew. He gave his head a shake and took a deep breath. The world slowly reassembled itself. He tried to reckon with the strange experience. He figured that he was discombobulated from oversleeping after a series of nights of insomnia. He thought some coffee might perk him up a little, so headed over to a nearby cafe.

Standing in line, he spied a blonde girl sizing him up. Her gaze made him self-conscious of the fact that he hadn't showered recently and was wearing old smelly clothes. Not that it mattered. As bad as Tyler could let himself go, he never had trouble getting women's attention. Julie told him that he had an "effortless" look to him. His bed head and shaggy clothes made him look confident, which was very sexy, apparently. He didn't pretend to understand what women found attractive. However, now that he was going to be back on the market for the first time in four years, he figured he'd better learn to start playing to his strengths.

From his peripheral, he considered the blonde. She was hot in a very high maintenance kind of way. Tyler didn't necessarily have a "type," though these were the sorts of women that seemed to be attracted to him. Julie was very anxious about how she looked in public when they first started dating. She grew more comfortable when it was just the two of them. Still, if they went out anywhere, even if it was just with friends, she still had to have her makeup and wardrobe on point. Whenever he listened to guys talk about women he was always surprised by their high standards, how easily they found certain flaws so repulsive (although, Tyler was confident they were full of shit). Nevertheless, he didn't want to be seen out and about with an ugly girlfriend. The blonde spoke loudly of personal matters with a much less attractive brunette. Tyler eavesdropped on their conversation. They seemed to be complaining about a mutual acquaintance. He deduced that they were co-workers who were on a lunch break from wherever they worked here at the mall, most likely a beauty salon judging by their conversation and appearance. Maybe someday soon he'd drop by for a haircut.

He ordered an extra large dark roast, which he took black. The girls' conversation paused as he walked by. He felt them watching him as he left.

He was smacked in the face by wind and rain just as he stepped outside. The sky was dark blue as night began to fall. Tyler threw up his hood and started walking. He stuffed the bag containing *Final Fantasy VII* into his coat pocket. He thought about the arguments he and Julie used to have about video games, usually their merit, and whether they could be considered art. Tyler argued that they could be. He used examples likes *Shadow of the Colossus* and *Bioshock*. Julie argued that while video games had artistic qualities, and she conceded that some did indeed have great narrative elements, they couldn't necessarily be considered art in the strictest sense of the word. Tyler thought this was very elitist of her. How could she not see that something like *Final Fantasy VII*, for example, wasn't art? Surely, the scope and sophistication of the story qualified it as such. Tyler never felt as immersed in a novel as he did playing a great RPG or other story-driven games.

As he thought of *Final Fantasy VII*'s protagonist, Cloud, a genetically-modified super soldier who wrestled with alien genes inside him, Tyler became nauseous again. His head whirled, and his chest was tight. The coffee was making him feel queasy. He threw the remaining half-cup into a garbage can. He took out a cigarette. His hands shook as he struggled to work his lighter against the wind and rain. Tyler bowed his head down against the elements and quickened his steps.

He got into his house and stripped off his wet clothes. He lay on the couch and tried to slow the Tilt-A-Whirl currently reeling inside his skull. He packed his bong and took a long rip. The bong water bubbled violently. He filled the glass chamber with yellow smoke then quickly inhaled. He closed his eyes and held his breath, letting the pot saturate his lungs. As he exhaled, he felt relief. He took a few more hits. The cycle was a meditation exercise. The burgeoning Zen was interrupted when he began coughing violently. He fell off the couch and rolled onto the floor, fighting to catch his breath. Stars shot across his vision. He lay on the floor another while as he sucked in air and composed himself. He started to laugh.

"Like a virgin," he said aloud.

He stood up and the nausea was gone.

He went to his room and dug around for his old PlayStation. He'd gotten it for his eighth birthday in 2002. By then he'd already internalized the fact that he was poor. His single mother was a secretary at the university.

She couldn't even afford a car. Most of the kids in the neighbourhood were poor, too. Their house was surrounded by housing projects in Rabbittown and Stabb Court. Only a few of the kids could afford something like a video game console and everyone piled into the rooms of the ones who did. Controllers and games were shared. The kids planned their birthday and Christmas wish lists strategically. Tyler asked for a Playstation 2, Shawn asked for a Gamecube, and Will an Xbox, so that they covered the entire gaming spectrum. They chipped together money so they could walk down to Allan's Video on Elizabeth Avenue to rent games over the weekend. They'd have sleepovers, playing *GTA, Halo,* or *Super Smash Bros* all night. Now Will and Shawn were living in Alberta. The rest of his old friends were also scattered, only coming home for brief visits. Sometimes they all got together for trips to Mexico or Cuba. They invited Tyler, but he never went. He didn't get the whole obsession with travel. It seemed like a big competition to make your friends on Instagram jealous or score a nice little profile picture hugging a skinning African child.

The only person he had left in his life was Julie, and now she was leaving too. He remembered that conversation with Nick at Julie's birthday party. "Are you going to be moving with Julie to Halifax?" Tyler understood now. She'd already made her decision to go to Dalhousie. She just hadn't told him yet.

He hated Halifax. The trip last summer was fun, but he didn't like the city or the people. They all had this superiority complex. Haligonians weren't from Nova Scotia, they were from *Halifax,* as if it were the only bastion of civilization east of Montreal. The night he blacked out, he and his buddies weren't allowed into a club because they had Newfoundland IDs. The bouncer claimed the club didn't admit out of province IDs. Tyler ripped into the guy. He cursed him, the city, and everyone in it. He was shouting from the middle of the street. A crowd began to form. Someone muttered "cops" and Tyler took off running. That was the last thing he remembered of that night, the smug look on that bouncer's face. Whenever Tyler thought of stuck-up mainlanders, looking down on Newfoundlanders, he thought of that guy's face. 'Fuck Halifax,' he thought. Even if Julie wanted him to go, he wouldn't.

He remembered falling in love with Julie, how quickly it had happened. Their first summer together, before university, was the happiest time of his life. They did drugs, had sex, ordered pizza, and repeated the process until they lost track of time and dates. Everything felt new with her. She was experiencing so many things for the first time and he rediscovered them with her. There was an insatiable hunger for newness in her. A whole different person was growing within her and it was thrilling for Tyler to behold and be a part of. But there was a conflict within her. There was also the old Julie that persisted in all this growth. The part of her that was like her parents and old friends. The Julie that would rather have a nice job with nice things and be surrounded with nice, successful people. All the talk about becoming a writer was just childish dreams. Tyler feared he was only a phase for her, that she would eventually leave him behind and become a yuppie just like her parents. Now, it seemed like that day had come and the other Julie had finally won out.

Tyler continued to dig around his closet for his PlayStation 2 to no avail. He could remember the look on his mother's face when he first tore at the wrapping to reveal its blue box. He could see the happiness in her eyes whenever she gave him something that brought him joy. Looking back, he understood the financial stress she was under. Still, he was surprised by how little it held them back. Even though she didn't have a car and they never took any trips, Tyler still had nice clothes, video games, and could afford to play house league hockey. And when she died, she left Tyler the house mortgage-free and funeral expenses paid. He wondered how she did it.

He went poking around the rest of the house, in the closet, around the living room, even in some of the kitchen cupboards. The last place it could be now was his mother's old room. He walked up to the door and slowly turned the knob. The wood and joints creaked from lack of use. The room was musty and the air was heavy. He switched on the light, but it didn't work. He took out his cell and used the flashlight function. A thin film of cobwebs and dust covered everything. His mother's old pictures lined her dresser. They were mostly photographs of Tyler as a boy and his grandparents. His mom only kept one picture of herself. It was a Polaroid of her outside the old Montreal Forum. She wore high-wasted jeans and a pastel shirt. Her wavy blonde hair was tied up in a scrunchie. Tyler thought she'd actually be fashionable today. He didn't look much like his mother, he knew. He'd never seen a picture of his father, and his mother never provided much of a description. His name was Joseph. That was about all that Tyler knew. Below the photo was written "Go Habs Go!" She'd gone to see game five of the 1993 Stanley Cup final between the Canadiens and the Los Angeles Kings. The Habs won it to take the Cup. She was a huge fan, never missed a game on TV, yet whenever Tyler asked her about the Stanley Cup game she only gave him the most perfunctory details. He couldn't imagine seeing the Habs win the cup in Montreal. It would be the game of a lifetime. "It was a long time ago," his mom would say when Tyler wanted to know what Patrick Roy looked like in the flesh, or what the Forum sounded like when Kirk Muller scored the winning goal. What did the seats feel like? What did the beer taste like? "It was a long time ago."

When he brought this all up to Julie, she pointed out something Tyler had never considered: he was born exactly nine months later, March 9th, 1994. He couldn't believe he'd never figured that out for himself. Surely his mother's reticence had something to do with his father. Maybe it was him who took the picture. He wondered what his mom would've thought of Julie. She would've liked her, he imagined. He wasn't so sure what she would've thought of how he turned out. He picked up the photograph and examined it. The only time he could ever remember seeing his mother smile like that was his eighth birthday, when he opened his gift and found the PlayStation 2. He rubbed the dust off the glass frame. He saw that there was a slight bulge in the photo. He took the frame apart. Two ticket stubs fell to the floor. Something was written on the back of the picture in a handwriting Tyler didn't recognize:

> *To many more nights together.*
> *And many more Cups!*
> *Love,*
> *-J*

"J" must stand for Joseph, Tyler realized. He moved his foot and stepped on something sharp. He scanned the floor with his flashlight and discovered a ring. He examined it and it looked like an engagement ring. So much for "many more nights together." The Habs haven't won a championship since, either. The entire affair was cursed. Tyler tucked the tickets behind the photo and reassembled the picture frame. He left the ring on her dresser.

He opened the closet. All his mother's clothes were still hanging there. He pushed them around and searched the spaces with his phone. He couldn't see the PlayStation anywhere. With his hands on her old clothes, Tyler suddenly felt like an intruder, that he was invading a sacred place. He backed away from the closet and left the room. He shut the door behind him and wandered out into the living room. He sat down on the couch and then remembered what he'd done with the PlayStation 2. Back in high school, when the PlayStation 3 came out, he brought it over to Traders along with all his old games and hocked it. He was focused on PC gaming at that point and was no longer interested in consoles. He used the bit of cash to buy some weed. Not only was he a failure of a boyfriend, he was a failure of a son.

He struggled to breathe. He tried to wipe the warmth from his face as tears rolled from his eyes. He stood up and walked around, trying to catch his breath. He opened the door and stepped outside on his back patio, half-naked. The cold wind and rain whipped his skin until he felt numb. His tears turned to uncontrollable sobs. He looked up in the sky and saw a full yellow moon watching him beneath the cover of clouds. A fist of despair punched him in the stomach. The nausea returned. Everything around him spun as his vision funnelled downward into an abyss. His face contorted and his jaw clenched while he was in the middle of a sob.

He stumbled back into the house and into the kitchen. He needed water. He tried to turn the faucet, but the joints in his arms ached. The world collapsed into an impressionistic soup of colors and shapes and stars. He fell to the floor and struck his head off the table. The taste of blood filled his mouth. Spasms shook his body like a lightning storm. He writhed in pain on the kitchen floor until he mercifully lost consciousness.

Over the past week, Julie was getting better at this. She didn't even get piss on her fingers anymore. This was her second test today. She left the little stick in longer than five seconds this time, to be thorough. After she was done, she laid it on the sink and waited. She checked her phone, nervously swiping through tweets and Facebook posts. After a few minutes, she checked the pregnancy test. Positive. They'd all been positive. She was two weeks late now and her breasts had nearly grown a full cup-size. She felt randomly nauseous. There was no point denying it anymore. She grabbed her phone and texted Tyler. *We need to talk.* She hated to be so cryptic, but hopefully this would grab his attention. Julie didn't understand what was going on with him lately. Up to her birthday, he'd been making such an effort and then all of a sudden, he became withdrawn. Nonetheless, she needed to tell him the truth of this and everything else.

Julie closed the door to the bathroom and held her hand to her chest, trying to steady her breath. Her mother appeared.

"Are you okay?" she asked.

"Yes," Julie replied. "I'm just having bad cramps."

"I'm not sure I feel comfortable leaving you like this," her mother said.

"Relax. I'm okay. Really."

"Alright, well, we'll be gone by the time you get home from work. We should be at the hotel this time tomorrow."

Julie went to her room to get changed. She put on her bathing suit then covered up with some track pants and a red hoodie. She threw a change of underwear into her bag. She came downstairs and wished her parents goodbye and hoped they'd have fun on their retirement cruise around the Caribbean and South America.

"I really wish you'd take the car to work," her father said. "It looks like it's going to start raining soon."

"I'll be fine," she said. "I hope your flight isn't delayed. Escaping Newfoundland can be such a pain."

She kissed her mother and father goodbye and left. Most people didn't understand Julie's love of walking. Her parents had bought her a Jetta when she graduated high school with the understanding that she'd use it to drive to school and work. Nevertheless, Julie insisted on walking anywhere that was within a thirty minute trek. She considered herself a *flaneur* like her favourite French poet Charles Baudelaire. An urban wanderer strolling the city streets. Not to mention that parking on campus was a nightmare. Unfortunately, St. John's harboured a great antagonism towards pedestrians. A lack of planning over the years had created a patchwork quilt of a city. The downtown core was pretty much just a bunch of horse paths paved over and from there St. John's sprawled out haphazardly like a drunk throwing development deals at a dartboard. If anyone needed so much as a hammer and nail, they needed a car to make the trip. In the winter, the sidewalks were rarely cleared. Julie had many close encounters with inconsiderate drivers who were infected with the city's anti-pedestrian venom.

But while the city's antiquated grid frustrated drivers with its unpredictable one-way streets and dead ends, it delighted walkers such as Julie. It reminded her of walking in the older parts of Europe. She even appreciated the exercise she got from the city's peaks and valleys. Walking somewhere was an opportunity for her to plug in her headphones and drift. In those moments she didn't think about work, school, or Tyler.

Walking its streets was the only thing that connected her with St. John's after coming home from Europe. It wasn't anything about the city or Newfoundland in general; St. John's was as good a place as any. It was her life here that bored her. She was very fortunate to have wealthy parents, but their safety net at times felt like a spider's web. She longed for a more authentic form of independence. They meant well, but at every twist and turn she was confronted with their charity. And she was honest with herself enough to know that she would never truly get out from underneath them unless she put a bit of real geographic distance between them.

And then there was Tyler. Julie had hoped that she could help him progress beyond his state of inertia. She wasn't looking for anything specific; she didn't care if he went to school or got a trade; she didn't even have an issue with the fact that he spent his time washing dishes, playing video games, and getting high. She liked getting high, too. The problem was that he never wanted to do anything more than that. He never wanted to travel, to experience new things, or to create anything. She suggested that he become a competitive gamer. He laughed and said he'd never be good enough for that. She suggested he try designing games or computers. He laughed and said he'd never get the opportunity to work at the big gaming companies.

Her: What about independent game designers?

Him: That was like winning the lottery.

Her: Then why not just do it for the satisfaction of it?

Him: What would be the point of that?

There was always some excuse. Most recently, he'd kicked around the idea of becoming a cook. He enjoyed working in a kitchen and had a natural talent for food. They loved watching food shows on Netflix and Anthony Bourdain's *Kitchen Confidential* was one of the few books he ever read. But, as usual, these ideas remained only half-baked.

She came home from Europe last summer feeling so full of hope and ambition, like she could achieve anything. Then she found Tyler in exactly the same state as when she'd left him. Their trip to Halifax only confirmed what she'd feared. Before leaving, she'd felt travel weary and considered backing out. But then she remembered that this was a big step for Tyler. Perhaps getting his toes wet with this little adventure would trigger an untapped wanderlust. Unfortunately, it was a disaster. It started out as a success. The show was great. Then they met a drug dealer who was sealing acid. "It's triple-dipped," he explained. The sheet had an illustration of a grim reaper, which Julie could only interpret as more than a little ominous. She took half a hit. Tyler took the other half, along with two others. This was typical Tyler. Because she was generally a moderate, he could confidently indulge with excess knowing that she would be there to babysit him if/when things got bad. She realized that she should just speak up and tell him to take it easy, but that felt like being too motherly. They hit up a couple bars and were having fun, until they tried to get into one spot that wouldn't let them inside because of their Newfoundland IDs. Everyone was pissed, but Tyler went on a rampage. He ran off, claiming he was gone to find a human rights lawyer. Clearly, the acid had kicked in. The group went looking for him. They found him screaming at the Old Burying Ground. "Fucking niggers," he kept screaming. Julie tried to calm him. They deduced that a couple black guys had mugged him. Some cops came by. They explained that he could make a report, but that they would have to get him somewhere to dry out for the night, otherwise they'd throw him in the drunk tank.

Julie got him back to their room. They were staying in the students' residencies at Dalhousie. She got Tyler into bed. His rage over the mugging had cooled off. But then he started to weep. Julie had never seen him cry. Not even when he talked about his mother. "What's wrong?" she asked.

"Why doesn't he want me?" Tyler kept repeating.

"Who?" Julie asked. "Your father?"

Tyler's cries then turned into a howl, like an animal caught in a trap. He cried and screamed until his voice was hoarse and he sounded like he was possessed and speaking some demonic language. He eventually exhausted himself and fell asleep. The next morning, he claimed to have completely forgotten the incident. He apologized for being such a state and didn't want to file a report or press charges. The only thing he claimed to remember was the bouncer who wouldn't let them in the bar. Everyone agreed that it was discriminatory and an awful shame. However, what Julie saw as a just an isolated incident of one particular asshole, Tyler saw as vindication of his belief that mainlanders don't want Newfoundlanders around, so everyone should just stick to their own part of the playground.

Julie understood then that Tyler was frozen in time, paralyzed. His pain was glacial. While he was justified in his righteous condemnation of that bouncer's discrimination, what he wouldn't admit though, which Julie could see, was that he was infinitely grateful the experience. It gave him an excuse. It gave him permission to stay holed away in St. John's. To say, "Oh well, they don't like our kind. Might as well not even bother." Julie was willing to let slide the fact that he had took too much acid and made an ass out of himself. She was also willing to dismiss the racist slurs as an isolated incident. But she couldn't let go of the sound of Tyler's crying. The deep anguish it betrayed. There was a pain deep within Tyler to which he could not give a voice. It wasn't that he was stupid. Julie never thought that of Tyler. To have grown up without a father and then losing his mother at such a young age was the sort of trauma few could recover from. It was commendable that Tyler could function at the level he did. Part of what made her love him was his refusal to indulge in self-pity.

When they'd first started dating, she was amazed at his independence. He was so much more mature than anyone their own age. To be frank, she was a spoiled princess, just like her friends. Everything had been handed to her. And here was Tyler, all on his own, fending for himself. She didn't even know how to work an oven. He helped her discover her autonomy. Now, she understood that it was a reaction to losing his mother, the only person he had in his life. In order to survive, Tyler matured overnight. But in many ways, he was still the same sixteen-year-old kid. And now he was petrified in that state.

Julie did not expect him to change for her. She knew it was too much to ask for him to put all that behind him. However, she also wasn't obliged to be his psychotherapist and pseudo-mother. She'd always believed him when he said he'd give university another chance or apply to trade school. He'd also toyed with the idea of building custom computers. He once rigged up an old tube TV to her busted laptop. "Hipsters would buy the shit out of this," he said. And he was probably right. There always seemed time for these dreams to come true. Now, in her final year as an undergrad, time had caught up them. Or at least for her. She was ready to move on, to become someone new. All she could see in Tyler was stagnation, a fear to move forward. She still nevertheless believed that Tyler could reach his potential at some point, she just no longer believed that he would with her.

She arrived at the pool. She went to the staff change room and took off her hoodie and sweat pants. She grabbed a towel and some flip flops. Chelsea was getting changed, too. She was one of the few friends she had in high school that she'd kept in contact with after she started dating Tyler.

"You okay?" Chelsea asked. "You're looking a little stressed."

"Lots on my mind," Julie said.

"How're your exams going?"

"I'm all done now, actually. Semester and undergrad totally finished."

"Congrats! I hear you're going to Dal in the fall."

"That's the plan. Do you have a work term this summer?"

"Yeah, I'm going to Aberdeen, Scotland."

"Wow, I'm jealous. Sometimes I wish I'd done engineering."

"I'm sure you'll do well with law. Will Tyler come to Halifax with you?"

"I don't know," Julie said after some hesitation.

"I see," Chelsea said, as they walked out onto the pool deck.

Julie was in the kiddie pool with the tots and their over-protective parents. Each time she stepped into the heated pool, she repressed the knowledge that it was full of children's piss. She resented the fact that if you were a woman working as a swimming instructor you were almost certainly going to have to teach tots. She looked across the pool at all the guys walking around deck, teaching breaststroke to the more mature kids. "They're just more comfortable around women," parents would say about their infants. Funny, Julie thought, because they screamed and bawled just the same.

One part she truly enjoyed about tots was the baptismal. That first splash of water. She'd take the child from its fawning parents and hold it in the water. The child would adjust and start kicking its legs. Then Julie would count down. "One, two, three!" and dunk the kid under the water. The child would usually emerge with a shocked look on its face that slowly turned into a grimace, exploding into tears. Its mother would scope the child up with a towel and try to comfort it as if this was some kind of traumatic experience. What did they expect when they signed the kids up for swimming lessons?

Julie watched a mother in the family change room, removing her baby's diaper and changing it into a swimsuit. It all seemed repulsively mammalian to her: these little sucklings that attached themselves to their mother's breast, crying when they were tired, hungry, or bored; parents having to carry them around like giant fragile eggs; cleaning up after their shit for years until they become ungrateful teenagers and then left (hopefully) without ever looking back--unless they picked the wrong undergrad (which is about all of them) and now they were broke and back in the basement. That's what Julie feared, falling back into that state of dependence on her parents. That's why she didn't want to go to grad school. She'd come to see academia as just another womb, a hiding place from the real world. So many of her profs had the emotional maturity of their students. She was disgusted by the sad, middle-aged man in the tweed jacket and Levi's jeans hitting on young girls, thinking they were like Rupert Giles from *Buffy the Vampire Slayer*. She resented the pint-sized epiphanies and mutilated Marxism students offered professors to ingratiate themselves. She especially resented the fact that she herself was no less guilty of the exact same thing. Profs were just more authority figures from which to cleave validation. This was her final step towards authentic independence. To no longer require approval from anyone other than from herself. She had no delusions that law school would be radically different than her undergrad, but at least there was a way out, a passport to other possibilities.

Swimming lessons were over now. Staff were getting the pool ready for the evening recreational swim. Julie grabbed a quick shower to rinse the piss-water from her body. She went to the change room and threw on a lifeguard tank and shorts. She checked her phone. Tyler had responded to her text. *Drop by after work*, he'd said.

The fact that he didn't ask, *about what?* told her that he'd been anticipating this. Where would she start? That'd she'd accepted an offer from Dalhousie months ago without telling him? That she was breaking up with him? Or maybe that she was pregnant? There didn't seem to be any favourable entry into this labyrinth. She went to a nearby Tim Hortons to get some supper. She considered a few angles and rehearsed some approaches. This was what happened when the truth is denied for so long, Julie realized. It grew into a monster. There was one possibility, however, that she had never considered. What if Tyler said yes? What if he said he wanted to come to Halifax, that he'd get his act together?

She mulled these questions as her cheap coffee cooled. Chelsea saw her and came over.

"Now you're definitely upset," she said. She pulled up a chair besides Julie. "Talk to me. Is it about you and Tyler?"

"Yeah. He's been acting so strange lately. Obviously, he knows something's wrong. I feel so guilty."

"I remember when you guys first hooked up. We all thought you were crazy. You said you liked his sad, puppy dog eyes. We thought he was a wolf in sheep's clothing. But you guys really balanced each other out."

"I still love him. I just don't see a future together."

"Everything he's been through is so sad. He needs help to get through that. But that doesn't mean it has to be you."

"I agree. I was actually planning on going over there tonight to end it. I have no idea what I'm going to do."

"It's going to be okay. Your intentions are good and I'm sure you'll find the words. I'm here for you."

Julie stood up and hugged Chelsea. She wiped a few tears from her eyes. They went out on deck. Julie went to her first position. She was standing by the kiddie pool, which had now been turned into a hot tub. Two kids were making out in one of the corners. Julie wondered what possessed people in the 1950's to write cute love songs about teenaged public displays of affection. "And they call it puppy love."

Julie blew her whistle and gestured at the kids to knock it off.

The lifeguards rotated positions. Next to her whistle, hung the gold Phaistos disc necklace that Tyler had given her for her birthday. That night he'd opened a door to a possible future for them. But then, soon after, he closed it. She held up her necklace and considered the strange hieroglyphs etched into the disc. It was very romantic to imagine that they communicated some deep spiritual truths, but in all reality, they were likely inventory for grain, fish, and other mundane concerns. Ancient Greece had always fascinated Julie. She loved reading mythology growing up and she took as many Classics electives as she could at university. Last summer, she finally had the opportunity to visit Greece. Perhaps the most memorable moment was visiting the Temple of Zeus at Olympia. There she saw the remains of the temple's east pediment, which depicted one her favourite myths, Pelops' chariot race.

Pelops was a fascinating character. His father, Tantalus, had chopped him up into a soup and tried to feed him to the gods. Fortunately, the gods perceived the trick and reconstituted Pelops, except for his shoulder blade, which had been eaten by Demeter. Pelops went on to found the Olympic Games as a tribute to the gods. In the race that is depicted at Olympia, Pelops cheats Myrtilus, who then curses Pelops and the House of Atreus. All of Pelops's subsequent sons died cruel deaths, right down to Agememnon until Orestes finally made things right. Julie used to think it was profoundly cruel of the gods to punish Pelops' heirs, that they should pay for the sins of an ancestor from generations ago. Now, Julie understood that the Greeks had actually managed to capture humanity's existential condition: that we all bore the traces of the past. History was a nightmare from which we could not awake.

Some kids were running on the pool deck. Julie blew her whistle and they stopped. She went over and gave them a stern lecture. She could remember once a kid slipped and cracked his skull. A slippery puddle of blood bloomed from his head across the deck.

Julie hated being a lifeguard and swim instructor. She hated having to be an authority figure in a job that no one respected. However, it was the best option available to her. She didn't want to go into the service industry or retail. The idea of supplicating to the hoi polloi was horrifying. That was why she wanted to go pursue a law degree. She needed something to fall back on if her dream of becoming an author didn't work out. The thought of grinding out a living while she developed her craft was exhausting even to consider. That would certainly mean more years of being trapped in her parents' circle of influence. Her decision to go to law school was a product of both her practicality and her insecurity. While she read widely and was a strong student of literature, she'd yet to produce anything of much promise. There were people in her classes winning competitions and getting published. She had a vision for her body of work. Unlike all those social justice warriors language policing on the internet, screaming "No!" at all the shitty little dweebs, she would be an overwhelming "Yes!" Her work would be a giant affirmation of feminism and post-colonialism and all her other post-modern politics. It would be a giant tidal wave that would negate by saying "Yes!". Yet, despite these lofty ambitions, the best Julie had managed to achieve was to get a weepy little poem published in the English Department Student Society's journal:

"snack"

i've heard that when
Inuit want to kill wolves
they hack at a sheet of ice
and pour blood over its jagged edges
the wolf comes and licks the blood
overcome with appetite
it cannot taste its own blood
and dies in its feeding frenzy

i've read that when
a person eats a dorito
the brain is tricked
by the chemical lies
we anticipate a filling feast
so we continue to binge
to compensate for the lacunae

the cruel dialectic
of poverty and plenty

She'd submitted it at Tyler's behest after smoking a lot of weed. She never expected they'd actually choose it. And now there it was, immortalized in ink. Or at least whenever all the copies of that little journal were wiped from the earth, which she suspected would be the near future.

Julie and the rest of the lifeguards blew their whistles to announce the swim was over. All the kids were herded out and the pool was cleaned up. She got ready to leave. She got dressed and checked her phone. Nothing else from Tyler. There was a text from Nick: *End of term drinks tonight?*

"Did you want a ride?" Chelsea asked. "It's pretty gross out."

"That's fine," Julie said. "I'll need the walk over to get psyched up."

"Call me after if you need someone to talk to."

"I will."

Julie walked outside. The wind and rain cut deep into her bones. She looked up and saw a yellow moon hiding behind the rain clouds. She cursed it for the weather. Fortunately, the walk from the Aquarena to Tyler's house was short. Even though she'd been thinking about breaking up with Tyler for months, she'd never visualized life without him. While Keith was technically her first boyfriend, that was so long ago and so chaste that it may as well have been a kindergarten crush. Tyler was the only guy she'd ever been with. She wasn't leaving him because she was eager to be with someone new. She'd be happy to stay together, if things were different. She couldn't imagine being with anyone else. The thought of entering the dating scene made her anxious. Tinder and thirst traps were foreign concepts. She knew that Nick was circling around her like a vulture. He reeked of desperation. She respected Nick and found his intelligence very attractive. However, she couldn't imagine sleeping with him. The humanities and social sciences were filled with nebbish dorks. The other end of the spectrum was even worse: the poseurs with their Bukowski and boutique neck tattoos. Then there were the Social Justice Warriors and their foes, the Men's Rights Activists and Free Speech Warriors, all locked in a battle over the internet that no one really cared about. They were all doomed to be perpetual undergrads, late-twenty-something know-it-alls splitting hairs and blogging think pieces. It was a new Dantesque level of hell. Julie considered herself a feminist and despised the casual racism and misogyny that oozed into every pore of this patriarchal society, but who had time to play language police and explain post-colonialism theory and third-wave feminism to every meathead with WiFi.

For the last four years, Tyler had been a respite from this nonsense. They often disagreed over politics, and she knew that he was often baiting her, but he was someone that she could bounce ideas off of without feeling judged. What she loved most about being with Tyler was that she felt like not only could she be herself, she could also try being new people as well. She was comfortable exploring new aspects of herself with him and he was always curious about what new ideas she was kicking around. However radical her feminism became or how socialist her politics, she knew that

Tyler had a firm grip on the core of who she was. It anchored her. While she felt self-conscious discussing unclear ideas with her classmates, Tyler challenged her in playful way. Theories and concepts took on more significance than means towards academic achievement or social capital. Many A+ papers came from workshopping theses with Tyler over a couple bong hits. These were the types of things that kept her from leaving.

She also wondered if she'd be breaking up with Tyler if the sex was still good. After Europe, she'd gained a sexual autonomy as part of her new self-confidence. Before she'd let Tyler take the initiative and followed his lead. There were also things that had bugged her that she no longer took in stride. For one thing, Tyler rarely came inside her. He preferred to finish himself off. It made Julie insecure and she told him. She was also tired of their old routines. She enjoyed being submissive, but most of Tyler's fantasies involved her being immobilized. However, Tyler was unable to step even an inch outside his comfort zone. He'd helped her grow into her own sexual identity, and now she'd outgrown him. Once Julie started making demands, he lost his confidence and spontaneity, things that Julie had loved so much about him.

Early in their relationship, when they lay in bed together, sweaty and tired, she often made jokes about the cellulite on her thighs. Or she'd complain jokingly that it was unfair that she couldn't just move the fat from her ass to her tits. She was always putting herself down. One night at Tyler's, she was standing in front of his closet mirror in her bra and underwear, and remarked that she looked like Peter Pan with smaller tits. Tyler stood behind her and took off her bra. He bent her forward so that she leaned on the edge of his computer chair. He pulled her hair and told her to look into the mirror. He slapped her hard on the ass. "Say you're beautiful," he said.

"I'm beautiful," she said. He repeated this a few times. He then peeled her underwear off and stuffed it into her mouth and sealed it shut with red bondage tape.

"Say it louder now so I can hear," he said. He slapped her ass, and she yelled through the gag. He took off his pants and slid into her from behind. They looked at each other in the mirror. "When you come," he said, "I want you to say 'I'm pretty' until you're finished." When they were done, she pulled off the tape and spat her underwear onto the ground. They laughed for awhile until she started to cry. He held her. They lay in bed and fell asleep without saying anything.

She put these thoughts aside and considered her strategy. Julie established that this would be a two-pronged attack. First: *I accepted an offer from Dalhousie. I didn't tell you because I don't want you to come. A long-distance relationship is not an option. Second: I'm pregnant and I'm getting an abortion.* The latter was non-negotiable. She wasn't going to be timid about wanting an abortion. It wasn't fair that women had to be ashamed. If abortion is murder, then shouldn't miscarriage be considered manslaughter? As far as Julie was concerned, a miscarriage was your body deciding pregnancy was a bad idea, whereas an abortion was your brain making the same decision. Why should the body be given privilege over the brain? Why is it that if something happens "naturally," then it is morally just? Even if unborn fetuses could be considered "alive," then that would necessitate all sorts of implications. People should no longer have any say about whether they get to be organ donors after they die. Bodily autonomy might as well be totally abandoned. She realized that she was getting distracted. His house was close and she needed to focus.

She came up to his door and knocked. She could see that all the lights were on, but there was no answer. She peered in through the window. His living room was in a state. She took out her key and let herself in.

"Tyler?" she called out.

No response.

She heard the back door banging against the wind. She went to the kitchen and closed it. There were torn clothes scattered around the floor. She went to his room. Along the corridor were scratch marks across the walls. She heard something from the living room. It sounded like an animal whimpering. She found a giant dog licking its paw in the corner of the room.

She stared at the mass of black fur and tried to understand what the hell was going on. Did Tyler take off somewhere and leave the door open only to have some stray dog wander inside and rip his place up? As she observed the animal, she was reminded of the creepy dog/wolf her and Tyler had seen the night of her birthday in the cemetery. Surely, it wasn't the same dog, was it? She then decided that she wasn't interested in finding out and the best idea would be leave immediately. She began to creep backwards slowly and stepped on a broken splinter of wood, snapping it in half.

The animal looked up and they locked eyes. It began to growl and faced her. It didn't have those otherworldly yellow eyes that she remembered. Instead, its eyes were brown and very human. Just like when that kid slipped and cracked his skull, Julie didn't panic. She took deep breaths and clutched to her composure. She again made a move backwards and the dog growled louder. When she took another step towards the door, the dog stood up on its hind legs. To her shock, it must have stood six-feet tall. It walked towards her with its fists punching the floor like a silverback gorilla. At that point she lost her nerve.

She made a move to get out of the living room towards the front door, but the beast anticipated this and cut off that exit. She turned and sped to the kitchen. The dog followed. She ran behind the Formica table and picked up a carving knife. The dog pounced and crashed into the table. Julie leapt to the side and dodged the attack. She slammed her back hard against the sink. The beast crushed the table and slid on the linoleum floor into the fridge. It flailed clumsily trying to get to its feet, kicking at the broken table and sliding on the floor.

Julie escaped the kitchen and ran to the corridor. The dog chased her to block her path to the front door. She turned and swung her knife wildly. She caught it across the snout. The dog yelped in pain. She used the chance to run to the bathroom. The corridor was too small for the beast to maneuver quickly. Julie got inside the bathroom and locked the door. She stood in the tub, her back against the wall, with her knife pointed towards the door. Outside she could hear the dog moaning plaintively, as if it were some puppy that had been denied its toy.

She stood there, catching her breath, trying to plan her next move. The wind and rain beat the window above her. The beast crashed against the door and started clawing. She dropped the knife and opened the window. It was a small opening, but she managed to pull herself up. The wind and rain were a relief to feel against her face. The door broke. She was halfway through when she felt it grab her leg. She kicked at its claws until she was loose.

She was out in the backyard now. She jumped over the fence and ran out into the park.

"Help!" she cried out.

From behind her she heard the beast howl. She looked back and saw that it was standing on Tyler's back porch. It sniffed the air and located Julie. She ran. She looked back again and saw it easily leap over the fence. She was running towards the softball field and saw another dog crouching there, just as big as the one at Tyler's. It ran towards her now. It was grey with a white strip going down its chest.

She tried to run in a different direction now, but her leg collapsed beneath her. There was a deep gash in her calf. She tried to stand up, but the pain was too great. She crawled as best she could.

"Help!" she continued to scream as the second dog was soon upon her.

She looked back and the other was also fast approaching. However, this new grey beast ran past her towards the other. They collided, banging tooth and claw. The black dog was bigger, but the grey one was wily and the better fighter.

Julie watched as they fought and realized this was her chance. She tried to run but her body betrayed her. Her calf screamed in pain until she fell to her knees. Her pant leg was soaked through with blood. She began to crawl when the black dog jumped out in front of her. Then the grey dog pounced on top of it from behind, and brought it to the ground, holding its throat in its jaws. The black dog squirmed until it wriggled free and ran off.

The grey beast crawled towards Julie on all fours. She shuffled backwards. It was upon her now. It stopped and stared at her, smelling the air. Its nose paused at her crotch and sniffed. The dog whined a little and began licking her face. Julie passed out.

CHAPTER FOUR (1963)

Outside of Lockwood Elementary, kids were running about, talking and shouting, as a few nuns and Brothers supervised. They formed little circles, expounding on their summers apart, then breaking apart to form new formations. Violet wandered amongst the clamouring children, unsure of what to do or who to talk to. She had never seen so many kids together before. There must have been over a hundred. They gave her curious looks as they took in her fuzzy, stitched up head and scarred body. She'd recovered just in time for the first day of school. She was excited that she wouldn't have to start late and could begin with the rest of the kids, but now she was wishing she'd had a little more time to grow her hair back. The nurses were sad to see her go and she was sad to leave them. They'd given her lots of ice cream and she did everything they asked her to do. She never picked at her scars or stitches and gave herself plenty of time to rest in bed. As sad as she was to say goodbye to the nurses, nothing could've dampened her excitement about starting school and meeting new friends. Now, however, she wasn't so sure. She had imagined things unfolding differently when she was in hospital fantasizing about her first day of school. Everyone would see her scars and want to know what had happened to her. She imagined regaling everyone with her story of how she'd been attacked by a pack of wild dogs. She'd managed to fight them off for awhile, but there were too many and they eventually got the best of her. Then her mom got her to the doctor just in the nick of time to save her life. There was some embellishment, yes, but Violet figured she was entitled to it. In her more fanciful moments, she'd considered throwing in a bit about defending her baby brother.

Lockwood Elementary was the biggest building Violet had ever seen. It was three stories high with rows of windows, through which she could see the classrooms, the dining hall, and the beds. Along the top story were the words *Suffer Little Children to Come unto Me*. It was a Catholic school, run mostly by nuns and Brothers. Violet hadn't been to church very much. Her parents taught her and her siblings how to pray. Each night, Violet recited the Lord's Prayer: "Our Father, Who art in heaven Hallowed be Thy Name; Thy kingdom come, Thy will be done, on earth as it is in heaven. Give us this day our daily bread, and forgive us our trespasses, as we forgive those who trespass against us; and lead us not into temptation, but deliver us from evil. Amen." Then she would thank God for all the nice things that had happened that day, apologize for anything wrong she'd done (like disobeying her mother, usually), ask Him to look over everyone she cared about, and would finish with a couple wishes of her own (maybe a few extra coppers for candy when her dad took her to the Hudson Bay store, nothing too outrageous). Every now and then a priest made his way to Spotted Island and the entire community crowded into the rec hall and had service. That happened once or twice in the summer. They certainly never had a priest in Roaches Brook during the winter.

Violet looked around for Cecilia, trying to locate her sister amongst the sea of children. There was a group of older girls talking to each other and Cecilia was with them. The sisters locked eyes, but then Cecilia quickly turned her attention back to her friends, pretending not to have seen Violet. Before Violet got a chance to run over and talk to Cecilia, a nun started clanging a bell. The kids fell silent.

"New children first!" the nun yelled.

Violet stepped forward with a few other boys and girls. She was still very self-conscious about starting school so old. However, the new kids were all different ages and she wasn't the oldest so she didn't feel out of place. Her smallness helped her look younger, too.

"Inside!" the nun yelled.

Violet was scared of the Sister. She looked very angry, which Violet didn't understand. It was only the first day, the first morning. No one had had a chance to do anything bad yet. Violet remembered Cecilia's warning about the nuns being very strict.

Inside there were a few Brothers and Sisters waiting. In the foyer there was a large wooden crucifix with a life-sized man attached to it. Violet surmised that it was Jesus. She'd never seen a crucifix so big and ornate. She'd also never seen a figurative representation of Jesus before. He had a long beard and hair. He was covered with wounds and atop his head was a prickly headband. He looked sad. And hungry. He was very skinny.

"My name is Sister Rosaline," the nun said. "Girls come with me. Boys go with Brother Kevin."

Sister Rosaline led them into the girls' bathroom. The unfamiliar scent of bleach shocked Violet. The overwhelming smell irritated her nostrils. She rubbed at her nose as she struggled to get used to it. The Lockwood bathroom had several gleaming white toilets. There were a couple showers and a big tub. Violet had only ever used a wooden outhouse. In the centre of the bathroom was a sack filled with white powder. Sister Rosaline stood beside it.

"Take off your clothes," Sister Rosaline said. "And pile them up behind you."

The girls hesitated. They looked at each other, confused.

"I said take them off!" the nun repeated.

Violet held her pair of sealskin slippers that her mother had made. She was reluctant to let them go. Sister Rosaline snatched them from her and tossed them on the pile.

The girls stripped down their underwear.

"Those, too," Sister Rosaline commanded.

Violet took off her underwear and threw them in the pile. She could feel the other girls gawking at her, at her scars. She starred straight at the wall. Sister Rosaline looked her over.

"You must be Mrs. Matthews' new girl," she said. "She didn't mention that you were a half-breed."

Violet was confused. What did she mean by "Mrs. Matthews' new girl"? And what was a "half-breed"?

"Most of you come from dirty homes," Sister Rosaline explained. She took a handful of white powder from the sack. "At Lockwood we expect your spirits as well as your bodies to be clean. Now, keep your eyes shut or they'll burn."

Sister Rosaline shook the insecticide on their heads. It smelled even worse than the bleach. Violet accidently opened her eyes and it stung. It stung so bad she started to cry and that made it worse. The other girls were crying, too. Sister Rosaline herded them into the showers and dosed them with scaling hot water. Her scars burned. She thought her skin was going to peel off.

"Stop that blubbering at once!" Sister Rosaline commanded. "Put on your new clothes."

The girls found a pile of new dresses to put on.

"For the rest of the year, these will be your clothes," Sister Rosaline explained. "They will be washed regularly, and you are to keep them clean. There are two sets for each of you. If you tear them or damage them in any way, you will have to repair them yourselves. Am I understood?"

The girls nodded.

"Now, some of you may consider yourself to be White, but as far as I'm concerned you're all savages. And here at Lockwood we believe that to save the man, you must first kill the Indian. We will teach you how to be civilized young ladies. If you act accordingly, you will be fine. If you do not, you will be punished. Am I understood?"

The girls nodded. Sister Rosaline lead them out and into the dining hall. They lined up at the kitchen to get their breakfast. The cook, a big hairy man with a hostile face and a thick black mustache, ladled out lukewarm bowls of what he described as porridge. 'Why is everyone here so angry?' Violet thought. She took the bowl of greyish slop over to a table with the girls. She lifted up a spoonful. The mixture oozed slowly from the spoon like snot. The emptiness in her stomach convinced her to give it a try. It tasted much the same as it looked. The other girls struggled with it, too. No one spoke. They were too shy. Violet could feel the shared embarrassment of what they'd endured. Best not to talk about it. Other kids started trickling into the dining hall, having gone through the same delousing and given new clothes. A few other girls sat beside them.

"Your eyes are red," Cheryl said. She was the same age as Violet, but she'd been coming to Lockwood a couple years now. "You guys must've opened your eyes."

"You won't make that mistake again," Vicky said, another veteran.

They all nodded. They introduced themselves to each other and they all started chatting. The older girls talked about having to get naked in front of the nuns. They talked about how painful and embarrassing it was. Violet felt good opening up and seeing that the others had similar experiences. She was also relieved to finally talk to girls her own age again. After the attack, she'd only had the nurses for company.

Apparently, it was even worse for the boys because Brother Kevin liked to tug at their peckers until they got hard. Some of the older girls giggled, but Violet and the younger ones were confused. Violet had seen her brother's and father's penises and knew that they were for peeing. Some of the kids on Spotted Island had explained to her that a man put it inside a woman's vagina to make babies. However, Violet did not realize that they got hard and stuck out like a twig.

The rest of the kids filled the dining hall. At the head table the Brothers and Sisters were eating eggs and bacon with freshly buttered toast. The smells wafted over to Violet and danced in her nostrils. It beat away the memories of bleach and insecticide. Maybe the cook would give her some bacon if she asked nicely--even though he did have that mean look on his face. It was worth a try. She started to get up from her seat.

"What are you doing?" Vicky hissed.

"I want some bacon," Violet said. "This stuff is gross."

"Sit down before they see you," Cheryl said. "You have to eat it, or you'll get the cane."

"The cane?" Connie asked, another new girl.

"They make you hold out your hands and they strike your palms with a wooden cane," Vicky explained. "And you got to hold your hands totally straight. If you curl your fingers at all, they give you extra smacks."

"There's a lot of things you're going to have to learn quickly," Cheryl said. "Whatever you do, don't make the same mistake twice, because the punishments will only get worse."

So this was what Cecelia had meant when she said Lockwood was strict. Violet was used to getting whacked with the spoon by her mother, her dad had even given her a few lashes across her bum with his belt before, but she couldn't imagine having to hold out her hands and get smacked with a cane. And she didn't want to know how it felt either, so she started in on her porridge. She closed her eyes and shoveled in spoon after spoon. She focused on her hunger. As gross as the porridge was, at least it was filling her belly.

"Why do you have so many scars?" Vicky asked.

"Yeah," Cheryl said. "And what happened to your hair?"

All the girls stopped what they were doing and turned their attention to Violet. She finally got the chance she'd been waiting for and she didn't disappoint. While she didn't embellish the story as much as she'd planned, she did omit the part where she fell down and punched herself in the face. The girls were rapt. They were especially impressed by the fact that she might have died had she not been so lucky that the doctor was in town.

"That was Dr. Hunt," Cheryl said. "He's very handsome."

"I don't remember ever seeing him," Violet said. But she did remember her dream of the wolf man stitching her up like a rug.

At another table, a boy got sick and threw up into his bowl. Violet couldn't blame him; she'd been fighting the same urge to wretch. The nun who'd been clanging the bell outside came over to check on him.

"And what do you have to say for yourself?" she asked.

"I'm sorry, Sister Sherry," he said.

"You're to finish that bowl, young man."

"Yes, ma'am."

He got up from his seat with his bowl in hand.

"And where do you think you're going?" Sister Sherry asked.

"I'm going to get another bowl of porridge, Sister," the boy replied.

"No. I said you're to finish that bowl." She pointed at the pile of vomited porridge when she said "that."

The boy slowly sat back down. Violet watched, unable to comprehend the reality of what was playing out before her. Sister Sherry wasn't serious, was she? He wasn't going to eat that, was he? Cheryl and Vicky kept their focus on their own bowls. The boy lifted up a spoonful of puke. He looked at the nun. She nodded. He ate it. Everyone gasped. Sister Sherry looked around and silenced the hall with her glare. The boy kept eating. He started to cry. Violet looked over to the head table to see if the other Brothers or Sisters would do anything. They kept eating their bacon and eggs, not really paying attention. They boy threw up again. The nun made him keep eating. Violet looked away after that. She was afraid that if she saw anymore, she'd throw up too and would have to eat her own vomit as well.

When the boy was finished, Sister Sherry returned to the head table to retrieve her bell. It was time to get to class. Violet wasn't sure where to go so she followed the girls her own age. In the classroom there were about two dozen little wooden tables. She sat near Vicky and Cheryl. On her table was a few sheets of loose leaf and a wooden pencil. Violet was eager to start filling up those blank sheets with numbers and letters. The girls were all chatting but hushed as soon as the nun walked into the room. She stood at the head of the class in front of the blackboard. A crucifix nailed to the wall hung above her.

"My name is Sister Margaret," she said. "This morning we will be working on a few simple sums to get started."

Sister Margaret picked up a piece of chalk and began writing out problems on the board in swift and tidy succession. The girls all started copying them down. Violet did the same. There were lots of problems. Once Sister Margaret filled up the board, she started erasing old problems to write new ones. They got increasingly difficult, too. Violet struggled. Her parents had taught her how to basic sums in her head. Her dad was very good with numbers. He was able to estimate very quickly how much profit he was going to make on each dollar he invested. Her mother was also good at holding together the sum of their inventory at all times and could ration out materials anticipating when times would get lean. Violet was used to doing this all in her head, though. She'd never really sat down and worked it out on pencil and paper. Her writing was slow and sloppy from a lack of practice. She couldn't keep up with Sister Margaret's pace. Her hand ached to the point that her fingers went stiff and numb. She had to take a couple of breaks to shake out her hand. But she tried her hardest, anyway. She skipped over a lot of the difficult problems and did whatever she could.

Outside in the hallway Sister Sherry was clanging her bell again. It was time for recess. The kids all shuffled their papers together and brought them up to Sister Margaret. Violet saw that most everybody had completed all their sums. When she handed her papers to Sister Margaret, the nun gave her a hard look. Violet wasn't concerned. It was only the first day. She had lots of time to catch up. This was all just very unfamiliar and would take time.

She followed everyone else outside. Behind Lockwood was a big stretch of grass for the kids to play. Beyond that was a wooded area, which led into the wilderness of the Labrador interior. Violet gazed into the darkness amidst the tall trees. Vicky and Cheryl explained that kids weren't allowed to go in there. Brothers and Sisters patrolled to make sure no one went on an adventure into the woods. There were stories of kids who ran away from Lockwood, who tried to run back to their homes through the woods. But they got lost and were never heard from again.

"What happened to them?" Violet asked.

"No one knows," Cheryl said.

"They were probably eaten," Vicky said. "There are bears and wolves out there."

The scars on Violets head burned as she thought of the dogs attacking her.

"Sometimes the boys sneak off and go smoke cigarettes in there," Vicky said.

"How do they get cigarettes?" Violet asked.

"Brother Kevin gives them to boys who lets him touch their pecker," Cheryl explained.

"He'll even give them booze if they let him do more," Vicky added.

More? Violet wondered.

"Brother Gregory likes to touch girls," Cheryl continued. "So you can get smokes and booze from him. But you shouldn't. Because then everyone will know that you let him touch you."

"It's not fair," Vicky said. "Everyone knows when a boy lets Brother Kevin touches him and it's a big joke. But when it's a girl she's a whore."

"That's just how it is," Cheryl said.

Violet didn't know what a whore was. She was about to ask when she saw Cecilia standing around with a group of older girls. She excused herself from Vicky and Cheryl and went to see her sister. Cecilia saw her coming and frowned. She quickly went over to intercept Violet before she got too close to her friends.

"You can't talk to me here," Cecilia said.

"Why not?" Violet asked.

"Because I'm with my friends."

"So what?"

"You're too young. And you're a new girl."

"I don't understand. Why is that such a big deal?"

Violet saw the older girls looking her up and down. They were giggling as if they were making fun of her.

"It's hard to explain," Cecilia said.

"Well, when can we talk?" Violet asked. "I haven't seen you since I had to leave Spotted Island."

"I'm not sure. But we can't talk now."

Cecilia left and went back to her group of friends. Violet felt tears swelling and her lip quiver. For so long she'd been looking forward to hearing some news about her family and how everyone was since she'd left. She was hoping Cecilia could help her figure out all these rules the teachers had. She also wanted to know what the Brothers did when they touched you. Especially the boys. Why did their bits turn hard? None of it made any sense.

Violet suddenly felt like someone was watching her. She turned and saw Ophelia, the girl that was with Mrs. Matthews at the hospital. She was staring at Violet and then started to giggle. She took off running over towards a group of younger girls.

Sister Sherry was clanging her bell. Time to go back inside. Outside her classroom, Sister Margaret was waiting alongside another nun. They stopped Violet at the door.

"This is Sister Rebecca," Sister Margaret said. "She teaches the younger girls."

"Hello, Sister Rebecca," Violet said.

"We think you'd be more comfortable in Sister Rebecca's class," Sister Margaret said. "You have a lot of catching up to do."

"Really?" Violet asked. Disappointment was welling up into her throat and glistening in her eyes. She looked inside Sister Margaret's classroom and saw Vicky and Cheryl at their desks.

"It's not necessarily permanent, my child," Sister Rebecca told Violet. "We just want to make sure you know the basics. Some of you come from such primitive environments that we often have no choice but to start from the very ground up. Don't fret. If you pay attention and work hard, you will be back among your peers."

Violet choked back the tears. She was angry at her parents for not sending her to school earlier. Now she had all this stuff to catch up on. It wasn't her fault. She wasn't stupid. There were so many things about Lockwood that she didn't understand. And why were the teachers always calling her "savage" and "primitive"? What did that mean?

Sister Rebecca led Violet to her new classroom. The seats were smaller than Sister Margaret's class. As tiny as Violet was, she was still uncomfortable in her chair. She looked around at all the young girls. They stared at her and her scars. They were too young even to have the sense to be polite. She saw that Ophelia was in her class, too, still smiling that strange grin. On her desk was a Bible. They were taking turns reading passages, one at a time. Violet was a good reader. She skimmed through the passages pretty quickly. They were reading from Isaiah in the Old Testament. Violet counted the girls ahead of her and figured out which passage she would have to read and started practicing. The other girls were slow. Sister Rebecca made them repeat each word they mispronounced and then read the entire passage all over again until they got each word down. Violet soon got bored. She looked outside through the window. It was a calm, sunny day. She imagined that her dad and brother were very content out fishing today. What was her mother doing? What was she cooking for supper? Surely something better than that porridge she had for breakfast.

"Violet?" Sister Rebecca called out.

It was her turn to read. Violet snapped out of her reverie and tried to find her passage.

"There shall be no more thence an infant of days, nor an old man that hath not filled his days: for the child shall die a hundred years old; but the sinner being a hundred years old shall be accursed."

Violet was pleased with herself. She'd read very well and pronounced all the words correctly. She'd be out of here in no time and back with her friends.

"You haven't been paying attention," Sister Rebecca said. "Your passage was supposed to be 65:25."

"Sorry, Sister."

"The wolf and the lamb shall feed together, and the lion shall eat straw like the bullock: and dust shall be the serpent's meat. They shall not hurt nor destroy in all my holy mountain, saith the Lord."

"Sorry, Sister," Violet repeated.

"Stand up, please," Sister Rebecca said. "Come up to the front of the class."

Violet stood up and walked up to the chalkboard. The girls watched. Some of them were biting their lips, looking away, others were smiling. Ophelia had a particularly giant grin. Violet saw Sister Rebecca take out a wooden stick.

"Hold out your hands, please," Sister Rebecca said.

"I'm sorry, Sister," Violet pleaded. "It won't happen again. I'm sorry. I'll pay attention. Please."

"I'm sure you will. Hands. Or I will have to fetch Sister Sherry."

Violet did as she was told. She lifted her hands forward as if she was about to receive Holy Communion. The first couple strikes weren't so bad. But Sister Rebecca hit with sharp precession, bringing the cane down along the same welt as the previous repetition. Violet's hands soon became enflamed. She remembered Vicky's advise and kept her palms straight. Sister Rebecca seemed to get frustrated that Violet wouldn't acquiesce, as if she wanted Violet to give in and loosen her hands so she could be an example to the class. Violet lost count of the smacks. As she focused on keeping her fingers from curling, she couldn't hold back the tears. They ran down her face freely. Satisfied with this display of submission and weakness, Sister Rebecca sent Violet back to her chair.

She floated through the rest of the day. They broke for lunch and came back for more sums in the afternoon. Violet struggled to hold her pencil. Luckily, the problems were easy and she managed to get through them with no issue. They had soup for supper. It was mostly broth with a few potatoes and the odd piece of rubbery ham. She struggled to keep the spoon steady as she lifted it to her mouth. She kept her red palms hidden from view. There were conversations going on around her and she may have contributed a word or two, but she didn't process anything that was said. She was thankful when it was time to go to bed.

Sister Sherry led them to the dormitory. It was a big room with cots lining the walls end to end. The girls got out of their uniforms and into the nighties, which the nuns had provided.

"Time for prayer," Sister Sherry announced.

The girls all kneeled at the beds, heads bent, hands held together at their foreheads. Some were silent, others whispered. This was nothing new for Violet. She and her family always said their prayers before bed. After asking God to look over her parents and siblings, she opened her eyes and was about to get into bed when she saw that all the other girls were still praying. Sister Sherry glared at her, as if to say that she wasn't done yet. Violet resumed the prayer position and tried to think of other things to pray for. She apologized to the huskies for getting to their mother killed and for causing so much grief for her family. She prayed that her dad would catch lots of animals on his trap lines and that the animals wouldn't suffer too much. After that, she ran out of things to pray for. She listened to some of the whispers. She could hear the girl behind her:

"I pray that even while I am asleep, I will bring back to Thee souls that offend Thee. I ask forgiveness for the whole world, especially for those who know Thee and yet sin. I offer to Thee my every breath and heartbeat as a prayer of reparation."

Violet didn't really understand what the girl was talking about. She was talking like a priest. Violet tried again, this time using words like "thee" and "offend" and "sin." After speaking in what felt like a second language, Sister Sherry finally spoke.

"Lights out," she said.

Once the dormitory door was shut, no one was allowed to leave, not even to use the bathroom. The girls chatted in mousey whispers. They had to be quiet; the nuns slept just across the hall. Violet lay in bed and thought about her day. She tried to remember the impulse that had made her want to go school so badly, that had made her so jealous of Cecilia. All her sister had told her was that the nuns were strict. Cecilia didn't say anything about the powder that burned your eyes or having to keep your palms straight so the nuns wouldn't hit you even more; she didn't say anything about getting naked in front everyone; and she certainly never said anything about having to eat your own puke.

Exhausted, Violet soon slid into a troubled sleep. She dreamt that she was running in the forest. Wolf people chased her. They wore habits and frocks. She managed to escape the woods. She was on a rocky beach. From behind her she could hear the wolf people bark, growl, and howl. In the distance she could see her father's boat. Her family was there. They were loading the boat with their stuff to move to Roaches Brook for the winter. Violet tried to run, but her feet couldn't get any traction on the ground. The wolf people were getting closer. There was sharp pain in her neck as one of them bit her.

She woke up in her bed. Her legs were warm and wet. She lifted up her blankets and saw that she'd pissed herself. The bed was soaked. She got out of bed and was about to get up and go ask the nuns to change her blankets when the girl in the bed beside her stopped her.

"What are you doing?" the girl asked. It was too dark for Violet to make out who she was.

"I have to get new sheets," Violet said.

"You'll have to wait until the morning. If you wake the nuns up, they'll be very cross."

Violet didn't think her hands could take any more punishment. She got back into bed. Her warm piss slowly turned cold. She shivered in her wet bed, her cheeks also wet with tears.

CHAPTER FIVE (2015)

Julie woke up but felt like she was still dreaming. She was in a room that felt familiar, yet she couldn't remember who it belonged to. The air was thick, and it smelled musty. There was a lot of dust floating around, which made her sneeze. To the right of the bed was a nightstand with a picture of a woman that she felt like she knew but couldn't remember how. She was standing outside a building underneath the letters "FORUM." There were also pictures of a young boy who Julie quickly realized was Tyler. She then understood that the woman in the picture was Tyler's mother and that she was in her bed. During the four years they'd been dating, she'd never stepped foot inside this room, only stole peaks and glances on the rare occasion Tyler left the door open. Now, she felt like she was trespassing in a sacred place, that she'd spent the night in a crypt.

She threw the blanket from her and swung her legs around. When she tried to stand up a sharp liquid pain sprinted up from her calf. Stifling a gasp, she sat back down. The bottom of her right leg was wrapped in a wasp nest of dressing. She was covered in scratches, bruises, and Band-Aids. She felt weak and woozy, as if she was hungover. Memories of the previous night shimmered weakly behind a veil of fog like half-remembered nightmares. She pushed through the haze, struggling to remember, but the images she conjured were outrageous and beyond belief: visions of giant apelike wolves chasing her. She figured that she must've been attacked by some wild pitbull on the way to Tyler's house. It bit her leg and she passed out. Tyler took care of her. But she couldn't make sense of why he'd put her in his mother's room.

The smell of fried bacon and freshly brewed coffee pierced the room's oppressive musk. By the door, someone had left a crutch. Julie hobbled over to it. She opened the door. The smell of breakfast filled the house. She made her way to the kitchen. A man she didn't know was standing at the stove. He turned and faced Julie.

"Good," he said. "You're awake. Please, sit. I'm afraid I had to throw out the table given the state it was in. There are a few TV trays kicking around if you'd like to have a seat in the living room."

He had salt and pepper hair and a big dark beard with a grey streak running from his chin. Despite this, the man had no wrinkles and his body had a youthful build, like he was some yoga instructor who'd discovered the secret of immortality. However, Julie could see in his dark brown eyes that he had an old, troubled soul.

"Who are you?" Julie asked.

"That's a doozy of a question," the man said. "First, how are you feeling? You had a nasty gash on your leg that I had to stitch up. Probably be a little tender to walk on for the next few days. I had to rinse out your wounds, otherwise you might've gotten an infection. I gave you some pain killers so you're probably feeling groggy and can't remember much of last night. Oh, and I hope you don't mind, but I had to throw out your clothes. You evacuated shortly after you passed out."

Julie looked down and noticed for the first time that she was wearing Tyler's clothes. "Evacuated." She had "evacuated." Not evacuated *from*, just "evacuated." She was pretty sure that meant she had shit herself, and this strange man changed her.

"What the hell are you talking about?" she asked.

"Don't worry," the man said. "I'm not some random pervert off the street. You have an impressive fight or flight mechanism. I can see why he loves you."

"What? Who? Tyler?"

Blurred images of a broken door and blood dripping from the teeth of a snarling dog crowded Julie's mind. She lunged towards the sink and dry heaved in painful jerks. Her throat was afire with the taste of bile.

"I'd suggest drinking some water," the man said.

"What's going on?" she demanded. "Who are you? Where's Tyler?"

The man collected his breakfast and sat down in a chair in the living room. He gestured towards the sofa for Julie to join him. She remained standing.

"Does this look familiar to you?" he asked, tugging at the white strip running down from his chin.

Julie remembered the strange beasts from last night, the giant dogs that walked upright like gorillas. There was a black one here in the house, and a grey one appeared at the park. They fought. The last thing she could remember was the grey one smelling her and licking her face. It had a long white strip running down the middle of its fur.

"I still don't understand," Julie said. "Where's Tyler?"

"Tyler's asleep in his room. Probably won't wake up for another while yet. He's pretty banged up. The first time can be exhausting. It takes some getting used to."

With the help of her crutch, Julie hopped to Tyler's room. She opened the door and found him snoring in his bed. From his left cheek bone, just below his eye, all the way down to the left corner of his lips ran a fresh scar trying to heal. It was stained orange from iodine. Julie tried gently to rouse him.

"Tyler?" she whispered.

He muttered something in his sleep.

"Tyler?"

He groaned and winced at the pain in his lips then went back to snoring. Julie left him there to sleep. She returned to the living room. The man was wiping egg yolk from his plate with a slice of toast. He smiled and nodded at the sofa. Julie stood looking at him.

"I want you to tell me who you are and what's going on," she said.

"Yes, of course. But, please, have something to eat first. It'll help you recover."

"Answer me goddammit."

"Okay. Just sit. Please."

Julie acquiesced.

"Tyler is suffering from what I believe is some kind of genetic disorder," the man explained. "It causes him to transform into that thing you saw last night. It's triggered by a full moon."

"So, you're telling me that was Tyler? The guy I've been dating for the last four years transformed into a giant wolf and tried to tear me to pieces?"

"Yes. And I was the other one."

"This is lunacy."

"Literally, yes," the man said, chuckling. "Although no pun intended, I'm sure."

"..."

"Sorry. He attacked you because he was scared and confused. Luckily, I was around when it happened."

Julie leaned back into the sofa and rubbed her forehead. The man got her a glass of water and brought her a plate of breakfast.

"So, what," Julie asked. "You guys are werewolves?"

"I prefer 'Lycanthrope.' The Greek is much more dignified."

"Oh my god, I gave him that cut on his face."

"Don't worry. That'll heal nicely. After the next transformation, there won't even be a scar. He's got some grit, let me tell you. But he's not quite ready to take down his old man just yet."

"Excuse me?"

"My name is Joseph Stevens. I'm Tyler's father."

Julie sat back into the sofa again like she'd been kicked in the chin. She looked at her plate of food. It was impossible to have an appetite while she tried to digest all this information.

"I imagine this is a lot to take in," Joseph said.

"Where have you been?" she asked.

"Nearby, actually. After Tyler's mother died, I moved into a house in St. John's so I could keep an eye on him. Before that I moved around a lot. I was in Montreal and Northern Quebec and then settled in British Colombia for a number of years. I've been researching our condition, trying to find a cure. As you can see, it hasn't been very fruitful."

"Do you know anything that might help?"

"Only hypotheses. It's all conjecture. There are too many lacunae in the data. Part of the problem is genealogy. I was adopted as a baby, so I had no contact with my biological parents. I have a pretty solid theory about who they may be, but, again, speculation. Until now, I hoped that mine was an isolated case. The fact that Tyler appears to have inherited my disease tells me it is likely genetic. I'm hoping to do some tests to see what I can come up with."

"You say it's genetic. What triggers it? Why is this happening now?"

"My hypothesis is that the men in our line pass down this disease and that it is first activated once we have impregnated a woman."

"..."

"To that affect, I must ask you an indelicate question. Is that Tyler's child you're carrying?"

"Yes. How did you know I was pregnant?"

"As a lycan, my sense of smell is like an MRI machine."

"Tyler was so wild, but it sounds like you can control yourself."

"'Control' probably isn't the right word. It feels like the whole world is on fire and I'm just an exposed nerve. I've managed to get a handle on it over the years, but at best it's akin to lucid dreaming during your most wildest nightmare. It's taken me a long time to get where I am. I'm hoping I can save Tyler a lot of the trial and error I had to go through."

"I see."

"You should try and eat something, even if you have to force it down."

Julie nibbled at a piece of bacon. The salty meat triggered something in her empty stomach and her appetite reared its head. She cut up the cold fried eggs. The yolk was congealed like jelly. She was too hungry to care. She washed it all down with lukewarm coffee.

Down the hall, Tyler groaned. Julie and Joseph exchanged looks. Julie stood up and used her crutches to get to Tyler's room. He was staring at the ceiling, softly probing his scar with a finger.

"Hi," Julie said. "Are you okay?"

Tyler looked at her then looked back up at the ceiling. Julie sat down on the bed and held his hand.

"I dreamt I killed you," Tyler said. His words were awkward as he tried to speak around the damaged portion of his lips. "In my dream I was old. A dirty old man with long dirty fingernails. I looked in a pool of water and saw my reflection. I had brown shark teeth. I looked across the pond and saw a younger version of myself. I felt ashamed. Not only of myself, as this ugly, old man, but of this weak little child. Then I got scared. Scared of the boy. I had to kill him. He ran into the woods. I chased after him and almost had him, then you stepped out in front of him. You had my mother's voice. You told me I couldn't kill him. That it was against the rules. That he was supposed to kill me and you had to protect him until he was strong enough. Behind you was a cave. I could hear him crying. I knew you'd hidden him in there. I slashed at you, cut you bad. You fell into the cave. I tried to follow you, but the cave turned into a giant pool of black goo, like tar. I was stuck, sinking. Then I was the boy, watching myself drown. You were on the ground, bleeding. All around us were wolves, circling. They circled around you and—then I woke up."

"That's quite the dream," Julie said.

"It was so vivid." Tyler took a deep breath. "There's something wrong with me. Like, really wrong. The last thing I can remember is freaking out in my kitchen then falling and banging my face. I guess that's how I cut myself."

Julie decided now wasn't the time to correct him.

"I think I'm losing my mind," he said.

"You're not the only one," she replied

"What do you mean?" he asked. He sat up and saw Julie's leg. "What happened to you? Why are you wearing my clothes?"

"It's a long, crazy story. There's someone out in the living room waiting to talk to you. He can explain everything better than I can."

"Who?"

"It's better if you hear it from him."

Julie led Tyler out to where Joseph was sitting. He stood up. He and Tyler looked at each without speaking.

"Hello," Tyler said. "Julie tells me you can explain what's going on."

"Yes, please, sit down," Joseph said. "I made some shepherd's pie. You probably won't be able to eat anything too solid while your mouth recovers."

"I'm fine," Tyler said, still standing. "First, tell me what's going on."

"You and Julie are both very much straight to the point," Joseph said. "My name is Joseph Stevens. I'm your father."

"Excuse me?"

"I realize this is overwhelming. But there's a lot we need to talk about. I wish there was an easier way. Alas, here we are."

"What the hell is going on?" Tyler asked Julie.

"He's telling the truth," she said.

"How do you know?" he asked.

"Just listen to what he has to say," she said.

"Why should we believe him?" he asked.

"I don't have any bone fides on me at the moment to prove what I'm saying," Joseph said. "But I saw a picture in Karen's old room. She's standing in front of the Montreal Forum. I took that picture. It was on June 9, 1993. The night the Montreal Canadiens won the Stanley Cup. I wrote something on the back of the photo. You can go check."

"Alright," Tyler said after an extended silence. "Say what you have to say. What's going on here?"

"Last night, you experienced for the first time a condition that I've been living with since before you were born. I believe it's something that runs through our family. I've made some strides trying to research our condition. With your help, I'd like to identify the cause and perhaps even discover a cure. However, in the meantime I will share with you what I've learned and coach you through this."

"And what is 'this'?" Tyler asked.

"Our shared lycanthropy," Joseph replied.

"What the hell does that mean?" Tyler asked.

"Every month, when the moon is full, we transform into werewolves."

"Is he shitting me?" Tyler asked Julie.

"No," Julie said. "I'm afraid not."

"So, last night I was a werewolf," Tyler said.

"Yes," Joseph said.

"Okay," Tyler said. "Obviously, I took some bad acid again, and you guys are trying to freak me out as some kind of payback."

"I wish that were true," Joseph said. "But I'm quite serious. I'm guessing that for the past couple weeks you've been experiencing mood swings, and the last few days they must've been particularly acute. I remember when it first happened to me. I still go through it. Difficulty sleeping, increased appetite. Anxiety, nausea. It gets easier with time. Or, at least you get better at coping. It takes a lot of discipline and focus. Trust me, I've had to find out the hard way."

Joseph paused. Tyler was silent. Julie could see the cogs turning in his mind.

"I don't know if you can remember much of what happened last night," Joseph continued, "but at one point a grey wolf appeared and wrestled you down and away from Julie. That was me. The last couple of years I've been keeping an eye on you. When you're ready I can show you my research."

"I think you should leave," Tyler said.

"Tyler, please—" Julie tried to interject.

"It's okay," Joseph said. "You're upset. You have every right to be angry at me. I understand. If you want me to go, I'll go. When you're ready, give me a call. I'll explain everything that happened to you, me, and your mother."

"Go," Tyler said. "Just go."

"Alright," Joseph said. "I'll leave."

He stood up and walked out to the door. Julie followed him out on her crutches.

"I'm sorry," Julie said at the door. "He's really upset."

"Of course," Joseph said. "I understand. Goodbye, Julie. It was nice to meet you."

"Nice to meet you, too," Julie said.

She went back inside. Tyler wasn't in the living room. She found him in his bedroom, at his computer. His bong was on the computer desk along with a dish of shepherd's pie. The room was full of smoke and the stink of weed. He hadn't bothered to open the window.

"Why did you kick him out?" Julie asked. "Don't you have like a million questions?"

Tyler didn't answer. He was searching discounted computer hardware.

"What are you thinking?" Julie asked.

"You have no idea," Tyler said.

"Can I ask you something?"

"Why do people say that? Just go ahead and ask."

"Do you remember anything from last night?"

"You mean, when I was a werewolf?"

"Yes."

Tyler emptied the exhausted weed from his bong's bowl. He ground up a fresh bud and sprinkled it with a liberal dash of tobacco and repacked the bowl. He took a few rips while Julie waited patiently.

"It felt like I was disappearing," he said. "I couldn't breathe. My whole body was on fire, like I was having a seizure and a mental breakdown at the same time. It was like I died and went to hell. I came to and everything was screaming at me. But then I felt you. It was your smell. You were everywhere but I couldn't find you. Then all of sudden you appeared in the doorway. When you saw me you were so scared. And then I lost whatever control I had. I don't really remember much else. I remember fighting with something or someone, which I guess was Joseph. That's about it. I don't understand it. I'm sorry I hurt you."

Julie was silent.

"What about you?" Tyler asked. "The last time I heard from you, it seemed like you had something on your mind. Well, here we are. What did you want to talk about?"

"I think there's more important things going on right now."

"Yes, so why don't you help lighten my load here."

"I don't even know where to start."

"Why don't we start with the fact that you didn't tell me you're going to Halifax."

"Yes, I'm sorry. I wanted to tell you."

"Seems like I was the last one to find out."

"Please don't make this harder than it has to be."

"Okay. I'll make it easy. You didn't tell me about Dal because you don't want me to come with you. You were coming here last night to dump my ass before you headed off to law school."

"It's more complicated than that."

"I'm not so sure it is."

"You don't know what you're talking about."

"No? Well, here's something I do know. Ever since you got back from Europe, you've had this real uppity attitude. Like, suddenly I'm not good enough for you anymore."

"It's not like that. Don't make me out to be some stuck-up snob."

"Then what's it like? Educate me."

"Yes, okay, when I got back from Europe, I changed. I felt like I grew as person. But you didn't. I realized that you're never going to change. You don't want to. You're stuck inside this bubble and I can't deal with it anymore. I can't deal with this fishbowl."

"Well, I've changed now haven't I? I'm a whole new species. Is that good enough for you? I guess it's one of those 'be careful what you wish for' stories."

"That's not funny."

"I'm right, though, aren't I? About Dal? About breaking up?"

"I wasn't just going to dump you. I wanted to give us another chance."

"You wanted to give me an ultimatum. Get on board or else. Which isn't really a choice because you knew I wasn't going to go to Halifax. Awfully manipulative of you. You're going to be a great lawyer, just like mommy and daddy."

Julie didn't respond. She cursed herself for underestimating his ability to see through her bullshit. She had been unfair to him and she knew it. He knew it.

"Well," Tyler said. "What else?"

"What do you mean?"

"There's something you're still not telling me. I know it."

"That can wait."

"No, tell me now."

"Jesus Christ, Tyler."

"Enough with the bullshit. Tell me."

"I'm pregnant. I'm not sure how far along. Probably at least a month."

Tyler laughed. It started as a small chuckle but then grew into something loud and hysterical. When he was done, he turned around and lit his bong. After a few rips he went back to browsing for computer hardware.

"You asshole," Julie said.

She left and got her phone from Karen's room and called a cab. The afternoon sun's rays glared at her through the window. She went outside and waited. It was a warm, sunny spring day, the St. John's equivalent of a unicorn. The cab pulled up and she limped over. The sun ricocheted off the remaining dirty snow banks. The taxi splashed puddles of melting snow as it made its way to Georgetown.

When Julie got home, she sat on her couch restless. It was times like these that she would normally go for a walk to clear her mind. And it was such a perfect day for it. But her leg was in no condition for that. She decided instead to go for a drive. She grabbed her keys and drove through downtown St. John's and up Signal Hill's steep twisting road. Being a beautiful day, the parking lot by Cabot Tower was nearly full. A car pulled out and she found a spot overlooking the city. The harbour was dappled in sunlight.

She thought about the first night she spent in Paris. For her first weekend in France, she took a train to la Ville Lumière by herself, needing to experience the city for the first time alone. She didn't go inside any museums, she just walked the boulevards and famous walkways. It soon became clear to her why the city had such a romantic gravitas. She certainly didn't experience the shock of "Paris syndrome" in which the city didn't live up to unrealistic expectations. It was humanizing to see that Paris was an actual city, that some corners stunk like piss and many of its citizens were rude. She felt the weight of all those great artists' ghosts nearly everywhere she walked. It was pretty ridiculous, though, that famous cafes charged exorbitant prices just because James Joyce and Ernest Hemingway used to get drunk there. Those guys were alcoholics. How many bars around the world have the great expat literati pissed themselves?

In the evening she bought a bottle of red wine and went to the top of Montmartre and sat at the steps of the Basilica of the Sacre-Coeur. She watched as night descended on Paris. The streets slowly began filling up with light, like blood flooding the arteries and veins of a giant heart. The wine gave her a pleasant buzz. No one seemed to think it was peculiar that a young woman was drinking alone in public. She remembered feeling like she was being torn in two. She was lonely and horny but relished the solitude. She wanted Tyler to be there, to experience the moment with her. But she also realized for the first time that he never would be there for these sorts of moments. It was then and there that she began to understand that Tyler would never venture far from his cave.

She also felt the swell of her literary ambitions but also the crushing weight of her insecurity. The trip showed her that she could be alone, that perhaps she needed to be. To be away from her parents' safety net and Tyler's neediness. It was terrifying and exhilarating to see that solitude was necessary but also possible. She began to formulate a plan. She could go to law school. That would give her options. With a law degree she could create the solitude she would need to develop her craft. She realized that "Plan Bs" weren't sexy, but things were different for women. The same opportunities wouldn't be available to her as her male peers. She would have to work harder, be better than them, she would have to be strategic. That didn't bother her. The magnitude of hard work never scared her. What scared her was the blank page. The white sheet of paper that stared her down and was unfazed by her hopes and dreams, so cruel and indifferent. But she would face that, and in time would wear down all those blank pages one by one and beat them into submission.

And she was almost there, too. She had been accepted into her school of choice and was resolved to sacrifice her relationship if Tyler couldn't keep up. But, within a span of just twenty-four hours, all that effort was threatened to be undone by this unfathomable new chaos. She now lived in a world where werewolves existed. And she was pregnant.

"Well," she said aloud to herself. "Maybe I'll have enough material for a good first novel."

CHAPTER SIX (1964)

Humbert Humbert was wrong to claim, "Nymphets do not occur in polar regions." They most certainly did, according to Dr. Derek Hunt. Humbert described them as "plump, glossy little Eskimo girls with their fish smell, hideous raven hair, and guinea pig faces." Firstly, they weren't "Eskimos"; they were Innu and Inuit. Or at least they were in Labrador. Derek thought "Eskimo" was an ugly, generalized word for a diverse group of peoples who happened to live in northern climates. Humbert was simply a xenophobic European snob in that regard. Derek considered himself more modern and progressive. Racism was for small minds. Secondly, Derek loved aboriginal girls for all the reasons that Humbert hated them. He loved their chubby, squished faces, and he loved that they smelled like fish and animals. It inspired him to ponder the vitality of nature. Modern civilization had forgotten what it's like to be an actual human, to smell like an actual human. He even felt a little guilty for impugning on their purity by bringing them the gift of modern medicine. And while he liked the aboriginal girls, Derek's favourite were the Métis. Their olive skin was like taffy and he just wanted to sink his teeth in. The presence of Caucasian genetic heritage gave shape and form to the softer aboriginal visages. A wonderful mix of breeding. He appreciated the affect in all inter-racial mingling. It had something to do with being predisposed to one's own race, he was sure. But the introduction of a new set of genes was like an exotic twist on a familiar theme.

It was the spring now, so he would soon get the opportunity to travel on the coastal boats to communities along the northern Labrador coast. It was too dangerous to risk the waters during the fall and winter. Even during the summer, he was hard pressed for time to visit the northern Innu and Inuit communities, so he took advantage of whatever opportunities came his way. Unlike Humbert, however, Derek never acted on his impulses. That was certainly a line he would never cross. He merely cropped a few feels whenever he could. The gift of modern medicine was not without its price. Being a physician afforded him innumerable opportunities to fondle nymphets. He'd mastered the mask of professional indifference so as to disguise his indecent lust. But it wasn't like any of nature's children knew what proper medicine looked like, bless their blameless souls.

Exotic nymphets aside, Derek was anxious to get out of Cartwright for a spell. Being a country doctor in Labrador during the winter was a claustrophobic experience. His days started and ended in darkness. His clinic was mostly full of old women clogging up the waiting room--any excuse to get in and gossip. The hospital at Cartwright was big for the town's small population, but it was a hub for the surrounding areas. It was so busy that Derek was required to hire two full-time nurses. He also had to make house calls. There was no telephone service, so he was often jolted from his sleep at all hours of the night with a loud bustle at his door. At these moments he would punch a hole through the house's gyprock to relieve his frustration. His walls were subsequently adorned with tapestries and animal skins made by local artisans to hide the holes. At this point he was running out of space, so he was going to have to start repairs or the house might soon fall down around him.

The locals idolized him and his industry. He never denied a request. He, in turn, admired the nasty, brutish, and often short lives of these fishermen. At least down south, around the Grand Banks off the eastern shores of the Avalon peninsula, the men had the warm, foggy water of the Gulf Stream. Up in the north, they had to contend with the cruel Labrador Current. The fishermen who hauled the nets from the frigid water were exposed to extreme coldness for hours, which could turn a man's hands black and green. By the time most of them got to Derek, their fingers were gangrenous from frostbite. Amputation was the best he could offer them. And he understood the significance of this operation. Everything these men did depended on a functioning pair of hands. A missing thumb meant the man couldn't fix nets, set traps, or hold an axe. The new welfare benefits from Canada helped, but not much. In Labrador, the difference between a difficult life and a doomed uncertain future lay along a small margin of error.

Of course, they weren't just fishermen. That was only for the six months of the year that weren't frozen beneath the overlong winter. For the other six months, they were trappers. And in-between they were also carpenters, lumberjacks, masons, and whatever other craft this punishing land demanded of them. Derek had made several excursions around Labrador during the winter on dog teams. He enjoyed these sorts of adventures, but there was only so much he could be expected to risk his life for his patients. He wasn't good to anyone dead in the snow, deep in the interior of Labrador. Now, though, it was early summer, and the days were finally starting to stretch out a little. Unfortunately, early summer also meant flies. Their volume was Biblical. Derek found the best solution was to add a dollop of repellant to his pulse points, like applying some vile cologne. Labrador thus only had two seasons: snow and flies.

Today, one of his favourite patients had come in for one of his customarily irregular visits. He sat on the examining table, fat seeping from his ragged clothes. Tom never made appointments. He simply showed up at the clinic and told the nurses he was on death's door and had to see Dr. Hunt immediately. At this point he wasn't fooling anyone. He simply didn't want to wait behind the gossiping hens. Derek couldn't blame him. His issues were always the same--typical symptoms of diabetes and high blood pressure.

"What did you have for breakfast?" Derek asked.

"Couple slices of bologna and toast," he said.

"Not a very good meal given your condition," Derek said. "Plenty of butter, too, I imagine." He sniffed Tom's breath. "Anything to drink?"

"Tea," Tom answered, grinning. Whenever Tom lied he had the same boyish smile. His nose and cheeks were scarlet from alcoholism. His wife was dead, and his children moved away. He'd alienated the few friends he had left. Derek couldn't imagine there was much left to Tom's life but to dwindle away his few remaining years with booze and cigarettes provided by his piddly dole.

"Ease up on the rum and salt," Derek said. "You need more vegetables, greens."

"I'll try, doc, I'll try."

Derek knew it was no use. He gave him some calcium and magnesium supplements and sent him off. His next patient hobbled over to the examining room. Derek knew that if Horace Hubbard had that look on his face it meant he was in a degree of agony few people could possibly divine. The pain threshold of some these men astounded Derek.

"Damned nipper got me," Horace muttered. His voice was weak and raspy. "Back of my neck. Can't even get out of bed."

Derek removed the bandages and had a look. On the back of Horace's neck was an angry carbuncle with a network of boils and abscesses. Everything from his hairline down to his shoulders was inflamed. In the centre of the carbuncle was one particularly cruel abscess hinting at the vile puss brimming at the surface.

"I wish you'd come here sooner, Horace," Derek said. "We could've treated it before it got this bad."

Part of Derek's mission was to preach the virtues of preventative medicine. It was not going well. He knew how much these men despised losing a day of work. They preferred to simply ignore problems in the hope they'd just resolve themselves. And if that failed, they might acquiesce to their wives' home remedies. And if that failed, they might drop into the clinic if they felt death was imminent. And it often was. If Horace had waited much longer, the wound likely would've gone septic. His wife had done as good a job as she could have. She didn't squeeze it, which would've caused worse irritations and scaring. She'd used a warm cloth to help drain it semi-regularly. Unfortunately, for that to work, Horace would've had to remain stationary throughout the day, so she could do it consistently. As it was, he was out working sun-up to sun-down, so she had gotten treatments in whenever she could. Derek imagined that even then Horace wasn't a very cooperative patient. It also didn't help that access to sterilized dressings in these communities was nearly impossible.

Derek used tweezers to remove the webbing of dried puss. Little droplets of blood leaked out, which he dabbed away with some gauze. Then he applied gentle pressure and the ooze really started to flow. Yellow and red pudding streamed from the abscess. Horace grunted in pain, but Derek could feel his body relax at the relieved pressure. The process became more painful as the carbuncle deflated. Derek had to be thorough, had to make sure it was all out. Once he was satisfied, he covered it up with some dressings and bandages.

"I want you to come in here every day for the next couple weeks to change those dressings," Derek said.

"You got it," Horace said.

"And please take a few days off."

"I'll try, doc, I'll try."

There it was again. *I'll try, doc, I'll try.* How many times has he heard that refrain? On long days such as today, Derek retreated as much as possible into the paradise within his mind replete with nymphets. It was often the only thing that kept him from losing his mind. He envisioned a French boudoir full of callow mixed-race girls from all niches of the world. They served him red wine and aged cheddar. A gramophone played Edith Piaf. As much as he loved the romantic Labrador landscape, he also yearned for the metropolitan splendor of the world's greatest city, Paris, where he'd finally consummated his dark appetite. At the time he was a medical student studying in England. Throughout his university years, he found himself increasingly uninterested in girls. As they aged, he longed for his young days back in high school, and especially junior high, when love and sex were new and exciting. As a handsome young man, he had no difficulty inspiring girls' attention. It was the springtime of his libido and there were many smiling flowers, and he gathered as many rosebuds as he could. But once he enrolled in his undergrad, at just sixteen, he soon became weary of it all. And by medical school, he was totally abstinent. The smiling flowers had all wilted and there were no more rosebuds left worth taking. He wondered if this was just a symptom of early adulthood, nostalgic for halcyon days. At his worst, he feared that he was transforming into a homosexual. He certainly didn't share his classmates' zeal to go hunt some birds at the nearby pub for a snog. He kept to himself and focused on his studies. The acquittal from the animal magnetism of young male sexuality was actually an advantage. Without those distractions, he rose to the top of his class. The boys took to calling him Sherlock for his ascetic lifestyle and focus.

Then, to celebrate the end of a particularly grueling semester, he and some of the lads took a trip to Paris. They boys wanted to visit a brothel. "Come on, Sherlock," they said. "Give it some air." He wanted no part of it, but by this point any further abnegation would have inspired undue suspicion in his peers, and Derek certainly appreciated the value of good stature. When they arrived at the chosen establishment, Derek was sickened. But it did manage to give him a better appreciation for the works of Toulouse-Lautrec and the artist's commitment to verisimilitude. The mademoiselle lined up the buffet, most of them over-perfumed Rubenesque cows, which made Derek feel like Gulliver among the Brobdingnagians. He considered them with ambivalence until his eyes fell upon Cheri. She was petit and ethereal, not vulgar and gargantuan like the others. She looked at him with a pure intensity devoid of experience and practice. He took her to a chalet and she opened a door deep within him that he hadn't realized was locked. It was like escaping Plato's cave.

When he came back to London, he started seeing them everywhere. These little cherubs that had previously glided by without his notice were now all he could see. Like a spell on his eyes had been lifted. But he dared not indulge his desires in London, so near his classmates and faculty. He began taking regular trips to Paris, a city full of establishments eager to satisfy his needs. It was a city that appreciated more refined aesthetics, after all. Part of him felt guilty for indulging in such an immoral act, but he justified it by telling himself that these were poor creatures who were at least better off than trying to survive as street urchins. And if he didn't hire them, then some uncouth pervert would use them all the same. At least he treated them with respect.

During one trip to Paris, he came across *Lolita*. The book had been causing a stir in literary circles. Derek bought himself a copy. It was a green paperback published by Olympia Press, known mostly for smut. He was surprised by its literary merit. Mostly, though, he was struck by how he'd found a kindred spirit in the book's protagonist, Humbert Humbert. For much of his adult life he felt tortured by this burden of a secret he lugged around. In Humbert he'd found a kindred spirit, and Vladimir Nabokov gave him *le mot juste*: nymphet. *Lolita* buoyed his soul. How could such an evil sin stir such beautiful prose?

In rare moments when he managed to eschew self-deception, Derek knew that his mild gropings weren't as innocent as he often told himself. But he was a sick man and these were just small vaccinations to inoculate himself of his disease's greater symptoms. He had no illusions about what he was. Some nights, when he was miserable, rocking and rolling with insomnia, he considered suicide or moving somewhere far into the Labrador interior to escape humanity and quarantine his perversion. But the world needed his talents. Only the wounded physician can hope to heal. This was simply his cross to bear. Coming to Cartwright was a form of contrition. When he came home from medical school in England to St. John's, he considered the many far-flung rural postings that struggled to attract long-term doctors. He settled on Cartwright because it seemed remote enough to engender a sacrificial gesture. Labrador was, after all, "the land god gave Cain." This was his bargain. He'd practice medicine in this obscure corner of the earth, so that he could make up for his perverse nature.

And it wasn't like he couldn't do great things and achieve glory. Look at Sir Wilfred Grenfell, Derek's hero. Grenfell was responsible for bringing health care services to Labrador, starting in the late nineteenth century. Derek's hospital was part of the Grenfell Mission. He'd even attended the London Hospital Medical School, the same as Grenfell. He fell in love with the Grenfell legend upon reading *White Eskimo* by Harold Horwood, who based the protagonist, Gillingham, on Grenfell. Much like Gillingham, Derek was dismayed by the influence of the Catholic Church in Labrador and the incursion of modernism. He harboured idyllic dreams of becoming one with the land and being embraced by the noble northerners. His greatest moments of pleasure were going out with the men on their excursions into the woods with dog teams, seeing the traplines, shooting game, and fishing the ocean. He marvelled at the old sea dogs who could navigated these treacherous waters. Hidden reefs and monstrous crags that lay hidden beneath fog, darkness, or the most shallow of waters, waiting to claim less scrupulous sailors. These men read the landscape the way Derek analyzed a sick person's body. He thought back to older times of wooden vessels and before radio and other navigational aids. How did they do it? As technology advanced, these ancient techniques retreated.

It was late now. The two nurses had gone home. He was alone doing paperwork still at the clinic. He didn't like being at home in that big house by himself, so he stayed in the hospital for as long as he could. Sleep rarely granted him any more than four hours of peace a night anyway. The only purpose for his home was to keep food and a change of clothes. He was researching fly bites and the bacterial infections they caused when he was interrupted by a knock at the front door. It was technically after consultation hours, but a country doctor didn't really keep a regular schedule. The knocking continued with an urgency that indicated panic. He had become familiar with the different rhythms of patients' knocking and what emotion they indicated. Derek got up to see what was the matter.

"Dr. Hunt," said the woman at his door. "My cow is perishing."

It was Alma Martin. Despite not being much a people-person, Derek had quickly memorized all his patients' names and their family histories and circumstances.

"Okay," he said, grabbing his coat. "Let's go."

He didn't like treating animals, but without a veterinarian anywhere near the responsibility usually fell to him. Alma led him to the barn behind her house. It was springtime so many of the men were out at the seal hunt, including Alma's husband. She explained that her cow had calved two days ago. This morning she went to milk her but found the animal lying down on her side, unresponsive.

"I'm the only one who can milk her," Alma explained. "My husband won't go handy to her. 'She's likely to give me a boot upside the head if I ever touches her again,' he said. 'That's on account of your hard, old calloused hands,' I told him."

Livestock represented a big investment for people here. To lose a heffer like this would be a blow to the Martins. More than that, it was clear that Alma shared a bond with the cow. Derek admired that. He could imagine Alma coming out each morning to milk her, probably having a small conversation with the animal. It was a little private meditative experience she didn't have to share with her family, who were constantly making demands on her.

They walked into the barn. The cow lay on her side taking small breaths, her tail still. Her stall was full of broken and splintered wood; she'd been kicking and struggling all through the night. There were two older men standing nearby. Waltham Coombes and Finley Lemaire. The only men left around Cartwright during the sealing were either too young or too old to be out on the ice.

"I didn't want to bother you, Doctor," Alma said. "So I asked Walt and Fin to help. After we ran out of ideas I came and got you."

"What did you try?" Derek asked.

"First we gave her a solution of Epsom salts," Walt said. "After that didn't work, we gave her the sweet spirits of niter."

Derek had only heard of spirit of niter when he came to Cartwright. As far as he was concerned it was just snake oil sold to unscrupulous rubes. He shook his head at these old baymen. Fortunately, he knew the pathophysiology of the cow's condition: parturient paresis. Calcium from the cow's body was pouring into her milk, inducing a state of hypocalcemic tetany. Not that it was any good to try and explain that.

"She got milk fever," Derek said. The old men nodded in agreement, surprised they hadn't figured that out themselves. "I'm going to inject her with calcium. I'll have to go back to the clinic to get what I need and I'll be right back."

Derek trudged back to the clinic. It gave him pleasure to quickly solve a problem that so baffled these folk. He grabbed what he needed to concoct a simple intravenous calcium solution and headed back to Alma's barn. The cow was a more amenable patient than he was used to dealing with, let alone most the animals he'd had to treat. Last week he got himself scratched to shreds trying to haul a fishhook out of the lips of Milicent Pardy's tom-cat.

"She should be fine soon enough," he said.

"I can't afford to pay you, doctor," Alma said. "But I can offer you some supper."

This was typical. While the job didn't pay handsomely, he was never wanting for food, clothes, or the arts and crafts he used to adorn his home. Women were eager to knit him clothes and invite him over for meals, especially when the men were out fishing or sealing. Derek often agreed as it was certainly a fine feast compared to whatever paltry dish lay waiting for him back at home. He wasn't much of a cook. Whenever he sat alone in his living room, eating reheated soup, reading, he thought that he ought to find himself a woman--a utilitarian, functional wife. None could compare aesthetically to a nymphet, so he may as well get himself a live-in maid. And if they had children it would certainly bolster his facade as well-adjusted man.

Like Humbert, Derek was well aware of his attractiveness to women. Added to the fact that he was the only doctor within miles made him an extraordinarily desirable bachelor. Unfortunately, being the most eligible bachelor on the coast of Labrador was like being the world's tallest midget. The women repulsed him, which wasn't necessarily a knock on Labrador women; he despised all grown women. The years and hormones bloated their bodies like laundry sacks filled with dirty clothes. Mothers were especially repulsive. Knowing that a woman had carried and delivered a child was a complete disenchantment. He'd been in enough delivery rooms. Nymphets--bless Vladimir for giving him such a perfect word--were free of all these natural blemishes. They were angels devoid of all our grotesque mammalian attachments.

Inside Alma's house, her brood of children were sitting at the table. The girls were too young to be considered nymphets. They were still grubby little caterpillars with no hint as to whether they would transform into butterflies or mosquitoes. The kitchen was full of the smell of salt fish. There was also some carrots, cabbage, and potatoes boiling on the stove, fetched from the root cellar.

"Had I known you'd be joining us, I would've put on a bit of salt beef or pork," Alma said. "I have some jam that we can have for dessert."

"That'll be lovely," Derek said.

The children were excited. Whenever the doctor came for supper it meant mom was taking out the speciality items. Derek sat down and Alma laid his meal before him. He could taste the family's adulation. It warmed his belly.

"Did you save our cow?" one of the children asked.

"He certainly did," the mother answered.

As Derek explained to them the science of the cow's condition and recovery, he felt like a missionary bringing the light of god to heathen savages.

CHAPTER SEVEN (2015)

Mornings were the easiest. Well, not easy per se. Joseph couldn't remember the last time he'd felt rested after a night's sleep. However, he wasn't suffocating under the dread the night brought, and that made things a little easier. Still in bed, he rolled over and grabbed an exercise book and pen from an upside down milk crate, which served as a nightstand. In the dim light he detailed his latest dream. He wrote cursively in his *grad student's* drunken chicken scratches. It was an automatic process. He allowed the words to come and did his best to just get out the way. He'd been dreaming a lot about Tyler lately, and the dreams were getting increasingly violent. A month ago, he began having visions of wrestling with Tyler at the baseball park behind Whiteway. That's how he knew to be there the last full moon.

Over the years he had learned to trust his dreams and visions. He recorded them, and once he identified a pattern he reviewed them closely and considered their significance. The spiral-bound Hilroy was full, fat with three hundred and sixty ink-filled pages. He had to write in small letters to cram all the words into the last page. He chewed through one of these every three or four months. When he was done writing, he got out of bed—a couple old mattresses stacked on the floor—and went to his desk. He took out a label maker and dated his exercise book, Jan-Apr 2016. He added it to a pile of similar Hilroys.

He went to the kitchen and mixed a scoop of protein powder with almond milk. He grabbed a banana and washed it down with the shake. His kitchen and living room were taken up with lab equipment and stacks of books. Microscopes, Bunsen burners, and centrifuges were interrupted by case studies in epidemiology and histories of werewolf folklore. Mice squeaked plaintively in their cages. Joseph refilled their water bottles and dishes. The apartment stank like rodent shit. He'd neglected to get fresh sawdust for some time now. He made a mental note to pick some up at the store later today.

He went back to his room. He pushed the mattresses up against the wall and unrolled a yoga mat. He grinned self-consciously as he arched into downward dog. He felt his spine elongate and neck loosen as he stretched the muscles. His back and hamstrings especially gave him trouble. In addition to the yoga, Joseph followed a bodybuilder's diet, consuming at least half a gram of protein per pound of body weight (a lean one hundred and fifty pounds) each day. Leading up to a full moon, he steadily increased his carbohydrates. Hundred grams per day was optimal. A metamorphosis was as hard on the body as completing an Ironman Triathlon. It took several days to recover. And then there was the matter of healing whatever wounds he'd sustained as a lycan that weren't taken care of during the transformation back into a human.

Joseph's morning yoga routine took about forty-five minutes to an hour, depending on how stiff he was. He followed that with an equally long meditation session. After the downward dogs and warrior posses, he lay flat on his mat, staring up at the ceiling. His lower back sang with relief. He closed his eyes and began his breathing drill. He inhaled for five seconds, held the breath for five, and then exhaled for five. He performed this process five times. He then settled into a regular breathing pattern and began scanning through his body. He imagined a soft golden ball of light that started at his ankles. He brought the light up slowly, to his knees, groin, chest, throat, and then imagined it hovering a few inches above his head. His focus waned as he started thinking about cleaning the mice's cages. He repeated the five-point breathing exercise and regained his focus. He then imagined a long staircase, five-hundred steps. He counted each one. Thoughts came and went. He passed them by without engaging, like strangers one might pass descending a high-rise apartment building, some quietly staring, others screaming loudly.

At the bottom, Joseph stepped onto a snowy forest floor. Tall skinny conifers reached towards a black sky dotted with a watchful yellow moon. Fat, lazy snowflakes drifted in the soft wind. Around him, wolves crept softly. They bowed their heads in submission. He came upon the body of a girl. Her neck was slit. As always in these visions, her face was obscured to him. She had distinct features -- eyes, nose, a mouth -- but he couldn't piece together the individual pieces into a coherent whole. His mind refused to retain any impression. He also couldn't prevent what happened next. He'd tried shooing the wolves off, scaring them away, he'd even killed them, but they always came back. He'd tried lifting or dragging the body, but it was impossibly dense. He'd tried digging underneath her, but the ground was frozen solid. Now, Joseph walked on, shielding his ears as the wolves devoured the corpse.

The path then led him to the Southside hills of downtown St. John's. He surveyed the remains of Fort Amherst until he heard a scream coming from the woods. Joseph had tried running into the woods to stop it from happening, but he never arrived fast enough or at the right place. By the time he located the scream, the woman and man are dead. She with her throat ripped out, he with his body covered with knife wounds. Again, their faces were obscured. However, Joseph believed he knew who these people were. They were his parents. This was how they died, the night he was born. There was nothing he could do for them now.

He continued on the path. This was a territory he'd been excavating now for the past year. The place was called the Drook, an old, resettled community where he liked to go sometimes during the full moon. It had presented itself during meditation. Joseph sought it out and discovered it at the tip of the Southern Shore. The houses stood like hollow tombstones, gazing out over the bay. He reached the end of the path. He focused and extended it further. From his memory, he expanded the harbour. Salt box houses and fishing stages spontaneously assembled as if they were being pulled up from the land and sea with invisible hands. Soon, after enough meditations, the whole community would form instantaneously just as the previous locations. Then, Joseph hoped, his subconscious would reveal why it had brought him here, and he could add another piece to this strange puzzle.

However, it turned out that he wouldn't have to wait so long after all. In the distance, he heard dogs barking and snarling. A woman screamed, which was followed by a long, mournful howl. A body lay by a house with a naked man kneeling beside it. A woman was standing near. Joseph ran to them. He looked down and saw that the body's throat had been ripped out. This time the faces weren't blurred. It was Julie and Tyler. The body was his. Blood leaked onto the grass, pumping from the gash in his neck.

A phone rang. The shrill noise shook the earth and sky. The harbour crumbled as Joseph's focus deteriorated. It was his cell phone, an unfamiliar sound. Joseph scrambled to answer it.

"Hello?" he asked.

"Hey. It's Tyler."

"..."

"You alright?"

"Yes," Joseph said, catching his breath. He wiped beads of sweat from his forehead. "I was just exercising."

"Right on. Are you busy? I think we should meet up. Have a chat."

"Okay. How about an hour's time? Meet me at Burton's Pond over at MUN."

"Sure. See you there."

The mice would have to wait for clean cages.

Joseph grabbed a thick binder. "After Dark Vapours" was written along its spine. He loaded it into a backpack. He also grabbed a bottle of Aspirin and stuffed it into his jacket pocket. MUN was a short drive from his apartment, but he preferred to walk. After a quick brunch, he left his apartment on Merrymeeting Road and made his way down Mayor Avenue towards the university.

It was a mild April day, something to be grateful for in St. John's. The weather was never much of a bother for Joseph. Having lived in various parts of North America, he thought there was something to be said for a place that made him feel like he was an organism inhabiting planet Earth. Thanks to home heating and air conditioning, most places felt like neutral vessels for people to squat on, like living on some kind of frictionless grid designed for theoretical physics experiments. Newfoundland refused to be neutralized. The Labrador Current pushed and punched its way into a person's daily life.

Memorial University's campus had grown since Joseph was a student in the early 80s. However, it had remained true to its East Berlin aesthetic. It didn't help that the campus was built in the ugliest part of the province. Even MUN's Oceans Sciences Centre, which was built on the muscular cliffs of Logy Bay, was depressing to behold. It was like a bizarre wooden spaceship, leftover from a 1960's space opera B-movie. It was quite a shock to Joseph in the late 80s when he left for Montreal to study at McGill. He'd never considered the possibility that a Canadian university could be beautiful. He figured all the nice ones were in Europe or the Ivy Leagues south of the border. The recent work on Burton's Pond was lovely, Joseph had to admit. There was a nice walkway surrounding the pond. He sat down on a bench and watched the ducks. A few feet away, a lady was tossing them food. Joseph hoped it wasn't white bread. The water rippled as bits and bites struck the surface. Mama duck came with her little ones in tow, all in synchronized form. They then broke apart and fought each other for their morsels.

Joseph had been a serious student. He realized early on that school was a portal he could use to transform his life into something better than the petit bourgeois family he'd been thrown into -- if he worked hard enough. He never got along with his adoptive parents. It's not that he hated them. He loved them and they loved him. They just didn't understand each other; they didn't speak the same language. Joseph needed something from them that was never in them to give. It wasn't their fault, and he'd made peace with all that. Joseph wasn't sure what he wanted out of life as a young man, but it wasn't working forty hours at a job he hated, buying stuff, and then dying.

It was in first year chemistry at MUN when he discovered Karen's curly orange hair. It radiated, calling to him like a lighthouse to a boat in a stormy night. Of course, he never had the guts to just go up and talk to her, so he admired her from a distance. He couldn't believe his fortune when she was in his lab group. Still, he was too shy to speak to her. He counted the freckles on her pearly face and was silent. Luckily for him, she struggled with chemistry's relentless conundrums. Joseph realized he'd been given enough lucky breaks and made his move, offering his services as a study buddy. When he found out she was a Habs fan, he read all he could about the Canadiens, his knowledge of French finally paying off. He read Ken Dryden's The Game and felt like he discovered a kindred spirit amidst a sport he'd long considered boorish.

Unlike Joseph, Karen was not a serious student. She worked when she needed to and maintained a respectable 3.5 GPA. But she personalized what she learned in a way he never could. She applied history and sociology to her everyday life. Like Joseph, though, she also didn't know what she wanted and certainly didn't want the petit bourgeois life from which she, too, sprang. She took joy in life in a way Joseph had never experienced. She laughed easily and dismantled all of Joseph's defences. They'd lie in bed and smoke weed and talk about all the places they'd travel when Joseph finished grad school. He'd be a field virologist and she'd be a photo journalist. They'd travel the world, healing people and documenting their stories.

A legion of dead dreams that would never come to pass.

Joseph heard someone scuff their shoes nearby. Tyler approached, carrying a Tim Hortons cup in each hand. He sat beside Joseph and handed him one.

"Black okay?" Tyler asked.

"Yes, thank you," Joseph said. "Do you know if these ducks fly away for winter? Or do they have their wings clipped?" he asked.

"No idea," Tyler answered.

They popped the lids of their coffees and breathed soft cool air into the holes.

"How are you feeling?" Joseph asked.

"I'm alright."

"Is your job taken care of?"

"Yeah, I told my boss I had a medical issue, didn't want to talk about it. He was cool about it."

"Good. Like I said, you won't have to worry about money while we figure this out. I have you covered."

"Okay."

"What about Julie?"

"She's alright. We haven't been talking much the last week."

They sipped their coffees and watched the ducks. A few students walked past. Joseph had decided he would let Tyler lead this exchange, let him make all the first moves.

"This is going to sound dumb," Tyler said, "but I thought you had to be bitten to become a werewolf."

"I guess not," Joseph said. "A pathogen can leap from an animal to a human in a variety of ways. Rabies, for example, is transferred from a dog bite. Perhaps some ancestor of ours was bitten and he passed the disease down the line congenitally. Seems unlikely to me, but this is unlikely territory."

"So, what's wrong with me? With us?"

"Honestly, I don't know. Any answers I can give you are theoretical and unsatisfactory."

"Do you have a plan at least?"

"In a few days, once you've fully recovered, I'd like to take some blood samples to examine. I doubt they'll reveal anything promising. Mine hasn't anyway. For the time being you're going to have to learn how to adjust."

"I can't deal with this. I have a life."

"You still do. Only now it's more complicated."

"Why don't we just go to the university," Tyler suggested. "Tell them everything. Get them working on a cure. I bet this shit would get all the best scientists in the world together."

"No," Joseph said. "I don't want anyone else involved."

"Why not?"

"Henrietta Lacks. She was a poor black woman living in Baltimore who died of cervical cancer in the 30s. Without getting informed consent from the family, they took tissue samples from her cancer and used those cells for research that would go on to build an incalculable medical juggernaut. I don't want our cells getting into the wrong hands."

"So what? If our cells, or whatever, helped cure a bunch of diseases, I'm cool with that. I don't want money. I just want a cure. Sure, look at you. You look like the healthiest man alive. Why wouldn't you want to help other people?"

"You're not hearing what I'm saying. Once it's out there, we can't stop it. Who knows what sort of research this could lead to. Before they tested the atomic bomb, some scientists feared that a nuclear explosion might ignite the earth's atmosphere and burn the entire world. They did it anyway. You don't know what these people are capable of."

"You think some mad scientist is going to create an army of werewolves with our blood?"

"Maybe not so melodramatic, but something like that, yes."

"I hate the government and big pharmaceutical companies just as much as the next guy, but I think you're being a little paranoid."

"I have no idea what could happen. That's the point. This stuff is dangerous."

They sat in silence again. A few puffy clouds drifted about, otherwise the sky was clear. A chilly breeze reminded Joseph that he should've worn a sweater under his jacket. The burning at the pit of his stomach reminded him why he didn't drink Tim's.

"I have something for you," Joseph said. He took the binder out from his backpack and handed it to Tyler.

Tyler opened it. The first page contained the eponymous poem by John Keats:

After dark vapors have oppress'd our plains
For a long dreary season, comes a day
Born of the gentle South, and clears away
From the sick heavens all unseemly stains.
The anxious month, relieved of its pains,
Takes as a long-lost right the feel of May;
The eyelids with the passing coolness play
Like rose leaves with the drip of Summer rains.
The calmest thoughts came round us; as of leaves
Budding—fruit ripening in stillness—Autumn suns
Smiling at eve upon the quiet sheaves—
Sweet Sappho's cheek—a smiling infant's breath—
The gradual sand that through an hour-glass runs—
A woodland rivulet—a Poet's death.

"What is this?" Tyler asked. "Your screenplay?"

"No," Joseph explained. "The design is a subterfuge, meant to look like the manuscript for a novel in-progress. I didn't want to have to answer any awkward questions in case I lost it. The information inside is the fruits of my research over the past twenty years or so."

Joseph turned his attention back to the ducks as Tyler leafed through the material. There were many pages of typed notes, along with diagrams of the lunar cycle and illustrations of werewolves. Towards the end of the binder were various newspaper clippings. Finally, there were a number of pictures of Tyler throughout his life. Pictures of his mother, too. And letters, signed by her.

Love, Karen.

Tyler reviewed a page containing a family tree Joseph had designed. Derek Hunt, the man who Joseph believed to be his father, was highlighted.

"Why are you focused on this guy?" Tyler asked.

"I believe it starts with Derek," Joseph replied. "The Hunt family were pretty successful from as a far as I can tell. Each patriarch lived long and comfortably until Derek. He's the only outlier. He was found dead along with his wife up on Fort Amherst. He was covered in knife wounds and she had her throat ripped out. The police believed they'd killed each other. But there were a lot of strange details that were unexplained. It was a winter night, yet he was found naked. She had just given birth to a baby the previous night and given it up for adoption. Unfortunately, I have no idea why."

"And that baby was you?"

"It's my birthday."

"But if you don't know for sure?"

"I don't. It's a theory."

Tyler continued to browse the binder.

"Says here he was a doctor. Like you. That's strange."

"Not quite. I was a virologist, so I worked alongside many doctors. But yes, I've thought about that a lot. It's purely coincidence, of course. Likely, it says more about the medical profession. That it attracts people of a certain temperament, which is in many ways genetic."

"I guess I didn't inherit that doctor gene."

"No, you're more like Karen. More free spirited."

Both were silent in her non-presence.

"I have another copy of all that for Julie," Joseph said. "She's very bright. We could benefit from her input."

"She's pregnant," Tyler said.

"Yes, I know."

"Says here in your notes that might have something to do with it."

"Yes, I first transformed when Karen was pregnant. My parents died the night I was born. I imagine my father followed a similar timeline."

Tyler closed the binder. He finished his coffee and tossed it in a trashcan then leaned back with his hands in his hoodie pockets.

"For the next full moon, we will travel to the Drook," Joseph said. "It's an isolated, resettled community. I like to go there during metamorphoses. There's lots of room to run around and no one to worry about. I'll show you how to better control your lycanthropy."

"Why don't you build a couple of big cages?" Tyler asked. "Just ride it out in there."

"I've tried that. I've learned that it's best to let the beast out of the cage, so to speak."

"If you go to this Drook place when you're a werewolf, then why were you in town this time? How did you know that I was going to transform?"

"I don't know. Intuition I suppose."

"Where have you been the last twenty years?"

"After I first started transforming," Joseph said, "I fled to Northern Quebec to hide. Once I got a grip on things, I used my background in chemistry to invest in pharmaceuticals and medical technology. I eventually had some success with that and settled in British Columbia for awhile. Now I live off the dividends."

"So, you're like *The Wolf of Wall Street*?"

"I have no idea what you're talking about."

"Never mind. What about Mom? Why didn't you come to visit when she was sick?"

"Your mother and I spoke intermittently over the years by mail or phone. I could never tell her what was actually happening. But she understood there was something wrong. She trusted me that I was doing the right thing. Even when she was sick."

"What about me then? You could've helped me. I was alone."

"When your mother's condition became worse, I came home and kept an eye on you from afar. I kept my distance because *I thought I would only add to your problems*."

"You could've done something. You didn't have to move in, but a little support would've been nice."

"I supported your mother financially. Who do you think covered the mortgage and financial costs?"

Tyler stared at his sneakers.

"Alright, fair enough," Joseph said. "I probably didn't handle everything has well as I could have. But that's the past. We have to deal with the present. Right now, I want you to reopen lines of communication with Julie."

Tyler paused as if he were going to reply, but then got up and left without saying anything. Joseph remained on the bench. The sky was clear now. The cold breeze intensified, sending chills up his spine. Tyler was right, Joseph knew. He should have been there for his son. The boy was only sixteen and had lost his mother with no family to help him out. I thought I would only add to your problems. That was a coward's answer.

Joseph's chest tightened. Breathing became difficult and painful, like his lungs were full of thumbtacks. His arms tingled. He pulled out the bottle of Aspirin. He popped two tablets into his mouth and chewed, extinguishing the fire inside his chest. Feeling returned to his arms. He leaned back into the bench and did his breathing exercises. His body was wet with sweat. The cold air felt like a whip.

He took out his phone and texted Lydia. *Are you available, mistress?* he wrote.

He breathed deeply. His phone buzzed. Lydia had replied.

Come, dog.

Joseph walked home to get his car. He cursed the elements now as the wind punished him while he walked up Mayor Avenue's hill. Lydia lived in the east end of the city, which Joseph considered to be the asshole of Newfoundland. It was a suburban sprawl of banal neighbourhoods and strip malls. It also happened to be where he grew up.

For as long as he could remember, Joseph knew that he'd been adopted. His parents never had a momentous conversation in which they revealed that he wasn't their biological son. It was something that he must have learned at a young age and he simply absorbed it as a part of his identity. How many people can remember when they learned what it was to be male or female? Black or white? It wasn't until later in his life that the question of his genealogy became somewhat of an existential crisis. He wasn't histrionic about it. Whenever he had fights with his mom or dad, he never pulled the "you're not my real parents!" card. It bothered him because it was a gap in his character that he couldn't account for. Steve Jobs said that the pique about being adopted is the loss of control; learning that you were left out of the loop during the most important moment in your life. Joseph disagreed. For him, the condition of being adopted meant being infected with contingency, the constant mental replays of "what ifs." What if he'd been raised by his biological family? What if he'd been adopted by scientists, rock stars, a travelling circus? Of course, no one has control over how they're thrown into this world. But for adopted children, the condition of this existential phenomenon is more tangible.

Joseph passed by his parents' old house whenever he went to see Lydia. Incidentally, it was along the fastest route there. But Joseph wondered if he did it to punish himself. They were both dead now. He hadn't spoken to them since the metamorphoses began. Occasionally he had visions of them grieving their missing adoptive son. He was often compelled to reach out to them and assure them that he was okay. However, he decided that it was better to remain silent, that the unanswered questions would only make things worse for them. He had treated his self-imposed exile like the act of a martyr, that he was sparing those he cared about, not hurting them. He saw now that it was all just cowardice.

Joseph pulled up to Lydia's driveway. He rang the doorbell. She answered wearing a bathrobe.

"I'm still getting ready," she said. "You can wait for me downstairs."

Joseph took off his shoes and went down to her basement. The room was lit with red bulbs. Whips and chains hung from the purple walls. The cat o' nine tails was Lydia's favourite. Joseph's dick hardened looking at the spanking horse in the centre of the room and the leather throne in the corner. This was where he came when his guilt threatened to overwhelm him, to get his mind right. He'd met Lydia on an online chat room for kink enthusiasts in the St. John's area about a year ago. He was searching for ways to release his psychological tension and was willing to try anything. She convinced him to try BDSM. She helped him explore his fantasies and achieve a catharsis that he now relied on every few weeks.

He heard the sound of latex crinkle from behind him. He turned and saw Lydia standing in the doorway wearing a black catsuit with a Pfeiffer-esque hood. She held a stainless steel dog bowl, which she laid on the floor. Joseph looked down at her feet.

"Strip," she said.

"Yes, mistress," Joseph answered.

He stripped naked.

"Get down on your hands and knees, dog."

"Yes, mistress."

Joseph squat on the floor as Lydia attached a studded collar. She led him around the basement by a short leash. He stayed in step with her six-inch heels. The hardwood floor was punctuated with velvet rugs; however, Lydia did not let him touch those. Occasionally she stopped and Joseph immediately sat up with his hands up to his chest and his mouth open. She rewarded him with a treat by spitting in his mouth.

Lydia sat down on her leather throne.

"Lick my boots, dog," she said.

"Yes, mistress."

He started at the toes and worked his way up to her knees, dragging his tongue across the crisscrossing laces. Lydia presented her soles. He licked those, too. She lifted up her heel. Joseph sucked on the spike like a popsicle. He coughed at the taste of dust in his mouth.

"Good job, dog. You may have a drink."

"Thank you, mistress."

Joseph crawled over to the dog bowl. He bent forward and lapped up the water with his tongue.

"Come, dog."

"Yes, mistress."

Lydia strapped Joseph to the spanking horse, clamping his wrists and ankles. She muzzled him with a silicone bone gag. His body sang with each strike from the cat o' nine tails.   "Bark!" she yelled.

Joseph drooled and spit through his gag as he woofed and growled.

"Do you want to be milked, dog?"

"Please, mistress."

Lydia rubbed lube over her hands. She slid two fingers up Joseph's asshole and jerked him off with her other hand. He whined as she worked him, his pitch rising. His body jerked wildly against the horse as he came onto the floor. He relaxed as Lydia released him from his restraints.

"Thank you, mistress," he said, recovering his breath.

"And thank you," she said. "I'm going upstairs to change. Would you mind cleaning up in here?"

"Yes, mistress."

Joseph got some paper towels and cleaned himself off then got dressed. He wiped his cum up off the floor. He used a couple Lysol wet wipes to clean the spanking horse. After he was done, he went upstairs. Lydia was watching television. On a mantel near the sofa was a picture of her with her husband at their wedding.

"Would you like something to drink?" she asked.

"No thanks," Joseph said. "I have to be heading out."

"So soon? Too bad. You don't look so well. Everything okay?"

"I'll be fine. Nothing to worry about. Tell Hank I said hi."

Joseph got in his car and turned on the radio. CBC Radio Two was playing Chopin. He tapped his fingers gently to the rhythm of the orchestra. Traffic was mild as the afternoon rush had yet to start. He parked his car outside his apartment and went inside. He stepped in through the door and was immediately hit with the stink of mouse shit. He'd forgotten the sawdust. He went back out into his car.

Joseph lived on a gentrified patch of Merrymeeting Road. Like much of Rabbittown, there was a haphazard intermingling of stately homes with shabby houses. Some of the homes had small gardens out front. The nice early spring weather brought out some blooming flowers. There was one lady who took great care of her front yard. She had three rows of tulips and bleeding hearts. Monet would be proud.

The Sobeys parking lot was filling up. Joseph grabbed a cart and did his best to dodge slowly moving shoppers like he was skiing moguls. The top left wheel insisted on pulling him into contact with other carts. The aggressive lighting bounced off the waxed floor. Joseph ignored the Dave Matthews Band playing from the speakers. He picked up some groceries to make the trip worthwhile. He got some fresh peppers and jalapenos to make spaghetti. He made his way to the checkout. The express line snaked out into the aisles. He tried his luck with the regular queues, even though the customers in line seemed to be preparing for the apocalypse given the amount of stuff stacked in their carts. He tried to relax as he watched an old lady split hairs with the cashier over the language of coupons. He did his best to empathize. Perhaps the old woman was on a fixed income and had to account for each penny. And obviously this pimply teenage boy working cash had absolutely no control over the pedantic stipulations corporate delineates in their coupons. The line moved glacially. Joseph strived to be the ideal customer: prepared, courteous, and all business. Air Miles and debit cards at the ready. Therefore, it was frustrating when said pimply teenage boy was rude. Joseph could appreciate that such a colossally monotonous task would drain even the most buoyant soul. Nonetheless, rudimentary manners didn't require that much emotional labour.

He dragged his stuff out to his car then deposited the cart into the smash up derby corral. On the drive back to his apartment, he noticed a guy with sagging pants and a Michael Vick jersey tearing flowers from the lady's yard. He got in through the door and put his groceries away. He then realized that he'd forgotten the sawdust. He was in no mood to go back to the store. The frustration, along with the stink of mice shit on a muggy day, ruined his appetite. He grabbed a bag of chips and sat down at his computer desk. He turned on Netflix and absent mindedly binged on a police procedural

Night time was the worst. He thought of Karen dying of cancer, her long orange hair falling from her head. Tyler alone in the house. The violent things he did as a lycan. His parents. After a few episodes of his cop drama, Joseph could no longer block it all out. From a locked cabinet he pulled out a leather bath kit. Inside were needles and some balloons of heroin. Joseph only needed about two milligrams to get to the place he wanted to go. The metamorphoses kept his body rejuvenated, so he was always a virgin. No collapsed veins and no track marks. He sprinkled the heroin on a spoon and added water. He liked having the hydrochloride salt form because it meant he didn't have to heat it up, which made him feel like a junkie. The needle piqued his arm. A few seconds later, a tide of warmth crept up on him. Heroin created a silent womb that he could crawl into and forget the noisy outside world. It was a warm coldness, a friendly type of solitude. Joseph rolled around with this paradox like a child's blanket. He stared at the ceiling and thought of nothingness.

CHAPTER EIGHT (1964)

The bed wetting got worse. Every night, Violet woke up in a cold puddle of piss. And every morning, the Sisters scrubbed her skin pink, then caned her palms red. Eventually they got fed up washing her sheets and made her sleep on a rubber mattress. She stuck to it like fly paper. She struggled to fall asleep on her uncomfortable bed, and when she woke up in the middle of the night, having pissed herself yet again, she couldn't get back to sleep, too anxious thinking about the inevitable punishment she'd face in the morning. She often prayed at night for God to give her the strength to hold her pee until the morning. But He never graced her with that ability.

The nuns taught her how to pray properly. And every week they had to go to confession with Father Mahoney. It took a while for Violet to decipher his thick Irish accent. Most of her confessions involved wetting the bed and being disobedient or non-attentive during class. Father Mahoney absolved her of her sins and directed her to recite the Act of Contrition:

O my God,
I am heartily sorry for having offended Thee,
and I detest all my sins because of thy just punishments,
but most of all because they offend Thee,
my God, who art all good and deserving of all my love.
I firmly resolve with the help of Thy grace
to sin no more and to avoid the near occasion of sin.

She started sneaking around at night. She'd lie in bed awake for a few hours until she was sure that everyone was asleep. Then she'd creep out of the dormitory, her little footsteps softer than a pair of moths. She'd go downstairs to the bathroom and sleep naked for a couple hours in the tub. When she awoke, she rinsed the tub, got a shower, then went back upstairs to bed. She didn't understand why the nuns had to use such scalding hot water when lukewarm did the trick perfectly fine. This was a manageable solution until the winter came and it was too cold to sleep naked in a porcelain tub. She was back in bed, pissing herself, getting scorched and flogged.

She was getting punished a lot in class, too. She found it hard to focus because she was so tired. She sometimes even fell asleep, which really agitated Sister Rebecca. Pretty soon, any enthusiasm Violet had for school evaporated. She didn't care anymore. She only looked forward to when she could hang out with Vicky and Cheryl. Her favourite moments of the day were when she was outside. She'd stand the edge of Lockwood's schoolyard and gaze into the forbidden forest. She projected herself in amongst the trees, running free. She wasn't even scared of the bears and wolves. They were preferable to the Brothers and Sisters. Mostly, however, she thought about her family. How they were doing in Roaches Brook. She pictured her brother and dad with their komatiks and the dogs, checking the traps. Her mother taking care of little Bobby and her newborn sibling. Their tiny cabin filled the smell of her cooking. That was the life she wanted, she realized now. A place where there was no need of grammar or arithmetic. Where your problems were there in front of you and had real application. She didn't care about where Mexico City was on a map. She cared about the shape of the waves in the morning and the size of the day's catch. She wanted a family of her own. Little babies for whom she knitted sealskin moccasins. And in the morning, she'd go into the woods and shoot a squirrel or a porcupine. Molasses and raisin bread every afternoon.

This morning, however, she woke up fully rested. She'd slept well and didn't even wet the bed, knowing that today she and Cecilia were going back to Spotted Island. She went down for breakfast and suffered through her porridge gladly. Even the grumpy cook seemed to be in somewhat of a good mood. No one spoke. They were all too excited for conversation, deep in their own minds thinking about getting back to their homes. After breakfast she lined up with the others to get her old clothes back. Her uniform had been another source of trouble for Violet. She was always getting little rips and tears in it. Luckily, her mother had taught her how to sew and she discovered that she'd also inherited her mother's predilection for it. Her tiny nimble fingers were well-suited for the exacting task. She often volunteered to sew for other girls who'd ripped their uniforms. She was eager to show her mom how much her skill had improved. Perhaps this summer she would be sewing pairs of moccasins and mukluks.

Sister Rosaline handed Violet back her clothes. They seemed so tiny in her arms. She'd grown a lot this year. It was a struggle to fit into them. Her feet stretched her sealskin moccasins to their absolute limit. Once they were on, she nearly cried. It felt like her mother was caressing her feet. This year at Lockwood had certainly changed how she thought of her mom. Compared to the nuns, she was as soft as a cloudberry. Mostly, she missed her mom's embrace. Oftentimes, when her hands were sore, and her bottom was wet, and she was shivering in her bed, she hoped so desperately that her mother would miraculously materialize out of thin air and hold her and tell everything would be okay. She also looked forward to her mother's cooking. The food at Lockwood was consistently terrible and she was always hungry, along with everyone else. If they served awful food, the least they could do was give the kids enough to fill their little bellies. Violet was small and skinny before she came to Lockwood. Now she could see her ribs and feel the vertebrae of her spine.

She walked out of Lockwood's doors. The warm sun and soft breeze embraced her. She turned around and looked at the school. She read the words *Suffer Little Children to Come unto Me* for what she hoped was the last time. The black flies teased her, but they didn't bother her. She breathed deeply the smell of early summer. She started to walk towards the harbour with the rest of the children. She passed by the small hospital where she'd spend the last weeks of summer past recovering from the dog attack. It was tempting to go in and talk to the nurses before she left, but she was far too eager to leave. The *Kyle* was docked. It was the biggest boat Violet had ever seen. She'd seen the ferry around plenty of times, but had never actually been aboard. Spotted Island wasn't far from Cartwright, but the trip would take a couple days because the ferry was slow and had to make many stops to get all the children home to their scattered communities. There was even a kitchen onboard. Violet hoped it was better than Lockwood's. Surely it couldn't be any worse.

She knew that the first thing her father would do when they got home was give them their spring tonics. He made it with sulphur and molasses and gave them a teaspoon every morning. It was meant to flush out any stomach worms. And in the evenings, he boiled spruce, juniper, molasses, years, raisins, and rice to clean the blood. It was a tasty drink, and she liked knowing that her father was taking care of her.

There were a few moments of joy during her year at Lockwood. For Christmas, Santa Claus visited the school. He brought oranges and little pieces of chocolate for all the kids. Then in April came the Easter bunny, something she'd never heard of before. The nuns also took time away from lessons to make decorations and crafts. Violet was really good at painting eggs. She didn't really understand what a giant rabbit and decorative eggs had to do with the death and resurrection of Jesus, and the nuns certainly didn't have any satisfactory answers whenever she asked, but she wasn't about to spoil the rare bit of fun they were allowed to have.

On her way to the ferry, she found Cecilia. She wasn't with her stuck up friends, so Violet ran up and gave her a big hug.

"We're going home!" Violet shouted, as she embraced her.

"Let go," her sister said.

"Aren't you excited? Violet asked.

Cecilia didn't answer. She seemed upset. Violet didn't pay much mind, though, because Cecilia was usually crooked about something or other. It took a while, but Violet had learned the social hierarchy amongst the Lockwood children. Cecilia was light skinned compared to Violet; she looked more like their father. So, she was allowed to hang around with the popular kids. The teachers let them get away with more stuff. Violet was in the middle crowd because she was darker. So were Vicky and Cheryl. That's why Cecilia didn't want to be seen with her. At the bottom rung were the Eskimos, or at least the kids that most looked like Eskimos. The teachers were hardest on the Eskimos; they never let them get away with anything. Violet was already in trouble enough between her poor scholastic habits and tomboyish behaviour, so she stayed away from them.

They got to the ferry. The kids were lined up to get onboard. There was a rope staircase leading to the deck. Two deckhands stood at the bottom taking children's names and checking them off the list. Cecilia went first. Then it was Violet's turn. She nearly shouted her name.

"Not on the list," the deckhand said.

"What do you mean?" Violet asked.

"I mean that you're not on the list, so bugger off."

"But I'm her sister," she said, pointing to Cecilia, who was making her way up to the deck.

"Sorry, love," the other deckhand said. "If you're not on the itinerary, we can't take you aboard."

"Cecilia!" Violet shouted. "Wait!"

Cecilia ignored her and kept walking. Violet started to panic. Tears welled up. She didn't want to spend one more moment in Cartwright or anywhere near Lockwood.

"You're holding up the line," the mean deckhand said.

Violet backed away and let the other kids come forward.

"If there's an issue, you'll have to fetch the headmistress," the friendlier deckhand said. "She gave us the itinerary. She should be able to sort this out for you."

Violet ran back to Lockwood. She drove her feet and pumped her fists. She found Sister Margaret.

"Sister Margaret," Violet said. "I need to talk to Mrs. Matthews."

"The headmistress is busy," the nun replied.

"Please," Violet pleaded. "There was a mistake with the ferry. My name isn't on the list."

"Of course it's not."

"What do you mean?"

"She hasn't even told you? Oh dear. I'll take you to Ms. Matthews at once."

Sister Margaret lead Violet to Ms. Matthews' office. On the way she was muttering under her breath. "Incompetent woman...little half-breed pets... absent minded...no respect...our mission...bleeding heart..." Violet could barely hear her and she was too absorbed by her own anxiety to make any sense of it.

Sister Margaret opened the door to Ms. Matthews' office and pushed Violet in. She then closed it, leaving the two of them alone in the room.

"What seems to be the problem, Violet?" Ms. Matthews asked. Her desk was full of papers and ledgers scattered about. There was a framed portrait of a man in a military uniform.

"I went to get on the ferry, but my name wasn't on the list," Violet said.

"Oh dear," Ms. Matthews said. She put down her pencil and covered her face with her hands. "I can't believe I let this get away from me."

Violet stood in the middle of the room, shifting the weight of her feet in her uncomfortable moccasins, waiting for Ms. Matthews to explain what was going on.

"Please, Violet," she said. "Sit down."

Violet did as she was told.

"I'm really terribly sorry about this," Ms. Matthews continued. "I have just been so busy trying to run this school that I never got around to having this conversation with you. But I shouldn't be making excuses."

Violet squirmed in her chair. Her old dress wasn't too tight because she'd lost so much weight, but it was short and her thighs were exposed. She kept tugging at the skirt to get it down over her knees.

"When you first came to Cartwright," Ms. Matthews explained, "when you were attacked by those dogs, I had a long conversation with your mother. She told me that you were very keen on coming to Lockwood but that your family couldn't afford to send both you and your sister. She told me about the stress at home, a little baby and another on the way, and your father struggling to make ends meet with the falling prices of fur and fish. So I suggested that I adopt you."

Violet stopped fussing at her clothes.

"What did she say?" she asked.

"Well," Ms. Matthews said. "She said yes."

Violet sat still. Her arms limp at her sides. She looked at Ms. Matthews blankly. "So, does that mean I'm not going back to Spotted Island?"

"No, my dear. You will be living with me now. Here in Cartwright."

Part of Violet knew that she should be upset, that should be screaming and crying, begging Ms. Matthews to let her go home. But she continued to sit and stare, unable to make a sound. All the information sat motionless in her mind, unable to be processed, like a dry lump of hardtack stuck in her throat.

"I know this is probably difficult for you," Ms. Matthews said. "And I can't apologize enough for not telling you sooner. I still have a lot of work I have to get done here today. Why don't you wait in the dormitory and then we can go to my house for our first meal together?"

Violet stood up and walked over to the dormitory. She sat down on her rubber mattress. She tried to imagine her family's faces, but they kept evaporating. Instead she tried to imagine what summer would be like in Cartwright, but her mind was blank. She couldn't project herself into the past or the future. She was stuck in this present. So many things that she had found confusing started to fall into place. She understood now why Cecilia was so distant and why her mother wasn't there when she woke up in the hospital. Everyone knew except for her and nobody had told her anything. She hated this world of rules and lists. Her desire to see her family felt so essential and natural, but she was prohibited because her name wasn't on a stupid list in the hands of a stupid deckhand.

Ophelia entered the dormitory. She came over and sat down on the bed across from Violet. She was carrying that strange little grin that she tended to flash whenever she saw Violet. This time, it made Violet angry.

"What do you want, you little creep?" Violet shouted.

Ophelia giggled and ran out of the room.

Violet stood up and walked to the window. She watched the ferry slowly pull away from the harbour, black columns of smoke billowing from its chimneys, leaving a white trail of waves behind it.

CHAPTER NINE (2015)

Looking out the window of Julie's Jetta, Tyler felt like he was cruising along the Sea of Tranquility. The Irish Loop took them from St. John's down to the southern tip of the Avalon Peninsula. Much of the Southern Shore was treeless barrens, patches of brown dotted with rocks and only the occasional break of green. While he drove, Joseph explained that the coastline contained fossils of the oldest complex organisms on earth, which made sense because, with the exception of telephone poles and wires, the stretch from Cappahayden to Portugal Cove South felt like a journey back in time, a glimpse at a primeval era shortly after meteorites bombarded the planet and beat it into something suitable for life. Tyler had never travelled much beyond the overpass, aside from the odd party out in Paradise and CBS. He could remember the outrage when Margaret Wente described the interior of the province as "the most vast and scenic ghetto in the world." He had to admit that he sort of agreed with her. He understood that when people talked about Newfoundland heritage and culture they were talking about the outports. The Drook, the outport where they were headed, had been abandoned some time ago. As far as Tyler was concerned, resettlement was a good idea. He rolled his eyes whenever he heard songs like "Out from St. Leonard's." He didn't get the romanticism of Newfoundland's hard scrabble past. Confederation was an obvious improvement. Baymen needed to stop clinging to the olden days. Most of these people were out here living on welfare, or working a of couple weeks a year, then coasting on EI. They didn't bring anything to the table. And if it was cheaper to centralize them in bigger towns, then so be it.

"My parents loved driving the Irish Loop when I was a little girl," Julie said. "Sometimes, we'd jump out and pick bakeapples and have a little picnic."

"Was never much of a fan of bakeapples," Joseph said.

"I remember when the caribou were migrating there'd so many on the road they'd hold up traffic. It's sad to see them gone."

"The brain worm was devastating."

Joseph and Julie were up front carrying on a conversation, he driving and she in the passenger seat. Tyler was in the back, leafing through Joseph's notes on the history of "lycanthropy," as he called it. One of the earliest werewolf myths came during the eighth century in imperial Rome from Ovid's *Metamorphoses*. King Lycaon tried to serve Zeus the roasted flesh of his son Nyctimus because he wanted to see if Zeus was actually omniscient. Tyler was mystified that this was the best idea Lycaon could come up with. Turns out Zeus was omniscient after all and didn't think very highly of cannibalism, which was understandable considering his own father ate all his brothers. As punishment Zeus turned Lycaon and his other sons into wolves. Nyctimus was restored back to life. Tyler figured Zeus owed him that much for letting that experiment go as far as it did. If he was omniscient, why didn't he stop it from happening in the first place? Gods had perverse ways of proving their points. Tyl-er turned his attention away from the text.

"What did you plan on doing with your PhD?" Julie asked Joseph.

"I wanted to work in medical research," he answered. "Virology, preferably."

"Are you bitter that you didn't get to do that?"

"My career ended before it ever began. To be honest, I got into it because I thought it would be a challenge, because I was ambitious, not because I wanted to help people. I had these grand ideas of finding a cure for a disease and becoming rich and famous. I find what I do now challenging enough. I know finance and investment probably doesn't sound sexy, but I enjoy it. I use my knowledge of science and medicine to inform my investments in pharmaceuticals, medical technology, things like that. And it gives me the flexibility to deal with my condition."

"Must be convenient to take a night off whenever there's a full moon," Tyler said.

"Yes," Joseph said. "That too."

They sat in silence then as the kilometres rolled by. Tyler snacked on a bag of chestnuts, which Joseph had roasted himself. He claimed they were a great source of carbohydrates, which would help with the transformation. When Tyler got bored of those, he helped himself to some homemade granola. Julie had suggested to Joseph that he publish a werewolf diet cookbook. His meal preparations were likely just as legitimate as paleo or Atkins. Tonight, Joseph had brought along a Coleman stove for breakfast tomorrow morning. There were two ziplocked steaks marinating in a cooler along with a dozen eggs in the trunk. They were going to need protein in the morning to help repair all those damaged and strained muscles. Tyler took some comfort knowing that he could at least look forward to steak and eggs. Joseph had totally revamped Tyler's diet. His fridge full of processed junk had been replaced with complex carbs, healthy fats, and clean proteins. Although he didn't appreciate the *Biggest Loser* treatment, Tyler didn't mind cooking whole foods. Now that he wasn't working full-time at a restaurant, he had rediscovered the pleasure of being in the kitchen, even though he was eating by himself these days.

Tyler didn't know what to do with all his free time. At first, with no job or girlfriend to bother him, he was looking forward to putting in some serious time on Steam. But he soon found himself bored with gaming. His focus and intensity wasn't there. He tried reading Joseph's notes, but again he found his attention drifting away from the words on the page. Instead, he spent most of his time watching porn, sleeping in late, and going for long walks around St. John's followed by coming home and staring at the wall. He did, however, have success with Joseph's lucid dreaming techniques. The ability to control his dreams became more addicting than gaming. It was like being an architect and player at the same time. He often slept twelve hours a night, staying in bed late into the afternoon, only getting up for the sake of bodily needs such as food and bathroom breaks. Joseph believed that practising lucid dreaming helped him stay in control as a werewolf. They'd certainly helped Tyler with his nightmares. Instead of falling, he could fly; instead of running in place, he could sprint; instead of feeling weak when fighting his enemies, he was powerful. Despite his anxiety about the pain that came from transforming, he was curious to see how much he could control his werewolf state.

"How about a pit stop," Joseph suggested.

They pulled into a gas station. Old analog pumps with rusted levers and latches stood like battered Greek columns. Joseph was the only one of the three old enough to know how to work the esoteric technology. Tyler and Julie went inside. The gas station was also a small grocery, hardware, and liquor store. They manoeuvred around the tightly crammed aisles to get to the washrooms. Some of the local men were standing around, chewing the fat, Canadiens and Leafs hats laid precariously atop their balding heads. They looked Tyler up and down. He knew they could tell right away he was a townie.

Tyler went up to the cash.

"Yes, honey?" the woman working asked.

"Pack of Macdonald's regular, please," Tyler said.

Her smile faded as she registered his St. John's accent.

Tyler paid for the cigarettes and went outside. He tore off the plastic and lit one. A young guy around Tyler's age pulled up in an ATV for gas. He was covered head to toe in Fox racing gear. Tyler couldn't imagine what his life would've been like had he grown up in an outport like this. A bay-man's life seemed bleak to him. What did people do around here besides drive around on their quads? There were no bars or restaurants or stores. His phone could barely get a signal. No wonder there were so many board-ed up houses.

"Ready when you are," Joseph said.

Tyler took a couple deep drags from his cigarette, then dropped the butt to the ground and rubbed it out with his shoe. He returned to the backseat and grabbed a banana from the cooler. Joseph pulled off the main highway and took them down a dirt road, which snaked along the coastline. Bronze grass clung to stony banks that slipped into the sea. Joseph manoeuvred the car slowly around divots and rocks. The road dipped then revealed the abandoned town of Drook. Shells of houses, left behind by the dozen or so families that once lived here, bleached and dilapidated, dotted the mouth of a river emptying into the ocean. Remnants of fishing stages stuck out from the rocky shore, bone white like the skeleton of a giant decayed dinosaur.

Joseph stopped the car. He and Tyler got out and grabbed their gear. Julie sat in the driver's seat.

"Think you can find your way back to St. John's from here?" Joseph asked.

"I have the GPS," Julie said.

"Thanks for the lift."

"Good luck you guys," she said.

Tyler looked down at his feet.

Julie rolled up her window. She turned the car around and drove slow-ly back towards the main road.

"That was rude," Joseph said.

"What?" Tyler asked.

"I can understand why you're so antagonistic towards me, but Julie hasn't done anything wrong."

Tyler shrugged.

He'd reached out to her on Joseph's insistence. Most of their commu-nication was carried out over text messages. They hadn't spoken much in-person for the past month beyond perfunctory small talk. It annoyed Tyler that she wasn't being hostile. Her calm demeanour was clearly a passive aggressive attempt to deflect focus onto him, to suggest that she was blame-less in all of this. Of course, it was her idea to drive them out here in her car and pick them up again in the morning. And it didn't take long for her and Joseph to hit it off, either. They were so comfortable asking each other such personal questions. *Aren't you bitter about not achieving your hopes and dreams of curing diseases?* He couldn't believe she'd asked that.

They walked up the river, looking for a decent spot to pitch their tent.

They were walking at only a brisk pace, but Tyler's heart was thrashing. He heard it above the surf rolling against the rocks. The town, the river, the wind, it all started to feel unreal. His mind became foggy. He tried to remember Joseph's coaching. Not to fight the anxiety, but to let it pass through him, like it was flowing through his body, down to his feet, and out into the earth. To create a space where he could observe the anxiety and note the sensations instead of fighting with them, like sitting inside and watching a rain storm as opposed to being caught in the middle of it. He breathed deeply. The feeling passed.

They set the tent up behind a house that shielded them against the wind. They unfurled their sleeping bags and tucked the cooler away. Joseph explained that it was important to have everything completely ready because once they transformed back into humans, naked and exposed to the elements, they'd be too weak to barely open the zipper door. Inside his bag, Tyler had cloistered a joint the size of a heavy flow tampon. It was secured inside an earbuds case, wrapped in elastic bands. He knew that he was going to need a serious dosage of weed in the morning if he managed to survive the night.

Once the tent was prepped, they made their way down to the rocky beach. Tyler sat down and wiggled his hips around to find a comfortable groove amidst the rounded rocks. Joseph collected kindling and fire wood. He made a tiny log cabin of small, dry branches and sticks. He surrounded it with big rocks. He lit the kindling with Tyler's lighter. The fire danced and spit. Tyler watched flankers burst, then disappear. As the flame grew, Joseph added larger pieces of driftwood. The smell of the fire mingled with the salt water. The crackling branches popped and leapt to beat of the rolling waves.

The sky was dark now. The moon neared its peak. Tyler felt it trembling in his gut. Joseph stripped naked, then covered himself with a thick blanket, which he pulled from his backpack. That's where Tyler's comfort zone ended.

"You're going to regret having all those clothes on when the transformation starts," Joseph said.

"I'll take my chances," Tyler replied.

"The fire will help you focus," Joseph said. "It's full of rhythms. Look into it and you'll find the beat of your heart. Once you've found it, visualize how you're going to control yourself while as a lycan. Imagine running through the forest, fast and powerful. It can be a joyful experience. But you must resist succumbing to animal magnetism."

"I've done plenty of mushrooms," Tyler said. "I think I got this."

"I'm trying to help you."

"I guess I don't go in for this *Kung Fu* stuff."

"You're making jokes because you're nervous. I understand."

"You don't understand shit."

The small log cabin collapsed into embers. Joseph added larger pieces to the fire.

Just a handful of clouds obscured the starry night. Tyler had never been in a place without streetlights where the sky could be so dark. He shivered and huddled closer to the fire. A patch of cumulus rolled by and exposed the full moon like a pale seashell washed ashore by a receding wave. Something bubbled deep within his stomach. A heat travelled through his chest and up into his throat. He struggled to breathe. Sweat dripped from his forehead. He tried to pull his clothes off, but his joints ached as he moved. He fell down onto the rocks and writhed in pain. The rapid beating of his heart filled his ears. He wanted to ask Joseph for help, but all he could do was grunt and moan while his jaw unhinged and bounced in all sorts of angles. New teeth tore their way through his gums. His muscles ripped as his bones popped into a new architecture. An explosion triggered at the base of his skull and found release in a long howl.

Hot yellow tongues licked from a bed of burning juniper. Behind it, everywhere, salt. Rolling on the rocks, pushing/pulling, in/out. Hot yellow tongues spat little bites. Too warm. Dusty throat, but water too salty. Rocks shifted and crunched. Another. Blood's blood. Challenger. Usurper? No. Not afraid. Show it: big chest, big teeth, big voice.

Old dog strength. Knew how to move, where to bite, but slow. Try again, harder, faster. Hard rocks slammed the boney spine wriggled on stones. Crunchcrunch. Old dog's teeth around the throat. No blood. Submitted, released.

Old dog sniffed. Something in the shaking black. Ran, chased. Smelled it, too. Little furry bouncing meat. Sweet and oily. Each hop left a scent. Blotches of light on the trail. Quick sharp movements, but dogs faster. Saw it now. Hot blood pumped; fear hopped in the nose. Gone suddenly. Smell pulled the nose down a tiny hole. Trapped, nowhere else to move, afraid. Dogs tried to dig it out. Rip the tree apart. Tear it from the earth. Nowhere to hide then. Crush it between the teeth then. Pull its sweet meat apart then. Muzzle wet with oily blood. Impossible. Tree fingers clutched everywhere too strong.

Old dog barked, barked. Whined. New scent, new game, big smell, big meat. Ran, chased. Big meat left wide strip of gold shinning through the woods. Big boney ears, a turkey flying between the trees. Dogs jumped on each flank, pulled it down, fought for its neck. Big boney ears knocked the teeth. Blood in the mouth. Old dog broke big meat's neck. Big easy dinner now. Meat not sweet and oily like little bouncing furry. Tough and lean. But meat is meat, happy jaws, happy teeth. Sometimes forgot to breathe even.

Big belly full of flesh, rubbed the back on grass. Old dog lay nearby. Heart beat jerky and rough against the earth. Tired breath. Nibbled old dog's muzzle. Let him rest. Ran to the hilltop. Treeless grassless knuckle. Winds carried many scents. Hers too, soft and fluttering, a tiny fish at the bottom of the sea. New signature. Usurper inside her. Nails scratched, hair standing, big growl, big voice. Rip the usurper from her guts and break its soft little bones. Tear it between the teeth.

Old dog rubbed up against the muzzle. Big pale face in the black mass above. Dogs howled together. Winds carried the song. Playtime. Charge old dog, take him by surprise. Pinned him down. Heart beat strong now. Got his throat in the teeth now, but won't submit. Wriggled out. Chased back through the green and the dark. Wind and leaves slapped the face happy. Darted out between big old wooden boxes. Pick up the scent and off again. Heart beat full of life pumping blood, yelpedyelped.

Big pale face fading, almost hidden, taking the world's smells with it. Old dog ran and followed. Back to stones and salt. World too full of edges hard and bright. The teeth ached. Heart's thumpthumping filled the ears. The body broke screaming, rocks bumping, no more fur in the egg-yolk-orange heat's light, teeth back into the jaw, body full of red and fire, smell suffocated, colours bursting, cold wind nipping raw skin. Thumpthump thumpthump thump thump. Thump, thump, thump.

Tyler could still taste raw moose meat and blood. He wretched and fought the urge to vomit. His clothes from last night lay torn on the beach besides the ashy remnants of the fire. Joseph threw a blanket over him. The cold dawn air racked Tyler's body. His muscles tensed as his body shivered. He grunted in pain. Joseph grabbed him and pointed towards the tent. Tyler's legs wobbled like a baby lamb when he tried to stand. He tried to ask Joseph for help, but all he could do was grunt and moan. His jaw was tight and his teeth and gums ached. Joseph wrapped their arms around each other's shoulders and they hobbled towards the tent. Tyler felt like he was walking on a giant canvas sack full of nails and broken glass. Joseph opened the tent and Tyler collapsed into his sleeping bag. His stiff clumsy fingers struggled with the zipper. He inched closer to Joseph. Their body heat filled the tiny tent. Tyler stopped shivering. Memories and sensations of the night crowded his mind, beating away the sleep he so desperately needed. He remembered Joseph's maxim that an anxious mind could not exist within a relaxed body. He took a deep breath, held it for five seconds then repeated the exercise five times. His tense muscles softened as sleep took over.

◯

The tent was filled with light filtered by the green fabric. Joseph was slick with sweat. He bent forward to reach for his backpack. Every muscle fibre protested. He checked his phone and saw that it was noon. Tyler snored loudly. Joseph unzipped the door slowly and crawled outside, careful not to disturb him. The sun greeted his naked body. He watched the light shimmer atop the ocean. The brisk wind was a relief after being inside that cocoon of body heat. He pulled a hoodie and track pants from his bag and got dressed.

Joseph opened the cooler and took out a jug of water. The feed of moose meat last night would make today a little easier to manage, especially for Tyler. Joseph looked at the steak and eggs in the cooler and felt his appetite twinge, but the thought of cooking food was exhausting. The idea of doing anything seemed exhausting. He closed the cooler and sat down on the lid. He wanted to crawl back into the tent and sleep. He wanted to wade out into the ocean and let the waves pull him away. Then he thought of Tyler asleep in the tent.

"The boy still needs you," he said to himself. "You're not done yet."

He reached into his backpack and pulled out his black leather kit. There was a tiny bottle of pills along with syringes and heroin. He took out a tablet of OxyContin and chewed it. Snorting was the preferred method, but he didn't have that luxury at the moment. The bitter taste used to make him wretch. Now, by virtue of Pavlovian conditioning, he enjoyed the taste in anticipation of the high. He chewed the pill down to a paste and washed it down with some water, then confirmed with his tongue that he'd gotten all of it. The pain in his body was replaced by a soft warmth that spread through his limbs. The cold wind felt refreshing against his radiating body. Joseph took a deep breath and tried to suppress the big moronic grin spread across his face.

He fired up the Coleman stove. First, he boiled a kettle of water to brew some coffee. Then came the steak and eggs. The smell of meat made him think of last night. After eating the moose, he'd felt a tremendous pain in his chest. He'd never experienced that during lycantropy. It was getting worse, he knew. He wondered how many moons he had left in him.

Tyler emerged from the tent. The first thing he did was dig for that joint of his and fire it up. Joseph almost launched into a lecture but stopped himself when he was reminded of the chalky taste of OxyContin still swimming in his mouth. Tyler came over and sat down on the grass, the joint sticking out of his mouth like a firecracker.

"Do you mind?" he asked.

"No," Joseph replied. "How do you feel?"

"Like I drank a barrel of tequila, then ran a marathon with a fridge strapped to my back," Tyler replied.

The smell of the steak, eggs, and coffee mixed with the salty breeze coming from the ocean and Tyler's marijuana. Joseph filled up two cups with coffee. Tyler drank it eagerly and poured himself another cup. Joseph took up the steak and eggs and served Tyler his plate.

"Did we kill a moose last night?" Tyler asked.

"We sure did," Joseph said.

"I can still taste it. You'd think I wouldn't have an appetite this morning, but I'm frigging starving."

"Can you remember much else?"

"Mostly running through the bush. I can only remember little bits and pieces. Feels like trying to remember a night after being blackout drunk."

"Would you say it's an improvement from last time?"

"Oh definitely. Last time it didn't even feel real. More like a dream. Or a nightmare, I should say."

"You should call Julie to let her know we're okay."

"You do it."

"No. It should be you."

"Fine." Tyler took out his phone. He wandered around a bit until he could grab a signal. It started dialing. "Hi, Julie, it's Tyler. Yeah, we're both good. Are you okay? Oh, okay. Yeah, see you in a bit."

"That wasn't so bad," Joseph said.

"Yeah. She's getting on the go now the once. I think she has morning sickness."

Joseph was lifting a chunk of steak to his mouth when his arm went numb. A fire burst inside his chest. He rolled onto the ground clutching his body. He fought to breathe but each breath felt like he was swallowing a line of barbwire. Tyler crouched beside him. He looked up and saw his son's face get blurry as the world dissolved.

Small waves rose, crashed, and then receded. Joseph opened his eyes to a cloudless blue sky, the warm sun beaming over his body. He stood up and brushed brown speckles from his body. The sand was soft and warm between his toes. Sunlight dappled the pale turquoise sea. The coastline stretched out over the horizon in both directions, behind him was a wall of thick green and khaki palm trees. He felt like he was inside a travel brochure advertisement for a Caribbean getaway. He'd never been to a place like this before. In the distance, he saw someone lying on the sand, a red-haired woman. She waved to him. He walked towards her. He soon recognized her, but struggled to understand how it was possible

"Hello, Joseph," Karen said. "It's been awhile."

Julie crested the hill coming down over the Drook. She saw Tyler kneeling on the ground, hunched over. He had his head tucked into his shoulder like he was talking on the phone. His shoulders were pumping. As she got closer she saw that he was leaning over Joseph, trying to perform CPR. She parked the car and ran towards them. There was a smell of burning meat.

"Hold on," Tyler said to the phone. "My girlfriend is here and she knows CPR."

"What happened?" Julie asked. She knelt down across from Tyler and checked Joseph's vitals. His pulse was weak and he wasn't breathing.

"I don't know. We were talking, cooking breakfast, and he just collapsed."

"Is there an ambulance on the way?"

"Yeah."

"Okay. First, turn off that frying pan so we don't start a fire. Then check Joseph's stuff. He might have some medication."

Tyler opened Joseph's backpack. He hauled out the clothes and first aid kit. He found a black leather kit that looked like it might contain medicine. He unzipped it. There was a bottle of Aspirin. He also found syringes, baggies of white powder, and vials of pills.

"Find anything?" Julie asked.

"No," Tyler said. "Just some Aspirin." He zipped up the kit and shoved everything into the backpack.

"Don't worry, Joseph," Julie said, driving her palms into his chest. "You're going to be alright."

Joseph clutched his fleece jacket. His mustache was stiff with frozen snot, bits of ice and snow clung to his beard. Smoke drifted from the lumber yard, obscuring just a sliver of the big starry sky. The moon was a crescent, its sharp edges digging into its blackboard. Joseph made his way to the lodge, which had the only phone on-site. Inside, the TV was airing a French broadcast of the Canadiens game. They were playing the New Jersey Devils. Some guys were drinking beers and chatting about the Habs. Damphouse and Roy were bright spots, but no one seriously believed they would repeat this year. Joseph didn't have any friends here. And that's how he wanted it. Oftentimes he sat alone at the bar, watched the game, and absorbed the conversations going on around him. He told himself that he enjoyed the solitude. Loners were common at these sorts of places. Guys respected anyone who wanted to keep their distance. It was an unspoken understanding around here that man could come and do his work and not have to reveal anything about himself. This place was full of guys with regrets, sorry pasts, and dark secrets, here to earn some money and put that all behind them. As long as Joseph kept his head down and did his work, no one asked any questions.

A burly bearded guy was using the payphone. Joseph sat nearby and listened to the music of the man's thick Québécois without eavesdropping. He hoped the guy would finish soon before his courage evaporated. He hadn't spoke to Karen since she told him that she was pregnant. That was over nine months ago roughly. On the TV, Bill Guerin scored for the Devils. The men cursed and swore. Roy was not playing well. Martin Brodeur, however, was looking like a great young goalie for the Devils. The burly man hung up the phone and joined his buddies at the bar. Joseph took a deep breath and stepped into the booth. He dialed the number. The phone rang half a dozen times. He was about to hang up, relieved that he wouldn't have to go through with it after all, and then she answered.

"Hello?" Karen asked.

The texture of her voice was magic even in this mundane exchange. Suddenly he realized that he'd been dying of thirst and had just been given a drop of water.

"Hello?" she repeated.

"Karen," he said, his voice scratchy and metallic from lack of use.

"Jesus Christ."

"Close. It's Joseph."

"Fuck you."

"Sorry."

"What do you want?"

"I want to know how you're doing."

"You mean me and the baby?"

"Yes."

"What do you care?"

"I'm sorry for everything that's happened. I realize this is hard to understand and I can't really explain it, but there's something terribly wrong with me. I'm not safe to be around. I'm a threat to you both."

"You picked a grand time to lose your goddamn mind."

He thought about what to say next when he heard a young woman speak to him. *Don't worry, Joseph.* He looked around the lodge, but didn't see anyone who matched that voice. *You're going to be alright.* A few men off in the corner playing cards eyed him suspiciously.

"It's entirely possible I'm psychotic," he said.

"Funny how these symptoms suddenly appeared when I told you I was pregnant."

"Yes, I believe there's some sort of connection there."

"I'm hanging up."

"Wait. Please. I know you're angry and you have every right to be. But I'm trying. I'm going to make things right. I just need time."

"..."

"Have you been getting my cheques?"

"..."

"I'll figure this out. I swear it. I'll make it right."

"Your son's name is Tyler."

She hung up the phone.

The ambulance bounced coming down the bumpy trail. Tyler ran out to flag them down. They pulled up beside Joseph. The paramedics unloaded the stretcher. They lifted Joseph up onto to it and strapped him in. Inside the ambulance, they wrapped a mask around his face to help him breath. They stuck stickers to his chest that were connected to a handheld device.

"It's a heart attack," one paramedic said.

"Do one of you want to ride with us to the hospital?" the driver asked.

"I will," Tyler said.

"I'll follow in my car," Julie said.

Tyler hopped in the back of the ambulance and sat down. Between the stretcher and all the equipment, there wasn't much space. The paramedics got aboard, and then they were moving. The ride back to the highway was rough. Tyler watched Joseph's face. He grimaced as if in pain then went slack and his head slumped.

"His pulse dropped," one paramedic said.

"Defib," the driver said.

Tyler kept his attention on Joseph's face as the paramedics read out numbers and readings. They strapped rubber pads to Joseph's torso, then shocked him with two paddles. Joseph's body jerked.

"Pulse is back," someone said.

One of the paramedics sprayed nitroglycerine into Joseph's nose. Some of the colour returned to his face. His brow furled and he shook his limbs. Tyler wondered if Joseph was dreaming.

Gunmetal clouds filled the sky, darkening the sea. Waves swelled and crashed on the surf. The sand beneath Joseph was now cold and hard.

"None of this is fair," he said. "What did either of us do to deserve all this?"

"Nothing," Karen said. "Everything about being a parent is unfair. But what are you going to do about it? You can either run away or do what needs to be done. What are you going to do?"

Out in the sea, a boy was struggling to stay above water. He flailed his arms, splashing.

"You have to go," Karen said.

"I know," Joseph said. "I miss you so much. I never told you that all these years. It hurt too much to say it. I thought that if I acknowledged the pain, I'd fall apart. I should've told you that I loved you. That I missed you, needed you. That I was empty without you. All that corny shit you hate so much. I was a coward."

"You did what you thought was best. Stop beating yourself up over it."

Joseph stood up.

"Will this all be here when it's over?" he asked, gesturing at the beach. "When I'm dead? Will you be here?"

"I don't know," Karen said. "You'd better hurry up and get out there. He needs your help."

"I love you."

"I love you, too."

Joseph ran out to the surf. The cold water bit his feet. Pain shot through his body. The waves grew with each recession. He looked back to the beach. Karen was gone. In her stead was a mound of sand with a crucifix atop. He turned back to the sea and was slapped in the face by an open palm of salt water.

◯

The welcome sign to Holberg, British Colombia, read "Be Prepared for the Unexpected." It sat atop a great felled cedar, which in turn sat atop a crushed car. Joseph passed by it as he ran his morning 5K jog. He breathed deep the fragrance of Douglas firs that lined the rough logging road. He finished at the top of his street and walked to his house to cool down. He stepped into the small wooden bungalow and took off his sneakers. He lay down on a yoga mat in his living room and did some stretches.

After his shower, he sat down in his office overlooking Holberg Inlet. Natural light filled the room. He opened his laptop and began reviewing a number of financial reports for various pharmaceutical companies. He was also researching "deep learning" systems that used algorithms to diagnose patients. These systems were actually beginning to outperform human experts. Joseph wondered if he was looking at the future of medicine.

When he was working in Northern Quebec, he'd read everything he could on investment strategies. Warren Buffet taught him to focus his energies where he had a competitive advantage, which was biochemistry and medicine. Joseph could consume mounds of dense research material to expertly analyze companies in these industries. He identified businesses that were incorrectly evaluated and poised to make great profits. He bought low, waited for them to grow, then sold high. A simple but effective method that allowed him to amass considerable wealth. These dividends were a gift he could bequeath to his son.

His phone buzzed. It was Karen.

"Hello?" he answered.

"The cancer has spread."

"Shit. How much time do you have?"

"Not much. You need to get your ass to St. John's. I don't care what's wrong with you. You have to come home and look after Tyler."

"I'm not ready yet. I need more time."

"You don't have it. It's time to keep your promise. Come home."

She hung up. Joseph laid his phone down. He watched an osprey circle the inlet. Green trees slid into the blue water. In the distance he could see snow capped mountains. It was a beautiful late-summer day. He closed the financial reports and looked up flights to St. John's.

The ambulance stopped outside the emergency entrance to the Health Sciences. The paramedics pulled Joseph out and pushed him into the hospital. They were still trying to pump oxygen into his lungs. Tyler followed them inside. He spoke with a nurse who told him that the doctor would come find him. Julie came in and sat down beside Tyler. She reached over and grabbed his hand. Tyler held it loosely.

"How is he?" she asked.

"Not sure," he said. "Touch and go, I think."

They sat in silence, holding hands. A doctor eventually came out to speak to them.

"Mr. Stevens has stabilized somewhat, but he's not out of the woods yet. He had a pretty serious heart attack, which is strange because he looks to be in great shape. A nurse will let you know when you can see him. Are either of you family?"

"I am," Tyler said.

"What's your relationship?"

"He's my father."

Lightning ignited the sky. Rain filled the ocean. Joseph struggled to breathe as he fought the waves. He retched at the taste of salt filling his mouth. The boy was near. Joseph could hear him crying. A big wave formed before him. He swam hard to get ahead of the crest. It lifted him up and drove him underwater. Everything was black and cold. Joseph drove his arms and legs to breach the surface. The sea had calmed, but he couldn't find the boy.

"Tyler!" he called out. "Tyler!"

He paddled around. There was no sign of him. All he could see was black water getting pushed around by the savage wind. The rain and frigid water punished his body. Everything was numb except the burning coal in the centre of his chest.

Something wrapped tightly around his ankle and hauled him under. He waved his arms uselessly as the force dragged him down hard and fast. The light of the sky disappeared. He was surrounded by cold darkness. Two bright globes appeared. They raced towards him until all he could see was yellow. And then there was nothing.

CHAPTER TEN (1964)

Things were going pretty well until she started to bleed. It had taken some getting used to, but Violet was starting to feel comfortable at Ms. Matthews' house, or Daisy as she insisted on being called. Violet was getting along with Ophelia, too. She discovered that Ophelia's strangeness was more so a product of her shy nature. Daisy explained to Violet that the reason Ophelia had been giving her strange looks all year was that she was excited to have a big sister. She was just trying to be friendly, in her weird little way.

Daisy gave them short lessons every day. She worked with them on subjects they'd struggled with during the school year. At first, Violet wanted no part of it. She'd gone through a hard enough time with the nuns and she certainly didn't want to have to do more studies in the summer. But Daisy was a patient and persistent teacher. Violet found herself relaxing to the point that she actually started to enjoy the lessons. She found it rewarding when she figured out a particularly challenging math problem or discovered a new word to add to her expanding vocabulary. This was what she had hoped she would experience at school back before she ever went to Lockwood: the pleasure of discovering new things about the world and herself.

As Violet progressed through her lessons, Daisy believed she might be able to rejoin her friends and start the fall with her own age group. Violet was pleased with herself and felt her self-confidence swell. She also surprised herself by getting lost in some of Daisy's books and magazines during rainy days. *National Geographic* was her favourite, seeing the beautiful pictures and reading about exotic people and places. She imagined discovering secret far away places, being the first person from modern civilization to tread foot there and speak to the locals. She devised a game with Ophelia called "Explorers." They took turns hiding around Cartwright, making up strange characters, while one had to "discover" the other. Violet put more effort into her characters than Ophelia, but it was still a lot of fun.

Violet enjoyed being the big sister for once. She thought about all the times when she wanted to play with Cecilia but was denied, so she wanted to do a better job. However, she began to appreciate how exhausting it could be to have someone constantly following you around begging for your attention. Aside from Explorers, Violet and Ophelia liked to play on the little swing set in Daisy's backyard. She managed to get the Cartwright kids to play a game of Alley Over but it wasn't very successful. They didn't chase the ball as aggressively as the kids on Spotted Island.

Every Sunday they went to church. Daisy dressed them up in pretty dresses and brought them to mass. She and Ophelia were expected to behave even though it was painfully boring. If they acted up, they didn't get any treats and weren't allowed to play for the rest of the day. It was one of the few things Daisy was really strict over. At the church, Violet often saw the Brothers and Sisters, but they didn't pay her any mind. They were all too focused on cleaning cups and bringing things for Father Mahoney. They looked down at the ground a lot. Father Mahoney talked mostly about temptation. There were a lot of those, apparently. Fornication, sloth, jealousy, greed. Violet wasn't sure about all the words he used. She was often nervous because she didn't want to have to spend any time in hell or purgatory for committing a sin she didn't know. Daisy told her not to worry and just do as she was told. Father Mahoney was especially concerned with collection. If you wanted to go to heaven, you had to donate your fair share to the church. There were a few families in Cartwright who had lots of money to give to the church. The priest spent a lot of time with them. Violet didn't think that was fair.

One thing that was, however, much better in Cartwright was Daisy's food. They often had bacon and eggs in the morning and plenty of ham and chicken for their other meals. Daisy had lots of cakes and sweets, too, even apples and oranges. If Violet and Ophelia behaved and did all their chores, Daisy would give them coppers to take to the Hudson Bay Company trading station. Sometimes, when Violet was sucking on a candy, shifting it around in mouth, moving it between the pockets of cheeks with her tongue, she forgot about Spotted Island, Lockwood, the dogs, and just about everything else that had happened to her this past year.

Then, one morning, she awoke to find her sheets stained red. Her crotch and thighs were slick with blood. She thought she was still dreaming. It seemed like a nightmare that combined her bed wetting days in Lockwood and the dog attack on Spotted Island. She screamed. Daisy rushed into the room and Violet soon realized it wasn't a dream. Daisy hugged her and reassured her that everything was alright. And, no, she wouldn't get caned for spoiling the sheets. Violet learned about menstruation, about tampons and pads and how to use them. She learned a lot of other things, too. Like why boys' penises stuck out like a branch and how sex actually worked. It was nice to finally have someone to hold her and help make sense of a world that only got more complicated each and every day.

In those moments Violet missed her mother. Daisy was a wonderful lady, but it was her mother who should've been teaching her these things. And whenever Violet thought of her mother and how much she missed her, she got all knotted up inside, because mixed with those feeling of sadness was anger. She was mad at her mother for abandoning her and giving her away to Daisy. There were many times early in the summer when she cried herself to sleep thinking about it. Daisy tried to explain that her mother had made a very difficult choice and that she certainly hadn't made it lightly. Darlene was very upset and crying when she spoke with Daisy. It was hard for Violet to understand now, Daisy said, but she was actually being a good mother by giving her daughter a better life. It was a sacrifice, really. Violet didn't see it that way at first. But as the summer went on, and her lessons continued, she started to see how she might be able to take advantage of her education. She could become an explorer like the writers and photographers in *National Geographic*. Only a short time ago all she'd wanted was to go back to Spotted Island and Roaches Brook. Now she thought she might leave Labrador to see the world and never return.

Violet quickly put the experience of her fist period behind her. The cramps, unfortunately, intensified. As her monthly shedding approached, her gut felt as if it were being twisted by a pair of ragged claws. Today, Daisy decided she needed to see Dr. Hunt. He was the one who stitched her up after the dog attack, although Violet had no memory of him, only that crazy dream where she was a pile of yarn and he was a wolf man knitting her into a rug. Walking to the hospital, Violet felt a swell of affection for Daisy. That she could come to Daisy with anything and she would help her. She now felt confident enough to talk to her about something that had been bothering all summer.

"Daisy," Violet said. "You're really nice."

"Why thank you," Daisy said, swatting away any flies that came near. "That's very sweet of you to say so."

"Why aren't the Brothers and Sisters more like you?"

"What do you mean?"

"They're all so mean."

"They can be awful, I know. Unfortunately, I don't have any control over how they teach the children. My responsibilities are getting money and making sure the school is up and running. It's really difficult sometimes. And, honestly, mostly we're just scraping by. The church contributes the most money, so they have a lot of control."

"But can't you fire some of them for being really bad?"

"I was caned when I was a young girl, too, and I turned okay. It might seem terrible now, but when you grow up you'll see that they were looking out for you."

"But some of the nuns make the kids eat throw-up. And there are Brothers who give boys and girls cigarettes or booze if they let them touch them."

"Oh, Violet," Daisy said with a smile. "You shouldn't listen to rumours like that."

Violet started to wonder if what she remembered had actually happened, or if they happened the way she remembered them happening. Had she exaggerated things? Maybe the Brothers and Sisters did have their best interests in heart and she was just being a sook, like Cecilia always said. Whenever they fought and Violet went crying to their mom that Cecilia had hit her, Cecilia said she was just making stuff up to get her in trouble and their mom never wanted to hear any of it. No one seemed to believe her about these sorts of things. Maybe she was imagining things and it was time to grow up and stop blowing every little thing out of proportion.

Violet and Daisy entered the hospital and sat down in the lobby. It was actually kind of nice to back, to see the nurses again. When Daisy explained what was going on, they smiled knowingly and took pity on Violet and brought her ice cream, just like old times.

"Violet?" a familiar nurse called out. "Dr. Hunt will see you now."

Violet went into the doctor's office and sat up on the bed and waited. The strip of paper along the bed crinkled under her bottom. Two metal arms stretched out from the foot of the bed. She wondered what their purpose could be. Dr. Hunt entered. He looked at her with his big, soft brown eyes and Violet felt blood swarming to her face.

"You're looking a lot better than the last time I saw you," he said.

"Thank you," she squeaked.

"Your hair is growing back, I see," he said as he stroked her head.

Violet smiled and looked down at her shoes.

"I'm told that you've moved here to Cartwright with Daisy. That's a lot of changes to deal with. How are you doing with that?"

"I'm okay. Daisy is super nice."

"She is. Do you miss your family?"

"Yeah."

"I bet. And how are you finding school? Those nuns can be wicked."

"They're okay."

"When I was a little boy I got the strap a few times, let me tell you. It wasn't fun."

Violet liked Dr. Hunt. Like Daisy, he seemed like someone who wanted to help her.

"So, what seems to be the problem today?" he asked.

"Well, I think Daisy explained it to the nurse, didn't she?"

"Yes, but I want to hear it from you."

Violet looked into Derek's eyes. They were brown like an animal's fur. Like Daisy, and very much unlike the Brothers and Sisters, they were full of kindness. She looked down and spoke softly, describing her first period and then the subsequent cramps. She spoke so low that she could barely hear herself. Derek got closer. She felt his ear getting nearer to her mouth. She could smell him. He was fresh and perfumey but there was a hint of body odour there, too, which reminded her of her father. Her face was so flushed that she thought her head might pop.

"Okay," he said when she was finished. "You'll have to take off your underwear."

He adjusted the two arms on the table. Violet hesitated. She felt like she was back at Lockwood when Sister Rosaline doused her with disinfectant.

"Don't worry, sweetheart," Derek said. "I need to have a look and make sure everything is fine."

He smiled. Violet wanted to trust him. She slid her underwear off and stuck her feet into the stirrups. Her head bubbled like a boiled kettle as she felt Derek touching her. She stifled a gasp when he pushed a finger inside her. It pinched a little. She feel him wriggling like a worm searching for something deep inside a part of her body that she didn't even know had existed. Then he took it out and the tension was released.

"I'm going to prescribe you birth control," he said. "You've probably heard some of the girls talk about 'the pill.' It doesn't mean you're going to be having sex. It just helps with the cramping."

Violet nodded. He handed her a slip of paper with scribbles on it that she couldn't decipher.

"Give that to Daisy," he said.

Violet walked out of the office and handed Daisy the prescription. They left the small hospital and walked back to Daisy's house.

"How was your check-up?" Daisy asked.

"It was fine," Violet replied.

"I can tell you're blushing," Daisy said.

"What do you mean?"

"It's okay. Dr. Hunt is very handsome. All the ladies in Cartwright have a crush on him, whether they admit it or not."

Daisy went to the kitchen to get supper ready. Ophelia was outside playing with some of the other children. Violet went and sat down in the living room. On the wall hung a big portrait of Daisy's husband. He was dressed up in a soldier's uniform. He died in France fighting the Germans. Daisy inherited his money and decided she wanted to use it to help children. She left her home in Boston and came to Cartwright to run Lockwood. Daisy didn't like to talk about her husband. Violet and Ophelia learned not to ask her about him.

On the table was a globe. Violet liked to spin it around and see where her finger landed. Labrador was a big chunk on the globe, but she knew that only a small amount of people lived here comparatively. She'd seen pictures of big cities like Boston, New York, and London. Even St. John's made Cartwright look puny, let alone Spotted Island and Roaches Brook. She found it hard to imagine that someone could leave an exciting city like Boston and come to live in Cartwright.

Daisy entered the room and saw that Violet was playing with her globe.

"Do you ever miss Boston?" Violet asked.

"Sometimes. Especially in the winter. It can be cold in Massachusetts, but nothing like here. And the nights aren't so long. It can be so bleak here sometimes. And the flies can be so bothersome."

Violet saw something in Daisy's eyes that she'd never noticed before. But she knew what it was: homesickness.

"Maybe one day we could all visit Boston," Violet said.

"Maybe," Daisy said. "Supper is ready."

They went to the kitchen. Violet was quiet through supper. She didn't have her regular appetite. After, she sat in the living room again and leafed through magazines, barely scanning the photos. She and Ophelia went to bed. Violet lay in bed staring at the ceiling. Across the room she could hear Ophelia's breath slow into a sleeper's rhythm. Something drove Violet to pull her nightgown up over her hips. She slid her hands underneath her underwear. She was compelled to feel the place where Dr. Hunt had touched. The beat of her heart filled her ears. She could smell him again now, see those brown eyes, hear his voice. Her thighs squeezed her wrists and her back arched sharply. Her fingers moved in furious activity. Then everything was suddenly clear as a calmness exploded inside her. She lay flat in the bed and starred at the ceiling breathing deeply. The physical pleasure of her experience was matched only by the sublime silence of her mind. She soon fell into a deliciously dreamless sleep.

CHAPTER ELEVEN (2015)

Julie could see the iceberg floating outside the Narrows from where she was sitting in the cafe. A little early in the summer to see one in St. John's, but climate change was not without its gifts. As a Newfoundlander, it was easy to take icebergs for granted. Nevertheless, Julie often reflected on their beauty whenever she saw one. When she was young, her family went on a trip around the island, staying at B&Bs in various outports. On a sunny afternoon in La Scie, they saw an iceberg flip over. They heard it crack all the way from their patio overlooking the bay. A chunk collapsed into the water, roaring and splashing. Then the berg rolled over, briefly exposing its electric blue underbelly, and then crashed back down underwater, kicking up whiteheads. Julie's parents' gasped. People around the community cheered, as if the iceberg had put on a show for their benefit. Julie remembered suddenly feeling alienated. She realized that nature performed all kind of miracles indifferent to whether people were there to bear witness. She'd always thought of beauty in utilitarian terms until then; the flower attracted pollinators with its colours; peacocks flashed their plumage to impress potential mates; girls wore makeup to get boys' attention. Now she saw that beauty could and did exist often without reason or function. Not only did this make her feel estranged from the world around her, but also from the people who didn't share her epiphany. It was her first moment of philosophical reflection.

The chimes above the door dinged. Julie looked to the entrance and saw a guy who was likely the one she'd been talking to over email. He was a PhD candidate in the folklore department, working on a dissertation about werewolves in popular media. Julie had emailed him and said that she was working on a novel about werewolves in Newfoundland. He was very keen on meeting in person. He looked like a typical guy in grad studies: shaggy hair, scruffy beard, khakis, boring shirt.

"Julie?" he said. She smiled and stood up to shake his hand. "Ron."

"Nice to meet you," Julie said.

After he got himself a cup of coffee, he sat down and reviewed her (mostly Joseph's) notes. She was researching Amarok, a wolf figure in Inuit mythology. Joseph had touched on Amarok in his notes, but hadn't found a satisfactory link between it and werewolves. Julie wanted to pull that thread some more to see if she could discover something he had missed. Unfortunately, she wasn't breaking any new territory. Joseph's research had just about exhausted the literature. Moreover, she didn't have a background in folklore beyond an introductory course she took and didn't particularly enjoy.

"This is pretty thorough," Ron said. "Why don't you tell me a bit more about your project and I'll see how I can help you."

"Well, like I said in the email, I want to really couch the werewolf in Newfoundland folklore. Amarok seemed like a great angle, but I can't really find anything that links it to werewolves."

"No, I can't think of any examples, either. I asked a couple people around the department without any luck. Usually the Amarok is a symbol of strength. A giant wolf that is often blamed for hunters going missing when out alone in the woods. There's a sense that nothing is hidden from the Amarok. If a hunter does something to offend it, then it will have retribution."

"What do you mean by retribution?"

"I know of one story where a couple hunters stumbled upon an Amarok's den and killed its puppies. The Amarok soon returned with food and the hunters tried to hide. The Amarok went to a nearby lake and pulled humanoid forms from the water. Each of the hunters then died of a heart attack. It stole their souls."

An icy current rippled through Julie's blood. She mimicked Ron's enthusiastic smile to conceal her dread. The image of a giant supernatural wolf made her think of the night she and Tyler saw that big dog in the cemetery. The idea that they were visited by a canine god was demonstrably outrageous, but at this point she was willing to suspend her disbelief. She hadn't brought up the dog because Tyler and Joseph would likely just dismiss it as coincidence, which it probably was. But she couldn't dismiss the peculiarity of seeing a strange dog the night she was inseminated by her werewolf boyfriend. Ex-boyfriend.

"If you're really serious about finding some folklore that might provide a basis for your novel, you could always travel to Labrador and see what you can find," Ron said.

"Really? How would I do that?"

"Just go around to different communities, see if anyone knows any stories about the Amarok or werewolves. You'll be surprised by you can find. That's how this stuff works, really."

She took a sip of her coffee. It was black and strong, still warm in the white ceramic mug. She rubbed the bridge between her eyes. Her left eyebrow twitched slightly. She wondered how Joseph and Tyler would react to that idea of travelling to Labrador to follow up on her hunch.

"So," Ron said. "Tell me more about your novel."

"There's not much to tell," Julie said. "I'm still just researching some ideas. I've never written a novel before so I'm just learning as I go."

Julie could feel herself blushing. Ron probably thought it was because of him. She felt uncomfortable talking about writing, even an imaginary novel.

"I'm sure it'll be great," he said. "Have you written much before?"

"A few stories here and there."

"Right on. Listen, I have a class I got to run to, but would you like to meet up some time for a drink? Talk about something aside from giant werewolves."

"Oh, thanks, but I actually have a boyfriend."

"Cool, cool. No problem. Sorry."

"Not at all. Don't be."

"Alright, well, if you have any other questions, don't hesitate to shoot me an email."

Julie was surprised at herself for not taking him up on his offer. And that she'd played the boyfriend card as an excuse. Wasn't that the whole point of being single? Going out and having fun? It didn't have to lead anywhere. There was, however, some slight concern that if she imbibed an increment of alcohol, everything that she was holding inside her would come bursting out in a vast and insane soliloquy. Surely, she couldn't drag some poor unsuspecting guy into this mad drama of hers, and certainly not Ron with his soft hands and collection of cardigans. But he was nice. She was expecting some stuck-up nebbish and he turned out to be pleasantly sensible. She liked that he just came out and asked her out, as opposed to trying to impress her with his many serious thoughts on Radiohead's discography. Maybe another time. Another life.

Single. It was a concept and word Julie was starting to get used to. Going all the way back to Keith, it'd been about six years since she was single. And aside from the regular sex, she didn't miss being in a relationship. She enjoyed waking up in the morning and planning her day without having to worry about another person's needs or wants. Every decision took twice as long when in a relationship. What to eat, where to go, what time to do what. It was exhausting. Nevertheless, here she was researching obscure folklore for Tyler's sake. She knew that she could easily terminate this pregnancy, leave for Halifax, and never look back at any of this madness. Surely most people in her situation would do exactly that. It was the most sane thing to do. However, a significant part of her was still bound to him. He was fighting for his life and she couldn't bail on him.

The stress was bleeding into her dreams. The other night she had a sex dream about Tyler, which were becoming more common the longer she went without getting laid; she also suspected the pregnancy was wreaking havoc on her hormones. She dreamt he was going down on her with the kind of hunger he had for her when their relationship was young. She reached down to rub his hair and felt the pointed ears of a wolf. It looked up her with a bloody maw and snarled. At that point she woke up. And that wasn't even the worst of it. She had reoccurring visions of Tyler crying over the body of a person he'd murdered, his face covered in blood.

There were also dreams of a strange girl in a dark forest. Julie chased after the girl, snow crunching beneath their naked feet. They were surrounded by huge trees reaching up to a bright starry night. The girl stopped in front of a big pond, the moon glistening off the frozen water. Wolves surrounded them, snarling behind the trees, their bright yellow eyes shining like the stars above. Julie caught up with the girl and turned her around. Her throat was slit and blood poured from a gash on her head. The impression of the girl's face always evaporated after she woke up, but she felt like she knew her intimately.

She took out her Kobo and loaded up *A Tale of Two Cities*. She liked her e-reader because it kept her reading anonymous. This summer she'd set herself the goal of plowing her way through Dickens' most notable works and she didn't like the idea of people knowing she was still ticking off the basics of the Western canon. She wanted to affect the image of a finished product, not a work in progress. Reading lesser-known works like *Little Dorrit* or *Bleak House* in public were okay. But *Oliver Twist* or *Great Expectations?* Someone might as well walk right up and revoke her Arts degree.

However, after her conversation with Ron she wished that she had Joseph's compendium of notes, "After Dark Vapours." She was going to need to consult it before building her case for their own little episode of *Mythbusters* up in Labrador. She loved reading Joseph's notes. They were full of spontaneous, speculative moments full of poetry. He had a deeply curious mind and considered every possibility. "Why wolves?" Joseph asked in his notes:

Modern dogs evolved from wolves that were sensitive to early humans. They hung around camps and tribes, salvaging whatever the humans threw away. They could understand the humans' cues and were able to co-exist. Eventually, the humans sought their company and used them as guardians. Does that suggest a certain bond that could be traced way back when mammals started to differentiate? Do primates and canines have some shared genes that never went away, which is what allowed dogs to become "man's best friend"? And, for certain people, the full moon triggered a monstrous mutation lying dormant in these genes thus creating werewolves? We know that there are kids that are born with vestiges of gill cartilage, a memento from our nautical ancestors. Humans have many unused olfactory genes leftover from when primates traded smell for sight. Our bodies house ancient DNA like time travellers stuffing their luggage with curios. The traces of our genetic heritage are everywhere. Is it so unlikely that an arcane lunar alchemy could unlock these genetic modalities?

Julie envied Joseph's imagination. She wished she could bring that into her own writing. He wrote from a position of wonder whereas she couldn't get away from a position of error.

Her leg demanded that she reach down and scratch it. The wound was just about healed now and was well into the itching stage. She couldn't work as a lifeguard while it healed. On top of everything else that was going on, she figured she may as well resign. Joseph offered to reimburse her losses, but she couldn't accept. She embraced her unemployment as an opportunity to spend the summer reading because she likely wouldn't be able to consume much literature once law school started in the fall. On the one hand, she was nervous about leaving for Halifax without everything with Tyler resolved. On the other, she saw it as the finish line for her commitment to him. Beyond it lay freedom. A new stage in her life and a continent of possibilities.

Dickens' words streamed by. Julie was distracted by the thought of the life form growing inside her belly. She estimated that she was seven-weeks pregnant now, although she could be further along. She knew that after fourteen weeks, getting an abortion would be more complicated. Yet whenever she resolved herself to call the clinic, her nerve abandoned her. She had absolutely no intention of being a single mother with an infant in law school. When she first learned that she was pregnant, "Morgentaler's Take-Out" was her first thought. Now, she'd become infected with indecision.

Her phone buzzed. A text from Tyler.

Wanna visit Joseph? he wrote.

Julie wondered if he'd reached out to her because he wanted to involve her or because it was raining outside and he needed a ride. However, she did want to check in on Joseph.

Sure, when? she wrote.

Now? he responded.

That was typical of Tyler, so last minute. It was precisely this type of thing that she didn't miss about relationships; someone else feeling entitled to her time. She felt like telling him to wait an hour because she wanted to keep reading, but she knew that she'd be distracted thinking of him and Joseph. She drank the last few gulps of coffee--never willing to waste caffeine--and texted Tyler back:

OTW

It was raining so hard that the drops splashing on the asphalt made it seem like it was pouring from both directions. Julie walked quickly to her car; running just created more splashes, soaking feet and legs. The car's seat warmer made her feel like a champagne socialist. She drove out of the harbour front and made her way towards Rabbittown. Poor souls were standing outside in the downfall waiting for the bus. Along with a haphazard schedule, to punish users of public transit even further, the city wouldn't even spring for shelters. Julie pulled up outside Tyler's house. She took out her phone to let him know she was here, but to her surprise he was ready at the door. He ran from his house to her car.

"Hi," he said as he got into the passenger seat.

"How are you?" Julie asked.

"Good. You?"

"I'm well."

Julie drove through Memorial's campus to the hospital. Parking at the Health Sciences was always fun. She reached out and grabbed a ticket from the gate and joined the conga line of circling cars searching for a spot.

"You can go inside while I look for a spot," Julie suggested.

"No, I'll keep you company," Tyler answered.

Her own frustration and impatience was mirrored in the expressions of other drivers. She hated car culture. She hated that it was nearly impossible to live in St. John's without a car.

"There!" Tyler said.

An old woman was walking towards her car, bundled up in her rain coat. Julie followed her slowly and closely to let the other drivers know that she'd staked her prey. The old woman got into her car and Julie took the spot. She and Tyler got out and walked hurriedly through the curtains of rain to the hospital. There was a blast of warm air as they entered the Health Sciences.

The rain itself wasn't so bad. The fact that it was eight degrees in June that got Julie down. And it wasn't just the number; the chill in Newfoundland had a way of getting into your bones. People who'd spent time on the mainland talked about the difference between dry versus wet cold. The difference was real and important. In a place like Alberta, a simple shift inside was sufficient. In Newfoundland, it required a fireplace and warm soup.

Tyler lead the way through the Health Science's byzantine halls, past the paint-chipped walls and the South East Asian orderlies. Joseph had sprung for a private room. He was lying in bed reading the latest issue of *The Economist*, looking a little more his age.

"Hi, Julie," he said. "Great to see you."

"How are you doing?" she asked.

Julie stood up by the bed. Tyler took a seat at the far side of the room.

"Better," Joseph said. "Turns out I had what's called a spontaneous coronary artery dissection. It's rare for a man such as myself. It's more common among young women who have recently given birth."

"But you're so healthy," Julie said.

"It is possible for men to experience it after intense exercise. The last transformation must have done a number on me. Seems like the metamorphoses rejuvenate just about every cell in the body except the heart. I believe the heart is the engine that drives the transformations. It remains constant throughout. So, the transformations must be very taxing."

"Probably doesn't help that you're shooting heroin," Tyler said.

"What?" Julie said.

"Yes," Joseph said. "I'm an opioid user. It's psychological addiction. The metamorphoses don't let the chemistry take hold. I use them to cope with the pain. Mental and physical."

"I guess I don't have much hope," Tyler said. "I'm pretty much addicted to weed as it is."

"That's why I'm trying to help you through this" Joseph explained, "so you don't make the bad choices I did."

There was a knock at the door. A nurse entered and smiled. She looked at Joseph's chart, fussed with the machines, and left. The dull grey sky hung outside the window. Rain pattered on the glass.

"What if there's still hope for a cure?" Julie said after an extended silence.

"How?" Joseph asked.

"In your notes you covered the literature around the Amarok. We know that Derek spent time in Labrador. What if there are stories about the Amarok that the research hasn't discovered? Stories about lycanthropy. What causes it, what can cure it."

"What are you suggesting?" Joseph asked.

"We go to Cartwright and interview locals," Julie said.

"I've been to Cartwright before," Joseph said. "I didn't find anything. It was a dead end."

"But you didn't know what you were looking for," Julie said. "I'll pose as a writer researching werewolf folklore for a novel I'm working on. After Dark Vapours."

Joseph smiled.

"Sounds like a waste of time," Tyler said.

"What makes you think the Amarok is a good lead?" Joseph asked.

"This is going to sound ridiculous," Julie said. "But one night, me and Tyler saw a really strange dog. It was over at the cemetery on Bonaventure. It had these bright yellow eyes. And it seemed like it was waiting for us, like it knew exactly who we were. And it also happened to be the night I conceived."

Joseph was pale. "Something very similar happened to Karen and I," he said.

"Oh c'mon," Tyler said. "It was just a big dog."

"I think it's worth a shot," Joseph said. "I should be out of here tomorrow. We'll leave as soon as possible."

Tyler leaned back in his chair, folded his arms, and looked to the side.

"Also," Joseph continued. "If I have another heart attack, I don't want you to bring me to a hospital."

"So we just let you die?" Tyler asked.

"If I die in hospital, I run the risk of exposing my cells to researchers. They probably already have vials now already."

"What's the problem?" Julie asked.

"He's afraid the government is going to make an army of werewolves with our blood," Tyler said.

"It doesn't matter," Joseph said. "It's my decision."

"So you want us to burn you on a pile of wood right then and there like Darth Vader in *Return of the Jedi*?" Tyler asked.

"Yes," Joseph said. "Something like that."

"You're insane," Tyler said.

"We don't have to worry about that right now, do we?" Julie said. Tyler and Joseph were both silent, looking in the opposite directions of each other. "Let's focus on getting to Cartwright."

"You're absolutely right, Julie," Joseph said.

The rain's rhythm on the window pane had slowed. Sunlight was burning through the sky's greyness.

"I guess we should get going," Julie said.

"I'll let you know about the itinerary when I've made the arrangements," Joseph said.

They left Joseph's room. Tyler was silent. Outside the rain was replaced by a throbbing drizzle. They walked to Julie's car and were soon pursued by a driver desperate for a parking spot.

"Are you alright?" Julie asked when they got into the car.

"Yeah, I'm fine," Tyler said.

Julie pulled out and drove towards the gate. She handed the clerk her ticket and paid the fee.

"I'm sorry I said your idea was a waste of time," Tyler said.

"That's okay," Julie said. "We're all a little edgy."

Julie drove to Tyler's. She pulled up outside and waited for him to get out.

"Did you want to come inside for a bit?" he asked.

"Sure," she said after some hesitation.

She stepped inside Tyler's house. The last time she was here she'd found him hunched over in the corner of the living room, whimpering and slobbering, a snarling werewolf. She remembered him crashing through the kitchen table, which was now replaced. And then running to the bathroom. Tyler had burst through the door as she was pulling herself through the window. The door had also been replaced. She also remembered the many nights she'd spent here, coming in after studying at the library until it closed, her brain a hardboiled egg. Tyler would have junk food and weed ready for her. She was surprised to see the place so neat and tidy. No empty chip bags and pizza boxes all over the floor and couches. The air was fresh instead of smelling like a dog's kennel. Tyler opened a window in the kitchen and packed his bong.

"Want some?" he asked.

"I probably shouldn't," Julie said, unintentionally rubbing her stomach.

"Right," Tyler said. He took a deep pull and blew the smoke out through the window. "How's that going?"

"Alright, I guess."

"I should've said this a long time ago, but whatever decision you take, I'll support you one-hundred percent."

"Thanks."

"I was going to grill some chicken for a salad. Want some?"

"That'd be great."

Tyler fired up the stove. Julie sat down at the table. She wanted to confide in him the uncertainty she was having about her pregnancy, that she'd wanted to get an abortion but now wasn't so sure anymore. She hadn't talked about it with anyone and it was burning her up. He was one of the few people who knew about everything she was going through. However, she was hesitant to re-establish that kind of intimacy with him. The bond between them was nearly shorn and she couldn't decide whether she wanted to continue tearing it. For months now, she'd thought only of getting Tyler out of her life, but now that she truly saw the void that it would create she was scared.

Tyler threw some spinach and kale into a bowl along with baby tomatoes, almond shavings, and berries. When the chicken was done he dropped it in with shredded cheese. He laid out some plates, cutlery, and glasses of water on the table. Julie dripped some raspberry vinaigrette over her salad. They sat together and ate.

"How did you know Joseph was using drugs?" she asked.

"When he was having a heart attack and you asked me to look through his stuff," Tyler said. "I found his stash."

"Why didn't you say anything?"

Tyler shrugged.

Julie stuck her fork through a chunk of chicken and wad of kale.

"You should have at least told the paramedics," she said. "That was really stupid and dangerous."

"Well he's fine now, isn't he? And, what, shooting smack isn't stupid?"

"That's not what I said."

Tyler attacked his plate. He shoved the salad into his mouth and chewed it with his mouth open.

"You're such a suck up to him" he said.

"What are you talking about?"

"He bailed on me and Mom. He didn't even show up when she died. And on top of all that he's a junkie. But I guess he's another authority figure for you to impress."

"Well, maybe if you didn't drop out of school, you could talk to people about something besides video games and drugs."

Julie saw the fury rising in Tyler's eyes. But it was quickly undercut by a deep sorrow. She waited for him to say rally with something equally hurtful. Instead, he stood up and walked to his room.

She left then. Her mind was clogged with competing thoughts. Thankfully, her leg was sufficiently healed to tolerate a short walk. She drove over to Fort Amherst. On Southside Road, she passed one of her favourite houses in the city. It was a Queen Anne style and reminded her of those old doll houses. If it wasn't so close to the harbour, she could imagine herself living there. She drove up to the visitor's parking lot near Fort Amherst and got out. The grey clouds had been completely burned off now and the sun shone over St. John's. The light shimmered on the harbour water. The iceberg sitting in the Narrows glistened. As she walked towards the old lighthouse, she began to understand the conflicted emotions Tyler was trying to contain. He had unresolved anger towards Joseph, but he also wanted to build a relationship with him. He was jealous that she and Joseph had bonded so easily. She should've reached out to him or at least made an effort to de-escalate the situation. Instead, she antagonized him. However, she refused to feel mad at herself. It was unfair that she was the one always tasked with diffusing these sorts of situations. She doubted that Tyler was doing any sort of soul searching.

He was right, though, she begrudgingly admitted to herself, when he said that Joseph was another authority figure from whom she sought validation. After four years of dating, she lamented that she hadn't absorbed at least some his defiance to counteract her approval addiction.

The cold air surrounding the iceberg brushed her hair. She breathed it in and allowed her frustrations to seep out through her exhalations. Tourists milled about the lighthouse, searching for the perfect picture that would frame all the signifiers of Newfoundland. A green light encircled the base of the iceberg, which was visibly melting in the heat. Growlers had broken off and drifted towards the rocks. Julie saw a crack in the berg's belly, exposing a sliver of electric blue.

CHAPTER TWELVE (1964)

When Violet came back to Lockwood in the fall, the nuns insisted she sleep on the rubber mattress. However, after a month without incident she was allowed to have a regular cot like the rest of the girls. She still had trouble falling asleep many nights, nonetheless. On nights when sleep refused to come, she lay in bed and waited until the dormitory was full of snores. Then her hands crept down into her underwear and got to work. She pushed her face into her pillow to muffle her moans. Once she was finished, her sandman came quickly. Oftentimes she delayed satisfaction out of guilt and fear. The nuns taught them that masturbation was a sin and that sex was meant to only be between husband and wife, and for the sole service of procreation. At night, when she tossed and turned and delayed respite, she ruminated on God and the devil and damnation and hell until desire overwhelmed her and she couldn't resist. She couldn't understand why God would give her such urges if he didn't want her to act on them. Surely God would understand if she had the opportunity to explain herself. Really, it was only meant to help her sleep, because if she didn't, then she'd be tired in class and then the nuns would get mad and then punish her. She wasn't doing it for the pleasure; she did it so she could be a dutiful student. Nonetheless, she was still too scared to confess these sins to Father Mahoney. Instead she admitted them to God privately during her nightly prayers and recited the Act of Contrition.

This morning, Violet was in class working on math problems. The summer tutoring with Daisy had paid off. She was back in class with girls her own age. Not only was she able to keep up with the material, she was excelling as a student. The Sisters were always pleased with her work. She wanted to tell Daisy all about it, but she had established firm boundaries between her and the girls. She didn't want it to seem like Violet and Ophelia were getting any kind of special treatment. Violet could understand that, but it was still frustrating that she didn't get to show Daisy how much she'd helped her over the summer. Whenever Sister Margaret gave her back her work covered with check marks and an "A+" written at the top, Violet felt a swell of pride. And love for Daisy.

Outside the classroom, Sister Sherry was clanging her bell for recess. But instead of going outside, the children were all led to the dining hall for a "special announcement." Inside, all the Brothers and Sisters were gathered. There was also a woman among them that Violet didn't recognize.

Daisy wasn't there, which she found strange. She looked around for Ophelia but couldn't see her, either. She hadn't seen her around school for the last couple days. None of the other kids knew where she was and Violet didn't feel like it warranted paying Daisy a visit. In all likelihood she was sick and had to spend a few days over at the hospital, which made Violet slightly jealous. Sometimes she wished she'd get sick just so she could go see Dr. Hunt. The image of his face in her mind made her stomach jittery. However, she wasn't sure how he'd feel if she told him that she'd stopped taking the birth control pills. The side effects were too hard to deal with. Instead of occasional cramps, she had constant nausea. And the irregular spotting freaked her out--not sure whether there'd be a bloodstain in her underwear made her anxious. It gave her flashbacks of the dog attack. She was also embarrassed about having to take them. She was afraid that the other girls would find out and then everyone would think she was a slut. The boys would certainly have a spree with that. They were all disgusting. And the Brothers weren't much better. She could feel their eyes all over her chest ever since her small breasts had started to bud. She wished more men would act like Dr. Hunt.

Continuing to scan the cafeteria, Violet locked eyes with Cecelia and they both immediately looked away. Whenever the two former sisters crossed paths at school they acted like strangers. Seeing Cecelia twisted Violet up inside. Feelings of sadness and anger coiled around each other like a big tangled fishnet. She also felt like that whenever she thought about her family. Her old family. She wondered if Cecilia felt as twisted up as she did. Cecilia was never very good at expressing her emotions. Violet didn't want to be angry at her. They weren't technically sisters anymore, but that didn't mean they had to ignore each other. Violet was curious to hear news about her family. Her old family.

"Attention students!" Sister Sherry yelled, clanging her bell. "I would like to introduce you to our new headmistress, Mrs. Roberts."

Violet had to run that sentence over and over a few times in her head before she finally understood what Sister Sherry had said. "New headmistress"? If she was the headmistress, then where was Daisy? Sister Sherry was still talking, but Violet couldn't absorb the words. Mrs. Roberts stood beside Sister Sherry. She was older than Daisy and had strands of grey intermingled into her long brown hair that was tied into a tight bun atop her head. When the introduction was over and the students were given leave, Violet rushed over to Sister Sherry.

"Hello there, little miss," Mrs. Roberts said with a smile. "And who might you be?"

Her smile wanted to signal warmth, but Violet hated her for the confusion she'd instantly thrust into her life. She was ugly and fat and her face was dumb.

"Sister Sherry," Violet asked. "Where is Daisy?"

"She went back to Boston," she replied. "Didn't she tell you?"

Violet stared at her waiting for more information. Sister Sherry looked annoyed at having to explain the situation.

"She left a few days ago," she said. "And she took that little girl with her. Ophelia."

Sister Sherry walked away after that and Mrs. Roberts followed. Her smile had briefly broken when Sister Sherry revealed that information, but then she quickly rediscovered it. Violet stood there unable to process what had happened. The situation steadily revealed itself despite Violet's attempt to deny its significance. Daisy was gone. She went home to Boston and she had taken Ophelia with her. That meant she hadn't wanted Violet. She only wanted Ophelia. This was the only explanation. Its brutality stunned Violet. Again, she had been dropped from a parent. And again, she'd been left out of the process. No one had even bothered to come talk to her about it.

The room pitched and shifted like a punt on a stormy sea. She needed to get out. She took off running. The nuns yelled at her to come back, but she kept going down the hall. She ran outside. A cool fall rain showered her bare arms and legs. Her feet kicked up pools of muddy water that splashed her skirt. The bitter raindrops mingled with her warm tears. Her legs pumped until her shins burned atop her cold feet. She ran all the way to the only place that she could think of, to the only person who seemed to care about her. She burst in through the doors of the hospital.

"Where is Dr. Hunt?" Violet demanded. "I need to see him."

"He's busy at the moment," Nurse Powers explained. "What's the matter, dear? You're soaking wet. Here let me get you a blanket and you can have a seat."

"No, I need to see him right away!"

Dr. Hunt came out of his office.

"What's going on?" he asked.

"Young Violet is very upset," Nurse Powers explained. "I tried to tell her that you were busy, but she won't have it."

"That's okay," Dr. Hunt said. "You can wait in the room, love. I'll be right in."

Dr. Hunt ushered her into the examination room. He handed her a blanket and closed the door. She paced around the room, fidgeting at her wet hair. Tears were fighting their way to her eyes, but she resisted. She wrapped the wool blanket around her shoulders and sat atop the bed. Her wet bum quickly soaked the strip of paper. She looked at the arms and stirrups sticking out from the bed and was reminded of her first visit, which warmed her more than the blanket ever could.

"What seems to be the problem?" Dr. Hunt asked when he came into the room.

As soon as the words started so did the tears. Between the sobs and shrieks, Violet explained what had happened. When she was finished, her body racked with sobs. Her shoulders bounced as she cried and she shivered from the cold dampness. Dr. Hunt hugged her. She wrapped her arms around him and was enveloped in his glow. There was a softly intense heat from his chest and he smelled so good. Violet felt like she was back in the log cabin in Roaches Brook with a steady fire cooking supper in the middle of a dark winter's night.

"So many awful things have happened to you," he said. "I wish I could make things better. All I can say is that sometimes people aren't who we thought and hoped for them to be." He released her and held shoulders and looked at her with his big, soft brown eyes. "Daisy made a terrible mistake. You're a wonderful little girl and anyone would be lucky to have you."

She leapt forward and kissed him. She wrapped her arms around his neck and pulled his face down to hers. Her tiny mouth was lost in his big lips. She could smell the tea and cigarettes off his breath intermingled with his cologne. The wetness of his mouth seeped into hers. He tasted minty, like those little candies she got at the Hudson Bay Company's trading post. His stubbly chin chafed her soft cheeks. She let go then, realizing what she'd done.

His brown eyes darkened. She could see what looked like anger in his face, like when some of the Brothers or Sisters when they were about to inflict their punishment.

"I'm sorry," Violet said.

He flipped her around and slammed her into the bed and bent her over. She lay on top of the paper cover as he threw her skirt up over her shoulders and yanked her underwear down to her ankles. She anticipated a hand to strike her cold exposed bum. Instead, he drove something big and hard deep inside her. She squealed at the pain.

"Shhh," Derek growled. "Be quiet."

Violet squelched her cries. Like when she got the cane, she didn't want to make Dr. Hunt angrier and receive extra punishment. She yielded and was as pliant as possible as he thrust into her again and again. Her hips bumped against the hard bed and her crotch ached. After an amount time that felt impossible to measure, Dr. Hunt finally collapsed onto her back, tired and breathing heavily in her ear. She felt him shrink and pull out of her.

"Are you okay?" he asked after he regained his breath. "Did I hurt you?"

374   *After Dark Vapours*

Violet shook her head.

"We have to keep this our secret," he said. "I don't think Sister Sherry would be very pleased if she found out."

Violet nodded.

"Good girl," he said. "You're on the pill, so you have to worry about getting pregnant. Now get yourself together and go back to school. Don't say anything to Nurse Powers."

Violet was afraid to tell him that she'd stopped taking the pills. Instead, she kept nodding and pulled up her underwear and fixed her skirt. She walked out into the waiting room. Nurse Powers saw her leave the room then quickly readjusted her gaze to a pile of papers strewn across her desk. Violet walked back towards Lockwood. It had stopped raining, but the wind carried a chill with a threat of winter. With each step she tried to correct her limp. The cold wind soothed her aching crotch and hips. It was like Derek had shoved a hot poker up into her stomach and tore out her organs. Lockwood came into view. *Suffer Little Children to Come unto Me*. She managed to will her legs into a gait that wouldn't draw any suspicions.

She opened the doors. A few Brothers and Sisters were at the entrance. They called for Sister Sherry. Violet stared down at her feet to avoid their eyes. She focused on concealing any sign of what had just happened.

"We understand you were upset," Sister Sherry said. She held a cane in her hands. "But that's no excuse to go running off like that. Hold out your hands."

The lashes were a welcome distraction.

"Now," Sister Sherry said. "You're to go straight to bed with no supper."

Violet was relieved at that. She had no appetite and doubted whether she could stomach Lockwood culinary right now. She walked up the dormitory and lay in bed, staring at the ceiling, hoping for the throbbing to subside. That night she realized that she had deserved it. All of it. Everything. Clearly there was something wrong with her. Why would her mother give away only for Daisy to abandon her. She was dirty little half-breed. Touching herself at night like a pervert. She was obviously going to hell. Having accepted her status, a numbness enveloped her that she welcomed. Having embraced this indifferent void, she soon succumbed to a half-sleep.

CHAPTER THIRTEEN (2015)

"You're from St. John's, is it?" the woman asked. She brought her axe down and cleaved the junk of wood with a quick smooth swing. It split with an easy crunch. Piles of chopped lumber surrounded her. She set up another junk on the chopping block with the swiftness and regularity of a routine that had been repeated thousands of times.

"Yes, ma'am," Julie said, swatting away the legion of black flies encircling her.

"Call me Josie, love. That's quite the drive." She paid no notice to the flies.

"Yes, my boyfriend and I have been driving around the province, staying at a few different places. Neither of us have really spent much time outside of the Avalon."

"And who's the older fellow with you?"

"Oh, that's my boyfriend's father," Julie said. "He's actually paying for the trip."

"Keeping an eye on you two, is he?" Josie asked.

"Yeah," Julie replied. "Something like that."

Obviously, word got around Cartwright quickly. Julie, Tyler, and Joseph had only checked into their motel the evening prior. Their journey took two days. On the first day, they drove from St. John's to Saint Barbe on the Northern Peninsula in a Jeep that Joseph had rented that could withstand Labrador's ragged highway. The next morning, they got the ferry to Blanc Sablon. The Quebec-Newfoundland border ran between Blanc Sablon and L'Anse-Au-Claire, but its only identifier was two large boulders approximately fifteen feet apart. The road was very hilly, and the Labrador highway barely clung to the elevations' ridges. The blue ocean threw white surf against gray granite cliffs. They made their way slowly across the largely unpaved road to Cartwright. Much of the drive was spent in silence punctuated occasionally by perfunctory conversation. Julie didn't like to read while driving, so she mostly stared out the window, taking in the scenery and trying to suppress her overwhelming anxiety. There were long stretches of landscape without any sign of human presence, or even vegetation outside of the odd stunted brush. The few bony towns hardly broke the illusion that this road was in fact a kind of journey back in time to Pangaea. She and Joseph had talked of getting to work as soon as they'd arrived in Cartwright, but they were far too mentally fatigued by the time they got there and decided on a fresh start in the morning.

"Alright then," Josie said. "Let's go inside for a cup tea."

She stuck her axe in the chopping block, then piled the junks of wood by the side of her house. Julie considered helping her, but she stacked them with such swiftness, finding just the right angle for the perfect fit, that Julie thought she'd just be interfering. Josie peeled off her gloves and dropped them beside the axe. Julie followed her to the back entrance of the house. In the yard was a large garden enclosed by a riddle fence. Green textures dotted the brown earth. Little signs identified what was growing in each plot: potatoes, Swiss chard, spinach, turnip, carrots, onions.

"Did you plant all these yourself?" Julie asked.

"Yes, love," Josie replied. "Been doing everything myself now these past twenty years since Carl passed away. He was my husband. Not that he was much of a hand around here when he was alive."

They stepped into the kitchen and took their shoes off on the floor mat. Josie filled up an electric kettle with water. Julie sat down at a Formica table that looked out over the bight from the kitchen window. Josie prepared her tea the old-fashioned way, putting the cream and sugar in beforehand. Julie drank hers black. The kettle squealed. Josie poured boiling water into two porcelain cups. Her brown hands were streaked by purple varicose. She recounted her daily life in Cartwright, planting crops, tearing down fences, chopping wood, and clearing snow. Her head was capped with a crop of wild grey coils. She smiled rarely, but her eyes were friendly and full of warmth.

"Doctor says I shouldn't have cream or sugar in my tea," Josie said. "I told him that I couldn't afford neither my whole life, so I'm going to enjoy them now while I can."

Julie smiled. She was in awe of this eighty-year-old woman.

"So, you're a student from the university," Josie said. "What do you study?"

"French and Classics."

"I see," Josie said. "And what brings you up here to Cartwright?"

"I'm researching legends about wolves in Labrador."

"You're doing school work on your vacation?"

"I'm actually working on a novel. I'd like to use some details from in and around the province to give it authenticity."

"Oh, a novel is it? What's it called?"

"*After Dark Vapours*."

"Hmmhmm. And why wolves?"

"Oh, it's something that's always interested me."

Josie drank some tea.

As the little white lies amassed, Julie struggled to maintain the ins and outs of this narrative she was presenting; Josie struck her as someone attuned to the odour of bullshit. Julie believed it was harmless and understandable given the circumstance—how could she possibly explain her situation—but she still felt guilty being even slightly duplicitous with Josie, a woman so hospitable and forthcoming.

"Pardon my prying, love," she said. "It's my nature. I'm right nosey. Can't be helped. I suppose the crowd in St. John's aren't like that."

"I don't mind," Julie replied. "I guess being inquisitive is how you learned all your stories."

When Julie asked the locals around Cartwright about folklore, they all pointed her to Josie. She had a reputation for being a living library of genealogy, mythology, and gossip. "No flies on her," everyone said. "Her memory is something else."

"I've always been starved for stories," Josie explained. "I got it from my mother. She was Inuit. I loved hearing her stories and she loved telling them to me. My father, who was mostly white, was a trapper and fisherman. He'd meet all sorts of folks and share their stories with me. If we had a crowd over, I'd soak up all the talk. Same thing when I married my husband. He was a trapper and fisherman, too. And my brothers. All the men were once upon a time. Now, my three sons have all scattered across the mainland. I'm afraid I won't have no one to pass along all my stories."

"You should write a book."

"I've thought of it. But, you know, the words don't come on pen and paper like they do when I'm chewing the fat."

"I understand what you mean."

They sipped at their tea. A few boats lulled in the harbour. The late-afternoon sun dotted tiny waves. A green, white, and blue Labrador flag billowed against the breeze.

"For my research," Julie said, "I'm looking at people transforming into wolves. Werewolves."

"Yes, I've heard a few of those," Josie said.

"I'll try to more specific. Are you familiar with the Amarok?"

"I am."

"Have you heard any stories of an Amarok turning someone into a wolf as a punishment?"

"Certainly. The first that comes to mind is a one my mother told me. A man took his wife and child far into the bush, a long ways away from the tribe. It was a harsh winter. He was convinced that he could find a caribou and feed his family. One day, he was out hunting, and he came across an Amarok. He begged the god to help him. The Amarok told him to return to his tribe. But the young man was proud and wouldn't listen. Weeks went by and he still couldn't find anything to eat. He went mad, and in his madness, he killed his wife and child and cooked their flesh on the fire and ate them. The Amarok approached the camp. The man wept and begged forgiveness. The wolf god said that the young man could keep his life but that his humanity had been forfeited. So the Amarok turned him into a wolf."

"That's incredible," Julie said. "Nothing remains concealed from the Amarok."

"Yes," Josie said. "That's what they say."

Julie was sloppily scribbling in her Moleskin as fast as she could. Her fingers were sweaty and her face was flushed with blood.

"Do you know of any stories where a family was cursed with a line of werewolves?" Julie asked. "Like, each son down the line became a were-wolf."

"Indeed I have. There's a story of a man who had his eyes on a young girl. Except that he was already married. The problem was that his wife couldn't give him any children. So, he figured he'd get rid of this one and go after the young one. One day, he took his wife into the woods to go fishing. He killed her and left her to the wolves. Told everyone that she'd gone off into the woods herself and must've been attacked. No one found the body. Well, he got his new wife and soon enough she was pregnant. All of a sudden, the man started acting strange. Every night of the full moon, he'd disappear into the woods, not to be seen for days, come home all beat up and wouldn't say what'd happened to him. Then, when the child was born, he and the girl disappeared themselves. Except this time, they found the girl's body. And shortly after that they found the man, stark naked and raving mad, yelling and bawling, covered in blood. Saying that he'd been transformed into a wolf and it wasn't his fault. The men knew then that he'd killed both his wives. They shot him right there. The girl's parents raised the boy. He was a gentler soul than his father. But when he grew up and was married, the same thing happened. His wife became pregnant and he started acting strangely, disappearing during the full moon. Then, one night, he went into the woods one night and never returned. This contin-ued all the way down the line until one of the boys decided he wasn't going to let the same thing happen to him. So he camped out in the woods and waited for an Amarok. When the wolf god appeared, the boy asked it, 'Why do the men in my family go mad?' The Amarok told him, 'You are being punished for the actions of a forefather.' The boy asked, 'How can I atone?' The Amarok said, 'It is too late for you. It is for your son to atone. He must offer your life to me as sacrifice. Only then will your blood be cleansed.' When the boy grew up and had a son, and the son became a man, he ex-plained to him that he would have to kill his father. The son didn't want to do it, but the man insisted. So, one night, they went out into the woods, and the son killed his father, ending the curse."

The words on Julie's notebook were smudged. She stopped writing. She thought of her dream, of seeing Tyler standing over the body of a man he'd killed, his throat torn out. Was the man Joseph?

"What's the matter, love?" Josie asked. "You've gone right pale."

"I'm sorry," Julie said. "I'm suddenly feeling a little woozy."

She picked up her mug of tea. The cup rattled as she tried to bring it to her lips, spilling over the top. She laid it back down on the table, the black tea quivering inside the white porcelain. Air stuck in her lungs as she struggled to breathe. A spiky ball of anxiety throbbed in her chest. When she thought of the mass of life growing inside her belly, the room spun violently. She tried to swallow her tears, but they gushed down her cheeks. Josie helped her up out of the chair and over to the daybed. Rapid thoughts populated Julie's mind, escaping her control. She lay down and tried to douse the forest fire inside her mind.

"I'm pregnant," she said, finally. "And whenever I feel light headed or sick I get a panic attack. I don't know what I'm going to do. I haven't even told my parents yet."

"Honey, it's an awful racket," Josie said. "I knew many girls who ran off when they got a man's seed inside them instead of telling their parents. Or they gave it away. Left town for a few months and told everyone they went to Boston or some such thing. There's no one who can tell you how to carry it. You got to do what's right by you and that child. And the only person can tell you that is yourself."

"Thank you," Julie said. "I think I'm going to go back to the motel and lie down. Thanks again for your help."

"Not at all, love," Josie said. "You go on and feel better. If you want to talk some more tomorrow just drop by."

Julie stood up slowly. Beside the day bed, she noticed a framed picture. A man was holding a baby. The baby had smudges of grease all over its face and had a defiant look on its face, scowling at the camera. But it was the man that drew Julie's attention. He looked familiar.

"That's me as a young child," Josie said. "I'd gotten myself burned playing around the stove. My mother smeared poultice all over the burns. That's what's on my face."

"Who's the man?" Julie asked.

"That was the doctor at the time."

"Do you remember his name?"

"I believe it was Dr. Hunt."

Julie imagined Joseph without a beard and could easily see the resemblance. She had to get out of the house then before another panic attack happened. They said their goodbyes and Julie walked out the door. The fresh air cleared her lungs and mind. Even the flies were a welcome distraction. The sun was setting over Cartwright. A maroon sky burnished the harbour. Julie walked along the rough road towards her motel, which sat at the tip of the equally rough highway. In the distance she could hear Josie return to the steady rhythm of chopping wood. The breeze was soft and cool. Each step and each breath brought her feet a little bit closer back down to earth. The story she'd given Josie about her pregnancy-induced panic attack wasn't entirely honest, but it was a confession of sorts. She felt like offering at least that morsel of truth compensated somewhat for her false pretenses. She understood then that sometimes telling the truth required fabrication, that sometimes it had to be a creative act. It was the only way to achieve the catharsis of confession. Fiction could be an act of redemption. First with Ron and now with Josie, she began feeling comfortable with the identity of a writer, even though it was actually a disguise. Despite all the drama in which she was presently immersed, an idea began to formulate: perhaps she could work with Josie to compile all her folklore. She would be Josie's amanuensis. Together they could write a compendium of local Labrador stories. It was clear the woman was sitting on a wealth of material. It was an opportunity to consider in saner, and hopefully soon, times.

The bells above the motel's entrance jingled as Julie opened the doors. The motel was about the size befitting a town of barely five hundred people. Julie had her own room. Tyler and Joseph shared another. When she got in, she lay down on the bed without bothering to pull off her shoes. She soon heard a rap at her door.

"It's me," Tyler said.

"Come in," she said.

She didn't move off the bed and kept her gaze fixed on the stuccoed ceiling.

"How did it go?" he asked. He came over and looked down at her face. "You look pretty spooked. Everything okay?"

"I'm fine," she said. "We have a lot to talk about. Where's Joseph?"

"He's outside meditating. He should be done soon."

"What have you guys been doing all day?"

"Just wandering around town. We went to the old residential school. Creepy place. Joseph kept talking about how there's a darkness at the edge of town, waiting to reveal itself. Very Springsteen."

"Yeah, well, I think he might be right."

Tyler sat down on the bed beside her.

"I want to apologize," he said. "Not just for how I've been acting lately, but for the last few years. I've been thinking a lot about what you said. About how I'm stuck in a rut and afraid to pull myself out."

"I shouldn't have said that," Julie said.

"No, you were right. I understand why you didn't tell me about law school. I needed to grow up. I still do. But I want to make something of myself. I want to go back to school. Get a degree, get a real job. Joseph said he'd pay my tuition. I realize things between us haven't been good for a long time, but if you'd give me another chance, I'd like to give it a shot. I can enroll at St. Mary's. Rent out mom's house while we're gone. And if you don't want to give us another shot, that's okay, I understand. But I'll support you and the baby if you decide to keep it."

Julie lay on the bed, unable to absorb all the things that were going on. It was clear that Tyler had changed. And not just a minor, shot-term adjustment. While not exactly ideal circumstances, the time spent with Joseph was healing. The black hole was receding. It was being eaten by the wolf. But what would happened when the wolf consumed it totally? Would only the wolf remain? She took a deep breath and was about to respond when Joseph entered the room. He saw the look on her face and knew she had something grave to reveal.

"Alright," Joseph said, sitting down. "What did you find out?"

Julie recounted Josie's two stories about Amarok and the werewolves. When she was finished there was a long period of silence as everyone tried to absorb everything she'd just said.

"Hold on," Tyler said. "You're telling me that I have to kill Joseph?"

"I'm not saying that," Julie said. "It's just a story she'd heard."

"Yeah, and it's obviously complete bullshit," Tyler said.

"But it might be our own only chance," Joseph said.

"Are you nuts?" Tyler said.

"Can't you see the symmetry?" Joseph said. "Josie's stories are like so many others. Think of Lycaon feeding Zeus his son."

"You're talking about fictional characters," Tyler said. "Zeus and Amarok aren't real."

"No," Julie said. "They might not be real in that Amarok walks around the woods like a wolf, or Zeus lives on top of Mount Olympus, but what if they're manifestations of natural forces, like some kind of primordial moral code. These personifications are just how we as human beings perceive them. We create myths to make sense of it."

"So, you're a pagan now?" Tyler asked.

"Think about Abraham and Isaac," Julie said. "God asked Abraham to sacrifice his son as a test of faith, but then spared him at the last moment. People have interpreted that as a message from God condemning human sacrifices."

"It seems like the roles of Abraham and Jacob are reversed here," Joseph said.

"My point is, what if it actually happened," Julie said. "That these sorts of miracles happen and they're meant to teach us lessons."

"Doesn't sound like a good system to me," Tyler said. "Why doesn't God just tell us what to do. How does He expect us to get the message?"

"We share it," Julie said. "We write them down and pass them around."

"Okay, fine," Tyler said. "All of that might be true. You're still not going to convince me to kill my father."

"I'm not trying to convince you of anything," Julie said.

"I am," Joseph said. "During my meditations, I've seen images of my death. You two are standing over my dead body. This feels right to me, like the endpoint of the curse's trajectory. It feels like a cure."

A chill prickled Julie's skin.

"I've had the same dream," she said.

She and Joseph looked to Tyler. She could see that he too had shared the dream, but didn't want to admit it. It wasn't fair. It seemed like they were teaming up to force him into committing patricide. He was looking for a way out.

"Why don't you just get an abortion?" Tyler said to her.

"Tyler!" Julie exclaimed.

"What?" he asked. "You said you wanted one. That should put an end to it. I'll get a vasectomy. No kids. I'm fine with that."

"What if that doesn't work?" Joseph said. "You'd still be a werewolf. And maybe it would upset the Amarok even more."

"What about Derek?" Tyler asked.

"What about him?" Joseph said.

"We still don't know what he did, or if it really started with him."

"I saw a picture of him at Josie's," Julie said. "He looked just like you, Joseph."

"But we still don't know what he did," Tyler said. "What could he have done that was so awful to deserve all of this? Missus would've heard something about it if he had, wouldn't she?"

"She didn't say anything," Julie admitted.

"We know that there have been many documented cases of abuse at Lockwood," Joseph said. "Maybe he was involved in something particularly heinous."

"But you don't know that for sure," Tyler said.

Joseph and Julie were silent. Tyler stood up and paced around the room.

"I'm ready for this," Joseph said. "With my heart the way it is, who knows how many metamorphoses I have left in me. At least I can make some kind of contribution, make my life and death meaningful."

"Fuck that," Tyler said. "I'm not going to be part of your assisted suicide."

He left the room. They heard the bells jingle over the motel's entrance. Julie stood up to go after him.

"Let him go," Joseph said. "He needs to blow off steam."

"Christ," Julie said, rubbing her eyes. "This is all so totally insane. I don't know how much more I can take."

"Did you notice that one extraordinary thing that just happened, though?"

"Just the one?"

"Tyler referred to me as his father."

"Yes. I suppose that was extraordinary."

"You had a long day. You should rest. I'll go back to my room and wait for Tyler. Good night."

Julie lay in bed. It was only around nine at night, but she was exhausted. She couldn't fight against the heaviness pushing down on her eyelids. When she opened them again, sunlight was pouring through her window. She was still dressed and her teeth were thick with plaque. She showered, got dressed, and went to get some toast and tea at the small buffet in the motel's lobby. She sat at the table in her room and read some Dickens while enjoying her light breakfast. Her mind was briefly free of all her worries and she wanted to take advantage of that. Gradually, however, concerns about Tyler and Joseph snuck in and distracted her. She finished her tea and put down her Kobo. She went to Joseph's room and knocked on the door. There was no answer. It was locked. She walked outside and found him sitting at a picnic table.

"Good morning," she said. "Did Tyler show up after?"

"No," Joseph said. "I asked around this morning. Apparently, he'd been looking for a ride out of town. I guess he found one."

"Where did he go?"

"I don't know."

"We need to get after him."

"We don't know where he's headed."

"What do we do?"

"I guess we head back to St. John's and hope he pokes his head up, wherever he is."

The morning was clear. A few clouds drifted near the sun. People were milling about the fish plant down in the harbour.

"How are you holding up?" Joseph asked.

"I'm okay," Julie said. "Yesterday, when I spoke with Josie about the Amarok, I was hit by this devastating feeling of dread. Like a hole in the ground tore open and I could see the flames of hell flickering. I guess the idea of gods and magic and all that is just so baffling to consider. Like the infinite is too great for a finite brain, you know?"

"To be honest," Joseph said, "it's kind of a relief. Knowing that something supernatural is at work here sort of lets me off the hook. I was never going to figure it out using the scientific method, so now I can just let it go. Obviously, I knew this was paranormal territory, but I didn't know how to come at it. You found the last piece of the puzzle and I'm very grateful for that."

"That's assuming we are right. Tyler wasn't wrong to be skeptical."

"No, but this just feels right."

"You always seem so sure that things are going to work out."

"Believe me, I'm not so confident. I guess this whole thing has taught me to trust my intuition. It was my intuition that told me to hang around St. John's the night you found Tyler in the house. And my intuition is telling me now that what you're saying is right. If something smells right, I just follow my nose."

"Maybe this is like Abraham and Isaac," Julie said. "Maybe we can hope for a last minute pardon, too?"

Joseph considered this thought. He looked out over the bight and took a deep breath.

"Let's get our stuff," he said. "It's almost checkout time."

CHAPTER FOURTEEN (1965)

Derek sat in his kitchen and enumerated for the innumerable time the advantages and disadvantages of marriage. It came down to this: on the one hand, he was very lonely and wanted a partner, but on the other he despised grown women. Time was running out for him. He could only be a young doctor married to his ambition for so long. He was an eminently eligible bachelor and the longer he waited, the more people would talk. He had learned quickly the power of gossip in a small town like Cartwright. People would soon suspect there was something wrong with him. First it would be harmless chatter, but then the stories would gradually turn dark. Little tales from little girls of Dr. Hunt looking at them funny and touching them funny would begin to amass gravity. All the strange theories and anecdotes would attract each other to form a lurid solar system of perverse planets, all circling around Derek's black star. A wife, and even better a child, could nullify all these concerns.

He went over to the stove and added another junk of wood. While many of his patients couldn't afford to pay even the small nominal fee, one of the many alternative payments was a full load of wood delivered to him at the beginning of each winter. It was a typically cold winter's night in Cartwright. There was a stone heating up atop the stove. He would take that into bed with him, which would provide at least a bit of warmth while he tossed and turned the night away.

He returned to the kitchen table. He held a letter from his mother professing the many virtues of young Kate Emberly, the daughter of their friends who was now ready to be married. Derek could picture the little girl. Not exactly nymphet material, but she was quiet and well-behaved. Someone, he suspected, who might blossom into a silent and obedient wife.

There was a knock on his door. It was strong and urgent, but sounded like it belonged to a small fist. House calls this late usually inspired an urge to go punch another hole in the wall, but he'd been working on controlling his temper. Instead, he got up from the table and opened the door. Little Violet stood outside, shivering in her nightgown. She brushed by him and came inside before he could speak. She walked over to his stove and held her arms out to the heat. Her tiny shoes were covered in snow. She tracked trickles of water along the linoleum floor.

"What's going on?" Derek asked. He laid a hand on her shoulder. "You must be freezing."

"Don't touch me," she said and recoiled from his touch.

"Okay," Derek said. He stepped back and sat down at his table. "Are you alright?"

She huddled closer to the stove and refused to look at him. He suspected he knew what she wanted. He'd thought a lot about their moment of passion--often it was the only thing he could think about, especially when he was trying to examine patients on the exact same table. But as amazing as that experience was, he'd crossed the line. He knew that. He'd gotten away with it then, but it was dangerous to risk doing it again. That was Humbert's mistake. The fool had actually tried to have a relationship with a nymphet. They were exquisite snowflakes that ought only to be admired. Once you tried to grasp one in your hand they just melted away.

"Listen," Derek said. "What happened that time at the hospital a few months ago was wrong. It shouldn't have happened. I should have controlled myself. We certainly can't let it happen again--"

"I'm pregnant," Violet interrupted.

Derek felt the room get too hot.

"How do you know?" he asked eventually.

"Because I haven't had my period since that day at the hospital."

"But you're on the pill," he said.

"I stopped taking them," she said. "Before you raped me."

The word shocked Derek. Where did she learn it? Most likely from one of those stupid boys or ugly older girls at Lockwood. *Rape*. It sounded so ugly coming from her little mouth.

"I didn't rape you," he said.

"Yes, you did!"

"Stop shouting. I only did it because I thought you wanted it."

"I didn't want it!"

"I don't remember you ever saying 'no' or 'stop.' And you kissed me first."

Derek watched as she struggled with this truth. She seemed so much older since the last time he'd seen her, that evening at the clinic. Physically, she was still a nymphet, but her eyes had that world-weariness the prostitutes had in Paris, which he so loathed.

"I guess it doesn't matter now, does it?" she said.

"Let me examine you to make sure you're actually pregnant," Derek said.

"No. I don't want you to touch me ever again."

"Fine. How do you want to handle this?"

"I want to go to St. John's and never come back here again. I'll give the baby away to someone."

"Okay. There's plenty of places that'll take care of you. But I don't know if I'm allowed to just take you out of Lockwood like that."

"What do you mean?"

"I guess your mom has to give permission for you to leave. I don't know who has custody of you now that Daisy left. The nuns are very strict about this sort of thing."

"I don't care. Just make something up. I can't stay there anymore."

"There's another way. I used to do it as a student for extra money. I can take the baby out. It's not even a baby at this point, really. It probably doesn't have a face."

"What? No. I told you, I don't want you to touch me again."

Derek stood up from the table and approached Violet.

"Let me explain," he said. "It's the best way to proceed. Trust me. Then, maybe in the spring, I can take you to St. John's and see about fostering with a family."

"Get away from me," she said.

She pushed him. He grabbed her wrists and tried to pull her towards him. She swung her arms wildly, trying to get out of his grasp. Her feet slipped on the wet linoleum floor. Derek tried to hold her, but he fell with her. There was a wet thud as she struck her head against the corner of the stove. She collapsed on the floor and lay still.

Derek knelt down beside her. The back of her head was bloody. Her skull was likely fractured. She still had a pulse and was breathing. If he brought her over to the clinic, he could operate--stop the bleeding, repair the skull. And while she was unconscious he could perform the abortion, as well. But how would he explain all of this? People would ask questions. What was she doing at his house so late? How exactly did such an accident even happen? And what would Violet say when she awoke? Derek felt her head again. In all actuality, there was little chance she'd survive. The injury was quite severe. And even if she managed to pull through, would she have brain damage? She'd spend the rest of her life as an invalid. And it wasn't like she had much of a life to look forward to anyway. She was miserable as it was. Best to put her out of her misery. She owed him her life, anyway. The only reason she survived that dog attack was because of him. She was living on borrowed time. He'd prolonged her fate and it was up to him to correct his mistake. People, however, wouldn't understand that he was performing an act of mercy. He had to hide her.

A little bouquet of blood blossomed on his floor, growing from the wound in her head. Her curly blonde hair was matted with blood. Derek realized that he had to end this the way it had started. He grabbed a flashlight and a knife. He bundled her up in a couple blankets and tossed her over his shoulder. He stepped out his backdoor and crept into the woods.

A full moon hung above the teeth of the treetops sawing into the night sky. Derek stumbled around in the darkness until he knew he was far away from the town, then turned on his flashlight. He searched for paw prints in the snow. A howl swam through the woods. He came upon a frozen pond and stopped. The moonlight glistened on the ice. He dropped his cargo. Relief flooded his back and shoulders. He hadn't realized how sore and tired he was and had no idea how long he'd been trekking through the woods. He unfurled the blankets-rolled-Violet onto the snow. He checked her pulse. Weak but still there. Good. He took out his kitchen knife. He looked up at the sky. It was a clear night. The moon and stars shone brightly. Ribbons of ghostly green light shimmered. The northern lights felt like a blessing. Keeping his gaze upon the night sky, Derek slit her throat. Her life poured out into the snow. He bundled up the blankets and started retracing his steps. Delicate footsteps surrounded him followed by growls. He quickened his pace when he began to hear the tearing of flesh.

He realized that he needed to get out of Cartwright, out of Labrador. The place was making him too wild, inflaming his basest desires. He needed to return to civilization. Surely, he'd paid his debt by now. He would go back to St. John's and settle down with a wife and start a family. That would put an end to all this nymphet nonsense.

He got out of the woods and made it home. As he was about to open his back door when he heard something crunching in the snow behind him. Near the edge of the forest was a gargantuan black wolf. It must have followed him. Derek waited, clutching his kitchen knife. The wolf crept closer and into the light of the moon. Its yellow eyes shone. Derek felt them evaluate him. An icy claw gripped his heart. The enormity of what he'd done became real and colossal. His guilt was overwhelming. It brought him to his knees. He was paralyzed. The wolf could have walked right up and killed him without a fight. Instead, it snorted, then turned around and darted back into the forest.

Derek felt his heart beat again. He stood up and went inside. The fire in his stove was reduced to gentle embers. He stoked them and added more wood. The kitchen warmed and his dread lessened. Once he'd regained his composure he began to laugh off that scene with the dark wolf. He reminded himself that what he'd done to that girl was an act of mercy. How many lives was he responsible for? All that would be endangered if he allowed a misunderstanding like that to get out.

He went and got a pen and paper. He sat down to his kitchen table and started composing a letter to his parents, saying that he was coming home and would love to meet Kate.

CHAPTER FIFTEEN (2015)

Joseph had discovered poetry late in life. He'd been a great reader of non-fiction his whole life--he particularly enjoyed pop science in fields where he was layman--but after he became a werewolf, he cleaved to literature as a means to alleviate his solitude and fortify his sense of humanity. It was an incredibly human experience to reach across space and time and touch the heart of another person. He loved particularly challenging poetry. The density of the language was like working with a puzzle, which unlike, say, a scientific or mathematical problem, overflowed with various solutions. If Chomsky was right, that language was a distinctly human attribute, then poetry was the supreme human activity.

He laid his copy of Wallace Stevens' *The Palm at the End of the Mind* on his coffee table and checked his phone. There was a message from Julie, *Any updates?* She was asking about Tyler. They hadn't heard from him since he left Cartwright. They were in regular contact, monitoring Tyler's house, and updating each other on their lack of updates. Joseph wasn't angry. He understood the appeal of running and was hardly in a position to criticize the son whom he'd abandoned. But tonight was a full moon and Joseph was going to have to get out of St. John's soon if he was going to find somewhere safe to transform.

He resolved to read one more poem and then he'd get ready and leave. He chose "Anecdote of the Jar," one of his favourites by Stevens. It was difficult for Joseph to dive into the great novels because he essentially lived life one month at a time; the idea of projecting his self beyond his next transformation was too far a horizon because he was never totally confident he'd survive. Poetry collections gave him smaller portions to snack on. He'd accepted that he'd never read *Ulysses* or *The Brothers Karamazov*. Such short term thinking ran counter to the fact that long term investing was his main source of income. Investing felt different though because he was also building for Tyler. He was amassing a fortune to leave behind for his son. And now that death was a very tangible outcome and not just a possibility, Joseph realized that it was Tyler who'd kept him alive the last twenty years. If it wasn't for his drive to redeem himself in his son's eyes, he would've given up a long time ago. It was therefore apropos that he'd happily die for his son, too. Most parents would. More than that, he was ready to die for himself. Tyler called it an "assisted suicide." There was a lot of truth to that. This wasn't just martyrdom; it was an escape from pain. Joseph was tired of the pain. The physical pain of the metamorphoses and the crushing burden of living with the imminent possibility of death for twenty years. He'd carried the weight for long enough. However, none of that was possible if Tyler didn't fulfill his role.

Joseph put down Wallace Stevens and was about to start getting ready to leave when his phone buzzed. It was a text message from Tyler, *I've changed my mind about your plan. Meet me at my place. Don't tell Julie.* Joseph felt an immediate sense of relief knowing that Tyler was safe. That quickly faded as he realized this meant they were now going to actually go through with what he'd been imagining for the past month now. His son was going to kill him.

Joseph pulled himself together. He considered whether he should tell Julie. In the dream they all shared of his death, Julie was there. But Tyler was at a critical juncture and a betrayal of trust at this point would jeopardize everything. He texted Tyler, *I'm on the way.* Then he texted Julie, *Haven't heard from Tyler. I'm leaving for the Drook now. Will let you know if I hear anything.* He rushed around his apartment, grabbing whatever he thought he needed. He was about to leave when he remembered that he'd prepared a sack of sandalwood and gorse, which Tyler would need. Unsure if he was ready, he left for Tyler's.

The evening sun was low, spilling red across a clear blue sky. Tyler had clearly waited until the last minute to make his decision. There wouldn't be much time to get down to the Drook and prepare before the moon was up. Joseph drummed his fingers nervously on his steering wheel. Tonight, he could realize his life's purpose and put an end to this disease. Although it was a curse, after all, wasn't it? Or at least, that was the hope. They were working off folktales and dream logic. Joseph would never even know if it worked. His whole life, he'd been a man of science and reason. He didn't believe in God or an afterlife, and yet here he was taking a leap of faith.

Joseph stopped outside Karen's old house. Tyler immediately came out and got in the car.

"Alright," Tyler said. "I'm going to do what I need to do to end this thing."

"So, you're going to kill me?" Joseph asked.

"Jesus Christ, don't say it like that."

"I'm sorry. I just wanted to be clear."

"What is wrong with you?"

"You still haven't given me a clear yes or no."

"Yes. Okay? Yes."

"I take it you have some idea as to how you'd like this play out?"

"I've given it a lot of thought. The only way I'm going to do this is as a werewolf."

"That's very risky."

"Yeah, but there's no way I can do it, like, execution style. I don't think I could live with myself after doing something like that."

"Fair enough. We'll do it your way."

"Did you tell Julie you were coming here?"

"No," Joseph said. As a sign of good faith, he took out his phone and showed Tyler his texting history with Julie.

"Alright. I guess we'll go to the Drook."

Joseph made his way through downtown St. John's towards Pitts Memorial Drive, which took them down to the Southern Shore Highway.

"Do you remember what we talked about regarding my body?" Joseph asked.

"Yes," Tyler said. "No autopsy. You want to be cremated on the spot. Don't worry, I Googled funeral pyres. I think I know what I'm doing."

"I have a sack of sandalwood and gorse in the trunk. That should help mask the smell of burning flesh."

"You are the worst."

Nice weather in Newfoundland was devastatingly seductive. It was amplified by the fact that the inhabitants had to endure to so much preceding and proceeding misery. It was like being in an abusive relationship. On days it was nice, one got fooled into believing the possibility of "what if it were always like this?", disregarding all the evidence stating that this was clearly an outlier. Classic denial.

Joseph drove through the outports of the Southern Shore. Longliners were on their way home from a long day of fishing. He thought of ghost nets, nylon mesh sometimes miles long that snapped off trawlers and floated around the ocean like zombies. They trapped sea life and gradually sunk to the bottom of the ocean as their catch grew. And when all their prey finally decomposed, the nets were free to rise up once again to collect some more victims, gorging and purging, gorging and purging, repeating the process for generations.

They passed Cappahayden and were into the barrens of the Irish

Loop.

"That picture Mom had framed in her room," Tyler said. "She's standing outside the old Montreal Forum. It was the night of the '93 Stanley Cup final. You took that photo, didn't you?"

"Yes, I remember taking it," Joseph said. "My old Polaroid. Wish I still had it. I hocked it early on after my first transformations when I wasn't working and desperate for money."

"So, what was the game like?"

"Oh, it was incredible. The crowd was louder than a plane taking off. It was like being at a party with nearly twenty-thousand people. I don't think I've ever seen your mother so happy. She was the real hockey fan. I was just along for the ride."

"Whenever I asked her about that game, she wouldn't really talk about it. She still had the two ticket stubs in the frame."

"It was our last happy time together."

"I was born nine months later."

"Don't do that. Don't blame yourself."

"Hard not to."

"You've had the misfortune of being born into a family line paying for the mistake of a guy neither of us met. And I have to tell you, you're handling this all so much better than I did. You've got guts. Everything you've been through? You're going to be a great father."

"Yeah, well, that's not going to happen."

"What do you mean?"

"I can't raise a child after what I'm about to do. Every time I looked at him, I'd be reminded of it. There's no what that would be healthy environment for a kid to be around."

"So, what are you going to do?"

"I'll go to the mainland somewhere and send Julie money. Like what you did."

"As an expert on that subject, I can tell you that's a terrible decision. Don't do it, please."

"It was different for you because Mom still loved you. Julie doesn't love me anymore. I'd just be a big black cloud in her life. And the kid's."

"You're crazy if you think she doesn't love you."

"She told me she doesn't want to be with me."

"That doesn't mean she doesn't love you. Look at everything she's done for you. Anyone else would've taken off after that first night. But she stuck around. Only love can make you do something that crazy."

Tyler was silent.

"Obviously I'm in no position to give you relationship or parenting advice," Joseph said, "but after all this is over, I hope you reconsider."

Joseph pulled off from the main road in Portugal Cove South and onto the rocky serpentine path down towards the Drook. He realized this was the last conversation he'd ever have with Tyler, or anyone for that matter. What should he say? What sort of wisdom did he have left to impart? Thoughts and emotions assembled then dissembled in a shifting and shapeless mass that words couldn't possibly pin down and process.

"What was Mom like?" Tyler asked. "Before everything happened?"

"She was funny, quick to laugh. She loved to have fun and pull pranks. Very playful. We didn't have much contact after I left, but whenever we talked I could hear in her voice that she'd hidden away that part of her that glowed. Her spirit, I guess you could say. I'm responsible for that. I broke her heart."

"I think she was happy knowing that you were going to show up. When she was sick, she knew you were going to pick up where she left off. She was peaceful in her last days. That used to upset me. I mean, how could she be so calm knowing she was leaving me alone. But I guess she knew you'd eventually come."

They crested the hill down into the abandoned town. The last remaining light of the day was slipping away. But there was enough to see Julie waiting there in her car.

"What the hell is she doing here?" Tyler said.

"I don't know," Joseph said.

Joseph parked the car and they got out. Julie approached them.

"Why didn't you tell me where you were?" Julie asked Tyler. "I was so scared."

"Are you crazy?" Tyler said. "You can't be here."

"I had to come," she said.

"You promised me you wouldn't tell her," Tyler said to Joseph.

"He didn't," Julie said. "I came because I know what's going to happen. We've all seen it. Why are you still denying it?"

"Whatever those dreams may mean, this is still a dangerous place for you to be," Joseph said.

"I don't care," Julie said. "I have to be here. I'm a part of this." She held Tyler's face in her hands. "I love you. Whatever happens, I'll be here for you. We'll face it all together."

They kissed.

"I love you, too," Tyler said.

"We have to get ready," Joseph said. Tyler let go of Julie and made his way towards the beach. Joseph turned to her. "Run around to all the house and scatter your scent as much as possible, then find somewhere to hide. If this doesn't work, Tyler will come after you and I won't be there to stop him."

"This is goodbye, isn't it," Julie said.

"I'm afraid it is," Joseph said. "It was a pleasure getting to know you. You're an incredible young woman. You're going to accomplish so many extraordinary things. Please take care of Tyler for me."

"I will. Thank you for everything."

Julie walked towards the houses. Joseph went down to the beach and joined Tyler.

"I'm sure you still have a lot of rage inside you," Joseph said. "I want you to embrace it. Let it all out. Totally give into the wolf."

Tyler nodded. He was looking down at his shoes, breathily sharply and heavily.

Joseph put his hand on Tyler's shoulder. "I'm sorry for this. For all of this. I wanted so much better for you. I wanted to cure you and I failed. I wish I could've been there for you when your mother was dying. I shouldn't have waited so long. I should've handled this better. I owed you so much more. Everything I've done has been a huge failure. But at least I can do this one last thing for you."

Tyler hugged Joseph. "Thank you, Dad."

"It's not going to be the same as last time," Joseph said. "Once I feel threatened, I won't be able to hold back. And you can't hold back no matter what. When the fury hits, you have to ride it."

Joseph felt the first painful bubbles of metamorphosis. He looked up to the sky and saw the full moon ascending. Time was up. He closed his eyes and took a deep breath of the salty ocean breeze, then quickly stripped his clothes off. As his muscles ripped and his bones popped, he noticed that something felt different. A numbness in his limbs hid the pain he'd become so well acquainted. A fire in his chest made it hard to breathe. Joseph knew then that his heart was giving out. He fought to get the oxygen into his body, hoping he'd level out once the transformation was complete.

His breathing turned into panting. The world revealed itself through his nostrils. He felt stronger, but there was still a ragged drill burrowing into his chest. He had little time to burn. He searched for Tyler, sniffing the air. A force crashed into him from behind. Powerful jaws bit into his neck. Tyler's scent was everywhere now. Joseph was happy to let Tyler maul him to death, but he feared that if he didn't put a fight Tyler wouldn't feel threatened enough to do what needed to be done. Joseph summoned what strength he had and pushed backwards, slamming Tyler into the beach rocks. Tyler yelped in pain. Joseph was slow to rise and Tyler was ready for him. He made a fast, hard swipe at Joseph's shoulder with his claws. Joseph collapsed in pain. Tyler crept close, growling near Joseph's ears. *Here it comes*, Joseph thought. Tyler, however, having sensed that his opponent was defeated, turned his attention elsewhere. He sniffed the air and howled then took off running.

Darkness edged in all around Joseph. His body felt like it had been filled with lead. *You tried,* he thought. *You tried and failed. No shame in that.* He lay on the ground and let the darkness swell. He could hear the waves crash. *Maybe this is good enough. Maybe Amarok or Zeus or Yahweh or whoever's calling the shots will find this acceptable.* He heard wood splitting and a woman's scream. *Julie,* he realized. *Come on, old man, you're not through yet.* He pulled himself up. Each breath felt like swallowing sandpaper. The metallic taste of blood filled his mouth. The injury to his shoulder was devastating. He made his way to the abandoned houses, limping.

Julie watched the boys walk down towards the beach. The night sky was clear. The moon and the stars kept the world from falling into complete darkness. She took out her phone and turned on the flashlight. She opened her car's trunk and grabbed the tire iron. Armed and ready, she circled around the houses, forming figure eights then splitting them, trying to create some kind of maze that would hopefully befuddle a werewolf's smell, at least momentarily.

She took off her hoodie and left it outside the house farthest from her car. She then ran to the house nearest to it. She walked around to its side to one of its boarded windows. With the wedge of her tire iron, she pried off the plywood. The wood was soft and decayed and was easily removed. She tossed the plywood through the window, then pulled herself up into the house. Once inside, she used the tire iron to hammer the plywood back onto the window frame as best she could.

She scanned the abandoned house with her flashlight. She was hoping to find some old furniture to prop against the doors, but the house had been gutted. A thick, rotted musk surrounded her, which she hoped would help disguise her scent. She tried not to think of the bugs and rat shit under her feet. All these concerns were soon forgotten when she heard wolves snarling followed by a howl. She crept upstairs, careful not to disturb the creaking wood lest it snap. She found an old room with a boarded up window. If Tyler managed to find her, she could easily knock out the plywood and jump out. It wouldn't be a long drop. Then she could get to her car and drive off. It wasn't a great plan, but it helped ease her anxiety. She shut off her flashlight.

After the howl, the night had gone quiet. She could hear the heavy footfalls of something running around outside followed by eager sniffing and frustrated whining. It must've been Tyler. Did that mean he had killed Joseph? Was it a failure? Joseph died for nothing after all? She could hear Tyler circling the house. It seemed that he could sense her presence, but couldn't deduce that she was inside. Perhaps the house was masking her scent as she'd hoped. She was standing in the middle of the room, breathing softly, trying not to panic, when she felt something small and furry glide between her legs. She gasped and leapt backwards. The rat squealed and scurried away. A floorboard cracked beneath her foot and her leg fell through the floor.

Outside, Tyler snarled and barked. Julie heard him clawing at the walls, searching for a way in. He knew she was inside now. She turned her flashlight on and got to work on the window, holding the phone between her teeth. Tyler slammed against the front door and attacked it with his claws. He was inside the house now. He ran up the stairs, but broke through the old steps, slowing him down. Julie had the plywood off but there was a second board, nailed on from the outside. She heard a growl from behind her. The phone fell from her mouth onto the floor, dimly illuminating the room. She could see Tyler's monstrous frame. He paused before her.

"Tyler," she whispered.

He growled and she braced for him to lunge. Then something else entered the house. It clamoured up the steps and into the room. It was Joseph. He pounced on Tyler. They fought in the shallow light. Julie could see them biting, clawing, snarling. The old wood snapped beneath them and gave way. The floor lurched. Julie snatched her phone up, then ran out into the hallway. The floor broke, spilling the two werewolves down onto the bottom floor.

Julie heard them run out of the house. The fight was moving further away. She made her way downstairs. She poked her head out through the front door and tried to find Joseph and Tyler. The noises seemed to be coming from a fair distance, so she decided to make a run for her car. She pulled her keys from her pocket, but dropped them on the ground. She searched for them until a mournful howl froze her still. The melancholy sound split the air then slowly evolved into a human wail. She paused and waited to hear any sign of a wolf. Instead, she heard a person crying. Julie ran to its location. Tyler was bawling atop Joseph's body, speaking incoherently. Julie saw that Joseph's throat was tore open, his eyes lifeless. She dropped down onto her knees beside them. She tried to pull Tyler off of his father, but he clung to the body.

"Tyler," she said. "It's Julie."

He slowly let go of Joseph.

"It worked," she said. "It's over."

Tyler leaned into her and she hugged him. He pushed her back onto her heels and sobbed into her shoulder. She could feel the wetness on his mouth. She stroked his hair, slick with blood. Together they cried.

Dawn was breaking over the Southern Shore. The ocean shone with pink and orange lights. The moon was retreating behind the aquamarine sky, like a great white whale passing from view. Tyler splashed gasoline over the pile of wood, stacked like a log cabin. Atop the pile was the door that held Joseph's body. He was wrapped in towels and blankets, also doused with gasoline. Tyler had arranged the sandalwood and gossamer as Joseph had instructed. He took out his lighter and sparked a flame. With a quivering hand, he lit the fabric. The pyre quickly ignited into a giant flame. Tyler backed away and watched the fire grow. The wood cracked and hissed. Julie squeezed his hand and leaned her head against his shoulder, wiping the tears from her eyes. He thought of what Joseph had told him about a fire's many rhythms. That he could find his heart beat in the movement of the flames. He searched for it as flankers danced upwards into the new day's sky.

EPILOGUE (1993)

Karen stood outside the Forum. Canadiens fans wearing *tricolore* sweaters milled about, speaking in thick Montreal accents, their joual dancing just beyond the comprehension of her ears. Joseph was across the street, directing her into the centre of the frame. She stood beside a small tree whose crown intersected the O and R of FORUM above the main entrance. There was a brief pause in traffic. Joseph darted into the middle of *Rue Sainte-Catherine* to get a better picture. Karen raised her arms, her Roy jersey hanging loosely from her arms. Traffic started again. Drivers announced their displeasure with a medley of horns and outstretched hands in mock outrage. Joseph ran towards Karen, pulling the picture from his Polaroid and giving it a shake. He handed it to her.

"Love it," she said and gave him a quick kiss. "Lunatic. You keep telling me how crazy the drivers are here."

"Had to get the right photo to commemorate the moment."

Karen dropped the photo into her purse as they entered the stadium. Every nerve in her body danced with anticipation. They handed their tickets to the usher, then went to find their seats in the second deck near centre ice. The shiny white ice gleamed with the two CH insignias painted at the face-off circle beneath the giant jumbotron. Flanking the jumbotron were twenty-three Stanley Cup banners hanging from the rafters. Karen hoped that tonight she'd be there to see number twenty-four. She'd only seen hockey games at Memorial Stadium in St. John's to watch the baby Leafs, a mere four thousand capacity arena. The Forum had over nineteen thousand seats. She struggled to comprehend the density of so many people under one roof. More than that, the Forum wasn't a mere building, it was a shrine; history oozed from every corner of the arena. It was the type of place that made Karen suddenly believe in all those silly sports superstitions, that there were indeed "Ghosts of the Forum" watching over the game, waiting to make a puck bounce implausibly into the Habs' favour just at the right moment.

When Joseph had called her and told her that he'd gotten tickets for game five, she was too afraid to ask how he'd gotten them and what he'd paid for them. He told her that it was a celebration for finishing grad school and successfully defending his dissertation – and who knew if they'd ever be in the position to see the Habs win the Cup again. As much as Karen was excited about the game and appreciative of the gesture, she couldn't help but feel wary about it all. Joseph was not the type for surprises or grand romantic spectacles. It was usually her who remembered special dates and was spontaneous or cutesy. It was a dynamic they'd both settled into. It wasn't that he was inconsiderate; he did all sorts of small gestures that made her feel loved. He was the absent-minded professor, always with his nose in a textbook, studying hard. She loved that about him. Moreover, he wasn't even a hockey fan. She saw right through him as soon as they started dating. In his typically bookish way, he'd memorized and recited all kinds of facts that were significant to the Habs in order to impress her. His fastidious preoccupation with figures and dates was rehearsed like some taking an oral exam, not a real fan immersed in the jargon like a second language. And yet, they were this far into the relationship and he was still keeping it up. Perhaps he'd ended up actually becoming a fan in his own strange way. Despite her bewilderment, she finagled some time off work last minute and bought a plane ticket and flew over. Suffice to say, both of them would be paying for this trip for a long time.

Karen's suspicions were only multiplied when she arrived in Montreal. Joseph was acting strangely from the get go. He was excessively quiet and withdrawn, even for him. Her presence seemed to frighten him, like he didn't know what to do around her anymore. He had to be hiding something from her, she concluded. The long-distance relationship had been a challenge. Often, Karen wanted to just move to Montreal, but she didn't want to give up her job at the university. However, that was all over now. Joseph was done his PhD and was coming home soon to St. John's to begin his search for a research position somewhere. Then who knows where they'd end up. This trip should've been one entire celebration, and yet it had been painfully awkward the entire time thus far.

"I'm going to go get us beer and popcorn," Joseph said.

"Thanks, love," Karen said.

She wondered if he was doing that just to get away from her.

The teams took to the ice for a short warm-up. Everyone cheered as the Habs came out of the dressing room. Karen read the names Carbonneau, Muller, Damphousse, and of course Roy on the jerseys but couldn't register that they actually belonged to those same people. At the other end of the ice, Karen shuddered as Luc Robitaille and Wayne Gretzky warmed up with the Los Angeles Kings, taking shots against Kelly Hrudey. However, her faith was immediately restored as she watched Roy handle pucks with his typical swagger. There was a sense all around that the Habs had this one in the bag. After the call on Marty McSorley's stick in game two, they'd taken over the series. Even though each of their three victories came in overtime, it was always clear that the Habs were the stronger team. Roy had a bad game one, but after that he'd been his usual dominant self.

Joseph returned with the grub. He handed Karen a cup of Molson and tucked a big sack of popcorn between them. He had a grave look on his face, like he was waiting for something awful to happen. Karen gave him a smile that was more of a question. Joseph answered with a smile that said, oh no, nothing's wrong. They settled into the seats and waited for the game to start.

The lights dimmed and the singers came out for the anthems. There was an uncomfortable silence during the "Star Spangled Banner" and a smattering of boos. Cheers grew before the singer started "Oh Canada." It was nearly impossible to hear her voice over the crowd singing along. When it was over, Karen heard the full voluble potential of the Forum. She felt it in her chest. Her heart climbed up into her throat and she had to choke back a few tears from the intensity of the emotion. She had never had a religious experience before and she wondered if this was what it felt like.

The teams lined up for the faceoff. Muller took to the centre to square off against Jari Kurri. The ref dropped the puck. Muller battled it back into Montreal's possession. The players moved with such grace, coalescing then breaking out like birds flocking in the wind. Each pass was quick and crisp, as if they had magnates drawing the puck to their sticks. Having only experienced AHL games, Karen thought she was watching a different sport. And for all the exquisite grace, there was a plenty of violence to go along, too. Contact along the boards shuddered throughout the Forum, as fans cheered whenever a Canadien hit a King with a solid body check.

It took fifteen minutes for Montreal to score. Big power forward John LeClair took out a Kings defenceman, creating a turnover. Leeman grabbed the puck and passed it to DiPietro, who blasted it past Hrudey from barely a dozen feet out. Hrudey never had a chance. The Forum jumped to its feet and roared. Later in the period, Damphousse used his great speed to get a breakaway. He tried to squeeze it through Hrudey's five-hole, but the Kings' goalie stacked the pads on him. The period was over. The shots had been pretty even, but Montreal were clearly the more organized team; the Kings only really getting chances on the fly. Gretzky hadn't even managed a shot yet.

"Should I go get more beer?" Joseph asked after the end of the first.

"No, that's okay," Karen said. "Isn't this amazing? Being here?"

"Oh yeah, incredible."

"I know you're not so much a hockey fan as me, so thank you so much for doing this. It's really one of the best things anyone's ever done for me. I'll remember it for the rest of my life."

"No problem," Joseph said. He gave her a quick kiss. "I'm going to get us some more beer."

There it was again. It was like he couldn't handle being around her in a moment of inactivity. She remembered then that the Habs were up 1-0 in the potentially deciding Stanley Cup game five and felt better. However, in each of the last three games, Montreal got off to an early lead only to see LA tie it and send it to overtime. Fortunately, the Habs had been unbeatable during extra-time thus far during the playoffs; they'd won nine straight overtime games dating back to the first round. The logical part of her brain told her that didn't mean anything, and there was no guarantee they'd keep winning. Yet, the Forum had that propensity to seduce her into believing superstitions.

She wondered what it must be like inside the dressing room for the players. It was impossible to imagine Roy being nervous. She guessed that he was probably eager to get back out on the ice. She also wondered how the Kings were feeling. Here they were in the same situation as the last three games. Were they frustrated? Hopeless? Would Gretzky finally step it up? He'd already won four Stanley Cups with the Oilers so maybe he wasn't hungry anymore. He certainly wasn't showing it in the first period. As much as she wanted the Habs to win, she was eager to see the greatest hockey player of all-time show off a little.

Joseph came back just as the second period was ready to begin. Karen wondered if he'd purposely timed his return to avoid talking. The Habs got a power play early in the period. They were buzzing in the offensive zone. Everyone smelled another goal. But the Kings killed it off. Robitaille skated it over Montreal's blue line and dropped it back for McSorley who snapped it past Roy with a weak one. Roy had clearly been caught off guard, likely unfocused from a lack of activity for the first few minutes of the period. The crowd was a little deflated by that one. History was repeating itself. It wasn't going to be so easy after all. Perhaps this was going to be another overtime affair. However, just over a minute later, Montreal was back in the Kings' zone looking dangerous. Damphousse wrapped around the back of the net and centred it for Muller who banged it past Hrudey just outside the paint. The crowd cheered. It felt like the Habs had an answer for everything the Kings threw at them. LA seemed lost and Gretzky continued to underwhelm. In the middle of the period, the Habs were on the power play again. Keane carried the puck over LA's blue lie. He had a two-on-one going with Lebeau. Keane passed it and Lebeau scored. The period ended with the Habs up 3-1.

"More beer?" Joseph asked.

"No, just sit down," Julie said.

"Something wrong?"

"Just sit with me."

"Think the Kings will come back this time?"

"I don't know. A 3-1 lead going into the third is always dangerous."

"Really? Why?"

"I don't know. The team with the lead is over-confident, but the other team feels like they still got a chance. Two goals in twenty minutes is totally doable. Plus, they've already scored once so that gives them confidence. Then they score one and the momentum shifts. They're flying and the leading team is back on their heels. Then they tie it up and they've taken over the game."

"Hmm that's an interesting dynamic."

"Yeah, I'm pretty nervous."

"Don't worry. This is Patrick Roy and this is Montreal. We got it."

Karen laid her head on Joseph's shoulder and held his hand.

The third period started. The Kings threatened but Roy turned them away. Then, twelve minutes in, Montreal got their insurance. DiPietro and Dionne had a two-on-one. Dionne passed it and DiPietro scored. For the final minutes of the game everyone was standing. Karen wasn't sure if she wanted the clock to run out faster or for time to slow down so she could stay in this moment indefinitely. As the final seconds ticked away, the Habs' bench cleared and they flocked to Roy.

Karen turned and kissed Joseph. They embraced and rocked back in forth, celebrating. He was trying to say something into her ear, but she couldn't hear over the noise of the Forum. He leaned back and mouthed the words *I love you* with exaggerated facials. Karen giggled and mouthed *I love you too* back. She saw that the tension in Joseph's face that he'd carried the last few days was almost instantly drained. His eyes were full of love for her.

On the ice, the recently-hired commissioner Gary Bettman presented

Patrick Roy with the Conn Smythe, unsurprisingly. This team was better all-around than the '86 winners, but it was still very much Roy's team. Then came the presentation of the Stanley Cup. Carbonneau hoisted the Cup and summoned Denis Savard, who was injured and not dressed to play. The players seemed to love Savard, although Karen resented him for being part of the ludicrous trade that had sent Chris Chelios to Chicago.

The players circled around the ice, each getting their turn to carry the Cup. Everyone cheered each time a new player picked it up. Eventually, the players retreated back to the dressing room and the faithful left their seats. Fans were still buzzing as they trickled out of the Forum and onto *Rue Sainte-Catherine*. Outside, cars inched forward as the crowd spilled out from the sidewalks onto the road. Drivers seemed happy enough; passengers were hanging outside of their windows, waving Canadiens flags. Bars were packed with rowdy people cheering and saluting their team. The craziness slowly waned as they made their way from the Forum. Karen and Joseph held hands as they walked up towards the top of Aylmer, where Joseph had an apartment in the "McGill Ghetto."

"Let's keep walking," Joseph suggested. "I don't feel like going home just yet."

"Sure," Karen said, sensing that Joseph was acting strangely, yet again.

The giant crucifix atop Mount Royal shone amongst the stars in the clear night. Above it, hung a full yellow moon. It was late, but there were a number of people out along the walkways. They saluted Karen and Joseph when they saw their jerseys. Some wanted to stop and chat about the game, eager for details. They could hear the partying going on down in the city centre. Karen and Joseph sat down near the George-Étienne Cartier Monument. An angel stood atop a tall column, her outreached hand seemingly blessing the drivers cruising along *Av du Parc*. Karen thought St. John's was heavy with Catholic imagery. It had nothing on Montreal.

They sat in silence. Karen was leaning back into the bench, Joseph hunched forward. She'd had enough of these awkward silences and was about to ask him what the hell was going on when he took a deep breath. He slid off the bench and onto one knee. He dug around in his pocket, his face strained. Karen thought he was writhing in pain and was in the midst of some kind of heart attack. Instead, he pulled out a tiny little box and revealed a ring.

"Karen," he said. "Will you marry me?"

All the blood and synapses evacuated from Karen's face and limbs and rushed to the pit of her stomach. She bolted off the bench with a squeal, her hands covering her mouth. She wanted to speak, but the words were stuck. Joseph looked at her, nervously awaiting an answer.

"Well?" he asked.

"Yes!" she said finally.

He stood up and slid the ring onto her finger. They kissed and embraced.

"Is that why you've been acting so goddamn weird the last couple days?" she asked.

"Yeah, pretty much," he said. "I was really nervous the Habs wouldn't win. Probably would've had to change my game plan."

"I would've said 'yes' anyway, dork."

"I guess I needed it to give me the confidence boost."

She admired the ring.

"We should go back to your place and celebrate," she said.

"Absolutely," Joseph said.

They stood up to leave when from out of the trees a big black dog emerged and made its way towards them. It seemed to be looking directly at Karen with its yellow eyes. It was the biggest dog she'd ever seen but she didn't find it scary, at first. It seemed like it was sort of sad, like it wanted to get close to them but was hesitant. As Karen looked into its yellow gaze, she felt the joy evaporate from her body. The dog howled pitifully, which startled her. She jumped back. The dog turned around and took off back into the woods.

"Are you okay?" Joseph asked.

"Yeah," she said. "I just got a little fright, that's all."

"That thing was huge. Do you think it was a coyote?"

"Who knows. Let's just get back to your place."

They made their way back down to *Aylmer*. Joseph's roommates were out, most likely partying somewhere along with most of the city. He grabbed some glasses from the cupboard and they went to his room, which was still a state with papers and textbooks strewn everywhere. From a drawer in his desk, Joseph pulled out a bottle of red wine and poured them each a glass.

"I've been saving this, too," he said.

Karen didn't drink much wine, but she liked the taste of this one. Joseph grabbed a cassette of Bon Jovi's *Keep the Faith* and stuck it into his stereo. He fast-forwarded to "Bed of Roses," one of Karen's favourites. Joseph pulled her up off the bed and they danced. When the song was over, they kissed. They undressed as "If I Was Your Mother" played. The music stopped as Side One ran out of tape. They made love in the silence. After they were finished, Joseph stood up and flipped the tape over. He poured them some more wine.

"Where's that picture I took?" he asked.

"In my purse," Karen replied.

Joseph got the photo and went over to his desk. He grabbed a sharpie and wrote on it. He handed it back to Karen.

To many more nights together.
And many more Cups!
Love,
-J

She read it and smiled, wiggling her fingers with the engagement ring. She laid the picture on the nightstand and Joseph joined her in bed. They made love again.

CARCHARODON

PAUL CARBERRY

CHAPTER ONE

The **Swift Current**
Near the Grand Banks
Off the Coast of Southern Newfoundland

The waves lapped off the side of the *Swift Current*. Each wave sounded like wet feet slapping against the surface. Jonah McGilvery tried to hold his hand steady, the cloudy liquid splashing over the rim of his cup. He cursed each wave as it jolted his yacht back and forth. A strong southerly gust carrying the unseasonably warm air from Maine over the icy Labrador Current formed a dense layer of fog that had sneaked in. Jonah was too drunk to acknowledge the sudden transition in the weather. The *Swift Current* sank further into the swell of the water as the tide began to surge. Disappearing behind a wall of fog, the coast hid beneath the mysterious midnight sky as the clouds masked the moonlight. White tips at the ridge of each wave were the only reference points Jonah could see as they rolled towards him.

Jonah fetched himself one more drink before heading back to the St. John's port. His company, Labyrinth Oil, had persuaded the federal government to sell him the rights to St. John's Harbour. Several factors had stumbled into place for him that favored the sale. Global warming had started to affect the island of Newfoundland; you could see the drastic changes in the ocean's erratic currents just off its shorelines. The waters surrounding the island had become unpredictable, making it too treacherous for any fisherman to make a living. The decline of the fisheries meant less money for the government, and the economy of St. John's had taken a hard hit. Labyrinth Oil developed a technique allowing them to extract the rich oil deposits deep underneath the turbulent currents of the Grand Banks without having to build an offshore oil rig. This would help generate jobs for the laid off fishermen who had become desperate for work.

Jonah stumbled down the ladder leading to the cabin of the *Swift Current* and nearly toppled over backwards as the ship sank deep into the trough of the rising waves. Jonah clutched the rail and waited until his legs got used to the swells underneath him. His bottle of dark spiced rum rested in a wine holder affixed to the marble counter. He was glad that the large waves hadn't knocked it loose. "One more drink," Jonah lied to himself as he stumbled forwards.

A loud crash rocked the *Swift Current* violently. Jonah lost his balance and crashed hard, face first, into the wooden bar. The glass flew from his hand and smashed against the hardwood boards sending sharp shards of glass scattering across the floor of the galley. A piece of his tooth cracked off, scattering across the bar counter. The room spun around in Jonah's blurred view; the warm, sticky tang of blood filled his mouth as his upper tooth bit though his cheek. He could feel the boat rise and fall with the waves, but somehow the boat was being held in place. Waves crashed over the yacht in a deafening rumble, and water cascaded down the companion ladder in rhythmic spurts.

Jonah figured the waves must have drifted the *Swift Current* against some rugged rocks. He reached up and grasped the forty-ounce bottle, taking a generous swig of rum. It burned as it rushed down his throat and splashed into his empty belly. Jonah walked back to the ladder and got a mouthful of saltwater as another wave crashed over the yacht. He stuck his head out of the hole just in time to watch the next wave roll over the deck. The force of the wave nearly knocked him back down, but he managed to hold on long enough for it to pass over. He pulled himself onto the deck and grabbed hold of the wheel, bracing himself against the crashing wave. There was complete darkness above and below, the fog making it near impossible to see the root of the problem. He took another long gulp from the bottle, wiping his lips with his wet sleeve leaving behind the bitter brine of saltwater.

He turned the ignition of the *Swift Current*, and the diesel engine roared to life as he pushed the throttle forward. The engine howled loudly, but the yacht remained arrested in place; a thick plume of smoke billowed from below. "Curse it," Jonah swore again as he eased back on the throttle. Another wave roared over the yacht and knocked Jonah off his feet, and he slid across the slick deck. His leg smashed hard into the metal railing, and an excruciating pain radiated from his thigh as his femur splintered into pieces. The *Swift Current* bobbed up and down in the raging waves, water crashing over Jonah making it hard to breathe. He reached back and tried to pull himself away from the railing, but his hands slipped in something oily. He glanced over his shoulder, and a chill shot down his spine. A giant tentacle full of suckers ran over the deck and down the side of the yacht. It must have been roughly twenty-feet long and nearly a foot thick. The massive tentacle of *Architeuthis dux* had been holding the *Swift Current* in place.

"Jesus Christ." Jonah tried to stand up, but the pain in his leg was overwhelming. He fell flat on the deck, dragging himself towards the steering column. The boat began to rise with the tide, but the giant squid held the stern of the vessel in place. Jonah reached out for anything to stop himself from slipping. Another wave crashed down on him. The force sent him hurtling towards the colossal squid, its shiny white beak waiting for him. "Help!" Jonah screamed out in vain. He was all alone in the vast ocean with no one around him for miles, the weather much too treacherous for anyone to venture out in. A giant, soulless eye stared back at him from the large pink body. Jonah could see only a sliver of light in its large black pupil. He closed his eyes and braced himself against the jagged beak of the *Architeuthis*.

A loud splash boomed over the thunderous roar of the waves, and a spray of thick slime washed over Jonah. He opened his eyes to find complete darkness over the edge of his yacht. The giant tentacle remained stuck to the deck of the *Swift Current*; everything else torn away. A dark slick covered Jonah's face and mixed with the water on the deck. The boat drifted with the waves now, but somehow the starboard side of the yacht turned towards the waves. Jonah looked on in horror as a giant wall of darkness towered over him. The wave pounded the *Swift Current* and sent him tumbling into the water.

As Jonah plunged into the icy cold waters, his muscles seized solid with shock. He screamed; air bubbles escaped his mouth, dancing around his face. He didn't recognize which way was up, water covering him like a black sheet pulled over his eyes. Jonah kicked his legs and thrashed his arms once the shock wore off, not knowing which direction the surface was. Darkness shrouded him.

Something powerful snapped closed over his chest, driving the remaining oxygen from his lungs. Razor-sharp teeth pierced his flesh, shredding the soft meat with ease. Jonah felt blood pumping out of his body through the jagged wounds. He peered down and came eye to eye with the cold dead eyes of his maker. With a brutal jerk of its body, the *Carcharodon carcharias* tore hunks of flesh from its prey, its jaw jutting forward to get a stronger grasp on the carcass in its mouth. The juice from the giant *Architeuthis* had sent the giant great white into a frenzied state. It devoured Jonah whole within a matter of minutes. This creature stalked the ocean for forty years now, and five years ago it was driven into the deepest parts of the ocean by orcas and over fishing. The frigid cold waters of the ocean had altered this shark into sizes not seen by humans before. Lateral lines, tubes that ran along the enormous creature's body, filled with fluids that helped it sense vibrations in any direction. These lines began just under the creature's snout and ran down the sides of its body, helping it to track down its prey. With every movement of its body, the muscles enveloping the canals warmed the fluids inside, allowing the shark to stay warm in the frosty depths of the ocean. Thirty feet long, weighing close to eight-thousand pounds, it wasn't the only great white shark cruising the Grand Banks of Newfoundland.

CHAPTER TWO

Newfoundland and Labrador

Five-hundred million years ago a warm equatorial water mass called the Iapetus Ocean covered the land mass that would form Newfoundland. The continents of Europe, Africa, and North America surrounded the Iapetus Ocean. Over the next one-hundred million years these continents drifted towards each other on a collision course by forces deep within the earth's mantle. This collision smashed the ocean floor into jagged rock formation, thrusting up huge land masses to establish the Appalachian mountain chain. We find this mountain chain throughout the British Isles and all the way to Norway. Once this tremendous collision ended four-hundred million years ago, it formed one giant land mass called Pangaea.

Then, 225 million years ago, the same forces that set the continents on a collision course ripped them apart. This left a piece of Africa on Signal Hill in St. John's, North America's oldest city. As the continents drifted apart, it created a large gap which filled with water, forming the Atlantic Ocean. Then, during the ice age, gargantuan glaciers formed across the earth. Once these giant, frozen masses of ice melted, they carved the landscape of the island that the people of Newfoundland call home. These sheets of ice reached upwards of a kilometre in thickness and carved the land to form lakes and cut deep enough to form rivers and lakes. Bays located on the western coast of Newfoundland resemble the fjords in Norway.

Over hundreds of millions of years, different species roamed the earth. Dinosaurs roamed across the land that is now Newfoundland during the Jurassic and Cretaceous period. Abundant aquatic life-forms filled the waters surrounding Newfoundland. The codfish, so plentiful, could block the passage of European ships. Seal hunting off the coast of Labrador had once been a thriving industry but now faltered because of different animal rights activists. Casting a bloody image over the industry, it soon faltered. Even the whale hunting industry boomed during the twentieth century.

Newfoundlanders have suffered over the last century. The people living here have seen great tragedies befall the citizens in unimaginable disasters. The sealing disaster of 1914 was the start of a long list of tragedies that shaped the harsh way of life in Newfoundland during the last century. During a wicked storm on the ice flows on March 30, 1914, the crew of the S.S. *Newfoundland* and the S.S. *Stephano* returned to the ice. They left to kill seals, despite the signs of worsening weather. Both captains thought the sealers were safely aboard the other vessel. The sealers, caught in the freezing rain and darkness, endured a night without shelter. Then, still soaking wet from the night before, a snow storm struck the next day. Only fifty-four men out of the 132 sealers survived the forty-eight-hour ordeal from hell. Captain Isaac Randell of the S.S. *Bellaventure* rescued them from their horrible fate. The survivors suffered life changing injuries from the extreme frostbite. Many sealers had lost limbs and fingers. This same storm claimed the lives of the entire crew of the S.S. *Southern Cross*. While official marine court of inquiry determined that the ship sank in the same blizzard, they could not find evidence to verify this. People believe greedy owners allowed the *Southern Cross* to sail with rotten boards, which succumbed to the pressures of the heavy sea. The storm took the lives of over 250 men from the three sealing ships, a collective tragedy known as the 1914 Newfoundland Sealing Disaster.

On the Burin Peninsula in November, 1929, a tsunami carrying giant waves at forty kilometers an hour pounded the shores. It washed entire homes from dozens of communities out to the sea, killing twenty-eight people and leaving hundreds more homeless. This destructive force of nature only compounded the economy of Newfoundland and Labrador during a worldwide depression. Back in 1929, the country didn't own a seismograph or tide gauge. This device could have warned the residents of the island the tsunami was approaching after an earthquake rattled the Grand Banks, registering a 7.2 on the Richter scale. At 7:30 pm on the eighteenth of November, residents along the Burin Peninsula noticed a severe and rapid drop in sea level. Unknown to residents, this was moments before the trough of the tsunami's first wave stuck. Portions of the ocean floor that had remained submerged for years was now exposed. This sudden drop in water levels caused docked boats to tumbled over onto their sides. Then just minutes later, three successive waves hammered the shores, flooding the coastline and raising the water up to twenty-three feet above normal. The swell in the peninsula's long narrow bays caused the water to rise as high as eighty-eight feet. There was no refuge that night, the storm only a fraction of the ocean's wrath that day. In only thirty minutes powerful waves ripped homes from their foundation. Motor boats and schooners swept out to the sea. The enormous force destroyed wharves and fish plants. Thousands of pounds of salt cod washed back into the ocean. In another cruel twist of fate, a snow storm damaging the telegraph wire isolated the entire peninsula from the rest of the world. It was not until three days afterward that the outside world learned of the fate of the Burin Peninsula.

A German submarine attacked the S.S. *Caribou* during the Battle of the St. Lawrence by a German U-boat on the night of October thirteenth in 1942. The night was pitch black with no moon. Under the command of Ulrich Graf, U-69 spotted the *Caribou* belching heavy smoke off the coast of Newfoundland. At 3:40 am, confusing the *Caribou* for a two-stack destroyer, Graf sent a lone torpedo into the starboard side. The explosion caused mass chaos, and, in a sadistic twist of fate, several of the lifeboats were unable to launch or were destroyed. This forced many passengers to jump overboard into the bitter cold Atlantic waters. Out of the 230 people aboard the *Caribou, 136* perished.

On the fourteenth of February, 1982, the Ocean Ranger received reports of an approaching storm caused by a major Atlantic cyclone. Neighboring rigs had received reports of a broken port light and water in the ballast control room. Stormy seas of up to sixty-five feet with winds gusting at one-hundred knots pounded the Atlantic Ocean. At 0052 local time on the fifteenth of February, the Ocean Ranger sent out a call noting a severe list to the port side of the rig and called for immediate aid. During the night, the adverse winter storm sank the Ocean Ranger. A crew of eighty-four lost forever.

The ocean has played a huge role shaping the lives of Newfoundland-ers. Waves eroded the rocky shorelines and claimed countless victims. With the effects of greenhouse gasses changing the world's climates and melting the ice caps, global warming will soon ravage the shores of Newfoundland and Labrador. The melting ice caps flood into the Labrador Current, carry-ing an influx of frigid water to the island of Newfoundland.

Bergmann's rule states that creatures with greater masses are better able to regulate their internal body temperature. Creatures who live in cold water will grow larger. Now with the waters off the coast of Newfoundland and Labrador colder than ever before, the creatures that inhabit the sur-rounding waters will increase in magnitude.

CHAPTER THREE

St. John's Harbour
Harbour Masters Quarters
Labyrinth Oil News Conference

The sun burned a golden yellow high in the sky, piercing through the haze of the mid-afternoon smog. Kevin O'Reilly remained in the cab of his old Dodge with the air conditioner turned up, staring at the temperature readout on the dash. Another sweltering day in the mid-thirties, an extraor-dinary occurrence for two straight weeks in September. This summer was the hottest on record, breaking last year's temperatures with ease. Global warming had wreaked havoc for years and there was nothing to be done about it.

Kevin parked outside of the Harbour Masters Quarters, expecting the news conference scheduled by Labyrinth Oil. He regularly discovered an excuse to escape home early. His marriage had been breaking down for years, and, with the increased pressure imposed on it, the less effort Kevin put into working on saving it. His wife, Amy, had tried desperately to conceive children, but the doctors had determined that he wasn't capable of reproducing. The marriage fell apart the day she told him she was pregnant; she claimed it was a miracle, but Kevin had his doubts. Rumors of his wife's unfaithful ways spread throughout town, making him a laughingstock. Paternity tests proved his doubts correct, but by that time he had grown to love the child as his own. Once his son had grown up and moved off to college, Kevin had no reason to stick around but he had lost his youthful good looks. His broad shoulders and muscular chest looked smaller now compared to his growing stomach. His hairline fading into a widow's peak with streaks of grey taking over his copper curls. People didn't look at him the same way anymore; girls no longer turned their heads when he walked into a bar. He generally spent too much time and money on an attractive lady at the bar before she left with a younger man. He yearned for those days.

An irate mob assembled outside in the parking lot, composed of two very distinct groups of protesters. Their common hatred united each with their own reasons to hate Labyrinth Oil. Burly fishermen comprised the first group, agitated by the blistering sun as they waited for the announcement. Even though everyone had known the rumors for months, people were still turning up expecting the crushing statement. Kevin had given up being a fisherman at an early age, instead choosing to work for the coast guard after struggling for years to make ends meet. The government had always kept the fishing industry in Newfoundland down even though everyone knew how bountiful the Flemish Cap was just off the southern coast. For hundreds of years until the cod moratorium in 1992, the Flemish Cap provided the fisherman of this province a living. For years other countries continued to reap the benefits of the fertile fishing grounds, while the hardworking people of this province had to stand by and watch.

It took years for the rights of the Grand Banks and Flemish Cap to be rewarded back to Canada and handed over to its rightful owners. Newfoundlanders were so close to bringing the fishing industry back to the top, but it happened about ten years too late. Labyrinth Oil had discovered an oil reserve so large they would stop at nothing to get their greedy hands on it. Their claim to fame was their revolutionary oil pumps that sucked the oil straight from the grounds off the coast of South Africa. The pipes contained suction pumps and motors within junctions every fifty metres, drawing the valuable fluids out with no oil rigs in the water. They had come under scrutiny from environmentalists who believed they altered whale migration routes, but they couldn't prove Labyrinth Oil had been directly involved. One thing was certain, the fishing industry in South Africa suffered when Labyrinth Oil placed their oil pipes.

The other half of the angry gathering were environmentalists, the brains to the fisherman's brawn. They were a mixture of university professors, students, and "hippies," as Kevin often said. Kevin didn't understand their plight. They weren't fighting for their jobs or money. They were fighting for the environment. Kevin looked around at their signs that read "Save the Whales," "Protect our Environment," and "Global Warming." They hollered out nonsense about how oil was ruining the planet. Kevin shook his head in disgust as he listened to their cries. Didn't they understand that the world ran on oil and without it they'd all be living in the dark ages?

It was time for the meeting to take place, but no one had walked onto the stage yet. Kevin grabbed a better view of the press conference. He turned off his truck and opened the door. A smothering heat smacked him in the face. Beads of sweat rolling down his back, Kevin thought about closing the door and cranking the air conditioning, but the electric crowd urged him closer. The angry grumbling and high-pitched fever that swept over the raucous assembly immediately infected Kevin, drawing him into the growing mob. Harbour security and the local law enforcement had assembled near the stage, working to keep matters under control.

"Get out here!"

"You're destroying our oceans!"

"Yellow-bellied coward!"

"Show yourself!"

"Trying to take away my livelihood!"

Men and women shouted at the empty stage, waiting impatiently for Jonah McGilvery to walk out of the Harbour Masters Quarters and onto the platform. "Where are you? You're a piece of shit!" Kevin screamed out, trying to push things further towards a confrontation. The crowd didn't need much of a push it seemed; it had been teetering on the brink of hysteria.

"You fucking prick!"

"I'll gut you!"

Police officers shouted out warnings to the mob, advocating for calmness. A wicked smile crossed Kevin's face as the officers' pleas fell on deaf ears. People hollered hateful threats at Jonah that fueled the crowd, each insult enticing another horrid remark.

The doors of the Harbour Masters Quarters opened, a hush fell over the parking lot as they waited for Jonah to show his face. A young Asian man dressed in a grey suit led the way. He slicked his short, dark hair back. A white dress shirt poked out beneath the grey tunic. His brown shoes shimmered in the sunlight. He was followed by a tall Asian woman in a maroon dress, her long black hair streaked with platinum blonde highlights. Her tanned skin caused the man to look pale in contrast. Her darkened features caught Kevin's attention. The door closed behind them without an appearance by the guest of honour, Jonah. They walked up the ramp, the woman's high-heeled stilettos clipping off the metal with each stride. Low rumbles and murmurs spread amongst the fishermen once again. They felt like Jonah had turned his tail and ran from the angry mob. People shouted out the word "coward" repeatedly, but Kevin fixated on the woman. Her dress hugged her curves, showing off her attractive toned figure. The man stepped up to the microphone, resting his hands on the edges of the podium. The woman strayed to the rear, just out of Kevin's view. He worked to force his way through the crowd, but people had stuffed themselves together trying to get close to the stage.

"I apologize, but Mr. McGilvery couldn't be here." An angry roar erupted from the crowd, drowning out the next words from the man's mouth. The man paused and patiently waited for the noise to die down before he continued. "I am Mr. Kurosawa, the chief financial officer of Labyrinth Oil." Mr. Kurosawa pointed over his shoulder towards the woman in the red dress. "And this is Miss Eguchi, the head lawyer for our company."

Unimpressed by their titles, the crowd grew more irritated. The extreme heat wasn't helping matters. The sun's brilliant rays igniting the mob's fuse. Security guards up front struggled to keep the angry protesters from pushing their way onto the stage. Police officers called for backup, realizing that a powder keg was about to go off. Mr. Kurosawa held up his hands pleading for order.

"Pipe down!" Kevin barked. "We need to hear what he has to say." Mr. Kurosawa nodded at Kevin, but Kevin wasn't interested in Kurosawa's approval. He tried to glimpse Miss Eguchi. He hoped that his command of the crowd would impress her but he couldn't see her through the giant mob of angry fishermen.

"I am proud to announce on behalf of Labyrinth Oil we have purchased the St. John's Harbour." Mr. Kurosawa shocked the crowd. Everyone stood with their eyes wide and jaws dropped. People expected the news of an oil pump, not the acquisition of their harbour. With the crowd hushed Mr. Kurosawa foolishly carried on, not understanding what was going through the mob's mentality. "We will establish several oil pumps into the territory of the Grand Banks and the Flemish Cap."

"What's happening with the harbour?"

"How's this going to affect the fishery?"

"What are the plans for the boats docked in the harbour?"

A chorus of questions erupted from the crowd all at once. Mr. Kurosawa looked over his shoulders to Miss Eguchi, covering the microphone with his hand as they spoke.

"Where is Jonah McGilvery?"

"Get that bastard out here! I demand answers!"

"I will kill you!"

Miss Eguchi approached the dais, and they could scarcely hear her delicate voice. She had to repeat herself. "There will be no further questions."

The two Labyrinth Oil employees fled the stage, but the crowd had heard enough. Security guards and law enforcement officers pushed back as the mob tried to force their way into their path. Angry shoves and curses accompanied death threats directed towards the fleeing employees. Two guards opened the doors for them as several more security ushered them past the mob and into the building. Fishermen slammed their fists into the Plexiglas, trying to break down the door and force their way inside.

Sirens blared as the squad cars pulled into the parking lot. Cops dressed in riot gear flooded into the crowd, trying to get them to leave without further incident. Kevin backed away from the chaotic scene and got back into his truck, watching the train wreck take place from the air-conditioned cab. The riot patrols hauled away the biggest trouble makers, sending a message to the unruly mob. Police officers slammed people down onto the hot cement, placing their hands in cuffs before moving on to the next angry participant.

A vibration in Kevin's pocket drew his attention away from the rioting crowd. He reached down and pulled out his cell phone. "Hello."

"Kevin, we have a call put in on a missing person." Ali spoke softly on the other end. She was the night shift supervisor for the coast guard, which meant if she was still at work someone important had placed the call. "How long before you arrive at work?"

"I'm at the Harbour Masters now. I can be there in ten minutes." Kevin gave himself enough time to grab a coffee on the way. It was only a five-minute walk, anyway.

"I picked up your coffee on the way in." Ali's voice was heavy with sleep. "Our new boss made the call."

"I guess that's why Jonah wasn't at the conference this morning. So, who's missing?" Kevin pulled his pickup around to the edge of the parking lot, parked vehicles lined both sides of the road, but the street was empty.

"It's Mr. McGilvery. His lawyer Miss Eguchi said he took his yacht out last night and hasn't returned. They haven't been able to reach him."

Ali's statement shocked Kevin. "Have they informed the police yet?" The angry mob outside of the Harbour Masters Quarters led Kevin to believe they wouldn't find Jonah safe and sound. He knew of a few fishermen that had rap sheets longer than their resumes and regularly acted without considering the repercussions.

"The police directed her to us," Ali said sharply. "I have already been in contact with the chief of police and we are organizing the search and rescue mission."

Kevin turned down the road that lead to docks. The Canadian Coast Guard Ship *Cape Spear* was teeming with activity as workers prepared the vessel for its search and rescue mission. The white cabin sat atop the bright red hull, the lookout tower darting into the sky far above the roof. They built the CCGS *Cape Spear* for speed while still having enough room for a crew of five. Waves gently slapped the side of the forty-foot rescue ship as the calm harbour waters rose with the tide. Kevin parked his truck in his designated spot as Ali walked towards him with two white cups of coffee in her hand. Her auburn hair was unkempt and fell over her shoulders in a tangled mess, the sun giving it a radiating red aurora. Dark bags formed under her blue eyes. The effects of a long night and no sleep exaggerated the worried look on her face. "Good —"

"I don't have time for your cruel jokes today," Ali cut him off. Her grey tank top clung to her body, her skin covered in sweat from the blistering heat. "You need to get aboard now." She shoved the coffee in his face.

"I haven't even checked…"

"Everything you need is already on board and your crew is waiting for you." Ali had gained a lot of confidence since stepping into the supervisor role. She turned to leave before Kevin could say anything else. She stormed away on a mission.

Not wanting to piss her off, Kevin opened the back door of his truck to retrieve his red and white duffle bag. He slung both straps over one shoulder and walked towards his ship. His crew went about their business at a frantic pace as they loaded the last bit of cargo onto the *Cape Spear*. The dock bounced underneath his feet as Kevin walked up the ramp.

CHAPTER FOUR

Gansbaai
West Coast
South Africa

Andy Grant sat on the wharf with his legs dangling over the edge and stared down into the frothy water. The rough, chaotic ocean waters off the coast of South Africa offered Andy a strange sense of calm he couldn't explain. Three-foot waves crashed into the wood pillars that kept the wharf sturdy; all the boats bobbed up and down with the swell of the ocean. A strong breeze whipped over the water sending a spray of sea water in the air, the salty drops leaving Andy's lips dry and cracked. The film crew that funded his research were late. If they didn't arrive soon, they would have to wait for the tide to come back before they continued filming their documentary in Shark Alley.

Shark Alley was infamous for its great white sharks. The treacherous alley lay between Dyer Island and Geyser Island. Dyer Island was the home to a dwindling population of African penguins, and Geyser Island housed a colony of thousands of cape fur seals. These two islands had remained untouched by humans, both nothing more than jagged rock formations in the ocean, leaving a flourishing alley teeming with great whites in the middle. Andy had been studying the sudden reappearance of the prehistoric predators in the area. The sharks had left when a pod of orcas decimated their numbers and sent them to New Zealand. Now, after several years, they had returned to Shark Alley, bigger than ever. No one had tagged a shark in the Alley for years, and the crew had hired Andy, the former US Navy Marine diver turned cinematographer and paleobiologist, for the job.

Andy heard their truck approaching, the gravel crushed underneath its massive tires. The small fishing village of Gansbaai was impoverished and was desperate for the sharks to return. People only visited Gansbaai now when pods of whales migrated along the Western Cape coastline. The waters around the village were rich with fish, but the costs of processing and shipping their products from the isolated location proved too big a hurdle for most businesses. Few villagers owned a car, and the presence of any vehicles drew the entire village's attention. Andy glanced over his shoulders and wondered how much longer they would be.

Bright sun rays beat down on Andy's neck as he stared off at the light house at the tip of Danger Point Peninsula. A bright blue sky offered clear visibility for miles around. The waters around Birkenhead Rock, located off Danger Point, were notorious for causing over 150 ship wrecks. Even the most seasoned sailor had to be extremely cautious sailing its waters.

"Andy, you have to come see this," Derrick called out from inside the research tent, interrupting Andy's thoughts. His research assistant was a constant pain, getting excited over every last-minute detail.

Andy stood up and headed towards the green tent, the wind whipping the flaps back and forth, the door zipper left half open. He ducked underneath and entered the temporary research lab. Derrick sat in front of his satellite laptop, the blue glow from the screen reflected off his glasses. The constant barrage of meaningless observations agitated Andy. "What is it?"

"We got a ping off the satellite tag *one five alpha*." Derrick said enthusiastically, oblivious to Andy's tone.

"We get pings off the tags all the time, Derrick. That's how we tracked the sharks from New Zealand to here." Annoyed, Andy turned to leave the tent.

"I know, but notice the region of the ping," Derrick was bursting with excitement. "It's originated from the Grand Banks of Newfoundland."

Andy stopped in his tracks. "It must be a mistake." He turned back, curious. "Who does the tag belong to?"

"It belongs to Joan of Shark," Derrick turned his laptop towards Andy. "Notice, she's been firing off signals all morning."

The bright glow of the screen was hard to look at inside the darkness of the pavilion, but the data didn't lie. Every time the shark reached the surface of the water the satellite tag would emit a signal to the receiver. Joan was active, and the receiver off the coast of Newfoundland picked up several signals over the last few hours. "Can you call the research station at the university there and make arrangements for us to get to St. John's?" Andy requested. He had first placed a tag on Joan three years ago just off the southern tip of New Zealand and followed her to Australia. They placed another tag on her there before she disappeared six months ago.

"The film crew won't be pleased with that," Derrick added.

"Well make arrangements for them too. No one ever tagged a *Carcharodon carcharias* there before." Andy had done a lot of amazing things in his career, but he had never been a pioneer. He had become an expert at tagging sharks, but he wasn't the first person. He had tracked the South African sharks to New Zealand, but wasn't the first there either. If he caught Joan of Shark in the frigid Atlantic waters off the coast off Newfoundland, maybe he wouldn't have such a hard time getting his research funded.

"What's the rush?" Derrick sat in his chair, moving sluggishly for the satellite phone. "I mean we already have a tag on her."

"The battery will die and Joan would be lost forever." A door slammed shut outside, alerting Andy to the film crews' arrival. "I'll go convince them to fund us, you make the call."

Derrick stood up, moving a little faster now as he picked up the phone. As Andy left the tent, the bright daylight forced him to squint. He instinctively held up his hand, blocking the sun from his eyes as he spotted the film crew. They had gathered in a small circle at the back of the truck as they gathered their equipment. "Hold up," Andy shouted out over the wind.

The director of the documentary turned towards Andy. "What is it?" Ellen snapped. A sour expression on her bronzed skin, her pink lipstick smeared into the corner of her lips. She must have been in a rush; her red dress shirt was untucked and her hair was tied up in a messy bun. "We're working behind schedule."

"We should travel to Newfoundland," Andy sputtered.

"Are you kidding me?" Ellen snorted, choking back laughter. "You can't be serious."

"Joan of Shark appeared just off the coast." Andy replied, studying the disdain on Ellen's face. His response didn't impress her. The scowl grew more intense as she glared at him.

"So what? Who cares about some shark you've already tagged?" Ellen shrugged her shoulders. Andy's enthusiasm didn't affect her.

"No one has ever tagged a shark in these waters." Andy sold his proposition. "Not to mention she's a shark from right here. This changes everything we know about great whites. If we manage to catch her on film, it would be extraordinary."

"What's so important about Joan of Shark?" Ellen still wasn't buying his sale pitch. Her film crew had already unloaded their gear onto the cart and was heading down towards the boat.

"Wait up, guys." Andy held out his hand, motioning for everyone to hold on. "Ellen, Joan of Shark should just be reaching the age of maturity. I think she went to Newfoundland to mate, and if we could catch her in the act, it would be the first time anyone has ever filmed it." While no one had ever filmed a *Carcharodon carcharias* mating, Joan of Shark didn't head into the frigid waters of the Atlantic to perform this ritual. Andy had to think of something to persuade Ellen to fund his trip, and he knew this would catch her attention.

Ellen motioned for her crew to stop. "What makes you think she would head into freezing cold waters to mate."

Andy had to think of something fast. "There's a reason no one has ever filmed sharks mating." Andy paused and waited for Ellen to nod her head. "I think it's because we've been looking in the wrong place. Get me to Newfoundland, and we can make the biggest discovery about great whites ever. People will throw money at us to watch this video. Research firms will pay through the nose to be part of this groundbreaking research." Ellen stared at Andy with a harsh expression, her pale blue eyes piercing into his. She was studying him to see if he was bluffing. Andy tried his best to keep a convincing look on his face. His heart stopped beating for what seemed like an eternity as she studied him intently, watching for any sign of deception.

"Get that gear back on the truck," Ellen ordered. "Mr. Grant, you better be right about this, or I'll make certain no one ever works with you again. Get your shit packed up, and I'll make the arrangements."

"I had my assistant book the flights. I need you to pay for them when we get to the airport." A childlike smile crept over his steel jawline.

Ellen shook her head. "I pray for your sake that shark is putting out." Ellen stormed off to the truck, slamming the door behind her as she took out her phone. She rolled the window down, a scowl on her face. "Get me some footage of Shark Alley while we wait for the flight to leave. At least we will have something to show for being in this forsaken village."

Andy headed back to the tent to pack up his gear. He needed to get a tag on Joan before the battery in her tag ran out of power; he couldn't risk losing track of the creature. His whole career hung in the balance, and now he may be in over his head with Ellen. A great white shark sighting off the coast of Newfoundland was extremely rare. He didn't know why he would gamble on finding another male in the area. For the second time in his professional career he ran his mouth. The last time it had cost him his job with the Marines -- hopefully Ellen wasn't aware of what led to his dishonorable discharge from the Navy. "Derrick, get the cage ready. We need to complete a dive before we leave this place."

Gansbaai
Shark Alley
West Coast
South Africa

The waters in Shark Alley were unique. The green, murky depths gave the semblance of transparency but still veiled the ocean's deadliest predators from view. These waters were the perfect arena for them, allowing them to ambush their prey from all angles. Glimmers of silver light sparkled brightly just below the surface, the light penetrating only a few feet below the surface. Andy looked around, concealed in a foreign environment where every shadow threatened you from just beyond your reach. The speed of the demons stalking these waters made any reaction pointless. If they desired, they had the ability to stalk and ambush you without your knowledge.

Andy reached out and grasped the metal bars of his pen. No matter how many times he made the dive, he would never get accustomed to the fear that awaited him. Every passing shadow and dark crevice hid danger from view; he could never pinpoint where the threat would emerge. All he knew was the sharks in this area were attracted to the cages and had grown unafraid of them. Some sharks had grown so daring they had earned the reputation for destroying the steel enclosures, turning them into tangled, splintered fragments of metal. If he stayed down here long enough, he would eventually capture footage of a great white shark, and if he stayed down too long, he would get himself eaten. He waited for what seemed like an eternity. Something was occupying the *Carcharodon* in this area. He heard the mechanical groan as the wench raised the cage topside.

"Did you get any footage?" Derrick bellowed.

Andy shook his head. "Not this time. Do we have any old film we haven't aired yet?"

"I'll scrounge up something to fool Ellen." Derrick chuckled. "It's time to go, we will be late if we don't get a move on."

CHAPTER FIVE

CCGS Cape Spear
Marystown
Southern Coast of Newfoundland

The CCGS *Cape Spear* cut through the four-foot swells with efficiency as Kevin navigated his course towards Marystown, the last known position of the *Swift Current*. Equipped with an S.O.S. system, an electronic ping sounded out to the satellite every four hours. The *Cape Spear* rose on the crest of the waves and sent foamy sprays of ocean water over the bow as it plunged back down into the next wave. Kevin kept a close eye on the radar read-out, but all that popped up were small schools of fish and smaller fishing schooners. The swelling waves kept the smaller fishing dories in the harbour's shelter, but some lucky fishermen, with sturdier boats, confronted the rougher waters.

Melvin was scanning the ocean from the crow's nest with a pair of binoculars, his reflective life vest caught every glimmer of sunshine that cracked through the clouds. Dark storm clouds were slithering in from the south and a steady warm breeze had rushed in. Kevin watched as the fog rolled in over the frigid waters fed by the Labrador Current that had met the warm Pacific air. If Melvin didn't discover the boat quickly, fog would make it impossible to spot the ship. Kevin didn't like the last ping from the S.O.S system. He knew the waters around Marystown like the back of his hand from his days as a fisherman. He knew Jonah had smashed his yacht along the craggy coast.

"I can see debris hard to starboard." Melvin's voice chimed in on the walkie-talkie.

Kevin eased off the throttle and spun the ship back towards the jagged shoreline. "Copy that. How far away?"

"I'd say about half a mile," Melvin responded. "It's hard to tell with these waves."

Kevin glared out the window as Melvin climbed down the mast. Now that Kevin was heading back towards the shore, the four-foot waves rocked the boat's hull. Vibrations rattled the entire steel frame of *The Cape Spear*. Kevin had to battle with the wheel to keep his course steady. "Make sure the guys are ready," he said. "I want to find Jonah before these waves get any bigger. They built this ship for speed, not for rough seas." Kevin cursed under his breath at Ali for picking this rescue boat. He realized that time was a factor, but the waters around the Grand Banks were erratic and the impending storm surge threatened to bring in the rolling waves without warning.

"You got it, Skip." Melvin headed through the cabin and down the stairs below to round up the others.

Kevin looked down at the radar, hoping to spot any signs of the *Swift Current* nearby. Filled with green and yellow circles, the radar picked up various marine life swimming around. The screen rattled as each wave crashed into the side of the boat. Kevin pushed the throttle a little harder. He preferred to get *The Cape Spear* in a better position to break the waves.

Kevin looked through the window of the boat, pieces of broken wood and fibreglass floated in the crest of the waves. "All right," he said. "Let's bring her in and get a closer view." Kevin steered the ship towards the wreckage as it bobbed up and down with the swell of the ocean.

"Have a gander at that." Lewis leaned his hand on Kevin's shoulder, a powerful smell of caffeine and liquor on his breath.

Kevin was annoyed by the young officer. "What am I looking at Lewis?"

"The *Swift Current* has washed-up right on shore." The young search and rescue diver's voice was pompous. He yanked off his aviator sunglasses and pointed at the beached yacht. Kevin should have been looking at the rocky shore towards the *Swift Current*, but he wanted to punch Lewis in the face. His spiked black hair and thin goatee screamed hipster, but his brawny frame demanded attention. His collared shirt was unbuttoned just enough to show his shaved chest and sterling silver chain that dangled loosely from his neck. "We can anchor the boat and investigate the wreckage from the coastline."

"That's a good plan," Kevin said mockingly, not trying to hide his disdain for Lewis. "It would take hours to port if we left now. I'll throw the anchor here and you can take the lifeboat in before the tide rises and washes more debris back out into the ocean."

Lewis shook his head in disgust, taking exception to Kevin's tone. He looked like he wanted to say something before Melvin walked back inside. "Looks like we got a storm heading our way."

"Melvin take Lewis on the lifeboat with you and have a look for Mr. McGilvery." Kevin took command of his crew, the tone of his voice growing confident with power.

"Come on, lad, help me lower it into place now." Melvin took notice of the tension between the two men.

Lewis Park stood a foot taller than Kevin, with near perfect posture. The two men locked eyes, testing each other's resolve. Kevin refused to back down. "Run along with Melvin." Kevin taunted him with a sly grin.

Melvin held the door open and lingered for what seemed like an eternity before Lewis walked past Kevin, brushing by him as he strode out of the cabin. Kevin could feel his blood boiling with rage. The newest member of his crew needed to learn his rank. He was already devising a plan to teach Lewis a hard lesson about working in the ocean. He was looking back down at his sonar to gauge his depth when he noticed a large blip on the screen that disappeared just as quickly as it flashed onto the screen. Kevin tapped the filter with his knuckles, checking to see if it was malfunctioning. Outside the window, Kevin looked at Melvin and Lewis as they lowered the orange rescue craft into the rough seas then back down at the radar. He couldn't help look back down at the screen, nervously waiting for the radar to pick up the object again, but it vanished.

***

The prehistoric predator swam through the frigid current, the cold waters suppressing her appetite. She was able to sense the heartbeat of the fish with pinpoint accuracy, able to detect one from the other with ease, the hunter's abilities toned to perfection over millions of years of evolution. Its snout was covered in tiny black dots called ampullae of Lorenzini, which detected the minute electrical impulses generated by moving muscles. A passing school of fish created a sensory overload. Smaller fish gave the *Carcharodon carcharias* a wide berth, making sure they stayed far enough away that the shark's efforts weren't worth the meal. The great white had the ability to look past all the signals it received. It focused on the strange electrical impulses being sent out by the CCGS *Cape Spear*. Vibrations from the vessel created a distraction too strong to ignore, but the size of the boat kept the shark in the shadows.

Global warming's biggest concern wasn't the rising temperatures on the land. It was the deadly impact on the earth's oceans. For thousands of years the great white navigated the oceans using the magnetic fields of the earth. Now that the temperatures of the ocean were changing and the water levels were rising, those fields had evolved. These signalled the sharks to Newfoundland instead of back to South Africa. She wasn't alone on her pilgrimage. Joan sensed the other male sharks closing in on her position. She was in heat and her scent attracted several suitors, but she was avoiding them for now. All she craved was her next meal. The colder waters of the Atlantic meant she required to eat more to maintain her body temperature.

As she got close enough to the boat to realize that it wasn't a whale, she lost interest. She swept her snout from side to side, probing for a meal that would be worth the expended strength. She headed back out to the deeper waters as a giant squid's beating heart grabbed her attention.

The thirty-foot *Carcharodon* raced along the rocky sea floor, her jaw left slightly ajar to allow the water to flow through her gills. Once she reached the drop-off she immediately descended into the murkier waters, getting ready to perform her assault on the giant squid. The colour of her skin allowed her to ambush her prey from below. The dark grey dermal denticles that covered her back like chain mail made her virtually invisible to prey looking down into the depths. The scales on her back resembled razor-sharp teeth. They were smooth to the touch if you ran your hand down her back, but if you went the wrong way it would shred the flesh on your hands to pieces.

Joan focused solely on the beating heart of the *Architeuthis* while still keeping track of any other signals sent her way. For now, she swam with a purpose out into the cold current around the Grand Banks towards her next meal. The powerful electrical signals from the giant squid's pulsating heart rang in Joan's head. Each heartbeat acted like a light house in the dark, lighting her way past all the other disturbances of the ocean. Sharks' survival instincts were far more sophisticated than people wanted to believe; they were not just mindless psychopaths who slaughter for sport.

The Swift Current
Marystown
Southern Coast of Newfoundland

"When is Kevin going to retire? He doesn't have a clue about what's going on out here." Lewis Park vented his frustration to Melvin.

"I don't think that Kevin's such a bad guy." Melvin looked back at the *Swift Current*. "I'm sure he could teach you a thing or two about these waters. He's been doing this for years."

Lewis let the swell of the wave take control of the orange life raft, forcing the small vessel towards the shore. The shore line was mostly jagged rocks. The trees that managed to survive the harsh winters had their growth stunted by the strong winds. The grass was burned yellow from the relentless heat of the sun. "That don't mean much to me, Melvin," Lewis said. "Just because he's been doing something for years doesn't mean he's good at it." Lewis had developed an intense disdain for his boss since his first day on the job. "He doesn't have a clue about the science. I mean he completely ignores the effects of global warming because he doesn't believe in science." Lewis spread out his arms at his surroundings.

Melvin shook his head slowly. "There's more to this job than understanding why the ocean acts the way it does. You have to know how to handle it when you're out in her." Melvin steered the life raft into a small inlet where the waters were calmer. "Do you understand what I mean, Park?"

Lewis blushed with embarrassment. He always respected Melvin because he was good at his job and a hard worker, but he wasn't the smartest crew member in the coast guard. Lewis was more than just a little surprised to be getting solid life advice from Melvin. "Yeah, I do," Lewis mumbled. "I still don't think he should be the captain, that's all," he added.

"Maybe you're right, young fella, but it is what it is," Melvin said as he steered directly towards shore.

The wreckage of the *Swift Current* was only twenty-feet away now. Planks of wood and broken fibreglass bobbed up and down in the water all around the life boat. It had run aground during high tide, and now it was nearly ten-feet aground, left behind by the receding currents. Lewis hopped over the side of the raft. The cold waters pierced his skin like tiny icicles poking at his flesh through his rubber boots. Melvin jumped out on the other side. Both men grabbed hold of the boat and dragged it up the rocky beach until it was far enough away from the crashing waves.

"I wonder what happened?" Melvin said dumbfounded.

"Let's get closer." Lewis unzipped his jacket and tossed it in the orange life raft. The sun was beaming down on them, sweat rolled down his backside. The temperature on land was a sharp contrast to the sea. Frigid waters from the melting ice caps could be felt directly out in the water, but once you stepped foot on land the sun controlled you. As they walked towards the wreckage, the rocks slid around underneath their feet, hitting against each other. Lewis could hear the caw of seagulls over the rolling waves as they flew overhead. He looked up at the sky as the dirty white birds flew past.

Lewis approached the *Swift Current* first. Something had torn a large hole in the hull, exposing the luxurious underbelly of the yacht. "Damn, what is that stench?" Lewis caught a strong whiff of booze as he poked his head into the large gap. There were shards of glass all over the floor of the galley, Lewis spotted one cabinet door open. "Jonah left his liquor cabinet open during the crash."

"I'd say he was fetching himself a drink when it happened." Melvin helped to piece together the puzzle. "The shore is so rocky we'd never see which way he went."

Jonah McGilvery was a notorious alcoholic, and it didn't take long for Lewis to form an opinion. "I'm guessing you're right, Melvin. I'd say he came down here to fetch a drink and wasn't paying enough attention to where he was and ran his yacht right into the rocks." Lewis bent down and picked up a fragment of the rum bottle that still had the label. "Cabot

Tower dark spiced rum."

"Mr. McGilvery's drink of choice." Melvin seemed to enjoy the sweet aroma of the liquor.

"I take it it's yours too." Lewis smirked. Melvin bent down to pick up a piece of broken glass, rubbing his finger over the sticky surface. He put his finger in his mouth once he had enough of the substance on it to taste. "Well what's the final consensus?" Lewis asked.

"Tastes like salt water and spiced rum," Melvin said with a sour expression on his face. "Not the way my woman mixes my drinks."

"To each their own I suppose," Lewis joked. "Can you get on the radio and let Kevin know we will probably find Mr. McGilvery in one of the bar's in Marystown."

"You think he ran off towards town?" Melvin questioned.

"Let's hope so. If not, the poor man got himself lost in the woods over there. I guess we will need to alert search and rescue just in case, but I'm guessing even if Jonah was loaded drunk, he would still see the lights." Lewis stepped inside the *Swift Current*, the glass crunching underneath his boots. Looking around the galley, Lewis searched for any signs of what happened to Jonah. The wooden bar had a small red stain that had dripped down over the side of the bar. Lewis walked over to get a better view and it became glaringly obvious that it was a blood stain. A tiny piece of blood-stained tooth had fallen into the sink. The sudden impact must have caused Jonah to smash his face into the bar as he was taking a drink. He looked down into the garbage can but there weren't any bloody rags or tissue inside. Whatever happened must have caused Jonah to run topside in a hurry. Flecks of blood led towards the ladder up to the deck. The bright red drops stained the shiny metal surface all the way up. Lewis headed back outside, not wanting to disturb the blood stains on the ladder in case the police needed to investigate.

Melvin was sitting on the edge of the orange life raft with the radio in his hand. The sun glistened off the white caps behind him, making his figure nothing more than a silhouette against the bright blue backdrop. The CCGS *Cape Spear* cut through the waves out in the rough seas as it headed towards the port of Marystown. Lewis walked around the yacht and searched for any more signs of blood against the rock in a vain effort. If Mr. McGilvery had abandoned ship, the waves would have washed any evidence away. The *Cape Spear* was tilted towards the water at a slight angle on its port side. Lewis could see the railing had been bent outwards, which caught his attention; every other sign of damage pointed to a crash except that one section of railing. He figured that it must have been from an earlier accident that had never been repaired in ages, but Lewis still got closer for a better look.

Something was lodged in the wood just below the rail. Lewis reached up and felt something jagged embedded in the decking. He was able to get just enough of a grip on it to dislodge it. He pulled down the object and held it in his hand. The sunlight glared off the surface of the giant two-inch tooth in the palm of his hand. The serrated tip came to a deadly point, and the edge of the tooth was razor-sharp along the outside. "What the hell?" Lewis said aloud. He tucked the tooth into his pocket for safekeeping. He needed to call his ex-girlfriend at the Marine Institute to identify which species of fish had left this massive tooth behind. Lewis looked back out towards the vast ocean as a chill ran down his spine at the thought of heading back out there in that tiny life raft. "Fuck me."

CHAPTER SIX

The Marine Institute
St. John's, NL

Kate Hamilton sat in front of her high-powered microscope looking at a slide of bacteria found in a codfish. A restaurant had claimed a local fisherman had sold them a batch of tainted fish caught off the shores of Cape Race. Her students had prepared the sample under her supervision during class earlier, but now she sat in the laboratory by herself. Her desk overlooked two rows of five workstations that ran down the middle of the classroom. Each workstation had its own wash sink, black countertops, and stainless-steel cabinets underneath. Two long countertops lined the walls that ran the entire length of the room. They had built shelves above and below the counters to store the various equipment needed to run the labs.

The room was eerily quiet, the students all gone to lunch in the cafeteria at the other side of campus. Kate didn't like being a teacher, but it was part of her duties at the Marine Institute. They agreed to fund her research on the cod fishery, and she only needed to teach two classes, but she didn't like being in front of so many people and having to speak. She looked down at the watch on her slender wrist and could feel her stomach tighten: only another twenty minutes until her next class. Once her final class of the day finished, she would be free of teaching for the weekend and left alone to work in her lab. While many considered Kate to be beautiful, she didn't have time for dating. She was happiest when she could immerse herself in her work; she knew what she was doing would change the way people viewed the oceans. Kate did her thesis on the effects of the rising sea levels caused by the effects of global warming and its effect on the marine ecosystem.

Her study had earned her recognition from the entire scientific community, and the grant at the Marine Institute here in St. John's. Kate theorized that the health of the Grand Banks off the southern coasts of Newfoundland was vital not only to the island's economy, but it was also a key indicator of the effects of global warming. As the polar ice caps melted into the Arctic oceans, the frigid water poured into the strong Labrador Current. This cold layer of water was changing the ocean's ecosystem, and there wasn't a better place on earth for studying the effects than right here. Species of fish only found in the Arctic Ocean drifted south towards the densely populated fishing grounds of the Grand Banks. Fisherman reported catching several new species in their cod fishing nets. Reports of Greenland sharks escalated to a daily occurrence. Whale migration patterns changed, bringing more whales down the Labrador Current than ever before.

Kate heard the murmur of students as they flooded back into the halls. Students started getting ready for their next class, opening their lockers and chatting about what their plans for the weekend. There was a time when she used to be just like them, but that seemed like such a long time ago even though she had only graduated three years before. Kate looked back down into the microscope. It was just another sample of tissue from a healthy cod. The owner of the restaurant didn't accept that they hired a shitty cook. She placed another slide underneath the microscope to confirm what the other twenty slides had already told her. The door creaked open. Kate didn't want to make small talk with any of her students right now.

"Hello, Kate." A familiar voice from her past sent her heart racing.

Kate looked over at her old boyfriend Lewis Park, standing in the door frame. "Hey, Lewis." Kate's voice squeaked like a teenager. Lewis was leaning against the frame, biting onto an arm of his aviator glasses, his features scrunched up nervously on his face. "I'm surprised to see you."

"You look good." Lewis stared down at the floor immediately after the words left his mouth, his cheeks turning red. "Long time no see."

Kate wanted to rush over to him, unable to decide if she wanted to hit him or hug him. "You never called." She wished she hadn't said that, but her anger muddled her thoughts. "I didn't think you wanted to stay in Newfoundland?"

Lewis fidgeted with his glasses. "Listen, I'm not here to talk about that."

"Then what are you doing here?" Kate cut him off. She had felt betrayed when he moved away, but it had devastated her when she discovered he moved back home without telling her.

"I need your help with a work-related problem." Lewis tried to change the topic, his deep blue eyes avoiding eye contact with her. "Would you examine something I found?"

The hallway grew louder with noise now as her students made their way back to their classes. Kate just wanted five minutes with him. She wanted to get an apology or at least an explanation. "Can you come back after class?" Kate offered in hopes he would agree.

Lewis walked over to her desk and took out a clear plastic bag with a tooth in it. "I'll come back later." Lewis placed the bag down on her desk. "When would be a good time?"

Kate looked down at the razor-sharp looking tooth and recognized it. "It belongs to *Architeuthis dux*." Kate picked the bag up and handed it back to Lewis, who had a confused expression on his face. "A giant squid common to the waters around Newfoundland."

"A giant squid left this tooth behind?" Lewis looked like he had seen a ghost, his skin turned a pasty white.

"Razor-sharp teeth line their beaks in rows." Students filed into the classroom. "My lab will be over in three hours if you need any further explanation."

Lewis tucked the bag back into his pocket. "Listen, I'll drop by sometime if you'd like, but I need to get back to work."

Kate wanted him to come back, but she refused to seem desperate. She sat at her desk in silence, glancing at her students as they settled away behind their stations. The room filled with the sound of zippers opening and closing, books hitting the desks, and chit-chat between the students. "Mr. Park, if you need to see me, I will be here in my laboratory during the hours posted on my door. Now if you will excuse me, I have a class to teach."

Lewis sauntered out of the room, pausing briefly at the door to study her timetable. He looked back at her as he put his sunglasses back on, an awkward smile on his face. "I'll talk to you later." Lewis stood head and shoulders above everyone as he joined the crowd. Kate's face flushed with embarrassment. She prayed that her students didn't notice. "All right, class, open your books to chapter seven. We will learn about the different diseases that affect our fish in the Atlantic Ocean."

CHAPTER SEVEN

Outer Cove
Logy Bay
Newfoundland

David stood on the edge of the bank, staring down at the rocky beach of Outer Cove wondering if he could drive his truck down to the beach. He didn't want to lug his kayak down the steep path, but he saw no alternative way down. His eyes moved back and forth from the rock pools that spread out across the shoreline and the breaking waves as they crashed against the rocks. He felt the rejuvenating energy of the sun against his backside warming his body. Seagulls sang their high-pitched notes from their perches along the jagged coast.

"Well, what's the verdict?" David's wife, Alice, called from the passenger seat. The natural cadence of of the sea mesmerized David, the salty smell of the water and the soft twinkling of sunlight glistening off the waves capturing his attention. "Earth to David."

"Park the pickup and we will have to carry the kayak's down," David answered without twisting around. The couple had heard about a pod of killer whales in Logy Bay and wanted to get a closer look for themselves, but found all the whale sight-seeing tours booked solid. They had used to kayak before the kids were born and didn't think it would too troublesome to take up again.

David returned his focus towards shore and observed the rushing waves as they collided with the jagged outcrops, sending sprays of ocean water high into the sky. Littered with pebbles, burnt logs and discarded campfires, the small beachhead below was a popular destination amongst the locals. The calm waters below were enough to launch their kayaks and give them time to get used to the swell of the waves. Whispers of the ocean breeze tousled David's long blond mane. He closed his eyes and took a deep breath of the poignant salty air.

"David, are you going to help me, or should I carry both myself." Alice had grown impatient, their daughter fraying her last nerve the night before.

"Coming, honey." David hopped over the tiny white fence. The chipped paint and splintered wood reflected years of neglect. "Sorry, why don't you head down to the beach and relax. I'll bring them down."

Alice stood with her hands on her hips, her blue and green wetsuit clinging to her slender frame. She tied her auburn hair into a messy bun atop her head. Her freckles seemed to multiply with the exposure to the sunlight. Her emerald eyes glimmered with the sparkle from the ocean. "Are you sure?" Her voice softened.

"Yeah, I'm sure, honey. We have lots of time." David followed his wife's butt as she strolled away with a sly smile on his face. "Not so fast."

Alice peeked over her shoulder; a playful grin painted on her lips. "You're sweet today." She giggled. "What do you crave?"

David winked at his wife, the intoxicating aurora of the sea lifting away his cares. "I see no one around."

"In your dreams, David." Alice walked down the bank and stopped just before she disappeared from view. "Isn't the ocean just dreamy."

David left the kayaks in the bed of the truck and ran down the bank after his partner.

Logy Bay
Newfoundland

David could feel his shoulders growing sore as he paddled through the growing swells protecting the cove. His kayak would ride up the crest of a wave and plummet down into the next, sending sprays of salty mist into his face. The strong breeze made the ocean choppy. He kept looking over his shoulders to make sure Alice was close by. She showed no signs of fatigue, keeping up with him as they headed towards the eighteen-foot whale watching boat. The owner painted the boat a sleek black with a deep red stripe along the top. Silver rails lined the back of the ship. A group of excited whale watchers had gathered on the far side, huddled against the rail. They were all taking pictures and pointing out to sea. It had to be the pod of killer whales.

"We're almost there." David tried to hide his fatigue, but he found it difficult to control his heavy breathing.

"You going to make it?" Alice said sarcastically. "I thought you'd have more energy after what I did for you."

"I would do that all day, but don't worry about me. I'll race you there," David called out playfully.

"Of course, you would do that all day, you did nothing." Alice paddled faster, gaining on David.

David churned his arms faster, the muscles in his shoulders growing tighter with every stroke. The kayak cut through the waves, icy cold water washing over David's lap. His neck muscles tightened. He lowered his head and forced his arms to keep moving. His lungs burned now and he couldn't catch his breath. Alice called out his name from behind. At least he wouldn't lose this race.

"Look up, David!" Alice screamed; her voice full of shrill panic.

David opened his eyes and saw nothing but the black wall of the schooner just feet in front of him. He wouldn't have time to turn out of the way now. His only chance of avoiding a collision was to stop. Without thinking, David drove the paddles into the water to slow his kayak. His boat turned sideways just as a wave crashed into the side, tipping it over. Trapped for what seemed like an eternity, David found himself upside down in the ice-cold water. He swallowed a mouthful of the salty brine. The frigid cold waters stung his skin all over. David opened his eyes, the salt burning into them. He tried to orient himself so he could roll the kayak back over, but he couldn't gather enough momentum to swing it right side up. A powerful blow struck his arm and David screamed out in pain. Bubbles of air escaped his mouth and floated up to the surface. His stomach twisted into tight knots as his mind raced with the possibilities of what had struck him. He twisted his neck to see a paddle thrust into the water. David reached out and grasped hold of the wooden shaft, and, before he knew it, he saw the burning yellow sun as he breached the surface. Gasping for air, David looked over at Alice. "I'm okay."

"You sure?" Alice asked, concerned. "You seem like you swallowed a lot of water."

Ocean water filled David's mouth with a bitter taste, his lungs burning from oxygen deprivation. "At least I won the race," David tried to joke as he spit up water. His whole body was shaking from the cold.

"I should have left you down there." Alice rolled her eyes at him.

"Everything all right down there?" The captain of the ship called out from behind a giant wooden steering wheel.

"Yes, everyone is okay, thanks for helping." Alice answered.

"Come around this side of the boat. The orcas are putting on a show for us." The captain pointed out towards the deep blue sea.

"Are you up for this?" Alice turned her kayak to face David. "We don't have to do this if you don't want to."

"We came all this way. It would be a shame to miss it." David mustered all of his remaining strength and paddled his way around the ship, Alice keeping right behind his slow pace.

As they rounded the nose of the ship, they saw three orcas breaching the water playfully, the water dripping from their slick black and white bodies, their giant black dorsal fins standing five-feet tall. They were playing with something, bouncing it high in the air amongst each other. They seemed to be putting on a show for the whale watchers. David's kayak rocked up and down from the rippled waves as the killer whales' bodies slammed back down into the ocean. The two larger males were over twenty-feet long and weighed over five tonnes, while the smaller female was about eighteen feet and four tonnes. They were playing with their food, a seven-foot shark with a pure white belly and grey back.

"Is that a baby great white shark?" Alice asked in astonishment.

"It can't be. I don't think I've ever heard of a white shark in these waters." David had grown up on the seas and never encountered a great white shark before. "It's a porbeagle." Killer whales were edging closer to them without either of them noticing before it was too late. The large male orca flung the dead fish high in the air straight towards David. A thousand-pound carcass crashed into his kayak, splintering the plastic and sending a flood of ice-cold water over him. "Jesus Christ!" David screamed, a wave of panic washing over him. "Get me the fuck out of here!" He abandoned the sinking kayak and swam towards the boat, looking over his shoulders as the orcas kept creeping closer to retrieve their prey.

The captain of the boat threw David a life preserver and pulled him in as soon as he got in it. Alice paddled her canoe quickly. Someone threw her a line to pull her up once she was close enough. Alice ran over and wrapped David in a bear hug once they were both on board. "It's not my day is it?" David groaned; his entire body ached.

Alice laughed. "It definitely isn't your day, sweetheart."

The crew of the boat threw a fishing net down to catch the shark, the green threads wrapped over the lifeless body as the net sank into the ocean. It took all four of the crew plus four more of the passengers to drag the corpse onto the deck.

Something had torn the shark's stomach open with extreme precision. The insides of the dead creature were still intact. Its wet black eyes looked off into the distance. Rows of razor-sharp teeth lined its jaws in a viscous looking smile. The shark had no visible scars aside from the clean cut that ran the length of the pristine white stomach. "Well, I'll be surprised if that isn't a great white shark." The captain stood at the pectoral fin of the lifeless shark. "It looks like a juvenile too," he said to one of his crew.

CHAPTER EIGHT

Marystown
The Fisherman's Landing

Cigarette smoke veiled the air of the primitive bar. The patrons of The Fisherman's Landing stood just outside on the deck overlooking the harbour. Kevin walked over to the bar and grabbed a stool. The bartender sauntered over; a dish rag slung over her shoulder. "What can I get for you?" A woman in her thirties, wearing a pink and blue plaid shirt covered in liquor stains leaned in to find out what Kevin demanded.

"I'm just here searching for a friend. Have you noticed him here?" Kevin brought up a picture of Jonah McGilvery on his phone that he'd found on the local news website.

The waitress reached into her slacks pocket and pulled out a pair of red-rimmed reading glasses. She had a look at the picture and shook her head. "Can't say I did, sweetheart." Her voice was dry and raspy. She drew up a glass of water and took a deep drink to clear her throat. "Is that the fellow on the news that people are saying went missing last night out on the water?"

Kevin nodded his head in agreement. "The same guy, honey." An intoxicated man bumped into Kevin's arm, spilling his white Russian all over Kevin's pants. "Excuse me," Kevin said, raising his arms in the air, revealing his displeasure with the man's clumsiness. The man didn't even seem to notice he wasn't alone at the bar. He stumbled his way towards the washroom, his trousers already unzipped.

"Could you excuse me a second. I need to call Gary's wife to come get him." The waitress excused herself to make the phone call.

Kevin walked through the dank bar, the floor boards creaking beneath his feet as he made his way towards the balcony door. The owners filled the room with round tables chest high; the dark oak wood hadn't aged well. The bar stools had no backs. Anyone that had stayed inside leaned into the table, slouching with their drink grasped desperately in their fist. With the fishing grounds around the Grand Banks closed, it sent the ability of the men to earn a living and their emotional status plummeting to depressing levels. Kevin was glad he had changed out of his work clothes before coming to The Fisherman's Landing. He would have been asking for a confrontation wearing his uniform here.

Pushing the door open, the sea air and smoke mixed into a comforting scent. Kevin closed his eyes, drawing in a deep breath. The sunlight glared off the water in the harbour, virtually blinding him as he opened his eyes. Angry fishermen filled the patio with angry conversations and despair for the future. No one paid him any attention, their faces buried in their drinks. Kevin pulled out a pack of smokes and stuck a fag in his mouth. "Can I borrow a light?" Kevin said as the cigarette dangled from his lips. A man flicked a yellow lighter and held it for Kevin, a tiny orange flicker lighting his cigarette as he puffed on the filter. "Thanks."

The tired-looking man stared at Kevin with bloodshot eyes. Dry ocean air chaffed his lips and his nose red from sunburn. "No problem, stranger. What brings you all the way down here?"

Kevin pulled up the picture of Jonah and showed it to the fisherman. "Have you seen this man around here?"

A scowl caused deep creases to appear in the man's thickened skin. "It's a good thing I didn't because I'd give that bastard a piece of my mind."

"What's going on, Al?" one of the other men inquired.

"This fucker is down here seeking for the man responsible for the closure of the fishery." Spittle flew from Al's mouth as his face turned rosy red, the veins in his neck popping out with the surge in blood pressure.

"They reported him missing last night, his yacht washed up just outside town." Kevin struggled to explain himself. Deep down he hated Jonah McGilvery just as much as they did. "I'm just trying to do my job, folks." Angry eyes glared at Kevin; the mob of unemployed fisherman began to surround him. "I don't agree with what he did either." Kevin glanced over his shoulder; an immense man cut off the doorway. His chest muscles bulged out of open plaid shirt, his forearms thick with muscles and swelling veins.

"I'd say you're searching in the wrong place for that son of a bitch." Al drove his index finger into Kevin's rib cage, driving him back with a slight jolt.

"Ease up, pal, I'm not looking for trouble." Kevin frantically searched for a way off the deck, but the drop was too far and the landing full of jagged rocks. The only way out was through the door and he didn't stand a chance against the behemoth blocking the way.

"I'd say Mr. McGilvery is a bloated corpse out there somewhere." Al pointed out towards the harbour. "Hopefully they never find his body."

"I couldn't agree with you more," Kevin stammered desperately trying to smooth over the situation.

"This is your only opportunity to leave." Al's breath was heavy with the smell of booze and stale stench of smoke. The gargantuan man held the door open for Kevin. "Anyone who's with Labyrinth Oil isn't welcome around here. Go on back to town and make sure that you spread the message around."

"I certainly will." Kevin left The Fisherman's Landing as quickly as his legs would carry him without looking back. He nearly tripped up in the uneven dirt parking lot. The sound of gravel crunching behind him, he threw open the door and jumped into his truck without waiting to see who was approaching. Kevin tried to grab his keys out of his pocket, but his jeans were too tight. A sharp knock on the window forced Kevin to look up.

"Don't mind that old fool. He's just had too much to drink and not enough to eat." The bartender had followed him out of the bar. The bright sunlight gave her dark hair a deep red glow.

Kevin allowed himself to relax enough to catch his breath. He stretched his leg out and forced his fingers far enough into his pants to grasp his keys. He turned on his truck and rolled down the window. "Does he always threaten people like that?"

"There's something you need to understand, young feller." She leaned against the door of the truck, resting her forearm on the window sill. "That man you're looking for stole something from these men that you can't replace."

"What's that?" Kevin asked foolishly.

"Their livelihood," the bartender said with a snarl. "That man got what he had coming to him if you ask me. Maybe it would be best if you left well enough alone if you catch my drift."

Kevin nodded in agreement. "I do." He put the truck into gear and eased out of the parking lot. Once his tires hit the paved main road, he pushed down on the gas. He looked in his rear-view mirror. The woman was still watching him as he drove out of sight. Kevin didn't know what happened to Jonah, but he was sure that they would not find his body. He knew he should tell the police about what had happened at The Fisherman's Landing, but his hands shook in fear of retaliation. He didn't want to join Jonah McGilvery as an ornament at the bed of the briny deep.

North Atlantic Ocean

The *Carcharodon* swam through the second largest ocean in the world, its waters covering twenty percent of the earth's surface. Bounded on the west by North and South America, this massive body of water was home to a vast array of wildlife. Frigid waters from the melting ice caps in the Arctic Ocean fed into the North Atlantic Ocean. These cold waters led the migrating packs of humpback whales further south to the shores of Newfoundland. The flutter of a whale's heartbeat alerted the apex predator to a source of food. Its muscles sending off signals as it beat its tail fin against the surface of the ocean. She continued to follow the continental shelf, keeping well below the surface of the water and staying hidden from view.

Nature built the great white for speed. Her triangle shaped snout allowed her to cut through the waters with ease. A thousand electrical impulses signalled from the sea floor, but her brain tuned them all out, her focus remaining on the whale's heartbeat. She cruised along the steep drop off, her body more accustomed the pressures of the deeper waters. Her stomach didn't demand as much nourishment down below. Rays of light from the yellow sun high in the sky ignited her appetite, but they failed to reach her down here. Able to turn her brain into cruise control, the shark could limit her energy depletion as she swam six-hundred metres below the surface, her mouth open in a sinister smile as she followed the electrical beacon towards the humpback whale.

CCGS Cape Spear
Marystown
Atlantic Ocean

"So, you're trying to tell me a squid killed Jonah?" Kevin couldn't accept what Lewis was telling him. "I thought you were supposed to be the smart one."

Lewis clasped the tooth in his fist. "I think it's an option we have to look at."

"I'm listening. I'm just having a hard time trying to figure out if you're trying to pull my leg or not." Kevin stared into Lewis's eyes but couldn't detect anything but the young man's concerned glare. "Tell me again where you found it?"

"I discovered it lodged it into the decking of the hull, right below the rail." Lewis held up the tooth between his thumb and index finger. "It broke from the creature's jaw." The light glistened off the razor-sharp tooth, the edges jagged and razor sharp.

Kevin didn't want to go to the police and propose a giant squid had ingested Mr. McGilvery. He was sure they'd laugh him out of the station. "Listen, Lewis, I recognize we don't get along but don't think I'm dismissing your opinion because I don't like you. I can't ever remember hearing about a squid that ate someone. It sounds fake." Kevin felt the swell of the ocean grow stronger as they left the safety of Marystown. "Just listen to what you're suggesting."

"I agree it makes little sense, but what else do you think happened?" Lewis raised his voice at Kevin, becoming frustrated that he wasn't listening to him.

"If you'd have been at The Fisherman's Landing with me, I know you'd come to the same conclusion as me." Kevin pushed the throttle forward. The engines rumbled below sending a wave of vibrations through the deck. "I suspect one of those fishermen may have seen his yacht last night and got rid of him."

"Are you kidding me? You're telling me somebody sailed out to the *Swift Current*, climbed aboard the yacht and killed Jonah." Lewis slammed the tooth down on the control panel. "And planted a fucking giant squid's tooth to cover their tracks."

"Listen, kid, you're not the one who has to get in front of the cops and tell them what happened. For now, we will file a missing person's report." Kevin reached out and snatched the tooth. "I'll mention we found this on board the *Swift Current*. But I ain't going to be the one to propose a fucking squid ate Jonah McGilvery!" Kevin yelled at his subordinate.

"Is everything okay in here?" Melvin asked, materializing out of thin air.

"Everything is splendid," Lewis muttered as he trudged away.

"What's the issue with you fellows this time?" Melvin stuck his nose where it didn't belong, trying to be the negotiator between the two again.

"We don't agree on something, that's all you need to know." Kevin was agitated.

"You don't say. Wish I had a nickel for every time that happened. I wouldn't have to work on this ship and listen to you two bicker at each other." Melvin didn't seem like he would leave soon, plunking himself down in the captain's chair.

"Why don't you make yourself at home, Melvin?" Melvin annoyed Kevin, but he hid it in behind a sarcastic tone.

"Saw no one else sitting in it." Melvin eyed the controls. "Ain't nobody watching the speed. We in a rush to get back?"

"Maybe we are, Melvin." Kevin leaned his head back to crack his neck, trying anything possible to mitigate the stress he was suffering.

"We are pushing the ship awfully hard, might burn out the engine in these rough waves." Melvin didn't wait for permission before easing off the throttle. "You're pissed off, but you still have to keep control of things around here."

"You're not questioning my decision-making skills, are you?" The accusation insulted Kevin.

"All I'm saying is everything is in the red and that ain't safe. You can take it whatever way you want to." Melvin met Kevin's glare with resolve, not backing down from his boss.

"You think Lewis should be in charge, don't you?" Kevin's blood was boiling, jealousy creeping over him.

"I expect he could handle this ship." Melvin paused. "I recognize you can when you got your head on straight. You won't be on the CCGS *Cape Spear* much longer, and this may be my last time coming out here. I've seen enough of the ocean to last me ten lifetimes. I've seen the sea destroy people's lives in all kinds of ways. I'm getting out of her way before my luck runs out. You can't beat her but many men have joined her."

"Melvin, what's your point?" Kevin had heard Melvin say he was quitting before, and he was expecting it. Every time they couldn't find a body or something bad happened, Melvin would always have second thoughts about his job.

"My point is we need to train people like Lewis. As long as people work in the ocean, people will get lost in it. They'll need rescuing. I'm on your side here. Lewis has a lot to learn, but, given the chance, he could do this job better than either one of us."

"Melvin, would you mind watching after things up here? I need to go take a break. I need to gather my thoughts." Kevin looked at Melvin who nodded his head in silence.

Kevin headed down below to the break room to find Lewis sitting at the table, playing with a deck of cards. When Lewis realized it was Kevin standing there, he went back to playing his game of solitaire without saying another word. Kevin walked over to the fridge and pulled open the door. The shelves were bare except for some bottles of water and packages of pepperoni and cheese. He grabbed a snack and sat directly across from Lewis.

"You have something you want to say?" Lewis didn't look up from his card game.

"I need something from you." Kevin waited until Lewis met his gaze. "I need you to investigate into this further." He placed the tooth on the table.

Lewis reached out and swiped the tooth off the table before Kevin changed his mind. "Why? Will the cops will be interested in it?"

Kevin still didn't feel comfortable going to the cops with this information, but he remembered they weren't the ones who issued the search and rescue mission. "People working at Labyrinth Oil will need to determine if they're putting their workers in danger. They have over fifty people getting ready to head down to the sea floor working on that oil line."

"You will still let the cops know about all of this right?" Lewis lowered his voice.

"Don't worry about it. You can do it yourself. I'm letting you take the lead on this, kid." Kevin tore open the plastic wrapper, a flood of relief washing over him.

"Are you kidding me?" Lewis was dumbfounded.

"I kid you not." Kevin tore a piece of pepperoni off with his back teeth. "I'll even help you every step of the way. It's long past overdue you start taking some responsibility around here."

"Uh… thanks, Kevin. I really appreciate this, and I won't let you down." Lewis held out his hand.

Kevin reached out and shook Lewis's hand, both men squeezing as hard as possible to prove their dominance. "You won't, Lewis." Kevin was glad to be free of this case. As soon as the news caught wind of the suspicious nature of Jonah McGilvery's disappearance the allegations would promptly follow. The police would start questioning some local fisherman, and Kevin was glad that he wasn't going to be linked with case.

Canadian Coast Guard
Dock
St. John's Harbour

Kevin sat alone in his office. A soft blue paint coated the walls. The lone window in the room faced the harbour, his view of the dark blue waters obstructed by the ships anchored just outside. On his glass desk rested a mountain of paperwork held in place by a whale-shaped paperweight. An air conditioner was blasting cold air at him from the corner as it swiveled back and forth. Kevin covered the wall with an oversized map of the waters around Newfoundland and the Eastern Coast of Labrador. The light in the ceiling was dim. The bulb flickered as the filament neared the end of its life.

Kevin had easily tricked Lewis into taking the bait. Now that the kid was going to be running the show and have his face in the media, Kevin was apprehensive of retribution from the fisherman in Marystown. He knew the best thing to do was to call in an anonymous tip, letting Lewis handle the media when they wanted an interview. This was almost too perfect. Lewis was so eager for control that Kevin didn't even have to convince him. He opened the bottom drawer of his desk and pulled out a silver flask. He unscrewed the cap letting out the oak-aged fragrance of whisky. Kevin gasped as the warm liquid took his breath away. The amber liquid burned the whole way down. The first swig of alcohol was always the hardest, but with every mouthful it got easier. He took another swig of the bittersweet drink, this time allowing the taste to linger on his tongue a little longer.

Picking up the phone, Kevin dialed the number to the police station. "St. John's Police Department, how may I direct your call?" a tired voice asked.

"I'd like to speak to the agent handling the McGilvery case." Kevin lowered the tone of his voice, trying to mimic an elderly gentleman.

"Just one moment please."

Kevin listened to the background music as he waited for his call to be transferred through to the detective handling the case. Kevin took another sip of the whisky and determined that he had built up enough liquid courage to follow through with the hoax. He felt his body temperature rising as the alcohol filled his empty stomach. He waited impatiently, thumbing through some paperwork he had left on his desk. His lips curled into a frown as he stared at the insurance papers requiring his signature. It still turned his stomach why he needed it. People had tried to sue the Canadian Coast Guard when they couldn't rescue their boats even though they had saved their lives. People could be so ungrateful.

"Hi, this is Detective Bowers. You possess information regarding the McGilvery case?" The young man's voice startled Kevin, bringing him back to the phone call.

"Yes, I have reason to believe a fisherman may have killed Mr. McGilvery." Kevin struggled to make his voice sound hoarse in an effort to camouflage his true voice.

"Now why would you suggest that, sir?" Detective Bowers sounded incredulous.

"Well, I overhead a guy from the Canadian Coast Guard talking to one of his employees about what he found below deck of the *Swift Current*," Kevin lied.

There was an abrupt silence. "Did you happen to catch the Coast Guard's name?"

"It was Lewis I think." Kevin made it sound like he was trying to recall. "Lewis Park."

CHAPTER NINE

20,000 ft above sea level
South Atlantic Ocean
Flight 148CC

Andy Grant looked out the tiny porthole window of the plane. The clouds parted just enough for him to see the glistening waters of the Atlantic Ocean far below. The cabin of the plane was darkened, the lights turned off for the lengthy journey from South Africa to New York. A scattered dull yellow glow from the overhead light dimly lit the cabin. Most of the other passengers on the flight were getting some shut-eye, sleep escaped Andy; he was too nervous. If they would lost track of Joan and this whole trip would be a failure. Derrick sat in the seat across the aisle from him, his head titled back and his jaw hanging open, drool sliding down his chin from the corner of his mouth.

Andy reached up and turned his light back on to study his notes on the migration patterns of the *Carcharodon carcharias*, working to slice the theory together. The words were barely visible from the dim glow. Luckily, Andy had them memorized, but he liked the visual keys that jogged his memory. Some scientists observed that sharks used not only their ampullae of Lorenzini to track prey, they also used their amplified sensory receptors to follow the earth's magnetic fields from place to place. The powerful force fields generated deep below the earth's crust kept them on track when crossing the vast oceans. Knowing this would help explain how Joan of Shark found her way back to her species' pupping ground. He needed to back up his theory with scientific data in case he was wrong about the reason Joan made her way to Newfoundland. Ellen would try to end his career otherwise.

He looked over to where she was sitting, her lustrous black hair drawn up in a compact bun and her perfectly pressed pant suit screaming professionalism. She was fingering the pages of a pamphlet, her head slanted down reading an article intently. Deep shadows cast across her face from the light above, smoothing out her harsh features.

A steward bearing a black vest over a white dress shirt pushed a grey trolley down the aisle, not bothering to wake the sleeping passengers. He paused next to Ellen, leaning in to ask her if she wanted anything in a hushed voice. She leaned in; her bright pink lipstick close to the nape of his neck as she whispered back to him. Andy felt a sudden twinge of jealousy wash over him, his blood pressure rising. At first, he didn't enjoy working with Ellen, but she gradually grew on him over months of work-ing, her beauty hidden behind an almost permanent scowl and disdain for struggling to make it in a male dominated industry. The steward poured a glass of water and handed her a small pack of cookies. He leaned back in; his lips close to her ears as he whispered something to her that made her giggle. Her face blushed underneath her tanned complexion, her pale blue eyes looked vibrant as they locked eyes. The steward handed Ellen a piece of paper and a pen. She scribbled something on it and handed it to him. He tucked it in his chest pocket, patting his chest to confirm it was in there before making his way to Andy.

"Good day, sir." The South African man leaned in close, his tone low but firm. "What can I get for you?"

Andy shook his head. "Nothing for me, thanks." Andy looked at his name tag. "Appreciate the offer, Will."

"Really? I'm sure I must have something that will interest you," Will said with a smile as he tugged open a tiny drawer.

Even though Andy had never showed any interest in Ellen before, he found himself jealous and resentful at the man. Will's black hair was styled into a tight fade, an impeccably groomed goatee on his chin. "I'm sure, pal," Andy said a little too loudly. Ellen turned her head towards them.

"I have coffee, everyone loves coffee." Will held up a silver pot and white Styrofoam cup.

Andy just wanted him gone, so he figured it be quicker if he agreed. "Fresh milk and one sugar."

"I knew it. I always aim to please my passengers." He poured the coffee into the cup, slowly adding the milk and sugar. The bitter scent of coffee filled the air, swirls of steam rising from the piping hot liquid. "Here you are, sir."

"Thanks," Andy said, the warmth from the coffee wafted over his face as he raised the cup to his lips. He blew on it, sending ripples over the sur-face.

"One last thing, sir." Will reached into his breast pocket and took out the folded piece of paper, handing it over to Andy.

Andy opened the paper and laughed. "Get some rest, you have a long day ahead tomorrow," he read the note out loud. "Thank you, Will." Andy wanted to deliver a note back, but he wasn't certain if Ellen was flirty or serious.

"Enjoy the rest of your flight, sir." Will pushed the trolley further down the aisle and out of view.

Andy looked back towards Ellen, and, much to his chagrin, she had her nose buried back in the magazine. He thought he could see a grin curve up on the corner of her face. Andy reached up, turning off the overhead light. He thought about going to sleep, but the steaming hot liquid in his hand suggested otherwise. Andy took a sip of the coffee and scrunched up his face. It tasted like dirt sifted through a sock, the vile drink sitting in his hands futilely. He didn't want to drink it, but the thought of spilling the steaming hot water over his lap was adequate to keep him alert. "God damn it, Will," Andy muttered under his breath, as he looked down at the coffee grinds floating in his mug.

"Since we both can't sleep, do you mind running me through why we left shark alley to find a shark in some place I've never heard off." Ellen startled Andy; he hadn't noticed her approach. He shifted over to the empty seat next to the window. He looked out the window to avoid showing too much interest in her presence, but his heart was beating a little faster now.

"Joan has reached the age where she will search for a mate." Andy had been tracking this shark for years now and was confident she had reached sexual maturity. "They discovered that great whites will always return to their birthing grounds when they are ready to find a partner. It would be a long road trip for nothing to cross the Pacific Ocean, to travel all the way to the northern shores of the Atlantic just to witness the sights."

"Maybe she got lost? What if you are wrong about her age?" Ellen didn't seem to buy Andy's story just yet.

"She's a big shark. I've watched her grow up around the island of Gansbaai for years. I'm not wrong about this. Look, the only way for sure is to check it out. As long as we can find her, we will make a scientific breakthrough. You have nothing to worry about."

Ellen stared forward at the back of the seat. "I hope you're right, for both of our sakes."

New York International Airport
New York City

Andy pushed his way through the crowd, doing his best to keep up with Ellen and her film crew. A jungle of people mobbed the food court of the terminal. They had a six-hour layover at the airport before their next departure and were keen to eat at a North American restaurant. Months of eating nothing but the local cuisine in South Africa had grown old; Andy craved a juicy burger and salty fries. His plan was to eat as much food as he could now and hopefully put himself into a food coma for the next five hours. The food court was enormous and had every type of cuisine you could ever want. There were local favorites, world-famous restaurants, and every fast-food chain imaginable. Thousands of people sat at tables, keeping to themselves as they devoured their food in a rush to catch their next flight. Ellen was already in line at Starbucks. Most of her crew had dissolved into the crowd and disappeared. Derrick was pacing back and forth between a pizza joint and a specialty bagel shop, the lineups getting longer and deeper as he struggled to decide.

The golden arches' yellow glow enticed Andy towards its counters, the long lineup moving swiftly. It didn't take long before Andy stood next in line, trying to decide what he wanted to get. "Good day, sir, how can I help you?" a young girl, no older than seventeen, said in a monotone voice. Her hair was a mess as it fell out from underneath her ball cap, the giant golden *M* faded.

"Yeah, I'll have the number three combo with large fries." Andy pointed up towards the menu hanging above the counter.

The girl didn't have to look up, instinctively punching in the meal. "Will that be all, sir?"

Andy tapped his fingers against the counter. "Better throw in a double cheeseburger and a shake." The server looked back up with a questioning look on her face. "And a ten box of nuggets with honey." The ebony skinned girl rang in the other items as quickly as Andy could rhyme them off. "Oh, and I should get a drink to wash it all down. Better throw in a coke."

"Mister, I'm glad I'm not sitting next to you on the jet," she snickered as she punched in his meal. "That will be $28.60."

Andy pulled out his wallet and took out a bundle of South African currency. Each bill had the picture of an animal brilliantly coloured on it. "Shit, I knew I forgot to do something." Andy looked down at the girl. "You don't accept the rand here do you?"

"No, I'm sorry, sir." She poked her head into the kitchen and called out to one of the hidden employees. "Hold up on that last order." She walked back over to the counter with an awkward grin on her face. "Do you have any other way to pay, sir?"

Andy had left his debit card in his suitcase. He hadn't used it in months while working in the port of Gansbaai. "Derrick, come over here." Andy called out over the crowd.

"I just got in line." Derrick was standing in line, waiting for an authentic slice of New York pizza.

"Do you have your debit? I forgot mine in my luggage." Andy held up the colourful bills to show he didn't have a means of paying for his food.

Derrick hesitated to leave the line, but as soon as he did the next person eagerly took his place. "Here, use the tap, bring it back. I'll be at the back of that line." Derrick pointed to the New York Bagels line.

"I thought you were getting pizza?" Andy showed the young woman the debit card. She stuck her head back in the kitchen and signaled out for them to go ahead with the order.

"You ruined it for me. Now I want a bagel. Just don't forget to bring me back the card." Derrick rushed back to get in the line, nearly knocking over a man's tray as he zipped by.

Andy paid for his food and it didn't take long before it was ready. The server piled his food onto his tray, struggling to find room to fit it all onto the single trey. Andy secured his food with two hands, making sure he wouldn't spill anything as he walked through the packed food court. He walked over to Derrick, who was standing at the back of a thirty-person deep line. "Here you go, Derrick." Derrick reached out and stole a handful of fries. "Hey, man, get your own."

"Them's the rules, man. You order a large french fries you have to share. I didn't make them up." Derrick stuffed the fries in his mouth. "You don't like it, too bad. Should've brought your own card."

"Thanks, mate." Andy didn't mind sharing his fries with Derrick but knew he wouldn't be able to stand there much longer without losing more. He could see Derrick already eyeing his fries, so he decided he would leave now before it was too late. "I'll be over there if you ever get served." Andy watched a man gather the trash from the family's meal onto one tray, the universal signal you were getting ready to leave. He rushed over and waited next to the family as they stood up, grabbing a chair as soon as they were all stood up.

Andy slid his tray onto the table and took a long sip of his pop, the bubbles dancing on his tongue. He tore the wrapper off his cheeseburger and took a giant bite, getting a taste of everything in one mouthful. He tilted his head back and closed his eyes as he savored the flavours, trying to distinguish them as he chewed. Ketchup, cheese, mustard, pickles, onion, the toasted bun, and a charred all-beef patty. "I missed you."

"Jesus Christ, Andy, you must really miss American food?" Ellen's voice startled him.

"Hey, you." He opened his eyes to see her sitting across from him with a coffee and wrap. "Hungry." He offered her the fries. Ellen reached over and grabbed the honey, tearing the lid off as she dunked a chicken nugget in. "Wow, you don't follow the rules of fast food?"

Ellen took a dainty bite of the chicken. "Can't say I ever have. Please explain." She dipped the nugget back into the sauce.

Andy shook his head. "My god, who raised you?"

"What?" Ellen looked confused.

"Well, for starters, you never double dip. Ever." Andy slid his tray closer to his chest. "And when someone offers you a fry, you can have a few, but you never just take a man's chicken nuggets." Andy tried his best to sound genuine, but his smile betrayed him.

Ellen laughed out loud, dimples formed on her cheeks as she smiled. "I've never heard of these rules before."

Derrick pulled out a chair and sat down, his plate had a cheese bagel toasted with cream cheese and a chocolate chip muffin with butter. "Andy, you didn't offer me a chicken nugget. I thought we were buddies?"

"You see what you started here." Andy held out the box as Derrick reached out and took one.

"Where's the honey?" Derrick asked. Ellen passed him the open pack.

Andy waited until Derrick dunked his chicken in the golden sauce. "She's a double dipper," Andy accused her

"You're not." Derrick seemed shocked, placing his nugget down on his trey. "You can't do that. Who raised you?"

Ellen laughed even harder. "Why didn't we have this much fun in South Africa?"

That was the question Andy was wondering. Maybe this break from the work was just what they all needed. They were all relaxed now, allowing themselves to joke around with each other a little more. It worried Andy that once they got to Newfoundland, if they didn't find the shark, Ellen would become distant again.

CHAPTER TEN

Labyrinth Oil Office
St. John's, Newfoundland

Kevin followed Lewis through the hallways of Labyrinth Oil. Expensive paintings hung on the walls by famous artists from all over the world. Most of them were abstract paintings which Kevin couldn't understand. He didn't agree that it was art, but there were millions of people who dished out hundreds of thousands of dollars for the mess. "Would you look at all of this art?" Kevin drew out the last word, trying to sound like a critic.

"I wouldn't call it art," Lewis said impatiently. "Isn't there supposed to be an elevator here somewhere?"

"The receptionist said it was at the end of this hallway." Kevin could sense that Lewis was nervous, especially after how the cops responded with laughter to his theory of a giant squid.

"We must be getting close now." Lewis quickened his pace. "I don't know why this needed to be done in person."

Kevin had told him that it was because that's how the Japanese did business, but he just wanted to have a reason to get close to Miss Eguchi. "It just does, Lewis. Nothing to worry about." The paintings on the wall were replaced by plaques and a trophy case, each one a major achievement for oil research and technological advances. The dark marble plaques had gold writing on them. The letters seemed to shine brightly, luring you in to read about why Labyrinth Oil was so great.

"Finally," Lewis grumbled as he pushed an onyx button on the wall. A chime beeped above, the digital display quickly descending from twenty all the way down to one. Two black doors with gold trim slid open to reveal a mirrored elevator. The two men stepped inside, and Lewis hit the button for the top floor.

"May I help you?" A voice came through the speaker.

"We are here to see Mr. Kurosawa," Lewis answered, taking charge before Kevin could answer.

"Do you have an appointment?"

Lewis looked at Kevin. "Do we have an appointment?"

Kevin shook his head. It had never crossed his mind to call ahead, but now he wished he had. "We are here on behalf of the Canadian Coast Guard. We have information about Mr. McGilvery." Kevin's years of experience allowed him to react quickly.

"Hold your issued identification cards up to the scanner."

Kevin took his ID card out of his wallet and held it underneath a card reader. Thin green lasers scanned the card. After a few silent moments the elevator started its ascent. "Looks like we solved the problem."

"Thanks." Lewis looked at his reflection in the mirrored wall. He brushed back the stray strand of hair and fixed the collar of his shirt.

"Just relax, Lewis." Kevin looked at his own reflection, fixing his shirt to hide his gut as much as possible. He pulled up his pants, trying to hide the bulging roll of fat hanging over his belt. The elevator doors pulled apart with a loud swooshing sound, opening into Mr. Kurosawa's private office. The far wall was a floor-to-ceiling window, giving a breath-taking view of St. John's Harbour. Mr. Kurosawa sat behind a giant slab of mahogany wood, a large bookshelf teeming with texts to his right.

"Good day, gentleman." Mr. Kurosawa stood up, buttoning his dress jacket in the process before walking over to greet his guest.

"Good day, Mr. Kurosawa." Lewis's voice was strong and confident. "I am Lewis Park and this is my boss, Kevin O'Reilly."

Mr. Kurosawa bowed his head. "How can I be of help today?" His English was strong, but you could pick up his Japanese heritage on certain words.

"Well, sir, we are from the Canadian Coast guard and we wanted to come see you about your boss, Mr. McGilvery." Lewis said politely.

"Please, come have a seat." Mr. Kurosawa walked back behind the oversized desk and sat in his leather chair.

Kevin sat down, sinking comfortably into the cushion. Lewis sat next to him and the three men shared a long, awkward silence. Mr. Kurosawa combed his jet-black hair straight back; his gel gave it a sleek shimmer. His pinstripe grey suit vest was left unbuttoned. A silver clip held his pale pink tie in place.

"Thanks for having us on such short notice, Mr. Kurosawa." Lewis sat with perfect posture, his large frame dwarfing the man sitting across from him.

"Please, you can call me Kal."

"So, will Miss Eguchi be joining us?" Kevin asked. Lewis shot him an angry glare, his eyes widening with rage.

"No, my sister-in-law will not be joining us." Kal's voice was sharp. "Should she be here?"

"I'm sorry, Mr. Kurosawa. I think Kevin just wanted her here because of any legal problems that may arise." Lewis's statement seemed to defuse the situation.

"Yeah, I mean if you have to file a missing person's report under suspicious circumstances." Kevin's tongue tripped over his words. He could barely form a complete sentence. "I think this situation needs to be handled with the utmost care."

"I will pass along any information that will apply to the report." Kal leaned forward in his chair and placed his hands on the table. They were balled into fists now. "Now, please, I'm a very busy man in Mr. McGilvery's absence."

"We believe Mr. McGilvery may have met an untimely death. His body was nowhere to be found, and we found blood all over the cabin of his yacht." Lewis spoke clearly but quickly. "Did Mr. McGilvery have any known enemies?"

"Jonah did not make many friends during his time here. Many of the fisherman wanted him gone, but that's nothing new for Mr. McGilvery. Being the owner of a major oil corporation afforded him few friends and a wealth of enemies." Kal's dark chestnut eyes glared at Kevin suspiciously. "I believe you were at the press conference yesterday morning with the mob of fishermen."

Kevin lowered his eyes to glance at the floor. "I was there, but I wasn't with the fishermen. I was just there wasting time before work began." Kevin continued to stare at the floor boards, admiring the red oak. Dark swirls ran through the hardwood creating an intricate pattern that screamed wealth.

"I see. I've been in contact with a Detective Bowers. He believes a fisherman from Marystown may be responsible for Jonah's death."

"Did he say why?" Kevin blurted out.

Kal eyed Kevin suspiciously. "Said he got a phone call from an anonymous source."

"There is another thing I found." Lewis hesitated; his hand clutched the plastic bag that was tucked away in his pants pocket. He pulled the tooth out and laid it on the table. "I found this embedded in the decking of the *Swift Current*."

Kal reached out and pulled the tooth inches away from his face, running his index finger over the ragged edge. He looked at it intently from different angles. "This tooth belongs to a kraken."

"A kraken?" Kevin asked.

"Growing up, my father told me tales of an ancient sea monster called a kraken." Kal placed his hands in his lap and leaned back in his chair. "My father told me tales of the giant squid. They would drag ships to the bottom of the ocean and devour the unfortunate crew."

"Someone told me this belong to the *Architeuthis dux*." Lewis remembered the name that Kate used.

"Arc a tooth us what?" Kevin felt left out of the conversation. Apparently the two men were speaking a different language.

"A giant squid, Kevin." Lewis was growing annoyed with him. "I believe those creatures are common around the waters of the Grand Banks," he added.

Kal nodded his head in agreement. "Yes, they are. We've had several ecological surveys done in the area and they are abundant, but we determined them to be harmless. I have workers getting ready to dive into those waters to get the pipeline laid. They will be down there for months. Labyrinth Oil cannot afford to have any more bad publicity come from this project. We are having a hard enough time dealing with the fishermen's union."

"What are you going to do about it?" Kevin asked, drawing the ire of Kal, his eyes flaring with anger.

"That is none of your concern." Kal stood up and buttoned up his vest. "Now, is there anything else we should know?"

Lewis shook his head. "No, sir, that is everything we needed to tell you."

"Then I must ask you two gentlemen to leave. I have a lot of work to do, so if you'd excuse me." Kal waved them back toward the elevator.

Kevin stood up first and turned to leave, not waiting for Lewis. The door opened as soon as he touched the button. He slipped inside and did his best to hide.

Lewis wasn't far behind. He lumbered into the confined space and waited for the door to close behind him. "What the fuck is wrong with you, Kevin?"

"Whoa, calm down, Lewis." Kevin wasn't about to take shit from Lewis.

Lewis paced back and forth, his face flushing red. "You really made us look stupid back there. I mean, what the hell was that? Why the hell did you ask about Miss Eguchi."

"That's enough out of you. It's over for us. We have nothing else to do with this now." Kevin ignored Lewis's questions. "The police will handle the matter now, and we will go back to patrolling the waters for the coast guard. End of conversation." The elevator beeped as the door slid open. Both men tried to push through the door at the same time. Lewis easily pushed Kevin back, shoving him deeper into the elevator as he stormed off through the lobby and out the front door.

7 Colonial Street
St. John's, NL
Kevin O'Reilly's home

Cramped in between the wall and the dining room table, Kevin's stomach pressed hard against the edge. One side of the dinner table had become ingrained into the drywall, the oversized table wedged into a small alcove just off the kitchen. It was a stretch calling it a dining room; it was just the place that his wife decided they would dine in. The cheap table was just big enough for the cramped space and it forced the married couple to stare at each other uncomfortably. Kevin enjoyed the sweet scent of apples in Amy's cinnamon coloured hair that hung in tight curls around her round face. Amy was dressed casually, wearing jeans and a hipster jacket pulled on over a blue dress shirt. Kevin looked at his own reflection, jealous over how little time had transformed her beauty while father time seemed to have declared war on him. Amy always had a shyness to her, a reluctance to show off her exceptional looks which is why it still shocked him to this day she had cheated on him. A picture of her son hung on a frame behind her, a perpetual reminder of her unfaithfulness. The ceiling tiles were old and sagged down in the center. A bare bulb hung from the ceiling. Kevin had broken the shade a month ago while changing the light bulb and hadn't bothered to replace it since. A narrow window with the drapes hanging down just above the windowsill offered a view of the neighbours' siding

Kevin stared down at his plate. The food didn't look appetizing and the portions were small. The batter on his fried cod looked wet. The steamed vegetables looked soggy and their vibrant colours had left with the steam. He scrapped his fork over his plate in disgust, wishing he had ate before he came home. At least he had grabbed a beer from the fridge before he sat down to his dinner. He picked up the brown bottle and took a long swig. Amy shot him a warning glare from across the table. Placing the bottle of Black Horse back down on the table, Kevin reached out for the salt and pepper, dusting an unhealthy portion of both over his fried fish. They ate in silence for what seemed like an eternity. Kevin reached for the television remote and flicked on the news. He needed something to distract him from Amy's look of disdain.

"I thought we agreed no television during supper?" Amy spoke in a disheartened tone.

"I want to hear the news, Amy. Is that all right?" Kevin let out a long sigh. Amy just glared at him with her deep blue eyes. He couldn't see the screen, but the sound was enough to distract him from his bland meal.

"So, you're saying that global warming has reached its apex?" a male reporter asked.

"What I'm trying to say," a woman's voice explained in a soft tone. *"We've already tipped the scale too far. There's no reversing the damage we've done now."*

"What effects will this have, Miss Northcott?"

"He can't be serious?" Amy mocked the interview.

Kevin pointed his fork at Amy. "Hey, I thought you said no television during dinner," Kevin said playfully, trying his best to connect on some level with her. Amy leaned towards the living room, listening to the answer as she cracked a smile.

"We've already experienced nasty storms around the world. The worst and most frequent storms have been happening off the coast of Newfoundland. The waves have pounded the shoreline with so much force they've registered on the seismometer. These storms are only the beginning. We will soon feel a drastic change in the world's temperatures. There will be an increase in natural disasters such as earthquakes, typhoons, hurricanes, tornados, and drastic flooding. That's when the real dangerous activity will start."

"Would you explain to the viewers what could happen, Madeline?"

"I believe that we will soon witness a drastic increase in the movements of the tectonic plates. There will be powerful actions where the plates converge and diverge. This will cause a drastic change in the structure of the continents and land masses all over the world."

"Is there anything we can do to stop this?"

"We can't stop it. We've set the earth on this course. All we can do now is adjust our actions so these effects won't last as long and hope we can survive through this ordeal. We need to stop using fossil fuels all together. Companies like Labyrinth Oil must be stopped immediately."

"That was a recording from earlier today in Washington at an emergency meeting about global warming. We will be back after the commercial break with the local news and the latest update on the Jonah McGilvery case."

"What a pile of crap," Kevin muttered.

Amy stared at him with blank eyes. "You must be blind if you can't see the effects of global warming all around us."

"It's the way the world works, Amy." Kevin took another sip of his beer, immediately regretting where the conversation was heading.

"But working out on the ocean you must see the terrible storms that woman was talking about," Amy said.

"Butts are for crapping, Amy," Kevin stood up from the table. His gut bumped the side causing the frail legs to wobble underneath. He walked over to the fridge and grabbed another beer. "I'll be in the living room." Kevin slumped down into his rocking chair, leaving Amy to clear the table and wash the dishes.

CHAPTER ELEVEN

Placentia Bay
Southern Coast of Newfoundland
The Mississippi

Peter Breau sat on the edge of his twelve-foot yacht with the air regulator piece pressed hard against his face, building up the courage to go spear fishing. The weight of his oxygen tank was drawing the straps deep down into his shoulder. The vivid yellow sun beat down on his balding head, scorching his scalp. Beads of perspiration rolled down his backside and formed a puddle in his Kevlar wetsuit. He found it tough to concentrate with the blaring heavy metal music pounding from the cabin of the *Mississippi*. Peter felt the deck of the new fishing boat vibrating underneath his feet as the base boomed.

The last time he went spear fishing was ten years ago in Costa Rica, and the waters were much warmer than in Placentia Bay. He decided he needed a break from the hectic city life, and began looking for a place to clear his writers' block. Ever since he sold his script to those damn television producers, he hadn't been able to get a single word out of his head and onto paper. He was lucky he had enough material written to stretch his show out over two seasons, but the first season had already aired and the network was hungry for more. Peter had to stimulate his brain. His only plan had been to take the ferry over from North Sydney and charter a car in Port aux Basques. Since then, he had been taking in all of what Newfoundland offered. He was trying to discover adventure, which led him all the way to Placentia. Now, as a struggling young fisherman blasted a heavy metal tune over his sound system, Peter was preparing to make the plunge into the ocean. The speargun clutched tightly in his grasp, Peter kept looking over his shoulder into the bleak waters.

"Please tell me there aren't many sharks out here?" Peter questioned his tour guide.

Looking up from behind the steering wheel, the young fisherman turned the music down just enough, allowing his voice to be heard over the obnoxiously loud music. "You might see a porbeagle, but I doubt it." The words escaped his mouth rapidly, weighed down by a thick accent. The captain had pulled his yellow hip waders over a stained white T-shirt. Long strands of curly brown hair fell over his eyes, and it looked like he hadn't washed it in days. Peter stared at the grime built up on his palms and underneath his fingernails as the fisherman lowered a rope over the side of the *Mississippi*.

"What is a porbeagle?" Peter asked, wondering why he was sitting on the edge of this boat. He should be seated in front of his computer writing the scripts for the third season. He looked down at seventeen notifications on his phone, all from the network producers looking for any progress from him. Peter never expected for his script to take off, but the overwhelming ratings demanded more.

"It's a smaller shark. Notting to worry bout, mate."

Peter wondered if the young man was putting on an act. This time his accent sounded Australian. "How often do people report shark attacks around here?"

The fisherman scratched his head with a confused look on his face. "I can't recall there ever being a reported shark attack in these waters here." He paused as if searching a database for the correct file. "Can't say I ever did."

A wave sent a spray of frigid water up Peter's back. Droplets streaked through the neck hole of his wetsuit, following the zipper all the way down to his crotch. He recoiled into a tight ball at the sensation. He hadn't realized how hot the sun was until the frigid ocean water splashed against his bare skin. Peter let out a surprised whimper, arching his back trying to escape the icy water inside his suit. The fisherman let out a genuine chuckle at Peter, enjoying his rigid reaction to the numbing waters of Newfoundland. "Anything else I need to know?" Peter asked.

"The waters round here aren't too deep, but you will want to keep an eye on yer air gauge." The fisherman reached out to the gauge on Peter's wetsuit. "You'll want to make yer way back up once this red needle reaches thirty." He patted Peter's shoulders with calloused hands. "You'll be fine, don't you worry bout nottin."

"What's your name again?" Peter had been so nervous preparing to get into the water, he was drawing a blank trying to remember his name.

"You can call me Felix."

Peter nodded before pulling the mask over his face and securing the regulator in place. He took a few steady breaths before giving Felix a thumbs up. He leaned back slightly, letting the weight of his oxygen tank do most of the work for him. Peter fell backwards off the side of the *Mississippi* and plunged into the freezing cold waters of Placentia Bay. His muscles constricted as the shock took hold of his body, his vision blurred by a massive swarm of air bubbles. For what seemed like an eternity, Peter sank deeper into the ocean helpless to defend himself against any predators. All he was able to detect was the booming vibrations coming from the music aboard the *Mississippi*, the thumping drumbeat echoing all around him.

The last air bubbles drifted past Peter's mask and floated away, allowing him a breathtaking view of the ocean floor. Years of erosion and sediment covered it in jagged rock formations. Seaweed and lobsters swayed back and forth with the strong current. Peter quickly adapted to the water temperature and rapidly pumped his legs, propelling himself downwards, deeper into the abyss. He looked back towards the surface. The sunlight struggled to penetrate the immense darkness of the ocean and reach the bottom. He looked around as a codfish swam past him and scurried off out of sight. Peter continued to dive deeper into unknown waters of Placentia Bay, completely cut off from all of his troubles for a brief moment.

Placentia Bay
Southern Coast of Newfoundland
One-hundred Metres Down

Joan swept her nose back and forth, sketching a picture of the ocean depths with pinpoint accuracy. She could sense the other male great whites around her. They had been pursuing her now for days. Every time she waded into the shallow waters around the coastline, she could sense the warmer waters changing her attitude. She moved faster near the surface and her muscles swelled with power, but with the newfound energy she required more fuel. Her stomach rumbled for sustenance as she continued her journey along the southern coast of the island, doing her best to remain ahead of the males seeking to mate with her.

A constant throb of electronic impulses echoed in the distance unlike anything Joan had ever heard. Felix had turned up his heavy metal music after Peter made his dive, and it taunted the prehistoric predator, daring her to investigate. Steady vibrations and constant thumping of the bass drum annoyed the shark, drawing her full attention. The foreign noise made it impossible to ignore; she had to find out what was causing the disturbance. Her brain's capacity to focus on a single source allowed her to ignore all the other distractions. She swam swiftly towards the source of the disturbance, raising up from the depths of the dark ocean to get a better idea of what was drawing her towards the surface. The *Carcharodon* sensed the familiar humming of a boat's engine entangled with the unknown sound. Joan kept her distance from the pounding source of electrical impulses that stimulated her lateral lines. Until she knew what kind of creature waited for her, she remained in the shadows of the murky water.

With her appetite growing stronger, her killer instincts took over, making her desperate for a meal. Her heart pumped blood through her veins, strengthening her muscles for an ambush if she discovered any prey to devour, anything able to keep her going until her next meal. She sensed the other white sharks closing in on the area, momentarily ignoring the hormones that Joan excreted. Whatever was making the commotion, it was considerably larger than the other predators in these waters, emitting powerful impulses throughout the ocean. Joan felt the beating hearts of the *Architeuthis dux* and the flutter of whales making their migration south from the Arctic sea. If the origin of the noise wasn't food, her ability to quickly locate her next meal allowed her the luxury to investigate. For the moment, the boisterous noise drew her attention towards *the Mississippi*.

Placentia Bay
Southern Coast of Newfoundland
Forty Metres Down

A freezing cold current of water marked the boundary of the drop-off. Peter looked off into the ominous blackness of the uncharted depths, a chill creeping up his spine. He wouldn't dare venture past the ocean floor that he could still see. The waters turned so dark they looked purple as the trickle of sunlight died in the depths on the other side of the cliff. Peter had followed a three-foot codfish for about twenty minutes now, the dark silver scales picking up slivers of fading sunlight as it swam near the ocean floor. He grasped his speargun in his hands now, making certain he secured the cable to his wrist. The ocean floor was teaming with crustaceans swaying back and forth with the strong currents. He could see an assortment of lobsters picking apart a cluster of starfish, stuffing morsels of flesh into their mouths with their claws. Peter had never seen so much activity underneath the water before. It was fascinating to watch. Years of gloom shrouded the rugged sea bed in algae. The remnants of wrecked ships littered about the ocean floor, left well preserved over the ages.

Peter checked his air gauge and his heart plummeted in his rib cage, disheartened to find it had dropped to forty percent. He had to make his move before he would have to return to the surface. He forced his legs to kick hard, churning up a barrage of air bubbles that drifted towards the surface behind him. The codfish banked hard to the left and then left again, attracted by the commotion that Peter was causing. The fish swam close enough for Peter to line up his shot, but it swam by him too quickly, passing him before he could pull the trigger. Peter twisted his body and took quick aim, squeezing the trigger before the codfish disappeared from view.

A low thump from the speargun echoed through the water as the spear pierced through the codfish's soft flesh. A faint mist of red blood trickled from the wound, clouding the fish from his view. Peter pulled the line in, hand over hand. The fish moved in jerky motions through the deep waters, leaving a trail of blood behind. Peter reached out and snatched the fish by the gills, drawing it in towards his body. He didn't want to lose his kill, but he didn't think he'd be able to get much flesh to eat.

A massive grey blur formed in the distance, appearing from nowhere like a ghost. The grey blur raced towards Peter, drawn in by the trail of blood. Fear gripped Peter's heart so hard that it ceased pumping, every muscle in his body tightened so taut it hurt. A sinister grin took shape as the grey blur came into focus. Before Peter realized what was happening, the grin opened wide, revealing an avalanche of razor-sharp teeth and pink gums. A black hole opened wide as the creature's jaws widened. Peter tried to swim away but was pulled inwards by the engulfing water. Raising his arm out of instinct, Peter tried to block the blow, but his efforts did little to stop the impact. A wallop more powerful than a freight train crashed into his chest. The shark slammed into him with its eight-thousand pound body. Three-inch teeth severed the human flesh with ease. An immense pressure washed over Peter as the jaw slammed shut with over four-thousand pounds of pressure per square inch. A crimson cloud engulfed Peter. He felt the pressure increase as the shark swam into the depths with tremendous speed. Peter's body quivered. His heart leapt into his chest as he found himself still alive but trapped in the creature's gullet. The creature opened his jaw and Peter's eyes focused on his own severed arm floating upwards, his fingers still clutching the speargun. With a jerking motion, the sharks jaw unhinged and jutted forward, its teeth tearing through Peter's flesh. For an abrupt moment, the creature relinquished Peter from its gnarled jaw. A soulless eye peered back at him. His mind trapped inside his mangled body; Peter was forced to witness slivers of his own shredded flesh stuck in the rows of razor-sharp teeth.

Peter found himself face to face with the pitch-black eye. Frozen in time, he saw flashes of his family playing on the creature's eye like an old projector movie. Loving memories played, images of Kelli, Dante, and Jaden flicked across the dark pupil. Peter was filled with a fleeting sense of happiness as the memory of his loved ones raced through his mind. Without warning, the movie ended abruptly. The black eyes rolled back into the creature's skull and its jaws hyper-extended without warning. An exploding shower of red burst into the sea as the jaws snapped shut over Peter's chest and neck.

Placentia Bay
Southern Coast of Newfoundland
The **Mississippi**

The bass drum pounded loudly as Felix leaned back in his comfy chair, pretending to play along to the beat of the song with his pencil in the air. Loud music drowned out the cawing of the seagulls and turrs. The song ended, and for a brief moment all Felix heard was the gentle sound of waves lapping off the side of the *Mississippi*. Sharp, piercing cries of seagulls overhead caught his attention. He watched the dirty white birds circling above his boat through the filthy windshield.

Thump thump thump thump

A rhythmic thumping caught his attention just before the next song kicked in. Felix sat up in his chair as something bumped against the hull of the ship. He reached out to his CD player and turned the volume down.

Thump thump thump thump

The rhythmic sound returned, and it only took Felix a moment to realize the waves had washed something up against the side of the boat. He got up from his chair and headed out onto the deck. He placed both hands on the metal railing that ran along the port side of his vessel and looked out into the vast horizon of the ocean. The deep blue sea met the light blue sky in tranquil transition.

Thump thump thump thump

Felix looked down into the waves, and it didn't take him long to spot the source of the sound. His stomach muscles convulsed, sending the contents of his tuna sandwich over the side of the rail. The vomit splattering off the water with a sickening sound. Felix wiped the half-digested food mush from his mouth and stared down at the chunk of arm severed just above the elbow. The ghostly white hand still clutched the spear gun as it bobbed up and down in the water with the waves.

CHAPTER TWELVE

The Marine Institute
St. John's, NL

Kate sat behind her desk with the door to the classroom closed, eating her lunch as she skimmed through her emails. There was nothing there except emails from her students pleading for an extension on their homework, or why they wouldn't be able to attend class on Monday. Stabbing a piece of hard-boiled egg with her fork, Kate frowned at the greenish colour of the yolk as she nudged the plastic tray aside. She anxiously awaited an email from the lab; they were supposed to let her know as soon as the shark carcass found in Logy Bay arrived. She needed to identify the species and determine the cause of death. Sharks had never been in her scope of expertise, or even something she was familiar with, but marine biology was her chosen discipline. Excited for the challenge and a break from teaching, this recent discovery would be a welcome change.

She opened her internet browser and searched for an expert in the field. Kate planned to document her findings, and if she encountered any problems, she would quickly contact a paleobiologist. She searched through all the names, many of them associated with other universities. Most of the experts listed lived in California, South Africa, and New Zealand. As Kate scrolled past Andy Grant's name, his picture caught her attention. His deep brown eyes drew her in, and his chestnut brown hair paired perfectly with his five o'clock shadow. Everyone had seen his show on television during shark week, and Kate still found it hard to believe his biography. He certainly did not act like someone that had their master's degree in paleobiology. She had always thought they had hired him because he was attractive, just an actor paid to play the part.

She jotted down his contact info for his office at the University of California and decided this may be a great opportunity to reach out to him. Without hesitation, Kate opened her email. Her fingers wandered across the keyboard. Her heart fluttered in her chest, and she felt her face flush with blood. The mouse hovered over the send button, her eyes reading the request for help to identify the shark making sure it was written professionally. Kate closed her eyes as her finger clicked the mouse. A bell chimed instantly alerting her that the email had been delivered successfully. Almost instantaneously, an email popped up on her dashboard from him.

"Damn it." Kate stared at the automatic reply, disheartened to discover he was presently in South Africa.

"Kate, we have the specimen down in the lab if you want to come look." Danielle startled Kate. She was in charge of the tanks in the basement, making sure she kept the salinity of the water at the proper levels for all the marine life. Her job was vital for keeping all the different species alive so that the institution could examine them.

"Thanks, Danielle, I'll be down once I'm finished reading this email." Kate closed her internet browser and powered off her laptop.

The Marine Institute
St. John's, NL

Kate walked into the visitors' section of the university. Tours ran through the basement daily between lunch and supper. They were the best source of income for the school because it was both an opportunity to educate and inspire young people, but it also served as an effective tool in teaching students. Students would practice what they learned in the classroom by answering the questions that would get brought up during the tours. There were interactive displays where people could learn about how the ocean tide worked and how the moon affected it. Kids could control the moon with a lever which would allow more or less water into the tank to show how the tides affected the landscape. There were three rooms that played movies about the various marine life found in the oceans around Newfoundland and Labrador. The biggest attractions were the fossilized displays of various fish found off the coast. The biggest display was the skeleton of a blue whale that had been reconstructed and hung from the ceiling, the massive fragments of bone held together with metal rods and screws. A tank with a preserved juvenile *Architeuthis dux* ran the length of one wall; its giant eye seemed to watch you wherever you went through the yellowed water.

They kept the basement of the Marine Institute extra cold to help stabilize the water temperatures. Large steel drums lined the back walls and water from the salt water tanks wet the cement floors. Each tank containing different marine life. They filled one with lobsters and crabs. If you looked closely enough you would be able to find the blue lobster donated by a local fisherman. Codfish swam in the largest tank and a net was thrown over the tank containing the wolffish so visitors wouldn't be able to get their hands close enough to the water. Someone had nicknamed the Atlantic wolffish the devil fish for good reason. Its jaws were filled with fang-like, conical teeth which it used to break the shells of molluscs and crustaceans. The final tank housed starfish, sea snails, and other fish which children could touch. Kate walked straight past those tanks and towards a door that led out back. A large yellow sign with red dashes warned visitors to stay out. The words *restricted access* scrolled across the sign in bold black letters. She pushed the heavy door open. A blast of ice-cold air carrying the heavy scent of salt and algae greeted her. They housed the filtration systems for all of the tanks in this area along with all the large display tanks that housed various species of fish not on display for the public.

"Over here, Kate." Danielle's voice carried over the hum of the pumps as they filtered water through the pipes. She was standing next to a large blue tarp that had been wrapped over the body of the deceased shark. She waved for two of her students to come over. The two young men and Danielle struggled to roll the dead weight enough to get the tarp out from underneath the one-thousand-pound shark.

Kate rushed over to help. The stench from the inside the tarp burned the hairs in her nose. It smelled like rotten salt and ammonia, something

Kate never would have dreamed of before today. Straining all of her muscles to help, she felt the incredible weight of the powerful sea creature roll over. The students pulled the tarp away once the weight shifted then stood behind Kate and Danielle to observe. The shark had a long slit that ran the length of its belly, but, miraculously, the contents of its guts remained inside. "Well, it's a male shark." Kate pointed towards two appendages hanging from the white belly. "We call those two organs claspers," she explained for the two students. Kate examined the pectoral and dorsal fins for any signs of damage. "It's a young shark, very young as a matter of fact."

"Why would you say that?" Danielle asked as she reached down to touch the skin. She recoiled in pain instantly as she tried to rub the creatures grey back. "What the hell?" Danielle's hand was bleeding from a nasty looking cut. She took a rag out of her pocket and applied pressure to the cut. "I'll go get a band aid."

"A shark's skin is made of dermal denticles woven together." Kate continued to explain to Danielle's students. "They act like armour and help to keep its skin clean. If you rub them the wrong way, the denticles will shred your flesh, but if you rub from snout to tail like this." Kate reached down and ran her hand along the sharks back without incident. "It's smooth. Give it a try."

The two young men hesitantly reached their hands out, afraid to touch the dead creature. "Don't be afraid, guys. She just showed you that it's safe." Danielle was back now with a ball of gauze taped to her hand. "I wish you had shown me before."

"Sorry, I thought it was common knowledge." Kate said bashfully.

"Anyway, you said that this is a young shark." Danielle made a fist with her hand, squeezing the wad of gauze. "Could you please explain that to us?"

"As I was saying." Kate pointed to the perfect dorsal fin. "You notice that the dorsal fin is almost a perfect triangle. As sharks grow older, they will encounter other sharks and predators, often they will fight each other to assert dominance. As they grow older, they will be involved in more of these confrontations. An older shark will have more battle scars on average than their younger counterparts. We can use the wounds and scratches on a shark's dorsal fin to identify the creature similarly to how we can identify each other using finger prints. Each dorsal fin is unique."

"Seriously? Like a finger print?" Danielle's lips curled up and wrinkles formed on her forehead as her eyebrows scrunched together.

"Yes." Kate moved towards the snout. "See these black marks that pepper its pyramid-shaped head. These are the ampullae of Lorenzini."

"I've heard of those. That is how sharks detect electrical impulses, right?" Danielle interrupted.

"That is correct. They can also detect the smallest amount of blood or urine in the ocean waters from extremely far distances. Thousands of metres away."

"That's incredible," Danielle added as she nodded her head in amazement. "So, what kind of shark do you think this is then?"

"I think it could be a great white shark." Kate found it hard to believe that she said that, but she was almost positive it was. "I must run tests on it. I'll need blood and skin samples before I can confirm. Do you think you could arrange your students to gather that for me?"

"Of course, Doctor Hamilton." One student was eager to help now.

"So, what could have caused the wound on its stomach?" Danielle asked.

"I don't understand." Kate had seen nothing like it. The cut had been made with surgical precision, clean as if made by the skilled and steady hand of a surgeon. "I think I need to make a phone call." Kate tried to get hold of someone in Andy Grant's office. Hopefully he would be excited to hear about the discovery of a *Carcharodon carcharias* in Newfoundland.

St. John's International Airport
St. John's, NL

Andy had fallen asleep during the last leg of the plane trip to Newfoundland during the in-flight movie. The steward had woken him up to buckle up his seat belt. He awoke in a dazed and confused state, forgetting momentarily where he was or where he was headed. He wiped the drool from the corner of his mouth, bumping elbows with the passenger next to him. The flight was crowded, and Andy had lost sight of Ellen a long time ago. Derrick was just two rows ahead of him, towering over everyone around him. His hair had grown long in the back and was straggly looking. The seat belt light was lit up, and they had turned the lights back on while Andy had fallen asleep.

He looked at the elderly gentleman sitting next to him. His snow-white hair was nearing the end of its life cycles as he was closing in on baldness. The dome light on the top of his head reflected off of his scalp underneath his thin hair. "I hope I didn't keep you up with my snoring," Andy said.

The elderly man shot him a vexed look; his eyes circled by two large dark ellipses from lack of sleep. "It wasn't only me son," he said with a gruff tone.

"Sorry." Andy's voice trailed off. He didn't know what else to say, but it wouldn't be much longer before they'd be off this plane. He could already feel the plane descending. His stomach seemed to be behind the plane's altitude. With every drop, the bile in his stomach sloshed around inside his empty gut. He grabbed hold of the barf bag tucked into the pouch on the back of the seat in front of him. He opened it and put his face down into the bag, waiting for the next drop in altitude. Normally he didn't get sick, but the strong winds had created a lot of turbulence, and now there seemed to be big pockets of air that the plane was diving into.

A sudden drop caused the bile to jump into his throat as the plane leveled out. The acidic fluids drained back down into his gut. "Come on, buddy, land this plane." Andy didn't want to throw up; he had way too much in his stomach for the tiny white bag he was clutching. Looking around at the other passengers, Andy noticed he wasn't the only one that found the flight a little too turbulent. Several people had their heads between their knees. The plane's landing gear was grinding below his seat, the mechanical arms of the wheel shifting around beneath the floor.

Another drop rattled the contents of his stomach, swishing around his insides. This time his lungs expanded against his rib cage as he held his breath and waited for the nausea to pass. Andy dry heaved, hoping to relieve some pressure building up inside, but it was no use. He looked out of the window but only a thick grey fog was visible. Beads of moisture ran across the window as the plane descended through the low ceiling. Not only was Andy sick to his stomach, now a wave of claustrophobia washed over him too. He didn't understand how the pilot guided the plane down towards the runway without being able to see. The pilot was only relying on his navigational instruments to guide the plane to safety. Blood drained from Andy's face. He looked down at the skin on his hands which were now pasty white. Beads of sweat dripped down his forehead and soaked into his beard, making the hairs prickly and sore.

A sudden rumble rattled the luggage compartments overhead as the wheels struck the ground. The whole plane shook as the breaks strained to slow the plane. Andy peered out the window once more, the yellow reflective paint scarcely visible on the runway. The immense fog seemed to swallow up everything on the ground. The terminal was ten feet away and was half shrouded by the sheer density of the grey mist. The plane's engine rumble faded as the twin turbine engines powered down, the plane slowly plodding down the tarmac.

"You made it." The elderly gentleman mocked him. "First time to Newfoundland, I guess. Most days are like this. You get used to it after time."

"I don't think I ever want to get used to that sensation." Now that Andy knew he was safely on the ground the blood slowly returned to his body, and the urge to vomit passed. Andy waited for the man to grab his stuff from the overhead compartment, taking a moment to gather his strength before standing. "Sorry I wasn't much company during the flight." The elderly man slung a satchel over his shoulder, giving Andy one last glance before sauntering down the aisle with the rest of the passengers. Andy noticed Derrick waving people past his seat as he waited. He looked around for Ellen, but she had vanished into the crowd as they shuffled off the plane. Andy was the last one to leave. His knees wobbled underneath him as made his way towards Derrick.

"We got a phone call from the office. They need you to check something out for them." Derrick held his cellphone in his hands. The tiny black phone looked like a child's toy in his giant paws.

"We don't have time for that. We need to check Joan's tracker and find her before it's too late." Andy clutched the seat in front of him as he stumbled past Derrick.

"They want us to head to the St. John's Marine institute." Derrick joined Andy in the aisle. "They think they found a juvenile great white. Doctor Kate Hamilton wants us to check it out."

"I will join her with the film crew. It will thrill Ellen to get footage of a great white shark here in Newfoundland." Andy could feel his heart beating faster with excitement. "You take the rest of the crew and get that satellite tag tracker working and charter us a boat so we can get out there and find Joan of Shark."

"Now joining us live from Signal Hill is Jody Baker."

Andy looked up at the television on the terminal wall as the local news played. Everyone had stopped to watch the report. As the camera panned over the blue ocean, a wall of fog rolled in towards land. The blonde-haired and blue-eyed reporter was wearing a light blue windbreaker. Strong gusts of wind blew her hair completely sideways, her coat ready to blow away with the wind as it pulled tight against her slender body.

"Thanks, Micheal. The waters off Newfoundland have always been considered by many to be treacherous, but now in the last three days two people have gone missing somewhere out here." The camera panned away to some footage from earlier of a news conference. A police officer was taking questions from behind a podium. *"Yes, Mr. Breau's arm turned up at the surface of the water but we could not find his body."* The officer leaned in as one reporter asked a question that Andy couldn't hear over the murmur of the airport crowd. *"No, we do not believe this case to be related to Mr. McGilvery's case. I realize that they have both disappeared under mysterious circumstances, but I don't believe we are looking for a serial killer. The two men have no known ties to each other. Next question."* A voice called out from the crowd. *"We believe someone has murdered Mr. McGilvery, but we are exploring other avenues of investigation."*

An outburst of chatter erupted from the crowd as people added their two cents to the situation. Some people sympathized with the man's situation while others agreed he had it coming. The television switched to a long shot of a fishing boat named the *Mississippi*. Then it showed a stock photo of Peter Breau on the screen before it changed to an interview with the captain of the fishing vessel. *"I heard a strange knocking against the side of the boat. When I looked over all I could see was his arm just floating there. That's all we managed to find."* The screen switched back to a live shot of Jody Baker. *"Police officers have said Mr. McGilvery's yacht the Swift Current was found, and there were signs of a struggle aboard. However, they have yet to find his body. As for Mr. Breau, all they have found was his severed arm, but an autopsy is being conducted now to find the cause of the wound. Back to you, Micheal."* The report went back to the studio. *"Thanks, Jody. We will be back after this commercial break."*

Andy wandered towards the luggage coral, waiting for his suitcase to come out on the track. There was definitely something happening off the coast of Newfoundland, but he wasn't sure what it was yet.

CHAPTER THIRTEEN

Atlantic Ocean
Cliffs of the Grand Banks

A bull humpback whale breached the surface, sending a sprout of sea water gushing from its blowhole. The massive, solitary whale was following the migration path south, chasing the capelin before they moved on to breed. The baleen whale was a brute, measuring just over fifty-feet long and topping the scales at over thirty metric tonnes. He had been around for eighty years now, and he had become adept at putting on layers of thick blubber that would sustain him during the warmer weather. Its giant head and lower jaw were covered with tubercles, giving it a bumpy look. Slapping the surface of the water with its fluke tail, the bull dove back into the deeper waters. The giant mammal sang a complex song, calling out to the other members of his species, warning them to stay away from his meal. The humpback pumped its tail and raced towards the capelin, getting ready to to feast upon thousands of the small fish. Whales would not eat once it reached the warmer waters, and it needed to make sure it had enough blubber to last him a long time. Once the mating ritual was over, he would gorge himself in the nutrient-rich waters of the Caribbean before making his migration back north.

The whale could sense a threat lurking in the depths, watching him from down below. Leaving behind the capelin, the whale headed back to the surface and slapped his tail off the surface, warning the would-be predator of its massive size. The humpback whale dove back down but could still sense the predator circling below, each rotation getting closer as it prepared to make its move. The whale sped towards the surface and breached, the entire thirty tonnes exploding through the surface waters as it jumped clear out of the water. It made an enormous splash upon re-entry, sending a thunderous boom echoing throughout the ocean. For now, whatever lurked in the shadows had disappeared.

Atlantic Ocean
Cliffs of the Grand Banks

Joan felt the shock wave as the humpback whale crashed back into the ocean, and dove back down to four-hundred metres. The whale would be more than enough to sustain her and the pack of male Carcharodons following her trail of hormones. She kept far enough away so that the humpback couldn't sense her, biding her time before she made her strike. She needed to disable the mighty whale's tail. One smack from its powerful tail would be devastating, even to a shark of her size. For now, she cruised along, her jaws slightly open in a mean snarl as she waited for an opening. She would be able to wound the whale if she managed to catch the bull off guard.

Joan sensed the smaller great whites closing in on her, sensing she was growing tired and weak from the chase. It had been days since her last significant meal. The odd creature that she found swimming in the waters wasn't big enough to sustain her for long. Her stomach was growling with pain as the muscles tightened from starvation. Her body had undergone a lot of changes since reaching sexual maturity. Her calorie intake had doubled to get ready for bearing pups. Joan continued along the drop off of the Grand Banks as the whale chased a school of smaller fish closer to shore. She wasn't going to be able to attack in these shallow waters. There wouldn't be enough room for her to escape if her attack failed. Her body was growing impatient with her, waiting for its opportunity to feed.

CCGS Cape Spear
Atlantic Ocean
Grand Banks

Kevin used his GPS to guide the CCGS *Cape Spear* towards the last sighting of a humpback whale the fisherman reported seeing near Cape Race. They estimated the giant whale to be well over fifty feet. The local news crew paid handsomely to hitch a ride with the Canadian Coast Guard. Lewis stayed behind on the docks, waiting to meet some marine biologist. Kevin was glad to have command of the ship without Lewis bothering him. Melvin poked his head into the cabin occasionally to preach to him about one thing then the other, but, like most of his crew, Melvin stuck around with the locally famous weatherman. What made things even worse was that his wife wasn't talking to him, making him sleep on the couch. His back ached from the old wooden beam that ran down the centre of the couch. He didn't get much sleep last night after a long fight about nothing. She thought he was cheating on her with some floozy he met at some bar; she didn't believe him when he said he was spending long hours trying to work on the McGilvery case. It was out of character for him and beyond his job description, but Labyrinth Oil paid him and Lewis a substantial amount of money to help keep things out of the media. Specifically, they didn't want the media to find out about the giant squid's tooth they had found. Mr. Kurosawa said it would give the activists a reason to shut down the pipeline. Since the *Architeuthis dux* was an endangered species, the pipeline would be shut down instantly if they decided to take up residence along the its path.

The camera man stood alongside the rail, taking footage of the large swells as the weatherman tried to explain how global warming was creating the large waves. He also predicted another foggy day because of the cold Labrador Current and the intense heat of the sun. Kevin had heard it all before, and he still wasn't buying in to the scientific concepts related to global warming. To him it just wasn't plausible. The way some people talked about the phenomenon, it would be the end of the world, an apocalypse to end all of humanity. The earth always found a way of balancing itself out. The melting ice caps and rising ocean levels would be balanced out later by something else, all part of the plan.

The nose of the ship cut through a four-foot swell, sending a spray of ocean mist over local weather man Edward Sheaves. Kevin laughed as the stalky man reacted like someone had slapped him in the face, terrified by some unexplained force. The saline water dripped down from his balding hair and over his microphone as he hunched over to shield himself from another blow. Kevin glanced at the ship's navigational system and found it hard to believe he was only twenty nautical miles from his destination. The fog rolling in over the waves made it appear like they were segregated from the land, trapped out in the middle of the ocean, isolated on all sides by nothing but blue water and groggy looking clouds. The ocean floor was just one hundred metres below. He hadn't even arrived at the drop off of the Grand Banks yet.

Melvin walked into the cabin; salt water soaked into his jacket, leaving behind white stains on the sleek black fabric as the heat baked it. "Hey, Kevin, Edward Sheaves wanted to do an interview with you about discovering the *Swift Current*."

"Did you tell him that Lewis is taking the lead on this one?" Kevin didn't want to be publicly involved, but it would help smooth things over with his wife if he was on news. It would give his story credibility.

"I didn't think that mattered," Melvin grumbled. "So, what do you want me to tell him?"

"It's fine, Melvin. I'll do it," Kevin called out, not wanting to miss his opportunity to prove to his wife he wasn't lying about working the McGilvery case. "Just give me some time to get my thoughts together." He didn't want to say too much. The police investigation was gathering intel as it heated up. They were closing in on two local fisherman that had motives and no alibi other than each other, and their story didn't seem to add up.

"Thanks, Kevin." Melvin softened his tone. "I'm proud of you for letting Lewis take the lead on this case." It had been Melvin's idea to let Lewis take control over the search for Jonah McGilvery. So far it had been working in Kevin's favor.

"Just let me get us to the humpback whale. Maybe they can get some footage of the whale during my interview. I know that would draw the ratings on the evening broadcast."

Atlantic Ocean
Cliffs of the Grand Banks

The bull whale thrashed its tail on the surface of the water, trapping the capelin in a net of bubbles. The small fish were caught in the shrinking ring, unable to find a way out of the closing trap. The mighty humpback whale opened his garage-door-sized mouth, the fish caught in the flow of water entering its stomach as it swam into the school of capelin. Thousands of the tiny fish disappeared down its throat to be digested in its giant stomach. When the bull's stomach was filled with fish and water, he swam to the surface to squeeze the excess water out through the baleen plates in his mouth. Finally feeling sated, the giant whale allowed half of his brain to rest, the other half taking control of his base instincts. The whale would drift with the tidal currents underneath the choppy surface waves. When he needed oxygen the mammal's primal instincts would take over and propel him to the surface to get the air he needed.

Atlantic Ocean
Cliffs of the Grand Banks

Joan could sense the lumbering giant drifting aimlessly through the waters. The electrical impulses from the enormous muscles had all but stopped. The whale's heartbeat had slowed to nearly a stop as he floated just below the surface. Joan rose from the depths quickly, closing the gap to one hundred metres. She circled directly below the creature, waiting for the electrical impulses from his giant heart to quicken, but her prey still didn't feel her presence. Joan dove straight down so she would be able to generate enough force to seriously injure the whale with one quick strike.

At two-hundred metres the *Carcharodon carcharias* rushed the whale, his giant shadow blotting out much of the sunlight from the surface. The massive silhouette didn't move until it was too late. The great white shark slammed hard into the whale's underbelly, her razor-sharp teeth grasping on to a large jawful of blubber. Joan thrashed her body from side to side. With her jaws clamped shut, she tore a hunk of meat off. A flood of warm blood washed over her as she extended her jaws to bite into the severed whale flesh. She sensed the whale's tail muscles exploding to life; she dove just in time to avoid the swift defensive blow from the giant appendage.

A flood of deep red blood poured into the ocean from the bull whale's wound. It wasn't dead, but it was severely wounded. The whale cried out in pain, bemoaning the effort it took to stay on the surface as it bled to death. The whale was far too strong for Joan to mount another attack. The piece of blubber she swallowed would have to be enough for now. She waited patiently for the humpback's electrical impulses to fade away before she would strike again. The scent of blood filled the ocean. The male white sharks that had been chasing Joan quickly closed in, no longer keeping their distance. With the strong scent of blood mixing with her estrus, the aroma drove them into a frenzy, making them brave. They took turns rushing the giant humpback, not getting close enough for a taste but close enough to make the bull defend himself. The dying whale had to spend a great deal of energy thrashing its tail in self-defence, causing its heart to pump harder. Gallons of blood spewed from the gnarly gash on its stomach. The whale struggled to keep its body right side up. His massive thirty-tonne frame rolled over, exposing the creature to a barrage of savage attacks from the snapping jaws filled with rows upon rows of teeth.

Joan sensed the last flicker from the creature's heart, ascending towards the carcass to fill her gullet with enough whale blubber to last her for days. An overpowering bouquet of impulses had sent the sharks into a frenzy as a giant pool of blood washed over them. Joan was just about to snap her jaws closed on the exposed stomach of the whale when one of the males took her by surprise, ramming his jaws into her gills to get a better grasp on her. Joan tried to fight the male shark off, but he held on long enough to commit the brutal ritual of mating. Once it was all over, Joan was exhausted from the ordeal and needed to feed. She made her way back to the whale carcass to eat.

CCGS **Cape Spear**
Atlantic Ocean
Humpback Whale Carcass
A giant blood stain floated around the humpback whale as he bobbed up and down in the water. Kevin could smell the coppery scent of blood

and the potent tinge of ammonia that flooded out of the creature and into the ocean waters. Edward Sheaves plugged his nose as he buckled over at the hips, clutching his belly as he suppressed the urge to vomit. "Jesus Christ, what the hell happened here." Kevin looked over at Melvin.

Melvin was using the binoculars to get a better look at the floating cadaver. "It looks like something tore it up," Melvin muttered to himself as he peered through the lenses. "Not that long ago that somebody reported seeing the whale here in the harbour. It was only three, four hours."

Kevin checked his watch. "Looking at just over three hours. Do you think it ran into the boat's outboard motor?"

"Not possible. We would have gotten a report from the vessel that collided with a beast this size." Melvin shook his head in disbelief. "Whatever did this is still down there somewhere."

"What the hell could have attacked a bull that size?" Kevin asked. "It could capsize this boat with a flick of its tail if it had the notion." Kevin slowed the engine down, not wanting to get too close to the dead whale's corpse. The image of a squid tentacle rising from the depths and clutching hold of his ship raced through his mind. Imaging a giant mouth filled with filed teeth opening wide as the tentacles dragged people into its mouth made Kevin's heart beat a little faster.

Edward flew to the rail and let the contents of his stomach drop overboard into the ocean. He leaned into the metal pole, a strand of vomit dangling from his lips as the breeze picked up. "You didn't get that on film, did you?" He looked over his shoulder with a defeated expression on his face.

"No, boss." The cameraman looked over at Kevin and winked, giving him a thumbs up. The red light on the video camera was blinking.

Melvin held up his finger to his face, trying to hush everyone on board. Kevin stopped to listen, all he could hear was the sound of the waves crashing against the shore and the weatherman heaving up his guts. "What is it, Melvin?" Kevin asked puzzled.

"Listen carefully. I can hear something tearing at the whale carcass." Melvin closed his eyes to enhance his hearing ability. The *Cape Spear* drifted towards the humpback whale slowly now, the boat entering the blood slick. "I can almost feel it."

Edward Sheaves suddenly jumped back from the rail and tripped up in his own feet, dragging himself backwards towards the middle of the ship. A horrified expression was plastered on his pale face. His jaw dropped open with astonishment. The cameraman kept the video rolling, getting his boss on film. It would probably never make it on air, but it would definitely be shown to his friends. A giant grin appeared on his face as he watched Edward shiver with fear.

"Sh… Sh… Shark," Edward stammered.

Kevin approached the railing to get a better look overboard. The water was thick with blood and guts, the whale's entrails floating on the surface. Something was churning up the water just below the belly of the giant humpback. Bubbles of air churned up through the bloodied mess making it hard to see. Then a grey dorsal fin created a ripple as it approached the whale. A dorsal fin kept rising from the water, standing nearly three-feet tall when the back of the shark finally emerged from the water. The shark's jaw snapped open and shut in an instant, tearing into a hunk of whale blubber. The shark's caudal fin thrashed from violently side to side as it shook its head, stripping the flesh from the humpback whale. When it finally tore off a piece big enough, it dove below the water. Another set of jaws clasped onto the whale to get its share of the food.

"What the hell is going on, Melvin?" Kevin had never seen anything like this before in his life. "Those sharks are massive." Every shark had to be at least twenty feet. Tall dorsal fins emerged from below everywhere as the sharks devoured the massive humpback whale in a frenzied state.

Melvin didn't wait for Kevin. He went into the cabin and put the boat in reverse. Some sharks were over half the length of the forty-foot search and rescue ship. Kevin grabbed Edward by the collar of his shirt and dragged him into the cabin without protest.

"Thank you," Edward said as he clutched the cabin wall.

"Get in here!" Melvin called to the cameraman who had moved closer to the rails to get a better shot. The boat sank into the swells and rose up on the crest of the waves, a bloodied sea splashing up over the decking of the ship. The cameraman held his video camera in one hand and braced himself against the rail with the other. "Hey, asshole, get in here before a wave tosses ya overboard!" Melvin barked.

"Come on, Sam, get in here. We got enough footage now." Edward's tone was full of dread for his daredevil friend, but he refused to leave the security of the cabin.

Kevin headed back outside. The clouds parted overhead, and the sun lit up the gruesome scene with visceral visuals. A giant puddle formed around the massacre. Bloodied water was saturated with scrapes of whale skin and guts, and tiny shreds of intestines floated in the water. The humpback whale's flesh was torn to pieces. No more blood flowed from the mammal's wound, but the body still shook as sharks pulled and tugged at the remaining blubber. "Come on, Sam…" Kevin started to say as one of the sharks slammed its tail fin into the boat, the vibrations rocking the entire hull of the *Cape Spear*. "Sam, get back in the cabin!" Kevin growled as he reached out just in time to catch Sam. A rogue wave crashed over the side of the ship, nearly sweeping Sam off his feet. He let the camera drop to his side as Kevin pulled him away from the railing. "That was too fucking close," Kevin said.

Melvin steered the boat in the opposite direction of the feeding frenzy and pushed the engines to capacity, leaving the grisly scene behind them. "Were those great whites?" Edward asked, his body still trembling with fear.

"I think so. What other species of shark gets that large?" Sam questioned.

"No one has ever reported white sharks in these waters." Kevin was still processing what he had just seen. "There must have been a dozen of them."

"I got some excellent footage." Sam sounded jovial.

"Too gruesome to air on the news, Sam," Edward added. "We won't be able to show that."

"I can edit the footage. We have to let people know what happened here," Sam protested.

"Melvin, how far away is the Labyrinth Oil pipeline?" Kevin remembered the divers started their work today. The blood in that water would attract all the sharks around for miles, putting them in a frenzied state.

"I'd say bout ten miles, maybe less." Melvin picked up the radio receiver. "Dispatch come in."

CHAPTER FOURTEEN

Labyrinth Oil Office
St. John's, Newfoundland

Kal Kurosawa looked down onto the street from his office window, shaking his head at the protesters. The crowd around the building slowly formed into a mob. First the fishermen gathered to protest the closure of the ports all over the southern coast, then the animal rights activists showed up to protect the migrating whales. Now a group of environmentalists led by Madeline Northcott joined in the protest to fight against the company. He observed as she rallied her troops. Madeline's fist pumped in the air as her fellow hipster friends lifted up their arms at whatever nonsense she was spewing against Labyrinth Oil.

"A message for you, Mr. Kurosawa," his secretary buzzed in through the speaker on his computer.

"What is it now?" Kal found himself growing frustrated with everything. The moment Jonah had gone missing, all the responsibilities had been thrust onto his lap. He didn't have time to deal with Jonah's obligations, he had his own agenda to carry out.

"It's from the Canadian Coast Guard. They say there is a pack of sharks close to the pipeline."

"Thanks. I'll deal with it." Kal didn't take his eyes off the growing mob. Their angry protesting rose above the sounds of traffic from twenty stories down, and the boisterous noise was growing louder. Jonah McGilvery hired Kal to handle one unique aspect of the organization. The analysts discovered something much more valuable than oil beneath the Grand Banks. A complex network of underground caverns underneath the pocket of oil contained something precious and unique. There was enough plutonium and uranium in these grottoes to sustain the world with clean energy for generations to come. The plutonium could also be used to power nuclear weapons. Jonah had always told him it wasn't up to him what the end-user did with the radioactive element. It was Kal's job to find the highest bidder. So far the United States government was hell bent on being just that, offering to add ten percent to the highest bid. Kal had the president of the United States bowing to his every command, applying the leverage from other offers to blackmail the entire country.

Kal couldn't afford to suspend production of the pipeline. He sat at his desk to make a phone call. If there were threats swimming around his workers they needed to be eliminated. He dialed the top-secret number that went straight to the oval office. The sharks would be dealt with one way or another. There wasn't a chance he would halt production now when they were so close to the caverns. For now, he needed to create a distraction that would draw people's attention away from the pipeline. Kal had to convince the police to arrest a suspect in the Jonah McGilvery case. That should draw the media's attention back towards the land and away from his operation. Kal headed into the elevator and put in his key that would grant him access to Jonah's private suite. He would plant evidence in some poor man's boat and pay off one cop to find it. He came up with a diabolical plot to kill two birds with one stone. That chirping birdie outside needed to be silenced long enough to finish this project.

Grand Banks
Atlantic Ocean

The *Carcharodon carcharias* could sense a vast array of signals, distinguishing small foreign objects that entered its domain. Joan could sense the exact moment when a ship dropped anchor, the reverberations alerting her lateral line of the slightest tremors even from immeasurable distances. Joan had learned that these objects were inedible. Normally she didn't bother to investigate, but she could sense the fluttering heartbeat of several creatures near these large sections of foreign metal in the ocean. She wasn't the only great white who took notice; a ferocious pack swam towards the mile-long pipeline being laid by Labyrinth Oil and the unsuspecting workers.

Labyrinth Oil Pipeline
Grand Banks
Atlantic Ocean

The turbulent seas slowed the progress of the pipeline. Darren Pike fought with the controls to keep his one-man submarine steady, the active currents knocking the sub around like a play toy when he didn't exercise caution. Divers welded the giant sections of titanium pipe together from the inside first. The opening of the pipeline spanned nearly ten feet in diameter with pumps at every junction to flush out the sea water once the pipe was finished being put together. One-hundred metre sections of pipeline weighed several tonnes and weren't affected by the current. Driving the sub proved to be treacherous, and entering the entrance of the pipe as the ocean current surged inside was problematic. Bright white lights from his underwater submersible illuminated the darkest depths of the ocean floor, sending the aquatic life scattering for shade. The odd fish would swim past occasionally curious about the subs, but nothing caused them any anxiety. Jagged rocks covering the sea floor were covered in dense algae and rusted out old metal parts. Seaweed drifted in the current, waving in the water as if blowing in the breeze. Beyond the reach of the bright lights all Darren saw was a blanket of darkness. Fish would appear out of nowhere as if by some magic trick as they drifted through the work zone and disappeared again into thin air.

Several of the workers had injured themselves as the strong current smashed them into the outer edge of the giant cylinders. Mr. Kurosawa insisted that production of the pipeline not be delayed. Several of the workers found themselves forced to work double shifts, not getting enough time in between dives. They had quickly depleted their workforce but were awaiting the arrival of another five hundred workers. The problem wasn't finding the laborers; transporting them from the airport to the work site unnoticed proved challenging. Mobs of angry fisherman begged for the work, but Mr. Kurosawa had insisted that the jobs be supplied by an American corporation.

Darren had worked on Labyrinth Oil's first pipeline, but something bizarre was going on here. When Mr. McGilvery built the original pipeline, safety first had been their motto. Now the demand to finish the task on time overruled all, the schedule rigid and strict. Mr. Kurosawa would not tolerate failure as an option. Darren had not seen a price too high to pay to get the job done. Several of the workers suffered severe injuries just to have another person take their place to do the same job. One poor soul had broken his back as the current slammed him hard into the titanium edge of the pipeline. Darren was one of the lucky few who got to control the one-man submersibles.

The Sea Welder Model Five or SW-5 was designed and modified from the older army model by Labyrinth Oil. Scientists at Labyrinth Oil originally designed the sub to make quick repairs to damaged war vessels when they found it impossible to make it back to port. They had modified the new design with four sets of arms, each with a unique ability to work underwater. One pair of arms could be used to pick up large sheets of metal. Another set functioned to weld the sections of pipe together, and a third set was used to cut them apart. The final set was designed to make precise movements that could be used for a wide variety of tasks normally saved for the divers. Darren's skills allowed him to use the arms to tie a knot in a rope if he wanted too. The whole cockpit of the sub was clear, made from a three-inch Plexiglas windshield able to withstand pressures found at depths up to 1,000 metres. The view was only obstructed by the flashing lights on his control panel, the bright LED lights reflecting off the clear glass.

Darren waited for one of the divers to give him the signal to weld the next section of pipeline together so the workers inside could move on. Paranoia crept over him, the vast depths of the ocean playing tricks on his mind as he stared off into the bleak surroundings. It had been about twenty minutes since the welders had made their way inside, but it seemed like an eternity to Darren. The pressures of the deep waters pushed down hard on the SW-5's hull, causing her to creak and groan in the eerie silence. At only 400 metres down the pressure was reaching dangerously high levels. Management should cut the divers' shifts in half, but Mr. Kurosawa insisted they stay down much longer until the next crew arrived. It was only a matter of time before there was another serious accident.

A pyramid snout poked through the dark veil and entered the light. Darren froze as the snarled, tooth-filled smile emerged from the darkness. Cold, black eyes peered at him as it turned its head back and forth taking in its surroundings. The shark's entire body drifted into view gradually, its grey body emerging from the darkness inch by inch. With minimum effort, the great white shark moved its tail fin gliding from side to side. Propelling the colossal frame through the deep waters with ease, it moved gracefully. Its two large nares guided the shark towards the opening of the pipe. Darren tensed up. His heart froze in his chest as he watched the white shark swim towards the crew trapped inside. For a moment, time seemed to stand still as Darren watched hopelessly. Instinct told him to turn and run. His blood ran cold and his body perspired profusely.

He snapped to his senses, realizing that he was operating a submersible, not swimming with the shark. He grabbed the controls of the SW-5 and pushed the throttle forward in an attempt to deter the *Carcharodon carcharias*. Momentarily forgetting the arms were still connected to the titanium pipe, his submersible banked at a sharp angle nearly causing a collision with the pipe. Darren flicked the release switch just before he ran out of space, sending the SW-5 into a tight barrel roll to avoid crashing. Turning back towards the opening to the pipeline, Darren saw nothing. The lights illuminated the sea floor but nothing else. Had he hallucinated the whole encounter with the shark? He had heard of other divers suffering from deep sea psychosis. Some people had called it the rapture of the deep, and others called it aberrations of the deep, but it was all caused by the same thing. Ambient pressure from the ocean mixed nitrogen into the divers' lungs causing nitrogen narcosis, a dangerous problem which could lead to these symptoms and worse: an unconsciousness which was often fatal at these depths.

Darren maneuvered his submersible towards the mouth of the pipeline, the bright lights illuminating the gates of hell. He rubbed his eyes and pinched himself but the demonic setting didn't disappear. Divers tried to swim past the massive shark as its jaws snapped shut on a man's leg. In a rapid motion, thrashing its head side to side, the shark tore the man's leg clean off, releasing a gush of crimson inside the enclosure. As people swam through the horrific blood-filled pipe, they immediately swam straight towards the surface in a desperate attempt to escape the shark's wrath. The blood had attracted more great whites, the scent of blood guiding them to the helpless swimmers. A shark set its sights on Darren, swimming straight into the Plexiglas of his sub. The powerful smack sent Darren spinning through the water. A thin crack formed in the protective glass. Darren held his breath as the water pressure slowly pried open the crack. At first a trickle of water poured into the cockpit before giving way to a flood of salty ocean water. Darren pushed the throttle fully forward and raced towards the surface. His lungs burned as the light of the sun seemed so distant. The surface seemed much further away as he struggled to keep conscious. Darren saw the white caps on the waves of the surface just before he blacked out. The sub broke the rough surface just moments after sea water filled his lungs.

Labyrinth Oil Office
St. John's, Newfoundland

"I understand. Make certain that no one finds out about what took place. I will handle the rest. You just keep this out of the news." Mr. Kurosawa slammed the phone down, nearly knocking the receiver off the table. The next crew wouldn't be ready to dive for another six hours, and now he would need an entirely new team to be flown in. Thanks to Jonah's death, he was already two days behind schedule, and he had already spent over half of the money given to Labyrinth Oil by the American government. Pressure from foreign sources increased. Building this massive pipeline had cost a fortune already, and now he would have to ask for another advance. He dreaded the thought of dishing out capital to the families of the deceased just to keep them silent.

The elevator door opened with a metallic swooshing sound. Miss Eguchi stepped out wearing a black dress with a wide silver ribbon around the midriff. The dress fell just below her knees but a long slit up the side revealed her toned thigh muscle. Her red high-heeled shoes clicked off the floor as she walked towards him. She was caring a beige file folder under her arm which she placed on the table, leaning her hands on the top of the folder as she leaned in towards Kal.

"What's all of this?" Kal asked, trying to avoid staring down her dress.

She opened the folder, spreading the sheets out over his desk. "It's a list of all the family members we need to silence." She held up one page. The worker's name was listed on top and below was his family members and contact info. "This is going to cost us millions of dollars."

"Don't you think I realize that, Hilary?" Kal raised his voice in frustration. "We can't stop now."

Hilary put the papers back into the folder and closed it. "What do we do if people aren't willing to take the offer?"

"We do the same thing we had to do the last time we had this problem." Kal pushed the folder away. "Do you need the number or do you still have it?"

"I still have it, but I won't be responsible for taking any more lives." Miss Eguchi snatched up the folder. "If you want it done, you can call yourself."

Kal avoided Hilary's scornful glare. "Just give me a list of the names of people unwilling to cooperate and I will take care of it." Hilary stormed out of his office; her slate-blue eyes welled with tears. It worried him, what his brother would say if he ever found out what he made his wife do. He had forced her to do horrible things for him since the first day they worked together. Over the past five years she had grown to loath him, but he threatened to kill her husband if she ever told him what they really did. The lies, deception, and cruel actions would bring shame upon their family.

Kal picked up the remote and turned on the sixty-inch high-definition television. The local news was just starting. The anchor was announcing the day's top stories for tonight's program. Kal's blood pressure started to rise as he saw the footage of great white sharks tearing into a deceased whale carcass. He threw the remote clear across the room as a clip of the reporter was getting ready to interview Kevin O'Reilly showed. "I don't have time for this." He was about to retrieve the remote and change the channel when he read the headline. *Labyrinth Oil to blame for the sudden presence of great white sharks.* Kal's blood pressure soared. Turning up the volume he listened as Kevin blamed his company for the sudden appearance of great white sharks in the coastal waters of Newfoundland. *"Since they started lay-ing the titanium pipe they've been showing up. They must be attracted to the metal they're using to build their new oil pipeline."* Kal slammed his fist against the table in a fit of rage.

Kal opened his desk drawer and took out a locked box as he cursed under his breath. Using the key, he opened the safe and dialed the num-ber written on the lone piece of paper that had been kept secure inside. He needed to silence Kevin O'Reilly before he attracted more attention to Labyrinth Oil's latest project. Not only would the investigation hold up the pipeline, it could potentially squash any deal they had made with the American government.

"I need another favor and I require it done now. Money won't be an issue."

CHAPTER FIFTEEN

The Marine Institute
St. John's, NL

The cab driver spoke the whole fifteen-minute cab drive from the air-port to the Marine Institute, no matter how hard Andy tried to avoid carry-ing on the conversation. Andy had been trying to gather his thoughts after that rough landing. His nerves were rattled. The grey-haired taxi driver spoke quickly, many of his words blending into the others, making it dif-ficult to follow what he was saying. His accent was heavy, and his voice was hoarse which didn't help matters. The backseat smelled like cigarette smoke and vomit from the night before. "Uhm…. How much do I owe you?" Andy asked.

"Dats gonna be eighty-four dollars." The cab driver leaned his head into the back of the car. His haggard smile was filled with yellow teeth.

Andy pulled out his wallet and handed him five of the twenty-dollar bills that Ellen had given him before they left the airport. "Keep the change." Andy didn't wait for a response. He threw open the door and dragged his suitcase right behind him as the taxi driver yelled out something. The sun was hiding behind the clouds, but its presence was felt. The air was hot and muggy. Andy couldn't wait to check into a hotel and get a shower. He could feel his shirt clinging to his damp armpits. He headed down a paved path towards the giant glass entrance to the building. Above the doors, in giant white lettering, the name of the building was displayed *The Marine Institute of St. John's University of Newfoundland*. The glass looked deep blue, mimicking the deep ocean waters. The large double doors opened into a giant reception hall. Rows of large white pillars and the marbled floor made it look like the lost city of Atlantis from the books he used to read as a child.

"Good day, sir. Can I help you?" a young woman sat behind the wicket asked gently.

"I'm here to see Doctor Hamilton."

"You must be Doctor Grant." The woman sprang to her feet and came out from her tiny office to great him. Her maroon tee shirt was embroidered with the university's logo in white letters. Her short blond hair was gelled into several sharp looking spikes that must have taken hours to get just right. Her white rimmed glasses made her look like the typical university hipster from some teen movie. "It's so great you could make it."

Andy reached out to shake her hand and was surprised by the girl's powerful grip, the knuckles on his hand cracking as she applied pressure. "Call me, Andy. And who might you be?"

"My name is Samantha, but my friends call me Sami." She blushed as she smiled at him.

"Nice to meet you, Sami." Andy looked around the room at the various plaques and statues strategically placed around the room. "So, should I wait here for Doctor Hamilton?"

"Don't be silly. I'll take you down right now if you'd like." Sami's emerald eyes looked longingly at Andy.

"Sure, that would be fine."

Sami turned right and started to point to the statues as they headed down a long hallway. "These are all the past deans of the university," she explained as she began to lead him towards a set of double doors. "This part of the university nearly closed a few years ago until we opened it up to the public. Now it is one of the most popular attractions on the east coast of Newfoundland. Which is great considering how important the ocean is to our existence." Sami nearly talked as fast as the taxi driver, but at least he could pick out all the separate words. "Doctor Hamilton's work has been featured in several scientific magazines. I'm sure you must have heard of her. Her thesis on the effects of the melting ice caps on the waters off the Grand Banks has been ground breaking." Sami continued to gush.

Andy chuckled a little. "I haven't heard her name before, but to be honest I don't read many of those magazines anymore." Andy was ashamed to admit it, but over the last few years he only focused on sharks so he'd look better on television. He devoted his life solely to learning all he could about the *Carcharodon carcharias* and hadn't taken the time to broaden his horizons. "Caught up in my own studies." There was an awkward silence for a moment, only their footsteps echoed down the hallway. Andy wasn't sure if the girl was being polite or shocked by his revelation, but now he wished he had just agreed with her. "This place is kinda quiet today huh?" They passed by empty classrooms and laboratories.

"A lot of our students are out on the water learning how take samples, and some are gone on a whale watching expedition," Sami said as they passed by the cafeteria. The smell of deep-fried foods made Andy's mouth water. "So, tell me what brings you to Newfoundland?"

"Well, actually, we have tracked a *Carcharodon carcharias* all the way from South Africa to here." Andy didn't want to mention anything about his theory of the sharks' mating ground. "Her satellite tag sent several signals from the southern coast of the island."

"That's so cool." Sami's voice was filled with awe. They turned a corner and a crowd of people were walking around admiring some sea life through the display tanks. "The exhibit is busy today. I guess word got out that a great white was brought here." Children pressed their faces to the tank making faces at the codfish as they swam by, ignoring the do not tap on the glass sign hung from the corner on a white sign.

"So, this keeps the university running, very clever," Andy said as he watched a little boy chase after another, running in and out of the displays as their mother buried her nose in her cell phone.

"Darnold could you at least try to enforce the safety rules," Sami yelled out to a gawky teen across the room. The young man looked up from the floor but couldn't see the problem, his glasses nearly sliding off his greasy face as he looked up. "No running, kids." The children didn't listen. Their mother, her face cast in the dull white glow of her phone, called out to them half-heartedly.

"So, you guys put the great white on display somewhere?" Andy looked around at all the tanks, trying to spot his fish.

Sami shook her head. "No, we kept the shark out back. Only staff are allowed out there. It's right this way if you'll follow me." Sami led Andy through a door at the back of the room and into a working cell of scientific holding tanks. The frigid cold of the ocean wrapped itself around Andy as two giant filtration systems pumped cold salt water through the pipes overhead. A young woman wearing a white lab coat was bent over the shark's carcass, kneeling down on one knee as she took a photograph. The light from the camera illuminated the pure white belly of the *Carcharodon* pup. The open jaw revealed the still developing teeth which were still an inch long just months after birth. Ellen's film crew was gathered around the seven-foot body of the shark, getting all of their equipment ready for Andy. Their cab must have arrived long before his, giving them a chance to set up.

"Doctor Hamilton, your guest is here."

The young woman was startled by Sami's voice, nearly leaping out of her black rubber boots. She turned around quickly as she regained her balance. Her cheeks were rosy red from the cold, and her eyes had such a light shade of blue they were almost grey. Her chestnut brown hair was tied into a messy knot atop her head, the light shimmering in the glossy hair spray she used to keep it under control. "You must be Doctor Grant." A jubilant smile crossed her face. She held the camera tightly to her chest.

"Nice to meet you, Doctor Hamilton." Andy extended his hand, but Kate ignored the gesture, staring at him like a school girl. "Please call me Andy."

"You can call me Kate." Her voice was high pitched. "I'm so glad you could make it here so fast."

"I was actually on the way here for research anyway. I see you met my crew." Andy waved to them. They nodded at him as they set up the camera.

"Ready when you are, Andy."

"So, you obviously didn't need me to identify the shark. This is a perfect specimen." Andy admired the great white shark's textbook perfect signs. The pure white belly, even the dark grey back side had no signs of scarring or indication of disease. The pectoral fins were nearly a foot long, its dorsal fin in perfect condition. "So how can I help you?" he asked.

"Well it's the cause of death." Kate pointed to the shark's belly.

"No signs of disease." Andy bent down and looked at the grey organs in its belly. "Have you opened her stomach lining? I've seen great whites try to eat things that are too big and block their throats off. They basically starve to death as they can't pass food down to their digestive track."

"I didn't open anything. I didn't want to touch anything." Kate kept looking at the camera as she spoke.

"Ignore the camera, just pretend it's you and me here." Andy motioned for the cameraman to push back slightly. "It looks silly on television." Andy looked around the shark's insides. "Are you sure nothing fell out when you cut him open?"

"I didn't cut him open." Kate defended herself. "This is how the shark was brought in to us."

Andy pushed his hand inside the slime-covered opening, pushing the organs around inside. "The shark's liver is missing. Do you know if there are any orcas around the area the shark was found?"

Kate picked up a clipboard and flipped through some pages. "The captain that brought the body in said that the killer whales seemed to be playing with the shark. Tossing it up into the air."

"Killer whales have been known to feed on the nutrient-rich livers of great white sharks. We still don't know how they are able to do it, but they can remove the liver with as much precision as a surgeon." Andy used his television voice for the camera, hoping to generate a great sound clip for the show. "I haven't heard of many great white sharks being discovered off the coast of Newfoundland. Do you get many?"

Kate shook her head and scrunched up her nose. "It's extraordinarily rare to discover them so close. I don't think we've ever encountered one so young."

"We certainly have stumbled across something here." Andy used his most mysterious voice, hamming it up for the camera.

"Cut."

"So how do you think the shark ended up in our waters? How old do you think it is?" Kate asked once the camera stopped rolling.

"Hey, guys, can we get the camera rolling again. This will be great for the show." Andy waited for the cameraman to hoist the heavy piece of equipment back onto his shoulder. "Kate, can you ask that same question again please."

Kate looked at the camera, dumbfounded. "So old do you think the shark is?"

"No, the other question, please." Andy was ready to divulge his theory. "We can edit this later right?" The cameraman shot Andy a thumbs up from behind the large piece of equipment.

"How do you think the shark appeared in Newfoundland?" Kate seemed uncomfortable in front of the camera now, her eyebrows furled.

"Well, Doctor Hamilton, I believe the pup was birthed here," Andy started to explain. "I have a theory that the *Carcharodon carcharias* are brought back to these cold Atlantic waters by instinct. They travel thousands of miles to mate and give birth near the Grand Banks. The nutrient-rich water is filled with abundant sources of food, and their natural predators are very rare in these waters." Andy stared straight at the camera. "It's the ideal nursery for a young generation to grow up and learn how to survive before migrating to other oceans."

"Cut," the cameraman said without much enthusiasm.

"Thanks for everything, Kate." Andy smiled wide, showing his bright white teeth. He felt like the interview went great, and it would make an interesting part of the documentary if his theory planned out.

"You don't actually accept that a great white shark gave birth to that pup here do you?" Kate questioned him. "I mean, that species of shark is not prevalent in these waters?"

"I actually do, and I have facts that back up my theory that the great white shark is perfectly capable of keeping itself hidden from humans if they choose." Andy defended his thesis.

Kate looked down at the shark carcass. "Wouldn't we have seen signs of them? Dead whales should have been more common than they are." Kate shook her head in disagreement.

"Maybe they have been eating other sources of food." Andy wasn't giving an inch. He was growing more confident with every clue. "We just have to find what they've been feeding on and I'll find them."

Kate stood in silence for a moment. "Do great whites eat squid?"

"Great whites will eat just about anything, but there would have to be a lot of cuttlefish in these waters to sustain their appetites." Andy knew that it was possible but highly improbable.

"What about a giant *Arcitheuthis dux*?"

Andy nodded his head in agreement. "That should do the trick. Thanks for the advice, I know that's going to help me find that shark nursery." Andy turned to leave but stopped when Kate's hand reached out and clutched his shoulder. He turned back towards her, her slate-blue eyes staring intently back at him.

"I'm coming with you."

CCGS Heart's Content
St. John's Harbour

"How much is this costing us?" Ellen complained as she carried her suitcase aboard the Canadian Coast Guard ship. The wheels got stuck on the rungs as she dragged it up the ramp, the bottom of the metal plank clanking off the wooden wharf as the waves rocked the boat side to side.

"Nowhere near as much as some of those private ships," Derrick answered as he carried a heavy metal briefcase in each hand. The satellite tracking equipment was heavy. The amplifiers needed to track the signal in the open sea weighed over fifty pounds each.

"It will all be worth it when we find Joan." Andy rubbed his fingers against his thumb, gesturing the universal sign for money with his free hand. "Besides, this is probably the only ship that can house all of us. I think we will be out here for a few days until we finally find her."

"And why is she here again?" Ellen stared back at the wharf as Kate Hamilton spoke with the young captain of the vessel. Her maroon university sweater made her look more like a freshman than a professor. "I'm not paying her for this."

"Don't worry about it, she's glad to come along as long as I agree to let the university capitalize on the newfound discovery of a shark nursery in their own backyard." Andy looked up as Ellen disappeared behind the gunwale of the ship, the rails obscuring her from his view. "Besides, I need her to help track down the giant *Arcitheuthis dux* in order to find out where the whites have been hiding all these years!" Andy yelled out.

"I thought you had a signal from your shark?" Ellen looked over the railing and down at Andy.

"She pinged on our system not two hours ago, but if she doesn't surface for another few days, then the tag become useless," Derrick piped up.

Andy reached the deck of the *CCGS Heart's Content* and was caught off guard by how luxurious the search and rescue ship was. The forty-eight foot long and eighteen-foot wide vessel was brand new, the crown jewel for the Atlantic's search and rescue fleet. The paint still hadn't faded from the salt sea mists. There wasn't a sign of rust anywhere on the sleek deck. There were four levels below deck on the ship. The bottom level housed all the mechanical rooms and the twin dual-diesel engines that could push the mighty ship to over twenty knots. Storage rooms filled the third level, along with a state-of-the-art infirmary and the kitchen. The crew's quarters were on the second level, each room with its own private bathroom and television. The mess hall was just below deck along with a bar and lounge straight across from the dining hall. Rescue equipment and life rafts littered the deck. They'd secured a deep-submergence vehicle to the stern of the ship by heavy chains and thick steel cables. The foredeck was mostly clear except for the Canadian flag fluttering in the wind. The bridge was two levels with a giant crow's nest stretching fifteen feet above the captain's room on the second floor.

"I will drop this equipment off on the bridge." Derrick's forearms were bulging, the sunlight shining off the layer of sweat covering them. His shoulders were tensed together as he hurried down the long corridor.

"I'm heading to my cabin." Ellen turned to leave in the opposite direction. "Once you're settled away, why don't you come see me so we can go over the plan again." Ellen winked at him.

"What room are you in again?" Andy called out.

"205."

Footsteps rocked the ramp behind Andy. He watched as Kate boarded the ship with a scowl on her face. She stormed straight past Andy and headed towards Ellen without saying a word. The ramp thumped as the Captain boarded his ship. "You must be Kevin O'Reilly," Andy said.

The young man glared at him with a disgusted look on his face. "No, Mr. O'Reilly seems to have gone into hiding. He isn't answering his phone so I'm filling in for him today." The Captain was an intimidating individual. His dark features amplified his angry snarl. "My name is Lewis Park. I'm going to be taking you out." Lewis brushed past Andy, nearly bumping into him as he hurried off towards his post. "We leave port in twenty minutes, so make sure you have everything you need. I don't plan on coming back to dock just because you're not ready."

Andy checked his watch and headed down to Ellen's room to make sure her crew had everything they needed. He was lucky enough that Derrick was able to take everything they needed in one trip. The camera crew would probably need to rush to be ready in time to leave.

Grand Banks
120 Nautical Miles South of Newfoundland

Joan's had gorged herself on the flesh of several divers, her appetite insatiable over the past few days. No matter how much she ate she couldn't satisfy her hunger. The juice from the humans was sweet, and their flesh had an awkward texture. The outer layer was troublesome to chew; she had to swallow the rubbery coating whole as she shredded the living thing's body apart. The creature's entrails were tender and rich with blood-filled organs that had left Joan wanting more. The bouquet of blood was unlike anything Joan had ever encountered. Now she scanned her head back and forth, picking up several heartbeats of the giant squids as they swam in the deeper waters off the banks' cliffs.

The *Carcharodon* was glad that her male suitors and stopped following her. The pregnant shark no longer attracted them. Her body had ceased to produce the hormone that guided them towards her. Her gills were still sore from the male shark's viscous bite marks, and the bright red wounds had grown inflamed. Her suitors now moved on towards other female sharks that had made the migration back to their ancient breeding ground. Joan needed to keep feeding in order to keep her energy levels high in the cold water. She descended into the deeper water, keeping her distance from the gathering of *Architeuthis dux*. She waited patiently for one of the squid to drift away from the others so she could isolate it and make an easy meal. She wasn't in dire need of food, her belly still full of human flesh and bones, which allowed the predator to be patient. This allowed the shark to carefully stalk her next meal, establishing her as the deadliest predator in the ocean.

200 Metres Deep
Marystown
Atlantic Ocean

Architeuthis dux began its ascent to the surface to feed. The swell of the ocean's current as the moon pulled the tide higher signaled to the creature that it was nighttime. The waters remained cool as the fifty-foot squid rose to the surface, the jet-black waters concealing her from the view of prey along the surface. She had fled the depths since the arrival of the *Carcharodon carcharias* into its hunting grounds and was being forced to the surface to feed. Normally the creature preferred to stalk the frigid, bleak waters of the deep, concealing itself in the purgatory of the ocean depths. Lately the creature found it was able to suffer the surface waters, which had cooled considerably over the years.

The *Arcitheuthis* used its giant eye to search the surface, able to see extremely well in the moonlit waters. It would never dare surface during the daylight. The bright yellow rays hurt its eye, but the soft white light allowed it to approach the surface. In the distance a shadowy object rocked along the surface, its vibrations mimicking the fluttering muscles of an injured whale, a trail of blood in its wake.

S.S. Harbour Delight
Marystown
Atlantic Ocean

Madeline Northcott awoke to find that her hands had been bound by tight nylon rope, and a soiled rag filled her mouth with the bitter taste of fish guts. She tried to stand up but found out the hard way that her wrist had been bound to a board behind her back. She nearly wrenched her shoulder out of socket against the ties that bound her to the small dory. The moon hung high in the sky, its soft warm light trickling over the waves revealing the choppy waters. A brisk breeze blew foamy salt water in her face, the aroma of the deep brine alerting her that she was out in the open sea. She was a prisoner to the swell of the ocean, rising up and crashing back down like the angry heartbeat of a bull. Madeline knew once the ocean died, the entire earth would soon disintegrate in its devastating aftermath. The boards underneath her creaked and groaned as the boat bobbed up and down, the rough seas threatening to sink the smaller boat.

The last thing she recalled was standing outside of the Labyrinth Oil headquarters, pounding her fist against the door demanding an audience. She had flown into St. John's from Washington on a mission to shut down the underwater pipeline. Now she had to find a way to survive this ordeal. She forced her tongue against the rag, pushing the vile mixture of blood and fish slime down her throat. Madeline tried to suppress the urge to throw up, but her stomach muscles clenched tight as the slurry entered her guts. The vomit raced up her throat, but the gag blocked its way. The immense force had nowhere to go but out of her nose. Thick globs of bile cut off her air supply. Her chest burned as she slowly choked on it. She tried to blow her nose, but the vomit was too thick and stars quickly entered her vision.

"Not yet." A man's voice startled her from behind. A mighty hand grasped a clump of her hair. Jerking her head back he ripped out the rag. Madeline gasped at the air. She had to spit out the mouthful of vomit and fish guts before filling her lungs with large gulps of oxygen.

"What the hell are you doing to me," Madeline cried out in between heavy sobs, tears cascading down her check. She strained her neck trying to glimpse her kidnapper, but he held her at bay, pressing her neck forward and pinning her chin to her chest.

"Relax, this will all be over soon."

"You don't have to do this," Madeline pleaded.

"Well if I want to get paid then sadly, I do," the man's gruff voice answered her. "Nothing personal, just some poor life decisions I made led me down this path, but at least it pays well." He laughed anxiously.

"Please spare me." Madeline choked out her words in between sobs. "I have a family."

"What does it matter?" the man asked. "If you took your own advice, the world is ending."

"The world's not ending, just going through some violent changes," Madeline replied in a hushed tone, realizing who was behind this. Labyrinth Oil needed her silenced, and it was pointless to struggle.

"I am sorry," the man said as he propped her up. "For what it's worth, I believe in your work," the man said regrettably as he gave her a sharp push.

Madeline tumbled head over heels and plunged into the frigid waters. She instinctively tried to kick her legs but her feet had been tied together. The cold water drove the oxygen from her lungs as a fire ignited inside them. She looked up at the dying moonlight as she found herself sinking into the darkness. Tilting her head up she could see a rope stretching out from the boat that had been tied off around her waist. A sudden lurch contorted her back as the rope tightened. Her spine nearly snapped in two as she was hauled to the surface. She forced her head back as she breached the surface waters, sucking in oxygen and salty sea water. Momentarily relieving the burning sensation from her lungs, the ice-cold water number her limbs. She knew she wouldn't have long before hypothermia set in. She thought about screaming out but decided it would be best to conserve her energy, praying that the delirious man was only trying to scare her away from Labyrinth Oil.

The man peered over the edge of the skiff, his ginger beard running wild over his face. He wore a black wool knitted toque. Strands of straggly red hair fell out from underneath. "Now if you'll excuse me, I have more work to do." He dumped a bucket of fish guts and severed codfish heads over her. As the mixture poured over her, the blood was colder than the water and sent chilling shock waves throughout her body. She watched hopelessly as the man cut the thick nylon rope and started the outboard motor, the dense scent of diesel heavy in the air as black smoke spewed from the engine. The dory slowly drove out of sight. Madeline waited desperately for a miracle as her mind raced with visions of some deep sea monster below coming up to devour her. Her head slowly drifted under the water as her muscles seized up. She sank slowly at first before something below her snatched her leg in a tight vice-like grip. She looked down in horror as an impossibly long tentacle dragged her deep underneath the surface.

Another tentacle appeared out of the obscurity, wrapping around her torso, taking complete control of her. A giant yellow eye slowly appeared from the darkness as the *Architeuthis* dragged her towards its snapping beak. Not waiting to feel the razor-sharp beak, Madeline opened her mouth and flooded her lungs with the ice-cold waters, praying to drown before the squid tore at her flesh.

CHAPTER SIXTEEN

Marystown
Town Wharf
The Queen Mary

Detective Shawn Bowers walked down the dock, the weathered boards groaning underneath his feet as he approached Al Patrick's berth. A twenty-five-foot schooner was anchored to the dock, the black and blue paint peeling from the hull. The name of the boat scrawled along the stern read *The Queen Mary*. Detective Bowers had taken a call from Kal Kurosawa and had greedily taken the bribe to frame the poor fisherman. He had received half of the payment into his account from an offshore company late last night, a one million dollar payment up front and another million once Al Patrick was in custody. Being a detective, he should have asked more questions, but he was desperate to retire at a young age and police work wasn't allowing him the lifestyle he had envisioned. When Shawn had first spoken to Mr. Kurosawa, he thought he would have offered a meagre bribe which he probably still would have taken, desperate for money and a one-way ticket off Newfoundland. He carried a rag covered in Madeline Northcott's vomit; the fabric torn from her alma mater sweat shirt. In his pocket was some of Jonah McGilvery's jewelry that he wore to all of his public appearances. All he had to do was plant them on the boat before he took Al away in handcuffs, leaving the personal items behind for the other police officers to find. Mr. Kurosawa didn't care if the conviction stood, he just needed to buy himself some time to complete the pipeline.

As Shawn approached, he could see the elderly gentleman asleep in his chair through a port window, his head slumped back and to the side at a painful angle. "This is going to be much easier than I thought," Detective Bowers said out loud. He peered through the windows to get a better look. The muscles in the man's neck look like they had been stretched beyond their limits, his head weighing too much to hold up. As Shawn approached the boat, he could hear the waves slapping off its side in a relentless rhythm.

He walked up the ramp that led to *The Queen Mary*, the old boards sagging down dangerously as he placed his weight on the frail structure. He reached out and grabbed the waterlogged rope that acted as a rail, preventing anyone from falling down in between the boat and the wharf.

Shawn gasped a sigh of relief as he placed his foot on the deck of the boat. He looked over his shoulder and down into the gap. The blue water looked much darker in the shadows, giving it an illusion of being much deeper than it actually was, and the short frequency of waves as they beat off the side of the wharf then the side of the boat made it look like a tempest. He crept slowly towards the captain's quarters, trying not to make any abrupt sounds as he approached the opening. A strange sound was coming from inside the enclosed cabin, an eerie sound that he couldn't identify. He laughed as the table came into view. Several empty brown beer bottles rolled back and forth with the waves. Al Patrick's filthy hands grasped a half full bottle of Jack Daniels whisky, held between his legs for better support. His green dress shirt was unbuttoned, and his sweat stained wife beater had seen better days. A putrid stench of vomit and urine caught in Shawn's throat, nearly making him puke up his coffee. Al had pissed himself sometime recently, his dingy blue jeans stained dark blue all around his crotch.

Shawn opened up a cupboard under the sink and placed Madeline's swatch of cloth under the sink, next to the bleach and cleaning supplies. Then he looked around the room, searching for a safe place to plant the jewelry before settling on the pocket of a yellow slicker that hung from an oversized screw in molding around the door. He let out a deep sigh, rationalizing that Al Patrick would be better off in jail than left to rot in this boat. The elderly fisherman was running out of time, and at least being in a cell back in St. John's he would get three square meals and a bed. Shawn took out his cell phone and called for backup.

"I need back up. I've arrested a drunken man aboard *The Queen Mary*, and I believe I may have found something."

Shawn put the phone down as the old man let out a long, anguished groan. Al batted his eyes open, squinting against the sunlight as he let out a disgusting belch. "What's goin hon ere. Who-tha fuck are ye?" Al slurred his words.

"Mr. Patrick, you are under arrest for the murder of Jonah McGilvery and Madeline Northcott." Shawn held out a pair of cuffs while hovering his hand over his service pistol, making sure that Al saw the gesture. *You're doing him a favor. The old fool doesn't know it yet, but he's better off this way.*

The Labrador Sea
Atlantic Ocean

A deep and cold water mass, the Labrador Sea is located between the Labrador Peninsula and Greenland. It was formed over sixty-million years ago, during the separation of the North American and Greenland Plates. The stretch of one-thousand kilometre sea reaches near three-thousand and four-hundred metres at its deepest depth and stays at near-freezing temperatures all year round. Nearly five-metre waves carry large icebergs down from the Arctic Ocean, making it a desolate and barren stretch of the earth's surface. People fish close to shore but avoid going out into the deeper waters.

Kevin O'Reilly woke up in a state of deep confusion, his brain throbbing against his skull as the inflamed brain matter pushed in all angles to escape the pressure. His arms and legs were bound together with thick ropes, his mouth was gagged, and his eyes were blindfolded. Kevin coughed repeatedly until the rag fell from his mouth. He sucked in large mouthfuls of fresh air, spitting out the oily sensation left behind in his mouth. He found himself unable to remember how he got here, and his body trembled with fear. The sour stench of sweat filled the air and mixed with the tangy metallic taste of hydraulic fluid. The floor of the helicopter vibrated as the blades slowed down. The change in elevation wreaked havoc on the pit of his stomach. The running boards touched down first. He had no idea where he was or how he got here. The roaring of the engine eased back, as the hiss of the hydraulics pierced deep into his skull. A metallic thud was immediately followed by a frigid gust of moist sea air. There was a taste bitter brine of salt left behind on his lips.

"Help!" Kevin cried out over the howling winds as they whistled into the cargo bay. No one responded. An ominous sound of footsteps crunching through the snow approached as someone lingered around outside.

"Please help me," Kevin begged desperately, praying for this nightmare to be over. "Why are you doing this to me?"

There was no answer. Kevin heard someone board the helicopter, their boots clunking off the metal floor as they jumped up. A powerful pair of hands grabbed him underneath the arms and dragged him away from the helicopter like a rag doll.

"Please stop this. You don't have to do this."

Bright light blinded Kevin as the blind fold was pulled down over his face, the sunlight burning through his eyelids. Squinting his eyes against the sun, Kevin saw only a silhouette of the man who stood towering over him. Once his eyes adjusted the man's features slowly came into view. The man's face was covered with a giant ginger beard that covered the neck of his jacket. His dark brown eyes stared down Kevin with a distant look to them.

"Who are you? What do you want with me?"

Kevin's antagonist reached into a breast pocket, pulling out a picture and threw it in his face. It nearly blew away with the wind, but the old Polaroid picture pinned to his chest by the steady gust. Kevin looked down to see a picture of his son and wife sitting on the living room couch. "What did you do to them?" Tears rolled down his face.

"I haven't decided yet," the man answered in a gruff voice. "That's up to you."

"I'll do anything you want, just make this stop." Kevin looked all around. The only thing visible was the rough waves and bright blue sky coming together far in the distance.

"I can spare them, but you have to agree to stay here."

"Where am I?" Kevin looked around at the sea of blue. There wasn't any land in sight.

"We are on an iceberg in the middle of the Labrador Sea. We are slowly drifting towards Newfoundland as we speak." The man took off his backpack and tossed it on the ground at Kevin's feet. "There's enough supplies in here to last you for days."

"You're fucking insane." Kevin strained against the rope, his efforts only managing to dig the fibres of the rope deep into the soft tissue of his wrist.

"I've been told you don't believe in global warming." The man let out a hearty chuckle. "And you think that I'm insane."

"What does any of this have to do with global warming?" Kevin's voice trembled, barely audible over the crashing waves as they sent tremors through the core of the iceberg.

"Nothing really. This is all about your little news clip. Labyrinth Oil is paying me to silence you, and I've just decided to get creative." The man took out a large nine-inch hunting blade. The serrated back of the knife looked like a set of razor-sharp fangs. "Normally I'd just shoot you."

"You're going to stab me to death." Kevin tried to back away, his feet slipping over the surface of the ice. He tucked his knees into the fetal position and waited for the killing blow.

"Nothing like that. Stabbing someone is too personal. I've got nothing against you so don't take this personal." The man threw the blade into the ice, the handle sticking straight up as the tip of the blade dug two inches into the thick ice with ease. "No, I'm going to leave you here on this iceberg and let science teach you one final lesson." The man knelt down and pulled the hood of his jacket over his head. His breath was heavy with the scent of coffee and cream. "Do you remember it wasn't that long ago that Newfoundland was famous for the large icebergs that would drift off our shores?"

Kevin didn't respond. He didn't know if he should make a move for the knife or take his chances in the ocean. He was paralyzed with fear, neither option giving him any hopes of survival.

"Well, thanks to global warming, most of the smaller ice floes like this will melt before it reaches the shores of Newfoundland." The man grasped the ropes that bound Kevin's hands together, yanking him forward like a rag doll. "If you make it close enough to land, you can try to swim to shore so you can warn your family. If you don't make it within five days, I'll pay that pretty little number of yours a visit."

"Fuck you. I'll never make it five days out here." Kevin spat into the man's face, the thick yellow phlegm dripping down his beard. "You have to spare my family. I'll do anything you want. Whatever they are paying you I will double it."

The man laughed hysterically as he reached for the handle of the knife. He cut the ropes with one strong movement before throwing the knife into the ocean. "You couldn't even come close to raising enough money. Trust me, I already checked into it."

"Please don't hurt my family." Kevin clasped his hands together in front of his face, pleading with the mad man.

"Maybe I will, maybe I won't. I just want you to think about it as you're out here drifting towards Newfoundland. It should take about four or five days depending on the currents. They are pretty slow now, but the wind has been picking up." The man kicked the giant bag that he had thrown on the ground. "Everything you need to survive for five days is in here."

"This is insane. You can't leave me here like this to die," Kevin called out as the man walked back towards the helicopter.

"You wouldn't be the first Newfoundlander to be left alone to die on the ice floes." The man jumped into the cockpit. Kevin tried to jump to his feet, but the ropes tripped him up, and he fell hard into the ice. His face smashed against the solid surface, a gush of blood pouring from his nose as he looked up at the helicopter blades gaining speed. Kevin reached down to untie the rope from his legs. The knots pulled into tight bundles making it near impossible to free from his legs.

Kevin eased himself to his feet, the warm feeling of blood running down his face made him sick. He could taste the coppery fluid as it dribbled over his lips and into his dry mouth. The helicopter lifted off from the iceberg as Kevin watched hopelessly. The aircraft got smaller and smaller as it faded away into the horizon.

Kevin sat down beside the duffle bag and unzipped it. A yellow Gor-Tex coat lined with faux fur was laid on top. Kevin pulled it over his shoulders and zipped it up. The jacket blocked the wind from chilling his bones, and he could feel the warmth quickly building inside. The stranger had stuffed a green knitted hat and a pair of green waterproof gloves into the pockets to help keep him protected from the wet weather. Bottles of water and brown paper bags filled with rations had been stuffed into the bag along with a Coleman stove. Kevin lay down on his back and stared up at the sun as he drifted along with the Labrador Current, basking in the sun's warm glow. His whole body shivered violently as the cold water from the melting iceberg seeped into his jeans. Kevin didn't know if he would make it through the night. He sat up and fumbled with the ropes. he worked patiently to free his legs. He didn't know how much longer this iceberg would last. He needed to be ready to swim for it.

CHAPTER SEVENTEEN

CCGS **Heart's Content**
42 Nautical Miles East of Cape Race

Andy looked at the chalkboard outside of the mess hall. He couldn't decide between the deep-fried cod and chips or the calamari rings for supper. The waves had been treacherous as the giant swells slowed the voyage, already putting them behind schedule. Derrick and Ellen had already grabbed their meals and were sat at a table with Kate, chatting about the wicked weather. "I'll have the calamari." Andy watched as the server ceremoniously dumped a scoop of the squid rings onto a plate. The worker pointed towards two large silver containers filled with fries or mashed potato, the staples of any sea voyage. "Potato please."

Andy walked over to the massive stainless-steel cooler to grab a bottle of water and a bowl of pudding for his dessert. He joined the others, sliding his tray across the table as he sat down. The waves rolled endlessly outside of the port window. Rough whitecaps peaked at the crest of the wave before rushing down into the valley's below. "So, have you been able to get the satellite tag up and running yet, Derrick?" Andy asked.

Derrick looked over at Andy with an annoyed look plastered on his face. "I did actually, no thanks to you."

"Sorry, Derrick, I made him stay behind to organize what the cameras were going to film," Ellen said, defending Andy. "We need to know what to be looking for."

Derrick stabbed his fries with his fork. "Whatever. I mean it's all set up now so I think I'll be heading down for a nap. I'm sick to my stomach." Derrick stood up and nearly lost his balance as the ship rolled forty degrees to the port side. His utensils flew off his tray and skittered across the fibreglass floor. He reached out and clutched the bench. "I'm still not sure why I need to be on this damned ship. It would have been the same if I set up on land and radioed you."

Andy felt bad for making Derrick board the CCGS *Heart's Content*. "I thought you'd be alright on this ship. It's much larger than the ones we are used to," Andy apologized.

Derrick waited by the table for a moment, waiting for his legs to adjust to the sway of the giant vessel. "If you need me, I'll be in my room." Derrick walked away from the table, grabbing onto the back of other people's chairs with every change of direction.

"I guess that's the reason I always found him in the tent," Ellen tried to joke, but Andy sympathized with Derrick.

"I haven't seen the seas this rough in a long time." Kate changed the subject. "Must be a storm approaching fast. Maybe we should consider heading back to port."

"This vessel was designed to operate in these conditions." Ellen was determined not to lose any more time. "We will reach the Grand Banks soon and once we get some footage of a pregnant shark; you can run back to your little classroom."

"Your documentary is pandering to the lowest common denominator," Kate retorted. "No offence, Andy."

Andy sensed the tension between the two ladies. Both of them were trying to show their superiority over the other. "Listen, as long as the captain keeps this ship out here, we must be safe. He isn't going to put us all in danger."

"Lewis is a fool." Kate snapped.

"So, you two do have a history. I guess that's the real reason you want off this boat." Ellen leaned back in her chair and giggled.

"None of your business."

"Alright, you two, there is no reason to be at each other's throats." Andy wanted to defuse the situation. "We've only been out here for four hours. We are going to have to work together." The three of them sat at the dinner table in silence. The waves ravaging the side of the boat, crashing into the hull with a thunderous roar. Vibrations ran through the entire ship. Andy watched the tiny ripples in his bottle of water.

"Do you mind if I sit with you." Lewis Park stood at the head of the table holding his tray with both hands.

"Please be my guest." Ellen offered him a seat much to Kate's dismay.

"So, is this weather going to force us to turn back?" Andy asked, ignoring the tension between Lewis and Kate.

"This ship was built to handle anything the ocean can throw at it," Lewis responded as if by automated response. "We wouldn't be able to do our job if it wasn't." Lewis let out cocky laugh.

Ellen leaned far back in her seat, stretching her arms above her head as she yawned. "These waves aren't even that bad. I wouldn't say they are over ten feet."

"The waves have been peaking at just over fifteen feet," Lewis added as he took a bite of battered fish.

Kate pulled her chair out and stood up. "Andy, I'd like to discuss your method of tagging sharks." She picked up her empty tray, her glass nearly toppling over.

Andy looked down at his plate and stuck his fork in the powdered potatoes. "Just let me finish up and I'll meet you on the bridge."

"I will be in my room." Kate winked at Andy as she brushed past Lewis. Giving Andy a sly glance as she walked away.

"How much longer until we reach our destination?" Andy asked.

Lewis checked his watch. "I'd say we got at least another four hours or more unless this weather eases up."

Andy took a bit of the flavourless potato mash and stared out at the pitch-black storm clouds approaching from the south. A thunderous boom rolled across the vast ocean, announcing the brooding clouds were ready to burst open. The ominous clouds outside block out the day's light, casting the sky in a premature twilight. Far in the distance a bolt of hot white light split the horizon in half, illuminating the giant waves as they rolled over each other. Thick sheets of rain poured from the sky, the bright white lights of the CCGS *Heart's Content* catching the rain drops in a brilliant display of mother nature's immense power. A flash river formed on the decks as the rain water gushed over the sides and down the windows.

"This storm looks bad. We won't be able to get much of a signal until the weather passes." Andy stood up to leave.

"I'll catch up with you." Ellen brushed Andy off as she rubbed her foot up Lewis's leg.

Andy walked away before his facial expressions betrayed his attempt to hide his jealousy. "Yeah, I'll see you on the bridge when the storm passes." Andy swayed back and forth, the sea rising like a great mountain underneath him. The water was turbulent and unforgiving as if it were angry. As he walked past the window, he witnessed flashes of bright white light on the dark horizon and the gregarious roar of booming thundering approaching them. Gale force winds carried salt water in the air sideways, the rain drops pelting against the hull of the ship. Andy decided that he would join Kate below deck to pass the time. He needed to distract himself from Ellen. His blood pressure rose. He acted like she was betraying him again. He cursed himself for not making a move earlier.

Joan of Shark

500 meters deep

Twelve nautical miles south of the Grand Banks

Jolts of dynamic electrical impulses jarred the great white's ampullae of Lorenzini, briefly overloading her senses with every strike. With every bolt of lightning the jarring force scrambled Joan's senses like a blow to the head. Mother nature forced the *Carcharodon carcharious* to dive deeper and deeper, abandoning her quest for food. Normally she would be able to pinpoint a single fish amongst a school, but the electrical overload fried her navigational senses. Joan still sensed the tremendous surges rushing through the ocean even at depths of five-hundred metres, forcing her to keep diving further down in a rush.

She hastily dove to seven-hundred metres to escape the overbearing signals. The inky black waters were filled with fantastic creatures. Prehistoric lifeforms adapted to life without light by developing the ability to produce light through a chemical reaction called bioluminescence. Different species of fish used the light in different ways. Several species of squid used this light to camouflage with the overhead light so they couldn't be seen from below. Some fish like the angler fish used it to lure their prey while others used it to attract a mate. Any of these tactics should not fool the great white shark. The creature's heartbeat gave away its position, but her senses still hadn't recovered from the overload of electrical impulses. The lightening from the surface no longer bothered Joan, but it forced her into danger. Before she could react, the long tentacle of a fifty-foot *Architeuthis dux* wrapped around her torso. The suction cups allowed the squid to gain a tight grip on her before she could swim out of the arms' reach.

The giant squid wrapped another suction-filled tentacle around Joan and began to pull its body towards her. Joan thrashed her tail fin and forced all of her energy into her muscular body in an attempt to sever her attacker's grip. The shark was able to pull the *Architeuthis* through the deep ocean waters with her but couldn't shake the creature's tentacles from her body. With every fleeting moment the squid managed to tighten its vice-like grip on its prey, its giant black eye staring at Joan intently. Joan had to keep moving. It was the only way she could keep breathing. She changed direction abruptly and hurtled her pyramidal nose into her assailant, generating as much force as a head on collision between two cars. The massive *Architeuthis* was caught off guard by the shark's powerful blow. The vice-like grips of its tentacle that had once been its greatest weapon would now spell the creature's doom. The suction cups couldn't let go of Joan soon enough, as her jaw jutted forward into the squid. A row of three-inch razor-sharp teeth sliced into the squid's soft flesh, tearing it apart with ease. Trying desperately to escape, the giant squid tore its tentacles from its own body as the shark continued to chomp into its flesh. Her mouth opening and closing, pieces of shredded flesh and dark blood spilled out from Joan's mouth.

Joan felt the lifeless tentacles slowly fall away from her body, leaving behind bright red circles from the powerful suckers. She swam back up to six-hundred metres with her mouth left slightly ajar in an evil grin, her jaw spasming as the water flushed through her gills once more. She could sense the powerful heartbeat of another squid nearby amongst the flutter of a school of smaller fish. Too exhausted from her fight and mentally drained from the storm, Joan kept her distance from the squid and the surface. The strikes of lightning on the surface were hitting faster now as the storm was passing directly overhead.

CCGS Heart's Content
Twenty-nine Nautical Miles South East of Cape Race

Andy knocked on the door, the shallow drumming echoing down the hallway. He heard Kate shuffling her feet across the floor, the door latch sliding open just before the door creaked open. Kate had let her hair down, the long strands of golden-brown hair falling over her shoulders. "Come in." Holding open the door, Kate removed her university sweater. Underneath she was wearing a charcoal grey tee shirt. She had tucked one side into her jeans while letting the other side hang loosely over her hip.

Andy stepped inside the cramped quarters and pulled out the single chair by the side of the bed. "Thanks."

Kate walked over and sat on the edge of her single bed. "I can't believe how quickly this storm sprang up." A steady flash of bright light lit up the dark waves outside the tiny porthole of her berth. "I don't remember the weatherman saying anything about this storm on the evening weather."

"They were too busy reporting on the whale carcass to worry about the weather." Andy recalled the weatherman bumbling through the weather, still rattled by the discovery of sharks shredding apart the dead humpback whale.

"I meant the university sonar station," Kate giggled. "I never listen to that guy, anyway."

"I've never seen waves so big before in all my life," Andy said as a wave rocked the boat, rattling the entire steel hull. "This is getting crazy. I'm just waiting for the captain to bring us back to port."

"Yeah, he won't be doing that. He's got too much to prove." Kate's voice was bitter and full of resentment.

"So, you two obviously have a history," Andy prodded, hoping for an interesting story or anything that would help pass the time.

Kate looked down at her feet. "We used to date before." Her voice was low, the pounding raindrops making it difficult for Andy to hear her. "I thought it was serious, but I guess I was wrong."

Andy stared straight ahead, not knowing what to say. He heard the hurt pouring out, but she didn't seem to want to elaborate. For several minutes they sat in silence, the raging storm outside offering enough distraction between them to not make it awkward. The cracking claps of thunder and howling hiss of the wind roared over the open ocean. Magnificent waves had their way with the forty-eight foot search and rescue ship. Through the tiny porthole, the sky vanished behind giant towering walls of water. Thick lines of white foam whirled around in the waves like spiderwebs. Every time the boat crested a wave the entire ship would be rocked violently as the nose dove back down into the next valley, the next wave slamming hard against the ship.

The sudden sound of the door opening to the adjacent berth startled both of them. Andy overheard Ellen talking to someone. He wanted to press his ear against the thin wall to hear what she was saying but wasn't sure how Kate would react. Thankfully Kate was just as interested as he was when a deep voice responded to Ellen. Kate leaned back on her elbows, the back of her head resting against the wall. The sound of heavy breathing and fumbling against the furniture brought a flustered expression to her face, and Andy felt his heart sinking into the pit of his stomach. The groans and moans grew louder, escalating quickly in Ellen's room.

"Would you like to grab a drink?" Kate stood up from the bed quickly as the entangled bodies fell into the bed, the frame thudding off the wall.

"What are the chances they're serving in this storm?" Andy asked before he caught on to the meaning of her question. She didn't care what they did, she just wanted to leave. Andy wasn't stupid but knew that he didn't want to stick around much longer either. "Let's go see."

They left Kate's room in a hurry. The sounds of Ellen's passionate moans spilled into the hallway as they rushed towards the exit. Andy turned the corner, trying his best to push the sounds out of his mind, but he still heard them no matter how hard he tried to shake it. He was jealous and furious at the same time. he wanted to break down the door and demand an answer from Ellen. He truly believed they had been hitting it off since the plane ride back from Africa, but he couldn't understand how quickly she threw herself at Lewis. He cursed at himself under his breath. They walked past the entrance to the dining hall and just a little further down at the end of the hallway were two giant double wooden doors with large brass handles. Andy checked the door handle. Relieved to find it unlocked, he held the door open for Kate.

The sharp smell of liquor wafted through the room, mixed with the stench of sick. The only reason the bar was open was to give access to the bathrooms. Andy could hear groans as people heaved their guts up from behind closed doors. Behind the teak bar there were only two shelves that had been stacked with every hue of amber liquid. Andy was glad to see members of the film crew sprawled out on the giant leather couches, their skin as pale as ghosts. A trio of dartboards lined the back wall covered in red and green patterns. There was a pool table in the corner, the balls clanking off each other with the sway of the boat in a never ending racket. The floor boards were made from light hardwood and given a sophisticated shine. All the furniture was made to resemble vintage pieces, like it had been pulled from the Titanic. The Victorian era pieces looked expensive and brand new. The colors were bright and vibrant, the fabrics spotless and plush looking.

"Swanky." Andy was shocked by how big the bar on the search and rescue ship was. "I've never seen such a large bar on a search and rescue ship."

"Yeah this is the government pissing away money trying to appear better off than they actually are," Kate replied with a disheartened tone. "They purchased this craft from a New Zealand cruise line company in order to save money."

"Where do you want to sit?" Andy asked as he scoured the room looking for a quiet place to talk. They spotted a leather love seat unoccupied behind a wooden coffee table and headed over. Andy sank into the soft cushion, the air seeping from underneath him slowly, lowering him down towards the floor. Kate sat down next to him; her leg pressed against his sending a warm tingle racing through his body. "I can't believe they didn't convert this into something more practical, but it is a beautiful place to come relax after a long day's work at sea."

"This ship is the one they use to entertain dignities that visit the island." Kate placed her hands in her lap, her fingers nervously fiddling with each other. "A false showcase of how well off the government is in this province."

"That seems like a huge waste of money for no reason." Andy leaned back, questioning himself about putting an arm around her but wasn't sure if he should.

"The government here likes to pretend we are doing better than we are, but they are nothing more than a bunch of crooks. Instead of getting something we needed, we asked for an outlandish ship to show off." Kate complained as she leaned into Andy, pressing hard against him as the boat began to change direction. The waves tilted the boat at thirty-degree angles as it glided up and down with each swell. She reached out to brace herself, her hand falling on his knees. "We must be making our way out towards the Grand Banks now," she said. Andy's stomach contents were rolling with the ship, the waves getting larger now as they entered the eye of the storm. He braced himself against the arm of the sofa, allowing Kate to fall into him with every crash of the stern. He embraced her toned, warm body as it pressed against his muscular frame. He fought the urge to puke his guts up, desperately wanting to stay on the couch with Kate he swallowed back a mouthful of bile.

The CCGS *Heart's Content* headed into the gale force winds head on. The twin engine ship struggled to stay on course as the wind buffeted the ship one way then the next. Outside, the wind continued to howl, pelting the window with rain mercilessly. The engines groaned under the pressure, billowing out two black plumes of diesel smoke behind her. The entire boat creaked as the wind relentlessly battered and tore at every crevice of the ship as it growled with the violence and raw power of Poseidon himself. The booming thunder cracked overhead with virtually no break, the flashes of lightening streaking through the sky.

"I'm going to be sick." Andy tried to stand up, but the boat rocked hard forcing him back down. He tucked his head between his legs, hoping that the nausea would pass.

Kate rubbed his back gently, her hands pressing lightly just between his shoulder blades. "You'll be fine. Just focus on the floor. Don't look out the window," Kate spoke calmly.

"How can you handle this?" Andy asked as he tucked his knees closer together. He had grown up on the ocean and spent most of his waking hours on a boat, but he had never gotten seasick before.

"I've grown accustomed to the harsh weather off our coast," Kate said gently. "This will pass soon enough."

Andy groaned in agony as the hull shuddered. He felt Kate's arm reach out and guide his head into her lap. "Just close your eyes and try not to think about it." She ran her fingers through his hair trying to soothe him. "So, tell me, how did you manage to get your own television show?"

"Well that's a long story." Andy swung his legs over the arm of the sofa, looking up at Kate. Her hair veiled her face as she stared out to the sea.

"Well we got nothing else to do, unless you have something better in mind?"

Momentarily forgetting about Ellen and Lewis, Andy could think of other things to do to pass the time, but the weather prevented him from making any moves. "I remember you suggesting this will pass soon."

Kate smiled. "You probably have time for one story."

Andy felt safe in Kate's lap. He focused on her slate-blue eyes and pushed out everything else. "Well, when I was working on my thesis for school, I invented a device that would deter sharks from populated beaches. I used underwater acoustic speakers to play orcas singing to each other. Great white sharks avoided killer whales because they had recently begun to feed on their livers."

"I heard about that. You set those up on the beaches of South Africa." Kate smiled as she looked down at Andy. "So, why don't we use your device in North America?"

Andy could sense the sea sickness passing as he lost himself in conversation. "As I'm sure you know, the *Carcharodon carcharias* have evolved differently all around the world. Whites in African waters hunt in murkier water than those on the western coast of California. They have acquired particular techniques to ambush their prey. They also face different enemies. Killer whales only hunted the sharks near the shores of Africa, so the great whites near California were not programmed to fear the orcas. We tried to use my method to deter them on the beaches of California, but it failed."

"So, your failure landed you a television show?" Kate looked perplexed.

Andy chuckled. "It was a scientific breakthrough. We discovered that we could assign subgenus classifications to the distinctive types of *Carcharodon*. That and the boat-load of money I made from the government of South Africa allowed me enough popularity and the means to fund my own research. The university loved me and thrust money at me, and the rest they say is history."

"I've watched your show a few times. I must say you're a better palaeobiologist than an actor." Kate grinned from ear to ear.

"Geez thanks, I guess." Andy closed his eyes as Kate played with his hair and the waves grew so large, they dwarfed the vessel. The storm showed no mercy. There was no grace in the waves only wrath and tempest. Andy felt comfortable in Kate's arms. "Can I tell you something I've never told anyone else?"

Kate let out a soft groan. "Sure, I mean I didn't realize this was an episode of *Degrassi High*, but if that's what floats your boat."

"Maybe I don't want to tell you now." Andy became defensive, sitting up and turning to face Kate. Her slate-blue eyes and wide grin allowed him to relax again.

"Oh, come on. I was only kidding," Kate pleaded, clasping her hands together in front of her chest, pretending to beg.

Andy laid back down. "It's about what I did before I got involved in all of this pageantry." Andy paused, building up the courage to continue. "I used to be a clearance diver with the Navy."

"Really?" Kate sounded surprised. "No offence, but I would have never pegged you as being patriotic.

"My job was to clear explosives we found underneath the water." Andy choked back an anguished cry; his throat as dry as sandpaper. "One day I was so intoxicated I could barely function, but I still cleared myself for duty. I found the explosive device and determined that it wasn't in our direct path. I told my superiors I deactivated the bomb, thinking we would avoid any danger."

"Did the ship change course?" Kate asked, invested in the story.

"No, we made it to port with no incident just as I predicted."

"Then what happened?"

"A research vessel charted by a high school science group passed us as we entered port. The scientists were showing the teenagers how to tag great white sharks in an effort to get them interested in a career in marine biology." Andy paused, warm tears rolling down his cheeks as he remembered his commander calling him into the office. "They hit the explosive device I said I deactivated. No one survived. I received a dishonourable discharge from the Navy."

Kate wiped away a tear from Andy's face. "I don't know what to say."

"You don't have to say anything." Andy closed his eyes. "Every time I enter the water with those sharks, I pray one of them will end my suffering."

The Labrador Sea
Atlantic Ocean

The piping hot yellow sun beat down on Kevin, sweat dripping down his backside. Looking down at his feet, he watched helplessly as tiny rivers of melting water flushed from the iceberg into the ocean. The sun was relentless in its attempt to melt the massive hunk of ice. Kevin couldn't sit down because the flood-waters were much too cold. His leg muscles were getting sore from standing in place, the surface much too slippery to walk around. His feet ached from the ice-cold waters that soaked through his boots and drenched his socks. It was amazing that he found himself so hot and cold at the same time. It brought with it a sense of dread.

A gale force wind threw the cold waters of the ocean into his face with a furious rage, the waves rocking the mighty iceberg in the rough current. The bright horizon began slowly fading away as the sun dropped beneath the water, casting looming shadows across the ocean. Kevin's mind raced with fear. He didn't know if he was more afraid of drowning or freezing to death. He remembered how his grandmother used to tell him stories about how her grandfather had been left behind on the ice floes during a winter storm to die during the great sealing disaster of 1914. He lost most of his fingers and toes to an extreme case of frostbite before he fell through the ice. Kevin began to imagine he would soon experience exactly how much his great grandfather suffered that day.

Kevin shuddered. Ominous grey clouds rolled in towards him far in the distance, bringing a brisk wind with them. He wasn't able to judge how much longer it would be until the storm reached him, but the atmosphere was already changing around him. The wind whipped into his face, carrying a chill with it. The vast storm front stretched across the whole horizon to the south, the creeping shadow heading his way. Unable to find any sign of land in any direction, his only hope was that the storm would miss him as it swept over the ocean.

His heart beat faster and faster and he started to hyperventilate. He sat down to catch his breath, the cold waters soaking through his jeans, sending a chill throughout his body. Kevin didn't want to face a night out on the open ocean in a storm with no shelter. Kevin lay back. A pool of bitter cold water pooled underneath him. His body shook uncontrollably as his muscles fought against the cold, his brain suppressing the instinct to move. He closed his eyes to wait for the cold to take him away.

CHAPTER EIGHTEEN

The Labrador Sea
Atlantic Ocean

Ice cold ice pellets tore at the skin on Kevin's exposed cheeks. He tried to open his eyes, but his tears had frozen them shut once the sun had disappeared beneath the waves. He tried to move his hands, but the muscles in his arms were numb. A thousand ice cold needles pierced his body sending shock waves of pain racing to his brain. He tried to kick his legs, but his feet were encased in ice. The melted water had refrozen and trapped him against the ice flow. He knew he should have been cold, but his body wasn't shivering anymore; his muscles had all but given up. He squeezed his eyes shut and tried opening them several times before the thin layer of ice finally broke. The perfectly dark sky was littered with a thousand white specks. A full moon above cast a shimmer across the waves. All he saw above his head was a clear night sky. He didn't see any clouds even though it was hailing.

Kevin tried to scream for help, but his throat was too dry. His tongue was glued to the roof of his mouth. He tried to make enough saliva to wet his tongue, the lump of flesh nearly choking out his air supply. Desperately wishing this was some terrible nightmare, he closed his eyes once more praying that he would slip back into a deep sleep. Kevin found no comfort. His backside was rubbed raw. Huge blisters had formed from the rough ice that glued him to the ice floe as the waves rattled the chunk of ice back and forth. He couldn't feel his toes. He tried to wiggle them but nothing happened. Images of his family raced through his mind. Horrible images of them dying in their own personal hell played against the back of his eyelids. The mad man who had left him to die on the ice floe had learned about his own opinion on the effects of global warming, punishing him ironically with death by the bold statement. His wife was deathly afraid of fires, and he worried that she would be burned alive. His son was deathly afraid of heights. He pictured him dangling from a tall building, suspended precariously from a rope that would give away at any moment.

"Hello."

A distant voice carried on the wind. Kevin opened his eyes and stared off into the oblivion of space. He moved his head to the left, his hair ripping from his head as it tore from the ice. All that remained in his field of vision was the flicker of moonlight kissing the crests of the waves. He rolled his head to the other side in one painful movement, but there was only emptiness no matter where he looked. He must have imagined the voice.

"Are you alive?"

The voice sounded closer now, more familiar than it was before. Kevin tried to clear his throat. A giant lump formed in his swollen throat. With his mouth wide open, he let the ice pellets fall into his mouth and melt inside.

"H… H… HE… Help." Kevin's dry voice cracked.

"Hello."

Kevin forced his arms to move, digging his elbows into the hard surface. He pushed down with all of his might, the skin tearing off his back as he pressed himself up. A painful yelp escaped his lips, tears streaming down his face. "Help me! I'm over here!" Kevin screeched.

"Can you get to me?"

Kevin looked in all directions but couldn't spot the woman's voice. "Please help me!" Kevin cried. Deep sobs cut his sentence into smaller chunks. Looking down at his hands, Kevin nearly vomited at his blackened fingers. The skin looked like it had been burnt in a fire and hurt just as bad. Kevin looked at the ice below him. The tip of his nose had fallen off his face and was stuck in the ice. "Just get me out of here," Kevin begged.

"You have to get up."

"I can't get up!" Kevin screamed in frustration.

"You have to keep us safe."

The voice screamed in his ears.

"This is your fault."

Kevin heard his wife's anguished cry, her calls for help choked with tears. "Amy, where are you." He frantically searched the vast ocean, the delirium setting in now.

"We are down here."

Kevin tried to stand up, but he had no sensation in his feet. He tripped up in his boots and tumbled down the slippery slope of the iceberg, the frigid waters rushing towards him to greet him. He plummeted into the sea face first, the world going completely dark as the jet-black waters engulfed him. The cold no longer affected him, but the salt water stung his eyes as he searched for his family. Kevin's arms and legs felt like cement as he tried move. He drifted deep below the surface. His lungs burned for oxygen. From the depths, Kevin heard Amy laughing maniacally. He opened his mouth to scream. What little air he had left escaped his lips and floated towards the surface, the salty water filling his lungs as he began his descent to the ocean floor.

CHAPTER NINETEEN

Joan of Shark
Four-hundred metres deep
Eight nautical miles south of the Grand Banks

Joan swam through the calming waters in a catatonic state, the closest thing nature would allow to sleep for the *Carcharodon*. Half of her brain rested as her pectoral fins kept rigid and stuck straight out by her sides to keep her upright, her mighty tail fin swaying side to side pushing the ocean waters through her gills. A vast change in her surroundings stirred her to wake. The animal lived her life in a constant state of movement, always pushing forward. Instincts guided the shark from one meal to the next, her stomach and brain linked together by the ocean's most complex nervous system.

The surge of electrical energy slowly rolled past, allowing Joan to venture closer to the surface. Surrounded by ink-black waters, Joan saw the ocean as a vivid map, the beating hearts sending bright signals to the shark's peppered black snout. Water rushed into Joan's golf-ball-sized nostrils, the bouquet of diesel fuel and smoke running through her nose. A giant vibrating source of electrical impulses on the surface caught her attention. The dull sounds of the creaking boat mimicked the sound of a dying whale. With a strong thrust of her tail, Joan changed directions quickly to investigate the disturbance. As she rose from the depths, the ocean changed from a deep violet into an emerald green as rays of sunlight reached out for Joan.

She scaled the rocky sea cliff at the edge of the drop-off that reached up from the depths. It was broken by fissures and caves that were inhabited by seaweed, kelp, and small fish that hid from predators in the tight confines in the rock. The bright morning sun had began to rise high into the sky, the storm clouds vanishing from view. As Joan approached the surface, she still sensed the static electricity left behind from the lightening last night. The ocean currents had returned to normal as the waves died down, letting Joan cruise through the waves with ease as her caudal fin cut through the surface.

A mighty heartbeat caught Joan's attention. The pulse was strong but calm; she turned her snout towards the beating muscles. As the water flushed into her nostrils, she could smell the predator; it was another female *Carcharodon*. All of Joan's senses alerted her to stay away. The vibrations she felt in her lateral line dwarfed even the largest whale she had ever stalked. The hormones that the female produced warned Joan to stay away, and she changed direction immediately. Her motherly instincts took over allowing her to quickly realize she would stand no chance against this new predator in the waters.

CCGS Heart's Content
Atlantic Ocean
Cliffs of the Grand Banks

Andy awoke to the rapid boom of hammering at his door. His stomach was still nauseous from the storm, but the gigantic waves had long died out. The knocking continued. The sharp pounding seemed in sync with the pulsing in his temples. "Who is it?" Andy groaned as the knocking grew louder.

"It's Ellen." Andy sensed the irritable manner of her voice through the door. "We're here. You need to get in the water now."

Deep down he had hoped it was Kate. Ellen was the last person he wanted to see right now. He rubbed his head, trying to comprehend getting into the water. "Did Derrick pick up Joan's signal?"

"Listen, we don't have time for this. The film crew is waiting and there's no way we are missing this." Ellen forced her way through the unlocked door. Her black hair was glued to her forehead, matted into clumps. A harsh light from the fluorescent bulb gleamed off the sweat on her forehead. She had on an oversized sweater. The neck was much too large for her, showing off the white flesh of her cleavage. Ellen must have sensed Andy's eyes lingering, she tugged at the neck to adjust the neckline. "Come on, we can't afford to miss this."

"I've seen a dead whale before." Andy swung his legs around, letting his bare feet touch the cold floor. He thought about protesting, but he knew Ellen wasn't going to let up. He had already convinced her to travel all the way to Newfoundland, and he wasn't about to press his luck. "What's the big deal," he pouted.

"Just throw on your wetsuit and meet us on deck." Ellen disappeared down the corridor before Andy had the chance to say anything else.

Rummaging through his messy suitcase, he found the vacuum sealed pouch that contained his wetsuit. It was constructed to withstand near-freezing temperatures and contained an electrical current that would distort his pulse from the ampullae of Lorenzini of the great white. He stripped off his sweat-soaked boxers and used a towel to dry off his body, making it easier to slip into his suit. Once he dried off, he put on clean underwear and socks. Stepping into the suit he pulled the arms up over his shoulders and wiggled his body to squeeze into the wetsuit. He grabbed his flippers and rushed down the hallway, fighting the urge to knock on Kate's door as he sprinted past.

As Andy opened the door, he couldn't help but notice the sky was glowing pink with hints of orange hues trying to push its way through the beautiful backdrop. The sun rose into the air like a burning ember shooting from a fire, its orange glow shining fiercely. The deck of the *Heart's Content* was buzzing with activity as the film crew eased the silver metal shark cage into the waters, making sure it didn't get entangled into the side of the coast guard ship or any of the wires that ran along the deck. Ellen stood near the edge of the rail holding a hand-held camera and a snorkel. She waved at him, her hands flailing frantically trying to catch Andy's attention. "Hurry up before we lose the shot."

Andy obeyed. Preferring not to have to look for a new career, he jogged over the wet deck, his bare feet slapping off the metal surface. As he approached the rail, he detected a hint of the rotting whale carcass on the breeze. He heard the water splashing all around as he saw the dorsal fins slicing through the water around the dead mammal. "Jesus Christ," Andy muttered out loud, his jaw gaping open at the ferocity below. He had never seen so many great white sharks at the surface at the same time.

"You sure you want to go out there with them all riled up like that?" Lewis cried out from above.

"He'll be fine in the steel cage," Ellen answered for him.

Andy's heart was racing, the adrenaline coursing through his veins as Ellen thrust the snorkel into his chest. "I'm not confident that I'm ready to do this?" He searched around for Kate, suddenly feeling the desire to say goodbye to her.

"Once people experience this footage, they will be all over you. You'll be a superstar. We won't have to worry about money anymore," Ellen said enthusiastically.

"What do you mean *we*?" Andy let the last word hang from his lips, questioning the interpretation of Ellen's definition of the term. It was only a few hours ago that Andy pictured them as a couple, but the man standing above him put that image in serious jeopardy. Did she mean business partners? A fury of emotions ran through his brain in a dash. Before he got a reply from Ellen, someone spun him around.

"Come on, before I lose my nerves." Derrick took the camera from Ellen in his giant hand making it look like a child play toy.

"Wait, what about the cameraman?" Andy questioned

"Are you fucking nuts?" one of the crew piped up. "No way I'm getting into that water with all those fucking sharks."

Andy stared at Ellen. The pink glow of the sky behind her made her appear even more beautiful than he had ever seen her before. Her bronzed skin and pale blue eyes basked in the radiating glow of the majestic morning sky. Andy spit into his mask, allowing him to get a better seal. He climbed over the rail of the *Heart's Content* and eased himself down to the cage without speaking to her. Derrick quickly followed behind him. As Andy opened the top of the cage and climbed into the ice-cold waters of the Atlantic Ocean, all he could think about was the old saying his father would say.

Pink sky at night, sailors delight

Pink sky at morning, sailors take warning

Andy kept telling himself he wasn't a sailor. He was a scientist, and he didn't believe in old proverbs. The colour of the sky had no bearing on the situation. The sky may as well have been bright blue. Either way it was a treacherous and stupid idea to climb into an untested cage with a herd of savage *Carcharodon*.

Shark Cage
Atlantic Ocean
Cliffs of the Grand Banks

As the cage lowered in the frigid waters of the Atlantic Ocean, Andy discovered the phenomenon of claustrophobia for the first time in the water. The pen had hardly plunged five feet below the surface, the blazing orange tinge of the sun still visible, but Andy found himself trapped inside those steel bars. He was sequestered in obscurity, inserted in an underwater prison cell with Derrick, powerless to communicate verbally with the man who was swimming shoulder to shoulder with him. As his eyes adjusted to the murky waters, the horrific scene folded out before him, making the cage resemble the gates to hell. Tiny steel bars were the sole defence from the snapping jaws waiting to twist his cage into his coffin.

Derrick reached out and patted Andy on the shoulder then pointed to the red light on the camcorder and gave him a thumbs up. Andy quickly reciprocated the gesture, taking his cue that he was now on camera. Andy began by pointing out an eighteen-foot great white shark as it swam past their cell not more than fifteen feet away. Its powerful body propelled the beast through the rough waters with practiced ease. The *Carcharodon* was forcing its way straight for the shredded whale carcass, joining in on the smorgasbord of whale blubber. Six sharks of approximately equal magnitude had already staked their seat at the dinner table, their razor-sharp teeth buried into the dead whale's flesh. As the eighteen-footer rammed its snout into the humpback whale, its body rattled from the impact as the powerful shark drove away its competition. Derrick panned the camera around, noticing at least another dozen great whites coming towards the whale from all angles. Andy looked down at his feet as a powerful current swept underneath. The largest *Carcharodon carcharias* that he had ever seen emerged from the depths. Its jaws must have been at least four-feet wide, its jagged white teeth a terrifying exhibit of its pure ferocity. Its grey back was littered with deep scars that had vivid red rivers running in their depths, its white snout peppered with black dots and two tangerine-sized nares. The horrifying form rose from the shadows. Andy's eyes grew wide and his heart skipped a beat as the impressive anatomy kept forming from the blackness, the cold dead eyes glaring at him as it rose. Its pectoral fins must have spanned ten feet as the trunk continued to widen. The jagged dorsal fin stood four feet from its spin hinting at the *Carcharodon's* advanced age. The body slowly began to thin as the pelvic fin emerged before the seven-foot caudal fin finally came into view.

The great white shark must have been at least twenty-five feet from the tip of its snout to its mighty caudal fin that swayed with an effortless motion. With ease the great white flexed its muscles, thrusting the shark forward as if on autopilot. The cage swayed in it its wake as the shark swam past; it headed for the humpback to claim its meal. The other sharks backed away from the feast as the shark clamped its mighty jaws into the flesh of the whale. The ancient predator's massive girth dragged the whale underneath the water as it thrashed its head side to side. The humpback popped back up to the surface as a four-hundred pound hunk of whale blubber tore off its frame. The massive female shark circled near her dinner, chewing greedily on her meal.

The other great whites started to circle closer to the cage making sure to keep their distance. They waited for the alpha shark to have her fill before they attempted to rejoin the feast. Andy kept his eyes glued on the monstrous shark, not realizing that he had been holding his breath since the creature first emerged from the depths. He wasn't paying attention to the other sharks, but they had finally taken notice of the two divers in their territory. They began to swim closer and closer to the cage, their circles tightening up as they evaluated the metal cage with their cold, dead eyes. Just as their presence registered with Andy, he realized why Derrick was poking him in the ribs. The cage rattled violently as an aggressive male shark rammed his snout into the cage. Derrick dropped the camera as he reached out to brace the cage as if that would help keep the steel bars together. Andy looked around as the *Carcharodons* buzzed around them, amped up on the smell of blood and the presence of the CCGS *Heart's Content* which sent electrical impulses to their brain, tricking them into thinking the coast guard ship was a predator.

Once the first shark bumped the cage and swam away unharmed, the others quickly lost their fear of Andy and Derrick. Andy ducked as an open set of jaws raced towards him, a hellish darkness set in between rows of jagged, razor-sharp teeth. The shark tried to take a bite of the steel; its jaw gaped open right in front of Andy. The inch-thick bars were the only obstacle between Andy and his demise. He found his muscles glued to his skeleton. Frozen in place, his heart stopped beating and his stomach twisted dreadfully as he stared into the blackness that awaited him. He closed his eyes as he heard the metal clang. Another shark smashed the side of the cage with his tale. The force was enough to send Andy toppling over into Derrick, and the two men were pinned against the far side of the cage. Andy looked up at the cable and winch, praying that someone would notice the peril they were in, but the cage swayed side to side. He sensed the vibrations from the metal cable groaning against the strain. With every attack from below, the only thing keeping Andy and Derrick from plummeting to their doom threatened to collapse. The booming, metallic twangs pierced into Andy's eardrum as the cage rocked violently from an unseen force below. One of the guide lines snapped on the cage sending out a shrill metallic roar as the cage dropped at an odd angle, pinning Andy on top of Derrick.

Andy looked on in bewilderment as the sharks seemingly disappeared into thin air. The twenty-five foot female released her death grip on the whale's hide and did one semi-circle near the humpback before fleeing into the distance. Andy could hear his heartbeat thumping inside his chest, his pulse thumping aggressively in his wrist. There was an eerie silence in the ocean. The humpbacks shredded remains swayed back and forth softly with the ocean current, the last of the mammal's blood long expelled from its ravaged body.

The mechanic roar of the boats wench finally rumbled to life, but the cage seemed to be stuck in place, the three remaining guide lines barely hanging on anymore. Something hit Andy in the back. His heart leapt out of his mouth as he spun around to see the camera floating carelessly inside the cage. A flood of relief washed over his body. He found himself laughing as a flood of bubbles escaped from under his mask. He reached out to nab the camera when he saw a soft white glow raising from the murky darkness below. At first it seemed small, but it continued to grow. The soft white glow was just a blob of light, but Andy could tell whatever created the glow was massive. He felt the cage bounce and rattle as the tension on the cable began to raise the cage. He looked up just in time to hear the powerful snap as the remaining guide lines tore from the cage. Suddenly he found himself motionless. Time stood still for a moment before the cage began its rapid descent into the briny depths.

CHAPTER TWENTY

Arctic Ocean

The smallest ocean in the world, the Arctic Ocean, is also the shallowest of the world's oceans. It is situated in the north polar region and is mostly surrounded by Eurasia and North America. The ocean has limited access to the rest of the world and has its own complex system of water flows. Because the density of seawater increases as it nears the freezing point, it tends to sink. While the top layer of water is covered with sea ice, the relatively warm ocean water keeps the temperature moderate. This is the big reason why the Arctic does not experience the extreme weather conditions seen in the Antarctic continent.

The strongest impact of global warming can be seen in the Arctic. Some of the oldest and thickest ice in the waters just north of Greenland, which remain frozen year round, have begun to break up. The sea off the north coast of Greenland had remained frozen since the last ice age, but warm winds and abnormal heat waves have caused the ice to retreat further away from the coast. The arctic ice pack is a large section of sea ice that covers most of the Arctic ocean. This ice melts in the spring and summer but returns in the fall and winter in a continuous cycle. Global warming is giving the spring and summer months an advantage. Each year less and less of the Arctic basin sea ice remains

Darwinism can be summed up by one picture. That picture that shows how man evolved from an ape. Everyone has, at one point in their life, seen the poster somewhere. The theory states that species who have the strongest ability to compete for food, survive its environment, and reproduce successfully will continue. Those species that are unable to adapt will be weaned out by natural selection. It has been often described as the survival of the fittest. This form of evolution is the most commonly accepted theory for new species. Another theory that was developed by Dutch geneticist Hugo de Vries added another layer to Charles Darwin's widely accepted theory. The mutation theory suggested that not all species evolved through the slow accumulation of variation over vast periods of time. Mutation theory suggested that some species were brought to life by rapid transformations, often caused by an extreme change of environment for members of a species that have been separated from the majority of its own kind. The one thing that both theories have in common is that these evolutionary changes are beneficial for the new species to survive. The problem with mutation theory that we chose to ignore is that sometime these mutations create dangerous monstrosities, an abomination within an already deadly species.

Carcharodon carcharias is not normally found in the Arctic ocean, the waters much too cool and the food source unable to sustain a thriving subspecies of the great white shark. Most of the great white sharks who have ever ventured into the unforgiving Arctic Ocean quickly leave. However, a *Carcharodon carcharias* birthed into the environment managed to survive even though its mother died shortly after its birth. Bergmann's law dictated that the shark grow exponentially in order to generate enough heat to survive. The cold waters were relentless, forcing the shark to grow far beyond its species' capabilities. The great white shark was already forty-two feet long and was still growing. It weighed over seven-thousand kilograms, its powerful muscles able to generate more force than any creature in the ocean. Its jaw was the size of a small truck, lined with six rows of four-inch razor-sharp teeth that looked more like steak knives sticking out of its pink gums. Its gnarled mouth contained over four hundred of these triangle-shaped, flesh-tearing tools in its unhinged jaw. Able to exert a bite force just over twenty-thousand newtons, it could quickly disable its prey with one devastating bite. The predator had never seen the light of day, keeping itself hidden underneath the ice floes. It feasted on stray walruses and smaller whales who dared venture beneath the ice floes with it. The grey pigmentation of its skin was no longer necessary and another genetic mutation took place, causing albinism over a few years. Its hide was as pristine and white as the ice above it. As with all creatures affected by albinism, its eyes had no pigmentation. Every vein that ran to the creature's eye turned the white iris blood red.

Now, over the years as the ice retreated, covering less and less of the ocean, the apex predator was quickly running out of places to hide. A strong magnetic force from deep within the earth had called the solitary shark back to its ancestors' breeding ground just off the shores of Newfoundland. The maturing albino *Carcharodon carcharias* could feel the urge to mate overcoming all of its basic needs except for one other. It had followed the frigid melting ice down the Labrador Current and all the way to the southern coast of Newfoundland where it waited patiently for the sun to set. Its powerful sense of smell picked up the scent of a large whale. Its ampullae of Lorenzini could sense that the creature's heart was no longer beating. Not wanting to miss out on an easy meal, the gigantic *Carcharodon carcharias* began its ascent towards the surface. It needed to feed.

CHAPTER TWENTY-ONE

Shark Cage
Atlantic Ocean
Cliffs of the Grand Banks

The pressure began to build in Andy's ear as the cage dragged him down into the blackness. The light blue waters quickly changed to a deeper shade of blue then purple. His mind raced faster than the steel casket that was bringing him to his final resting place. Derrick's arm bumped his head, reminding Andy that at least he wouldn't have to die alone. The white light continued to glow as the cage plummeted past the ghostly figure that was now hovering above them like a malevolent spirit. Andy was in agony from the pressure building inside of his cranium. If he didn't stop his descent, his skull would implode at any moment. His brain was being forced at from all angles. His eyes felt like they were about to erupt out of their sockets. Suddenly a force reached out and caught Andy by the arm. He watched the steel cage continue its descent until it dissolved away into the shadows.

Derrick had opened the top of the cage, and the two men floated next to each other encased in darkness, unsure of which way was up or down. Derrick shook Andy until their eyes locked. He stared into his friend's eyes full of panic. The left eye was completely blood shot leaving only traces of the white iris behind, the pressure bursting a vessel. Andy knew they were far too deep. They had to act before the crushing force surrounding them was too much to bear. Kicking his legs, Andy and Derrick both started to move in the direction they prayed was up. Andy started to claw his hands at the water above his head, trying to grasp the water and pull himself towards the surface faster. Soon the purple water faded, and the deep blue water signalled that they were on the right path. Every muscle in Andy's body began to cramp, his legs as useless as two lead weights, his quad strings growing tighter with every kick. His shoulder and back muscles were tense, acute pain shooting up and down his arms, the pain threatening to shut them down. A knot developed in his neck, forcing him to look down. Shadows seemed to be churning in the blackness beneath, preparing to reach out and drag him back down at any moment.

The deep blue slowly turned a softer shade, the glimmers of sunlight invigorating him enough to keep his arms and legs churning. Andy broke the surface and ripped his mask off, sucking in enough fresh air to fill his lungs. The orange sun beat down on him, thawing his chilled soul.

"Get out of the water!" frantic voices screamed from behind Andy.

A loud splash startled Andy, his heart sank to the bottom of the ocean expecting a set of jaws beside him. He was relieved to find Derrick had breached the surface. "Let's get out of here." Andy began to laugh uncontrollably after cheating death. Derrick pulled off his mask and joined in and nearly choked on a mouthful of salt water as a wave splashed over both men, the briny water stinging Andy's eyes.

"Hurry up!"

"Come on, swim!"

"Move, you fools!"

Andy turned towards the sound of the delirious shouting. The CCGS *Heart's Content* towered over them, its sleek black hull about thirty metres away. Andy raised his arms and waved before giving a thumbs up, signalling that he was okay. He couldn't pick out the distraught faces or agitated voices from the distance, the sun burning brightly behind them, obscuring their features.

"Holy fuck!" Derrick roared, his arms and legs thrashing in the water as he broke off, swimming towards the coast guard ship.

"You have to move, Andy!"

"Don't look, just swim!"

"Move, you fucking idiot!"

Andy turned left towards where the humpback whale should have been to find that it had disappeared. He kept turning around, expecting to see that the great white sharks had returned, but his mouth hung open when he saw it. A five-foot, pure white dorsal fin sliced through the water leaving a three-foot wake behind it. Andy froze in place, not from exhaustion but from the terrifying realization of why the other sharks had fled. A predator much larger had staked its claim over these waters and was now patrolling the area for intruders. The dorsal fin slowly slid underneath the waves. Andy watched as the impossibly large albino *Carcharodon* slipped beneath the surface, its ghastly white glow more terrifying than any shadow that had ever crept up from below. Andy turned and started to swim towards the CCGS *Heart's Content*, the ungodly glow circling beneath him.

CCGS **Heart's Content**
Atlantic Ocean
Cliffs of the Grand Banks

Kate didn't believe her eyes. The albino abomination's mammoth jaws had exploded from beneath the humpback whales carcass, the sheer force that the shark had generated sent the creature soaring above the blue waters. The forty-two foot anomaly hovered out of the water for what seemed like an eternity before gravity reached out and brought it back down. The alabaster shark landed on top of the remaining whale, and the two creatures disappeared underneath an enormous upsurge of salt water. When the vast aftershock of waves finally dissipated, the two giant creatures had vanished from view as if they had never existed.

Then she saw the dorsal fin grow from beneath the waves. The ghost-white hide of the creature glowed brightly beneath the water. The creature was headed straight towards Andy and Derrick as people urged them to swim towards the boat. Now the ethereal glow circled beneath the two men, their arms and legs thrashing wildly through the rough seas straight towards them. "Oh, my god!" Kate stammered as she realized that the creature was getting ready to strike. She rushed down the metal stairs, skipping two at a time, and dashed towards the rail of the ship. "Lewis, you have to get them out of the water now."

Captain Lewis Park turned around; his soft blue eyes filled with terror as he acknowledged his ex-girlfriend. "Grab a life ring and throw it in." Lewis pointed towards the white and red flotation device along the sterling silver wall. He had already tossed one of the rings overboard, but there wouldn't be enough time for Lewis to rescue both men. Everyone else fled in panic, cowering at the sight of the monstrosity that was nearly the same size as their boat.

Kate grabbed the rubber ring and dragged it towards the rail, the length of rope tied off to a hitch on the wall made it much heavier than it looked. She struggled with it. Lewis rushed over and grasped hold of it, dragging Kate across the deck with it.

"Let go!" Lewis barked as they reached the metal railing.

Kate let go just before Lewis hoisted the life ring up to his chest and flung it overboard. Kate couldn't stop the forward momentum that Lewis had generated, and she tumbled over her own feet trying to stop on the slippery deck. Her face narrowly missed the rail as her hand darted out in front of her to brace her own fall. Her fingers bent backwards at an awkward angle, and she felt the calcium in her knuckles pop as they twisted back towards her wrist. Lewis gently placed his hand on her shoulder and helped her up. "Thanks." Kate's voice was faint. The pain welled up in her hands instantly.

The rope hanging over the rail tightened suddenly. Kate looked over and saw Andy had raced past Derrick, reaching the life ring first. The smile that crossed her face quickly fled. A sense of dread curled the corner of her lips as she watched the white blur grow larger as the alabaster great white swept underneath both men, disappearing beneath the *Heart's Content*. Kate tried with all of her might to pull Andy up, straining with every last ounce of strength to move him. Andy reached his arms over his head, grasping at the rope and pulled himself up the side of the hull hand over fist.

"I need your help," Lewis urged. The strain of pulling Derrick up had turned his face bright red. The veins in his taut neck stuck out like mighty rivers running over rocky mountains.

"What about Andy?" Kate braced herself against the side of the rail with her feet, trying desperately to get some leverage.

"He'll be on board before Derrick," Lewis barked at Kate in a voice he ordinarily reserved for their fierce arguments when they dated. "We need help over here!" Lewis cried out in vain. The rest of the crew were scrambling around, much too frightened to approach the edge of the ship.

Ellen appeared seemingly out of thin air Kate noticed her hands had clasped hold of the cable. Ellen's hand lay just over the top of where Lewis had grabbed. The bright glow appeared once more. This time the shark's form was clear enough that Kate could pick out the different fins on its body. The *Carcharodon* turned its snout directly towards Derrick. The shark could sense the panicked flailing of his limbs as he thrashed wildly in the water. The five-foot dorsal fin emerged from the water for a moment then dove straight down twenty metres before reaching its intended prey. Cries of agony and distress could be heard from behind the chaos, people too afraid to help but unable to turn away from the nightmarish scene. A wave left from the wake of the shark's ascent caught Derrick in its flow, sending his body crashing into the hull of the boat. The loud bang as his back smashed into the boat made Kate cringe, the sound echoing up the hull.

"Hold on, Derrick!" Ellen called out in between staggered breaths.

Kate finally let go of Andy's rope and got behind Ellen, hauling the rope with all of her might. They watched as Derrick slowly began to rise out of the water. Everyone breathed heavy, grunting loudly as they grappled with the dead weight. Derrick's body dangled precariously three feet over the surface when Kate noticed the white-hot glow directly below him.

Andy's hand reached up and clasped the rail. His forearm muscles looked like they were about to burst out of his skin. "Andy!" Kate cried out as she watched him pull himself over the rail. Andy toppled over the top and fell hard onto the deck, his chest heaving up and down from exhaustion. "You're okay," she said. Andy laid on his back, resting his hand over his stomach.

Kate kept tugging on the cable. The three of them were finally appearing to generate some actual progress getting Derrick out of the water when the white glow rushed towards the surface, a black hole opening in the center. Before anyone was able to react, the rope slackened, and they all tumbled backwards, falling over each other. A giant spray of foamy white water swept over the deck as the albino shark breached the surface, soaking Kate to the bone. She looked up as the giant shark rose above them, its belly, as pure white as fresh fallen snow, blocking out the sun. Kate shuddered and closed her eyes, waiting for the immense body to crush them as it fell back down. After what seemed like an eternity, she heard a giant splash as the shark fell backwards into the water. Giant waves rocked the boat violently, a force generated by the seven-thousand kilograms slamming back into the ocean.

A loud scream forced Kate to open her eyes. Andy's cries of anguish jolted her senses, forcing her to gasp at the gruesome sight. Derrick's arms were tangled around the metal rails, grasping on for dear life. The blood had drained from his face, his eyes stuck open in a permanent shocked expression. His lips quivered as he struggled to speak, scarlet blood trickling from his mouth. Bubbles formed from the corner of his jaws as he tried to breathe. Derrick's upper torso ended just above the hips, the lower half of his stomach spewing blood and entrails as his innards fell into the water below. Kate wanted to throw up as she listened to the soft contents of his stomach plopping against the surface below.

Ellen choked back a cry, the deep sobs catching in her throat nearly cutting off her supply of oxygen. Andy was the first to his feet. He ran over to comfort his friend in a vain attempt. "You're going to be alright." His voice trembled. Derrick stared at him with a sorrowful expression on his face, not accepting what Andy had claimed. Andy tried to haul Derrick onto the deck, a frivolous endeavor to prevent his friend from becoming shark food. Andy slipped in the blood that had spilled over onto the deck, his face falling inches away from Derrick's severed torso.

"Get away from me." The words sputtered out of Derrick's throat in a gargled, wet sob, the blood blocking the words from escaping his mouth.

"I need help." Andy struggled to move his friend; his body was pinned against the rail. The rope from the life raft had wrapped around his mangled body and restrained him against the cold metal. Ellen and Lewis rushed forward, nearly pushing Kate out of the way as she tried to help Andy with the rope.

"Move," Lewis demanded, pulling a large knife out of the sheath attached to his black leather belt. The sunlight reflected the blazing sun along the razor-sharp edge. The blade looked sharp enough to split atoms. Lewis grabbed a length of rope and sliced through the rope with ease. The binds holding Derrick in place loosened enough for Andy and Kate to lower his body onto the deck of the *Heart's Content*. The last of his life blood flooded out of his body. His spine had been snapped clean in half from the vicious bite. All the colour had drained from Derrick's face. His eyes remained open, the terror bulging them outwards as if they were about to pop out of the sockets as any moment.

"Thanks," Andy mumbled as he knelt over his friend's corpse. Lewis patted Andy on the shoulder, unable to find any comforting words.

Kate reached out and pulled Andy into her body, his face buried into her neck. Warm tears fell from his cheek and formed a puddle in the nape of her neck. Andy's body convulsed as he began to weep passionately. Kate ran her fingers through his hair as he let out a surge of emotions and frustration. Ellen and Lewis began to untangle the rest of the rope from Derrick as Andy grieved the loss of his friend. Kate watched Ellen step into a coil of black rope that they had thrown overboard for Andy, the life ring still floating on the surface of the ocean.

"Ellen!" Kate began to scream, but a loud twang cut her off. The rope went taut, and the coil tightened around her ankle. A loud metallic pop echoed through the air as the hook holding the rope burst off the wall. Ellen's eyes grew wide and her jaw dropped as the back of her head slammed into the rail with a loud crack. Then, as the rope continued to tug at her leg, yanking her up and over as her body flipped over the rail. Her limbs flailing around as the impact knocked her unconscious. Her body disappeared over the side and plunged down into the ocean, the length of rope dragging her into the dismal abyss.

Lewis leapt over the side of the ship after her, the knife clenched in his jaws.

Open Water
Atlantic Ocean
Cliffs of the Grand Banks

The water frothed up, sending out ripples from the spot where Ellen had plummeted into the cold waters. As Lewis dove headfirst into the disturbed water, he saw Ellen reaching up towards the surface, almost as if she was reaching out for his hand. The salt water stung Lewis's eyes as he broke through the rough ocean. He forced himself to keep them open. He wouldn't risk losing sight of Ellen. Her jet black hair blended in with the ink-black waters, exaggerating the brightness of lipstick and bronzed skin. The white glow of the shark was rapidly drawing away at and odd angle. Lewis couldn't tell if the shark was descending or going straight. All he knew was Ellen was plunging deeper. Her hands fidgeted with the ropes in a frivolous attempt to loosen the constraint it had over her ankle. She was pulling away faster than Lewis could swim. His lungs began to burn as he tried to hold on long enough to reach her.

The rope pulled tighter and the force of the shark had finally taken its toll on Ellen's ankle joint. A loud pop reverberated as the ball joint tore out of the socket. All the flesh, muscle, and sinew below the rope ripped clean off. A large red cloud burst into the air. Ellen screamed out in anguish as a torrent of bubbles danced over her face. Lewis pumped his arms and legs harder. The white glow shifted direction abruptly as the aura of blood circulated throughout the salt water. Ellen's head lurched back, her dying gaze fixed on Lewis. Her arms and legs stopped moving as the cold, saline water filled her lungs and abdomen, causing her to sink down into the abyss like an anchor. Lewis started to kick his legs, recognizing that he'd never be able to reach her before he would be obliged to accompany her at the bottom of the ocean.

Lewis looked down one last time, wishing that he hadn't. The albino shark barreled towards Ellen faster than anything Lewis had ever seen in the ocean. It's massive, snarled-tooth jaws snapped open wide enough to swallow her whole. As the alabaster *Carcharodon* clamped its jaws shut, the razor-sharp teeth severed Ellen's outstretched arm. A detonation of blood erupted like a blossoming flower, draining over the shark as it rushed past. Lewis turned his head towards the surface and swam with all of his might, a trickle of light from the blazing sun above him. He wouldn't dare look down, knowing that if he saw the *Carcharodon carcharias* coming for him, he would freeze in place. The shadow of the CCGS *Heart's Content* loomed over the surface, close enough now that he was able to distinguish the mast and cabins resting on the deck.

Lewis embraced the warm air kissing his hand as it breached the surface for a brief moment, like a lover's tender embrace. The sensation of swimming in quicksand took over, as an unseen force tugged at his legs, holding him in place. The water began to flow like a violent river, the force pressing in on him from all around. The warmth of the sun was snatched away without warning as he began to sink deeper into a dark void racing up from beneath him. A force stronger than a freight train erupted beneath him. The sun disappeared in an instant and everything was cast into complete darkness. Gravity seemed to have no effect over him, he felt like his body was soaring through the air. Lewis hung weightless in a void of pitch black. A putrid, sour stench overwhelmed him. The smell of decomposing fish and flesh churned all around him. Lewis realized that the alabaster shark had swallowed him whole, and now he was left alive in this hellish nightmare. He reached to his pistol, pulling back the safety, and decided he wasn't going down without a fight. He fired twice, the booming sound echoing off the shark's thick hide. As the muzzle flashed, his own grotesque casket was brought to life, like the flash on a camera taking pictures in the dark. Hunks of Ellen's flesh caught in the jagged, four-inch teeth lined the creature's death trap.

A surge of water as the shark opened its mouth dragged Lewis down. Murky blue water sparkled brightly against the pure darkness enveloping him for a moment. He tried to swim towards the opening, his lungs burning with excruciating pain. His body was now drained of the energy required to fight the current pulling him deeper into the shark's stomach. The light disappeared in a violent snap. A colossal force snapped his spine clean through as the razor-sharp teeth clamped together, severing Lewis Park in half.

CHAPTER TWENTY-TWO

CCGS Heart's Content
Atlantic Ocean
Cliffs of the Grand Banks
Andy watched in horror as the ethereal glow rushed towards the CCGS *Heart's Content*, the snow-white dorsal fin slicing through the three-foot waves. The Carcharodon swam with fierce grace. Her body moved with ease through the waters as her powerful torso and caudal fin pumped savagely. The shark closed the distance quickly, moving through the rough seas at over forty knots. Not one of the crew knew what to do; the boat was laying directly in the path of the monstrous great white shark. A giant cloud of black soot filled the air. The ship's engine rumbled much too late. Andy could smell the heavy, choking fumes sputtering from below deck as someone tried to force the *Heart's Content* to move before its time. Andy could feel the vibrations shuttering through the hull.

"Grab on to something sturdy." Andy turned towards Kate. The brilliant glow of the sun caught in her hair, and for a moment Andy wondered if he had already died and was now looking up at an angel.

"What?" Kate asked confused, her body trembling with fear. Her bottom lip quivered as she spoke.

Andy grabbed Kate around the waist, pulling her towards the center of the boat by her belt. They reached the rail of a staircase leading up to the helm. Kate tried to run up the stairs but Andy held her tight. "Wait here and hold on." Racing up the stairs, bounding up them two at a time, Andy moved towards the main deck. He burst through the door and looked around at the terrified faces buried into their computer screens. Their faces were illuminated by a pale green from the monitors. "Where are the keys to the submersible?" No one answered him. Everyone was waiting for the boat to move. Andy knew they couldn't outrun the giant shark in this giant ship, but he may out-maneuver the creature. He had to stay on top of his game, keep the creature guessing his next move. "Hey can someone..."

SMASH

The albino *Carcharodon carcharias* rammed the stern of the CCGS *Heart's*

Content, sending a vicious shock wave throughout the ship. Andy fell face-first into some computer equipment as the ship whirled hard to starboard. The vibrations of the engines had enraged the great white. Now they sputtered and choked. The whole room filled with the loud bangs of equipment crashing to the ground, glass shattering, and the anguished screams of the crew. A loud metallic groan wailed from the engine room as the gears struggled to keep turning.

"Turn the engines off!" Andy called out as he climbed back to his feet. "You need to turn them off now!" He barked, but no one listened.

"The shark is attracted to the vibrations from them. If you don't turn them off, it will keep attacking us," Kate stated calmly. There was a bright red gash across her forehead spilling crimson blood over her face.

Andy rushed to her side. "Are you okay?"

"Turn off those fucking engines!" Kate screeched, her voice shrill and full of anger.

BOOM

An explosion rattled the entire ship as the engine blew up, sending a shock wave through the ocean. Every computer screen that hadn't been destroyed during the impact a moment ago now lost power. The red emergency lights flicked on overhead as a loud siren rang overhead. The acidic scent of fire and fuel soured the air. Andy started sweating as a wave of heat from the fire below deck washed over him.

"Close off the engine room," a woman spoke into a walkie-talkie. "Flood the ballast to douse the fire."

"It's swimming away!" A sailor called out gleefully, his finger pointing out the window.

Andy walked over and watched in disbelief, the dorsal fin slicing through the waves with ease. Kate's warm breath sent a riptide of goosebumps through his body. Her lips inches away from his neck as she leaned against him. Her body went limp, her weight crashing down over him as she collapsed into him. "Kate." Andy caught her underneath the arm just before she slammed face-first in front of him. He eased her down, the blood flowing from the deep gash on her forehead that ran into her hairline and disappeared beneath a wet clump of her hair. He placed his finger on her neck, and a flood of relief washed over him as he found her faint heartbeat still pulsating in her neck. "Wake up, Kate." Andy shook her gently, her chest rising and falling slowly as she breathed.

"We are taking on water," a static filled voiced came in over the walkie-talkie.

"It's circling us."

"It can sense we are sinking."

"What do we do, Ali?" Her crew looked to their supervisor.

A loud metallic groan echoed beneath them as an incessant torrent of water threatened to sink the *Heart's Content*. It crippled the ship. They were a sitting duck in the middle of the Atlantic Ocean. The biggest *Carcharodon carcharias* ever encircled them, waiting for its prey to enter the water with it. Andy stared down at Kate's ghastly pale face; the blood spattered over her gorgeous eyes.

"Get the life rafts in the water," Ali ordered.

"That thing will pick them off. You won't stand a chance out there with it waiting to strike," Andy objected.

"We will sink before help can reach us and there's no fucking way, I'm getting into the water with it," Ali argued, ignoring Andy's warning.

"Call for help and you may get off this ship alive." Andy stood up and turned his back to Ali, looking out of the window as the dorsal fin patrolled the water just one-hundred metres away.

"Are you deaf or just plain stupid? We won't stay afloat long enough." Frustration ripped through Ali's throat, each word spitting out in anger. "Unless you have some plan, I'm lowering those life boats."

"You're right, you do have to get those life boats lowered but not yet." Andy continued to marvel at the snow-white dorsal fin as it cut the waves in half.

"I'm not waiting for that thing to get closer. We need to go now while it's still far enough away. We may have a chance if it doesn't catch us leaving."

"That shark will sense the exact second you place anything into its domain. Its radar senses work much better than what you have on this ship." Andy let out a chuckle. "I'll grab its attention and you can make a run for it once the shark is entertained. I'll lead it away."

"How do you plan to do that, cowboy?" Ali mocked him.

Andy spun around to look at Kate. "Get me the keys for that submersible."

CHAPTER TWENTY-THREE

CCGS **Heart's Content**
Atlantic Ocean
Deep Sea Submersible Pegasus

Andy climbed into the cockpit of the two-man deep-submergence vehicle *Pegasus*. The inside of the cockpit reminded him of something he would have seen on *Lost in Space*. There were over-sized buttons, dials, toggles, and an LCD display screen that emitted a pale green glow. A musty smell from beneath the seat suggested that it had been a while since anyone had done maintenance on the deep-submergence vehicle. Andy cursed under his breath at the crew for neglecting the extraordinarily advanced technology in favor of their daily routine. The swathes of stainless steel ran into the polished black floor, the light gleaming along the outline of the component of his high-tech dashboard.

Clink clink clink clink

A metallic squeal rang out overhead as the chains lowing the *Pegasus* struggled against the rust and grime buildup, threatening to break and send Andy careening down into the deep blue ocean. As each link passed through the pulley system, the sub bounced, held in place for a moment before dropping back down until the next stoppage. Andy powered up the twin-turbo engine. The power of the engine surging throughout the entire cockpit sent jitters through his whole body. The submarine was only designed to go thirty knots, so he couldn't outrun the albino *Carcharodon carcharias*. His best chance of survival would be to outmaneuver the speedy shark. When the sub finally reached the water, the waves lapped over the acrylic glass dome, the crystal clear sky slowly fading into the murky mess surrounding the boat. The CCGS *Heart's Content* damaged engines were spewing oil into the Atlantic Ocean. The remains of the humpback water floated through the water like a heavy haze. Andy looked at the sonar screen and immediately picked up two giant blips. The behemoth shark had closed the gap to just fifty metres now. The movement of the dominant great white was too much for the radar to keep track of. A brief delay in reporting the creature's position could prove catastrophic. "Come on." Andy slapped the screen with an open palm, hoping that would solve his dilemma.

He turned the bright white lights on. His heart dropped in his chest as he couldn't see much more than ten metres ahead of him, enclosed by the carnage next to the ship. He ran his fingers along the toggles until he found the release switch for the chains. The submarine floated freely in the water, bobbing up and down in the waves. The bright blue sky overhead was tarnished with tall pillars of jet black smoke from the *Heart's Content's* burning engines. The white dorsal fin changed directions now, cutting its tight circle in half to investigate the electronic impulses sent out by the *Pegasus*. His natural instincts took over. The desire for self-preservation pushed the throttle forward. Andy sent the sub into a sharp spiral downwards, trying to find an escape from the thick slurry of blood and oil that clouded his vision. Every passing moment was sheer agony. Dark shadows followed him at every turn, waiting to reach out and take hold of the sub.

The light finally broke into the ink-black waters of the depths as the *Pe-*

gasus sped down the shelf of the Grand Banks two-hundred metres below the surface. Now Andy was able see forty metres ahead of him, the light seeping into the blackness ahead of him. Checking his radar, Andy wasn't shocked to find that the great white had closed the gap to twenty metres and was now following the *Pegasus* from behind. Andy craned his neck and looked over his shoulder through the crystal-clear glass. The white glow shined like a bright light at the end of a dark hallway. "Fuck," Andy said to himself as he pushed the deep-submergence vehicle further down into deep waters, not wanting to afford the *Carcharodon* the opportunity to strike from below. With the ability to gather the force of a locomotive, it would certainly prove to be a devastating blow. Even the tiniest puncture to the acrylic dome would allow the pressures of the deep into the cockpit, crushing Andy's skull like Gallagher hitting a watermelon with that hammer. The *Pegasus* soared through the abyss, the white hot glow trailing his every move as Andy deviated left and right. He was desperately trying to keep his pursuer off guard long enough for the crew of the *Heart's Content* to make it to safety.

As Andy pushed deeper into the blackness, white particles drifted past the clear glass, giving him the illusion he was flying through space. The tiny white dots reflected the sub's own light back at it, like stars in the Milky Way. "This is insane," Andy laughed as the alien form behind him kept pace with him through every twist and turn. The ocean floor came into view, the rocky bottom covered in barnacles and underwater vegetation that hid hundreds of species from predators. Andy maneuvered the *Pegasus* as closely as possible, hoping that would deter the giant beast stalking him. The pure white belly of the alabaster shark passed over head. Andy banked sharply to port, narrowly avoiding a giant outcrop of rocks as he twisted the controls of the submarine. He found himself upside down, the ocean floor now a ceiling. Andy was trapped in a confined space with the evil monstrosity. Its blood-shot eyes pierced through the light beam, following it to the *Pegasus*. Flops of sweat formed in an instant on his forehead. A wave of heat rushed through his body as the weight of claustrophobia washed over him. Andy cringed as a crushing sound echoed all around him. The cockpit was being squeezed shut. His breathing came in short gasps and fear's fingers dug in between his ribs, holding his chest in place with anxiety. Andy began to lose consciousness as the jaws gaped open and jutted forward. Rows of jagged, razor-sharp teeth sprang out past the shark's snout as its jaws unhinged. Andy stared into the darkest void; a blackness so intense there was no escape from its reach.

Life Rafts
Atlantic Ocean

Ali cradled Kate's head in between her thighs, the blood from the deep gash on her forehead soaking into her pants. Ali felt the sticky fluid against her skin, the heat fusing a bond between the fabric of her pants and her legs, using the blood as a bonding agent. "Sheldon can you locate land yet?" Ali asked, her back pinned against the rubber side of the life raft.

"Not yet," Sheldon answered in a disheartened voice as he leaned on the edge of the raft.

The yellow life raft had a built-in motor. Melvin had intuitively taken command of it when the four of them first got in the raft. The roaring buzz of four other engines could be heard as the twenty surviving crew members raced towards shore. Each one of the rubber bottoms slapped off the water as they hopped over the waves. There was enough room in their raft to fit all twenty people, but they came to an agreement to take five life rafts. If that shark decided to pick off one of the boats at least the rest would still make to land. "We will find it soon, I can tell," Melvin said excitedly.

"I can't believe this is actually happening," Ali whispered to Kate, looking down at the extensive wound. Ali tilted her head back to scan the horizon, expecting to see the five-foot, pure white dorsal fin streaming towards one of the life rafts at any moment.

"The worst part'all this is over now," Melvin reassured her. "Just put your faith in the lord. He'll lead us home yet."

"How can you be so sure?" Sheldon asked pessimistically.

"We're still here, ain't we?" Melvin pointed his finger over Ali's shoulder. "Well ain't that a sight for sore eyes. I've never been so happy spotting land."

Ali looked over her shoulder as the land began to come into plain view, poking out through a thin veil of mist from about two kilometres away. The green trees blended together, making the island appear like one giant shrub sticking out of the water. "We are still here." Ali gave Kate's shoulder a tight squeeze. She used her index finger to find a strong pulse pumping in Kate's neck, her jugular throbbing underneath her skin.

"Where are we?" Kate's voice was muddled by confusion. Her eyelids batted open and closed as she struggled to block the sun out of her eyes while trying to search for a prominent landmark.

"We are safe now," Melvin reassured her.

"We are almost back to land," Ali added.

Kate looked around the raft, her face wrought with anguish. Her lips writhed into an expression of torment. "Where is Andy?"

There was nothing but the rumble of the outboard motors as the five life rafts raced across the water. Everyone was rendered speechless. Ali sought to figure out something to say other than *I don't know*. She didn't want to upset the poor girl in her lap; she had been through enough already. Ali watched as Kate's chest rose and collapsed back into itself more rapidly now. The realization of what she had just witnessed began to come back to her. "Andy took the sub and led that demonic abomination away long enough for us to get to land."

"He'll be right behind us," Melvin chimed in. A wave rocked the boat, and everyone lost their balance except Melvin. His sea legs were much stronger than everyone else. His years on the water gave him a strength far beyond years of lifting weights could have. With practiced ease, Melvin set the raft back on course before the ocean had a chance to claim another soul.

"Would you look at that," Sheldon whined, his chin hitting his chest in defeat. "So much for taking separate rafts. They're enough of those things out there now that we are completely screwed." He pounded his fist against the raft and started to bawl.

Cliff of the Grand Banks
Atlantic Ocean
Deep-Submergence Vehicle Pegasus

Andy awoke, his body shivering from the extreme cold. His chest hurt from the savage beating of his heart. Twisted knots in his intestines forced stomach acid back up his esophagus. He choked on the burning bile on the back of his tongue. He rubbed his eyes, trying to make sense of where he was. His skull weighed down like it was full of rocks. A dark cloud hung over him. A groggy sensation combined with sharp jolts of pain firing from every synapse in his body clouded his thoughts. It was hard to fathom what he was looking at. Several teeth had punctured the glass dome of the *Pegasus*. Two inches of razor-sharp teeth had broken through but remained lodged in the acrylic glass dome. The long, white teeth were the only things keeping the pressure of these depths out of the cockpit. The sound of water rushing past gave Andy the illusion that he was stuck in a river, but he knew that he had fallen to rest on the ocean floor far below the Grand Banks. Red warning lights flicked across the screen displaying various system failures, the dull glow reflecting off the acrylic dome.

Life Support Failure
Heat Pump Failure
Engine One Failure
Engine Two Malfunction
Navigation System Failure
Buoyancy Balance Failure
Pressurization System Stable
Light System Off

"Goddammit." Andy smacked the monitor in front of him. "Give me one piece of positive news." He was losing consciousness as the carbon monoxide burned into his lungs, and he was starting to become light headed as the oxygen level plummeted. He searched under his seat, his fingers discovering the rubber mask. He pulled out the regulator that was attached to a pony tank. In a swift motion, he yanked the elastic strap over his head. Instinct told him to rotate the handle to the right. Fresh oxygen flowed into his mask and he thankfully sucked in a mouthful of air. After a long and deliberate deep breath, Andy no longer suffered from the ill effects of the carbon monoxide, the poisonous gas leaving his body. He pressed random buttons on the keyboard, hoping that some miracle might take place. He let his fingers dance across the keys, not really knowing what he was expecting to happen. Then he noticed it, a diagnostic image of *Pegasus*. Almost all the different systems of the deep-submergence vehicle were coloured red except for one engine that was a hope-bringing yellow. It was just as bright as the sun, and it warmed his soul in the same way that a warm summer's day would.

Andy turned the engines off and then tried to restart them. This time the yellow changed to green and he heard the power surge through the *Pegasus*. He could feel the raw energy coursing throughout the cabin, an incessant rumble as the engines growled to life. The diagnostic display slowly began to fill with yellow as some systems came back to life.

Life Support Critical
Heat Pump Warming
Engine One Failure
Engine Two Ready
Navigation System Searching for Signal
Buoyancy Balance Steady
Pressurization System Stable
Light System Ready

A steady flow of warmth began to spill out of the vents, fighting off the glacial chill of the abyss. He analyzed the oxygen gauge on the small tank and calculated that he had about thirty minutes or so to reach the surface. Everything would be okay as long as that hellish nightmare had returned to its domain. Turning on the lights, Andy's chest burned with pain, his heart failing to beat. With his jaw hanging open, the bright white beams revealed that the creature hadn't returned to hell. Andy found himself trapped in the jaws of the Albino *Carcharodon carcharias* as it glided through the depths. He powered up the engine and tried to burst clear from the monstrous jaws of the snow white *Carcharodon*. The lights illuminated the ghastly insides of the demonic creature as the *Pegasus* shifted, the nose of the submarine now pointing straight down into the creature's unfathomable gullet. Andy gagged at the flecks of flesh still caught in between the creature's jaws. A swatch of fabric that had belonged to Ellen's jeans was stuck on the jagged edge of a tooth. Andy covered his face with his hand, preventing the bile from spilling out. Vomit burned his throat as it filled his mouth. He ripped off his oxygen mask just in time. Andy threw up into his own lap. The hot liquid splashed against his legs and promptly turned cold again.

Spitting out a mouthful of reddish brown slime, a bitter, metallic tang filled his mouth. Andy wanted to turn away from the carnage, but he needed to force his way out of the beast's mouth. The radiant light beam flickered, and the surge of the engine rattled obnoxiously as the deep-submergence vehicle began to run out of electricity. At this rate, his oxygen would last longer than the battery cell. He didn't want to die down here in the dark, waiting for the unknown to come take him. Andy pulled his mask back over his face then he peeked down at the control panel once more. Specks of spittle had spattered onto the screen. He wiped it away with the sleeve of his arm and turned off the heat pump in an effort to conserve battery power. A tear rolled down Andy's face as he flicked through the diagnostics system, unable to find a solution to his dire dilemma. He pounded his fist against his thighs in exasperation over and over until his legs were numb, unable to take it anymore. The bones in his hands ached, and his knuckles were white as his fists clenched in anger.

"Come on, you bastard!" Andy screamed out at the top of his lungs. "Finish me." His voice reverberated off of the acrylic dome, the roar of rushing water drowning him out. Andy smashed his fist into the monitor. A spider-web pattern spread across the glass but did not break. Andy laughed breathlessly. He didn't want to suffocate, but he didn't want to be devoured whole into this demon's belly. He searched around the cabin with tear-filled eyes, his will to live silently losing the battle to the realization of his dreadful situation.

Eject

The word stood out in bright reflective tape on the side of his left leg, the lever surrounded by a plastic case.

For Emergency Use Only

"Well, this will probably be my only chance to experience how this actually functions," Andy joked, struggling to come to terms with his decision. He ran through all the scenarios in his mind; none of them involved surviving this. He reached out, lifting the case up. His fist hovered above the red lever.

Pull Out   Twist Counter-Clockwise   Pull Down

He studied the directions internally, mulling over each word as if he was to be interrogated on the procedure.

"Fuck me," Andy whispered as he placed his hands on the lever. It seemed to be connected to a formidable force. He could barely pull the handle up and twist it into place. "Here goes nothing."

Andy closed his eyes and tried to picture the sun on his face one last time, but all he could see was the sinister smile of the alabaster ghoul. He didn't know what was about to happen, but Andy slammed the ejection lever down with no regrets.

CHAPTER TWENTY-FOUR

Life Rafts
Atlantic Ocean

"Quit your bellyaching, ya fool." Melvin let out a hearty chuckle. "We will be just fine. Take a gander over there,"

Sheldon raised his head up and scanned the horizon. He raised up a balled fist, slowly raising each finger. "One… Two… Three… Four… Five." He waved his hand at Melvin. "I count five dorsal fins."

Kate let out a soft whimper. "The great white sharks must have fled to the cove to get clear of that creature." Pushing herself with her elbows, she strained her neck to look into the direction of the sharks. A broad smile stretched across her face.

"What's so fucking funny?" Ali snapped at Kate. "I've had enough of this bullshit." Ali pouted like a child, letting her arms flop to her side in defeat.

"Those dorsal fins belong to orcas," Kate said, her voice full of joy. "They've come to bring us home."

"You think those things would even attempt to stop that white freak?" Sheldon said smugly. "They wouldn't stand a fucking chance," he accused Kate as if she had screwed up.

"The orca is the natural adversary of the *Carcharodon carcharias*. Millions of years of evolution will keep that creature out of this harbour. It's hard-wired to avoid these creatures." Kate's grin reached from ear to ear as the orcas circled the life rafts, guiding them towards the shore.

"You couldn't make this shit up," Melvin said as he buckled over laughing, his palm slapping off his leg as he let the fear drain out of him. "We are going to make it."

Kate nodded her head in agreement. "We are going to make it." His laughter infected Kate, and she felt a flood of relief relax her every muscle. The sharp pain in her head faded away into a dull throb that she was able to ignore, the joyous sensation overwriting the pain.

"We are going to make it?" Ali still didn't believe what was happening.

A killer whale breached just ten feet from the life raft, its sleek black skin rising into the air as it matched the speed of the boat. It continued to dive in and out of the water alongside the raft. A fine mist sprayed from the whale's blowhole every few jumps.

Cliff of the Grand Banks
Atlantic Ocean
Deep-Submergence Vehicle Pegasus Escape Pod

Andy spun out of control. The escape pod rushed towards the surface, gathering speed with every passing moment. Different shades of blue raced past his vision as the uncontrolled ascent twisted him in all directions. The hot white glow remained in the deeper blues. The sound of metal being crushed echoed through the deep water, the metallic groaning piercing into his ears. Andy was disoriented, the rapid ascent and spinning tossing him around like a wash cycle. The tension built up in his ears as the pressure changed faster than he could adjust. His stomach churned inside out, as his body rattled against the violent rocking. The seat belt tore into his shoulders, the straps threatening to break his collarbone. His neck rattled from side to side. The muscles ached as they were being stretched too far apart. The fibres and sinew ripped underneath his skin.

The escape pod burst through the ocean surface. Andy felt weightless as he soared ten feet into the air. As gravity took back over, it pulled the pod crashing down hard into the choppy blue surface. He re-entered the ocean face down, the darkness of the ocean staring back at him. He tumbled into the dashboard as the pod rolled back towards the surface. The yellow sun bobbed high above him against the blue sky. The ocean current quickly took its hold over the escape pod. Andy sensed that he was drifting aimlessly across the surface. He embraced the warmth of the sun kissing his skin like the embrace of an old lover, the sensation washing over him instantly. Andy's blood pressure dropped. The whole ordeal took its toll, sending him crashing into despair. Water lapped against the acrylic glass pod. The sound of a seagull in the distance and a strong breeze lulled Andy into a deep sleep.

The deep blue ocean surrounded the escape pod on all sides, the horizon a melting pot of blue hues. The white glow of the albino *Carcharodon carcharias* was visible underneath the escape pod, the vicious predator circling far beneath the surface. It remained hidden, waiting for the opportunity to finish its prey.

Life Rafts
Cape Race
Shipyard

The ancient wooden dock was a sight to behold, although the weathered grey boards were in desperate need of repair. The salty spray and years of negligence had withered them down to virtually nothing. The dilapidated wharf was slanted towards the depths, some boards submerged beneath the water as they descended towards the bottom. Only a few scattered boats were tied to the few remaining sturdy poles that were closer to shore, connected by colourful nylon ropes. Up on the hilltop, the Cape Race Lighthouse stood tall and proud. The white cylindrical body towered into the sky, the red top standing out against the deep blue horizon. The sight sent a shiver down Kate's spine, the image a stark reminder of the albino Carcharodon towering out of the water with its bloodied jaw. For a moment, Kate shuddered in fear, but the rocky cliffs that rose high above the ocean were a welcoming sight.

"I can't believe we made it." Ali stood up as the boat neared the dock.

"I told you we would," Melvin said matter-of-factly as he slowed the engine and let the momentum carry the life raft towards the submerged boards. "Now someone race up to that lighthouse and tell them Andy is still out there." Melvin jumped over the side, his feet splashing in the water before thudding against the dock beneath. He grabbed the guide line for the boat and held it in place, offering his hand to help people onto the wharf.

Still clouded by a deep haze, Kate was propelled forward by a surge of adrenaline flooding into her bloodstream. She leapt over the side, the cold water shocking the skin on her leg. She nearly slipped on the algae-covered boards. It was difficult traversing the treacherous dock, but her legs kept spinning until she launched herself out of the water and her shoes slapped against the weathered boards. She raced towards the rocky beach as the dock groaned beneath her. Once her foot touched solid ground, she got down on her hands and knees, kissing the soil. Euphoria washed over her. At that moment she swore she would never set foot in another boat as long as she lived. She could hear the others boats reaching the cove, their engines rumbling like thunder as the sound reverberated off the cliff faces on either side of the harbour.

Kate got back to her feet and followed the rocky path up a steep slope. Her legs shook uncontrollably underneath her, but something kept her moving. A voice in the back of her imagination reminded her of the will to get help for Andy. It also screamed at her to get as far away from the water as possible. A giant red barn crept into view at the base of the lighthouse as she crested the hill. An elderly woman knelt in a flower bed at the foot of the barn, her long silvery hair being tossed around by the breeze.

"Help."

Kate tried to yell, but the words tumbled silently out of her parched mouth. She swallowed hard, trying to draw some moisture back into her mouth. The woman looked up at the sound of rocks scuffling underneath Kate's feet, an expression of concern crossed her tanned skin. The sun had burned her skin, causing the wrinkles underneath her emerald green eyes to be that much more pronounced.

"Help." Kate managed to spew the word out, her voice shrill.

The woman jumped to her feet with a quickness you wouldn't expect from someone her age, but the terror in Kate's cry could have raised the dead. "My dear, what's the matter?" Her voice was soothing and softer than a cashmere blanket.

"My friend is out there with a monster." Kate broke down and began to whimper, her legs finally giving out as she collapsed into the ground.

"Harold, honey, you better signal for help!" she called out towards the lighthouse.

Cliffs of the Grand Banks
Atlantic Ocean
Sea King Rescue Helicopter

Blue skies raced by, the cabin shook, and the metal door frame rattled by the rotating blades while Chad gripped the edge as he peered out over the ocean. They were responding to the operator of the Cape Race Light-house, who had called in a distress call, giving the Coast Guard the direction of a sinking ship. The CCGS *Heart's Content* had been abandoned by all hands. Chad glanced down as they passed over the coast guard ship. The capsizing boat had rolled over onto its port side and only the underside of the hull remained above the crashing waves. Reports of a forty-foot, albino great white shark attacking the boat deterred all other ships from heading out on a rescue mission. Luckily the majority of the crew had made it to shore in the life rafts, but now the *Sea King* was searching for an electronic signal from an escape pod that had led the monstrosity away.

"We got a signal!" the pilot called out from the cockpit as he abruptly changed directions in an instant, nearly sending Chad hurtling into the ocean below. A carabiner fixed to a bar in the ceiling attached his harness kept him inside the helicopter.

"Can you give me a heads up before you do that again!" Chad yelled out, his heart racing inside his chest.

"Sorry!" the pilot called out sarcastically.

Chad shook his head as he looked out towards the horizon. The Atlantic Ocean seemed to go on forever. They could see a man, floating above the water. Chad had to look twice, rubbing his eyes to make sure his eyes weren't playing tricks on him. As the chopper approached, and as the man came into view, his features became more distinct. Sun rays beaming off the acrylic glass once the angle was right forced the pilot to adjust his approach.

The sub pilot must have ejected the escape pod and was now drifting alone in the ocean. The man waved as the rumble of the *Sea King* hovered about twenty feet above the escape pod.

"I will lower the harness now," Chad informed his partner.

"Roger that."

Chad dragged the metal framed harness to the edge and gave it a tiny shove over the side. The harness fell about five feet before the slack ran out. Chad used the wench to lower it down towards the stranded man, hoping that he was healthy enough to get into the harness without assistance. A white glow formed directly beneath the acrylic escape pod from the depths. The man was frantically moving his arms and shouting, the rumble of the engine drowning out his voice. Chad quickly realized that the man wasn't trying to draw their attention to him, he was trying to warn them to get out of here.

Before Chad could react, the white hot glow opened into a dark chasm, a giant black vortex sucking in the water beneath the hovering *Sea King*. A mouth full of razor-sharp teeth exploded in a fury of destruction, swallowing the escape pod whole. The gigantic jaw continued straight up, the darkness colliding with the helicopter. Chad fell backwards as the impact sent the *Sea King* spiraling out of control. The smell of diesel and smoke filled the helicopter. Mechanical hisses and metallic groans screamed all around as the world spun into a blur. The *Sea King* smashed into the ocean with a thunderous impact. The cold ocean waters quickly filled the helicopter and pulled it down. Chad was tossed outside of the door, his mouth and nostrils filled with salt water, his body still strapped into the harness as the weight of the helicopter dragged him down with it. He tried to detach himself from the harness but couldn't reach the carabiner in time. The blue ocean quickly faded to black as he lost consciousness.

CHAPTER TWENTY-FIVE

Arctic Ocean

Joan felt her stomach turn over itself as she swam further north, the waters frigid and cold. She could still detect the scent of the large predator no matter where she went. She had followed it up through the Labrador Current and into the Arctic basin for days, hoping that she could find somewhere to give birth to her pups. She cringed, her abdominal muscles constricting as her pups writhed around inside of her belly. The time finally arrived, they were ready to come out and face the harsh waters of the freezing cold sea. Joan was exhausted. She had lost her appetite, too afraid to eat ever since she first picked up the apex predator's scent days ago. She wanted to put as much distance between them as possible, afraid that the monstrous shark would devour her newborns without blinking an eye.

This was the first time Joan found herself this far north. She kept close to the surface, basking in the warmth of the sun. The nights were almost unbearable, her muscles barely able to generate enough heat to keep her alive. Joan didn't know why, but she was following a signal buried deep beneath the ice floes. Something was drawing her there, the same signal that once brought her mother there years ago. While Joan had been birthed in the waters just above the Grand Banks, her mother found her way back to give birth three years later. A deep-rooted instinct to evolve drew Joan into this frozen hell. Now, as Joan's belly burned with the pains of child birth, she forced herself down deeper into the frigid depths of the abyss. She lost control of her stomach muscles, no longer able to hold back the pups from bursting out. Giving birth in the harsh environment would force the pups to adapt in the same way as Joan's sister had evolved.

Her stomach burned with intense pain as her body pushed the pups out. The first pup that managed to escape her womb hurt Joan the most. The other two pups passed through virtually unnoticed. Joan's body was drained from the ordeal. She floated towards the surface in a daze, leaving her children to fend for themselves. Their instinct would soon take over, allowing them to gorge on the slow moving prey drifting aimlessly along the bottom. Her pups would easily adapt to the frigid waters of the Arctic ocean because they had been born into them. Joan was not so lucky. The cold waters drained the remaining energy from her exhausted muscles. She wasn't able to keep moving forward anymore. Unable to force water through her lungs, Joan drowned. Her body sank to the ocean floor for her young to feast upon. She slowly suffocated as she suffered the razor-sharp teeth ripping into her flesh.

CHAPTER TWENTY-SIX

St. John's International Airport
Terminal
St. John's, NL

Kate sat in a hard plastic chair, her feet folded up beneath her. She rested her open laptop on her thigh, the screen tilted down at an angle making her uncomfortable. Her clenched fist was mushed into her check, and her elbow dug into her knees as she glared at the screen. Another rejection letter from a magazine refusing to publish her work. No one accepted the tale of the forty-foot albino *Carcharodon carcharias*; not even the tabloid newspapers would bite. No one ever recovered any evidence substantiating that the creature even existed. There were no reports of any sighting of the great white shark in over two months now. Kate wasn't able to find any evidence of the destruction it had wrought. The official cause of the sinking of the CCGS *Heart's Content* recorded by government officials was that it ran up against an outcrop of rock nearby and damaged the engine. They also revealed it to be the same location that Jonah McGilvery ran into when he sank the *Swift Current*. All the lives lost at sea that day were linked to the hallucination of a mysterious creature emerging from the abyss. Collective post-traumatic stress disorder developed amongst the survivors, and the true explanation of their deaths was never disclosed to the public, just the delusion left to blame in order to cope with the overwhelming catastrophe.

Labyrinth Oil had made billions of dollars since they began draining the oil out of the Grand Banks. The corporation also discovered plutonium underneath, but Kate's gut feeling led her to expect that they knew about it before they announced their pipeline. Kate discovered that Mr. Kurosawa had paid off the media to cover up the true tragedy. With no more sightings of any great white sharks along the coasts of Newfoundland, the breaking news of the discovery of plutonium caught the nation's attention. This made it easy for the media to make it seem like the only reason the sharks caught on the evening news was an anomaly. They believed the only reason they gathered off the shore in the first place was the dead humpback whale. They were drawn into Newfoundlands' shores during their journey back towards Africa from Nova Scotia. Kate tried to use her position at the university to warn people about the giant monstrosity, but her colleagues ridiculed her, discrediting all of her work she had produced trying to prove the albino abomination actually existed.

She sat alone in the airport, waiting for a departure to Alert in Nunavut, the northernmost settlement with a permanent population year-round. She resigned from the university in St. John's after they declined to fund her exploration into the shark. Unable to find anyone willing to pay for the frivolous expedition, her only chance of finding clues to the genetic mutation would be found from working at the research facility located in Alert. The military was conducting experiments with deep-submergence vehicles underneath the Arctic ice cap. She knew if there was any evidence of the albino predator it would be found somewhere in the vastly unexplored Arctic Ocean. She couldn't let all those people die in vain, to let people think that these people simply disappeared with no explanation. She owed it to Andy to prove that *Carcharodon carcharias* was still evolving, growing much larger to adjust to the earth's ocean's declining temperatures. Soon the *Carcharodon carcharias* would evolve into the world's most destructive predator. *Carcharocles megalodon* roamed the oceans before the last ice age and would soon be brought back into existence, but this time they would be prepared to survive the impending ice age.